MW00800034

GIVE US THIS MARS

GIVE US THIS MARS

by

Thomas W. Cronin

Book 2 Of The Saga Begun In

AS IT IS ON MARS

Tharsis Books

The characters in this book are entirely fictional, and bear no relation to any person, living or dead. The stealth spy spacecraft of the CIA and U.S. Air Force is also fictional.

The places on Mars are real, described as accurately as allowed by data from NASA's Viking, Pathfinder and Mars Global Surveyor missions.

Mars place names used in the book are those set forth by the International Astronomical Union, except for names of local features, named by characters in the book. These local feature names are entirely fictional, and are in no way intended as proposals for official names.

Times and dates on Mars, with respect to Earth times and dates around 2048, are believed to be as accurate as current computational technology and astronomical data allows.

Kasei Valley image on back jacket courtesy of NASA and U.S. Geological Survey. Mars global image on front jacket courtesy of NASA.

ISBN 0-9687502-1-4

First Published March 2003

Canadian Cataloging in Publication Data
Cronin, Thomas W. (Thomas William)
Give us this Mars / by Thomas W. Cronin

ISBN 0-9687502-1-4
I. Title
PS8555.R61118G58 2003 C813'.6 C2002-911241-9
PR9199.3.C6682G58 2003

THARSIS BOOKS
P.O. Box 55, Saanichton (Victoria)
B.C., Canada V8M 2C3

Printed in Canada by Friesens, Book Division, Altona, Manitoba
10 9 8 7 6 5 4 3 2 1

Dedicated to those engineers, scientists and others,
who have worked on missions to Mars.
Without their spectacularly productive efforts,
this book could never have been written.

We could steal away in the rovers soon,
beneath a dawn-red sky,
And flee along the valleys wide,
between escarpments high;
Escape ere the drifting ice fog lifts,
dispersed by the morning sun,
Ere the deep blue hue of the dawn clouds fades,
and a new day is begun.

They seek to drag us off this world,
from all that we have here,
This world for men who strive like Gods,
for men who know no fear.
But we will not yield before this foe.
Let no man say we fled.
We'll fight and strike the hammer blow,
and force them to flee instead!

From *Flight or Fight*, an entry in
the Second Part of the Book of Mars.

JURGEN EINDORF, the mission's chief flight engineer, was as good as his reputation, and on Friday, July 10, 2048, he engineered a safe landing, on a flat, sandy surface on Elbow Plain. In the Martian calendar, it was Sunday, Alpha-October 14, just a few weeks past the fall equinox.

The third manned landing on Mars was so smooth it was hardly felt by the twelve astronauts inside. Computers, guided by radar beacons on the ground, brought the squat cylindrical lander in automatically.

Had it not been for the silence after the ear-splitting roar of the rocket engines, and then a monotone computer announcement of a successful landing, the twelve could not have told for sure that they were down, and that the European Space Agency had succeeded in safely landing a rescue mission on Mars—where NASA had failed just two years earlier.

Minutes later, when that monotone computer announcement of the successful landing reached Earth, cheers and shouts of elation erupted at Mission Control just south of Toulouse, and indeed, all over Europe. But in high places in the United States, the feeling was very different.

After touchdown, Captain Richard Derk, his two first officers, and three others, remained seated around the circular edge of the lander's lower personnel floor. Each of the six had a small view port to the right, but none of them could see anything outside except for dense, swirling clouds of orange dust. The lander's powerful rocket exhausts had created a blast crater under the lander, throwing up enormous clouds of dust in the process.

Nobody said anything. They were mostly experiencing a feeling of relief, mixed with curiosity and even elation—they had landed safely on Mars, only the third set of humans ever to do so. For the present they were content to remain seated and watch the drifting dust outside.

The mission commander, Captain Derk, calm and collected, lay back in his severely reclined seat. He was used to command, descended directly from a long line of aristocrats, all of them leaders in their time, right back to the infamous Norman Duke Gilbert D'Erque, whose army had laid bloody waste to large parts of Saxon England during the Norman Conquest. Captain Derk was a man it did not pay to cross.

At that moment, this twenty-first century Norman aristocrat was experiencing a certain exuberance, both at the prospect of new lands to conquer and control, and at the prospect of becoming the first governor of a lucrative Mars colony.

The dust settled quite quickly. Captain Derk looked to the northwest. He expected to see a red, rock-strewn valley floor, with the famous Stem Gap in the distance, ten miles away. This was the huge, mile-wide gap in the northwestern escarpment wall of Kasei Valley, and the entrance to the sanctuary of Leaf Valley. It had been clearly visible during the descent, until just before touchdown and the clouds of orange dust.

But now, with the dust settled, the Captain was surprised to discover that he could no longer see anything remotely like the famous landmark.

He ordered his crew to stay seated. Seconds later, he was out of his seat, checking the view through each of the six view ports in turn. What he saw through each was much the same, and not at all what he had been expecting.

He suppressed feelings of anger. They had promised him a sheltered landing site—as good as inside Leaf Valley. But this was just a hole in the ground. They'll pay for this, he thought to himself. They'll not put me in a hole in the ground.

But they had put him in a hole in the ground, at a strategic disadvantage, well outside the sanctuary of Leaf Valley. And they had another surprise waiting for him too.

Not enjoyment, and not sorrow,
Is our destined end or way;
But to act, that each tomorrow
Find us farther than today.

From *The Psalm of Life,*
by Henry Wadsworth Longfellow

All warfare is based on deception.

Hence, when able to attack, we must seem unable;
when using our forces, we must seem inactive;
when we are near, we must make the enemy
believe we are far away;
when far away, we must make him believe we are near.

From *The Art of War,*
by Sun Tzu

CHAPTER ONE

High Stakes

EVERYBODY HAD been convinced. There could be no doubt. The survivors of the first manned missions to Mars had all died of starvation.

So it came as a complete surprise six years later, in August of 2044, when NASA discovered they were still alive. When further inquiry confirmed that they were not merely alive, but flourishing, and had built a prosperous settlement in a place called Leaf Valley, the world was stunned. And when the settlers revealed the extent and sophistication of their settlement, in a remarkable video recording they sent to Earth, there was even shock, and envy too.

Before that August, nobody had ever heard of Leaf Valley, but a careful NASA study of the video recording showed it to be a natural sanctuary, a kind of Martian Shangri-La, and an ideal place for human settlement. Because it was low down, it was usually warmer than the high, cold, wind-scoured plateau surrounding it, and it had higher pressure air for the same reason; it was protected from severe dust-storm winds too, by its enclosing precipices and escarpment walls; and, most importantly, it had a water supply.

The sheltered valley lay in the western Kasei Valley region of Mars, and was about sixteen miles long, running north-south. The main entrance was at its southern end, through an impressive gap in the escarpment wall of the far larger Kasei Valley.

Leaf Valley, as one might expect, had the shape of a leaf. The converging walls of the two long sides of this leaf ran northward, but did not quite meet at the leaf tip. Instead, they ended in a complex of narrow canyons, with very high walls. These walls shaded the canyon floors from the sun, even in summer, in the process preserving life sustaining frozen water underground.

The dominant feature of Leaf Valley was a lone mountain, lying only a few miles south of the valley tip. The video recording showed it rising abruptly out of the red, rock-strewn valley floor, in front of the converging valley walls. The settlers had called it Mount Tip.

On the southeast side of Mount Tip, there was a broad shelf, about fifty feet up, with a panorama view of the valley. On this shelf lay a large enclosure of glass slabs set in copper frames, rising out of foundation walls of orange Martian concrete. Inside this enclosure grew a wide assortment of green plants, surrounding a pleasant garden home, in which all but one of the settlers lived.

Down on the valley floor, just south of this glass-enclosed oasis on the mountain shelf, the video images showed an array of four huge rectangular greenhouses, mostly for food production. The greenhouse floors, covered in green plants, were sunken well below ground level, and only the tops of the orange-concrete side walls were visible above ground; sunlight came in through flat roofs, made of glass slabs set in strong copper frames. A sunken, plant-lined walkway, also roofed by glass slabs, connected these greenhouses to the glass enclosure containing the garden home.

The video images also showed an industrial complex, source of the construction materials used in the settlement. It lay down on the valley floor, about a half mile east of the glass enclosure on the side of Mount Tip. It held a workshop, a glass works, a cement works, a copper foundry, an aluminum works, and an iron works. It also had chemical plants that could make rocket fuel and oxidizer from Martian air and water, and the water needed came from an ice mine in the main canyon at the valley tip.

If all that was not enough to stir imaginations on Earth, the video also revealed a Zen monastery in Leaf Valley, at its southern end; it was the home of a Japanese Zen master, sole survivor of the failed Japanese mission of 2038. The monastery lay high up, at the edge of a precipice, with breathtaking views over the valley below.

In the upper echelons of Government, in both the United States and the European Union, the reaction to the images of this Martian settlement, and the unique valley that sheltered and nourished it, was initially more shock than surprise. That shock soon gave way to envy at what the settlers had accomplished, and that envy soon gave way to desire—and even lust—for possession and control. A later revelation of very large copper deposits, conveniently close to Leaf Valley, intensified these feelings.

It was obvious from the video images that copper had been used extensively in the construction of the settlement, and the source of this copper very quickly became a matter of engaging interest on Earth. NASA geologists were soon searching for it, carefully scrutinizing Mars terrain data, sent back to Earth by survey satellites in earlier decades. And well before the end of 2044, they found it.

The copper was coming from what appeared to be exceptionally large deposits in a mountain with a ridge summit, which the settlers had called Chiselhead Mountain. The mountain lay within Kasei Valley, only about ninety miles south of Leaf Valley.

It quickly became clear to both NASA and the European Space Agency, ESA, that the assets of the Leaf Valley region were of enormous value. Shortly after the discovery of the settlement in 2044, NASA estimated a value of at least a trillion dollars for the valley.

Initially, the great value of the settlement lay in the simple fact that it drastically reduced the cost of a mission to Mars—to less than a tenth of the cost of the disastrous 2038 NASA mission. It was no longer necessary to ship a greenhouse, tens of tons of food, habitat, Mars rovers, or an extra Earth return rocket that would make its own fuel on Mars. A single mother ship, equipped with a simple landing craft, carrying maybe a Mars buggy or two, was now sufficient.

The lander would just need rocket engines powerful enough to get it back up into orbit at the end of its stay on Mars. It could be light weight, and could land with only half its rocket engines firing for only a few seconds, because its large fuel and oxidizer tanks, needed to get it off Mars later, could be close to empty for the landing. Once down on Mars, the lander could get fuel and oxidizer from storage tanks filled earlier by the Leaf Valley chemical plants. During the visit, the crew could make use of the Leaf Valley living quarters and greenhouse facilities.

Both NASA and ESA soon realized that the original trillion dollar estimate for the value of the Leaf Valley region was too low. That estimate had been based only on the hundreds of billions of dollars the settlement would shave off the cost of a mission to Mars.

By late 2044, after scientists found out about the very large copper deposits at Chiselhead Mountain, it was easy to believe that in years to come, with advancing technology, a way might be found to bring copper economically from Mars to Earth. There was thus the additional possibility that a Leaf Valley colony could one day pay for itself, as well as enormously benefiting the mother country. And who knew what other treasures remained to be discovered? It was no wonder that envious, lusting eyes were directed at Leaf Valley. Its true value was incalculable, probably in the trillions of dollars.

Before 2044 ended, both the U.S. and the E.U. were drawing up rival plans for taking control of Leaf Valley, for the purpose of founding a potentially lucrative Mars colony.

There was just one problem: What to do about the settlers in Leaf Valley. They were no longer employed by any space agency on Earth, so you could not order them to come home. Even worse, no space agency had any legal right to their facilities, which they had built themselves. The Earth's space agencies had even turned the surviving equipment from the failed Mars missions over to them in 2038, when it was thought that they would all soon die of starvation on Mars. And to top it all, the settlers showed no desire for a rescue, and every indication that they were quite happy to stay put.

Within the United States, there was some division of opinion on this matter, although none at all high up in both Government and NASA. Opinion there was firm in the belief that the interests of the United States must take precedence over those of a few individuals, especially when only one of them was a U.S. citizen. There were a few dissident factions in NASA though, and more than a few in some Mars societies, who were rooting for the settlers on Mars versus Big Government. The power elite in Europe, of course, believed that the interests of the E.U. should take precedence over those of the settlers on Mars.

There was also the matter of rights to the land on Mars. An international Mars agreement had given ownership of Mars to the people of Earth, through the United Nations, administered by the U.N. Mars Office. The U.N. Mars Office had the power to transfer property rights to any nation occupying land on Mars for the purpose of building a colony—at a modest price for the land. Legally, the settlers on Mars had no right to the land their settlement sat on; they were squatters, paying no rent to the rightful owners.

This meant that all a government on Earth had to do to get control of Leaf Valley and the surrounding region was send a mission to Mars to rescue the settlers, and maintain a presence in the Leaf Valley region after they were off the planet. It could then negotiate with the U.N. Mars Office for transfer of title to the land.

*

Not long after the discovery of the settlement in Leaf Valley, a new administration came to power in the U.S., after the Presidential Election of 2044. The new administration soon became convinced that it could get control of Leaf Valley by sending a rescue mission that would both persuade and pay the settlers to come home.

Some in the U.S. Government, particularly among the Joint Chiefs, even argued that the U.S. should use more than persuasion and payment to get the settlers back to Earth; but use of armed force, which NASA was dead against, was ruled out by the President.

The President was a clear-headed man when it came to matters of principle, unlike his predecessor. Although his Joint Chiefs believed that force should be used as a last resort, he was not yet prepared to use force against an American citizen, who not only had done no wrong, but was a hero in the United States. The President was convinced that peaceful persuasion, sweetened with both patriotic appeal and an offer of one hundred million dollars in hard cash for each of the settlers, would be sufficient to win the day.

In early 2045, the urgency of the situation was apparent everywhere in the U.S. Government, for the E.U. had already taken the first steps toward a Mars mission of its own. The U.S. could not afford to have the E.U. get there first, and snatch the prize. At the urging of both NASA and the President, Congress agreed to fund a low-cost NASA mission, to take advantage of the April 2046 opposition. An opposition occurs every twenty-six months, when Mars and Earth come closest, and is the best time for a Mars mission.

Of course, the NASA rescue mission would need the cooperation of the settlers, since Congress was providing funds for only a low-cost mission. The mission would not have Mars survival facilities with it, such as a habitat, rovers, food stockpile, greenhouse, or fuel for the return journey, and would be dependent on the settlers to supply these necessities.

That meant two things. First, the settlers had to be convinced that the NASA mission had no intention of dragging them off the planet against their will, for otherwise, why would they be interested in receiving the NASA visitors? And second, NASA would have to pay the settlers for the services it needed, in advance. In other words, the settlers would need to see the NASA rescuers as harmless visitors, who had paid in advance for a stay at a Martian hotel, equipped with a restaurant and gas station.

Early in 2045, NASA did convince the settlers of its peaceful intentions, and succeeded in negotiating a satisfactory mission-stay agreement to cover the projected 2046 visit. The agreement stipulated that NASA would pay for its stay with relatively inexpensive items the settlers currently could not make themselves. This would save the Space Agency hundreds of billions of dollars.

The European Space Agency was understandably very interested in this interplanetary agreement, and managed to get hold of a copy, which was carefully analyzed at ESA headquarters in Paris.

In keeping with the mission-stay agreement, NASA sent some low-cost landers on ahead. They carried three new portable nuclear power plants, two of them for the settlers' rovers, as well as a new chemical plant for manufacturing fuel and oxidizer. NASA also sent new electric motors and batteries for the rovers and buggy. The landers also carried medical and dental supplies, additional batteries and solar panels, sheet rubber, some of the latest computer hardware and software, communications equipment, and other useful items.

NASA also sent the settlers many technical items to enable them to refurbish the habitat from the 2038 mission. That habitat had been wrecked by flying rocks in the explosion of the mission's return rocket, and had been lying derelict at the old NASA landing site, over a hundred miles south of Leaf Valley. It was still intact, having miraculously survived one of the worst dust storms ever, in 2040. Now that there were good metal working facilities in Leaf Valley, it made sense for the settlers to tow the habitat to their valley, repair the punctures in the walls, and replace all the damaged parts.

The result was a new, functioning habitat for fourteen persons, and thus a further valuable addition to the settlement in Leaf Valley. One of the new nuclear power plants NASA sent provided electric power for the building. It was in this refurbished habitat that the NASA rescue crew planned to stay—at least until NASA had control of the complex.

As well as sending all those relatively inexpensive supplies to the settlement in Leaf Valley, NASA also put some essential satellite infrastructure into orbit around Mars.

About five months prior to the arrival of the rescue mission, the U.S. space agency got three communications satellites into high-altitude areostationary orbit. A satellite in areostationary orbit goes around the planet in exactly one day, so that, to someone on the ground, it appears to stand still in the sky as the planet rotates, which is ideal for communications.

The settlers in Leaf Valley could now use the comsats to communicate easily with NASA. The communications equipment NASA sent included a dish antenna to link with one of those comsats. The settlers installed the dish up on the slope of Mount Tip, above their glass enclosure.

There was also a need for new ground survey satellites. NASA had always had at least one ground survey satellite in polar orbit around Mars, between 1999 and 2039. However, when the last ground survey satellite failed in 2039, NASA did not replace it. The excuse then was that NASA already had detailed terrain data for the entire planet. Collecting further terrain data seemed unnecessary.

Now the U.S. needed to keep track of what was going on in Leaf Valley, and after the comsats were successfully installed, NASA also put two new ground-survey satellites into low-altitude polar orbits.

The two new survey satellites, supplied by the Air Force, with the latest in high-resolution ground imaging facilities, were really spy satellites. They soon sent back data encouraging the belief that the Chiselhead copper deposits were truly enormous.

The survey satellites also revealed something quite unexpected—a new building the settlers had put up, right beside their greenhouses. It looked like a laboratory, and the settlers later admitted that it was. This raised some eyebrows at NASA, especially when it was recalled that, as part of the mission-stay agreement, the settlers had been sent computer hardware and software that gave them access to all the large scientific databases in the U.S.

NASA was at once concerned about this laboratory, in case the settlers were up to something that could negatively affect the rescue mission. With the help of the CIA, NASA investigated the settlers' use of the U.S. scientific databases. This investigation pointed to a clear genetics research activity, for there had been significant access to the Master Genome Database in Washington. When asked about this, the settlers would say only that they were working on some biochemical problems peculiar to Mars.

The CIA was not satisfied with this, and continued to investigate. But NASA could not see how such research could affect the coming rescue mission, and was content to view this new lab positively, since it made the settlement even more desirable for the U.S. Each time the settlers added something to the settlement, it became more valuable. Nevertheless, the CIA would one day be shown to be right in its suspicions.

*

The NASA rescue mission, with a crew of ten, got underway in December 2045, carefully monitored by the European Space

Agency. The mission's mother ship was similar to the one used on NASA's Mars mission of 2038, except that it was nuclear powered, with the thrust coming from high-velocity steam propellant, heated by a fission nuclear reactor.

The mission did get to Mars, in the spring of 2046, but only as far as initial Mars orbit. Then it went very badly wrong, and could not land, to the great relief of the power elite in the European Union. Fortunately, nobody got killed, largely because of what the settlers on Mars did to help.

Essentially, the accident in Mars orbit happened because the restricted budget for the mission forced NASA to skimp. NASA had used an older, cheaper, and less reliable type of nuclear reactor to power the mother ship, instead of a new, much better reactor type. The newer type was both stronger and lighter, but would have cost an extra billion dollars, which NASA could not afford.

Just after the ship entered initial orbit around Mars, during an aerobraking procedure, it was subjected to very strong G-forces, which caused a catastrophic failure in the ship's nuclear reactor.

Aerobraking is where the ship goes into a pronounced elliptical orbit around Mars on arrival, so that each time around, it grazes the planet's upper atmosphere. This enables a spacecraft to slow down gradually without using up precious propellant, and so maneuver itself into a low-level, near circular orbit. The procedure is not without risk. In the past, a considerable number of unmanned spacecraft had been badly damaged, and even lost, during aerobraking.

On the first braking trip through the upper atmosphere, the ship tumbled out of control for a few minutes. This subjected it to unexpectedly high G-forces that badly damaged the reactor's control units. The result was an uncontrolled nuclear chain reaction.

The crew then had to abandon ship before the inevitable reactor meltdown. Fortunately, they were just able to get out of the crippled mother ship, and into their Mars lander, and pull away, before the reactor went critical. Things looked bleak for the ten in that lander, stranded in a highly elliptical orbit, with food for only a few days, but it was help from the settlers on Mars that saved their lives.

The lander had too little fuel to land on Mars, given its high-energy elliptical orbit. The only chance for the ten was to use the fuel and rocket motors on the lander to maneuver into an orbit where they could dock with the old abandoned mother ship from the 2038 NASA mission.

It was a tricky business. It took eight days. The problem was that the high-energy elliptical orbit of the lander was badly mismatched with the low-energy circular orbit of the 2038 mother ship. This required the lander to slow down and switch orbits at the same time, using a succession of carefully timed rocket burns.

The computing resources on board the lander were not sufficient for computing the timing and intensity of the rocket burns, and NASA could not help them with the real-time computations needed, because of the near twelve-minute time delay communicating between Mars and Earth.

In the end, it was the computing resources of the Martian settlers that saved the day. They gave the helpless crew nearly all their time during that week, using all their computers to help. NASA also uploaded essential software to help them do the job.

Once the ten were safely on board the old 2038 mother ship, they had to leave for Earth at once, for there was unspoiled food on the old mother ship for only about five months. Unfortunately, the only way home was a nine-month long trajectory that took them well inside the Earth's orbit around the sun. As a result, they were half-starved when they got home, but they did get home, to the relief of all. NASA also got the old mother ship from the 2038 mission back, even if it had lost its new, nuclear-powered mother ship.

The Martian settlers now showed themselves to be a farsighted and canny lot. They had stipulated, as part of their deal with NASA, that if for some reason something went wrong and the NASA mission could not show up, then NASA would have to pay a penalty equal to the supplies sent. The settlers had not been prepared to accept being in American debt, just because NASA screwed up. But, as things turned out, it was a fair deal. Without the settlers' help, the crew of the 2046 rescue mission would not have survived.

There was one other positive. It would have been a disaster if the derelict nuclear-powered mother ship had been left abandoned in that elliptical aerobraking orbit. Eventually, it would have slowed down enough to crash on Mars, and spew highly radioactive material over quite a large part of the planet's surface.

Fortunately, the abandoned nuclear mother ship did have emergency auxiliary chemical rocket motors. On reaching the old mother ship from 2038, the ten survivors were able to send instructions to the main control computer on the abandoned ship. The computer then turned on those auxiliary motors at just the right time to push the ship out of Mars orbit. Its new trajectory would take it out of the solar system in about twenty years, and out of everybody's way.

As a result, NASA could call the whole fiasco a successful failure, like the Apollo-13 mission to the moon in the previous century. Nevertheless, neither the President, nor the Joint Chiefs, nor the Congress, were impressed by NASA's second manned Mars mission failure in less than ten years.

*

The failure of the 2046 rescue mission was a major blow to both NASA and the U.S., although it did not cause the President to abandon his goal of a U.S. colony centered on Leaf Valley.

Then came worse news. Ten days after the departure of the crippled NASA mission from Mars orbit, on its long starvation voyage back to Earth, the European Space Agency announced approval of a twelve-man rescue mission to Mars. It would land near the following opposition, which was in early June of 2048.

This was a further blow to American pride. The U.S. had tried hard to be first to Mars to rescue the settlers, but had failed, and now the Europeans were going, with the prize just sitting there, waiting to be snatched.

The reaction of the U.S. President was 'over my dead body', or words to that effect. The projected European mission made him even more determined. He would not allow the E.U. to get control of Leaf Valley, even if he had to use the military to prevent it.

And that is precisely what he decided to do, within days of the announcement of the European rescue mission. A secret military Mars mission, born of necessity, and the first ever, was in the works shortly after. It would be armed, and scheduled to arrive on Mars in 2048, but one month before the ESA mission. Neither NASA nor ESA was aware of its existence.

*

After the discovery of the settlement in Leaf Valley, in the summer of 2044, the E.U. had been just as interested as the U.S. in rescuing the settlers on Mars and gaining control of the valley. Unfortunately for the Europeans, the bureaucracy that runs the European Union is even more cumbersome than the one that runs the

United States. The Washington bureaucracy is a streamlined machine by comparison. Because of this, the E.U. had simply been unable to organize a Mars mission in time for the 2046 opposition, in direct competition with the U.S.

It has to be understood that the E.U. is run by the European Commission, which has a large staff at its headquarters complex in Brussels. At the top is the Commission President, and a roster of Commissioners. The Commission President more or less corresponds to the U.S. President, and each Commissioner corresponds more or less to a U.S. Cabinet Secretary.

The Commission is the executive arm of the E.U. Government, and is usually responsible for all new initiatives that lead to E.U. projects. But like the U.S. executive arm, led by the U.S. President, the European Commission cannot just do what it wants. It has to get the approval of the Council of Ministers, which more or less corresponds to the U.S. Senate. It also needs the approval of the European Parliament, which more or less corresponds to the U.S. House of Representatives.

The Commission President and Commissioners each tend to act in the interests of the entire E.U. In contrast, the individual members of both the Council of Ministers and the European Parliament, like their counterparts in the Congress of the United States, have little pan national vision. Instead, they fight hard for their particular regional interests.

It was the European Commission, following strong input from the European Space Agency, that in late 2044 began pushing for an ESA rescue mission, in time for the opposition of 2046. Unfortunately, the Commission's first Mars mission initiative got stuck in the Council of Ministers, which was unable to agree on which member country would get which slice of the Mars mission pie. As a result, the E.U.'s 2046 Mars mission initiative never got approval, while the U.S. rescue mission forged ahead.

The Commission President did get something from the Council of Ministers, however, in early 2045. At its Paris headquarters, ESA had been carefully studying the American rescue mission plans, and had presciently concluded that the U.S. mission was under funded to a level that subjected it to considerable risk of failure. The Commission President soon became aware of this ESA conclusion, and used it to influence the Council of Ministers. As a result, he got permission to initiate planning and research for a twelve-man ESA rescue mission in 2048, to put ESA in a state of readiness, should the U.S. mission in 2046 fail.

So, well before the U.S. rescue mission ever left Earth, the European Commission had provided the European Space Agency with the funds needed to carry out important planning and research directives. In addition to the planning for a rescue mission in 2048, the Commission directed ESA to carry out strictly secret research on the economic viability of a future colony in Leaf Valley.

This directive placed particular emphasis on research into the possibility of profitably transporting copper from Mars to Earth.

The director of the European Space Agency, Dr. Roger Riddleby, an expert in transportation economics, was very clear about the importance and urgency of this research, as well as the need to keep it secret from the Americans.

A great deal of the research work was farmed out to university researchers, who received generous ESA research grants, in return for willingness to publish their research results only in an ESA scientific journal with restricted circulation.

One such grant went to a professor of structural engineering at the University of Uppsala in Sweden. This professor had a young graduate student named Astrid Larsson, who was both a qualified geologist and structural engineer. She did the completely unexpected. In early 2046, she came up with a bold and novel idea for getting copper off the surface of Mars cheaply, and in enormous quantities. Astrid Larsson's work consisted of computer simulations of a fundamental engineering structure only, but the bold idea underlying it stirred imaginations in both the upper levels of ESA and the European Commission.

Of course, Astrid Larsson could not be publicly recognized for her work. That might alert the Americans, who still thought that the necessary technology was at least half a century away. ESA would find another way to reward her.

Copper now gave the Europeans an even more compelling motivation for building a colony on Mars. Nor was there any doubt that the copper was there, for in the winter of early 2046, the new NASA ground survey satellites had returned convincing evidence for a truly enormous copper deposit at Chiselhead Mountain.

Europeans have a long colonial tradition, and the European Commission was now tantalized by the possibility of a Mars colony that might pay for itself quite soon, instead of in the distant future, by exporting copper back to Earth. After all, Astrid Larsson had shown how this could be done economically, at least in principle.

The European Commission now had an irresistibly strong motivation for getting control of Leaf Valley, and when the news of the nuclear accident that crippled the American rescue mission reached Earth, in late spring of 2046, the Commission President had everything ready. He had a detailed, well thought out rescue-mission proposal ready to send to the Council of Ministers for approval.

He also had a proposal for a prototype construction project at a secret location inside Europe. This was a prototype of a novel transportation facility that might one day be built on Mars, based on Astrid Larsson's bold idea.

This time, the E.U. Commission saw to it that there was something in its proposed Mars venture for every member nation of the European Union, and the Council of Ministers unanimously approved the proposals after less than a week of debate. A few days later, the European Parliament also voted its approval.

An ESA rescue mission to Mars was in the works at last, and in the early summer of 2046, European engineers could start putting the mission together.

Dr. Roger Riddleby, the Englishman in charge of ESA, now showed himself to be a much more able space agency director than anybody had anticipated when he was first appointed as only interim director in 2044. Indeed, it was largely because of Riddleby's initiative and determination, in lobbying and persuading the powerful European Commission, that the ESA rescue mission to Mars ever got final approval.

Riddleby got the mission hardware built on schedule, and the ESA mission left for Mars in January of 2048, with a crew of twelve that had been selected with unusual care. One of the twelve was the young Swede, Dr. Astrid Larsson, her bold engineering idea still a secret. She had completed astronaut training with distinction, enabling her selection as a member of the historic mission to Mars. Her selection was partly as a reward for her work so far, but mostly it was due to the desire to further exploit her geological and engineering skills on Mars.

The mission left Earth on schedule, for arrival on Mars in July of 2048, just after the 2048 opposition. Riddleby made sure that ESA took no chances with the design of the mother ship and Mars lander, and spent the extra funds to eliminate all risks.

Of course, just like NASA in 2046, ESA had to pay the bill, in advance, for the projected Mars mission stay at the Leaf Valley habitat. Officially, the mission was a good-will visit of exploration and research, prepared to rescue the settlers, but only if they desired it. That was the basis on which the European Space Agency negotiated a mission-stay agreement with the settlers for the projected visit. The settlers had been happy to make a deal, overjoyed at the prospect of a friendly, non-threatening visit from Earth.

Not all the details of the deal that ESA negotiated were made public, although the CIA made it its business to know everything about the mission. It was public knowledge, though, that ESA sent on ahead three more portable nuclear power plants, batteries, new rover and buggy parts, sheet rubber, medical equipment, and communications equipment. The settlers could now also install an ESA communications dish part way up the slope of Mount Tip, above the glass compound, beside the dish NASA had sent. This latest dish pointed at an ESA communications satellite in areostationary orbit.

The ESA rescue mission went as planned, and on Friday evening, July 10, 2048 in Washington, Sunday afternoon on Mars, an ESA lander arrived safely on the ground on Mars, with the mother ship parked in a safe, stable orbit around the planet.

Although the news of the successful ESA landing on Mars resulted in euphoria in Europe, it was not well received in Washington. That evening, less than an hour after the President received the news at the White House, he ordered his Chief of Staff to arrange a high-level meeting for the following morning.

The President had a serious problem. The ESA rescue mission had got to Mars before his secret military mission, run by the Air Force. His military mission would not be in final orbit around Mars for another four weeks. It had been delayed two months, by the discovery at the last moment of potentially lethal bugs in the mission's software, to the exasperation of the President and the Joint Chiefs. It had taken two frantic months of repair and testing, prior to departure, to put things right.

*

It was Saturday, July 11, the day after the ESA landing on Mars, and not many months before the Presidential Election of 2048. That summer morning, the Cabinet Room in the West Wing of the White

House was full. The media people were there, transmitting the scene to the nation.

Seated at the long, curving conference table were the President, six members of his cabinet, the Director of the CIA, the Chairman and members of the Joint Chiefs of Staff, and the NASA chief.

The President sat at the middle of the long table. Shafts of summer sunlight slanted through the east windows behind him. He looked tired, and worried too, for the successful ESA landing on Mars the previous day, contrasted with NASA's rescue mission fiasco of two years earlier, would not help his reelection as President.

Then security people ushered the media people out, and the President got things moving with a short speech.

"As you all know," the President began, "the European Space Agency's first manned Mars mission landed safely yesterday in Elbow Plain. This success for the Europeans is very bad news for us. In fact, it's a threat to the national security of the United States."

"There's even worse news," he went on. "According to the CIA, the crew of this Mars lander is armed. That's a violation of the international agreement prohibiting weapons on Mars." He paused here, his eyes scanning those around the table.

Even more worrying for the President was a CIA report that the ESA mission was armed with nanoguns, whereas his military mission was not, but he did not mention this. As for the treaty banning weapons on Mars, he could hardly accuse the E.U. publicly, since the U.S. was intending to violate it too. The President took some satisfaction from the thought that the E.U. had violated it first.

"Some of you may be wondering if the classified Mars project we have in the works can be of any help," he continued. "So far, it's been a matter only for myself, the Secretary of Defense and the Joint Chiefs, and the Director of the CIA, but you've probably all heard rumors about it. Unfortunately, it looks like it got started far too late. Its earliest possible arrival time is nine months from now."

He paused again, looking across the table at the NASA chief, Dr. Judy Campbell, sitting well to his left. The NASA chief was frowning. She could not know that the secret military mission would reach Mars in less than four weeks, not nine months. The CIA chief had persuaded the President that not only was Dr. Campbell to be kept in the dark, she was to be misled. The CIA feared that ESA agents would be quick to spy out anything NASA knew about the project. A great deal could depend on the element of surprise.

"Ladies and gentlemen," continued the President, "it looks like the E.U. has outmaneuvered us. We have no national policy in place to deal with what may be about to happen on Mars. We need to come up with one quickly. But first, we need to be properly briefed on the latest developments. The Director of the CIA will fill us in."

The CIA director sat on the President's side of the table, but well to his right, almost at the end. He was a small, bald man in his fifties, with an unemotional face.

"It may look like everything's gone without a hitch for the Europeans," the CIA chief began, "but that's actually not the case. They do have some problems. I'll talk about that later.

"First of all, let me say this is a very serious situation. Of the twelve on that lander, five have a strong military operations background. Three of these even have Special Forces training. That means people selected primarily because of their ability and willingness to get things done using methods most people couldn't stomach. I'm talking here about the mission's leader, Captain Richard Derk, one of his two first officers, Emma Grant, and a junior member called Karl Mannhardt.

"But it's Derk we're most worried about. He's a good-looking, aristocratic type—he looks down his nose at just about everybody, but he's good at public relations. He's not out for money—he's got plenty—loads of inherited wealth. It's power and prestige he's after. He usually appears as the charming, not too clever, harmless, well-bred upper-class type. But, in reality, he's one of the most cunning and ruthless of men, and a strategy mastermind. It's many years since Derk was in Special Forces service, but that training makes him an even more formidable military strategist.

"His mission has two faces. The official face is a mission of good will, exploration and research, willing to rescue the three in Leaf Valley only if they want rescued. That's just blather, but it's what the European public believes, and some of the mission's scientists too. The true purpose is to get those settlers off the planet, with the least possible embarrassment to the E.U., and take over their facilities.

"ESA news releases are playing up the scientific qualifications of the five military types, but for the most part they're minor. The European media don't know what's really going on. Only two of the five military people, Jose Montoya and Monique Montpellier—the two without Special Forces training—have the equivalent of a graduate degree in science or engineering from a reputable American institution. Montoya also has desert warfare experience in North Africa. He's next to Derk in the military chain of command.

"Of the seven non military people, Jurgen Eindorf's the most senior. He's the chief flight engineer, but he seems to be aware of the true nature of the mission. He's a disciplined type, obviously selected because he's both a brilliant engineer and a person who rarely questions orders—only when he sees technical problems.

"On the scientific and engineering side, the most important are Dr. Donald Carruthers, the chief geologist, and Claude Bertrand, probably Europe's best known structural engineer. He's designed a lot of Europe's engineering landmarks. We're not sure about Dr. Astrid Larsson and Dr. Vincenzo Cassoni. These two are qualified both as geologists and structural engineers. But the presence of these four must mean the mission has big engineering plans.

"Then there's Dr. Sheila Bell, the mission's doctor and dentist. She's a charming Irishwoman, with a very media-friendly personality. We're certain she has no idea what this mission's really about. She's doing her best to find out though. She's very inquisitive. We think she's secretly gathering the materials for a book. That's no surprise; the Irish are a nation of writers. She's a very different kind of doctor from Denise Lavoisier in Leaf Valley. Denise is regarded with respect and even awe in Europe, but I doubt if she's much loved. She's too coldly rational for that. Sheila Bell has the common touch. She gives the mission a human and friendly face.

"Finally, there's Dr. Ursula Schneider, a biologist from Austria. Like Sheila Bell, she's completely harmless. Neither of these two women have ever fired a gun in their lives." The CIA chief paused here, and drank some water.

"You may wonder how we know so much about this mission," he continued. "Well, some of our information comes from the normal intelligence gathering methods we use in Europe. But most of it comes from listening in on the mission itself. How we did that would surprise most Americans—and probably shock the Europeans. So would what we've been able to find out."

He paused. Everyone around the table was staring at him.

"We too had a mission to Mars this year," he explained, "to keep the ESA mission company. The Air Force was in charge of the logistics, and the Air Force Chief of Staff will give you the details."

Eyes opened wide around the table. This was a surprise. The Air Force doing surveillance in space for the CIA? Even the NASA chief was surprised. Is this a big part of the secret, military-run Mars project, she wondered? But in this conjecture, Dr. Campbell was far from the mark, although she could be forgiven for the error. She was a civilian, and had no understanding of the size and extent of projects connected with the Defense Department.

The Air Force chief was sitting at the end of the table, beside the CIA chief. He scanned a thick dossier in front of him for a few seconds, and then spoke: "Our mission used a small, unmanned, stealth spy ship, launched by the Air Force. This stealth spacecraft had a very low radar profile—nearly impossible to detect. It was crammed with the latest electronic spying and surveillance equipment. It traveled to Mars over the last six months, together with the ESA mother ship, but running about fifty miles ahead. Just far enough ahead to prevent those on board the ESA mother ship from detecting it.

"Our spy ship did not go into orbit around Mars with the ESA mother ship, but just flew straight past the planet. Once the ESA ship got to Mars, we had no further use for the spy ship."

"During the voyage to Mars, this spy ship monitored all conversations in the rotating torus at the front of the ESA mother ship," the Air Force chief continued, "and relayed them back to us. Its imaging equipment was also able to monitor just about every human movement in the rotating front, which had a lot of transparent structures to let the crew see out up ahead. Those transparent structures also let us see in."

Once more the eyes of all those around the table opened wide in astonishment, as the Air Force chief, proud of the success of his new toy, closed his dossier and nodded to the CIA chief, at his left.

"We didn't need the spy ship to monitor the ESA mission's transmissions to Earth," added the CIA man. "We lease time on NASA's big dishes to pick those up down here as they arrive. Everything the mission sends to Earth is encrypted, but it's no problem for us. As a result of this intelligence gathering, we understand the true nature of this ESA mission. We also know the problems the mission has, and the kind of people we're dealing with."

"You may recall," continued the CIA chief, "that the main terms of ESA's mission-stay agreement with the settlers were that the mission gets food, fuel, accommodation, and the use of a buggy, in return for supplies sent in advance.

"The settlers were also contracted to help the ESA mission land near the industrial complex, but not where there was a risk of being toppled in a bad wind storm. ESA assumed this meant that the landing site would be somewhere inside Leaf Valley. It couldn't be on the high plateau around the valley, because that plateau's just too exposed to high winds. The only other possible landing place nearby was just south of the valley, in Elbow Plain, but that seemed ruled out too. Elbow Plain can have dangerous winds in a bad dust storm. Those winds could easily topple a lander—like the three hundred mile an hour winds in the big dust storm back in 2040.

"But, about a week before reaching Mars, the mission got a surprise message from the settlers. It informed them that the landing site would be out in Elbow Plain after all, and not in Leaf Valley.

"Derk was upset, to say the least. Apparently, a Leaf Valley landing site wasn't put in the agreement explicitly. ESA just assumed that the settlers would have to bring the lander down inside Leaf Valley. But now, at the last minute, Derk discovers differently. The settlers' message also assured him that the new landing site in Elbow Plain was well sheltered and quite safe—no possibility of his lander being toppled by high winds.

"But even if this Elbow Plain landing site was safe, it meant that the ESA mission would now be at a disadvantage. They would be landing about twenty-five miles from the complex they wanted to get control of. And they had no rovers with them. They just had two open buggies, although they would also have the use of a third buggy. That's the buggy from the JSA mission in 2038, which the settlers have agreed to place at the ESA mission's disposal.

"That left Derk with only two options: Accept what the settlers offered him, and land safely, under radar beacon guidance, at a prepared landing site in Elbow Plain. Or ignore the safe landing site, and land without radar beacons, and no prepared landing site, but where he had originally intended to land—inside Leaf Valley, within about a mile or two of the industrial complex.

"The flight engineer, Jurgen Eindorf, strongly objected to the second option. He maintained that trying to land without a prepared landing site and landing beacons would be far too risky. He told Derk he couldn't guarantee the lander would function correctly for launch later as a return vehicle, if it were to land on an uneven surface without landing beacons.

"In the end, Derk gave in and accepted the Elbow Plain landing site. He couldn't say the settlers hadn't kept to their side of the agreement. It was just not what he had wanted. Things would have been a lot easier for him, if he had landed close to the industrial complex inside Leaf Valley.

"Of course, all this happened because we told the settlers that the ESA mission was probably armed. They're clearly not anticipating a friendly visit any longer. They're obviously worried that the ESA mission is not what it appears to be, and have been taking precautions. That suits us just fine."

The CIA chief now continued: "The ESA mission landed on Mars yesterday, as we all know. Although they landed safely, they sure got a surprise. The safe landing site in Elbow Plain was just a big hole in the ground. Derk also got another surprise. His habitat was sitting out on Elbow Plain too—not inside Leaf Valley, as he was expecting. I'd like to have seen his face when he found out."

The Marine Corps Chief of Staff, sitting beside the Air Force chief, now had a question. "I don't understand the significance of landing in a hole in the ground. Could you explain?"

"The settlers have clearly decided to keep the ESA mission out of their valley as much as possible," explained the CIA chief. "That's the reason for the landing site and habitat out in Elbow Plain. But that means the landing site has to be sheltered well below ground level, to prevent dangerous winds toppling the lander.

"But Derk must see it as a deliberate snub. He can't appear on the European video networks as the valiant commander, landing triumphantly in Leaf Valley, surrounded by the spectacular Leaf Valley scenery and facilities, welcomed with open arms by the settlers, and setting up shop there as if he were already in charge. Don't forget he craves power and prestige. Instead, he's landed well outside Leaf Valley, in a hole in the ground, and has to set up shop outside. Makes it hard for him to show off. In fact, it makes him look like a beggar, shut out of Leaf Valley."

"I see," said the Marine Corps chief.

"It's early fall on Mars in the Northern Hemisphere right now," continued the CIA chief, "and winter won't begin officially for five months. But don't take that to mean that the ESA lander's going to spend the fall, winter, and spring seasons on Mars, until the months before the next opposition, like the NASA mission in 2038. It's not. It'll stay only a short time on Mars."

"So it's to be quick and dirty," said the Marine Corps chief.

"Right," said the CIA chief. "They intend to stay only three weeks, and avoid an eighteen-month stay by taking the long way back around the sun, actually coming inside Earth's orbit, just like our failed rescue mission in forty-six. A three-week stay is all that's provided for in the mission-stay agreement with the settlers.

"The ESA mission planners think a short stay on Mars is the key to success. They believe it's important to get the settlers off the planet as quickly as possible. But they're not intending for all of the ESA crew to come home after a three-week stay. Eight of them will stay behind in Leaf Valley to take charge of the complex."

"You're sure about this plan to stay only three weeks?" asked the President. This greatly bothered him. If it was true, and the ESA plan succeeded, his secret military mission would arrive a week after it was all over.

"Yes, we're very sure," said the CIA man.

The President was now even more anxious than at the start of the meeting. He had had some disquieting conversations with U.S. business leaders recently, about their intentions concerning both Leaf Valley and campaign contributions for the forthcoming Presidential Election. He found it hard to believe that these two issues could suddenly have become so inextricably linked.

"Do you know what plans they have for the complex when they get control of it?" the President now asked, probing for some ESA weakness.

"No, we don't," said the CIA chief, "certainly not in the short run, although ESA seems to be planning something spectacular for the long run."

"Have you any idea what that might be?" persisted the President.

The CIA chief hesitated, and then said: "We have some idea, but we don't have the full picture yet. It'll be about a week before we can get you a complete report."

"Can you tell us anything about these plans right now?" asked the President, impatient for facts that might help. He had confidence in his CIA chief though, and understood why he hated to deliver a report full of holes. He, the President, was the one who had to decide courses of action, and good policy decisions depended on sound and complete factual information.

The CIA chief hesitated again, thinking about just how much he could safely reveal.

"We think it's something to do with a new type of space vehicle or space installation connected with Mars," he said at last. "There's something very big and secret going on in a large facility ESA and Aerobus Aerospace have built in an isolated mountain peninsula at the southwest tip of Ireland. ESA has taken up almost the entire peninsula. Before ESA moved in, it was almost uninhabited, except for a few sheep farms. We have the complex under constant surveillance, but still don't know exactly what they're developing. It's a very cloudy place most of the time, which hampers our spy satellites. But we recently succeeded in penetrating the installation. We should know exactly what it's all about in less than a week."

"You mentioned Aerobus," said the Commerce Secretary, who had been hearing disquieting rumors of a commercial nature. "Are any other large companies involved? Any subsidiaries of U.S. corporations?"

Once more the CIA chief hesitated, and then decided to open up just a little more. "We've uncovered a quite large network of corporate involvement. The British Woomegong Group, and all the big European space companies. Our own Condor too, and the subsidiaries of our big Generals."

"Generals?" queried the Joint Chiefs Chairman. He recognized only the name Condor, which was Condor Copper Inc., the world's largest copper mining and refining concern, rivaled only by Woomegong, the second largest.

"The European subsidiaries," explained the CIA chief, "of our General Space, General Propulsion, Fusion General, General Software, and General Transport."

"But if Woomegong and Condor are involved, as well as all those space companies," said the Commerce Secretary, "that would imply that the E.U. is planning to mine copper on Mars in a big way."

"Unfortunately, we do not yet have the full picture," said the CIA man, anxious to put an end to this line of inquiry. "I can't reliably reveal any more right now. As I said, in about a week, I should be able to give the President a full report."

"But from what you have revealed so far," persisted the Commerce Secretary, who had just had confirmation of many of the rumors her staff had been hearing, "it would seem that U.S. multinationals are hedging their bets. Could it be they're intending to profit from the development of a Mars colony, even if it's the Europeans who get control of Leaf Valley and not us?"

"Probably," said the CIA chief, who actually knew this to be the truth.

The President stared at the CIA chief for a moment, feeling even more concerned. Then, seeing that everyone around the table had a question for the CIA Director, he decided to rescue him from any more probing questions by initiating the next phase of the meeting. He would get his CIA chief's report soon, and a complete picture.

This phase of the meeting then ran on for another hour, during which the situation as it was developing on Mars was analyzed and discussed in detail, but with no mention of the military's secret Mars mission.

*

In early afternoon, after a working lunch, served in the conference room, the President initiated the final phase of the meeting.

"Thank you all, for these insights," said the President. "Clearly the situation is very bad. The settlers in Leaf Valley are badly outnumbered, and they are unarmed, with no experience in military matters. I admit it looks hopeless. Nevertheless, we still must decide the best policy for how to deal with this situation going forward, especially what we release to the press. Has anyone any ideas?"

There was silence around the table. The President glanced at the NASA chief, the CIA Director, the Secretary of State, the Secretary of Defense, the Chairman, Vice-Chairman, and members of the Joint Chiefs of Staff, and the other members of his cabinet present. But none of them would look him in the eye.

It was obvious what they were thinking. The Leaf Valley region was now certain to fall into the hands of the countries of the European Union—the old colonial powers—who would soon have a thriving new colony to administer and grow, in a new New World. The European colony's future growth would be enhanced by the participation of the European subsidiaries of large U.S. multinationals, working under E.U. regulations, to the exclusion of the Government of the United States.

The United States, the greatest power on Earth, through the short-sightedness of its leadership, in never being willing to pay for what it took to do things properly on Mars, was now about to lose the greatest of Martian treasures, and suffer a galling humiliation in the process.

The thoughts of those around the table varied in detail, but in substance they were all the same. The extent to which the Government of the United States had been devoid of foresight and vision with respect to Mars, throughout the twenty-first century, was now clear to all of them.

Mars had sat there, waiting to be settled, for a cost well within the reach of their technologically advanced nation. Yet, for the first decades of the century, the country had done very little—just inexpensive robot missions—even in the face of pleas from the presidents of those Mars societies ardently promoting the human settlement of Mars.

Many of the leaders of those societies, from early in the century, had persuaded, argued, lobbied, and written books, all to no avail. They had grown old and died, frustrated, and broken in spirit. They had spent their lives watching huge national budget surpluses being dissipated uselessly, or so it seemed to them. These large surpluses inevitably accumulated in the business cycle upswings, but were all too often wasted, it seemed, either on politically motivated tax cuts, or on military adventures abroad, in vain attempts at creating a better world on Earth.

Meanwhile, a whole new world lay waiting to be created on Mars from the ground up. The huge surpluses would easily have paid for a well-equipped Mars mission, decades before the first under funded manned mission ever took place.

The early Mars mission proponents, out of sheer frustration, and against their better judgements, were then reduced to proposing very low-budget manned missions, in the hope of tempting the Congress to open its purse. They knew full well that such low-cost manned missions would be risky, likely to fail. But they were desperate, and in those barren years, anything was better than nothing. Nothing, however, was what they got.

Then, in the 2030s, when the U.S. Congress grudgingly approved a manned Mars mission, it under funded it by nearly a hundred billion dollars, forcing NASA to run risks. This was the ultimate cause of the disaster of 2038, when the mission's return rocket exploded at the landing site one morning, killing everyone except John Erway and Denise Lavoisier. And it was whispered, but never proven, that it was the then President himself who had committed the ultimate in mean-spiritedness toward Mars, by getting his CIA to sabotage the seventh lander of that mission, in order to save the cost of rescuing the two survivors. The seventh lander had been carrying food to the stranded and starving pair.

Finally, when the 2044 discovery of the Leaf Valley settlement revealed that survivors of the missions of 2038 had not died of starvation, but had built an enormously valuable resource in Leaf Valley, that mean spiritedness had continued. The nation had skimped yet again, by sending the low-cost 2046 mission to Mars, powered by a cheap, unsafe nuclear reactor, the direct cause of the resulting fiasco and failure. The folly of the national policy of neglect and meanness with respect to Mars over the century was now all too obvious.

Such were the thoughts of those around the table.

In a few weeks at most, they would know the outcome. If all went as expected, the United States would be humiliated, and would be left with only two options. Either pay the enormous price to build an entirely new settlement of its own, or, the unthinkable, take Leaf Valley back from the European Union by force, which could mean a hot war. They could only pray things did not go as expected in the coming weeks.

One thing the President knew for certain. If the E.U. mission succeeded, he would not see another four years in the White House. In the coming U.S. Presidential Election, he would get the blame for the U.S. humiliation, blame he knew he deserved. Sealing his fate would be the inevitable cutting off of campaign contributions and support from all those U.S. multinational corporations, whose European subsidiaries would participate in the E.U. development of the Leaf Valley region.

Business and industry representatives had relayed the message to the President, loud and clear. U.S. business wanted a piece of the action. It intended to participate profitably in the development of Mars, and preferred, even demanded, that it take place under U.S. auspices. But if the President could not deliver control of Leaf Valley and surrounding regions, then U.S. business, through its European subsidiaries, would become involved under E.U. auspices, and would support the sitting President's opponent in the coming Presidential Election.

Nevertheless, in spite of all the hard thinking, analysis and discussion directed at the question of control of Leaf Valley and surroundings, there was something those at the helm in both the U.S. and the E.U., and in their large corporations, were not taking into consideration. It was something only the settlers in Leaf Valley had learned to take carefully into account. It was Mars itself.

On Mars, nothing was for nothing. The small settlement on the Red Planet had succeeded only because the settlers had been willing to pay the enormous price the planet had demanded. The leaders of the U.S. and E.U., with their educated and industrious peoples, and powerful corporations, had not yet accepted that they too must pay the full price. Indeed, they were determined not to pay.

The leadership elites in both the U.S. and E.U. still had a lot to learn about settlements and colonies on Mars, for there was another possibility for the outcome of the current race to gain control of the Martian prize. It was an outcome that no one in the two Great Powers would ever have dreamed possible.

*

The meeting in the White House dragged on for another hour. But no satisfactory policies could be found. When it was obvious that they had done the best that could be done, the President made an unconvincing closing speech, and adjourned the meeting.

He made no further mention of the secret Mars mission run by the Air Force, due to arrive in just under four weeks. Everything there depended on secrecy and surprise, and on the settlers being able to hold out, a now unlikely eventuality, until the U.S. mission arrived. Even if the U.S. military mission did arrive in time to prevent the E.U. taking over Leaf Valley, everything would then depend on the settlers, fresh from a conflict with the E.U. mission, being positively receptive toward the U.S. mission, also a matter in doubt.

The only positive was that the President had learned the bitter lesson about the futility of skimping when it came to Mars missions. Ample funds for the military Mars project were coming from generous military appropriations, approved by a Congress unaware of exactly what lay behind the activities being funded. The Department of Defense had an annual budget some fifty times the size of NASA's. The technical reliability of the project was thus assured—it was its strategic relevance that was now very uncertain.

CHAPTER TWO

Face To Face

AT THE unique elbow of Kasei Valley, where its northward flow turns abruptly to the northeast, the valley floor broadens to form Elbow Plain, enclosed by high escarpment walls.

Eons ago, when the planet was warmer, and water was plentiful on the surface of Mars, it used to flow down Kasei Valley for over a thousand miles, cutting the valley ever deeper below the surrounding high plateau. At that time, Elbow Plain would have been a lake. Today, like most plains on Mars, it is dry, red, rolling, and rock-strewn, and studded with the eroded remains of small impact craters. At its widest point, Elbow Plain is about thirty miles across.

Near the middle of Elbow Plain there is a small hill, called Elbow Hill, about a mile across at the base. And on the northwestern side of this hill, there is a flat shelf, about one hundred feet above the level of the plain. On this shelf, a small group of human onlookers were awaiting the arrival of Richard Derk's mission.

There was more than just the waiting onlookers on the shelf, however, that Sunday afternoon in the early Martian fall. There was something installed there that would surprise and upset Richard Derk when he arrived—the refurbished habitat that his mission had contracted to occupy during its visit.

The onlookers were sitting in vehicles parked in front of this habitat, watching the sky. The lander was due any minute.

Its landing site lay down on the plain, a mile west of the shelf, which was not where Derk had originally expected it to be. Nor was it the kind of landing site he was expecting, for it was actually a partly man-made crater, or landing pit, built quite recently.

From their vantage point up on the shelf, the onlookers could see not only the landing pit below, but well beyond, as far as the distant orange escarpment wall at the boundary of Elbow Plain, some ten miles away to the west. The late afternoon sun was descending toward this distant boundary wall, in a pink sky that was almost completely clear, except for an occasional wispy, white ice cloud.

Looking in a direction northwest of the shelf, the waiting onlookers could easily make out an imposing gap in the boundary wall of the plain. This was Stem Gap, the entrance to the natural sanctuary of Leaf Valley. Richard Derk had originally expected to land inside this sheltered valley, and not in Elbow Plain, and he was still expecting to find his habitat installed there. Leaf Valley was also the site of the first human settlement on Mars, and the homes of the onlookers waiting in the vehicles parked on the shelf.

The onlookers were survivors of the disastrous Mars missions of 2038, ten years earlier. Their Mars vehicles had survived too, and that afternoon, they were parked facing the landing pit: two nuclear-powered rovers, side by side, and an open, battery-powered buggy. Each rover was a light blue color, with six large yellow wheels.

The low sun shone through the front windows of the two rovers, directly on the faces of the two adults inside. They both sat in the driver seats, wearing light blue body suits, in expectation of having to go outside soon in pressure suits, to greet their guests.

In the driver seat of the rover to the right sat an American, Dr. John Erway, a geologist and structural engineer, formerly of NASA. He was a trim, medium tall man, just past forty, with dark brown hair. He had an intelligent, confident face, with a slightly cleft chin.

His red-haired French wife, Dr. Denise Lavoisier, a geneticist and medical doctor, formerly of ESA, sat in the other rover. She was almost forty years old, and good looking, with a distinctive bell-shaped upper lip; her good looks were enhanced by a happy disposition, a healthy lifestyle, and a good nature. She had a penetrating and inquiring mind, and had a wondering look that softened her decisive and confident face.

Two small children were standing up in the front passenger seats of Denise's rover. They were a boy and a girl, twins, soon four years old, both red-haired like their mother, and born on Mars.

To Denise's left, Dr. Ichiro Sato, the elderly Zen master, wearing a white Mars pressure suit, sat in his open buggy, under its radiation protecting roof rack. Dr. Sato was both a physicist and master craftsman, and a former member of the Japanese Space Agency. He was seventy-six years old, in excellent health, the years still touching him but lightly. As a Zen master, he had practically eliminated his ego, and was a man of great internal peace. He was also the most present-minded of men, possessed of an awareness of his Martian environment that his two companions had never learned to match, and for which they had the greatest respect. He was perhaps also the very antithesis of Richard Derk, a man driven by a powerful ego.

Both John and Denise were searching the sky to the west through field glasses. Dr. Sato, holding a video camera, was ready to record the historic event—the arrival of the European Space Agency's first manned Mars mission, officially both a rescue mission and a mission of exploration and research.

Two Earth years earlier, in 2046, these three had negotiated a mission-stay agreement with ESA. This agreement gave the ESA mission temporary use of certain settler facilities during its stay on Mars, in return for shipping the settlers a relatively inexpensive range of items they could not make themselves. The agreement saved the ESA mission hundreds of billions of dollars, by eliminating the need to bring most of the necessities normally required for a manned mission to Mars.

An important clause in the lengthy agreement stipulated that the ESA mission would rescue the three, and return them safely to Earth, but only if they so desired.

This assurance had been especially welcome to both John and Denise, for they had grown very attached to Mars over the years. They were determined to remain on the planet, happily settled in their beautiful valley. As a result, there had been feelings of joy, and eager anticipation, at the prospect of this apparently friendly first visit from Earth.

Unfortunately, the initial feelings of joy had since changed to feelings of disappointment and anxiety. During the ESA mission's six-month long voyage to Mars, the settlers in Leaf Valley had become aware of evidence that pointed to treachery. They now had good reason to believe that the ESA mission's primary objective was to rescue them, whether they wanted it or not, get them off the planet, and seize control of the lands and resources they had worked so hard to develop.

The evidence had come from the CIA, anxious that the settlers resist the ESA mission, at least long enough for a secret U.S. military mission to get to Mars, and seize their lands instead. The three knew nothing of this secret U.S. mission. They had no definitive proof of ESA-mission treachery either, but they suspected the proof was hidden in the ESA lander's cargo hold.

Suddenly, the unmistakable fiery trail of an in-coming space vehicle appeared beyond the escarpment wall to the west. The twelve-man ESA lander was streaking across the sky, heat shield glowing, as it burned its way down through the upper atmosphere.

The onlookers on the shelf watched in awe, as four large colored parachutes suddenly blossomed in the pink sky, further slowing the machine's continuing descent.

Soon the lander was near enough for the onlookers to make out its shape. It was a squat cylinder, with six tall rocket cylinders equally spaced around it. There was a cluster of three rocket motors in each rocket cylinder.

The onlookers now witnessed the spectacular sight of the lander approaching the Martian surface, with its silvery metallic surfaces gleaming in the sunshine, and three of its six rocket motor clusters blasting long jets of flame downward, powerfully braking the final stage of the descent. Each rocket cluster sent out its flaming jet, with exactly the right thrust, and at exactly the right angle out from the vertical—precision thrust vectoring—to keep the craft stable in the critical landing phase.

Then, a hundred feet above the landing pit, the lander stopped for some twelve seconds, hovering, its rocket motors blasting.

"Why is it hovering like that?" Denise cried, puzzled and anxious. "Is something wrong?"

"No," answered Dr. Sato. "The flight engineer's doing it exactly as it needs to be done. He's burning up the excess fuel in the tanks, so that, when he lands, there'll be only a few seconds of fuel left. He'll burn that up on the ground. That way he'll have empty tanks and no chance of a fire or explosion after the landing."

"I see," Denise said, impressed, for a few moments reliving the memory of the explosion of the fully fueled return rocket that had destroyed the NASA mission, ten Earth years earlier, in 2038.

The Zen master's assessment was correct. As the lander dropped gently into the landing pit, guided in by radar beacons, the rocket engine exhausts threw up clouds of orange dust, lit up by the exhaust flames. The enflamed, billowing dust continued to shoot up above the rim of the pit for some two seconds after the machine disappeared from sight, in full view of the onlookers. Then the flames extinguished, and the billowing dust began to settle.

The settlers watching on the Elbow Hill shelf, with a grandstand view of the landing, and a long string of Martian firsts to their credit, were now also the first humans to have witnessed and recorded a manned landing on Mars.

But far more significant for the settlers would be the long-term impact of the landing of Captain Richard Derk's mission. It would change everything. The old days, when the settlers had the planet to themselves, were now gone, never to return. Before very long, another Mars would be born of the agony they would have to endure, and the searing pain of that birth would reach across space and affect millions of people on Earth, high and low, rich and poor.

*

The habitat intended to house Derk's mission lay directly behind the three vehicles on the shelf. It was a shiny metal building, long and telescope-like, on eight wheels. The long building, gleaming in the sunshine, sat in a north-south orientation, almost on the north side of the hill. It had three sections, getting larger from north to south—like a three-section telescope. Each section was semi-rectangular in cross-section. There was a quite large motor-controlled dish antenna on the roof of the northern section, for satellite communications, along with an assortment of wire antennas, for surface radio communications. The habitat's three sections could actually collapse into each other, just like a telescope. It was in the collapsed form that it had arrived on Mars nearly eleven years earlier.

This building was the original habitat from the now abandoned NASA landing site in southwest Kasei Valley. That landing site lay over one hundred miles to the south, further up the valley. The habitat had been badly punctured by flying rocks, in the rocket explosion of 2038 that had wrecked the landing site, and six NASA astronauts had died in it. It had lain derelict for eight Earth years, until NASA's attempted rescue mission in 2046.

Anticipating the arrival of visitors from NASA, the three had spent nearly a week towing the badly damaged building along the road from the old NASA landing site to Leaf Valley. There, they had repaired it, with the products of their industrial complex, the great craftsmanship and metal-working skills of Dr. Sato, and some essential high-tech components sent by NASA, to help pay for the visitors' anticipated stay.

The building was now as good as new, and although the expected NASA visitors had failed to show up in 2046, it would serve as the Mars habitat for the twelve visitors from the European Space Agency, who had just landed.

From where the three sat on the shelf in front of the long building, looking out over the plain below, they could see a road to their right. This road began at the shelf, and wound down along a ridge to the plain, in a northwesterly direction. The lone ridge protruded, spur like, from the north side of Elbow Hill, curving to the northwest as it gradually descended to the valley floor. When the winding ridge road reached the plain, it headed for the landing pit, about a half mile farther along. It went in a reasonably straight line, in a westerly direction, rolling a little, occasionally forced to wind around a few of the ever-present small craters on the valley floor.

The ridge road down from the shelf on Elbow Hill had a very shallow gradient, and the three had built it mostly by bulldozing rocks and stones to either side. The road had made it possible for them to tow the habitat up to the shelf, some four weeks earlier, using the combined power of the two rovers and Mars buggy.

After the three had refurbished the NASA habitat in 2046, it had sat unused in Leaf Valley for two Earth years, near the home of John and Denise. They had intended it to remain there permanently, as a hotel for guests. That was also where Richard Derk was expecting to find it when he arrived on Mars. However, the three had towed it out of Leaf Valley, to the shelf on Elbow Hill, after they had learned from the CIA that their ESA guests would likely arrive armed with automatic weapons that could fire nanocomputerized bullets.

When John and Denise had learned that the ESA mission was likely coming armed with such powerful weapons, their feelings of joy and eager anticipation had instantly changed to anger and shock, which soon gave way to disappointment and anxiety. When they had recovered enough to think rationally again, they had concluded that they had better take precautions, just in case the CIA had told them the truth. The three had agreed to a plan, and, as part of the plan, had decided to position the habitat—and the landing site for the ESA lander—well outside Leaf Valley, in Elbow Plain.

Since then, John had grown steadily more determined to do something to remove the risk posed by the weapons. He had already developed a plan, which he would set in motion very soon, but not before he had his guests safely settled into their habitat, for he was also convinced of the wisdom of strict compliance with the mission-stay agreement with ESA. He understood that any breach of contract on his part might justify open action against them on the part of Richard Derk. Part of John's overall strategy was to keep it difficult or impossible for Derk to so act, given that the public on Earth believed the ESA mission to be one of good will.

The long habitat was ready for their visitors. It lay on the Elbow Hill shelf in such a way that its south end was recessed into a dug-out shelter, excavated out of the north-facing slope of the hill.

Elbow Plain could experience ferocious three hundred mile an hour winds from the south on rare occasions, during certain types of dust storm. Such winds were extremely dangerous, especially if they were carrying a lot of fine dust, which they usually did. Recessing the refurbished habitat into the north-facing hillside ensured that it could not be blown over, even in the worst possible dust-storm wind from the south.

But John had done more. Beside each of its eight wheels, he had sunk a copper stake deep into the ground, and embedded it in concrete, and had attached the end of each wheel axle to a stake. This meant that the building could not be toppled by strong dust-storm winds from any other direction either.

The other major hazard to the building's occupants had also been taken care of—radiation storms. Before installing the habitat, John had excavated a radiation shelter under the habitat, with the shelter ceiling more than six feet underground. The roof of the habitat was also covered in white plastic sand bags, to protect those inside the building from the normal high daily levels of radiation on Mars.

Although John Erway had left Earth for Mars as a structural engineer with only limited experience, his years on Mars had caused him to develop unique skills. He had become a skilled Martian structural engineer, experienced in putting up and installing safe and secure Martian structures.

He was a person who did not run risks on Mars—if there was something he could do to prevent or avoid the hazard. His cautious policy had paid off. He, his wife, and Dr. Sato, had now survived for ten Earth years on the hostile planet, and had even prospered.

John had learned to treat the planet with the greatest respect. He was convinced that if the day ever came that they forgot this, the planet would strike back, without warning, and destroy them. He was determined not to give the planet the opportunity to do this, either to himself, his family, the Zen Master, or their guests, even guests like Richard Derk, who might be secretly bearing arms.

"Well," said John, lowering the field glasses, "looks like they made it down in one piece."

"I suppose we can be thankful for that," said Denise, looking at her husband through the side window to her right, the sun glinting on her red hair. "I've been imagining all kinds of nightmare scenarios—like a serious accident with a large number of injured, and the habitat turned into a hospital, with me in attendance night and day."

"If you'd said that a few years back, I'd have asked you to get a grip on that imagination of yours," said John, "but after what happened to our NASA visitors in forty-six, I can imagine just about anything going wrong."

"At least they all got home safely that time," said Denise, thinking back to the dramatic events of 2046, when the lives of ten NASA astronauts hung in the balance, after being forced to abandon ship in orbit around Mars.

"Well, now that they're down safe," she added, "what do you think? Has the plan got a chance?"

"Fifty-fifty maybe," said John, looking at the landing site.

"Is that all?" said Denise, staring at her husband.

John nodded. "Don't ask me to list everything I can see going wrong."

Denise looked very worried. "This is terrible. It should have been a day of celebration and joy. Instead it's been turned into a day of sadness and worry, and all because there could be guns on board that lander. I still don't want to believe it's true."

"It's still possible it's not true," said John. "Maybe the CIA lied. I don't think so though. My gut tells me the CIA told us the truth. Well, there's a good chance we'll know by tonight. If it's true, then we'll know for sure that our visitors' intentions are quite different from what they're supposed to be officially."

"Which means intentions quite different from what the ordinary people in Europe believe them to be too," said Denise, "and probably even different from what the scientists on the mission believe them to be as well."

"Very likely," agreed John. "Well, if the guns are on board, and our plan works this evening, Dr. Sato will have some destructive metal work to do tomorrow."

"A noble task," put in the Zen master.

"In some ways it's better to have to deal with a real enemy," said Denise philosophically, "instead of with people who act like your friends, and who make deals with you, but who might become an enemy in the future, if you refuse to do certain things."

"If we knew for sure they were an enemy, all of them out to kill us, it would certainly make things a lot easier," admitted John, "at least in the short run. They wouldn't survive twenty-four hours. I'd blow up the habitat tonight while they were asleep. But right now, such an act is unthinkable. At least six people on this mission are innocent scientists. But there are two, maybe three, whom I think would harm us, if we seriously got in the way of a successful mission, assuming the true intentions of this mission are what we think they are. It's those three I'm most worried about."

"You mean Richard Derk and Emma Grant, and maybe Karl Mannhardt," said Denise.

"Yes," said John. "Let's hope the CIA's wrong about them. I still can't believe Derk's as dangerous as the CIA makes out, although his guns are doing a good job of convincing me. Nanoguns even! We definitely have to do something about weapons like that."

"I agree," said Denise. "This lander reminds me of the story of the Trojan Horse. Anyway, isn't offense supposed to be the best defense?"

"Look, Denise, I'm an engineer, not a general," said John. "I can't guarantee anything."

He raised the field glasses again.

"Guess it's about time we drove down and said hello to our guests, and made our acquaintance with Captain Derk," said John, as he lowered the field glasses. "Dr. Sato, I think you should lead the way into the landing pit, as a man of peace."

The clouds of orange dust had disappeared from the landing pit, and the blunt silvery top of the main cylinder of the lander could now be seen sticking out of the pit.

*

Shortly after, a three-vehicle procession was winding along the road on top of the curving ridge, as it made its way down to the plain.

Once on the plain, the vehicles went quite fast along the road, and reached the exit to the landing pit in only a few minutes. Here they turned off the road, to the right, onto a trail that led down into the pit. The trail into the landing pit was simply a fairly steep reddish cutting down through the eroded rim of a former crater, which John had gouged deeper with the minicat.

The landing pit floor was about one hundred and fifty meters in diameter, covered in loose, red, sandy, and dusty soil. The pit floor was in bright sunshine, and was large enough for the three vehicles to park well away from the lander.

The lander looked enormous compared with the rovers. The main lander body was a vertical metal cylinder, about thirty-five feet tall, rather blunt at the top. A few parts of it glistened in the sunlight, but mostly it was covered in fine red dust, deposited only minutes earlier, as the clouds of dust settled.

A panel at the top had slid back just after the landing, and a dish antenna had emerged; it now pointed at an ESA communications satellite in stationary orbit to the south.

The main cylinder was some twenty-five feet in diameter, and had six rocket cylinders attached regularly around it. Each rocket cylinder was about six feet in diameter and about thirty feet long.

Higher up the hull of the lander, two rows of view ports circled the main cylinder, betraying two personnel floors. Each view port was between two rocket cylinders. Below the lower personnel floor, at the bottom of the lander, there was clearly room for a cargo floor.

The lander sat on landing pods at the end of six landing legs, each stretched out about twelve feet from the main cylinder, each pod in line with a view port, between a pair of rocket cylinders.

Each of the tall rocket cylinders had twenty feet of fuel and oxidizer tanks at the top, and then a cluster of three independent rocket motors at the bottom—six feet of rocket engine combustion chambers and four feet of flexible exhaust nozzles. A rocket cylinder could thus hold about twenty tons of fuel and oxidizer. Right now, all six sets of tanks were completely empty.

To refuel the lander, the three settlers would have to hand over about a hundred and twenty tons of fuel and oxidizer, which they had manufactured in their industrial complex—in accordance with their mission-stay agreement with ESA. At launch, the six full tanks would weigh far more than the empty lander.

The bottom floor of the three-floor lander, the cargo floor, was only about three feet above the floor of the landing pit. Barely a minute after the three vehicles entered the pit, a panel in the wall of this cargo floor slid open, to reveal a cavity. In this cavity was a folded staircase in front of an airlock door.

Suddenly, the metal staircase arched out, five-feet long, and descended to touch the ground beside one of the landing legs. The airlock was close enough to the ground to permit cargo containers to be unloaded easily.

John had driven his rover quite close to the lander, facing the airlock door, stopping only about forty feet away. He was now examining the door intently, and committing the details to memory. He was soon satisfied that the airlock-door control buttons lay behind a small sliding panel door, to the right of the airlock.

These details memorized, John reversed the rover a little. Then he got up from the driver's seat, walked back through the rover to the pressure suit closet, and began putting on his pressure suit. Denise, in the other rover, was also preparing for going outside. John's action in driving close to the lander, to study the lander's airlock-door controls, had not gone unnoticed, however.

Five minutes later, the two were outside, standing in front of John's rover. Denise stood at John's right, between him and Dr. Sato, whose video camera was recording the proceedings. All three wore radiation protection umbrellas, as they usually did, when outside during daylight hours. The two children remained in Denise's rover, under its front roof overhang, sandbagged for radiation protection. They were looking on, eyes wide open with curiosity.

They did not have to wait long. In a few minutes, the outer airlock door opened. A figure in a light green pressure suit emerged, and backed slowly down the stair, holding onto the stair's hand rails. Once the figure was out of the airlock, the outer airlock door closed again. As the figure reached the ground, the airlock door opened again, and another figure appeared, and began to back down the stair.

It quickly became clear that the first figure was a man. He waved to the waiting three, then turned around to watch the second figure descend. This one, a woman with dark blond hair, carried a video camera, suspended from a strap around her neck. A short time later, all twelve crew members were standing in a small crowd at the base of the stair. None of them wore radiation umbrellas.

While the woman with the video camera recorded events, transmitted live to Mission Control via the ESA satellite, the one who had come out first then walked over to the waiting three, bowed slightly, and spoke. He was a fairly tall, lean and handsome man, about forty-five years old, with a confident, military bearing. He had a mildly protruding chin, cold blue eyes, and close cut, thinning, slightly waved, sandy hair.

"I'm Captain Richard Derk, the commander of this good-will mission of exploration, research and rescue," he said, smiling, in a clear, upper-class English accent. "We thank God for the safe journey that has allowed us to stand before you on this historic day. We're happy to see that you all look well. We've been very worried about you."

He paused, eyes searching John's face, a face that expressed a solid confidence, and one that did not flinch under Derk's shrewd, penetrating gaze.

Probably anyone other than Derk would have been somewhat awed by the moment, and would have said something that reflected the deepest and truest feelings of humanity. Words like: We are honored to have the privilege to stand before you; in the whole history of mankind, no living persons have ever been held in greater esteem on Earth, than you three.

But Derk said no such thing. He merely continued with: "Let us all shake hands, and introduce ourselves." The high esteem in which the three were generally held on Earth would not last much longer—Derk intended to see to that.

"We are honored by your visit, and thank you for your concern," said John politely, but without any obvious expression of joy in his face—he was wondering where the guns were hidden. "We congratulate you on a successful voyage and landing. We hope you'll be happy with the arrangements we've made for you, and wish you success in your exploration and research activities." He tactfully ignored Derk's mention of a rescue. There was no point starting an argument in the first ten minutes.

"Thank you," said Captain Derk.

Then, one by one, the twelve filed past the three, shaking their hands and introducing themselves. As they filed past, each one gave his or her name, the European country represented, and function on the mission. In all, there were two from Germany, three from Britain, two from France, one from Austria, one from Italy, one from Spain, one from Sweden, and one from Ireland.

Captain Derk was first. He was followed by Jurgen Eindorf and Emma Grant, the mission's two first officers.

Jurgen Eindorf, chief flight engineer, from Germany, was a medium tall man, quite thin, about forty, with short, straight, dark fair hair, and blue eyes, and a plain, but very intelligent, thoughtful face. Emma Grant, communications specialist, was the one holding the camera. She had short, straight fair hair, green eyes, and a tight-lipped, sharp face, which gave her a determined, ruthless look.

After that came Jose Montoya, a determined-looking field engineer, and also the second flight engineer, from Spain. He did not mention that he was also the senior military man on the mission, after Derk, and would be in charge of any operations in the field of a military nature.

Five of the twelve were women. As well as Emma Grant, from England, the one with the camera, there was Monique Montpellier from France, Dr. Ursula Schneider from Austria, Dr. Astrid Larsson, from Sweden, and Dr. Sheila Bell, from Ireland.

Sheila Bell was a rather strongly-built woman, about thirty, quite tall, with short, wavy, brown hair, matching light brown eyes, and a broad, smiling face. She was the mission's doctor and dentist, but also a biologist. When she shook hands with Denise, there was a longer exchange.

"Sheila Bell, at your service," said the big-boned Irishwoman with a broad smile, and a pronounced Irish accent, "and a very good day to you."

"Welcome to Mars," said Denise, smiling in return. "You're just the person I need to see. As soon as you're settled in, I need to make a dental appointment. I've taught my husband to do minor dental work, but I think I need a professional."

"Well now," said Dr. Bell, still smiling, "we can manage a thing like that. They brought me along to keep everybody healthy and well, and I intend to do just that. Maybe tomorrow or the next day, as soon as I get organized. Now would you be in any pain?"

"No, not at the moment," said Denise. "But I've been having some problems. Thank you for your concern."

Then Captain Derk approached the three again, with Emma Grant standing close by, video recording, and said to John: "The radar beacons you set up worked perfectly, although we weren't expecting to land in a hole in the ground. I must say you took me by surprise there, old chap."

"We thought you should land here in Elbow Plain," said John, "so you could have more privacy, without us all getting in the way of one another. So to be on the safe side, just in case a dust storm should blow up, it was best to use a recent crater as a landing site. We just dug it out a bit more. There's no way a strong wind could topple your lander down here."

"Privacy?" queried Captain Derk, eyebrows raised. "Does that mean we're not going to be staying in Leaf Valley?"

"That's right," said John. "You've a habitat with a view, on a hillside, but only about a mile from here—within walking distance."

"I see. That is a surprise, old chap," said the Captain, smiling, and suppressing the feeling of anger that arose within him. He had not been expecting this, but understood the strategic and logistical implications immediately.

"Mars is full of surprises," said John, also forcing a smile. He felt uncomfortable in the presence of this man. "Now I've got another surprise for you. I'm going to recommend that you all take the one-mile hike to the habitat—there's a road all the way. If you unload your personal gear into these trailers, we'll take it up to the habitat for you."

"You really think a hike's necessary?"

It was Denise who answered. "Speaking professionally," she said, "it's a good thing to do, after being cooped up in a spacecraft for six months. It'll get you used to walking in Martian gravity without any risk. Just don't leave the road. You're not used to Mars, or walking in a pressure suit in its lower gravity. You can easily stumble, and a stumble against a sharp rock can be fatal. A good hike will also give you a chance to look around, and an appetite for supper. Yes, I strongly recommend it. Oh, by the way, we advise only sanitary conversation when out walking or driving on Mars—no talking unless it's about some aspect of the local terrain that might be dangerous. If you have to talk about something interesting, stop first. Another thing, although you're not intending to stay long, I would recommend you all wear radiation protection umbrellas while outside. You'll find several boxes of them in a storage cubicle at the habitat, from both ESA and NASA."

There was silence, while Derk considered this. He did not like to appear to be taking orders. On the other hand, Denise was a doctor, and far more knowledgeable about Mars than either him or any of his crew. He decided he would probably look worse if he ignored her professional medical advice, especially if things were to go wrong later as a result.

Captain Derk turned to his crew. "You all heard the lady. She's a doctor, and I'm accepting her professional advice. We're going to have a hike before we eat. Let's get our gear unloaded."

"And I think I should unload my dental case too," said Sheila Bell. "I was going to leave it until I needed it, but it seems I'm going to need it right away."

Some twenty minutes later, there was a heap of gray plastic belongings containers in each of the trailers, two for each mission member, and the extra dental container.

Then Captain Derk ordered his crew to fall in three deep, and the procession began to make its way up the cutting at a brisk pace. Captain Derk, Emma Grant, and Jurgen Eindorf led the crew, walking behind the last rover.

*

Soon they were marching along the winding road across the rolling, red, rock-strewn Elbow Plain to the habitat. It was now after five o'clock, and the sun was not that far above the escarpment wall behind them to the west.

The gleaming habitat was clearly visible, about a mile away, nestled on the side of Elbow Hill, which itself glowed orange red in the light of the evening sun. As the crew walked along, behind the rovers, their heads turned this way and that, drinking in the red landscape of Mars.

Soon they were walking on the stretch of road along the ridge leading up to the shelf and the habitat. On this stretch, they got an even better view of their surroundings. The height enabled them to better make out the many small craters, most of them with well-eroded rims, on the floor of Elbow Plain.

Twenty-five minutes after leaving the landing pit, all fifteen of them stood in the shadow of the east side of the habitat, in front of the building's airlock door. The habitat airlock was in the middle section of the long, three-section building, at the south end of its east wall.

"Well," said John to Captain Derk, "did you all enjoy your first hike on Mars?"

"I'm sure we all did," said Derk. "It was just what the doctor ordered."

At this point, the magnificence of Mars, as well as John's obvious straightforwardness, caused Derk to be less on the defensive for a moment, and he expressed his true feelings.

"I think we're all somewhat overwhelmed by this place," added Derk. "It's simply magnificent." As he said this he put out his right hand, and swept it around him as he turned, gazing at the view across the plain to the southeastern escarpment wall of the valley.

"Yes, it is overwhelming," agreed John. "It takes a few days to get used to it, although we've never stopped being overwhelmed by it. But business first. I think we should show you around the habitat now. Then we'll get out of your way, and leave you to assign the space as you think fit. Dr. Sato also has some video of the landing. You'll probably want to send it to Mission Control. He'll copy it into one of the habitat's computers for you while I'm showing you around."

Soon, John, Dr. Sato, Captain Derk, Emma Grant, Jurgen Eindorf, and Jose Montoya had negotiated the habitat's airlock and were inside, while the others unloaded the gear. The airlock, about five feet by four, could easily take two at a time, and John and Jose Montoya went in last. They did not take off their pressure suits inside—each of them just removed the helmet, and left it dangling on the short air tube connecting it to the suit's backpack.

Denise did not go inside immediately, but talked again to Sheila Bell for a few minutes, as she helped her unload her dental and belongings containers from a rover trailer. Denise was determined to get her dental appointment as soon as possible.

*

The habitat had fourteen personnel cubicles, a storage cubicle, a combined kitchen and eating area, a meeting room, two washrooms with laundry facilities, a small laboratory, a workshop, a computer and communications room, pressure suit closets, and a surgery cubicle, all carefully packed into its eighteen hundred square feet. The visitors were already familiar with the habitat layout. They had studied it on their computers during the long journey to Mars.

A very great deal of thought had gone into the design of the long habitat, which was one hundred and twenty feet long and averaged fifteen feet wide. It lay in a north-south orientation, and had three connected sections, each forty feet long.

It's internal layout was remarkably simple.

The airlock was in the central section, at the south end on the east side. This central section contained only two rooms, the smaller airlock room at the south end, some fourteen feet long, and the kitchen/eating room at the north end, nearly twice as long.

In the airlock room, the airlock was in the southeast corner. Directly opposite, in the southwest corner, was a large closet, almost a small room, four feet deep by five wide. This was the facilities room, from which all habitat facilities could be controlled. The remainder of the two outside walls of the airlock room were taken up by pressure suit closets. The airlock room had no windows, but the general color was light orange—no doubt to remind the building's inhabitant, about to go outside, that outside was very different.

To get into the adjacent kitchen/eating room, or living room, from the airlock room, you entered through a doorway in the dividing wall; the doorway was not in the center, but nearer the east side of the habitat. The living room was some twenty-six feet long, and had windows on both sides. It was bright and cheerful, and generally a blue-gray color.

Along the west wall were the kitchen facilities, with red counter tops, and three small windows in the wall above. Sticking out about six feet from the opposite east wall were two blue-topped dining tables with chairs, and at the head of each table was a small window. Denise had placed a small green plant in a pot on each table.

There was an entrance from this living area into the main hallway of the northern section—the command section.

The command section was split in two by a nearly three-foot wide hallway running the length of the section. As you entered the hallway, the communications room, ten feet long, lay to the left, and thus along the habitat's west wall. The meeting room, some fifteen feet long, lay to the right of the hallway, and along the east wall. In this room, twelve persons could sit comfortably around a long table, which had a small potted plant at its center.

Next along the hallway, on the left side, came a washroom and laundry room, adjacent to the communications room. Then came small cubicles, each about six feet long, with four on each side of the hallway. A cubicle could be an astronaut's room or a storage room. The cubicle adjacent to the meeting room was a foot longer than the others, and was intended for the habitat commander. Each cubicle had a small window.

At the south end of the central section there was an entrance from the airlock room into the main hallway of the southern section—the science section.

Like the command section, the science section was split in two by a hallway running the length of the section. On entering the hallway from the airlock room, there was a small workshop immediately on the left, along the east wall, ten feet long. Along the opposite west wall was a fifteen-foot long laboratory. Next to the lab came a washroom and laundry room. The remainder of the space, on either side of the hallway, was taken up by cubicles, three on the west side and five on the east side. The cubicle beside the workshop, on the east side, was the habitat's surgery. Each of the cubicles had a small window.

All in all, the habitat had fifteen cubicles to serve either as rooms for astronauts or storage rooms. It was designed to take fourteen people. All the thin aluminum walls inside were modularized, and had been shipped to Mars in boxes inside the habitat.

There had been no lab or workshop in the original habitat, as landed by NASA, just extra cubicles and storage space. These new facilities had been structured into it during the refurbishing in Leaf Valley, at the request of NASA.

*

As Captain Derk and Jose Montoya, accompanied by John, inspected the sections in the long building, Denise helped Sheila Bell bring her dental container to the habitat surgery in the science section, just round the corner from the airlock room.

Meanwhile, Emma Grant, Jurgen Eindorf, and Dr. Sato had walked through the living area to the communications room, in the command section. Almost at once, they began transferring a copy of Dr. Sato's video of the landing to the main communications computer's video library. This would make it possible to transmit a copy to Mission Control in Toulouse.

Dr. Sato and Jurgen Eindorf talked easily together, and it was not long before both the flight engineer and Emma Grant, the mission's communications specialist, had a pretty clear idea of the communications and computer facilities available at the habitat.

Emma Grant said very little, but listened intently as the Zen master explained the system, pretending in her mind that she was responsible for this mission. Emma was a quiet but very ambitious woman in her early thirties, intent on command one day. Although technical communications and public relations were Emma Grant's official mission specialization, she had Special Forces training and experience that would make her indispensable for military operations. She accepted that Captain Derk would require her to function under the command of the more field hardened and experienced Jose

Montoya during such field operations. This did irk her somewhat, since she was Jose's senior in the official mission command structure. Nevertheless, she was unquestioningly loyal to Derk, on whose good offices her advancement depended.

Although most people would have been overawed at the prospect of setting foot on Mars, as most of those on the mission were, especially the scientists and engineers, Emma Grant cared nothing for Mars. To her it was just another place, and an inconvenient place too, where you could not breathe the air. Derk had selected her for her competence and loyalty, not for her interest in Mars.

Emma was quick to demonstrate her mastery of the communications system. It took her only five minutes to run a check on the habitat's dish antenna, and lock it on to the stationary ESA communications satellite in the southern sky. A few minutes later, she had completed sending Dr. Sato's video recordings of the landing to Mission Control in Toulouse, where it was the middle of the night. It would be some fifteen minutes, at least, before they got a reply.

Just then, John, Richard Derk, and Jose Montoya came back from their tour, and stood at the communications room entrance.

"Well, I'm sure you all have a lot to do," said John. "I think we should leave you to get settled in and get yourselves organized. You'll no doubt want to get your two buggies assembled as soon as possible too, and your other cargo unloaded. I assume you've got the buggies in the lander's cargo bay. By the way, if you find you're missing some buggy parts, Dr. Sato may be able to make them for you in his workshop."

"We do indeed have the buggies in the cargo bay," confirmed Jurgen Eindorf, speaking very correct English, with a pronounced German accent. "Two three-seater buggies, each with eight-hour batteries and a satellite link. There are no parts missing. I checked the crate contents myself before we left. Nothing was forgotten. I expect we will be down in the landing pit tomorrow, to get them assembled." He looked at Derk for confirmation.

"Tomorrow morning, first thing," said Derk, as they walked back through the living area toward the airlock room, which had now filled up with the other members of the mission.

"Good," said John. "And we leave you our Mars buggy for your use during your stay too, as we agreed with ESA. We've added four collapsible copper seats with rubber seat cushions to the trailer, as you've probably noticed. So it'll carry six of you plus some gear. It's good for about eight hours on the new batteries ESA sent us, but probably not when it's carrying six people. Don't forget to plug it into the power plant outside. If you want to go a long way in those eight hours, stick to the valley roads, which I advise you to do anyway in the beginning. Our buggy's got no satellite communications dish, unfortunately, so it's not good for going a long way alone. I guess that's it. You've got plenty of water and food in the kitchen—nearly all vegetarian I'm afraid, but that's Martian food."

"Thank you," said Captain Derk, impressed at how everything necessary for their stay had been taken care of, something he had no intention of ever admitting to. He wondered if John knew more than he was letting on, for if he did, John betrayed no sign of it. On the surface, at least, John was the perfect host, seeing to the needs of his guests.

The Captain then said: "We certainly have no cause for complaint, as far as the technical facilities are concerned. NASA did a good job in sending up what it took to get this habitat operational again. As for the vegetarian food, each of us has a few dozen cans of meat, fish and cheese in the gear, to give us some variety, in case we get tired of the rice and beans. And you've done everything ESA asked you to do...." It was on the tip of his tongue to add 'and you've done it well', but he caught himself just in time. He would not be seen to praise the three in front of any of his crew, even for work that organizations on Earth had asked for and paid for, and he would certainly never praise anything that had resulted from the personal initiative of the three on Mars.

It was Denise who responded. She and Sheila Bell, returning from the surgery in the adjacent science section, had entered the airlock room at about the same time as the others, coming from the communications room in the command section.

"Thank you," she said politely, a little taken aback at how he directed praise everywhere except at them, considering the effort the three had expended on behalf of their visitors. "We thought we should leave you alone tomorrow, to give you a chance to get your buggies assembled, and look around a bit for yourselves too. We would be happy to have you and your two first officers to dinner at our home the following evening—Tuesday evening, arriving about five, if that's convenient."

Captain Derk's eyes opened wide. Of course it's convenient, he thought, and you three are going to be on that lander out of here very soon. This spectacular place, and everything in it, is to come under my control. "We'd be delighted," he answered. "Five o'clock, you say?"

"Yes, five o'clock. That'll give us time to show you around before dinner," said John. "After the dinner, we can discuss getting your lander refueled."

"I take it we just follow the road through Stem Gap and up Leaf Valley," said Derk.

"Yes," said John. "You can't miss us. It's just under an hour's drive from here. Oh, I almost forgot, we have rules of the road, which we ask you to follow. They're in the computer, along with the other safety tips. There's not a lot of traffic, but an accident is still possible if you don't follow the rules, which we found out once—the hard way. You drive and pass on the right. There's a speed limit too—thirty miles an hour by day, twenty by night. Most of the time the roads wind around old craters too much for it to be safe to go much faster. If you miss a bend and go off the road at high speed the rocks will wreck your axle housings pretty quick. If you're in a buggy, they'll probably tear your suit and kill you as well."

"We promise to look up the rules and follow them," said the Captain, "and to take care of your buggy. Jurgen will be our chief Mars buggy engineer."

"Good." John then looked at Jurgen Eindorf. "If you do anything near as good a job with our Mars buggy as you did getting the lander down safely, we can have no cause for complaint."

John turned back to look at Derk. "One other thing. Don't ask me to explain why just now. But do not leave the road going through Stem Gap, either in a buggy or on foot. It's very dangerous."

"We'll remember that," said Derk, puzzled. He wondered why, but could not guess that John, as part of his precautionary efforts, had hidden some hazards of a military defensive nature at Stem Gap, just in case.

Then Denise turned to Sheila Bell, who had been standing in the background listening. "We'll have you and some of the others to dinner another evening," she said. "But I'll be seeing you tomorrow morning anyway, for my dental work, if Captain Derk has no objections."

"I've agreed to treat Dr. Lavoisier in the surgery tomorrow morning, at nine thirty," explained Dr. Bell to Derk, "if I'm not needed for anything else."

Derk thought for a moment. "That'll be all right," he said. "It'll help you get your surgery set up and working properly. I presume Dr. Lavoiser is very familiar with it."

"Yes, I am," said Denise, "although I doubt if Dr. Bell needs much help."

John turned to Captain Derk: "Well, we're off home. It's supper time. We'll see you Tuesday evening. Enjoy the habitat, and Kasei Valley. You can watch your first Mars sunset shortly—about six twenty-five. Sunrise about six fifteen." He paused here, and then looked at Derk, with a very firm expression on his face. "And one last thing," he said. "We would also ask you to respect our private property in Leaf Valley. We would prefer if you came into the valley only on invitation."

Captain Derk had the greatest difficulty keeping control of himself at this last request. But he could not think of an appropriate answer on the spot, and just nodded. Later he thought: Private property. So that's how they see it. Well, it'll be their turn for a few surprises soon.

CHAPTER THREE

Preemptive Strike

JOHN AND Denise, their eyes accustomed to the darkness, could just make out the valley floor ahead, and the distant silhouette of Elbow Hill against the star-filled sky.

Earlier that evening, after returning home from greeting their guests, they had eaten a hasty meal, and had set out in a rover again, headed for Stem Gap. Dr. Sato, who had grave reservations about what they were planning to do, had agreed to stay home with the two children.

It was now just before nine in the evening, and the two were sitting in the rover on the main road from Stem Gap, about two miles from the ESA landing site. They had very carefully crawled the nearly eight miles from Stem Gap in the dark, with no headlights on, and only the stars to see by.

There were no lights on in the parked rover, and John was looking through field glasses at the habitat, three miles away on the side of Elbow Hill. Nearly all its windows were lit up.

"Let's hope Derk's crew are tired and go to bed early," said Denise. "The sooner we get this over with the better. I never thought that one day I'd have a career as a cat burglar."

"If it's any consolation," said John, "I'm the burglar. You're just the look-out."

"All right," said Denise. "I've a new career as an accessory to burglary."

"There's no sign of them going to bed early," said John, putting down the field glasses. "Heaven only knows what time they were on before they came down. Maybe they won't get sleepy till something like three in the morning."

"On the other hand," pointed out Denise, "if Derk's as competent a military man as the CIA thinks he is, he'll have had his crew on Kasei Valley time well before they landed."

"That's what I figure too," said John. "But if he's that competent, and if the lander really does have weapons on board, then he could be planning a midnight visit to the lander too. If so, his soldier boys will have to sneak out while the others are asleep. His six scientists don't know the lander has weapons on board. He'll have to get them out of the lander and back to the habitat, without them knowing about it."

"How are they going to keep them concealed in the habitat?"

"I don't know, but I'm sure it's been carefully thought out," said John. "My best guess is that they'll keep them in a storage cubicle, disguised as something else. They're military people, and won't be happy unless they have their guns close by. They'll also want to keep them secret as long as possible. Bringing them to Mars violates an important international treaty on Earth."

"Have you any idea how they're intending to use them?" asked Denise.

"No, afraid not," said John. "It's probably impossible to predict their plans in any detail. Maybe they've some cunning scheme we don't expect. Maybe they don't even have a plan yet. Don't forget they were expecting to find their habitat right next door to us, in Leaf Valley. Finding it out here, in the middle of Elbow Plain, must have put a few crinkles in any plans they'd already made."

"But you think they're really intending to use those guns against us?"

"I'm sure they'd prefer not to have to," said John. "But I'm also sure they'll want them handy, in case they run into a situation where they feel they've no other options."

"But sooner or later the scientists on the mission will find out about the guns," said Denise thoughtfully. "How's he going to deal with that?"

"I'll bet they've that all thought out too," said John. "Maybe some excuse to do with weapons research."

At that the conversation ceased.

Denise was very worried—more than that, nearly sick with worry. For ten years, she had been without any feeling for Earth, neither like nor dislike. She just loved Mars, and everything about it, especially her home and family, and the sheer magnificence of the Leaf Valley region. She was determined never to leave Mars, not without a fight at any rate. But now she was beginning to develop a dislike for Earth and the aggressive ways of its peoples, the product perhaps of both the CIA's attempt to kill them ten years earlier, and now the probable attempt of the E.U. mission, disguised as a friendly good-will mission, to force them off the planet at gunpoint, or perhaps arrange for them to have an accident if they refused to go.

Actually, Denise was wrong about that last possibility, for Derk had no such plans. He did have plans, but Denise, a forgiving person who had never deliberately harmed anyone in her life, could have no concept of the devilry Derk was capable of.

Her husband did not have exactly the same feelings as his wife. He still harbored a liking and a deep respect for the blue world, especially for its technological genius. He also still admired his own country, the United States. He had grown to love Mars though, and his home in Leaf Valley. He especially loved and respected his wife, and loved his children. He knew Denise would never willingly leave Mars. And if she would not, he could not, for he understood only too well that he could not live without her.

Deep inside, Denise was close to feeling despair. It did look hopeless. Still, she had great faith in her husband. She knew he could manage risk better than just about anybody, and, she felt certain, better than any of the twelve in the habitat three miles away. She knew that if there was any hope, it had to be with her husband.

Perhaps it was just as well at that point that she had not grasped that although her husband might be a brilliant engineer, in matters of strategy he was no match for Captain Richard Derk. She would get a foretaste of that before the evening was out.

*

Meanwhile, at the habitat, Derk was busy with an interview video, which Emma would send to Mission Control that evening, for release to the European media.

In the first part, Emma Grant interviewed each of the crew members in their cubicles, while Jurgen Eindorf held the camera.

In the second part there was an interview with Derk, sitting in the communications room, surrounded by the complex electronic gear, with Emma Grant posing questions sent up by journalists on Earth, along with a few extra questions added by Derk. The camera now sat on a table, with Derk and Emma Grant in front of it. Jurgen Eindorf was not present.

In the images, both Emma and Derk looked tidy, professional and friendly. They wore clean, light brown ESA shirts and pants, and both appeared smiling and good humored during most of the interview. Near the end of the interview, the questions turned to how the trio on Mars had received them.

"And now," said Emma, speaking with a southern English accent, "perhaps you could tell us if you think the three were happy at our safe landing, and at the prospect of being rescued."

This question seemed to pain Derk. His smile vanished, and he adopted a more somber and saddened expression.

"I don't think they were at all," said Derk.

"Why do you say that?"

"Just an impression, that's all," said Derk, his face now in a frown. He was apparently thinking deeply. "But it's not for me to say anything negative about these three, given the deservedly high esteem in which they are held by everyone on Earth."

"Didn't they express any gratitude for the effort and expense needed to get this rescue mission to Mars—entirely on their behalf?"

"No, I'm afraid not," said Derk.

"Didn't they understand that the taxpayers of Europe could well have spent the funds for the mission on their own needs, instead, or on the needs of the poor and disadvantaged?"

"No, there was no sign of that," said Derk.

"Didn't they appear to appreciate that twelve men and women had put their lives at risk to rescue them?"

Derk's brow furrowed again, and he managed to appear very sad at the same time, even hurt. Then he said: "That's the hardest thing to...." Then he forced a smile. "No, they did not, but perhaps they've just been isolated too long."

"So you think the isolation may have affected their minds?"

Derk hesitated, frowning. Then he smiled weakly: "Perhaps, although it would be wrong of me to say that right now."

"Can you give us an example of any behavior you found strange? I'm sure the psychologists on Earth will be very interested. After all these three are unique—they've been alone on Mars for ten years."

"Well," said Derk. "There's one thing. They've a crackpot notion that they own Leaf Valley. They've asked us not to come in without permission. Of course that's preposterous—a sixteen mile long valley owned by three people, or just two people! And Mars, as every sane person understands, belongs to the people of Earth, as represented at the United Nations and the Mars Office."

"Any other examples?"

"Actually, there is," said Derk. "I was very surprised to discover that Denise Lavoisier seems to be jealous of Sheila Bell. It was very obvious from her behavior today, as you noticed yourself."

"Yes, I did notice that," confirmed Emma, frowning. "Do you have any idea what could be causing the jealousy?"

"I know it's hard to believe, but I think she may be upset that there's another doctor on Mars, and a very competent one too, who could detract from her prestige, and a doctor that's very popular everywhere in Europe as well. Sheila Bell certainly doesn't think she's better than everyone else. Of course, Sheila is so good natured she would never believe anyone could be jealous of her. And I think John Erway may be jealous of Claude Bertrand too—for all the fame and acclaim Claude has gotten around the world for his civil engineering successes."

"So you think Denise and John may have become somewhat delusional, suffering from an excess of pride?"

"It could well be," said Derk.

"Do you believe the three will come round in time, and see things more normally, as they mix more with the mission members?"

"Yes, yes," said Derk, "I'm sure they will. At least I hope so." But he looked worried as he said this.

"One final question," said Emma, "What are your exploration plans for the mission tomorrow?"

"We'll be getting our Mars buggies unloaded and operational first thing," said Derk, his cheerful and optimistic expression from earlier in the interview back again. "In the afternoon, after we've tested them out, I'm intending to have the three buggies go out on a trip down Kasei Valley, to the east. They'll be on a road the whole way, so there won't be any risk. It's just a routine trip to help us get acclimatized. The two buggies we brought with us each have an array of small satellite communications dishes, so that they can stay in touch with the habitat via our communications satellite, even when the buggies are in motion. We want to test that out too. As you know, Emma, normal radio communications on the surface of Mars is line of sight. That means you can't communicate very far with surface radio, because the high escarpments and mesas around her would block out the signal. But with the dish arrays on our buggies linked to the satellite, we'll always be in contact with base, and even with Mission Control, no matter how far away we are, or how rugged the terrain. That's a big safety feature.

"The following day, late in the afternoon, we'll both be driving into Leaf Valley, along with Jurgen, to inspect the facilities there. We hope to make use of them when the rescue is complete. There isn't space on the lander for us all to go back to Earth in a few weeks. Some of us will have to stay on until the next opposition."

"Thank you," concluded Emma. Then turning directly to the camera, she smiled and said. "This is Emma Grant signing off, on this Martian Sunday evening, wishing good morning to all of you, from the European Space Agency's mission habitat in Elbow Plain on the Red Planet. God Bless."

Jurgen Eindorf, had he still been present, would not have been happy about this first interview with Derk on Mars. As an engineer, he preferred reality and the control of it, and disliked any distortion of it. In contrast, Derk considered the most important reality to be in people's minds, something he could and would manipulate, to his own ends. Emma was not in the least troubled by the deliberate distortions in the interview.

*

At 10:15 John put down his field glasses. "All lights out except one," he said. "Looks like you were right. They're on Kasei Valley time. We should be able to get moving soon. Let's go a mile closer."

The rover crawled forward in the darkness, for about fifteen minutes, at a speed of only a few miles an hour, as John and Denise watched for the road, with only starlight to guide them. Patches of ice mist had formed here and there.

"That wasn't much fun," said Denise, after they had stopped, now only about a mile from the lander. They were still on the main road leading south along Kasei Valley, but at the junction with the short side road up to Elbow Hill. This side road led past the landing site, and then directly up to the habitat.

"At least there was no risk to the rover," said John. "The worst we could have done was go off the road for a bit, and over a few rocks at very low speed. This machine can easily manage that." He looked out toward the habitat as he spoke. The remaining light was still on. "Come on," he muttered impatiently. "Go to sleep."

Five minutes later, the last light went out.

"Action stations," said John, as he turned into the road that led past the landing site, and then continued the slow crawl, with no lights on.

Another fifteen minutes later, they turned to the left, off the road. In less than a minute, the rover stopped at the top of the cutting through the crater rim, on the trail down to the landing pit. Denise was already beside the airlock door, backpack on.

"Good luck, John," she said. She put on her helmet and went through the airlock, outdoors field glasses dangling from her neck. A minute later, she was standing on the trail, as the rover carried on down the cutting, vanishing in the darkness.

She carefully made her way off the trail onto the rock and boulder covered terrain of Mars. This was a dangerous thing to do in the dark, given that a stumble against a sharp rock could rupture her pressure suit. She had practiced what she had to do many times though, even in darkness, well before the lander arrived. She knew exactly where she was, and where all the dangerous rocks were.

The dim light from the stars helped, and she made her way carefully to the rim of the dug-out crater, right beside the cutting, and the highest point around.

She reached the rim safely. From this vantage point, she could see down into the landing pit ahead. To her right, she could see across the plain to the habitat, on the side of Elbow Hill. There were no lights on in the habitat.

There was now a dim light down in the landing pit, coming from the rover's parking lights. It was blocked by the crater rim from being seen from the habitat. In the dim light, she could make out patches of ice mist in the crater.

She watched as John came out of the rover, his headlamp on, moving quickly toward the lander's staircase. He seemed to spend an interminable time at the top of the stair, but eventually he disappeared inside. Denise heaved a sigh of relief. So far so good.

She raised her bulky outdoors field glasses to her helmet, and focussed on the habitat, a faint silver rectangle, barely visible in the starlight. The outdoors field glasses were designed for use with a pressure suit on, and had come to Mars with the disastrous 2038 mission, ten years earlier. Until that evening, however, they had never had a use for them.

She put down the field glasses, and gave most of her attention to the lander again. She could now see dim lights, varying in intensity, coming from the view ports on the lander's lower personnel floor. Then these lights disappeared, only to be replaced a few seconds later by lights from the view ports of the upper personnel floor.

Just at this point, a light appeared at the habitat. In was from a cubicle in the command section. Denise straightened as if stung. She studied the habitat through her field glasses. Then a second light came on, and then a third. The two new lights were also in the command section.

Denise now felt anxious. Although she was a person who could experience strong emotions, in a crisis situation she could be perfectly cool and rational. She controlled her feelings and spoke to John in a low voice, via the radio connection. "John, be quick! Three lights on in the hab!" But as she had expected, there was no reply. Radio waves could not penetrate the metal hull of the lander.

She waited patiently. She knew John would appear at the airlock every so often to communicate with her, in case of any threatening activity at the habitat. It was part of the plan. Please hurry up, she thought.

Then more lights came on at the habitat, in the three kitchen windows in the central section. Denise became very anxious.

A few minutes later, she saw a light moving outside, beside the habitat. She studied it through her field glasses. It was a helmet light. Now she became alarmed.

She focussed on the habitat again. Now the lights were gone from all the cubicle windows in the command section, but not from the kitchen windows in the central section. But there was still no sign of John.

Then she saw a second light moving on the shelf beside the habitat. "John!" she cried. "Trouble! Two outside at the hab!"

"I found them. The CIA was right. The bastards brought guns," came John's voice back, as his helmet light appeared at the airlock door. "Can you make out what's going on at the hab?"

"No," said Denise, feeling too concerned about the lights at the habitat to have any time for feeling a sense of outrage at the lander's cargo of weapons. "Wait! The moving lights have both disappeared, but there are still three lights on in the hab—central section, kitchen windows."

"They could be coming to get their guns," said John. "I thought there was a risk of that. I found twelve odd-looking gun cases in a floor compartment in the cargo bay, disguised as sample containers, I think. Nine have weapons and ammunition inside, and three are empty—the empty three on top—decoys obviously, in case their scientists found them. I need time to get it all out—the best I can do is carry out what's in two cases at a time. I'm going in for the first lot now. Are the moving lights still gone?"

"Yes," responded Denise. "Please be quick. I don't like this."

At this, John's helmet light disappeared. A few minutes later, he appeared again. She trained her field glasses on him. In the rover parking lights she could see he was carrying two large, ugly-looking guns in one arm. They resembled submachine guns.

Around his neck there were two belts, each containing a holster and what looked like a machine pistol. In the other arm he was carrying several bulky rectangular boxes of different sizes. Must be ammunition, she thought.

Loaded with the weapons and ammunition boxes, it took John almost a minute to get down the staircase. Once down he ran toward the rover trailer, only a few meters away. He flung his burden in, and ran back to the stair. As he did so, Denise trained her field glasses on the habitat again. There was still no further sign of any helmet lights. She breathed a sigh of relief. Maybe they forgot something outside, she thought, although she could not imagine what that might be.

But just at that instant, two powerful lights came on outside the habitat. She recognized them at once. They were the buggy headlights, and now they were moving away from the habitat.

John had just finished climbing the stair and was about to enter the airlock door. "John! John!" Denise almost screamed. "They're coming! The buggy's just left the habitat!"

John could think fast.

"It's night," he said quickly. "Twenty miles an hour on that road at most. Here in three minutes. No time to get the rest of the guns. Might just have time to get the empty gun cases back in the floor compartment. Better do it. Maybe they don't know how many are supposed to be full."

He disappeared through the airlock. A minute and a half later, he was out again. He spent ten seconds manipulating the airlock control panel, and then almost jumped down the stair and raced for the rover airlock, as Denise focussed on the buggy. A minute later, he was in the driver seat, sitting awkwardly, his backpack still on.

"I'll hide, John," cried Denise. "There're no time to pick me up. Come back for me later. They're not doing more than twelve miles an hour. But they'll be here in minutes. Drive, John! Drive! Now!"

John pressed the accelerator, and the rover shot up the cutting out of the pit. He had made the cutting himself and knew it in detail, even in the faint starlight. Twenty seconds later, the rover was racing along the Elbow Hill road, in a direction away from both the habitat and the landing pit, toward where it met with the main Kasei Valley road in a T-junction. The main Kasei Valley road was the first major road built on Mars.

John went quite fast along the mile toward the junction—about fifteen miles an hour in the dark, several times narrowly averting running the rover up onto rocks at the side of the road. John groaned each time that happened. He knew that the rover's flexible elbow joints where the wheels were attached were very strong, but twelve miles an hour over rocks was all they were designed for.

A cairn of light-colored andesite stones marked the road junction. He reached it safely at last, and turned right and headed along the main road back toward Stem Gap. A half mile further on, in a slight hollow of the road, he stopped, turned off the road onto the rocks, and brought the rover right around to face the way he had come. He was just in time to see red tail lights disappear down the cutting to the landing pit. Thank heavens for that, he thought; looks like they didn't see us. But now he had to wait for a chance to rescue Denise.

*

Denise had been left standing on the outside of the crater rim, on sandy, rock-free ground, facing into the landing pit. Her back was to the Elbow Hill road, with the habitat to her right and the cutting to her left. As the buggy headlights got close, she got down on her hands and knees and crawled carefully over the crater rim and down the inside slope of the pit for just a few feet, far enough to shield her from the buggy headlights.

The buggy was now coming along the short trail to the pit. As soon as she could see the headlight beams shining down the cutting and onto the lander, she carefully crawled back up the slope, over the crater rim and down the outside a few feet. Then she stood up, turned, and peeped over the rim.

The buggy had stopped, facing the lander's airlock, its lights still on, a few faint wisps of ice mist reflecting the light. She was close enough that she could easily pick up any conversation in the landing pit, but so far there had been none. Five figures got out of the buggy and trailer, and disappeared into the lander.

John was right, she thought. He had predicted the military types would come for their guns on the very first night. She was sure three of them were Derk, Emma, and Karl Mannhardt. She wondered who the other two were. She knew that those three had Special Forces training.

Ten minutes later, the five emerged from the lander, each carrying a large gun, and what looked like ammunition. Denise now saw for the first time that the guns were unusually large. They each had two separate barrels, one above the other, and a large stock.

The five walked a few meters from the lander, stopped, and began readying their guns. Denise was now surprised to see them separate each of the large guns into a pair of guns, a larger one and a smaller one. Composites, she thought. She had heard of such weapons. You could use the two guns separately or together.

Each of them now placed the larger of the two guns on the ground. Denise then observed the five insert what looked like large L-shaped magazines into the feed wells of the somewhat smaller guns. Denise could now see that they were automatic rifles. Then she heard Derk's voice.

"Wait here," said Derk. He walked quickly toward the edge of the crater, to Denise's right. He went a few meters up the slope, stopped, and with his boot ploughed out a large letter X. Then he walked back the forty meters or so to where the other four were standing watching. One of the four got in the buggy, and turned it around, so that its headlights shone on the distant X, partly obscured by wisps of ice mist.

Derk now bent down and placed a small square object on the ground in front of him. Then he dug the toe of his right boot deep into the ground, and knelt down, with his right knee on the square object, and the toe of his right boot still deep in the ground. Then he raised his weapon, the butt against his shoulder. Orange-blue flashes spat from it, and a shower of bullets raised the dirt at the center of the X. Denise was actually able to hear a faint machine gun rattle in the thin Martian air.

"Hardly makes a sound here," said Derk. "All right, one at a time," he continued, hand signaling to one of the others. "You next, Emma. Dig your right boot in very firmly, and kneel on the kneepad. The ground's too cold—it'll affect your aim."

One by one, each of them dug a hole with the right boot, knelt down on the kneepad, and took a turn shooting at the target. Every one of them hit the target first time. Denise shuddered. She had never handled a gun in her life, much less fired one, but she was sure that hitting that target in the dim misty light with a pressure suit on took skill, a skill neither she nor John possessed. She was puzzled by the emphasis on the right boot in a hole in the sand though.

Then a reassuring thought struck her. They don't seem to be aware we took two sets of weapons, she thought. Maybe we'll get time to practice before they find out. I know just the place.

Derk now picked up one of the larger bulky guns lying on the ground, and attached what looked like a large T-shaped magazine to the weapon.

"I'll set it for two thousand meters," he said. "That should be safe. Let's see if it works."

Derk then dug in his right foot and kneeled down as before. He aimed the gun just above the rim of the crater, to the north, away from the habitat, and away from Denise. He fired. A large red flash came from the gun barrel, and Denise was able to follow the bullet as it streaked away. Four seconds later there was an explosion in the sky to the north.

"Good," said Derk, "it works."

Denise knew she had just witnessed a nanobullet explode, like a grenade. John had witnessed it too, and knew exactly what it was. Inside the large bullet was a tiny nanocomputer, a computer on a semiconductor nanochip that could explode the bullet after it had traveled a set distance. The bullet's shrapnel could thus kill an enemy sheltered behind a wall or rock. On Mars, a single exploding bullet could kill a dozen people by puncturing their pressure suits.

Then Derk said something Denise could not make out. He and two others then got in the buggy, carrying automatic rifles. In a few seconds, the buggy was shooting up the cutting, out of the pit. The remaining two turned and faced toward the part of the rim behind which Denise stood, hidden from view. Their helmet lights were turned on, and were dimly lighting up the slope below the rim.

Denise's heart leaped into her mouth, as suddenly she realized her predicament. She could not crawl down the inside of the crater rim to hide from the headlights as she had done before, without being seen by the two in the pit. All she could do was try to crouch down low, on her knees, on the freezing cold Martian ground, as the buggy emerged from the cutting.

She was puzzled though. Why was the buggy driving out of the landing pit with only three of them? Where was it going?

Suddenly she had the answer, as the buggy stopped, turned toward the crater rim where she was crouching. The buggy was only about fifty meters away, and its headlights lit up the terrain all around her, and her light-blue pressure suit too. Her heart pounded.

It's not possible, she thought. How could they know? She groaned inside. They must have spotted the rover leaving the pit, she thought, or maybe picked up the last of our conversation. They must have been closer than we thought. But the range of the helmet radio was not more than about a hundred and fifty meters, and she and John had kept their voices low—or had they? But maybe they knew we were here all along—could be they're a lot smarter than we gave them credit for. Maybe they saw the faint light in the landing pit.

Then she remembered practically screaming to John to get moving, just before the buggy arrived. That must have been what alerted them, she concluded, still in shock.

"You can come down now," said the voice of Captain Derk.

Denise did not respond. She was almost petrified. She simply did not know what to do. Could it be they were talking to someone else?

But they were not. They were talking to her. "Now please come down," repeated Captain Derk. "I'm sure you would not like us to come and fetch you down. Which of you is it? Dr. Erway or Dr. Lavoisier?"

Then Denise recovered her wits. She thought about the guns. They wouldn't dare, she thought. She couldn't see in the glare of the headlights if any of them were aiming their guns at her.

"It's Denise Lavoisier," she answered. "Please put down your guns. I'll come down."

"Guns?" responded Derk, in his flawless upper-class accent. "Why would we point guns at you? We did indeed bring a few weapons. But it was merely to test them out for a manufacturer in Munich, in the low air pressure and low gravity. That's all. There's an international treaty that prohibits the use of guns on Mars, which the E.U. countries have signed, and will make every effort to comply with. But experimental weapons are allowed for purposes of testing. We naturally wanted to keep our testing of weapons a secret. Many ordinary people in Europe, and around the world, would likely not approve, even if it's perfectly legal."

Denise walked slowly down the slope, and a few minutes later stood on the trail beside the buggy, out of the glare of its lights.

"Oh, I think I'm beginning to understand now," Derk continued. "You must have thought we had brought the guns to use against you. That's what you've been thinking, isn't it?"

"Yes," answered Denise. She was devastated, embarrassed, and now she was being made to feel like a schoolgirl caught in the act of some petty theft.

"That's why you and your husband tried to remove the guns from the lander on the very first evening," said Derk, "isn't it?"

"Yes," answered Denise. She was sure Derk was enjoying this.

"So where's your husband now?" asked Derk. "A few miles down the road, waiting for us to leave, so he can come back for you?"

"Yes," said Denise, for the third time. She almost wished the ground would open up and swallow her. What would John say?

"Well, this is not a nice situation," said Derk, "but understandable, I suppose." An understatement, thought Denise.

"Well, we'd better clear up this little misunderstanding at once," he continued. "Please get in beside me. I'll drive you to your husband. You must be about to freeze. The temperature's nearly minus sixty." He now sounded sympathetic.

Denise actually was beginning to feel very cold. She obeyed, as the one beside Derk vacated the passenger seat, went round the back, and climbed up onto the trailer. Denise thought it was Emma Grant. The figure did its best to conceal the fact in the shadows, but she was sure it was carrying a gun.

The buggy then headed down the trail from the landing pit, and turned right at the Elbow Hill road. They had traveled barely a quarter mile along this road, when the rover came into view, heading toward them at speed, headlights full on. John had seen his wife's predicament on the crater rim through his field glasses, and had headed back at once to come to her assistance. John slowed down as the buggy approached. Then he drove carefully off the road to his right, headlights aimed at the road. Shortly after, the buggy stopped on the road adjacent to the rover.

Captain Derk did not turn off the buggy's headlights, nor did John turn off the rover's. Wisps of ice mist reflected the light. John was relieved at the sight of Denise in the buggy, apparently unharmed, field glasses hanging from her neck, her blue pressure suit standing out beside the light green of the other three.

"Dr. Erway, I'm so sorry, but I'm afraid there's been a misunderstanding about weapons," began the Captain. "Looks like you've both been letting your imaginations run away with you. Somehow you've been misled into thinking that our weapons were to be used against you. Preposterous idea, I must say. Of course, I can understand how you might come to think that, especially if our American cousins, our CIA friends in particular, were the ones who informed you we had guns on board." He paused here, as if to catch his breath, but waiting to see if this would bring some response. It did not.

"As I just explained to your wife," continued Derk, "we brought the weapons with us merely to test them in a Martian environment—low pressure air, low gravity—that kind of thing. You know how military people are—always wanting tests carried out in every environment imaginable. As I explained to your wife, test weapons are allowed under the Mars treaty." He paused again, and then continued. "Well, it's late. I'm sure you and your wife would like to get to bed, and we've a busy day ahead tomorrow, getting our buggies unloaded and assembled. Before we all go home, if you would just be a good fellow and let us have our test weapons back. The ones you removed from the lander. I presume they're in the trailer."

"Yes," said John. "You'll find two sets in the trailer. If the whole thing was a misunderstanding, as you say, they're your weapons. Just take them."

Derk raised his right hand and the two figures sitting in his buggy trailer slid down the back of the trailer and moved to the back of the rover trailer. Denise did not move. Inside she was terrified. In spite of his cultured and sympathetic voice, Derk frightened her. She was afraid to make any unexpected move. The two soon returned to the buggy carrying the weapons and ammunition cases.

"I think you should get home now, Dr. Lavoisier," said Derk, as his two crew members climbed back into the buggy trailer.

Denise got down and walked toward the rover airlock.

"Good night," said Derk. "We're looking forward to the dinner on Tuesday evening."

"Good night," said John. At that, Captain Derk drove a little off the road to his right, to turn the buggy around. He was soon back on the road, and on his way back to the landing site, red tail lights receding in the darkness.

John was waiting for his wife as she came through the airlock. He helped her remove her pressure suit and stow it in the suit closet beside the airlock. Neither of them spoke. John had a worried expression on his face.

A few minutes later, she followed her husband forward through the eating area, and down the steps to the driver area. But as she sat down in the passenger seat beside him, her right foot hit something solid.

"What's that?" she asked, as she flicked a light switch on the dash. She looked down. It was the large stock of a composite automatic weapon.

"I had time to collect just one more set of weapons that time I went back inside the lander to tidy up," explained John. "Got some ammo too. To save time in getting away, I took them straight through the airlock, instead of throwing them in the trailer."

Denise said nothing. Her mind was still swimming.

"We bwought the weapons heah meahly to test them," said John, imitating the Captain's accent.

"Who does he think he's kidding?" he went on, in his normal voice, but sounding angry. Then his tone changed again, as his thoughts turned to his wife. "I guess you've had a shock, Denise. You can't be feeling too well."

"I'm all right," said Denise. "We did our best. But I don't think I was ever cut out to be a burglar."

"I didn't enjoy it much myself," said John. "But you're right. We did our best. There's nothing we could have done to get all those guns out. Derk was just one jump ahead of us."

"I know," said Denise. "I think he knew we'd try to get into the lander this evening. But let's not talk about it any more. Done is done. Right now I just want to go home."

"Home in an hour," said John, as he turned the rover around. He then drove back to the junction of the Elbow Hill road and the main Kasei Valley road. At the junction he turned right and headed across Elbow Plain toward Stem Gap, at twenty miles an hour, as the potato-shaped moon Phobos rose above the western wall of Kasei Valley, almost straight ahead of them.

CHAPTER FOUR

Canyon Road

EARLY NEXT morning, John and Denise were in a rover, advancing up Tip Canyon. Denise was driving, and the attached trailer carried the spoils of the previous night's foiled burglary attempt.

The early morning ice mist had not yet lifted in the canyon, and visibility at ground level was poor. The huge rover advanced only slowly in the drifting mist, as the road wound around the barely visible remains of small craters on the canyon floor. High up to the left, the top of the northwestern wall of the canyon was clear, and glowed bright orange in the morning sun.

They had built this spectacularly scenic road six years earlier. It entered Tip Canyon at the northern tip of Leaf Valley, and proceeded northeastward on the canyon floor. When it emerged from the canyon, after about fifteen miles, it first bisected the southern reaches of the treacherous but unbelievably beautiful chaotic terrain or labyrinth area of western Kasei Valley. Then the road entered a wide valley, running east-west, which they had named Hazard Valley, and with good reason. The road went on east along Hazard Valley and finally made a junction with the main east-west Kasei Valley road, about eighty miles northeast of Elbow Plain and Stem Gap.

The Tip Canyon and Hazard Valley roads, together with the east-west Kasei Valley road, allowed a spectacular drive all the way around the high plateau country east of Leaf Valley, a circuit of about a hundred and eighty miles.

They had not built the road through Tip Canyon for its scenery, but for easy access to mineral deposits in the many exposed cliff and escarpment surfaces along the route. They had learned, the hard way, however, to keep out of the beautiful labyrinth, with its multitude of small, intersecting valleys, most of them filled with sand dunes.

Late one afternoon in the fall, years earlier, Denise had ignored all advice about avoiding the labyrinth. As she drove along the eastern stretch of Hazard Valley, headed for Tip Canyon, she had found her way blocked by sand dunes. Four separate tongues of dunes, slowly crawling west along the valley, had locked themselves together, with the front and rear ends of the complex jammed against mesa walls on either side of the valley, blocking it completely. To get around the blockage, Denise had ventured into the labyrinth—only to become completely lost by the time darkness fell.

Denise, who had a natural inclination to run risks, had not blamed herself—after all, she recalled thinking, she had been only about twenty-five miles from home.

Unfortunately, the rover's global terrain database for navigation could not help the unwary traveler much in the enticingly beautiful labyrinth terrain, and could even mislead. Many of the short labyrinth valleys, breathtakingly sculpted, looked very much alike. This fact, combined with the spectacular sand dunes on the valley floors, and either blowing sand and dust when there was a wind, or late morning and early evening ice mist when there was not, made it all too easy to mistake where you were, lose track of the way you had entered, and end up lost in the labyrinth. And because the many mesa escarpment walls easily blocked surface radio signals, you could not radio for help.

Fortunately for Denise, when she had got lost that fall afternoon, years ago, her rover had been well provisioned. She had spent the night in the labyrinth, although exactly where, in that plethora of beautiful dune-smothered valleys, she had never been able to figure out. Next day, she had succeeded in extricating herself, to the relief of her husband, who had been searching through the night for her, along with Dr. Sato. She had never ventured into the labyrinth again.

On that occasion, the seductive labyrinth had failed in its first attempt on the life of a human being. The time when it could try again was drawing ever closer though. Next time it would not fail.

*

They had traveled only about twelve miles along Tip Canyon, when suddenly the ice mist cleared and they were in bright sunshine.

There was a dead-end side canyon to the right, running to the southeast for about two miles. The early morning sunshine was filling this side canyon, and there was also sunshine in the adjacent part of Tip Canyon and the road along it. Here the warming sun had already dispersed the ice mist on the canyon floor.

"This ought to be far enough," said Denise, "if we're to be back by eight."

Denise's appointment with Sheila Bell was for nine thirty.

John nodded. "I agree, it's far enough. A nice sunny spot too, and those dunes look just about right."

Denise turned the rover to the right, off the road, and onto the rocks and stones of the canyon floor. She then proceeded over the reddish, rock-strewn terrain to the sunlit side-canyon entrance.

The side canyon was about a quarter mile wide, and the sun was just above its shallow northeastern escarpment wall, near its eastern end, two miles away. About a mile up this side canyon, they could clearly see sand dunes, huge dunes of orange and red sand stretching right across the canyon, and blocking their way.

Dunes were common not only in the chaotic terrain or labyrinth region of Kasei Valley, which began less than five miles away, but also in side canyons of Tip Canyon, especially side canyons with anything approaching an east-west run.

When they first explored this region, years earlier, they had been puzzled by the prevalence of such large dune fields in small valleys and side canyons, but had eventually discovered the explanation. The fine sand and dust to form the dunes was borne on the strong winds scouring the vast, exposed, high-plateau regions surrounding the canyons, the labyrinth, and Leaf Valley. When the wind direction matched the run of a small side canyon or labyrinth valley, cut down below the plateau, the wind speed would drop locally, since the air now had more space in which to flow—a kind of negative funnel. The lighter wind would then be forced to drop its load of fine sand and dust into the valley, from which it could not blow out, so that sand and dust just collected in the small valleys. Over time, centuries probably, stronger winds forced all the sand to one end of a dead-end valley to form dunes.

They went along the red floor of the side canyon at only about ten miles an hour. They kept to the southwest side, until they reached the first dunes. Then Denise took the rover up onto the lower reaches of the orange-colored escarpment to her right, at a very low speed, bypassing the dunes.

She drove along the edge of the shallow escarpment for about another two hundred meters. Then she drove the rover back down onto the floor, right between two massive dunes, and stopped. The orange-red sand between the dunes was less than a foot deep. Here and there, the darker rocks and stones of the canyon floor could be seen sticking out.

Five minutes later, they were both outside in the early morning sunshine, wearing overshoes, but neither overgloves nor radiation umbrellas. John was out first. He went immediately to the back of the trailer, and pulled out the set of weapons he had succeeded in getting out of the lander the previous evening.

John gave Denise the pistol and ammunition boxes to carry, while he took the composite weapon. Then they walked about a hundred meters away from the rover, keeping between the two dunes.

They stopped about fifty meters from the steep slope of the dune northwest of them. The dune was at least thirty feet high, and ran right across the canyon floor.

John then took the composite weapon apart, laid the much larger nanogun on the sand, and carefully began to examine the automatic rifle.

"At least it's a standard type," he said, "according to the knowledge base, anyway. Made by a weapons company in Germany, but modified for a person wearing a pressure suit glove. Shoots six millimeter rounds at two hundred a minute, and three-round bursts."

"As long as you're sure you know what you're doing," said Denise, looking uneasily at the quite large, dark weapon. "It looks ugly and dangerous. I think I'd rather give it to Dr. Sato to cut up."

"I studied it very carefully against the computer specs last night," John assured her. "Everything matched except for the extra large trigger. I'm certain it's a modification of the standard type for use on Mars." He paused here, looking at the weapon. Then he said: "I'd prefer to have the Zen master cut it up too, Denise. And if we'd got all of them last night he'd be hard at work right now. But when we've got just one set of weapons and they've got eight, we've no choice but to learn how to use what we have—just in case."

"I suppose so," said Denise, still uneasy, "although how to kill people with an automatic rifle is something I'd rather not have to learn. But if we have to defend ourselves, then we must learn, I suppose." She paused, and then added: "John, there's something else bothering me—it's Derk. He obviously didn't miss this set of weapons last night. He obviously assumed that four of the twelve weapons cases were empty decoy cases, and that there were only eight full weapons cases in the cargo bay, when in fact there were nine. But that man is very clever. Don't you think he'll send a message to Earth to find out exactly how many full weapons cases were actually on board?"

"Maybe," said John. "He'd have a problem though. We may not have the codes and software to intercept messages between the hab and Mission Control, but the CIA does. So he'd have to encrypt the message in a very special code, something the CIA didn't know. He wouldn't want to blabber a message like: 'Hey you guys, how many sets of guns are we supposed to have up here?' all over the solar system. He doesn't know if the CIA knows for sure he has guns."

"I see," said Denise, "and if he did code his message in some special way, he knows the CIA would wonder what was in it. And in no time at all the CIA would have their computers running hot to break the code, and would eventually succeed."

"Right," said John. "So, if he's smart—and there's no doubt he is—he won't send any messages, but try some more devious way to find out if there were more than eight sets of weapons."

"But wait a minute," said Denise. "Why would he be worried about the CIA finding out now? He knows we know he has weapons, and could tell NASA?"

"He doesn't know if we would do that," said John, "and if we did, he could always accuse us of lying. He'd prefer that risk, to being caught red-handed sending a message asking how many guns he's supposed to have."

"So what way will he use to find out if there were more than eight sets of weapons?"

"Don't know," said John. "But if he suspects he's missing a set, I'm sure he'll think of something. But maybe he doesn't suspect."

He kneeled down, and carefully opened a box of ammunition. "Let's get this over with," he said, as he got up again. "Watch me carefully while I load."

Denise watched, as John slid a large magazine into the rifle's feed well. Then he showed her the safety catch on the weapon. Then he placed it on the sand.

"Wait here," he said, and walked away to the northwest, to the edge of the nearest sand dune, about fifty meters away. The sand was fine and not very compacted, and he was able to walk only about a meter up the steep side of the huge dune. Then, like Captain Derk the previous evening in the landing pit, he wrote a large X on the side of the dune with his boot.

Back beside Denise, he lifted the rifle and gave it to her.

"Release the catch," he said.

She did so, as he walked behind her.

"Now fire just a few short bursts, and try to hit the X," he said, standing behind her, with the sun at his back to his right.

Denise raised the weapon slowly to her shoulder. It was not all that heavy in the low Martian gravity. She sighted the X carefully, waited a few seconds, and then fired a few three-round bursts.

Spent shell casings spewed from the side of the gun, as spurts of sand jumped out of the dune, about ten feet to the right of the target, and Denise lost her balance and flew backward. She did not hit the ground, for John had been prepared, and caught her in time.

"My goodness," said Denise, as she got back on her feet, "I wasn't expecting a kick like that... and I wasn't much of a shot either."

She looked at her husband, who was grinning.

"You knew," she accused him. "You knew it would knock me off my feet."

"Guilty," said John. "But I thought it would be better if you learned from experience. Now you know why those military types knelt down and dug in last night to fire these weapons, and why they were out practicing first thing. It's much harder to fire a gun on Mars than on Earth. When the gravity's low, the turning force on the upper body, or the torque, when you fire a weapon, is much greater than on Earth. So it's easier for the weapon recoil to topple you. And this gun has a pretty good recoil force anyway—two hundred rounds a minute—almost like a small rocket motor. And our backpacks make the torque effect even worse."

"All right," said Denise, "I got the message. Can I try again? This time I'll kneel down and dig in, just the way Derk did last night."

"All right, but I'll stay just behind you."

Denise dug her right foot down into the soil below the sand, and then spent a few minutes getting into a good kneeling position. She could feel the freezing cold of the sand on her knees.

"We really need a kneepad," said Denise. "Derk had one last night. The cold on the knee is distracting."

"Be quick then," said John. "And keep it short. We'll get something for a kneepad if ever we need this gun in earnest."

Denise fired a burst. This time she did not fall over, and the sand spurts were only a few feet from the target.

"Not bad," remarked John. "Another way to avoid the high torque effect is to lie down. Try that."

Denise did so, and managed to hit within a foot of the target.

"Good," said John, "now it's my turn."

John dug in and knelt down. He too felt the cold in his knee at once. He fired a short burst, but did not do any better than Denise.

"We're probably just a bit tense," said John, "but that's supposed to be natural when you first fire a gun. Anyway, I reckon we've enough ammo in the magazine for about twenty more bursts each. We can't afford to waste any more. There were only six mags in the case. Let's just take turns until we exhaust this mag and see if we get any better."

They did that, and gradually their marksmanship improved, both kneeling and lying down. By the end, each of them was getting some hits inside the X.

They repeated the procedure for the pistol, closer to the target this time, but again kneeling down and dug in. They each used the left hand to reinforce the right hand holding the pistol.

"Good," said John afterward. "Now let me try this nanogun."

"I've never seen a gun like this before," said Denise, "although I've heard of them. Do you think you can use it?"

"I'm going to try," said John. "According to the computer specs it's not difficult. You use the laser range finder first to find the distance to your target area. Then you set the computer for the shell to explode so many meters back of the target. See that small crater with the deep shadow further along the escarpment. It's about sixteen hundred meters away. I'm going to try and explode the shell about ten meters beyond it."

John carefully attached a T-shaped magazine to the weapon. The shells were big, sixteen millimeters. Still standing up, he aimed the weapon, got the range, and after manually injecting a shell into the firing chamber, adjusted a distance setting on a small display screen. Then he knelt down, as before, pointed the weapon at the crater again, and fired. The shell streaked out, and just over three seconds later, it exploded exactly ten meters beyond the crater.

"Very good," said Denise, impressed, "but I'm going to leave that canon to you. I'd probably kill myself if I tried to use it."

"Fair enough," said John, satisfied, as he carefully detached the magazine from the gun. "It's been a good morning's work. But I see we really do need a kneepad. My right knee's freezing. Let's get inside, and go home and have breakfast."

"Yes sir, general, sir," said Denise, raising her right arm in salute.

"Some general," said John, "in charge of a two-man army with about a half hour's training."

They both laughed as they picked up the weapons and ammunition boxes and headed back across the sand to the rover, although inside John had a decidedly sickening feeling about the thought of his wife engaged in a shoot-out with Special Forces military personnel. We must be crazy, he thought.

Soon they were both seated in the rover, ready to go.

"Our wonderful Martian peace is gone," reflected Denise. "Now we're involved with guns, in a struggle against other human beings, as well as the usual struggle with Mars. Somehow I prefer the battle with the planet. Are we going to tell the Zen master we have a set of firearms, and are intending to keep them, instead of destroying them, as we all originally agreed?"

"Do you think we should tell him?" responded John.

"I'd rather not," said Denise. "As a devout Buddhist, I'm sure he'd want to have nothing to do with guns, apart from the job of cutting them up."

"How do you think he'd react if we told him about them?" asked John.

"I really can't say," she said thoughtfully, "but it does worry me. On the surface he'd probably take no notice. There's a chance though, that it could give him a negative impression of us, deep inside whatever's left of his ego, and perhaps turn him slightly against us in some subtle way."

"And maybe accept the offer to return to Earth with the E.U. people, without a fight?"

"Maybe. It would certainly weaken our position here if he did that," said Denise. "It would increase the pressure on us to give in and go too."

"It could be a rough trip back for somebody at his age," observed John, "and the long way back too, right around the sun, and inside the Earth's orbit. Nine months or so in space. Do you think he's up to it—medically speaking I mean, if he did go?"

"Yes, I think he would be," said Denise. "He's led a stress-free existence and is still very healthy as a result—although most people wouldn't call what he's been through stress free. But his lack of any significant ego just about eliminates the normal stress reaction. In Japan, Zen masters have a reputation for longevity—in a country whose people have a reputation for longevity. I don't think the trip back to Earth would be much of a stress for him—certainly not more than it would be for us."

"But he's happy here," said John. "And he has his monastery on a site like nowhere on Earth. Every time I'm up there, the view blows me away."

"He's also a Zen master," Denise reminded him. "That means he's neither happy nor sad—just neutral. He doesn't really care where he is. One place is as neutral as another to him."

"All right," said John, now somewhat worried himself at the thought of being deserted by Dr. Sato, "suppose we just don't tell him we have a set of weapons. I don't mean we should lie to him. Suppose we just never mention it."

"I wouldn't advise doing that," said Denise. "His Zen awareness would detect our concealment of something important. We'd risk losing his trust. And remember we once all promised to treat each other honestly and with respect in all matters. Let Derk and his soldiers be devious. We can't."

"Maybe that's the answer," said John. "It's how I prefer to operate anyway."

"How do you mean?"

"We tell him the truth," said John. "We tell him we got caught last night, but managed to get away with only one set of weapons. We try to make him understand that although we hate to deal with guns, as long as a superior force threatens us, we have no choice but to keep the few weapons we have. We would hope we never have to use them, and would use them only as a very last resort. That way at least we keep his trust. If what you say about his Zen awareness is correct, he'll detect the devious nature of Derk and his soldier pals quite quickly. He has to prefer those he trusts to those who can't be trusted."

Denise said nothing for a while. "I think you're right," she said eventually, in a quite decisive tone. "Good thing we discussed it. The right thing to do is to tell him everything. Perhaps you should do it after breakfast, while I'm visiting Sheila Bell." She paused, looking vacantly through the front window at the glowing orange sand outside. "Just one other thing, I don't want those guns in our house. We should hide them somewhere safe outside."

"Agreed," said John, without hesitation. "I know just the place …in the cement plant. Now let's go. The kids will be wondering where we are. I'm hungry too."

The ice mist in Tip Canyon had cleared in the forty minutes they had spent in the side canyon, and once they reached the Tip Canyon road, it took less than twenty minutes to complete the drive between its high walls to Tip Valley, at the tip of Leaf Valley.

As they passed their ice mine at the exit from Tip Canyon, the orange-brown, round-topped Mount Tip came into view about three miles to the south. Their eyes were drawn at once to the sunlight reflecting on the glass walls surrounding their magnificent home, on its shelf near the mountain's southeast base.

*

Just after nine fifteen that morning, Denise was again in the rover, driving up to the habitat, along the ridge on the northwest side of Elbow Hill. The sky had changed since early morning, and was now largely covered in thin, white, wavy, washboard clouds. The sun could shine through the thin ice clouds, but quite weakly, and the temperature was still well below freezing. If this cloud doesn't clear off we won't get above freezing today, thought Denise, as she parked in front of the habitat. She knew that it probably would clear off though.

The daytime sky on Mars is mostly clear of cloud cover, but nights with cloud cover are fairly common in the fall in the western Kasei Valley region of Mars. Light cloud cover can occur even in the mornings, on rare occasions.

As Denise came out of the rover and walked to the habitat airlock, there was no sign of life, and the buggy was gone. But Sheila Bell was home, and had seen Denise coming. She greeted Denise as she came out of the airlock.

"We have the whole place to ourselves, except for Emma," said Dr. Bell, as she helped Denise remove her pressure suit, and place it in a closet in a wall of the airlock room. "They've all taken themselves down to the lander to put the two buggies together. Emma's working in the communications room, looking after the link with Earth. She's certainly the most patient woman you could ever meet. Says very little now, but does more than anybody to keep things shipshape. You wouldn't believe the amount of blarney that keeps coming in from Mission Control. Most of it would bore you stiff. They want to know every little wee thing we do. I do think indeed they're all scared stiff that something terrible will happen to us all, like this habitat blowing up, and killing us all, or something like that, just like what happened to that NASA mission away back in 2038.

Would you believe they want all the technical data from the habitat sent to them every twelve hours for analysis, and sample data every two hours?"

"The habitat's very safe," said Denise, detecting a slight nervousness in the big, brown-haired Irishwoman with the large, cheerful face. "My husband knows what he's doing when it comes to things like that. And the lander can't blow up, because there's no fuel in it. You'd even be safe here in a bad dust storm, and you've a radiation shelter under the hab if there was a radiation storm. You just have to be careful outside that you don't stumble and rip your pressure suit on a sharp rock—that's about the only danger around here right now. You can feel very safe."

"Well, it's nice to hear that," said Sheila. "It's very interesting to come to Mars, but I'd like to go home one day too. Now come on into the surgery, and we'll see what's the matter. I've everything ready for you."

They walked from the airlock room into the hallway of the science module, past the workshop, to the small surgery.

Dr. Bell had soon examined Denise's teeth and announced the verdict. "You're teeth are in excellent shape for a woman your age. I suppose it's because you're safe here from all the temptations we have on Earth. Now I can't stay away myself from the cream chocolates. I'll give you a few to take back with you when we've finished. No. I can't—the low pressure outside would make a tidy mess of them. We can have some for coffee instead, when we've finished. A few won't do you any harm. Well, that's the good news. The bad news is not so bad at all. You have two cavities, one hardly worth bothering with, but I think I should fill it, to be on the safe side. The other one's the real thing—it needs to be filled at once. That's why you've been getting the pain sometimes, when you eat sweet foods. All in all, you're doing just fine. I can do both cavities this morning, and I'll give your gums a good cleaning too. I'll have you right as rain in a few hours."

Dr. Bell did the job in an hour and a half. Denise had no reason to question Dr. Bell's competence, but after suffering the dental treatment, she concluded that the Irish doctor would have made a much better veterinarian. Dr. Bell was quite tall for a woman, had a strong muscular build, and was consequently completely in control of her patient. Actually, Dr. Bell did have skills in veterinary medicine, another reason why she had been selected for the mission.

Denise also concluded that the Irishwoman did not know that the mission was armed, or that its initial objective was to get the settlers off the planet, and seize control of Leaf Valley. She also discovered that Sheila had an unusually inquisitive nature, which had led her to become puzzled about some features of the mission.

The young doctor talked as she worked, in the manner of most dentists with a captive audience, in her lilting Irish accent. She entertained Denise with the goings on in ESA, and with funny stories about the small Irish space agency ("Now did you hear the one about the ..."). She even told some stories about the local politics surrounding the secret ESA project in the peninsula in the southwest of Ireland. She did not know what was going on in that peninsula, except that local rumor had it that the project concerned 'reel launches'.

Afterward, they had coffee together in the kitchen/eating area in the central module, sitting facing each other at one corner of a table, each eating a cream chocolate from Sheila's apparently secret store ("Now not a word to Captain Derk—I don't believe he'd approve."). The eating area had two blue-topped tables, each protruding from the east wall underneath a small window, so that everyone sitting at a table could see out. Each table was capable of seating six or seven. Denise had her back to the door into the airlock room.

They talked about the ESA mission for a short time, and then Sheila turned the conversation to the activities of Denise, John, and Dr. Sato on Mars. Sheila asked a lot of questions, and soon had Denise convinced that here was a woman with an insatiable curiosity. Denise spent some time telling her of her experiences in the pivotal years 2038 and 2039, when their survival was very much in doubt. She did not mind talking to Sheila. There could be no doubt her interest was genuine.

It soon became clear that Sheila was also very curious about the kind of person Dr. Sato was, and in Zen, as this had excited much interest on Earth in the West, especially in Europe, where knowledge of Japan and Japanese culture was very limited. Denise had actually written some reports explaining Zen in a Martian context. She had transmitted these reports to NASA, and they had been widely read, particularly in Europe.

"A person like Dr. Sato almost comes across like a Christian saint from medieval times, except that a Zen master doesn't believe in God," said Sheila. "That's what bothers me about Zen."

"I take it you're a convinced Christian," said Denise.

"Yes," said Sheila. "It's how I was brought up, although I never gave it much thought till I was selected to go to Mars, and I read your reports on Dr. Sato and Zen. Then I began to wonder."

"Whether or not there really is a supreme God?"

"No," said Sheila. "I've never doubted that. I can't imagine living without that belief. Nothing would make any sense. No, I began to wonder how a Zen master could not believe in God and yet be so serene and content."

"I think I explained that the source of a Zen master's serenity lay in not feeding the ego, in fact in starving it to the point where it practically disappears," said Denise. "Then 'you' can't be bothered or upset by adversity, because there isn't any 'you' to be bothered. This causes all the statements in your unconscious memory about what 'you' like and dislike, what is good for 'you' and what is bad for 'you', to be erased or at least marked as void…"

"I think I understand that," said Sheila. "Your own emotional system keeps checking what it sees in the environment against that list of statements about what you like and don't like. It'll give you good or bad feelings, depending on whether what's in the environment is good for you or bad for you, according to those statements you carry around deep in your head. And those statements are just your very own values. So if you have no statements with 'I' or 'me' in them, everything you see will give you a good feeling."

"Quite correct. So what's bothering you?" asked Denise. "You seem to understand the basis of Zen quite well."

"Well, now," said Sheila slowly, "it seems to me that if your emotions are reacting only to everything around you with good feelings all the time, then what you are having good feelings about, all the time, is God's creation all around you. Is not the entire environment, both on Earth and on Mars, God's creation?"

"If you believe that a supreme being created the universe then yes," said Denise, "a Zen master would be continuously experiencing God's creation with good feelings. So what are you driving at?"

"Well then," said Sheila, "it seems to me that you could be both a Christian and Zen enlightened at the same time. Now could that be the case?"

"No, I don't think so," said Denise. "But you could be a Christian and have a partial Zen enlightenment."

"But not a full enlightenment?"

"No," said Denise.

"Why?" asked Sheila.

"Because to be a Christian you'd have to have some significant ego," said Denise. "You have to believe that 'you' will go to heaven when 'you' die, that Christ died to redeem 'your' sins, that 'you' can commit sin, and so on. As well as that, you'd have to accept a lot of Christian beliefs that involve concept words and phrases with no basis in reality, like 'Holy Spirit', 'soul', 'the Trinity', 'Son of God', 'angel', 'devil', and so on, what proponents of Christianity call having faith."

"So you think the two really are incompatible," said Sheila, looking a little disappointed.

"Yes," said Denise, "but a shallow Zen enlightenment is certainly possible for a Christian. That would allow him or her to be less bothered by adversity, and more appreciative of God's creation, as you put it, or just the reality of the universe, all around, as a scientist would put it. It would help you be a much happier and contented person. On the other hand, you could argue that a person with a full Zen enlightenment, and no ego at all, would never have any need to be a Christian. He or she would never need to have 'sins' forgiven. A person without an ego could not possibly commit 'sins'. All 'sins' are unjust acts committed for 'your' benefit at the expense of someone or something else. A Zen master, fully enlightened, would never act in a way a Christian could call sinful. If every human being who ever lived on Earth were like Dr. Sato, Christ would have had to stick to his day job as a carpenter. There would have been no 'sins' for him to redeem."

"Dr. Sato must be a saint then," said Sheila.

Denise could not restrain a sudden feeling that arose within her, or stop a tear from glistening in one eye, and duly noted by her medical companion. "Yes," she said. "He is."

"Have some more coffee," said Sheila, getting up and walking across the room, to fetch the coffee pot from the kitchen. "I think this conversation has gotten too serious for this time of day. Better for a cold winter's evening around a blazing fire—not that anyone's ever likely to have a blazing fire here on Mars." A look of homesickness came on her face as she said this.

Denise accepted the second mug of coffee and they talked on for a while in a lighter vein, returning no more to Zen. As they talked, the subject of conversation came back to the plans and activities of the European Space Agency, and touched again on the secret ESA project in the remote southwest corner of Ireland.

"You don't happen to know what a reel launch is?" asked Dr. Bell, with hopeful look. "I do believe our structural engineers know, and the Captain too, but none of them will talk about it. When the Captain found out I'd been asking about that, he told me not to concern myself with engineering research projects. 'Leave that to the engineers,' he said. 'You stick to your medicine and biology. That's what you're good at,' he said."

"No, I never heard of reel launches," said Denise, "but I'll ask my husband. If it's anything to do with space, I'm sure he'll know."

"No, don't do that," said Sheila, now with an anxious look on her face. "I don't think the Captain would like that."

"This all sounds very mysterious," said Denise, her curiosity aroused. She thought for a moment. "Now you've got me puzzled too. If what ESA has going on in Ireland is as big a project as you make out, shouldn't there have been a big discussion in Europe about where to put it? I seem to recall the E.U. member countries arguing forever about which country would get even the smallest E.U. project. Shouldn't there have been a big political fight over where to locate it? And why would the Irish get it? They must be nearly the smallest member state in the E.U.—no political clout worth talking about, compared to the big members."

"Now there's a point. Indeed, I never thought of that," said Sheila, frowning. "Now that you mention it, there never was any discussion at all about where to put it. It was just set up in the southwest of Ireland. No political fights at all about it."

"The local politicians must have been happy about all the jobs it would create," said Denise.

"Happiness indeed," confirmed Sheila. "Every pub in the area is overflowing with liquid happiness ..."

Her voice trailed off. They could hear voices in the adjacent airlock room. Then Derk entered the room, and stopped at the table. Had they been watching out the window they would have seen him drive up with three others.

"How is the patient, Sheila?" he asked.

"Oh, I think she'll live," said Sheila. "It was just a few fillings she needed, that's all."

"Good," said Derk. "The buggies and trailers are all working, and we're going out on our first expedition this afternoon. There's been a change of plan—we're going south, up Kasei Valley. I want you to come. There are ten of us going. Monique and Jose will stay here to mind the fort and handle communications. They'll get to go on the trip tomorrow—the other direction, east, down the valley. There's a briefing at twelve—in fifteen minutes. We leave at twelve thirty at the latest—with all three buggies."

He said nothing to Denise, but merely nodded to her with cold eyes and walked out of the room, into the command module.

Denise had a recurrence of the feeling of fright she had experienced the evening before at the landing pit, when Derk had trained the buggy's headlights at her, and, she felt sure, his automatic rifles as well.

"Monique and Jose?" said Denise. "I'm afraid I've forgotten what they do. There are so many of you."

"Monique Montpellier's a biologist from France," explained Sheila. "Jose Montoya's a field engineer, and the second flight engineer, from Spain."

"Monique Montpellier?" said Denise. "That's not a well known name in the biological sciences field."

"No, I don't think it is," said Sheila. She lowered her voice. "Maybe I shouldn't be telling you this, but most of her biology work was in the French military—something to do with survival and fighting in extreme environments."

"I see. Well, I'd better be going," said Denise, "and let you get to that briefing. Thank you for the dental work. I've been very worried about something going badly wrong with my teeth—no joke if you're on Mars without a dentist. You've taken a load off my mind."

"Not at all," said Sheila. "Maybe one day I'll need you to do some work for me."

"I hope not," laughed Denise. "I'd rather find some other way to repay you. Anyway, have a good trip south today."

"You know, I thought we were going the other way, down the valley to the northeast, toward what you call Dune Narrows," said Sheila. "So we were told yesterday evening. The change of plan must be because of a message from Mission Control this morning. The Captain doesn't usually change his plans without good reason." She sighed. "And now the time I spent studying the terrain database this morning will all have been wasted. I spent all my time on that part of the valley to the northeast of here. I won't know a thing about the land at the south end of the valley."

"I wouldn't worry," said Denise, as they got up from the table. "If it's an unexpected change of plan, many of the others won't be any wiser. But your geologists will know where they're going."

"Well, as long as somebody knows where we're supposed to be going," said Sheila, standing up, but not moving from the table. "Do you know, when I was studying the maps this morning on the computer, I noticed there's a back door into Leaf Valley. You just go down Kasei Valley to the northeast, then you take the fork to the left about eighty miles from here, and then come back on the road along Hazard Valley and through Tip Canyon. Is that a real road—into Leaf Valley through Hazard Valley and Tip Canyon?"

"It certainly is real," said Denise. "It took us over three weeks to build it. It's a proper road—with beautiful scenery, and radiation shelters all along it. But the scenery is spectacular everywhere in this region. It's especially spectacular as you go south from here—huge escarpment walls quite close by the road, on either side of Kasei Valley. You'll enjoy today's trip. Do you know how far you're going today?"

"I'm not sure now, but at breakfast I heard some of the others say we would definitely visit Chiselhead on our first trip south," said Sheila, as they walked into the airlock room. "I'm afraid I don't know where that is."

Denise was startled at this, and although she tried, was unable to prevent Sheila from noticing. "Is there something wrong about going there?" asked Sheila anxiously.

"No," said Denise, recovering. "It's just a good trip from here, that's all, about eighty miles, just under three hours each way in a buggy. But the buggies are good for eight hours without a recharge, so I suppose it'll be all right. There's a road all the way, with radiation shelters all along it too, just in case. Might be a bit cold in a buggy today though, if the cloud doesn't blow off and let the sun shine a bit brighter."

"Is there anything special about this Chiselhead place," persisted Sheila, "that you'd want to build a road to it?"

There's no limit to this woman's curiosity, thought Denise to herself, but decided she'd better tell Sheila the truth, especially since she would find out anyway that afternoon.

"It's a mountain with a ridge top, Chiselhead Mountain, where we mine our copper," explained Denise. "That's all. You can pick raw copper up off the ground there."

"Oh, I see," said Sheila. "It was two of our geologists—Astrid and Don—that I heard talking about Chiselhead at breakfast. That would be interesting to them."

"You'll have to forgive me again," said Denise. "But who are Astrid and Don?"

"Dr. Astrid Larsson's a structural engineer and geologist, from Sweden," said Denise. "She's a real cold fish. You met her yesterday—rather tall and thin, the one with the curled fair hair and the long, serious face. Hardly ever smiles, but very clever, and very polite too. I've never seen her treat anyone unkindly, but she doesn't go out of her way to be helpful either, although she sometimes is. Dr. Donald Carruthers is a geologist and geochemist. He's the mission's chief geologist. We have another geologist too, a structural engineer with geology skills—Dr.Vince Cassoni, from Italy. Don Carruthers is from the north of England, a Yorkshire man. He's the exact opposite of Astrid Larsson. He has a happy face, and he's always smiling. He's a very helpful and considerate man too. I like him a lot."

Denise nodded, as Sheila helped her with her helmet. She wondered if there was something going on between Sheila and Don Carruthers. Sheila's eyes had lit up when she talked about him. As for the copper, a lot of other people besides Astrid Larsson and Don Carruthers will be interested too, thought Denise.

Chiselhead Mountain was where raw copper had been extruded from the interior of the planet, into cavities in the basalt rock of the mountain. Years ago, when he had first discovered the deposits, Dr. Sato's original estimate for the amount of copper there had been for up to ten million tons of it, worth about $100 billion at the current price of copper on Earth. Since then, they had revised their estimate upward. John now believed that there was at least twenty times that amount of copper there, or at least two trillion dollars worth.

Although NASA knew from satellite surveys where the copper find was located, and knew the deposit was very large, as far as Denise knew, no one on Earth knew just exactly how much copper was there. The E.U. is about to find out, by the looks of it, she thought.

"Oh, there was something I meant to give you, for the children you know," said Sheila, as Denise was about to enter the airlock. "Just a minute. I'll fetch it from my cubicle."

Denise waited as Sheila disappeared around the corner, into the hallway of the science module, where she had her cubicle, next door to the surgery. A minute later, Sheila was back with a small plastic object in her hand. "It's just a little thing to amuse the children," she said. "It's a funny little Irish video recording for small children—about fairies and wee folk, nothing scary—I'm sure they'll love it."

"Well, thank you very much," said Denise, touched by the doctor's good nature. Suddenly she could see why Sheila was so popular in Europe.

"I'm sure the children will enjoy meeting you when we have you up to dinner one day," she added.

"Now that's something I'm looking forward to," said Sheila. "I'd really like to meet the children, and visit that wonderful Mars house you live in."

Denise smiled and nodded. A few seconds later, she was in the airlock.

She did not know then that she had just talked to Sheila Bell for the last time, and that if she had expanded the conversation just a little more in one direction, she could have prevented her death, and the devastating sequence of events that would follow it.

*

Denise felt anxious and depressed as she drove home on the familiar road across Elbow Plain toward Step Gap, but got the usual feeling of safety and security once she was through the gap and driving north inside Leaf Valley. The generally duller red and gray color of the valley floor that day added to her depression. High white washboard clouds still stretched across the sky, partly obscuring the noon sun.

In spite of her feelings, Denise was still observant of the activities of Nature around her. You learn to be that way on Mars, especially when you are good friends with a Zen master, and she noticed that the clouds seemed a lot thinner than earlier in the day. There was clear pink sky far to the east too, promising the usual sunny skies for the afternoon. These observations cheered her a little.

One of the things bothering her was the thought that ESA would be even more determined to get rid of them, once they had confirmed that the region possessed not only the facilities for a Mars colony, but a fortune in copper to boot. The only consoling thought was something John had said about it being worthless to anyone on Earth—it was impossibly expensive to ship it off the planet. Still, it was very valuable to any future Mars colony, as an inexpensive source of a metal with a multitude of uses.

The other thing bothering her was the notion that the finders of mineral deposits ought to own them—not those who came later, no matter how powerful. Although she had already given the matter a lot of thought, this would have to be thought about again, she concluded. She could not help her thoughts turning to what John had done to assert their ownership of the copper find, just before NASA's 2046 rescue mission had been scheduled to land, two Earth years earlier.

Thinking about John then reminded her to ask him about reel launches.

There was also a load of work waiting for her—the greenhouses needed tending, among other things. She felt despair about that too. There was really no need to bother if they were all going to be shipped off to Earth in a few weeks. But deep inside she was still determined not to go. This had to be thought about too, but she could not see how she could possibly resist her rescuers if five of them knocked on their door one morning armed with powerful automatic weapons.

It was a very anxious woman who drove her rover up onto the shelf at Tip Mountain a little later, to her home in the glass-enclosed compound she loved so well.

CHAPTER FIVE

King's Ransom

IT WAS just before three o'clock that Monday afternoon, and the clouds that had covered the sky for most of the morning were now gone. The afternoon sun shone brightly on a train of three buggies, each one pulling a trailer, as the train emerged from Kumar Gap, and approached a road junction, after an almost two and a half hour journey south. The sun had warmed the ground sufficiently for the air temperature to climb a bit above freezing, and the ten occupants of the three buggies had not suffered from the cold.

The lead buggy was the one on loan from Leaf Valley. Jurgen Eindorf was driving, with Captain Derk beside him, both of them sitting under the buggy's sand-bagged roof rack. Dr. Astrid Larsson, and Claude Bertrand, the forty-five year old French structural engineer, sat behind in the trailer seats.

Dr. Donald Carruthers, the mission's thirty-four year old chief geologist and geochemist, from England, drove the next buggy. He was trim in build, of medium height, with a boyish look. He had dark fair, wavy hair, hanging over his forehead, and a pleasant, broad face, that smiled a lot. Sheila Bell and Emma Grant sat beside him.

Dr. Vincenzo Cassoni, a forty-year-old Italian geologist and structural engineer, was driving the last buggy. Vince was a lively man, of medium height, with a sense of humor and a good-natured but rather sharp face. He had fine, slightly waved, dark hair, neatly cut, and combed sideways. Beside him sat Ursula Schneider, the Austrian biologist, and Karl Mannhardt, the German field engineer.

Astrid Larsson and Claude Bertrand, in the trailer seats of the lead buggy, wore radiation umbrellas, about three inches thick, filled with sand and water. The six in the other buggies had no need to, sitting under sand-bagged roof racks. They all wore overshoes and overgloves, to protect against the slightly corrosive Martian soil.

There was an array of small satellite communications dishes sitting on top of the roof rack of each of the two ESA buggies. The dishes, each about the size of a small saucer, were arrayed in almost a half sphere, about two feet in diameter, twenty-four dishes to an array. A dish array looked like a giant, rounded lilac flower.

The idea was to have at least one of the dishes of the array pointing at the ESA communications satellite, high in the sky to the south, no matter which way the buggy was turned. This avoided the need to stop the buggy and point the dish at the satellite, which you would have to do if there had been only one dish. It also avoided the mechanical apparatus for steering the dish in search of the satellite. Such an apparatus was likely to go wrong, or not work well, when subjected to the rigors of buggy travel over the rough terrain of Mars. In contrast, the half-sphere array of small dishes never had to move. A computer just selected the dish, or small group of adjacent dishes, currently pointed at the satellite. It did this in real time, so that the satellite link was always maintained, when the buggy was moving, changing direction, or rolling over rocks and stones.

Nothing is for nothing, however, and the price of this powerful and convenient satellite link was that you had to use very small dishes, in order to have an array of them. This meant that you had to use not just very high frequency radio signals, but what engineers called *ultra extreme high frequency* signals. These were even higher frequency radio signals than those commonly used on Earth for satellite communications, with a much larger dish.

The ultra extreme high frequency radio beam from a small buggy dish had one disadvantage. It behaved much like a light beam, and could be badly scattered or reflected by ice clouds. As a result, a buggy's radio beam up to the satellite would find it hard to get through even a thin cloud layer. So when the sky on Mars was cloud covered, the communications link could be poor, or even out.

Buggy engineers had not believed this was a significant disadvantage, since the buggies were intended for use in daylight on Mars, when cloud cover would be very uncommon. Nevertheless, that morning, this minor drawback to the satellite communications system had bothered Jurgen. On his very first morning on Mars, as he directed assembly of the ESA buggies down in the landing pit, the sky had been cloud covered.

During the long drive south up Kasei Valley that afternoon, however, the sun had dispelled not only the cloud of the morning, but also Jurgen's initial concern that the buggy satellite links might sometimes not work as intended. Just before two o'clock, Emma Grant had used the satellite link to call Jose Montoya, some forty-five miles away at the habitat, while the buggy was in motion, and the system had worked perfectly.

A final test, involving satellite transmission of video images, had also been a success. With the buggy in motion, Emma had video recorded images of the scenery along their way, and had used the satellite link to send the images back to the habitat in real time, and to Mission Control on Earth as well. Karl Mannhardt had sent images from his moving buggy too, all without a hitch.

Half an hour after Emma and Karl sent the images, the buggy train arrived at the road junction lying just beyond Kumar Gap. It had taken two and a half hours of scenic travel south on the main Kasei Valley road to reach this important junction.

At first, for over an hour and a half, they had driven south on the stretch of road between the high escarpment walls of southwest Kasei Valley, at about thirty miles an hour. Their route along the valley floor had continually wound around eroded craterlets, and rolled over small ups and downs. The scenery had been spectacular.

Then they had come to a five-mile long gully, called Finger Gully, that led up to the southern, much higher level of Kasei Valley. They had climbed up the gully road, which John Erway had improved in recent years, at only fifteen miles an hour.

Finger Gully was one of five adjacent gullies, laid out like the fingers of a hand, all leading to the upper level.

The original road up Finger Gully had twisted a great deal, and John's improvements had involved using his mini bulldozer to straighten the worst bends. The motivation had been the derelict habitat at the old NASA landing site, to the south. The roadwork had allowed the three Martians to tow the long building north for repairs.

From the gully top, the ten ESA astronauts had continued south on the road. After about eight miles, the road turned east, or left, through a gap in a line of low hills, called Kumar Hills. It came out of this gap, Kumar Gap, at a road junction in an adjoining valley that also ran north-south. This adjoining valley was thus the eastern of two twin north-south running valleys, separated by Kumar Hills.

Derk ordered a stop only a few hundred meters beyond Kumar Gap, as they approached the road junction. A large mesa, Funnyface Mesa, now lay about twelve miles dead ahead to the east. The mesa's huge escarpment wall was in full view on the horizon, pock-marked with small impact craters. The mesa wall marked the eastern boundary of Kasei Valley, on this higher valley level.

They could also see an imposing mountain, lying somewhat to their left, northeast of the road junction. It was black, brown, and red in color. The summit was a ridge, several miles long, running to the northeast, so that the mountain was wedge shaped. It was quite steeply sloped on its southeastern side, but was gently sloped on its opposite northwestern side. The usual small, scattered impact craters decorated both slopes of the mountain.

"That's Chiselhead Mountain," said Derk, with a tone of satisfaction, as Emma video recorded the sight.

The drive south had gone without incident, and it pleased Derk to know he was now sitting in front of a king's ransom in copper. The key question was whether or not that ransom was large enough to justify the E.U.'s ambitious plan for developing the region, and his future as the person in charge of it all, the ultimate authority over a very profitable Mars colony.

"Well, this is as far south as we go today," Derk went on. "The right turn ahead takes you further south for only another twenty miles or so, as far as the old NASA landing site. There's nothing there except the graves of the eleven dead from the 2038 mission, I should remind you. We take the left turn, and the road to Chiselhead Mountain. Only another five miles and we're there.

"You may recall from the briefing that the road doesn't end at Chiselhead Mountain, and that we're not coming back this way. The road goes on past the mountain, and then turns back toward the north by a different route. It goes down a different gully too—quite a steep one—to get back down to the lower level of Kasei Valley. And it comes out of the gully in a different small arm, called Chiselhead Canyon. We came past the entrance to it about an hour ago. We'll take that shorter route back, after we've done the survey."

"Mission Control has sent us a long way on our first day out," ventured Sheila. "They must think this survey's very important."

"Mission Control thinks it's important that the mission find out how much copper Chiselhead Mountain has," said Derk.

"Are we going to be back before dark?" asked Sheila. She was feeling concerned for the safety of the expedition. She thought they had all come rather far. If something were to go seriously wrong, they could not survive even till midnight, since their air supply was good for only about eleven hours, until about eleven thirty, as were the batteries that kept their pressure suits warm and functioning.

"Absolutely," said Derk. "It'll be just getting dark when we get back. Remember, the mission places a premium on safety. We can't afford accidents. So we're not going to end up driving in the dark on our first major trip. But we also have to do the job we were sent here to do, and that will involve some risks. If you were worried about a delay causing us to run out of air, Sheila, remember that these buggies are super reliable, and that the chance of three of them going wrong is remote. If we did have a problem with one of them, the other two could get us all back safely."

"It was indeed our air supply I was worried about, sir," admitted Sheila, "since we've come such a long way with only buggies."

"I'm well aware of that, Sheila," affirmed Dirk, "but there's no need for concern. We've a wide margin of safety. This is only a seven hour trip, allowing for nearly a two-hour survey. That means we can easily comply with the basic safety rule—no one outside more than eight hours at a stretch. The air in your main air flask will last ten hours, and there's another hour in your reserve flask. As well as that, there are duplicate air pumps, and duplicate air valves in both flasks, just in case. There's practically no chance of anything going wrong with the air supply. We'll not be out long enough to come anywhere near emptying even the main air flask in your backpack. And if by some remote chance you were to lose the air in both air flasks, you could borrow the reserve flasks from a few of your companions. That would be enough to see you safely home."

"I see, sir," said Sheila, feeling a little less concerned. "Maybe I'm just not used to having to worry about margins of safety when you go outside."

"Margins of safety are my responsibility as mission commander," said Derk confidently, "but as mission doctor it's your duty to bring any matter to my attention that might endanger the health or safety of the crew." He had been happy to expound at length on the safety of the air supply, for he suspected that Sheila was not the only one feeling concerned.

Derk did not turn around as he spoke, but appeared to be studying the mountain to the northeast, as if quite unconcerned about the air supply issue. Actually, he did have some concerns of his own about that issue, given that they were using buggies and not rovers. He knew though, that an enormous amount of engineering development and testing had gone into ensuring that the air supply in their suits was sufficient, reliable and safe. He meant it when he promised he would maintain a good margin of safety. He did not intend to relax his concern until he had succeeded in getting control of the two rovers in Leaf Valley, to allow risk-free, long-distance trips.

"Right ho, let's carry on," he added.

Ten minutes later, the road began to climb up the shallow slope of the northwest side of Chiselhead Mountain. It climbed up very gently, going mostly transversely across the long slope, in a northeasterly direction.

About six hundred feet up, they came to a reasonably flat shelf, to the right of the road. Derk ordered a halt here. On the shelf was a cleared area of about two hundred by two hundred feet, obviously cleared by a machine. There were no rocks lying about, except for six large piles of stones. The stones were big and quite irregular, and were mostly brown in color, but with some black material attached—raw copper embedded in dark basalt rock.

Beyond the cleared area, the road continued on, but turned down the mountain slope. When it reached the bottom, it veered left somewhat and then headed due north across the plain below, in the general direction back to the habitat.

"All right," said Derk, as he scanned the terrain round about, "this spot's as high as the road goes. It's obviously where the three in Leaf Valley stockpiled their raw copper. It'll serve as a base for our survey. We haven't got a lot of time. We should be gone from here in an hour and a half, two hours at the latest."

Then he said: "Don, Vince. Listen carefully. I want you to survey all the way around the mountain if you have to. And since this will be the first time you've driven the buggies on rock-covered terrain, I want you to be extra careful. Don't forget the slope on the other side of the mountain is very much steeper than on this side.

"Each of you is in charge of your crew. You can coordinate what you do between you, but remember: You've two goals. First, and most importantly, you are to get an estimate on the total amount of copper. Second, you are to determine the extent of the deposit and stake it. You have the stakes. You should each make your own independent estimate of the size of the deposit, and keep it to yourself. You can discuss your estimates with me when we get back to the habitat. Any questions?"

"No," said Don Carruthers, "Vince and I have already figured out a good way to divide up the work. It should save us a lot of time." The English and Italian geologists got on well together.

"Good," said Derk. "Now, you two may be the geology experts, but remember, you need help to get this job done in less than two hours—you've a lot of survey equipment to get in and out of the trailers. Make sure you use that help." He turned to Emma and Sheila. "You two are to help Don in every way possible. You do what he asks without question. We have to get this survey done today."

"Now you don't have to worry," said Sheila. "Emma and I will do exactly what Don asks."

"And you two are to do everything you can to help Vince," he said, looking at Ursula and Karl, sitting in Vince's buggy.

"I can help Vince set his equipment up," said Karl. "We practiced it in training. That should save us some time."

"I can help with setting it up too," added Ursula.

Karl Mannhardt was a forty-one year old field engineer, with Special Forces background. He was a fairly large, strong man, with a square, determined jaw, and wavy fair hair, which he kept close cut, military style. Although he was technically very competent, something on which he prided himself, his face seemed cold, even heartless. He lacked both imagination and any sense of humor.

Ursula Schneider, thirty-three years old, had long, straight, light-brown hair, and a flat, wondering, but kindly face. She had major skills in plant and animal biology, and minor skills in geology, with enough knowledge of human biology to be Sheila Bell's backup.

"Excellent," said Derk. "And one last thing. Emma and Karl: I want you both to video record as much of the survey as you can, but be careful not to transmit the video to Earth. If you have any technical problems, help one another." Derk had decided not to run the risk of the CIA intercepting that particular transmission.

"No problem," said Emma. "We can easily save the recordings."

"Good. Well, you'd better be off," said Derk. "We won't be very far from here. We're going to do another small survey. And remember the safety rule: No talking while out driving or walking, except to point out something important about the immediate terrain. Keep your minds on what you're doing. If you must discuss, stop first."

The two survey buggies set out, and soon were just two specks in the distance, crawling along the side of the mountain.

Meanwhile, Captain Derk, Jurgen Eindorf, Astrid Larsson, and Claude Bertrand set out on a walk around the northwest slope of the mountain. All four of them wore radiation umbrellas now, and Astrid carried her buggy's video camera. The four walked for just over an hour, on the lookout for anything interesting. They never strayed more than about half a mile from where the buggy was parked on the cleared area, with its heaps of raw copper.

The thirty-one year old Astrid Larsson was primarily a structural engineer, but was also a qualified geologist. During the walk, even the normally imperturbable Swede sometimes got quite excited at what she saw. As well as the large quantity of copper and basalt rocks, in all shapes and sizes, littering the slope everywhere, every so often they came across an exposed copper-filled fissure in the dark basalt bedrock of the mountainside. Some of these fissures were quite enormous, hundreds of feet wide and many feet thick.

"Molten copper must have simply squeezed up everywhere it got a chance," explained the Swede once, in her sing-song Swedish accent, as she stood looking at a huge copper-filled fissure, making a video of it. "The total deposits have to be enormous."

"How can you be so sure?" asked Jurgen Eindorf.

"The same way Columbus was sure he had discovered a large continent when he saw the mouth of the Mississippi River," answered Astrid.

"Because only a continent could supply such a lot of water, I suppose," put in Claude Bertrand, the structural engineer. He spoke very correct English with a mild, cultured French accent.

Claude Bertrand was a strongly-built, medium-tall man, quiet and well mannered, with a serious face. He had thinning, straight, dark brown hair, cut short and combed to one side, and balding at the temples. He was probably Europe's best known structural engineer.

"Yes," said Astrid. "Likewise there has to be a frozen river of solid copper underneath this slope. The copper rocks we see on the surface are just some of the twigs and leaves of a very large tree. The river of copper is the trunk of that tree. It is well out of sight; but it has to be there."

Eventually they all came back to the buggy and sat down in its seats, which were designed for occupants wearing backpacks. They sat facing out to the north, but kept an attentive eye to the southwest, where they expected the other two buggies to appear, coming around the southwestern side of the mountain after their survey trip right around it.

Although none showed it, each of them, Derk included, was experiencing a faint feeling of anxiety. An accident this far from base could be a calamity. They all understood though, that the survey job had a very high priority. The amount of copper under the mountain would determine the level of investment in any future colony for decades to come.

The late afternoon sun was to the southwest, but still quite high in a pink sky that was now completely clear of clouds. The deserted northwest-facing mountain slope, on which they sat, lay in bright sunshine. The copper everywhere imparted a rich brown glow.

They had a magnificent view from where they sat, some six hundred feet above the floor of the upper Kasei Valley level. The valley floor all around below was littered with the usual partly eroded small craters, found everywhere on Mars. The mountain slope was badly pockmarked with small meteor-impact craters too. It was the meteor impacts that had shattered the basalt surface of the slope, with its many protruding copper-filled fissures, in the process littering the slope with copper and basalt rock fragments.

From their vantage point, they could easily see over the top of the final range of the low Kumar Hills to the west, as far as Finger Gully on the horizon to the northwest. Due north, another set of gullies could just be seen on the horizon. There were only two, but they seemed much more pronounced than the five gullies making up the Finger Gully complex. The road to the north made for the rightmost and nearer of these two gullies.

In the terrain database in each buggy, and at the habitat, there was a detailed map of the region, with place names. John Erway had constructed the map, and on it this rightmost gully was marked Chiselhead Gully. The narrow arm of the lower level of Kasei Valley, which the gully led down to, had been marked Chiselhead Canyon.

"We'll get to explore that canyon on the way back," said Derk, observing Jurgen Eindorf studying the terrain to the north.

"I was thinking about the road," said Jurgen. "Those three have managed to build a lot of good roads. NASA was obviously thinking when it sent a small bulldozer on the 2038 mission."

"Does anyone know why they built two roads to this mountain?" asked Claude Bertrand.

"I would imagine it was because the way we came up, along Finger Gully, has a very shallow grade," answered Astrid Larsson. "The shorter route back, down Chiselhead Gully, has a much steeper grade—easy for going down but not for coming up."

"Makes sense," said Claude Bertrand slowly. "So you think they would have taken their copper out through Chiselhead Gully?"

"Yes," said Astrid. "I would think so."

"Could you build a rail link down to Elbow Plain through Chiselhead Gully?" asked Derk.

"I do not think so," said Astrid, "at least, not with the steep grade Chiselhead Gully has at present, but I would have to see it before I could be sure. I can give you a better assessment this evening, after we have been through it."

"Even if the grade is too steep, it might still be possible to blast out the whole tip of the gully to get a lower grade," said Claude, thinking about the problem professionally. "Whether or not that could pay would depend on the volume of traffic. If it is big enough, it can pay to do anything."

Derk said nothing, but thought to himself that it might well be big enough. Never in his life had he seen so much copper.

Just at that moment they spotted the two survey buggies to the southwest, lower down the slope, well separated, about a mile away. All four of them experienced an immediate feeling of relief, as they watched the progress of the buggies.

Suddenly one of the buggies stopped—the one lower down—and its three occupants got out and stood around something nearby. They were too far away for Derk and his company to hear what was being said over the helmet radio.

Then the other buggy drew up beside the first and stopped. Its occupants got out too, and now all six were standing in a circle, obviously discussing the object of interest. Derk studied the group through outdoors field glasses, but could not make out what was causing the commotion. Then one of the six got back in a buggy. An instant later the radio alert came on in Derk's buggy—a light started blinking on the dash, and a beeping sound came on in their helmet radios.

Derk took the radio cable from the dash and plugged it into a socket on his breast plate. He could now communicate via the buggy's surface radio, over a much wider range.

Vince Cassoni's voice came through, with his unmistakable Italian accent. "Captain," said Vince, in an animated tone, "we would like you to come down and see this. It looks like something for you."

"On our way," said Derk.

*

Monique Montpellier handed the field glasses to Jose Montoya. Monique was in her early thirties, and was reasonably good looking.

She had wavy, brown hair, cut quite short. There was a decisive and determined look to her round, serious face. She was a biologist by training, but had spent eight years in the French military, specializing in extreme environment survival and combat.

"What do you think they are up to?" she asked, frowning, and speaking very correct English with a mild French accent. "They seem to be staying well clear of the landing pit."

"Hard to tell," said Jose, as he lowered the field glasses, "but if we wait, I am sure we will find out. Just keep watching." Jose also spoke very correct English, but with a quite strong Spanish accent. "I am sure the Captain would like to know too," he added.

Jose Montoya, thirty-five years old, the second flight engineer, was a handsome, strongly built man, fairly tall, square jawed, with thick, straight, very dark brown hair, but close cut, military style. Like his companion, he had a decisive and resolute face. Although a competent flight engineer, he had had extensive military experience as a field engineer, and was no stranger to military field strategy. He looked tough and resilient. Had he had a pointed beard, and had he been wearing an old-style Spanish military helmet, he would have looked the image of a conquistador of old. He gave the impression of a man who would let no obstacle stand in his way.

Jose and Monique respected and understood each other, and got on well together. The two of them were standing by a small kitchen window, on the west side of the habitat's central module, looking down on the region of Elbow Plain around the landing pit, about a mile away to the west. It was close to five o'clock, and the sun was now above Stem Mountains, to the left of Stem Gap. The distinctive gap in the northwest wall of Kasei Valley was easily visible in the distance.

What they had been observing was a single rover. It had driven up the Elbow Hill road shortly before, to a point about fifty meters past the entrance to the trail down to the landing pit, and had stopped there for a few minutes. Then it had started up again, but had left the road, and was now slowly making its way over the stony terrain between the landing pit and the habitat, but only about a hundred meters from the rim of the pit.

Then the rover stopped. A few minutes later, two figures came out of the airlock and went to a spot adjacent to the back of the trailer. The two figures appeared to be looking at something on the ground. Then they bent down, and lifted a box-like object, with a small dish-shaped piece of metal attached to the top, and carried it to the back of the trailer and pushed it in. Then they got back in the rover. The rover then continued on, but veering to the left, keeping about a hundred meters from the pit edge.

"Now we know," said Jose. "That was a radar beacon. There are two more. They should be at 120 and 240 degrees around the pit from the first one. Just watch."

Jose was right. After circling the pit by 120 degrees, the rover stopped again, two figures got out, and removed a similar object.

"See," he said. "I wonder why they want to collect those."

"Could they be expecting another ESA lander?" asked Monique.

"ESA has nothing in the short run," said Jose. "Maybe they are worried about the possibility though, and are taking precautions."

"What about the Americans?" asked Monique. "Could they have a lander coming we have not heard about?"

"I think we would have heard something, if that was true."

"Maybe they just want to feel in control."

"Could be. If they have the beacons, they certainly keep control of all landings. Landing without them is very risky."

"Are they ESA beacons?" asked Monique.

"Most likely," said Jose, "although NASA sent them beacons too, in 2046. The question is whether or not they were meant to be returned to ESA. This is definitely a matter for the Captain."

"But by the time he gets back, the beacons will be gone," said Monique. "Maybe we should be doing something to stop them."

"We could shoot them easily enough," said Jose. "They are within range. But I have strict orders not to open fire unless attacked."

"So you think there is nothing we should do."

"It looks that way. The Captain did say we have to make allowances for these two. He thinks they are a bit crazy—suffering from too much isolation. A few screws loose, as they say. Anyway, our mission will need that rover once they are off the planet. The Captain would certainly not want us to shoot holes in it. And you can hardly justify shooting people over a few landing beacons."

"Should we call the Captain?" asked Monique. "We can reach him with the satellite link."

"No," said Jose firmly. "There is nothing he could ask us to do. We have no buggy. We could not even drive down and challenge them. All we can do is tell the Captain when he gets back."

Jose was in charge. It was his decision.

Monique and Jose did nothing except watch from the habitat, as the rover stopped at the third radar beacon, and John and Denise got out and loaded it into the trailer.

A short time later, the rover was back on the road, driving toward the main road that ran across the plain to Stem Gap and the sanctuary of Leaf Valley.

Monique and Jose continued to keep a lookout in turns, as instructed. Derk had been concerned that yet another break-in attempt might be made, this time on the habitat, where the mission's illicit guns were now safe in a storage cubicle.

The rover did not return. At about seven twenty, when it was almost dark, almost an hour after the sun had set behind the stretch of Stem Mountains directly to the west, and with patches of ice mist on the floor of the valley, Jose Montoya spotted the train of buggies, some five miles away. The buggies were coming up the main road from the south in the fading light, with headlights full on.

Soon the buggy train turned right at the Elbow Hill road junction, and now Jose could just make out ten upright figures in the three buggies. Two hours earlier, he had had a message from Emma saying they would be back just after seven. Nevertheless, he heaved a sigh of relief at the sight of the ten. Back safe. Thank God, he thought. He went at once to the communications room to send a message about the safe return to Mission Control, where it was nearly four thirty in the morning. Many had stayed up, waiting impatiently for news. Sheila Bell had not been the only one concerned about the ten being so far from base in only open buggies.

Soon all three buggies were parked on the shelf outside the habitat. The ESA mission's first major surface expedition on Mars had been successfully completed.

*

Captain Derk did not have the estimates for the size of the copper deposit at Chiselhead Mountain, when the expedition got back to base. He had decided to be patient, and wait till later in the evening, before meeting alone with his two geologists. He did not want it generally known how important the estimate was, and what was hanging on it, at least not yet. Only Jurgen and Emma, and his structural engineers, Claude, Astrid, and Vince, knew exactly what was depending on it. Don Carruthers, the chief geologist, did not.

Later that evening, after a private meeting with the two geologists, Emma Grant interviewed Derk once more, and transmitted the video and audio of the interview to Earth. Derk sat at the corner of the long table in the meeting room, with a kindly, smiling face.

Most of the interview was about the trip south that day, and Emma included some of the video recordings she had made.

Derk spent some time explaining the workings of the buggies' satellite communications system, the first of its kind ever used on Mars. He talked about how it had worked flawlessly that day, and how it would help reduce risk for the team when out in the field. The habitat, and thus Mission Control, would always be in contact.

When asked about Chiselhead Mountain and the copper, Derk was very positive and enthusiastic. He said that they had successfully confirmed the existence of a large copper deposit, which would certainly be very useful for any future human settlement in the region. Some rather restricted video of copper deposits on the mountainside followed.

Later in the interview, when asked about Denise's visit to the habitat that morning, the expression on Derk's face became saddened and pained.

"She seems to be full of her own importance," said Derk. "She practically bullied poor Sheila into giving her dental treatment at once, when Sheila had so much to do for the mission, including getting her surgery up and running. Of course, Sheila is just too kindhearted to say anything negative about her, but Denise Lavoisier had little or nothing wrong with her teeth. There was certainly nothing that needed immediate attention. Sheila did two fillings, and from what I can gather, at least one of them did not have to be done at all. And then Denise Lavoisier walked out, without saying one word of thanks. And when I came back from the buggy assembly work this morning, and asked how things had gone, Denise Lavoisier wouldn't say a word to me."

"What do you think the problem is?" asked Emma.

"I'm no psychologist," said Derk, "but I think it's just pride. They've just grown used to feeling superior to everyone else, because they think they've been able to manage here on Mars so independently. They never admit the contribution of the hundreds of billions of dollars that were spent to get them here, and bring all the equipment needed for them to build their fine house and greenhouses. Denise Lavoisier seems to have no gratitude for the enormous expense the taxpayers of the United States, and Europe and Japan too, were put to on her behalf."

"Is that just your opinion," asked Emma, "or do you have anything that might confirm that?"

"I have some evidence people back on Earth will find quite shocking," said Derk. "The fact is: John Erway and Denise Lavoisier have no scruples at all. I know it sounds incredible, but last night, just as I was about to get in my bunk, I noticed a light down in the landing pit, about a mile away. Five of us went down in the buggy to investigate, and caught the two of them red handed, in the act of burgling the lander. We caught them unloading test equipment from the lander's cargo floor and stowing it in the trailer of their rover. It was experimental equipment we had brought to Mars to test out for a manufacturer in Munich. When we confronted them, they did hand it back, but never even said sorry."

"What did you do with them?" asked Emma.

"What could we do?" asked Derk, looking worried and pained. "On Earth I suppose I'd have called the police. It certainly looks like criminal behavior to me. But here, well, I just told them to go home. We knew there was a good chance that these two might be a bit peculiar, after so many years alone on Mars, but nothing like this."

"And that's all?"

"Well, not exactly," said Derk. "We decided we'd better take precautions. While we were away today, I left Monique and Jose to keep an eye on things, and keep a lookout for another attempt to burgle the lander. I didn't really expect anything after we had caught them red-handed the night before. But I was wrong. While we were away, they came and took the landing beacons from around the landing pit. What good they could possibly be to them, I can't see. But the beacons are the property of ESA. These two must surely have something badly wrong up top."

"Are you going to try to get them back?"

"I don't know," said Derk. "We don't need them in the short run. I think we have to accept we're dealing with people who are a bit mentally unhinged. I think we'll just humor them, and wait for a chance to get the beacons back later. If we were to ask for them, they might well destroy them. Who knows what they might do?"

"Aren't you going to visit their Mars house tomorrow evening, and eat a meal there?" asked Emma. "Are you intending to take precautions for the visit?"

"It's hard to see how," said Derk. "It's just one more risk we have to face here on Mars." He sighed and opened out his hands.

The questions then shifted to the geological survey trip down Kasei Valley to the northeast, planned for the next day. Derk's worried and saddened expression was at once replaced by the enthusiastic and positive expression of earlier in the interview.

*

Late that evening, with the habitat quiet and everyone retired to their cubicles, Sheila Bell came to the cubicle of her friend, Don Carruthers. Both their cubicles were in the science section of the habitat, at the south end, which was partly recessed into the hillside.

Don had been expecting her, and gave her a huge hug as she came in. He was very fond of Sheila Bell, and happy to spend some time alone with her. Actually, he had fallen in love with her, but did not yet know it, for she was always around, and he tended to take her for granted.

"I'm afraid it's still cramped," began Don with a smile, speaking with a northern English accent, "but it's a lot better than on the trip out. You've got three choices. You take the chair while I take the bunk, or the other way round, or we both sit on the bunk."

"If we both sit on the bunk, we can't both stretch out," said Sheila. "I want to put my feet up for a bit, after that buggy trip. You take the bunk—I'll take the chair if I can put my feet up on the bunk beside yours."

"Fair enough," said Don, as they made themselves comfortable. "Do you have any of those chocolate creams with you?" he asked, with a look of anticipation in his face.

"One each," said Sheila, as she pulled a small box from her pants pocket. They were both wearing standard ESA shirts and slacks, light brown in color, but now rather dark in the dim light from a small lamp on a tiny desk beside the bunk. The bunk, chair, and desk, with a computer on top, and a few shelves to one side, were the only items of furniture in the tiny cubicle, only six feet by six.

"Well, what do think of Mars?" asked Don. "You certainly got to see a piece of it today."

"It's unbelievably beautiful," said Sheila. "I always thought a really beautiful place had to be green, and rolling, with hills and valleys and lakes, and the sea pounding on rocks and beaches—"

"You mean like Ireland?"

"All right, I'm prejudiced," said Sheila. "I always thought a place had to be something like that to be really beautiful. But this is an altogether different kind of beauty, a rare red beauty, and so quiet and peaceful too."

"I agree," said Don, "it's one continuous pleasure just to look at it. I could stay here forever."

"But pleasure isn't the only feeling I get looking at it," said Sheila. "I also feel I'm like a fly that's just landed on an exquisitely beautiful spider's web—waiting for the spider to show up."

"You sense the danger, that's all," said Don consolingly. "Mars is a dangerous place."

"Yes," said Sheila. "The danger's very obvious. You only have to make one stupid mistake here and the planet will kill you. Take today's trip now. I know it wasn't likely, but just suppose something had gone wrong with the buggies, so that we couldn't get back as planned. Our air would have run out by about eleven thirty this evening. A problem like that would have been enough to kill us. Back on Earth it would have been just a wee bit of bother. I'm still not sure it was wise to go so far in buggies. I think—well, it seems to me that a trip like that is better done in a rover."

"Don't you think you're exaggerating a bit?" asked Don. "What could have happened that would have caused all three buggies to be delayed so badly that we all ran out of air before we could get back? I can't imagine anything doing that. One buggy might just possibly have gone wrong, it's true. But the others could have towed it home. That might have taken a few hours longer, but still well inside margins of safety, as the Captain said. As well as that, although the Captain didn't mention it today, if all of the buggies had gone wrong, we could still have used the satellite link to contact the habitat, and Jose could then have contacted John Erway, and asked him to come for us in his rovers."

"I understand that, Don. Doesn't my head say the same thing?" said Sheila. "I can't imagine myself how it could go wrong with all the buggies together, and with those three in Leaf Valley with their big rovers ready to help as well. I just don't feel easy in my mind, that's all, and I don't know why." She was silent for a few seconds. "What about if there had been a radiation storm?"

"There were shelters set out along the road," said Don, "and it's close to the low point in the sunspot cycle, so a storm is not likely.

But if there had been one, we would have gone into a shelter, and stayed there till after dark."

"But then we might not have been back till after eleven," pointed out Sheila. "You can't drive as fast at night. Now wouldn't that have been a wee bit too close for comfort?"

"All right, Sheila," said Don. "You have a point. I suppose we just have to accept that Mars is a dangerous place."

They were both silent for a while, thinking about this. Then Sheila asked: "Do you have confidence in the Captain, Don? Do you think he always knows what he's doing?"

"He's got a better head for strategy than anyone I've ever met," said Don thoughtfully, "and he really does take care to make sure nothing happens to any of us. I just don't think he cares about us personally. He's a very ambitious man, and maybe I shouldn't say it, but I think he's a heartless man too. He's like the captain of a ship, who needs every one of his crew to achieve his objectives, but wouldn't hesitate to sacrifice one of them, if he suddenly found out that it was the only way to get the job done. But maybe he can't afford the luxury of caring personally for everyone under him. I don't know. I'm just certain Captain Derk doesn't care two hoots about any of us personally—and doesn't care whether or not he's liked by any of us either. Sometimes I even think he prefers to be feared."

"He seems to care a lot about the copper at Chiselhead Mountain," said Sheila, "almost as if it belonged to him. Did you see the way he reacted when he drove down and saw that last copper stake, and discovered you and Vince hadn't staked the find because John Erway's stakes were there already? All he could say about that stake was: 'Pull it out, pull it out at once'."

"I'm not a lawyer, but I don't think it was legal to pull it out," said Don. "I've read my fair share of Westerns. In the days of the Old West that was called claim jumping—good way to get yourself shot or strung up. I'll never forget the look on his face, though, when we dug down and discovered that particular stake was stuck in at least a half ton of concrete."

"I saw it too," said Sheila. "And did you see his red face? I thought he would burst a blood vessel when he realized we wouldn't be able to get it out."

"I didn't have the courage to refuse to try and get it out, and tell him I wanted no hand in any claim jumping," said Don, feeling a little ashamed of himself.

"Do those stakes mean that the copper belongs to the three in Leaf Valley?"

"I doubt it," said Don. "There has to be a law allowing the staking of claims, and a land office run by some legal authority in which to register a staked claim, and the legal authority has to have sovereignty over the land. I've never heard of such a law for Mars, and there are certainly no land offices on Mars."

"So John Erway could not possibly have registered a claim."

"No, he could not."

"So his stakes are just symbolic then," said Sheila, determined to get to the bottom of this.

"Most likely," said Don. "But you never know. There's a chance his stakes could give rise to an ownership dispute one day, when the proper laws are in place, which is probably why the Captain wants them pulled out. But two things are for sure. The Captain will have those stakes out before long, and there's going to be no love lost between the Captain and John Erway."

"But if the Captain has them pulled out, what's to stop John Erway putting them back in again, in even bigger blocks of concrete? He has rovers and a cement factory."

"He may not get that chance," said Don slowly. "I have a feeling the Captain is intending to rescue those three, even if they don't want rescued, and by force if necessary, and send them back to Earth, especially given the size of that copper deposit."

There was silence, as Sheila considered this. Like most people, she had been persuaded that the three would want to be rescued, if not initially, then certainly after they made contact with the ESA mission. After all, nobody could possibly want to stay on Mars forever. But the possibility of a forced rescue bothered her. And now the copper find seemed to be related. Her curiosity was strongly aroused. She decided to pursue the objective from another angle.

"By the way, did you have that meeting with the Captain and Vince this evening?" she asked.

"Yes, we did have a short meeting," said Don. He smiled, knowing what was coming next from his always curious friend.

"A moment ago, you seemed to be saying that the copper deposit was very large," said Sheila. "I don't suppose you want to tell me just how much copper there is up there."

"You don't suppose correctly," said Don. "You know the Captain asked us not to say a word about it."

"But you know you can tell me, I won't say a word to anyone."

"No, I'll keep my word to the Captain," said Don. Then he added: "I could confirm an estimate you made on your own though, without saying a thing."

"Could you now?" said Sheila. "I heard you say this morning that copper is worth between ten and sixteen euros a kilo on Earth, depending on the market. That means at least ten thousand euros a ton."

When Don did not deny this she went on: "So if there was a million tons it would be worth ten billion euros at least—about ten billion dollars. Now would that be a big find?"

"It would be a big find for the purpose of building a Mars colony, but a very ordinary copper find, nothing special, as far as Earth was concerned," said Don.

"Well now, if there was a hundred million tons of copper, it would be worth a thousand billion euros. Isn't that a trillion euros?"

"It is," said Don.

"So I can suppose a trillion euros worth of copper is far too high?" said Sheila.

Don shook his head, but almost imperceptibly.

"Now then, isn't that something to think about? Well then, two trillion would have to be far too high, I suppose?"

Again Don shook is his head slightly.

"Then four trillion would be too high?"

This time Don nodded slightly.

"Then I'll make my own estimate that it's worth about three trillion euros," said Sheila. "My God, that's a powerful mountain of money. Wouldn't the Americans get excited if they knew? Three trillion dollars!"

Don nodded again. "Anybody would get excited. That's why it has to be kept secret, and you know you're not supposed to fish things like that out of me," he said. "Let's just agree it's worth enough money to start the equivalent of a gold rush if it were on Earth, or even a major war. But it's worth very little here. You couldn't use even a tiny fraction of the copper in that mountain. So it doesn't really matter whether there's a hundred million euros worth—or a billion—or a trillion."

"Now wouldn't it make a big difference if there was a way to get it down to Earth?" said Sheila. "Is there any way a thing like that could be done?"

"In theory it could be done, but in practice it couldn't, at least not in this century. Maybe in centuries to come, when technology has advanced way beyond where it is today."

"Now you're making me curious again."

"It's a bit technical."

"Try me. I'm not stupid you know."

"All right," said Don, giving in to his friend's curiosity. "Make yourself comfortable. Here goes. Suppose you have a loaded cannon. The explosive goes off, and the cannon ball flies out. What happens to the cannon?"

"It recoils back a little."

"Right. Some of the explosion energy goes to the large motion of the light cannon ball and some goes to the small motion of the heavy cannon, and action and reaction are balanced. But motion energy goes up with the square of the speed, so most of the energy goes to the cannon ball, and only a little to the slow moving cannon."

"I understand that," said Sheila.

"But if you made a small cannon out of very light-weight metal," said Don, "it would go flying back at much higher speed. So now a lot more of the explosion energy would go to the motion energy of the cannon, and a lot less to the cannon ball."

"Fair enough, which is why cannons are always big and heavy," said Sheila.

"Right, but a rocket's like a cannon ball coming out of a very light weight cannon. When the fuel burns in the rocket motor, the energy goes partly to the rocket going one way, and partly to the very light exhaust gases going the other way at very high speed. Again, action and reaction must balance. When a rocket is lifting off the launch pad, most of the energy of the fuel is going to the high-speed exhaust gases and very little to the rocket motion. So you need an awful lot of fuel and oxidizer to get even a small payload into orbit. That's why the weight of the payload is always a very small fraction of the weight of the fuel and oxidizer at launch."

"Now, are you telling me that it would be very wasteful to try to lift a copper payload off Mars in a rocket?" said Sheila.

"Right," said Don. "You'd have to find a way where all of the energy went to the lifting vehicle, whatever that was."

"And you say there is such a way in theory, but not in practice."

"Yes. The concept's well known. It's even been used in science fiction stories about Mars. But it's out of the question in practice. It's the space elevator concept. You put a big asteroid in stationary orbit around the planet and build a cable down from it to the surface. Then you run an electrically powered elevator up and down the cable. Because the elevator always pushes on the cable, which is attached to a big asteroid at one end and Mars at the other end, it can't move, and all the energy goes into moving the elevator. When the elevator gets to the top of the cable it's moving around Mars at exactly the speed of the planet's rotation—at areostationary orbit distance out. That's about three thousand miles an hour, about eleven thousand miles up from the surface. At that speed, it would take very little further energy to shoot an object out of orbit and back to Earth.

"If you had a space elevator lifting the copper off the planet it would become economic to ship it to Earth. It's downhill from Mars to Earth, gravitationally speaking, once you get up off Mars, into areostationary orbit. You could probably lift off a hundred tons for the same as it would cost in energy to lift off one ton in a rocket."

"It does sound like science fiction," said Sheila. "But you say it's impossible in practice."

"Yes, because of the weight of the cable. The cable has to hang there, thousands of miles of it, under enormous tension, being pulled down by the planet's gravity. It would snap under its own weight. There's no material known that could do the job."

"Could that be what ESA is working on in that secret project in southwest Ireland?"

"Now you're letting that imagination of yours run away with you," said Don. "Absolutely not. Nobody's trying to solve that problem anywhere. It's a century away if there is a solution. You'd have to find something that could be done with today's technology, but with the energy efficiency of a space elevator."

"Is there anything?" asked Sheila.

"Actually, there is a candidate," said Don slowly, his eyes opening quite wide, as if something had just occurred to him.

"Now could that be what they're working on in the project in Ireland?" persisted Sheila. "I've a feeling you know just a wee bit more about that project than you're letting on."

"Now Sheila, it's getting very late," said Don, suddenly looking very firm, "and you know the Captain is very insistent about not gossiping about ESA projects, especially that project in Ireland. I admit I do know a little about it. But I'm not supposed to know. I found out only by accident. I'm afraid I can't tell you, Sheila. I'm sorry."

Sheila looked at her friend thoughtfully. She was thinking that she hadn't done badly for one evening. She was sure she would soon solve the mystery of ESA's Irish research project. She had certainly made progress in satisfying her curiosity, however, for now she had good grounds for suspecting that the project was connected with the copper at Chiselhead Mountain. It was about something equivalent to a space elevator, she suspected, and that something was something to do with reel launches.

"All right, tomorrow's another day," said Sheila. "Now did the Captain talk to you about tomorrow's trip?"

"Yes, he did. We'll both be going, leaving about one, after a late morning briefing, provided it's a calm day, with little or no wind. A high wind could be a problem where we're going."

"I don't like leaving so late," said Sheila, frowning. "I do think it's safer to leave early in the day, so that we'll have more daylight if things go wrong."

"The Captain has his reasons, I think," said Don. "We'll be coming back through Leaf Valley, and he want's it to be getting dark when we do."

"I think you mean we'll be going down Kasei Valley, and then back along Hazard Valley, and into Leaf Valley through the back door, at Tip Canyon?"

"That's what he's got in mind," said John. "The Captain's not coming, so there'll be just two buggies on the trip. He and Emma and Jurgen are leaving at four for dinner at the Erway compound. They're to get to look around too, and decide on how the lander's to be refueled."

"Did the Captain get permission for us to enter Leaf Valley?" asked Sheila. "I did hear John Erway say we were not to come in without permission—I don't think the Captain was very pleased."

Don shook his head.

"Well, for myself," said Sheila, "I would prefer to respect the privacy of those three in there, if they really don't want rescued. After all now, they must surely have worked very hard to build that garden house they've got. I've seen some pictures of it. It can't be right at all for us just to barge in and behave as if we owned the place."

"I agree," said Don. "But I don't think the Captain does. He says they don't own the land. He says the U.N. Mars Office owns it, and will soon grant the E.U. title to the whole region. That's why I think he's intending to rescue those three by force if they refuse to leave.

Anyway, we're not supposed to cause any trouble on the trip tomorrow. The Captain says he wants the geology of the region explored. We're supposed to just drive down Leaf Valley at dusk, with our lights off, while they're all inside the house having dinner. That way, John Erway will not find out. He's not supposed to know."

"So that's what it's all about," mused Sheila. Then she added: "It does look a bit longer than today's trip. Do you think it's safe?"

"I would say so. It's shorter in terms of time," said Don, "and it should be safer too, since we don't have to spend nearly two hours surveying off the road, like we did today. The road trip's only about five miles longer—about a hundred and eighty miles. It's six hours driving altogether, but less than five hours from here to the entrance to Leaf Valley. That's why we're not leaving until one. The Captain figures it's safer that way, since we'll use less air. We should reach the entrance to Leaf Valley by six. We're not supposed to drive down the valley till about seven. If we left here at twelve we'd be at the Leaf Valley entrance at five, which is far too early. We should be back here by eight thirty at the latest. We'll be outside for only about seven and a half hours at most. That still means a very good margin of safety, since our air supply is good for eleven hours."

"I see," said Sheila, reassured.

"By the way," Don continued, "the Captain was very interested to hear what you told me this morning after Denise Lavoisier left—I mean about the road through Tip Canyon. Earlier he wasn't sure about the road through that canyon, and was undecided about whether or not we should try to come back that way. When I told him you said that Denise Lavoisier had said there was a good, safe road that took over three weeks to build, with radiation shelters all along it, he seemed quite relieved. He decided on the spot that we'd come back that way."

"Do you know why they gave the name Hazard Valley to that big valley between Kasei Valley and Tip Canyon?" asked Sheila, feeling concerned once more.

"No, I don't," said Don. "But the terrain database shows all the small valleys around there covered in dunes—obviously no place for a buggy to leave the road, but it should be safe enough in a big wide valley as long as we stay on the road. Hazard Valley is as much as three miles wide at the far end. I suppose that's what was worrying the Captain, before he knew for sure there was a good road through there."

"Then I suppose it'll be all right after all," said Sheila slowly, "although I still think trips like these are for rovers, not buggies."

"We don't have rovers, Sheila," said Don. "ESA's doing this mission on the cheap, for a fraction of what a proper mission would cost. Look at this big habitat we're staying in. It would have cost ESA far more than the whole mission to get something like this safely down on Mars, if we'd had to do it ourselves. We just have to run some risks."

"Now I seem to recall an interview with John Erway about risk on Mars," said Sheila. "It was published in a magazine a few years ago. He said that on Mars you must never run a risk, especially if it threatens your life. If you find a risk in whatever you have to do, it's best to get rid of the risk first, before you go ahead, he said."

"Hmm, did he really say that?" said Don, thoughtfully. "I suppose he must know what he's talking about. We've hardly been here two days and he's still around after ten years on Mars. But look Sheila, old girl, don't you think we've talked enough shop for one evening? I'm getting lonely over here. Come and sit beside me. I need to hold you a little."

A minute later, they were both sitting on the bunk, in the dim light. Don's arm was around Sheila, their backs to the wall, with two sets of feet resting on the small chair beside the bunk. Above their heads was a small window, already covered in frost from inside the habitat. They had no more serious discussions that evening.

Outside, the fast moving, potato-shaped moon Phobos had just risen, and was not yet in the planet's shadow. It shone its feeble crescent light down on the solitary habitat, on that lonely shelf part way up Elbow Hill, in the middle of Elbow Plain. Already a paper-thin layer of fine white frost lay on the long building, glistening in the moonlight, under a starry sky.

CHAPTER SIX

The Glass Compound

THEIR THREE guests had arrived in Dr. Sato's buggy, a little before five, and John and Dr. Sato had spent nearly an hour showing them around the industrial complex that lay just east of Mount Tip, at the tip of Leaf Valley.

Denise had insisted on staying home, to make final preparations for the dinner that evening. It was to be a special dinner. Not only did she want to show off her Martian cuisine, she wanted to awe her guests, and drive home the idea that guests was what they were—visitors to a wonderful place, and not heroic rescuers come to save them from some dreadful fate. She still had some hope remaining that the splendor of the house, and the beautiful, enclosed garden surrounding it, would serve as a convincing salvo in this initial psychological war.

It was now just after six that evening. In the previous hour, high white wave clouds had drifted in over the valley from the east, and had been getting steadily denser. They were not yet dense enough to completely obscure the setting sun, which could still be made out, shining through the thin clouds, just above the escarpment wall at the western edge of Leaf Valley.

As John drove his rover up onto the shelf on the southeast side of Mount Tip, the Mars buggy followed close behind, driven by Jurgen Eindorf. Captain Derk sat beside Jurgen, and Emma Grant sat in the trailer behind. The other two ESA buggies had gone off on the survey trip down Kasei Valley to the northeast. All three in the buggy had noticed the high washboard ice clouds drift in, but had given no thought to the implications, so absorbed were they by the visit to Leaf Valley.

The two vehicles stopped on the mildly sloping shelf, at the east side of a huge compound, enclosed in orange concrete and glass. A glass slab wall in front of them rose out of an orange-concrete foundation wall. Inside the enclosure, shrubs and plants could be seen, some with quite large green leaves, and even flowers. Greenery inside grew right up against the glass, blocking the view of what lay beyond, except at one spot, where a bench was visible.

The upper wall of glass slabs was two slabs high, or about twenty feet, with the six foot by ten foot glass slabs embedded in heavy copper frames protruding from the low foundation wall.

The concrete and glass wall on this side of the compound was about two hundred feet long, and ran north-south, but curving away from them to the west at the lower southern end of the shelf. The top of the orange concrete foundation wall stayed level on the southward sloping shelf. It was only about three feet high nearer the north end, but was some eight feet high farther away at the lower south end.

Near the north end of the orange foundation wall, just to the right of where John stopped the rover, there was a gently sloping driveway running down to a lower level, about twelve feet below the level of the shelf. The sloping driveway was paved with large flat stones. There were steeply sloped orange concrete retaining walls on either side of this sloped driveway.

The orange concrete foundation wall was some fifteen feet high at the bottom of the driveway, and there were two copper doors in this high wall. The door to the right, at the north side, was very large. The other one to the left was much smaller. These were the airlock doors into the compound, the large one capable of taking a rover.

"You can't bring the buggy in," said John. "Park right where you are, and walk down the driveway. You go in through the small airlock. It can take four at a time. You'll find a pressure suit closet on the other side, to your right. It's got some light inside footwear. I'm taking the rover in through the big airlock."

John drove the rover down the driveway, with its trailer attached. The broad airlock door slid to the right, and he drove the machine inside. The door closed behind him, a valve opened, and normal air from inside the compound began filling the airlock's interior.

In front of him was another huge copper door, as big as the outside door. This was the airlock's inside exit door, large enough for a rover. When the airlock had filled, this inner door opened, sliding to the right. It revealed a large exit, opening onto a stone-paved parking pad, inside the compound, surrounded by greenery.

John did not take the rover through this open inside door, but left it parked inside the airlock. There was no space to park on the pad beyond the airlock—the other rover sat parked there.

The huge airlock was designed to double as a rover garage as needed. To make this possible, as the inner door to the parking pad opened, another large copper door, or perhaps skylight shutter, in the roof of the airlock, also slid open, just above the back of the rover, where the rover's heat shunt radiators were. Waste heat from the rover's nuclear power plant could now rise through this open skylight, and circulate into the compound, helping to keep it warm.

John and Dr. Sato were soon out of the rover. They walked around the front of the machine, and went through the huge exit door, emerging onto the parking pad. Turning left, onto a small entrance patio beside the south wall of the rover airlock garage, they were in time to see their three visitors emerge from the door of the small airlock.

They gave the visitors a helping hand with removal of helmets and backpacks, and waited on the patio while the three finished removing their pressure suits. They helped put the pressure suits in a closet on the south wall of the airlock garage and then helped their guests select some light sandals, recently manufactured by Dr. Sato. Each shoe was made simply but elegantly, from a thin strip of copper, fashioned in the shape of the sole of a foot, with a strip of rubber on both sides.

The entrance patio on the south side of the rover garage, as well as the rover parking pad, and the airlock garage floor, were all sunken some twelve feet below the general garden and shelf level, even below the level of the bedrock on the shelf. John had used explosives to blast out the sunken space.

Two sets of stone steps, both lined by greenery, went up from the entrance patio to the garden level, which was at about the same level as the original surface of the shelf before it had been built on. One set of steps went up to the south, to the garden. The other went up to the west, toward the house, and as it climbed, it overlooked the rover parking pad to the right, in front of the rover airlock garage.

"We take the west steps—here," said John to Captain Derk, pointing the way. "They take us almost directly to the house. Those other steps on your left—up to the south—bring you to a path that takes you round the edge of the garden compound. Maybe you'll get time to walk around it later. You can easily spend half an hour walking round all the garden paths we have here."

Derk did not reply, and merely nodded. He was impressed and surprised by what he had seen already. Although he had studied what was known about the house on Mount Tip, using the video recording John and Denise had sent to Earth, the exact layout was not known on Earth.

They went up the steps to the west, with John leading the way, the visitors next, and Dr. Sato at the rear. At the top they could see over the roof of the second rover, parked below to their right. There was also a path straight ahead to the west. They could see the upper story of the house ahead.

"This way," said John, leading them westward, along the top of the embankment sloping down to the parking pad to their right. Where the embankment ended, the path turned right and north, coming quite quickly to a four way junction. To the right was the head of another set of steps, leading down to the west end of the parking pad. John took the path to the left and west, directly to the house.

Soon they were on a patio, at the northeast corner of the house, outside the main entrance. It was one hundred and forty feet, in a straight line, from this corner to the outside door of the rover airlock.

Derk now asked: "How big is this compound?"

"It's about sixty thousand square feet," said John. "That's about an acre and a half—and the house has three thousand square feet on the lower level. The upper level has about two thousand square feet plus a thousand square feet of balcony around it on the south, east and west sides—on the roof of the lower level actually. Both levels are rectangular, with the long sides running east-west. This patio we're standing on runs all the way around the lower level. It becomes a balcony on the long south side. Come I'll show you."

They walked south on the shorter east side of the house, along the patio balcony, passing a copper staircase to the upper balcony. John stopped at the southeast corner of the house.

Because the garden sloped downward to the south, at this corner the patio was some three feet above the garden level. It had a low orange concrete and stone wall at its edge, so that it was now a balcony. At this corner, the balcony turned and ran east-west along the full length of the lower floor of the house. At the far end was a garden table and chairs, with a sun umbrella, surrounded by large orange pots in which a variety of long leafed plants grew.

The low stone wall at the edge of the balcony was quite thick and filled with red soil, and an assortment of plants grew out of it. Some were low flowering shrubs, but many were flowering creepers that fell down over the wall onto the balcony, or in the other direction, into the garden.

The long balcony wall was interrupted one third of the way along it, by a set of stone steps down to a patio at the lower garden level. This central garden patio was stone and orange concrete, and was surrounded by large leafed plants, most of them looking tropical. In the middle of the central patio was a swimming pool.

"You can get a better view of the garden from the upper balcony," said John. "Come."

They walked back along the balcony on the shorter east side of the house, but only as far as the copper staircase to the upper level. This took them to the balcony at the next level.

This upper level balcony was also surrounded by a low orange wall with plants, just like the one on the balcony below, except that now the plants trailing from the balcony wall fell down the wall of the lower level of the house. The upper balcony was on the roof of the lower house level.

They walked south along the short, upper, east-side balcony, and then turned right, and walked westward to the middle of the upper east-west balcony. They could now survey the whole garden from above, so that the overall shape of the garden compound could be seen clearly. It was an odd shape in plan.

"Exactly what shape is this compound?" asked Jorgen Eindorf.

"It's best described by how to make it," said John. "You start with a rectangle running east-west, about one and a half times as long as broad. Then you shorten the south side at each end. Then you round all the corners, rounding the southern corners more than the northern corners. The northern side is about three hundred and thirty feet long and the southern side is about two hundred. The compound's about two hundred and fifty feet wide, from north to south, at the widest point. The house is quite close to the long north side of the compound—not in the middle—more to the northwest corner, because of the space taken up by the rover airlock and parking pad in the northeast corner."

"We built the enclosure in this odd shape for both technical and esthetic reasons," added John, as they surveyed the garden below.

They could see an outer path through the shrubs and plants that went right around the compound, close to the perimeter. Next came a middle path that also went right around the compound. Paths also ran outward from the swimming pool patio, in different directions, like spokes from a wheel hub, to intersect these encircling paths. There were six such spoke paths, two running to the west, two to the south and two to the east, more or less. In the southwest corner there was a small pond, filled with salt water, which John explained was for growing sea weeds, as a source of essential vitamin B12, which could not be obtained from ground plants. The pond also had fish.

Every so often, arranged regularly, there was a thick, square, orange concrete pillar, mostly covered by climbing plants, that went almost up to the glass roof. Near the top of each pillar was a set of four solid copper posts, each fanning out, palm-tree style, to attach to the lower copper framework of the roof, in which a lower layer of thick glass slabs was embedded. Each central copper pillar continued on up, through the lower layer of glass slabs, to attach to the upper copper framework of the roof, in which an upper layer of lighter glass slabs was embedded, five feet above the lower layer. Water circulated between the two glass slab layers. The climbing plants on most pillars had partly covered the copper posts at the top. There was a concrete pillar for about every sixteen glass roof slabs, or one for every thousand square feet of garden floor area. The pillars were massive, each about two feet by two feet.

John noticed Jurgen Eindorf studying the orange support pillars. "They're heavily reinforced concrete," John explained, "to hold the roof down. We're inside a glass and copper balloon. Nine tons, Earth weight, of pressure per square meter."

Jurgen was impressed by the sheer size and apparent solidity of the structure.

"I was always led to believe people would live in inflated, transparent plastic domes on Mars," he said. "I never imagined anything like this."

"Science fiction," said John.

"Why?" asked Jurgen.

"It's the air pressure," explained John. "With a dome, the tearing stress on the transparent plastic, where it's attached to the support wall, goes up with the radius."

"You mean that a small dome would be possible, but a big one would not."

"Right," said John. "For example, a small inflated dome five meters in radius would be possible. The ripping force along the edge would be only about twenty-five tons per meter of length. You could get transparent plastic that could take that. But with a dome fifty meters in radius, the tearing force for each meter around the edge would be ten times greater, or two hundred and fifty tons per meter of length. No transparent material could take that. That's why the idea of a large city under a plastic dome is just science fiction."

"Which explains why you have all these pillars," said Jurgen thoughtfully, his right hand stroking his chin, "not to hold the roof up, but to reduce the stress at the edge of the compound. Obviously, if you sawed them all through, the pressure would simply rip the upper glass structure right off the surrounding support walls. So the basic principle is that enclosed structures on Mars have to have very strong support pillars, to hold the roof down, no matter what kind of building you put up."

"Yes, but of course, only if it's a pressurized building," said John.

"A lot of the books I read about settlements on Mars had everybody living underground," added Jurgen. "That was the cheapest way to solve both the radiation problem and the high air-pressure problem inside. Did you ever consider building your home underground?"

"Not for a minute," said John, "and you wouldn't have either if Denise was your wife. I've never seen her really angry, but I suspect that suggesting a monstrosity like that would be a good way to get her to erupt. Don't even mention it, if you want any supper. She won't accept breathing air made by a chemical plant. The plants in the garden are not just for decoration. They make the compound's oxygen."

It was perhaps a good thing that Denise did not hear this conversation about underground living quarters. It was something that had been more than just discussed by the ESA mission planners.

Underground living quarters were far cheaper to construct, in terms of man hours, than structures like the above-ground, oasis-like enclosure that John had built. The ESA planners, limited by the usual budget and time constraints, had concluded that the best way to grow the Leaf Valley colony, after its founders were safely off the planet, would be to put up, or rather down, such underground structures, right underneath Mount Tip. Colonial headquarters could remain above ground, of course, in the former home of Denise and John. A few additional low cost structures, as a perk for senior personnel, could be placed in the garden area surrounding the house. Since these few additional buildings would be inside the pressurized garden compound, there would be no need for the expensive engineering required for pressurized buildings.

The guests showed no inclination to move from where they were, as they studied the scene. There was not just the enclosure structure and the view over the garden to marvel at, but the sight beyond, through the glass walls.

From where they stood, they could see down Leaf Valley, with the top of Stem Mountains at the end of the valley just poking above the horizon. To the east, in the distance, the high escarpment wall of the valley, some two miles away, was still bright orange, even in the restrained light of the cloud-veiled setting sun. To the west, above the now darkened west wall of the valley, the veiled sun was forming a very weak, gray-blue sunset fan.

"How long did it take to build all this?" asked Jurgen. As an engineer, he was the only one of the three ESA visitors who could appreciate the construction effort needed to put up such a large structure.

"It took three of us nearly two Earth years, excluding the time to get the water for the roof," said John. "We learned how to work with glass slabs and copper frames from the experience of building the greenhouses. Do you want to hear a bit about it?"

"Yes, indeed," said Jurgen, failing to notice the annoyed expression on his chief's face, "I am curious."

"With the first greenhouse we weren't very efficient," explained John. "The best we could manage was two glass slabs in their frames each day. But we got better at it. We did between eight and ten slabs a day with this compound. The compound has just under twelve hundred thick glass slabs. There's another thousand glass sheets above the glass slabs in the roof, with five feet of water in between for radiation protection."

They all looked up at the roof. If you looked carefully you could see that there was clear water circulating above the glass slabs.

"We had to build the concrete foundation wall around the compound in sections—we didn't have a construction tent big enough for the whole compound. You understand that water just boils away in the low pressure Martian air. If you put out wet cement or concrete on Mars, the water boils away before the cement can harden. You have to do it inside a tent blown up with higher pressure air."

"Yes, I know that," said Jurgen. He thought for a moment and then asked. "So how did you join the sections of the perimeter wall together? I do not see how you could put up an airtight tent just to cover a missing part of a wall."

"You'd make a good structural engineer," said John approvingly. "For a long time I couldn't see how to do it myself, and had just about come to the conclusion that a glass-slab structure this size was impossible—which made my wife very unhappy."

"So how did you solve the problem?" asked Jurgen.

"I didn't," said John. "Dr. Sato did. As you may find out one day, our Zen master has a knack of coming up with very simple solutions to apparently unsolvable problems. Dr. Sato, perhaps you would explain."

The Zen master bowed, and then said, "The solution was to let the whole compound supply the higher pressure air needed for putting out the wet concrete and cement for the missing short sections of the perimeter wall.

"When the building project first got under way, enough of the perimeter support wall could be built, in large disjoint sections, to enable the upper glass slab walls and the roof slabs to be put up. Once this was done the whole compound was now enclosed—except for one meter gaps left in the perimeter concrete support wall every twenty meters or so. So the answer was to place some plastic sheets up against the wall at each gap, on the outside, and bulldoze soil up against these sheets, closing off the gaps …"

"Oh, I see," said Jurgen, suddenly grasping the idea. "If you bulldozed enough soil up against the sheets at each gap in the wall, that would seal the compound well enough temporarily to let you pressurize it to a low level, maybe ten percent of normal pressure. That would be enough to pour cement and concrete inside the compound to seal the gaps in the wall."

"Exactly right," said John. "Simple, once you see it. I'd been thinking about how to build the structure for months before we started, and this problem had me stumped. I mentioned it to Dr. Sato at dinner one evening, when we were still living in the Japanese habitat. It took him about five minutes to come up with the solution."

"Was the design of the structure yours?" put in Emma Grant. She really wasn't interested to know, but she wanted to be seen to say something intelligent, and impress her boss. Derk would have preferred her to have said nothing, however.

"Only partly," said John. "The layout design is Denise's. She wanted a garden home. I wasn't so sure originally that such a massive place was worth the effort to engineer and build."

"And what do you think now?" asked Captain Derk. How John felt about being on Mars was what really interested Derk, not his obvious engineering expertise.

"It's one of the great joys we have here on Mars," said John. "The proverbial wild horses wouldn't drag us away from it. But you must see the inside of the house. It's time to go in anyway. Denise will be waiting for us. We could go in from several places on this balcony. There are quite a few sliding glass doors opening out onto it. Same goes for the lower level balcony. But I think we should go in through the main entrance, since you're our guests, here for the first time. We go back down the way we came up."

They walked back along the upper-level south balcony to the southeast corner, and then went along the shorter east balcony to the copper staircase down to the lower level. Then they walked back the short distance to the northeast corner of the house, where they had first approached the house on the path from the airlock.

Here there was a large sliding copper door in the east wall, through which they entered the house.

Inside there was a long, wide passageway, with walls of gray stone set in orange cement, with a light stone-tiled floor, and with large windows to the right, set in copper frames. On the left side of the passageway there were four doorways. The doors were made of a light-gray, fiber-glass material. Potted plants sat on the sills of the windows to the right. There were pictures in copper frames on the wall to the left, all of them pictures of spectacular Martian scenes.

"The first door is into the master control room for the whole complex," said John, as they walked along the entrance hallway. "Next is the computer and communications room. We've surface radio links to the monastery on Outlook Shelf, to your habitat in Elbow Plain, and to the rovers as well. We're also linked to Earth via both the ESA comsat and the NASA comsat. The two satellite dishes, one from ESA and one from NASA, as well as some surface radio antennas, are up on the mountain slope behind the house."

"It's a far cry from the way it used to be," he added. It would be even better, he thought, if we had the codes and software to let us listen in on communications from Mission Control to the habitat.

He paused as they continued along the hallway. The CIA can also send us messages via the NASA comsat, he was thinking, but no way I'm going to mention that. He continued aloud: "This room is the downstairs washroom, with a small laundry room at the end of it. The last room is the children's playroom—always in a mess I'm afraid. All these rooms except the bathroom open out onto the main balcony on the south side—bright sunny rooms by day."

At the end of the passageway there was a large opening to the left, into a living area, while straight ahead, in a continuation of the hallway, a copper staircase led to the upper level.

The living area was bright and spacious, well endowed with potted plants, and opened out onto the south balcony. The south wall, at the balcony, was mostly glass in copper frames, with a wide sliding glass door to the outside.

Against the east wall was a sofa. There was a set of comfortable chairs in the corner of the west wall and the staircase. There was a quite large, but low, round glass table near that corner, with three more comfortable chairs facing into the corner. There were more pictures on the walls here too—all of Martian scenes.

There was no southwest corner, for the living area just continued along the glass south wall, past the kitchen. As the party entered the living area, Denise left the kitchen and appeared at the southwest corner of the room, her two children following, and hiding a little behind her. She was wearing a long yellow dress, and an intricate copper necklace.

"Welcome," she said, hiding her true feelings. She disliked Derk intensely, and the sight of him reminded her once more of her experience two evenings ago. "I heard voices. Dinner will be in about ten minutes. I still have a few things to do in the kitchen first. You've time to see the upstairs. If you want to freshen up, there's only one bathroom on this floor. There's another upstairs—children's bathroom—which you can use—I tidied it just half an hour ago. But come and see the kitchen and dining area first."

She led them out of the living area along the south wall, and stopped before a spacious, open kitchen to the right, evidently the center of operations at that moment.

"Better not go in the kitchen just now—too much going on in there," she said.

Then she led the visitors past the kitchen, still walking along the south wall, to the dining area.

The dining room occupied the whole western end of the house. It had two large windows in its west wall, and also a large window, reaching to the floor, in both the south and north walls. There were drapes beside each window, light green in color. There were more pictures on the east and north walls—more Martian scenes.

Up against the kitchen wall at the east side was a serving table, covered in a white table cloth—part of a parachute—and laid out with plates, utensils and already a great deal of food. In the center of the room, arrayed north-south, was a quite large dining table, also with a white tablecloth, capable of taking eight, but laid out for six.

The sun had now set, but a purple gray light from the still cloud-covered western sky lit up the room in a vivid purple hue.

"It's nice to sit here in the evening," said Denise, "with the sunset sky to the west—Nature in all its glory. It's not usually so cloudy though."

The three visitors said nothing, but were clearly impressed with the spacious house. John noticed Jurgen Eindorf studying the stone tile floor, with a puzzled look on his intelligent face.

"The tiles are on top of two layers of very porous concrete blocks and several layers of glass fiber for heat insulation," explained John, reading his thoughts. "The ground is extremely cold. Air is still the best insulator—trapped air in the glass fibers and porous concrete. The whole compound is solid underneath, with the garden soil on top of that."

"The whole compound?" said Jurgen, looking surprised. "Did you not say earlier it was sixty thousand square feet in area, six thousand square meters? You must have used a fortune in cement."

"We don't measure in money here—just man hours," said John. "Actually it's not concrete under the whole compound. We're on a mountain side, so all we had to do was clear away the loose top soil, or regolith, down to bedrock. The bedrock's about four feet down on this shelf, except near the south edge where we had our habitat originally—it's far enough down there to let you dig a radiation shelter.

"If there had been no bedrock we would have had to put out concrete about a meter thick over the whole compound. That would have needed the equivalent of about seven thousand bags of cement. And would have taken about four years to do, if you include the time to manufacture the cement and haul about seven thousand cubic meters of sand and gravel. In practice, it would just have been beyond us. We didn't have to do that, thank heavens, because we built up here on the shelf rather than down on the valley floor. The underlying bedrock saved us. We simply drilled into the rock where we needed to make reinforced concrete connections to the perimeter wall and the concrete support pillars."

"I see," said Jurgen, in astonishment. "I would have thought it impossible for three people to put up a structure like this on Mars in two years."

"Being able to find a way to do the impossible is a necessary condition for survival on Mars, in our experience," said John.

"So a rock foundation is very useful for building pressurized structures on Mars," said Jurgen, "provided you have drilling equipment to make a strong connection to walls and pillars."

"Absolutely."

Richard Derk had asked no questions about the structure, but had listened sporadically—with displeasure. He too was mostly thinking about the garden compound, but along completely different lines—lines of power and control.

He was a man who never did anything himself. He never used his hands for work, other than to hold a gun or drive a vehicle when he had to, nor did he ever do technical work with his head, which he reserved for strategy considerations involving people. He believed in using the hands and technical brains of others.

He believed in commanding others, and in having them do the actual physical work. He was actually inclined to despise those who worked with their hands, as was common among those of his class. This did not mean he was ineffective, for he had the capability to select and surround himself with men and women who not only could but would do at his command.

Every single person in his crew was highly effective, and could do things very well. Jurgen Eindorf, for example, was a first class space flight engineer, and possessed a broad knowledge of all fields of engineering. But unlike John, Jurgen preferred to be commanded, and have others decide what needed to be done. Once the project was decided, however, Jurgen could and would deliver.

Derk was thinking it was a pity that John Erway would have to be sent back to Earth. Here was a man who clearly could do—on Mars. John was obviously a man he could use, when he became the governor of the E.U.'s first Mars colony in Leaf Valley, which he expected to become, just as soon as the original trio on Mars were safely off the planet. The pity was that John was not a man who would do, at least for him. He was obviously far too independent, and would do only for himself and those depending on him.

Erway was even a bad example to his crew, for Derk liked to have those around him believe that technically competent people were no good at deciding what should be done overall, that only people like him had the ability to decide correctly what should be done, even if he depended on technically competent people to do it. For this reason he hated to make a wrong decision, and worse, have it known among those he commanded that he had made a wrong decision, with its attendant loss of face.

He was very careful about his decisions for that reason, and bad ones were rare. When he did make a bad one, he was always quick enough to put the blame securely on one of his underlings and make him or her pay dearly for the alleged error, as an example to others. And where he believed there was a serious risk of a wrong decision, he always arranged things so that there was a fall guy, somebody who could be legitimately blamed if things went wrong.

Derk was the leader administrator who, although he preferred to dole out largesse, had no scruple about doling out pain and punishment, even if undeserved, when it was necessary to maintain his leadership ascendancy. The only kind of democracy he believed in was one where people like himself controlled the media, and presented the common people, whom he did not trust, with a small slate of candidates like himself; the people could then choose from among this list, thinking they were in charge, when in reality they were not. He also preferred to maintain himself above those around him, and to be seen to be above those around him. This, of course, he was having difficulty doing within the garden enclosure, in the presence of John, Denise, and Dr. Sato.

Derk had already begun to hate being in the home of John and Denise—while John and Denise were the occupants. The message the house and garden sent was all too clear: People like Derk can be done without, or worse, are better done without. The more the trio on Mars accomplished the less Derk liked them, although the more he wanted control of what they had accomplished. Of course, when he did gain control, he would assert his superior decision making ability at once, by ordering work to 'correct' all the 'errors' in the useful but still rather 'amateur' construction efforts of the original founders of the complex in Leaf Valley.

He had become extremely jealous of the enormous prestige and respect these three had on Earth, a prestige and respect he was now engaged in undermining at every opportunity. He craved similar prestige, fame, and respect for himself, as the man who directed the establishment of Earth's first Mars colony, a flourishing and productive enterprise, with him as its governor, living in a splendid colonial residence—the former home, since improved, of Denise and John. What he would do with the Zen monastery on Outlook

Shelf he had not yet decided, although he was sure of one thing: It would not remain a monastery for long.

The prestige and respect the trio enjoyed among the general public on Earth, even in his own country, Britain, meant that he had to act with extreme care. He had to get the three off the planet without any appearance of anything untoward, that could damage his standing in the eyes of his fellow countrymen and the world. He knew his fellow countrymen only too well—they would not stand for any attempt at a blatant injustice against the three on Mars, and the two children.

The British Government, at the highest levels, was well aware of the opinions of its citizenry, and although that government was anxious to see Derk in charge of the first E.U. colony on Mars, it was also aware of the risks if the public ever found out the lengths to which it, and the E.U. Commission, would go to achieve that end. The E.U. Commission and the British Government were relying on Derk, the only man, it was thought, who had any chance of doing the job—if the trio on Mars decided they wanted to stay put.

This reliance on Derk was not misplaced. He was probably the best man for such a task. A supreme strategist was needed, a man who, like Derk, reserved his brainpower almost entirely for strategy considerations. And now that Derk could see the lie of the land with his own eyes, he knew that it was only a matter of time before a highly original strategy for accomplishing his goals would bear fruit. Although this strategy was still steadily evolving in his mind, a good deal of it was already quite clear to Derk, and was already being acted upon. Indeed, although his hosts were unaware of it, that very evening his men were already conducting a strategic operation that would help him complete his plans.

Nevertheless, strategy required a knowledge of the planet on which the strategy would be used, and on Earth this knowledge could be taken for granted. It could not on Mars though, for Derk did not know Mars, not the way John, Denise, and Dr. Sato did, and this deficiency would soon make itself apparent, that very evening in fact. Had he thought more about those clouds covering the evening sky, he would have realized the danger.

"I see just about everything is stone, glass, and metal," Jurgen was saying, looking around the dining area.

"Yes," said John. "Our main building materials are concrete, stone, glass, and copper, with some aluminum and iron. Those drapes we made from parachute fabric, and most of the chair and sofa fabrics too—which reminds me, we have to go hunting for the parachutes you used on the way down. We've got all kinds of uses for them—"

"John," interrupted Denise, "I'm sure our guests aren't very interested in all the things you can do with parachute fabric..." She paused, thinking. "... although I'm even wearing parachute fabric this evening," she added laughing, looking down at her long yellow dress. "But I'm going to have the food ready in about seven minutes," she went on. "I don't want it to get cold. So why don't you show them the upstairs at once? That'll give them enough time to freshen up before we eat. I'm just going to put the children to bed."

"We'd better do as she says," said John, as he shepherded his guests back past the kitchen to the living area and toward the stairs at the end of the hallway. "She can be a holy terror if you mess with her plans for food—although she means well. Sometimes I think she was meant to be a chef in a big Paris restaurant and not a doctor."

At the top of the stairs the party turned left, and emerged into another living area, considerably smaller than the main living area immediately below it. It had a very comfortable atmosphere, and looked as if it was heavily used. The south wall was mostly glass, and a sliding glass door opened out onto the upper east-west balcony. There were more pictures on the walls, all of Martian scenes.

There were no sofas in the room, but an assortment of comfortable chairs around two small round corner tables, one in the southeast corner beside the glass sliding door, and one in the northwest corner near the head of the stairs. The tables had thick glass tops mounted on copper frames.

There was a door near the southwest corner. It opened into the master bedroom, which was quite spacious, with a mostly glass south wall, and a sliding glass door, also opening onto the balcony. There were two large windows in the west wall, on either side of the large bed. A door in the north wall led to a bathroom and laundry room.

On the other side of the living area was a hallway that split the eastern end of the upper floor in two.

"These three doors on the right are for bedrooms," explained John. "The first two are the children's bedrooms, and the last one is a guest bedroom. It only ever gets used by Dr. Sato—he's staying in it right now. It has a door out onto the balcony, and a window facing east as well, so that it gets the early morning sun. Our bedroom gets the evening sun." He paused; then he added: "The ideal would be a bedroom that gets both morning and evening sun—but that's just about impossible to design into a large house."

They went down the hallway and had a look at each of the three bedrooms.

On the north side of the hallway there were four more doors. One was to a bathroom and small laundry room, opposite the guest bedroom. Next came two small workrooms, opposite the children's rooms, one for John and one for Denise. Beside Denise's workroom was a small surgery, nearest the upstairs living area.

The floors were all light-stone tiled, with the tiles set in light orange cement. The ceiling was orange concrete. As they came back along the hallway to the upstairs living area, John noticed Jurgen studying the ceiling with a puzzled expression on his face.

"We can't make them white, unfortunately," explained John, reading his thoughts. "You'd need white sand and white cement to do that. We can get the white sand—it's just quartz sand, which we use for making glass. But you'd need gypsum, calcium sulfate, to add to the cement clinker to make white cement, and so far we've not been able to locate any pure enough deposits. We do have some gypsum for medical purposes—for making plaster of Paris, but we can't afford to use that for ceilings."

"That was not what was puzzling me," responded Jurgen. "I was wondering how much radiation protection you have. What would you do for protection if there was a radiation storm? Where's the radiation shelter?"

"You're in it," said John. "The whole house is a radiation shelter. In fact the whole enclosure is safe from a radiation storm."

"But that must mean you have two meters of concrete or soil in the roof," said Jurgen. "I don't see anything that could support such a weight."

"You'd make a good structural engineer, as I said earlier," said John. "The roof of this house doesn't need to be supported in any conventional way. There are no glass slabs above the roof, just about six feet of concrete and Mars soil and gravel, so that the roof is exposed directly to the low pressure outside. The weight of the roof is less than the force upward from air pressure inside the house, so that, in reality, the house structure is holding the roof down, not supporting it. The walls are in fact strong enough to support the roof though, in the low Mars gravity, if it ever became necessary because of a loss of air pressure.

"The rest of the enclosure is protected by a roof made of nearly six feet of glass and water. The water circulates between the lower thick glass slabs of the roof and thinner outer glass sheets. The glass slabs take the high air pressure inside the compound, about nine tons a square meter. The upper glass sheets are just to contain the water and let the light in. They only have to be strong enough to take the vapor pressure of water, which is only a small fraction of the pressure inside this compound at normal temperatures."

"How do you keep the water from freezing at night?" asked Jurgen.

"That's the biggest technical problem as far as a greenhouse enclosure on Mars is concerned," said John. "It's expensive to do. We don't have radiation protection for the four big greenhouses down on the valley floor for that reason. It's cheapest to simply accept losing the entire crop if there's a radiation storm. But since we produce more food than we need each year, we can afford to run that risk.

"But with this big enclosed garden up here on the shelf we don't have that luxury. If we had a radiation storm we'd lose the entire garden—plants and bushes that took years to grow. And Denis insisted on a garden home. The only solution is five feet of water between the glass in the roof. But as you point out, now there's the problem of keeping the water from freezing at night, and even by day during the winter. You have to heat the circulating water, and you need a lot of heat. Solar heat exchangers heat the water by day, as well as heat from inside the garden enclosure itself—the greenhouse effect. The heat exchangers are made of thin copper sheets and sit in the roof of the house. The rovers are usually parked inside at night, so there's waste heat coming from their nuclear power plants too. There's also a nuclear power plant in the roof of the house that heats the water day and night. And just in case that's not enough, we've got battery powered heaters that will kick in. The batteries are charged by solar panels during the day."

"Was getting enough clear water a problem?" asked Jurgen.

"It was sheer drudgery," said John. "It took months to transport all the ice and clean the water, although we didn't do it all at once. Denise figured that once we had three feet of water in the roof it would be safe enough to start planting."

"What about dust falling onto the glass sheets on the roof and blocking the light?"

"You think of everything," said John. "Unfortunately, it's really an unsolved problem. The glass roof's too big to just blow it off. I have to go up on the frame about every six weeks and both sweep it and vacuum it. Takes all day. It's a job for a robot, but we don't have one. But I'm not complaining. On Earth you have to cut the grass. Here you have to vacuum the dust."

"Impressive," said Jurgen. "But now I see why planners on Earth think that surface dwellings on Mars are just too expensive, and why the common opinion is that a future Mars city should be built underground."

"As I told you earlier, don't say that to Denise," said John, "at least not before your dinner is safely eaten. Speaking of which, it's dinner time. You all know now where the upstairs and downstairs bathrooms are, if you want to freshen up for a few minutes. Everyone in the dining room in a few minutes. I want to freshen up too."

CHAPTER SEVEN

Forlorn Cry

THEY HAD just finished the first course of the dinner—a rich vegetable broth, and had begun the main course.

A large lamp hung low over the dining table, imparting a warm and comfortable light. Another smaller lamp hung low over the serving table against the east wall of the dining room. The meal was self serve.

There was still some light in the clouded sky, above the western escarpment wall of Leaf Valley. It was a dull gray purple, visible through the windows of the west wall of the dining room, against the copper and glass slab framework of the garden enclosure. The sky light coming through the large window in the dining room's south wall, at the balcony, was now so feeble that the glass mostly reflected the six seated around the table.

"Please excuse me a second," said Denise suddenly, rising. She walked to the south wall and pulled across the long, light green drapes.

"That's more pleasant," she said, as she sat down again, at the north end of the table. Dr. Sato was sitting to her left, and Jurgen Eindorf to her right. John was sitting at the south end, with Emma Grant to his left and Captain Derk to his right.

"May we offer you some wine?" said Denise, gesturing to three clear plastic containers of wine on the table. "We have a French wine and a California wine, sent by NASA two years ago. This one's a Martian wine. We made it from our own grapes, according to an old French recipe."

Both Jurgen Eindorf and Emma Grant looked interested, but waited for their chief to respond. Derk looked at his hostess and then at the wine containers. He thought for a moment, smiled to Denise, and then decided. "I'll have some of the French wine," he said.

Jurgen Eindorf raised his eyebrows a little, but enough for Derk to notice. Jurgen was aware of the slight to Denise. He would have tried the Martian wine.

If Emma Grant was aware of the slight too, she did not betray it. "I'll have some French wine too," she said.

"And some for me too," said Jurgen, trying to conceal his interest in the Martian wine.

"John, will you do the necessary?" asked Denise. She was quite taken aback, and even hurt, although she did not show it. Her Martian wine was actually very good, and the particular container on the table was the best of her best. She had expected Derk to be polite, at least, although she had to admit that Derk had been rude in such a polite way that she could have no cause for any rejoinder.

"Certainly," replied her husband, "and I'll open the Martian as well, if you'll join me, Denise. I actually prefer your Martian wine."

After that there was small talk for a time, although it was a while before John got over Derk's behavior. He was sure that Derk had known exactly what he was doing and was just being petty.

Unfortunately for John, he did not understand Derk, whose type was rare. He was the first of that kind John had ever encountered. Being out of contact with the wide range of humanity for ten years did not help his judgement either. Had he known the extent to which Derk was not being petty, but was acting consistently, from much deeper motives, he would have been more worried than upset. Derk simply could not and would not do or say anything in front of Jurgen Eindorf or Emma Grant that would show him conceding that the three survivors could perform any task well, without the supervision and guidance of a person like himself.

Eventually the topic of conversation turned to the voyage to Mars, then to the landing, then to the lander, and then to the lander's refueling.

"It'll take forty-five tons of fuel and seventy-five tons of oxidizer to get us back up again," Jurgen was saying.

"It's ready and waiting for you," said John. "It was meant for the NASA lander two years ago, but now it's all yours, as we agreed with ESA."

This was a technical matter, but also a logistical one, and Derk was interested.

"Do you see anything going wrong?" he asked, turning to John. "Isn't your having brought the lander down out in Elbow Plain going to complicate things?"

"Somewhat," admitted John. "We've a longer distance to transport the fuel and oxidizer, but that's all. If we're careful, nothing should go wrong. But we do have to be very careful, especially with the oxidizer."

"How long do you expect it to take?" asked Derk.

"About eight full days," said John. "That's with all five trailers in use, the two behind the rovers, the two you've brought, and the one behind Dr. Sato's buggy."

Details of how the fuel and oxidizer would be transferred from the storage tanks near the industrial complex had all been worked out, well before the ESA mission had ever left Earth, as part of the agreement between ESA and the settlement. Every detail of the refueling process had been considered.

It had been agreed that the cargo hold of the ESA lander would bring twenty-four small fuel and oxidizer tanks to Mars. Each tank would be about twenty-five inches square, and be capable of holding a quarter ton of either fuel or oxidizer. These portable tanks would be used to transport the fuel in the rover and buggy trailers.

The portable tanks were made from a special alloy, not because of any problems with the fuel, which was essentially a kind of kerosene that could be held safely in a tank made from just about any metal, but rather because of the liquid oxidizer. The oxidizer was extremely dangerous. It was highly corrosive. Any plastic object coming in contact with it would become inflamed immediately. Fuel coming in contact with it, of course, would burn at once. Human skin in contact with even a few drops of the oxidizer would suffer severe burns. To make matters even more dangerous was the fact that the oxidizer was highly volatile. Even in the Earth's high pressure atmosphere it would boil away at temperatures above about 20 degrees Celsius. On Mars it could not be exposed to the Martian air at temperatures above minus 60 Celsius, without immediately boiling away.

"I would like to start the refueling operation tomorrow," said Derk. "We don't expect the lander to stay more than three weeks. We also want to make a detailed survey of the escarpment walls of Elbow Plain before it leaves. It's to have survey samples on board."

"We've no problem with a start tomorrow," said John. "The fuel and oxidizer's sitting in tanks we took from the landers at the old NASA landing site. I assume the portable tanks you brought for transporting it are in order."

"They are," said Eindorf. "I checked them out this morning. We have also got the pipes that connect to your fuel tanks as well as pumps for the fuel and oxidizer. We can easily put four portable tanks on each trailer—one ton of either fuel or oxidizer. We could probably double that, but two tons of fuel or oxidizer in the trailers would mean some risks I suppose you would rather avoid. If we do three trips a day with each of the five trailers we can transport fifteen tons a day. I agree with your estimate—we should be able to do the job in just over a week, at one ton per trailer trip."

"Why don't you just agree on a time to start tomorrow morning?" suggested Denise, anxious to shift the conversation away from the refueling operation, and on to what really interested her. "Why not arrange for the two rovers and the buggies to be at the lander tomorrow morning? That way you could load the empty tanks up on the trailers first thing, and all the connection pipes and pumps too. Isn't that all you need to get things moving?"

"A bit more than that," said Jurgen, turning to Denise, at his left, "but not a lot. We have to have people at the storage tanks to fill the portable tanks, and then people at the lander to fill the lander tanks. And we must do the fuel first. But it's true we can get all that arranged in the morning." Turning to his chief, across the table, he then said: "How about that? Why not agree to be at the lander at seven thirty tomorrow morning to get things started?"

Derk said nothing for a moment, and then said: "I'd prefer an even earlier start. Let's say seven, if Dr. Erway is in agreement."

"Fine," said John. "Denise and I will handle the rovers. Your people can handle the buggies. We'll be at the lander at seven tomorrow morning." He looked at Denise, who nodded.

"Good," said Denise. "Now that we've sorted that out, I have a question for Captain Derk. The stated purpose of your mission, as laid out in our agreement with ESA, is to carry out exploration and research, and to rescue us, but only if we so desire. And that's what everyone in Europe seems to believe. But there are twelve of you and only twelve seats in the lander. So just how were you intending to bring us back to Earth, assuming, of course, that we wanted to be rescued?"

"Simple," said Derk. "Surely you didn't think that ESA would send twelve astronauts to Mars for just a three-week stay? We need only four of the twelve on board the lander for the return trip. That leaves room for eight, so there'll be plenty of space on board for the three of you and the two children, and for important rock and soil samples. ESA expects to send space vehicles to Mars every two years for the foreseeable future, to carry on research and exploration, and further develop this region. So most of the eight who stay behind will be relieved after about eighteen months. Those eight will have plenty to do."

"Are you one of those who will stay behind?" asked John quietly, but making an effort to keep his voice steady.

"Yes," said Derk. "Somebody has to run things. Jurgen and Emma will also be staying behind. Our second flight engineer, Jose Montoya, will get the lander safely back into orbit. I'll need Jurgen's engineering skills here on Mars, and those of Claude Bertrand too."

"Claude Bertrand?" queried John.

"Claude Bertrand is our civil and structural engineer, from France," explained Derk.

"I take it then that the further development of this region you mentioned a moment ago involves some serious construction," said Denise, who had already looked up Claude Bertrand in the knowledge base. "Monsieur Bertrand is not known for designing doll's houses."

"Yes," said Derk, "we do have construction plans, but I'm not at liberty to divulge what they are."

Denise glanced at John, but he seemed intent on eating.

"What about Sheila Bell?" asked Denise eventually. "Will she be staying too?"

"Yes, Sheila will stay behind," said Derk. "We obviously have to have a doctor and dentist, and she's also a very good biologist. You'll be the doctor on the trip back to Earth."

"Sheila mentioned something yesterday morning about a secret ESA project in southwest Ireland," continued Denise, "something to do with reel launches. What's that?"

"I can't tell you," said Derk, hiding his annoyance at the Irish doctor for even mentioning the secret project. He would have something to say to her when he got back to the habitat. "The project's secret."

Denise had been in ESA herself, and had resigned from the agency in 2038, to die on Mars in private. Back then, a secret ESA project was unheard of.

"There were no secret projects when I was in ESA," said Denise. "Why the secrecy now about this project?"

Derk hesitated. "Because it's in the interests of the national security of the European Union that it be kept secret for the time being, probably till it's either a success or a failure," he said eventually. "I have no wish to talk any more about it."

He knew in detail what the project was all about. He also knew how important it was that under no circumstances were the three survivors on Mars to find out about it, particularly about how it related to ESA's planned colony in Leaf Valley. He made a mental note to have his mission be very discrete about the reasons for planned survey work on the northwest escarpment wall of Elbow Plain, as long as the three survivors were still on Mars. That survey work was intimately related to the secret ESA project.

He now knew John and Denise well enough to realize that if they ever got an inkling of what ESA was planning, it would likely be even more difficult to get them to leave Mars. Given the copper deposit estimates he had received the previous evening from his geologists, Don Carruthers and Vincenzo Cassoni, he could now be certain that ESA and the European Union would have really big plans for Leaf Valley. The planned developments would be in the immediate interests of Europe, and certainly not in the interests of those living on Mars. A major task for Derk would be to see that these plans bore fruit.

They ate in silence for a while. Then Denise said: "My husband and I have no interest in leaving Mars. We're happy here. Won't that affect all your plans? While you're all very welcome as visitors, under the terms of our agreement with ESA, you can't expect to stay here indefinitely—at our expense."

"We don't believe you really want to stay," said Derk. "We've been expecting that you would be more or less like many people on Earth, who were lost in remote places, and weren't found until many years later. Such people have often resisted being rescued. There haven't been cases of that in this century, but there were many such cases in the previous century, and in earlier centuries. In the last century, for example, some Japanese army residues were lost for many years after the nineteen forties war ended, in the jungle, or on uninhabited islands. When found, they often had to be forcibly brought back to civilization."

"We don't normally think of ourselves as lost," said Denise. "And we're also certain that we live in a very civilized place—even if we had to create it ourselves."

"ESA would not agree with that assessment," replied Derk coolly, "nor do I."

"Are you saying then that we will have to be rescued by force, if we are not willing to return to Earth willingly?" persisted Denise.

Derk hesitated. He had hoped to avoid a conversation like this, especially in the early stages of the visit. "We do not think in terms of using force with any of you," he said, "but you are expected to return to Earth in three weeks. We expect that, by the time the lander is ready to launch, you will all have come to your senses and accepted it, as the best possible thing to do."

John had been listening intently to this exchange, and now decided it was time to back up his wife. "I'm afraid it will not be us who have to do the accepting," he said. "It's you and the whole ESA crowd who'll have to do it—all of you who came up with this idea of bringing us back to Earth, while eight of you stay on and take over all the facilities we've worked our guts out to build."

"Let's get something straight right now," he continued. "We're Martians now, and we're staying put. You and your crew will have to return to Earth after your three week stay is up. There's nothing in our agreement with ESA about us having to provide for you after that time, apart from humanitarian help in case of an emergency."

"Of course, if some of your scientists wanted to settle here," added Denise, "we'd be happy to sell them some land, and give them a loan to get them started."

Derk remained cool and collected, almost ice cold. "I understand how you feel," he said, with feigned sympathy. "You've obviously worked very hard to create what you have here. But let's not fall out about this rescue. Let's just say that we shall do our utmost in the coming weeks to persuade you to change your mind. Don't forget you've two small children to think of. It can't be right for them to grow up alone on Mars, without other children to mix with."

Then he turned to his right. "We've not heard your opinion, Dr. Sato. How do you feel about returning to Earth? Surely you would like to see your native Japan again, and your old monastery at Kamakura." Derk was thorough when it came to dealing with people. He knew a very great deal about the characters of the three survivors on Mars. He understood nothing of Zen, though, for otherwise he would have phrased the question differently. The answer he got told him nothing.

"Circumstances themselves always decide such matters," said the Zen master, "when the time is ripe."

Sensing that any reply to this would be pointless, Derk just smiled weakly and began eating again. But John was not ready to let Derk off the hook so easily, and decided to continue the attack.

"I agree there is no need for us to fall out over this," said John, "just two days after you got here. But let's suppose that, in spite of all your persuasive efforts, three weeks from now, when the lander is ready to leave, we're still determined to stay here, in our homes in this valley. What would you do then? Would you still be prepared to leave peacefully, when all persuasion had failed?"

Derk was silent, thinking. John and Denise looked at him, waiting. At last he said: "We would be prepared to leave as we came, in peace, if this was truly your home. Unfortunately it is not."

Denise sat straight up. "What do you mean?" she said. "This is most definitely our home. We built it ourselves, with materials we found and worked ourselves. And the monastery on Outlook Shelf is Dr. Sato's home too, for the same reason."

"Isn't there a rather important matter you're overlooking?" said Derk calmly. He was very sure of himself. There was no backing down now. The issue would have to be confronted that evening. He was well prepared, however. ESA had left nothing to chance, aware of just what it was dealing with, in its plan to remove the three from their settlement in Leaf Valley. Derk had discussed the core issue at length with the leading brains at the Space Ethics Division of ESA in Berlin. It was also an issue with which he was thoroughly familiar, for personal reasons connected with the family seat on lands in the rolling county of Gloucestershire, in the southwest of England. He had a wife living on that family seat, for whom he cared nothing, but his eldest son would inherit those lands, just as he had done, and as had his ancestors, right back to the Norman Conquest a thousand years earlier, when the land had been taken by force of arms.

"Exactly what are we overlooking?" said Denise, suddenly worried. The overlooked, as she knew only too well, destroyed arguments, led to incorrect conclusions, and often led to disastrous actions.

"You do not own this valley, nor any part of it, nor any of the resources you used to put up the buildings here," said Derk. "You are squatters on land that does not belong to you, living in homes built with material taken without permission, from land that does not belong to you."

John could hardly contain himself. "Well, if we don't own it, who does?"

"It belongs to the people of Earth," said Derk quietly, "since all of Mars belongs to the people of Earth. In actual practice it belongs to the United Nations Mars Office, in compliance with the Mars Agreement of 2016. The U.N. Mars Office acts in land questions in the interests of the nations of Earth. It is empowered to sell land to governments of countries that can start settlements on Mars. The money will be used to make some payment to the poorer nations on Earth that do not have the resources to settle and exploit the planet."

There was silence. Derk smiled. Let them chew on that for a while, he thought. It will not have occurred to them that legally they are squatters, he thought, with some satisfaction.

He was wrong, however. These matters had been carefully thought about by Denise, but not by John. Although John was undoubtedly a brilliant engineer and risk strategist, with a capability in that sphere far exceeding his wife's, in the arena of ideas and concepts he could not match his wife. Unbeknownst to her husband, she had delved deeply into the issue of ownership of real property, using the computer knowledge bases and the access to Earth's knowledge bases available to them for the past few years. As usual, being on Mars, in a continual struggle for survival on a planet never intended to support humans, had sharpened her mind, and given her an insight keener than that of almost anyone on Earth.

"Ownership of property is a collection of rights," said Denise, ready for battle. She detested Derk, and would nail him to the floor if she could.

"I agree," said Derk. "And your rights here are quite minimal."

"Could you explain that?" asked Denise.

"I can explain by example," said Derk, "an example widely used in ESA ethics circles in discussing your situation here."

"Interesting," said Denise. "I'm sure we'd all like to hear." John nodded. Dr. Sato said nothing. He had stopped eating, and appeared to be studying the ceiling.

"Suppose we have three travelers," began Derk, "in a remote part of the United States. Let's say in the American southwest, in a desert area of very large ranches, all privately owned. The travelers are two men and a woman. One of the men is an old priest. The travelers lose their way in a dust storm and end up traveling over a dirt road far from civilization. Suddenly their vehicle runs into quicksand, and disappears. They escape the quicksand, and continue on foot. Soon they are starving and without water.

"Then they come upon a small creek valley, where the creek forms a small pool that never dries up, where they can get water and some food from wildlife. There is no sign of human habitation for miles around, although the land is actually part of a very large ranch. Search parties are sent out to look for the missing travelers, but no trace of them is found, and they are assumed to be dead. The travelers build a shelter by the creek pool, and eventually improve it, to found a small settlement. They cultivate the land near the creek too, and use the creek water to irrigate it, and so have enough food, but have no way to return to civilization.

"In time their small settlement becomes reasonably comfortable and prosperous. The priest marries the young man and woman, and they have two children.

"Then one day they are discovered. The rancher himself is among the party that goes to greet them and bring them back to civilization. But now the three refuse to be rescued, saying they are happy where they are, and intend to stay. The rancher, who is a good man, is appalled. Instead of being grateful to him for the free use of his land, which enabled them to survive, the three want to take the land from him as their own. They even tell him and the other rescuers to get off their land.

"The rancher applies to the courts, and succeeds in his case against the three, for after all, it's his land. The police arrive, armed, but still the three refuse to move, determined to fight for their 'rights'. There is a skirmish, and one of the policemen is killed. The police bring in reinforcements, and the three are forced to flee. They are pursued, and are eventually cornered in a canyon. Still they refuse to give up. There is a big shootout. More police are killed, as are two of the three squatters and the children. The remaining one is captured. It's the young woman, a very vocal person with red hair.

"She is tried in a courtroom drama, where the defense tries to show that she had a right to fight for her rights. She is found guilty, and is eventually executed for the murder of a police officer. Initially, throughout the United States, there was admiration for the way the three had survived, and even some sympathy toward them for having to give up their home, which they had worked so hard for. But when the police officers are killed, all such sympathy disappears. The dead officers all left fatherless families behind." Derk stopped, glanced at Denise, and resumed eating.

"Not bad, as parables go, and quite biblical," said Denise. "Lots of action and drama, and a moral too. Make a good movie. Is anyone making such a movie?"

"Not to my knowledge," said Derk. That was a lie. The European Union Information Commissioner in Brussels, aware of the effectiveness of propaganda by dramatic story telling, was actually secretly funding such a movie. Galaxy Century Inc., the big Hollywood movie maker, currently owned by the large German conglomerate, Tuetonmann AG, recipient of the E.U. subsidy, was currently shooting such a movie in New Mexico.

"I take it that we three on Mars are analogous to the three lost travelers, settling on someone else's land," said Denise.

"I'm glad you see that clearly," said Derk.

"So that if we were to resist being rescued, and one of the rescuers was killed trying to get us to come back to Earth, all sympathy for our position would be lost on Earth, and we could even be charged with murder, and brought back to Earth to stand trial."

"More or less, yes," said Derk. "Now do you understand why your rights here are minimal? The three travelers did have the right to build their survival shelters on another man's land, but only as long as they were lost and unable to do anything about it. Once they were found, those rights disappeared. Their error was in assuming that those rights would continue indefinitely."

"I'm afraid I still don't fully understand why our rights here are minimal," said Denise. "When the rancher resorted to the courts, to have your squatters removed from his land, I would presume he would have had to show the judge the title deeds to the property, to prove his ownership."

"Of course," said Derk.

"So who on Earth has title deeds to this valley?" asked Denise.

"No single person," said Derk, a little taken aback. "But the people of Earth collectively have title to all the land on Mars. Mars belongs to the people of Earth. This was asserted quite clearly thirty-five years ago, in a United Nations resolution, passed unanimously, and is inscribed in the Mars Agreement of 2016. Any nation that has founded a settlement on Mars can claim title to the region involved, although final approval must come from the Mars Office of the United Nations, in return for a suitable payment."

"The price of the land, in effect," said John, frowning.

"Precisely," said Derk. "The people of Earth, through their representative body, the United Nations, are the owners of Mars, and are willing to sell a portion of the planet to an interested nation, provided the nation maintains a presence on the territory involved. In this way a nation can acquire title to the territory. A settlement nation can then, in turn, sell off portions of the territory to which it has acquired title, to individuals and corporations as it sees fit. The European Union will soon apply to the Mars Office for title to Leaf Valley and surrounding territories, in return for a suitable payment to the U.N. In time, the E.U. will sell portions of that land to business corporations, both European and American, for development."

"So you're saying that the people of Earth own Mars, and have all the rights to Mars," said Denise.

"Yes," said Derk. Get around that if you can, thought Derk. Denise, however, was determined to do just that.

"Why?" she asked. "Why do they own Mars?"

Derk hesitated. He had not considered that point. He thought hard, and then answered: "Simply because they have the rights to Mars."

"Let me be more precise," persisted Denise. "What is the source of those rights? Isn't all the people of Earth have done is assert, via their representatives at the U.N., that they have the rights?"

"True, but that's sufficient," said Derk "If the people of Earth say they have them, if they simply assert those rights, then they do have them."

"You're certain that's sufficient," said Denise, "and that all the people of Earth have to do is assert their rights to Mars, in order to have the rights?"

"Yes, I am certain," said Derk. "And the finest legal brains in Europe think so too."

Denise did not respond at once. Not only was her reason operating in high gear, but her fertile imagination too. Derk returned to his food, finishing off the plate. He was feeling satisfied, certain he had got the better of her.

Suddenly Denise excused herself, got up, walked to the west windows, and pulled the drapes. The light in the western sky had completely faded, leaving only their reflections in the windows.

"I see you have all finished eating," she said, standing by the table, smiling, her composure returned, and looking quite radiant in her long yellow dress. "Why don't you help yourselves to some dessert? It's a fruit dish—strawberries and blueberries in a chocolate and fruit juice dressing. It's John's favorite."

"I do recommend it," said John, aware that Denise had more than dessert in store for Derk.

"Thank you," said Derk, smiling to himself. Score one to us, he thought. He got up with the others, and served himself an extra large portion of dessert, which he felt he had earned. The dessert looked delicious, and although Derk would never have admitted it, he had thoroughly enjoyed Denise's food so far. Denise was an excellent cook, quite knowledgeable and skilled in French cuisine, the product of her upbringing in a well-endowed orphanage in eastern France. For Derk and his two first officers, the fresh food had been particularly welcome, after the months of monotonous canned and frozen meals on the long journey to Mars.

One by one they sat down again. There was silence for a while, as they concentrated on the dessert.

"A while ago, Captain Derk," began Denise, some time later, "you said that the finest legal brains in Europe are of the opinion that all the people of Earth need to do to own Mars is assert their right to the planet, through their representatives at the U.N."

"That's correct," said Derk, a little surprised that Denise wanted to continue the topic. He had thought that Denise had been defeated. The others stopped eating, anxious not to miss anything.

"But just suppose," said Denise, her green eyes flashing, "that a fleet of spacecraft from some alien civilization were to arrive on Mars next week, and build a large settlement, defended with far more advanced weaponry than anything known on Earth. Suppose these alien people were then to assert that they owned Mars and had all rights to the planet. Would you still maintain that the people of Earth owned Mars? Please just don't say that such an alien invasion of Mars is completely unlikely. Just suppose for the moment that it were to happen."

Derk was silent. He understood at once what Denise was driving at, and its implications too—getting these three off Mars was going to be even more difficult than he had supposed, he suddenly realized.

"The alien invaders would own it," admitted Derk eventually.

"Why?" asked Denise. "First the people of Earth have asserted that they own it. Then these aliens come and assert that they own it. Surely at least the Earth made the assertion first?"

"If there are others who are not party to the original assertion by the people of Earth," said Derk slowly, "as would be the case with the aliens, the others must either agree to the assertion, or not be in a position to negate the assertion by occupying the property and demonstrating they are capable of defending it."

"So, since the aliens would be in a position to negate the Earth's assertion of its right to Mars, by force if necessary," said Denise, "the aliens would become the owners."

"Yes," said Derk. "But of course the whole idea of aliens taking over Mars is preposterous."

"I'm missing something here, Denise," said John. "What you seem to be saying is that it's not enough for a people to assert ownership over a piece of territory, they must also occupy and be able to defend that territory."

"Not quite," said Denise, "but I can explain it quite simply, if you want to hear."

"Yes, I would," said John, looking around the table. "I'm very interested." Derk said nothing. He did not want any explanation. He understood the source of property rights only too well, and was shocked, although he did not show it, that Denise understood too. He could not refuse Denise's offer however, and eventually nodded to Denise.

"You told us your story about the squatters on the rancher's land, Captain Derk," said Denise, "to show us why we had no right to any land on Mars. Now, let me tell you another story that shows where the right to land comes from."

"Suppose we have a ship carrying ten refugee families on a wide ocean, but with nowhere to go," she began. "One day they come on a fertile but uninhabited island, previously undiscovered. As a group they assert ownership of the island, and as a group agree to divide the land up into ten equal parcels, one for each family. Each family then gets the right to a parcel of land, in return for conceding the rights to the rest of the land to the other families. They also agree that these property rights can be passed on to their heirs, and can be sold to others. Assuming that no other persons ever come near the island, the source of the property rights for each family is thus a deal, or a transaction: each family head agrees to getting the rights to a parcel of land in return for giving up the rights to the other parcels.

"But now suppose that after many years of working the land, when the island has become prosperous, another boatload of refugees arrive. The boat people are armed, but so are the islanders. The islanders tell the boat people there is no room for them, that all the land is taken up, and that they are the owners, in possession of all rights to the land. The boat people, not anxious for a fight, accept this and sail away in search of some other land. In other words, the boat people acknowledge the islanders' property rights.

"Later another boatload shows up. These people, unlike the first boatload, are armed to the teeth, and are cunning and aggressive. They get the same story as before: No land here, it's all already in private hands. They too sail off, but only over the horizon. That night they sail back, and attack the island at dawn, taking the islanders by surprise, slaughtering them all.

"These new arrivals, like the first lot, then assert their ownership of the land, and divide it up among the families, let's say ten families once more, so that once more each family gets the property rights to a parcel in return for giving up the rights to the other parcels.

"These new islanders are different from the first settlers in one important respect though. Like the first settlers they work hard and prosper, but unlike the first settlers, they devote an unusually large percentage of their efforts to the defense of their island. And over the years, more armed boat people arrive, even pirates, prepared to take over the island, but end up acknowledging the islanders' property rights when they see how well defended the island is. The descendants of the islanders are not inhumane, however, and every so often they accept a small boatload of newcomers on the island, provided the newcomers are willing to accept the existing islanders' rights to its land, including the right to pass it down from generation to generation. And, of course, from time to time a parcel of land is sold by one islander to another.

"The point is this, internally among the members of a people in possession of a piece of territory, property rights come about by agreement between free men and women, where one person gets the right to one parcel of land in return for giving up the right to the other parcels. But externally, between the people and other peoples, property rights come about by one people acknowledging another people's right to a territory, either by simple agreement: we people get this territory and you people get that one, or by acknowledgement extracted by force of arms: this territory is ours, and we'll blow you people away if you try to take it from us."

"And that is the source of the right to land," concluded Denise. "Not a pretty picture, and not one that even the most right-wing philosopher would be happy to admit to, because it points the way to revolution, where the landless, if they have the military strength, invade another people's territory to take their land, or massacre the current property owning elite to take the land and redistribute it. Examples are the French Revolution, where the peasants cut off the heads of the land-owning aristocracy and redistributed the land, or the case of Tasmania, where the Europeans arrived and slaughtered the original inhabitants of the land, to then redistribute it among themselves. In the case of the Americas, the European arrivals either slaughtered the native Indians, or moved them wholesale off good land to less attractive land, or confined them to small reservations—which allowed the newcomers to divide most of the land up among themselves. In a few cases, they did a land deal with the Indians.

"You can always blame the newcomers, and accuse them of stealing the land, but, as a famous philosopher once pointed out, since nobody ever made the land, it is not possible to steal it. But equally to blame are those who were in possession of the land, such as the French aristocrats, or the American Indians, or the Tasmanians, for not defending it. In the case of the French revolution, the growing numbers of the impoverished peasantry became too great for the aristocrats to defend their land against them, and the revolution swept them away. In the case of the native populations of Tasmania and the Americas, their weapons were too primitive and their numbers too small to keep out the hoards of Europeans, hungry for land.

"The moral is clear. Ownership does come from asserting your rights to the land. Such assertion is only a claim, however, unless you also occupy the land and are in a position to have those rights acknowledged by all other interested people, either by agreement or by force of arms.

"And that's why, if aliens were to arrive on Mars next week with superior weapons, any assertion of ownership of Mars by the people of Earth would be merely an unenforceable claim. The aliens, occupying the planet, and able to defend it, would be the owners."

Denise stopped here, and finished off her dessert. There was dead silence around the table. Nobody asked for clarification or tried to dispute what Denise had said. It was so obviously correct. Derk was shocked. He had assumed that it was John, with his superb engineering skills, who was the master mind of the Martian settlement. It hit him now that he had been completely wrong. The true driving force and master mind was Denise, and for the first time Derk began to understand why it might be impossible to get this witch off Mars alive, unless at gunpoint—which would leave him with very few options.

"I see we've all finished eating," said John, rising from the table. "There's coffee and tea and cookies in the kitchen. Let's go and sit down around the table in the living room. We'll be more comfortable there. Maybe we should talk about something else too." John was still very interested in the subject of property rights, but he needed time to digest what his wife had just said. He could see clearly that it had important strategic implications. After all, what they were discussing was something unheard of, although still a very practical matter for the three survivors on Mars, namely the property rights to a planet.

Derk could see that too, and as he rose from the table, had not yet decided whether or not to continue this exchange with Denise. Unlike John, he needed no time to digest what Denise had said. He understood all too well, since he was directly descended from that infamous Norman baron, the grand Duke Gilbert D'Erque, part of the invading Norman army that had come to England from French Normandy, an old Viking settlement. The Duke had helped lay waste to Saxon England in the eleventh century, destroying its Saxon culture, and driving the Saxon noble families from their lands. The Normans had asserted their title to England, had extracted its acknowledgement from the Saxons by force of arms, and had divided up the land among the newcomer Norman aristocracy.

One of those Norman noblemen was Derk's infamous ancestor, whose land the Derk family held to this day. And those Normans, completely clear in their minds as to the source of title to their new lands, had built enormous stone fortresses and castles throughout the land. They had defended their blood won titles to the land of England so well against all comers from then on, a tradition carried on right down to the present day, that never again in a thousand years of history was England successfully invaded and conquered.

Soon, the six were seated in the living area, in the northwest corner below the staircase to the upper level. Derk had selected a seat with his back to the west wall, from which he could see down the entrance hallway. Dr Sato sat quietly with his back to the adjacent staircase wall. The others had the outside chairs.

There was a silence for a while. All of them were thinking. Derk quickly concluded that he needed to know just what Denise had in mind about resisting return to Earth. He was in no doubt now that she did intend to resist departure to Earth in three weeks. What he needed to know was how, and how much of his intentions she had guessed.

"That was rather an extreme point of view you put forward in that little story of yours, or should I say speech, Dr. Lavoisier," he began. "I'm wondering how it affects what you think you should do about our offer to bring you all safely back to Earth."

"Well, obviously," replied Denise, "it shows that the people of Earth's assertion that they own all of Mars is merely a claim to ownership, if that ownership is not acknowledged, and agreed to by all, particularly by those already on Mars. Since we do not acknowledge Earth's claim to ownership of this valley, which we explored and developed, nor ownership of the many mines we have developed for obtaining essential raw materials, Earth does not own this valley, although it is free to claim it. We assert our ownership of it instead, and we, unlike the people of Earth, are in possession of it."

"But if Earth doesn't acknowledge your ownership of the valley, likewise you have only a claim to ownership," said Derk calmly. "I'm certain that there is no way the U.N. Mars Office will ever acknowledge your claim to this valley and its adjacent lands."

"Perhaps not," said Denise, "but our conversation has clarified the situation immensely. Obviously, 'white man has spoken with forked tongue'."

Derk stiffened. It was all he could do to keep control of himself. His hostess had just about called him a liar.

"I'm rather afraid I don't follow you," he said quietly. Another little matter that would have to be paid for, he thought.

"I wasn't implying that you were the only one who had spoken 'with forked tongue'," answered Denise, aware of Derk's reaction.

"And who else, may I ask?"

"The whole ESA leadership, and those governments in Europe who maintain ESA," said Denise. "They did everything they could to mislead us, and the ordinary people of Europe, into believing that you were coming here as our guests, to rescue us only if we so desired. But that was not the real reason why you came here, was it?" It might have been better if Denise had stopped here, but inside she was seething with animosity toward Derk, and could not stop herself. The two glasses of wine she had drunk did not help either.

"Like the boat people in the story I told you," she now continued, with passion in her voice, "who came to the island that was already occupied, your true purpose was occupation of the land of this region of Mars, and removal of the existing occupants from that land. And just like the boat people in the story, you knew that your assertion of ownership of that land might not be acknowledged, and might be resisted. So like the boat people, you came armed to the teeth, prepared to use force, and deception too. Those weapons you have with you were not brought to Mars for purposes of testing, were they, as you so innocently maintained? They were brought to subdue us by force if necessary, to ensure our removal from our land.

"And, of course, even if that removal turned out to be a bit messy, the full government propaganda machinery, together with the media, would be brought to bear to support your side of events. A few right-thinking people in Europe would understand what had happened, and would be upset. But they would have little influence on the minds of the general population, misled by their leaders. And anyway, those few decent people would be in no position to do anything about the E.U. occupation of this land. In time, with government help, the messy way in which it was accomplished would all be forgotten, and become just boring history, just like what happened with Tasmania. Isn't that the way of it?"

Instead of answering Denise's question, Derk turned to look at John, who was looking grim faced, and partly shaking his head in disbelief, as the truth of his wife's words sank in.

"I see your wife has an overly active imagination," said Derk. "I must say. I really don't know whether to be angry, or just burst out laughing." He feigned a laugh, but not very successfully. John said nothing.

Actually, although Derk truly was in no mood to laugh, he was not at all angry. In fact, he was feeling rather pleased, for he had achieved his objective, unbeknownst to either John or Denise, and was now happy to turn the subject to more trivial matters. He now knew the mind of his enemy, and understood that although Denise had guessed his ultimate goals correctly, neither she nor John was in any way prepared to deal with the devilry he was prepared to employ to achieve them. The mind of Dr. Sato bothered him a little though, for that mind he could not penetrate.

He turned back to Denise, smiling politely. "I see I made a mistake. I should have had a glass of your Martian wine after all. It certainly seems to have had a stimulating effect on the—"

WHEEEE—WHOOOO—WHEEEE—WHOOOO....

The pitching whistle sound came from down the hallway. Derk sat bolt upright in his chair, almost spilling the coffee in his cup. He put the cup down. "Isn't that a communications alert?" he asked. He had a worried look on his face, which puzzled John.

"Yes," said John, unconcerned. "Probably a message for us from NASA. We've been getting one about every fifteen days recently. We have the alert set all the time now, except during the night. We'll check it out later. We can send messages to NASA only on Sunday evenings—time on their big dish antennas is scarce."

"A message from the habitat in Elbow Plain could also trigger an alert, couldn't it?" said Derk. He was obviously very tense.

"Yes," said John, "but only if an alert were coded into it, which I presume would be the case only in an emergency. You look worried. Could something be seriously wrong at the habitat?"

"Yes, it's possible," said Derk. "I'd appreciate it if you'd go and check out that message."

"Certainly," said John, who got up and disappeared down the hallway to the communications room. Derk said nothing, but sat facing Denise and the hallway, his back to the wall, forgetting himself a little, with his hands joined together in front of him, so that opposing fingers and thumbs just touched, cage like. He often did this when he was very concerned about something.

A few seconds later, John was back, walking very quickly.

"It's from the habitat, all right, for you," he said to Derk. "It's from Dr. Vincenzo Cassoni. He says it's urgent. Please come with me."

John led the Captain down the hallway to the communications room, showed him the controls, and then came back to the living area, and sat down, leaving Derk alone. He picked up his coffee cup and drained it. Now John was worried. His intuition told him something had gone very wrong. The man at the habitat, obviously the Italian member of the ESA mission, had sounded very fearful.

"Anyone want some more coffee?" John asked. "I think I need some."

"One for me, please," said Jurgen, who was frowning. He too looked very worried. The others shook their heads. Emma Grant too was looking very anxious. They all know something I don't, thought John to himself, as he walked round the corner of the living area to the kitchen, to fetch the coffee jug.

He was sitting down again, drinking his coffee when Derk returned. Derk's face had changed completely. All the color had left it, and his brow was deeply furrowed. He did not sit down, but remained standing beside his chair, shaking slightly, and trying to reassert control of himself. He had obviously had a shock.

Both John and Denise jumped up, quickly followed by Dr. Sato. Something told them, all three, that danger lurked. Although they had just been having a rather philosophical conversation, during a pleasant dinner in a pleasant home, this home was on Mars, and on Mars danger lay everywhere.

"For heaven's sake man," said John, catching Derk's arm, "please sit down. You look as if you've just seen a ghost. What's the matter?"

Derk sat down. "I'm all right," he said, his composure returning somewhat. "Just some unexpected bad news. I'd like another cup of coffee, please."

"I'll fetch it," said Denise, hurrying to the kitchen.

Meanwhile Derk was breathing deeply. Normally he could keep control of himself in an emergency, but the news he had just received was not merely bad. It was worse than anything he had ever envisioned happening.

Denise had soon poured Derk his coffee, which he drank down quickly.

Eventually, apparently mostly recovered, he spoke, looking at Jurgen and Emma: "Could you two leave us alone for ten minutes? I need to talk to these three alone. Perhaps you could go for a walk on the balcony above. But don't go far away. I think I'm going to need you."

Surprised, Jurgen and Emma stood up, looking around, wondering which way to go.

"You can go out directly onto the south balcony," said Denise helpfully. "Come. I'll show you. There are outside lights too." She led the pair over to the south wall of the living area, and slid back a glass door. "The light switch is to your left, on the outside wall," she said, as the pair walked outside.

"Listen chaps, I'm rather afraid I've some unpleasant matters to discuss," said Derk, as Denise returned to the living room corner beside the stairs. "For obvious strategic reasons I needed to know about the entrance to Leaf Valley via what you call the Tip Canyon road. Today was the only opportunity, since tomorrow, and for the rest of the coming week, we would all be busy with refueling the lander. I realize you asked us not to come into Leaf Valley without permission. I had to ignore that, since anyway the E.U. does not recognize your right to this valley. So I sent out a reconnaissance mission today, ostensibly as a geological survey mission—six people, in the two three-seater buggies we brought with us on the lander. Dr Donald Caruthers, the mission's chief geologist, is in charge.

"The six had instructions to travel down Kasei Valley on the main road to the east, and then turn off to the north just before what you call Dune Narrows, into what you call Hazard Valley, and then take the road back along Hazard Valley, and then the road that comes back through Tip Canyon. Their orders were to wait at the exit from Tip Canyon until about seven, when it would be dusk. They would then drive out of the canyon and down Leaf Valley, past this compound, while we were inside having dinner. They would get back to the habitat just after eight. I was sure none of you would be aware of their trip if they did that. We thought that was the best way of avoiding any unpleasantness at this stage of our visit."

John frowned. Then the frown was replaced by an angry expression. "I'm very sorry, sir," he said, barely able to control his anger, "but, apart altogether from your attempt to deceive us, that's far too dangerous a trip to attempt in open buggies. You need rovers for a trip like that."

"I realize that now," said Derk. "I didn't believe there was any significant danger when I ordered the mission, for the maps showed a road all the way around that plateau to the east, and a distance of only a hundred and eighty miles. And Dr. Bell said yesterday that your wife had confirmed that there was a good, safe road back down through Tip Canyon to this valley. And the buggies have a range of about two hundred and forty miles, or eight hours at thirty miles an hour, before their batteries run down. Given all that information, it did not appear that there would be any risk if both buggies went." He paused here, and then said to Denise: "Can I have some more coffee, please?"

Denise poured another cup, and Derk drank half of it almost at once. "I'm not finished, and I don't quite know what to say to you," he said.

"They haven't come back, have they?" said John, very quietly. His anger was gone now, as he began to understand the implications. He could see too that Derk was a very clever strategist, and that

Derk's sneak plan would have worked, had it not been for the fact that he lacked the experience on Mars to make good judgements.

"No," said Derk. "They were to be back about eight fifteen or so. It's almost nine o'clock. Both Karl Mannhardt and Ursula Schneider are outside the habitat, scanning the roads with field glasses, but have seen no sign of them. The worst is the buggies have not communicated with the habitat since just after four o'clock. That was just after they were at the junction on the Kasei Valley road, where there's a road north to Hazard Valley. Karl blames the cloud cover for the communications break-down. The buggies have very small satellite dishes, and use ultra extreme high frequency radio. The radio beam up to the satellite behaves like a light beam and is easily blocked by a cloud layer."

"I understand," said John, "although the fact that tonight's clouds are blocking the signal doesn't necessarily mean there's any problem. But if I remember correctly, from your habitat you can see the valley floor at least ten miles down the valley, and you can see across the valley to Stem Gap. So if the buggies were on their way back, you could see their lights half an hour away at least. That means there's a problem."

"Yes, something's obviously gone wrong," said Derk. "They're nearly an hour and a half overdue. We need your help. You know Mars, and you must know the road, since you built it. They left at one fifteen this afternoon, so as to have plenty of time to do the trip, but that means their air flasks will give out in about two to three hours if they don't make it back."

"Oh my God!" cried Denise suddenly, whose imagination had been busy generating possible scenarios. "The labyrinth!"

"Labyrinth?" said Derk, startled. "What do you mean?"

"The last forty miles," explained John. "The road goes through a labyrinth of chaotic terrain—lots of small intersecting valleys, all looking very much alike, and filled with sand dunes. It's one of the most dangerous places on Mars—very easy place to get lost."

"I was aware of those small valleys in that region, but isn't there a safe road through?" said Derk, clutching the arm of his chair.

"Yes and no," said John. "That road can get blocked by dunes sometimes, when a pair of dune tongues lock together. If they could and did stay with the road, the labyrinth would pose no danger."

"And if they couldn't and didn't?"

"God help them," said John.

There was silence now, as they all contemplated what had the potential to develop into a nightmare scenario, all except Dr. Sato that is, who merely listened and reasoned.

"But on second thoughts, we don't know what they did," said Denise, "or even where they are. It could be they're nowhere near the labyrinth." But intuition told her that in the labyrinth, somehow, was exactly where the missing six were. She continued: "We have to find them quickly. Otherwise there'll be another disaster like 2038."

"Let's all calm down," said John, "and try to reason this thing out. We've got only two to three hours to find them alive, if they don't show up on their own, and they could be anywhere on a one hundred and eighty mile long road. We can get the rovers out, but we can't do more than about twenty miles an hour in the dark. So if they're more than about fifty miles away, we can't reach them in time. And then there's the question of which direction to go to search for them—up through Tip Canyon, or out through Stem Gap and northeast down Kasei Valley, or both. We'd better think this—"

WHEEEE—WHOOOO—WHEEEE—WHOOOO....

"It's probably for you," said John to Derk.

Derk disappeared. A minute later he was back, but looking no less shaken.

"No good news?" asked Denise.

"It was Vince again," explained Derk. "Mission Control in Toulouse tracks everything that's going on up here. They know we're here having dinner with you, and they know those six should have been back an hour ago, and that they've not come back, and have to be back in less than three hours. Vince says the story's already all over the media on Earth."

"I sympathize," said Denise, temporarily overcoming her dislike for Derk. "The last thing you need in a crisis like this is Mission Control breathing down your neck." She turned to her husband. "Am I right in assuming the communications system at the habitat does not use that ultra extreme high frequency to link up to the satellite to talk to Earth?"

"Yes, you are," said John. "The habitat dish is big and never has to move, except for minor orientation, so you can use a lower radio frequency, otherwise that link would be out too. It's only the link between the buggies and the satellite that the clouds could affect."

"I see," said Denise. "So there's really no way to get in contact with the buggies to ask them where they are."

"Not unless the cloud clears off," said John. "Surface radio couldn't reach them. Too many natural obstacles. A satellite link's the only way, and that's blocked." He paused, looking very grim. The others waited, both Derk and Denise looking very worried. Derk was thinking about his future. He had trouble seeing how ESA would forgive such a mistake, if it turned out as badly as it looked. Denise was thinking about Sheila Bell, the only one of the missing six she knew well, and even liked.

"We had better get moving, quickly," John went on, "but first we have to come up with a strategy—and if we do it wrong we'll have six dead bodies in the morning. Our chances of doing it right are low, I'm afraid. You'll be doing even better than the 2038 NASA mission, Captain Derk. It took two months to kill eleven that time. This time you'll have managed to kill six in two days."

Derk looked at John. John could see the cold fear in Derk's eyes. "You must be able to do something," said Derk, almost in a whisper.

"I don't know if I can, but I'll do my best," said John. He stared at the coffee table, deep in thought, his brow deeply furrowed. Then, suddenly, he turned to Dr. Sato. "What do you think?" he said. "Have you any idea what we should do?"

"It would appear," said the Zen master, in his usual unperturbed voice, "that it's like a doctor with a patient about to die in about three hours from a specific disease. The only problem is that it could be any one of about six diseases, all quite similar in symptoms, but each quite different in the treatment needed. And the doctor has time to treat for only one of those diseases. If he diagnoses the disease wrongly, he'll select the wrong treatment, and the patient will die."

"So what you're saying," said Denise, thinking about the problem along the lines of this medical analogy, "is that everything depends on a correct diagnosis of what went wrong for those six."

"Yes," said the Zen master.

"You're right," said John, nodding. "Right, as usual. We're being forced to run the risk of making the wrong diagnosis. All right, let's do the diagnostics. Let's all sit down, and see if we can figure out what most likely went wrong. We're going to get only one chance to save them."

CHAPTER EIGHT

The Labyrinth

ABOUT AN hour's drive from the habitat at Elbow Hill, the road east down Kasei Valley ran along the southern side of a great eight-mile long rupture in the valley floor, which the settlers had named Snakepit Crack.

The road ran quite near to the edge of the crack in a few places, and it was at just such a place that Don Carruthers ordered a ten-minute halt, for a brief survey. The ESA mission's chief geologist was in charge of the six-man expedition that Tuesday afternoon, and was driving the lead buggy.

There was nothing comparable to this eight-mile long rupture anywhere on Earth. The whole structure was generally snake-like in appearance, seen from above. The distance across the crack varied, but typically it was about a mile, except for a few places where there was a large embayment in the north side. At such an embayment, the distance across was as much as two miles.

The depth of the monster rupture varied along its length too, and Don Carruthers estimated it to be at least half a mile deep. The actual pit bottom was fairly narrow along most of its length, and was quite inaccessible. If you fell in, you would not only be killed, but your body would never be recovered. Instead, it would in time be buried by the prevailing east wind that often blew fine sand along the floor of Kasei Valley, and over the edge into the pit.

There was generally no clear edge to the giant chasm, on either side, nor were the poorly defined edges in any way straight. They just meandered along, snake like, like the bottom of the pit, but the meandering of the edges of the crack and the meandering of the pit bottom were almost never the same.

Most places there was no straight drop down to the bottom either, but a sequence of precipices, each with a shelf at the bottom that usually sloped down to the next precipice. The width of each shelf varied along the entire eight-mile length of the crack too, and the meandering of each shelf, and the meandering of each precipice, was usually different from the meandering of each of the other shelves and precipices.

At places along the length of the crack, one or more of the precipices in the sequence would be merely a very steep slope, and this was frequently the case with the uppermost precipice, which made the crack very dangerous. The number of precipices you had to go down to get to the bottom varied too, from one or two to about five, for sometimes the shelf between two successive precipices was almost non existent, resulting in a very large drop straight down. Such drops were more frequent on the north side of the crack, which was generally much steeper than the south side, where the road lay.

At the place where the buggies stopped, Snakepit was just under a mile wide, and if you looked across to the north side, you could see only one large precipice that dropped all the way to the pit bottom.

If you looked even further away, beyond the far edge of the giant crack, the red and gray terrain of the boundary escarpment of Kasei Valley rose up to the north, visibly pockmarked with small craters. The escarpment went up gradually at first, beginning at the opposite edge of the crack. Further from the edge, it rose more steeply, getting steadily steeper, finally merging into an almost sheer escarpment wall, about four miles away.

The huge crack in the valley floor meandered northeastward, more or less between this orange escarpment wall lying to the north, and the road lying to the south.

"My God, what a pit," exclaimed Sheila Bell, completely absorbed by the sight, her curiosity strongly aroused. To her left, the terrain on the north side of the road sloped away quite gently at first, with many rocks and boulders embedded in the red soil. Then, quite quickly, it began sloping away ever more steeply, with fewer and fewer rocks visible, finally disappearing into the abyss, about a hundred meters away.

The sight was so awesome that it pushed Sheila's earlier concerns for the expedition's safety completely out of her mind. The concerns were those she had expressed to Don Carruthers the previous evening, about the day's expedition traveling some ninety miles distant from the habitat, with only eleven hours supply of air.

Sheila was in the lead buggy, beside Don Carruthers, who was sitting to her left. She was standing up to get a better view, her helmet bumping against the buggy's roof rack. She was looking at the crack through outdoors field glasses, over Don Carruther's head.

"Just look at that cliff wall on the other side," she cried. "Look how far down it goes. The devil himself could live in that hole."

"No, no, Sheila. There are no devils on Mars," said Claude Bertrand confidently. He was next to Sheila in the lead buggy, on her right, and was standing up too, straining to see down to the pit bottom through field glasses.

There was no reply from Sheila, or any of the others, as they all stared at the pit.

Claude Bertrand's structural engineering mind was already analyzing engineering possibilities. But had he thought more about devils instead, he might have realized that he was wrong about there being no devils on Mars, and might have concluded that where there was a devil there was bound to be devilry. Indeed, although he could not know it that pleasant, sunny afternoon, he himself would be one of the first victims of that devilry, not very far in the future.

"This crack, it is not so bad," he observed at last, still looking at it through the field glasses, and speaking in his cultured French accent. "It has possibilities, has it not? If you were to put a transparent roof over it, you would have a very nice sheltered enclosure, twelve kilometers long. You could even plant trees in it, and have running water."

"Do you really think it would be possible to do that?" asked Astrid Larsson, in her sing-song Swedish accent. She was standing up too, in the buggy behind, recording the view with a video camera. "It could well be getting wider every year." Astrid was both a geologist and a structural engineer.

Her video recording was simultaneously being transmitted to the habitat and Mission Control on Earth, via the ESA satellite to the south. The signal was beaming up to the satellite from one or more of the twenty-four small dishes of the buggy's hemispherical dish array on its roof rack. The signal's ultra extreme high frequency allowed the enormous amount of information in a video recording to be transmitted easily.

"Certainly, it would be a big project," replied Claude to Astrid's question. Claude Bertrand loved the limelight, and was always on the lookout for engineering projects that would further enhance his reputation as one of Europe's most daring structural engineers. "But I can think of a way to do it, even if it does get wider by a centimeter or two each year. Of course, first you would have to make careful measurements of any widening."

"My friends," interrupted a voice with a heavy Spanish accent. It was Jose Montoya. He was the driver of the second buggy, sitting beside Astrid Larsson. “We should get moving. We have a long way to go. We should not forget we left the habitat fifteen minutes late. This place is just one more danger to watch out for. It means you do not leave the road around here after dark.”

They had originally planned on setting out at one o’clock, but there had been a delay at the last minute. Captain Derk had decided that the covert nature of the expedition would be less obvious to their audience on Earth, if they made a fuss about bringing along some light geological survey equipment in the buggy trailers.

Derk had not been concerned about the resulting fifteen-minute delay. He had prudently allowed six hours for the estimated five-hour trip, first eastward down Kasei Valley, then back westward, along the more northerly Hazard Valley, then through Tip Canyon, and so covertly into Leaf Valley after dark, at its little-used northern entrance at the leaf tip.

Monique Montpellier, sitting beside Astrid in the second buggy, nodded in agreement with her friend. She also made a mental note of an image of a buggy driver making a mistake in the dark, leaving the road, and driving over the edge of the half-mile deep rupture. Then, in correct English, but with a mild French accent, she said: “We have seen enough. Jose is right. We have too far to go today, to waste time looking into this worthless pit. We have been sitting here ten minutes already.”

“Now there, I don’t agree,” said Sheila Bell, in her lilting Irish accent. She was still awestricken by the giant crack, and her insatiable curiosity was now even more strongly aroused. “It isn’t every day you come to Mars. We can’t really see down to the bottom from here. We’re too far away from the edge. I’d like to see rightly down into it. Look! On up the road—about two hundred meters—there’s a place that’s a bit higher and closer to the edge. Now couldn’t we stop when we get there? I’m sure we could see down properly from there. And don’t you think all the people on Earth would want to see down too? Now, wouldn’t that be all right, Don? Just a few minutes for a better look?”

Don Carruthers, as a geologist, was just as curious about the mile-wide crack in the valley floor as Sheila. It amazed him too. He had never seen anything like it, and would have been happy to spend a week investigating it. Unlike Claude Bertrand, fame did not interest him much. Curiosity was his motor—curiosity about how Nature worked, and how she worked inside planets in particular.

"Well, let me see," he said, looking at his wrist display. "It's twenty past two, and we have a hundred and twenty miles to go to get to Leaf Valley. That's four hours at thirty miles an hour. So if we stop up ahead for another ten minutes, we should still reach the entrance to Leaf Valley by about half past six. We're supposed to be there by seven at the latest. All right Sheila, we can afford the time for a better look at this pit. I'm curious myself about what's down there. We should still get to Leaf Valley half an hour early. And I don't believe it would matter much if we didn't get there until after seven, except maybe for driving down the valley in the dark."

"But we are not just on a geology mission today," objected Jose Montoya, frowning. "An important goal of this expedition is to check out the road into Leaf Valley from the northeast, through Tip Canyon. I think we should allow more than just half an hour for unexpected delays. And I do think the Captain meant it, when he said we are to be there by seven."

Jose Montoya had wanted to be in charge of this expedition, since its true purpose was to reconnoiter the back road into Leaf Valley. As both an experienced military field strategist and engineer, he knew he was much better suited to this task than Don Carruthers. He certainly possessed the determination and discipline to see any expedition through, his determination constrained by a caution that made him a good survivor.

"Those aren't my orders, Jose," said Don Carruthers. "You're right we're to check out the road. But we're also to make note of all geological formations, especially anything that could be either useful, or a potential hazard, or just interesting to the people on Earth who are paying for this Mars mission. This pit qualifies on all three counts. As for unexpected delays, it's my understanding that there's a decent road all the way, like the one yesterday, and we have strict orders not to leave it. Sorry old chap, but it's my decision. I'm in charge on this trip. We'll stop up the road for ten minutes, and Astrid will do some more video recording. The video will make eyes pop on Earth, I'm sure. All right, let's carry on." He waved to the other buggy with his right hand as he pressed the accelerator.

When they stopped again, Jose Montoya's concern persisted. His concern was genuine, for although Don Carruthers might be a brilliant geologist, in Montoya's opinion he was not a good expedition leader. Carruthers was just too much the scientist, in his opinion, fascinated more with how Nature worked on Mars than with logistical matters. Jose had said as much to Captain Derk, that morning. Jose would even have been happy with Monique Montpellier in charge, whose instincts he trusted. She too had a military background, as well as being a biologist experienced in extreme environments, and she had a decisive but cautious nature.

Privately, Derk had been in complete agreement with Jose. But Derk had tactfully refused his leadership request, explaining that he had to have the respected and good-natured English geologist in charge, since he wanted the trip to look like a genuine geological expedition for the benefit of the public on Earth. Don Carruthers it had to be.

Where they made the second stop, there was a much better view down to the rugged bottom of the giant pit, and Astrid Larsson made some spectacular video recordings, which she transmitted to both the habitat and Mission Control. Although they could now see sand patches on the pit floor, far below, there were no obvious sand dunes, clear evidence that the wind never blew down there. Nor were there many impact craters to be seen, indicating that the giant crack was of relatively recent origin, in a geological sense.

The sight even impressed Jose and Monique. Nevertheless, both of them, largely because of their military training and cautious natures, remained uneasy about the further delay. Although neither of them voiced any additional objections, they were both keenly aware of their level of exposure to danger. They were to journey far from base with a limited air supply, in buggies with limited battery power. They both knew there was a distinct possibility of delays that could force them to deal with unfamiliar terrain in the dark, before reaching the northern entrance to Leaf Valley.

Even these two could have no inkling, however, of just how well founded their concerns were. They were unaware of how treacherous Hazard Valley could be, or of just how dangerous was the labyrinth region lying in wait at the western end of Hazard Valley, through which the road passed, on the final stretch of their journey.

Neither Captain Derk, nor any of the six European astronauts on the expedition that sunny afternoon, had taken the trouble to find out why Hazard Valley had its strange name. Had any of them understood why, the nightmare scenario that lay ahead might have been averted.

The second stop to view Snakepit Crack lasted fifteen minutes. If Jose Montoya had been in charge, they would have stopped only once, and would not have spent more than five minutes viewing the giant pit.

*

Just after four, they came to a T-junction in the road east along Kasei Valley. Here they were to turn left and head north on another road, and cross some fifteen miles of broken terrain, to gain access to the east end of Hazard Valley. From that end of Hazard Valley, the road then ran back westward along the valley floor, to the narrow Tip Canyon entrance at the northern end of Leaf Valley.

Don Carruthers called a halt at the road junction for a few minutes, to survey the terrain. Astrid Larsson did some more video recording, which she sent to the habitat, along with a message specifying their current location. Vince Cassoni was doing communications duty at the habitat and took the message. He wished them well on the rest of the journey, at the same time urging them to get a move on. Astrid promised they would report again around six.

The road straight ahead continued on eastward down Kasei Valley to Dune Narrows, some forty miles away. There, as far as they knew, the road ended—at one of the narrowest parts of the valley, a place subject to strong funnel winds that had once caused dunes of very fine sand to block the valley floor. In recent years, the sand had slowly drifted on, and the valley floor at Dune Narrows currently was sufficiently clear of sand to allow a rover to pass through. Also, unbeknownst to these six, some further work had gone on in that part of the valley, before their mission landed, to extend the road much further east, well beyond Dune Narrows.

To the south lay the boundary escarpment wall of Kasei Valley, sheer at the top but declining ever more gradually as it sloped down to the valley floor. The orange-brown wall marched off eastward over the horizon, stretching away somewhat irregularly at first, but very irregularly in the distance. In the late afternoon sun, the top of the wall was already in shadow in many places.

To the north, there was no longer a high escarpment wall to mark the edge of the valley floor. Instead, there was a series of rough, ascending terraces, a few miles away. Behind the top terrace lay broken, orange-red country—a jumble of high mesas to the west, giving way to very rugged red hills to the east. The road north to Hazard Valley climbed up the rough terraces, heading for the boundary between the high mesas and the rugged hills—seemingly impenetrable terrain.

The sun was already fairly low in the western sky, and long dark shadows were creeping across this rugged red landscape to the north. High, white washboard clouds had recently begun veiling the pink of the sky to the east too. The clouds were slowly drifting westward, threatening to dim the westering sun, and hasten the darkness of the approaching night. The clouds also posed a threat of a very different kind, far more serious, but this did not register with any of the six.

The road north, that late afternoon, had a foreboding appearance. It was not quite what any of them had been expecting, given their experience so far on roads on the broad floor of western Kasei Valley. Those roads had to contend with only the usual eroded craterlets everywhere, and with the minor ups and downs typical of the gently undulating floors of large Martian outflow valleys.

Had this trip been merely a casual exploration expedition, there was not a single one of those six souls who would have voted in favor of taking this northern route back to their Elbow Hill habitat that late afternoon. Each of them would have been content to call it a day, turn about, and head back to base the way they had come.

"Well, chaps, it doesn't look too cheery, but I'm sure it's all right," said Don Carruthers encouragingly. "The road goes through this rough country for only about fifteen miles. On the other side it comes out right at the east end of Hazard Valley."

"Have you found out yet why they called it Hazard Valley?" asked Sheila.

"No, not yet," replied Don. "Do any of you know?"

"Probably because it can be dangerous," said Jose Montoya.

"We are wasting more time," said Monique Montpellier. "We must keep moving, and be extra careful when we get to this Hazard Valley."

"This time I agree with you, Monique," said Don, "on both counts. Let's carry on." Although his voice did not show it, Don Carruthers was beginning to feel concerned, and he was beginning to regret that they had spent so much time viewing Snakepit Crack. His geological mind did not like the look of the terrain they were about to enter.

*

The road through the rough terrain between Kasei Valley and Hazard Valley was quite different from the roads they had been used to on the floor of Kasei Valley, both earlier that day and the previous day. This road did a lot of climbing, especially in the beginning. Then it was full of quite large ups and downs, winding a great deal at the same time. This required that they drive much more slowly, and with very great care. It was rarely possible to do more than twenty miles an hour along it, and often they could do no more than ten miles an hour.

As they proceeded slowly through this rough country, the road gradually turned to head northwest.

The scenery everywhere was spectacular, as they traveled along short valleys between the mesas on their left and the rugged hills to their right. Every so often, a gap between two hills to the right opened up an additional spectacular view.

Astrid faithfully recorded these sights, during the first twenty minutes, and dutifully transmitted them to the habitat, while the buggy moved along. The buggy's hemispherical array of twenty-four small satellite dishes, on top of its roof rack, continued to work well, allowing transmission while the buggy was moving. A computer continually selected the dish, or small group of dishes, currently pointed at the satellite.

Astrid soon got tired of making the video recordings, for the sights did not change much in character, and soon she put the camera away.

The six were largely unmoved by the scenery. The lengthening shadows, and the faint wisps of ice mist beginning to form in hollows on valley floors, were not exactly conducive to any feelings of enjoyment.

It was late in the afternoon, and the air temperature was dropping fast. Pockets of air in valleys and hollows were already below the Martian frost point, allowing the thin hair-like, ice mist to form, as water vapor condensed out of the thin air onto invisible dust particles and froze.

Only once, when an opening to the left between two well-separated mesas caused all of them to think that they were about to enter the wide, westward running Hazard Valley, was there any feeling of relief. This proved to be a false alarm, and their somber feelings returned. The road did not turn left into that valley. Instead, it continued on through even rougher country, winding treacherously through another set of interconnected short narrow valleys, with a high mesa blocking any turn to the west and the way home.

*

It was nearly five fifteen, about three quarters of an hour later than Derk would have expected, when at last they came through a final gap between two small hills, and saw the wide Hazard Valley spread out below in the sunlight, running due west.

The sunlight filling the valley from the sinking sun was quite weak, for in the past hour, thin washboard ice clouds, drifting in from the east, high up, had completely covered the sky. They were similar to the clouds of the previous morning. The air temperature was already very low too.

Don Carruthers called a brief halt, as he surveyed the three-mile wide valley before him, and the road down to it. This road descended gradually to the valley floor, down a long, gentle, rock-strewn slope; it veered to the west as it descended, but continued to wind, mostly around small craters.

The number of small dune fields littering the valley was a surprise to all of them. There were small dune fields everywhere, on both sides of the road along the valley floor, often reaching up to the lower reaches of the escarpments marking both edges of the valley.

Astrid Larsson made a brief video recording of these sights, but did not transmit the video to the habitat. Enough for today, she thought; they can have the rest when we get back. She gave no thought to the possible effect of the cloud cover on the buggy satellite communications system.

None of the others did either. None of them were communications experts, although Jose, an experienced military field engineer, did have substantial skills. They had all forgotten that those small dishes that made the buggy's twenty-four dish array possible, and thus satellite transmission while the buggy was moving, required ultra extreme high frequency radio signals. The signal beam behaved like a light beam, and thus, like light, had difficulty penetrating ice clouds on the way up to the satellite.

The dune fields lying on the valley floor were mostly in the shape of long serpentine tongues of sand. Some of these tongues just seemed to be immobile, lying filling in long hollows, and some of them seemed to be very slowly slithering along the valley floor toward the west, although at that moment there was no wind that could propel them.

"At least that's the Hazard Valley road down there," said Don, in a somewhat forced tone of encouragement. He was experiencing mild feelings of fear at this first glimpse of Hazard Valley, feelings he was unable to explain. Purposely, he decided to ignore his feelings. "Looks like a good, flat, straight road—a lot better than what we've just been on. Maybe now we'll make up some of the time we've lost."

"I was not expecting all these dune fields," said Astrid Larsson, in a puzzled tone. She was experiencing feelings of fear too, but was determined not to show it. "Were you, Don?"

"I was expecting to see some large dune fields in this region," said Don Carruthers, in a matter-of-fact tone. "Don't forget this valley is narrower than Kasei Valley, and it's got boundary escarpment walls that are still very high, even if they're only about half as high as those in Kasei Valley. So, since the prevailing wind is from the east, and since the valley runs due west, you're going to get funnel winds, and some drifting sand." He should have said lots of drifting sand. If he had, he might have understood his feelings better.

"I studied the maps and some of the terrain database images yesterday," said Sheila, also feeling very concerned, but like the others, reluctant to reveal the true extent of her concern. "I did see a few large dune fields, well away from the road, but I never saw anything like this."

"Most dune fields are not marked on the terrain database maps, since they're not fixtures," said Don. "I saw some large dune fields myself in the satellite survey images used to construct the terrain database. But I'll admit that there are many more small dune fields down there than I was expecting."

"They may have drifted onto the road in some stretches," said Jose Montoya. "That means we may have to drive off the road sometimes, which means we may be delayed even more." It was only with an effort that he kept an accusing tone from his voice. It was obvious now that he had been right about not wasting time. But he was more concerned now about getting safely to Leaf Valley than about causing trouble. He was a military man and his cautious nature knew the value of discipline. He too had been experiencing some feelings of fear, but had decided to ignore them, follow his expedition leader, and do everything possible to help things along. He knew it was important that the expedition be a success, regardless of who was in charge.

"You may well be quite right, and we might have done better to have heeded your advice earlier," admitted Don Carruthers. He was not one to protect his ego by covering up his mistakes. "Sorry, old chap."

Jose said nothing. He was feeling very concerned. Being sorry will not help us much if I am also right about what lies further down the road, he thought to himself.

"Now that may be why they called it Hazard Valley," ventured Sheila Bell, her tone betraying some of her fear. She was thinking that it might be better to turn around, and go back to base the way they had come, but could not bring herself to suggest it.

"Could be, Sheila," admitted Don, his tone now betraying his own concern. "We've no time to waste." He now knew though, as did Jose, that there was no chance of making it to Leaf Valley by seven. It was five fifteen and it was still sixty miles to the entrance to Leaf Valley at Tip Canyon. Some further small delays seemed inevitable. Seven thirty was more likely—if they were further delayed by no more than fifteen minutes. But that meant driving in the dark in unknown terrain. That might delay them further.

He waved his right hand, and the small convoy began the gradual descent down to the valley floor.

Sheila Bell's survival instincts were right, however. This was their last opportunity to turn back safely, and they were letting it slip by. If only they had attempted to communicate with Vince at this point, and discovered that the growing cloud cover was killing their satellite link with the habitat, they might have decided differently. From now on, they would be driving deeper and deeper into a Martian trap.

*

Soon they were driving east at thirty miles an hour, on the relatively flat but winding valley road. The road was only relatively flat, for Hazard Valley, like most Martian valleys, was full of gentle ups and downs. As was usually the case with valley roads, this road also wound gently, to circumvent the remains of small eroded craters on the valley floor. The usual scattered angular rocks and boulders lay everywhere too.

The rapidly sinking sun was now low in the sky ahead, but was partly obscured by the washboard clouds. The thin clouds were coming from the east, where they seemed to be denser.

Dune fields were common on both sides of the road, between the escarpment walls. The great tongues of sand always seemed to run in a southwesterly direction, and their dunes cast long blurred shadows to the east. There was a distinct possibility that one of these tongues would cross and straddle the road obliquely, requiring that they detour around it. So far, that had not happened.

The orange escarpments on each side of the road were developing long shadows, and were riddled with small impact craters lower down, like escarpments everywhere on Mars. The valley here was still about three miles wide, although they knew it would narrow gradually as they progressed.

The apparently clear road, and the absence of any obstacles to complicate or impede their progress along the valley floor, soon served to dispel some of the uneasy feelings and fears they had all been experiencing earlier. The constant sight of the sun in the thinly clouded sky ahead was also reassuring. They thus made steady progress, for about half an hour.

By just before six, the valley had narrowed to about two and a half miles wide. The sun, very low in the sky ahead, was now barely visible through the cloud cover, which had been getting steadily more dense. They were still over forty miles from the northern entrance to Leaf Valley.

Suddenly, Jose Montoya's earlier fears became a reality, as they came upon a stretch where very fine orange sand, from a dune tongue beside the road to the north, had drifted over the road. The depth of the fine sand varied from about four inches to as much as eighteen inches, and their wheels sank easily into it.

The sand forced them to slow down, and they barely averaged ten miles an hour. They could have left the road to the south and carried on over the rocks, to get around the sanded-over stretch of road, but Don judged that staying on the road was the lesser of two evils. After some twenty minutes of fighting the sand, it got too deep to travel any further on the road, and they were forced to stop.

To complicate things even more, they could now see an even more formidable obstacle lying about a hundred meters ahead. The dune tongue to the right of the road, with thirty-foot high dunes, had been getting ever closer to the road, as they traveled west. Up ahead it stretched right across the road, curving away in a southwesterly direction on the south side of it. As far as they could see, it was a quite long tongue of dunes, lying obliquely across the road. They could not see the end of this dune tongue to the southwest, and could not even be certain if it eventually reached the escarpment wall at the south edge of the valley, to possibly block their way completely.

By now the sun, almost completely obscured by washboard clouds, was just above the tops of the dunes in the distance. Patches of ice mist were forming in shallow hollows on the valley floor to their left, and in the troughs between the dunes to their right. Faint, wispy strands of ice mist drifted on the road in front too.

Astrid Larsson had little heart for making a video of the scene, but she did anyway. After that, she stowed the camera away in a dash compartment. The light had already faded too much for any more recordings.

"We'd better reverse a bit," said Don, studying the terrain ahead through the thin mist. "That looks like a very long dune tongue up ahead. They must have cut through it originally to build this road, but now it's filled in again. We obviously have to go off the road to the left to get around it. That could mean as much as a three-mile trip over the rocks. It could cost us another twenty minutes."

"We should keep the buggies about thirty meters apart, with tail lights on," suggested Jose, "in case the lead buggy runs into quicksand or something. The sand inside small craters is very fine. If we get moving we might just make it round before dark." As he was speaking, the barely visible setting sun disappeared behind the dunes ahead. Don switched on his tail lights, as he led the way off the road to the left.

The buggies now traveled over rock and boulder covered terrain, gently rolling up and down, as the sky above began to slowly darken. The washboard cloud cover meant it would be dark earlier than usual.

As they progressed southwest, with the dune tongue to the right, Jose was fully alert to his surroundings—far more alert than Don Carruthers. He was much more used to wilderness terrain than Don. He had done extensive military training both in rough terrain in the Pyrenees in northern Spain, and in the desert Atlas Mountains region of North Africa. That part of North Africa, with its rocks and stones, mountains and sand dunes, bore a remarkable resemblance to the region they were now passing through.

As he drove behind the red lights of Don's buggy in the gathering dusk, Jose also kept careful note of the exact outlines of the valley edges on the darkening skyline. Every so often, he also checked the map, or the terrain perspective, on the small screen of the portable navigation unit attached to the buggy dash. He kept careful note of the odometer readings on the dash too.

It took them a full twenty minutes to get to the tip of the tongue, which by now had curved around to run almost parallel to the road, about a mile south of it. There was barely a quarter mile between the southern escarpment wall of the valley and the tip of the dune tongue.

Once around the tongue, Don pointed his buggy due north, to travel the one-mile distance back to the road as quickly as possible. There was now no dune tongue to the right to guide them, however, and the fading skylines of the valley edges all seemed very similar in the deepening dusk. By now, the light was rather dim, and they decided to switch their headlights on.

Once Don drove too much to the northwest without realizing it. But Jose had been doing his homework, memorizing the skylines, and was able to advise Don as to the correct direction. Don, now very concerned, did not argue with the advice.

It was six forty when they reached the road again, having progressed only about six miles in the past fifty minutes. Jose reckoned they were still thirty-five miles from the Leaf Valley entrance.

"Maybe now we'll have better luck," said Don Carruthers, as they started out along the road once more.

There was no response from any of the others. They were all doing the same calculation. The light had faded too much to go faster than twenty miles an hour, so that even if they had no more bad luck it would take almost two hours to reach Leaf Valley. They could not be there before about eight-thirty, and could not reach the habitat before about ten. Their air supply would not last much past eleven thirty. They had been outside since about twelve thirty, even though they did not get away till one fifteen. Their main air flasks each had ten hours supply of air—which would last until about ten thirty. After that, each of them would have only the one hour of air in the reserve flask. They all understood now that another serious delay could put them in danger of their lives.

"It is six forty-five," said Jose, suddenly. "We said we would contact the habitat at six. Vince will be worried."

"Sorry, chaps, I completely forgot," said Don. "We've been too busy concentrating on not making any mistakes. No harm done. Astrid, can you do it? Tell Vince we're going to be delayed about an hour an a half, maybe two hours."

Astrid, in Jose's buggy, turned on the buggy's satellite communications system, as they traveled along the road. A display on the dash in front showed: *Receiving satellite identification signal. Transmission poor.* The buggy's antenna array had locked on to the satellite, and had successfully received a digital signal in which the satellite identified itself. Then they heard Vince's voice repeating the message: *Kasei-73 habitat calling buggies. Do you read?* The message could barely be made out. The signal was very weak, and noisy, with intermittent fading, and a peculiar distortion. The term Kasei-73 meant Kasei Valley at the 73rd meridian of longitude, close to where the habitat was located.

"Astrid Larsson calling Kasei-73. Do you read?" responded Astrid.

The display on the dash changed a second later to: *Satellite not receiving. No confirmation response.*

Astrid tried again, and got the same non confirmation response. She tried a third time, with the same response. Then Vince's voice came through again, even weaker, and badly distorted. *Kasei-73 habitat calling buggies. Do you read?* It was clear that Vince had not received Astrid's message.

"Don, maybe there is a bug in the system," said Astrid. "I can not transmit. Try yours."

Don got Claude to try. Claude did not know the system as well as Astrid, but he could not get through either, and got only the same weak distorted request from Vince.

"Isn't this terrible?" said Sheila. "The first time we really need this system, it lets us down."

"It is not the system, Sheila," said Jose. "It is the cloud cover. Our signal cannot penetrate up through it, and the cloud layer is also scattering the signal coming down from the satellite. You heard how bad the reception was. Remember the system was working perfectly earlier in the day, before these clouds blew in."

"Now I don't understand how Vince can reach us, but we can't reach him," said Sheila, sounding very anxious, but still curious.

"It's because the satellite broadcasts over a quite wide area," explained Jose, "and we are sending up just a narrow beam. It is as if the satellite was floodlighting the ground, and we were replying with just a flashlight beam."

"Do you mean the signal from the satellite is being scattered from many different parts of the cloud layer," asked Don, "and so comes down to us from many parts of the sky? If that's the case, we must be picking it up with quite a few of our small dishes at once."

"That is what I think is happening," said Jose. "It explains the distortion. The computers try to assemble the bits of the signal from all the different dishcs that are receiving. If the cloud cover gets much denser they will probably give up, and we could lose that signal too."

"Don't I remember reading somewhere that in the autumn you have to expect a bit of cloud cover every so often in this part of Mars, especially at night?" put in Sheila. "How did it happen that nobody remembered this? Now that's right, isn't it, Don?"

"Yes, it's right, Sheila," said Don. He knew that he should have thought of it, as the planetary expert. He had little heart for explaining that in the early Martian fall, the prevailing east wind brought air from the low lying Plain of Gold, a thousand miles to the east, air moist after a long summer of evaporating ice at the northern polar cap. That meant that since western Kasei Valley was high up relative to the very low lying Plain of Gold, ice clouds were likely to form in the cold of the evening and night, as the moist air was pushed up. For ice cloud to form high up, not only was very moist air needed, but an air temperature below about minus seventy Celsius, or minus ninety-four Fahrenheit, which you could easily get at night.

"Well, we can do nothing about this right now," said Jose, "except try and get through later, if the clouds clear away. Meanwhile, all we can do is concentrate on getting to the end of this road as soon as we can."

"I agree," said Don. "Let's just keep moving. We can do without the link to the habitat."

Maybe, thought Jose to himself, aware that loss of the link had made their situation even more dangerous.

As they progressed, the road gradually changed direction. Eventually Don Carruthers estimated they were now traveling more to the southwest, judging from the position of the point of maximum sky brightness, where the sun had set. That point of maximum sky brightness was but a faint purple gray color, just above the silhouette of the top of the escarpment wall, up ahead to the right.

There was still enough light in the washboard-clouded sky for them to discern that the escarpment walls on either side were getting closer, and the valley narrower.

They did not manage twenty miles an hour. It was more like fifteen. The narrower valley floor did not mean less sand. It just meant that there was less space to hold the sand. As a result, to their dismay, every few miles they had to travel off the road, to the left or right, for a few hundred meters, either because sand from an adjacent dune field was too deep, or because some small dune tongue obliquely straddled the road. These new dune tongues were minor, compared to the big one they had encountered earlier. The next fifteen miles took an hour.

Wide gaps in the faint skyline were now more frequent too, to both right and left, indicating gaps in the escarpment walls on either side of them, leading into tributary valleys, just as wide as the one they were in. In the past hour, these broken walls had continued to get closer.

Although they could not see the valley walls clearly in the dark, the navigation unit's terrain map confirmed that there was no longer a continuous escarpment wall on either side of the valley. There was only a jumble of mesas with a variety of shapes. Sometimes the nearest mesa wall was quite close, sometimes farther away. The terrain here was so complex it almost defied description.

They did have a sense of that complexity from the navigation units, and were thankful for the road. Without it, they could not have found their way. They were now journeying through the labyrinth region of western Kasei Valley, a bewildering maze of small interconnecting valleys, all of them looking very much alike, and more filled with sand dunes than anywhere else on Mars. This was clearly no place to be after dark in open buggies, especially on a cloudy night, with no satellite link, nor any stars to help with navigation.

*

The valley had become much narrower, only about two miles wide. They could just make out the tops of very high and broken escarpments, on either side, against the faint glimmer of gray light that remained in the sky. They could see only one star, whose light was just strong enough to penetrate the washboard clouds that still covered the sky, or maybe it was a fainter star shining through a less dense part of the cloud cover. It would give them little assistance in navigation, were they to need it, and the cloud cover practically guaranteed that buggy to satellite communication was still out.

It was very dark on the ground, and they were completely dependent on the buggy headlights to see the road. This was another worry, for the headlights were using up precious battery power. The road was now sometimes veiled in patches of ice mist too.

It was now seven forty-five, but they were only twenty miles from the entrance to Leaf Valley. According to the navigation units, they were on the last lap, on the Tip Canyon road, and had safely passed through Hazard Valley, whose name they now understood only too well. They were still journeying through the labyrinth, however. Their situation was not good, but now there was every reason to believe that their difficulties would soon be behind them—only twenty miles to civilization.

"It'll be nearly nine before we get as far as the Erway compound," said Don Carruthers. "See if you can get through now, Astrid." He was feeling a little consoled, as were some of the others, by the thought that in a worst-case scenario, if they were delayed further, they could stop there for sanctuary. Captain Derk would not be pleased, but he would prefer that to the alternative. If Astrid could get through to the habitat, the Captain could be prepared.

When Astrid tried to get through, all she got was the display message: *No satellite signal detected. Satellite could be down or atmospheric conditions could be unfavorable.*

Jose Montoya was now very concerned, and had begun thinking along entirely different lines. "We should forget about satellite communications until we see some stars in the sky," said Jose. "Anyway, Vince and Karl will understand that the communication problem is temporary, because of clouds, but will not understand when we are late. We are due at the habitat just after eight—eight thirty at the latest, and our expedition is being followed by Mission Control. Toulouse will want to know what is wrong when we do not arrive on schedule. They worry all the time. There will definitely be an alarm raised."

"But the Captain will be at the Mars house, having dinner," said Sheila. "Are you certain John Erway and Denise Lavoisier don't know we're out on this trip?"

"I am certain they do not," said Jose. "That is why we were supposed to be at the tip of Leaf Valley no later than seven, so that we could get past the compound before it got completely dark, without lights, and without being seen."

"Well, if you are right about an alarm, Jose, they are going to find out about us now," said Astrid Larsson. She was not comfortable with the realization that she was on a covert expedition, whose intent had been to sneak past the Leaf Valley complex without its owners being aware of it. She had been tempted to add 'as well they should' to her remark, but decided not to. Derk might hear of it. Her structural engineering abilities meant she also had a mind for strategy, even if she had no military experience.

"I am certain I am right," said Jose. "Karl and Vince know their business. They will raise the alarm for sure. And you are right, Astrid, about John Erway finding out about us now."

Although Jose was very close to Monique, he had a soft spot for Astrid Larsson, but she, while respecting Jose, had no interest in giving her affections to a military man. She preferred Don Carruthers. Unfortunately, since Sheila Bell had captured Don's affections, Astrid's inclinations in that direction had never come to anything. Astrid bore Sheila no grudge on that account. She even liked Sheila. She was convinced that, in Don's shoes, she too would have been inclined to prefer the vivacious, kindly, and inquisitive Irish doctor over her relatively cold and dull self, even if she was reasonably good looking. Right now, however, Astrid's thoughts were entirely on their dangerous situation.

"I take it you mean that the habitat will send an alarm to the Captain at the Erway compound, Jose," said Don Carruthers, "which means the Captain will have to tell John Erway that six of his crew are missing."

"That makes sense," said Claude Bertrand, who had a very good head for strategy. "And if I know our Captain, he will persuade John Erway to help find us. His two rovers are long range, and nuclear powered. They have the capacity to circumnavigate the planet. That means that most likely we will meet them coming the other way, well before we reach Leaf Valley."

"I hadn't thought of that," said Don Carruthers, suddenly feeling better. "Perhaps I've been more worried than I should have been. Not only are we only about twenty miles from safety, but help will be on the way if—Oh my God!"

He braked hard. He should not have been talking while driving, for a thin ice mist lay on the road at that point, reducing visibility by reflecting the headlights and causing a glare. He had run into the steep side of a huge dune tongue, glowing bright orange in the headlights, and completely straddling the road ahead. The buggy's wheels were deep in sand. Jose, ever cautious, had been far enough back to stop without running into Don's trailer.

"Not more sand dunes," groaned Sheila, aptly reflecting everyone's sentiment. "Which way this time? Left or right?"

With much effort, Don managed to back his buggy out of the sand. He then turned it to the right slightly. The headlights revealed a sea of dunes, stretching away on the right side of the road, but in the backward direction. Meanwhile, Jose had pointed his buggy to the left. There were more dunes stretching away to the left at an angle to the road, but in the direction they were headed.

"Looks like we go left," said Don, in a despairing tone. "Any objections, Jose?"

"No," said Jose. "We have no choice."

The edge of the dune tongue seemed to curve to their right as they traveled beside it. They did not have to travel far, before reaching the place where the dunes ended, a bit over a mile from where they left the road. The dunes were right up against a quite steep and rough escarpment wall. It took them ten minutes to get to it, for they could not do much more than six miles an hour off the road in the dark.

"Maybe we can still get past," said Jose. "Request permission to get out and look."

"Granted," said Don Carruthers, as Jose took a flashlight from the dash of his buggy and then picked his way carefully up the steep escarpment slope beside a huge orange sand dune. The headlights of the two buggies floodlit both the escarpment slope and the adjacent dune. When Jose was a few feet above the height of the dune, he shone his flashlight along the edge of the escarpment. It revealed dunes packed against the escarpment, shadowy and ominous, with shrouds of ice mist lying in the dune troughs. The dunes stretched away to the darkness beyond the range of the flashlight beam.

"Impossible on this side of the road," reported Jose. "We have to try the other side."

They turned and traversed back the way they had come, through mist patches lying in hollows in the gently rolling terrain, and over the shadowed rocks, stones and short stretches of sand littering the valley floor. Ten minutes later they reached the road safely, crossed it, and set off across the valley floor again. As they drove, both Sheila and Astrid were thinking of just how warm, comfortable and safe were their tiny cubicles in the habitat on Elbow Hill. There were no stars at all in the sky now. The cloud cover meant still no satellite link with the habitat.

This time it took fifteen minutes to reach the end of the dunes, which curved steadily around to their right, forcing them to continually veer to the right, in a direction away from their Leaf Valley destination. Where the dunes ended, the situation was clearly even worse than at the other side of the valley. The dunes climbed quite far up a very rough escarpment embankment. Jose got out anyway, climbed up the escarpment, and did his inspection.

"Absolutely impossible," he reported, as he shone his flashlight over the sea of dunes, clutching at the rugged escarpment slope. "This is very bad. Why do these escapements here have to be so steep and rugged so low down?"

Don Carruthers knew the answer to that question, but saw no point in explaining. Because the valley at this point lay between the two mesas not much more than a mile and a half apart, it was a wind funnel. Sometimes dunes lay piled up in it. More often, the valley was scoured clear of sand, as sand-laden wind funneled through it, functioning like a massive sand blaster low down. The scouring wind cut away at the lower escarpments on either side, as would a fast-flowing, sediment-laden river, making the bottom reaches of the escarpments steep and rugged, and more like river banks.

"Well, Dr. Carruthers," said Jose, after scrambling down the rough slope, and getting back in his buggy, "the Captain put you in charge. What do you recommend we do now? Our lives will depend on what you decide."

"I'm sorry, Jose," said Don, "but at this moment, I'm not sure what we should do. I'm not even sure if we should try to drive back to the road. All I can suggest for now is that we take ten minutes, twenty if necessary, to discuss it. We put our heads together—a kind of survival committee, to see if we can come up with some strategy. And we should switch off our headlights while we're doing it, to save the batteries."

Trust an Englishman to propose a committee to solve a problem, thought Jose. He did not voice the thought. He was disciplined, and knew there had to be a leader. He also understood that if they were to find a solution, everybody would have to contribute his or her best. The Englishman's committee suggestion is probably right, he admitted to himself, as he switched off his lights.

"All right," said Monique, whose survival-oriented mind had anticipated the problem, and had been searching out their options, as they drove along the edge of the dune tongue, "we have only three choices. One: we abandon the buggies and try to walk through these dunes. Two: we go back a little, turn into a side valley and try to go around the dunes using another adjacent valley. Three: turn about and drive back the way we came, all the way back along Hazard Valley and round into Kasei Valley."

"Number three is out," said Jose. "We have come a hundred and forty miles, both on and off the road, since we left the habitat. The buggy batteries are good for about only about eight hours driving or two hundred and forty miles on a—"

"I don't understand," interrupted Sheila. "That means we've a hundred miles left on the batteries. Couldn't we still do one hundred miles of the way back? That would take us to within forty miles of the habitat. We might be able to radio for help from there."

"No, Sheila, number three is definitely out," said Jose. "There are a hundred miles left in the batteries in theory only. We did a lot of ups and downs, and did a lot of traveling over sand and rocks, and we have had the headlights on a lot. I reckon we have used up over a hundred and sixty miles of battery power at least. That leaves only about eighty miles of power at most for a return trip—on a flat road in daylight. But if we allow for driving in the dark with our lights on, we have probably only power for fifty to sixty miles—less than three hours of driving time. We would run out of battery power before we even reached Kasei Valley, somewhere in that rough terrain between Kasei Valley and Hazard Valley."

"You are absolutely right, Jose," said Claude Bertrand. "And there is another problem with trying to go back. The time is now eight twenty, and it has taken us seven hours, six and a half hours of driving, to come this far, and most of that was in daylight. Not only would we run out of battery power after about three hours driving in the dark, we would run out of air. We have just a bit over three hours of air left, two in the main flask and one in the reserve. Number three is completely out of the question."

"What about a number four?" suggested Sheila, feeling somewhat chastened, but also desperate and very anxious. "Couldn't we just call for help from here with the surface radio?"

"No," said Jose. "These high mesas and precipices everywhere would block our signal, not to mention the blockage from the rampart on top of that escarpment wall north of the habitat."

"I wasn't thinking of reaching the habitat by radio," objected Sheila. "It was the Erway compound I was thinking of reaching."

"Sheila has a point," said Don Carruthers. Communications was not his area of expertise, however. It was not Jose Montoya's either, but as a military field engineer, he was more expert than anyone else on the expedition. Communications was Emma's specialty.

"The signal would still be blocked," maintained Jose. "The only way would be to transmit from the top of a mesa—but that is just not possible. Anyway, even if we could get a message through, how would any rescue party reach us? The road is badly blocked ahead."

"Then let us examine choice number one," said Astrid Larsson, who had been thinking hard about that choice. "You have had desert experience, Jose. Could we walk across those dunes? If what you said a while back about an alarm being raised soon is true, there is bound to be help on the road on the other side."

"I'm nearly certain we couldn't," said Don Carruthers, before Jose could answer, "although there's always a chance. Because the air is so thin here, it can lift only quite fine sand. So blowing sand on Mars is much finer than blowing sand on Earth, and there's less gravity to compact it once it piles into a dune. We'd just sink into the sand. Don't forget we're in pressure suits, all right for walking on clear ground, but not for scrambling through sand dunes. Scrambling is what we'd be doing, not walking.

"On top of that, we could easily tear the suits on sharp rocks hidden just below the surface of the sand in the trough areas.

"And if that's not enough reason, it could take up to three hours to get through this blockage on foot—if it was even possible. It could be several miles across, although it is probably just a pair of extra wide dune tongues that have locked together, head to tail. And there'd be nothing to guide us either. The valley's about a mile and a half wide here, and we could go in circles. Right now there's not a single star visible we could use as a guide."

"There's another problem too, you know," said Sheila, always mindful of air supply considerations, "if what you say about scrambling is true. We'd be using up a lot more oxygen scrambling about, than just sitting in the buggies. Maybe twice as much. Our air would run out a lot sooner, maybe before any rescuers could find us."

"I had not thought about that, Sheila," said Astrid. "But Jose, you still have not answered the question I asked you. What does your desert experience say?"

"It says that even in a desert on Earth, with more compact sand, walking across those dunes would be a hazardous undertaking on a cloudy night," said Jose. "And even if by some miracle we were to succeed, there could still be another bad blockage further up the road. According to the navigator screen, the valley gets even narrower further ahead, and there is plenty of sand in this region. It is more likely that there is a further blockage on up the road than that there is not. I would not recommend it. That point you made, Sheila, of expending a lot of energy, and using up our air twice as fast, is probably the most telling objection. We have only a bit more than three hours of air left. I prefer that to one and a half hours. Let us examine number two, but if it is worse we will have to try and walk through. Has anybody thought about number two?"

"I have been thinking about that choice too," said Astrid Larsson. "It is not good, but—"

"Wait a minute," interrupted Claude Bertrand. "I have not had my say. We are not finished with number one. What about the escarpments? We might not have to walk across the dunes. We could walk along the escarpment slope instead. You have been up there to look, Jose."

"I did not mention that because it was something I would not even consider, Claude," said Jose. "We have been on Mars for only a few days, and our experience of walking outside is mostly on cleared roads. We have very little experience walking outside even on rock-covered ground that is flat, and even that is dangerous. You can tear your suit on a sharp rock easily if you are not careful. Do you think we have any chance walking across a steep, rocky slope in the dark, with lots of loose material that could cause us to slip or slide and tear our suits? They would have hysterics at Mission Control at the very thought of anybody trying such a thing, even in daylight—but in the dark, on a starless night, and for maybe a mile of it."

"All right, Jose," said Claude. "I see the point. Sorry, Astrid. What were you going to say about number two?"

"Number two seems a better bet than number one," resumed Astrid Larsson, "even if it is not very good either. This area is full of valleys on both sides of the road, but according to the terrain map, the valleys on the northwest side are bigger. We can be sure there are sand dunes in them, but there is a good chance that the valleys are too wide to be completely blocked by dunes anywhere. According to the navigator unit, a few miles back there is an opening out of this valley toward the northwest. If we drive back along the edge of this escarpment, we must come to it. If we drive into that opening, and keep generally left, we should be able to travel right around this mesa we are sitting beside. If we stick to the escarpment edge the whole way round, we should come back into this valley well past the blockage. We could hit the road two or three miles nearer to Leaf Valley. It is about ten miles all the way round the mesa, judging from the terrain map, but we might be able to do five or six miles an hour, and come back out onto the road before ten thirty."

"And by that time," said Sheila, with a sense of relief, "Denise Lavoisier and her husband will have found out about us for sure from the Captain. I would think they'd go out on the road looking for us at once. I'm sure they could reach these sand dunes in less than an hour in their rovers. This is certainly the best plan. What do you think, Don?"

"I'm inclined to agree with you, Sheila," said Don, "although we're running the risk of getting completely lost. What do you think, Jose?"

"I agree we could get lost," said Jose, "but at least we would have buggies to ride in, and would be able to go a lot quicker than on foot. That way we would last a lot longer. Compared with trying to walk through the dunes from here, it seems the less risky of the two. It's not a good option, but it looks like the best one we have."

"I also agree," said Claude Bertrand. "It is our best chance."

"Monique," asked Don Carruthers, "what do you think?"

"Suppose we do get lost," said Monique. "We could end up with no battery power, and almost no air, maybe only a half mile from the road, and not know it. The rovers could be driving up and down, not able to find us on the road, and not able to see us off the road."

"But we could have the surface radio on," said Astrid, "calling for help."

"That would not help if we were just round the corner of some mesa escarpment or down in some hollow," said Monique, "we—"

"Stupid!" interrupted Jose suddenly. "Sorry, Monique, I did not mean you. We forgot about our emergency radio beacons. Each buggy has one, with its own independent power supply. It sends out a distress signal every ten seconds, even if the main batteries are dead. The distress signal is very short. It transmits for only a few seconds, but it has a signal strength higher than the full strength of the buggy's normal surface radio, and that radio gets its power from the main batteries. The emergency beacon has about a five-mile range on clear flat terrain, but obviously not in terrain like this. Still, a rover on the road should be able to pick up the distress signal from a buggy a mile away or more in this kind of terrain. Jurgen will remember about the beacons. Any rovers out searching for us will be listening for distress signals."

"All the more reason then," said Don, "why we should not abandon the buggies and try walking across the dunes. I hope it doesn't come to it, but those emergency beacons may turn out to be our last hope. We should turn them on when we get near the road again. If what you say is true, Jose, besides getting a stronger signal from the beacons, we also conserve the main batteries a bit at the same time. That little bit of battery power saved may make a difference. You're sure about the stronger signal from the beacons, Jose?"

"Dead certain," said Jose. "I remember it distinctly from field training we did."

"Good. That's at least something positive," said Don.

"Flare guns would have been useful too," observed Monique, "but nobody seems to have thought of that. And emergency beacons on our suits would have been a help as well. All right, I agree that going round this mesa is the best plan. I think now we should get moving. It is nearly eight thirty. We have three hours air left at the most."

"Before we go," said Don, his voice suddenly trembling with emotion, "I want you all to know something, in case some of us don't come out of this. I'm very, very sorry. This mess is all my fault. I was placed in charge, with the primary responsibility of keeping you all safe. I failed my charge. It's obvious now that I should have made a very different decision when we first set eyes on Hazard Valley, and saw that it was full of sand dunes, with a prevailing wind from the east. As a geologist, I should have realized that there would be even more sand further west, and that the responsible thing to do was turn around at once, and report back to Captain Derk that this road was too dangerous to attempt by buggy."

Jose, always the military man, came to his support. He realized that Carruthers was close to the breaking point, and understood the danger of the disintegrating morale that would follow a breakdown. "With respect, Dr. Carruthers, that is cow manure. If what you say is true then I am at fault too. I did not argue that we should turn back when we first saw Hazard Valley. Nobody else did either."

"We were all too afraid to admit we were afraid," diagnosed Sheila. "I was thinking it was just too dangerous to go any further, and that we should do the right thing and turn back. I just didn't want you all to think I wasn't brave enough to be out on Mars."

"I was thinking the same thing," admitted Claude.

"So was I," said Astrid.

"*Moi aussi*," said Monique, lapsing into her native tongue.

"All right, all right. That is enough," said Jose. "We are not in a religious confession. But I admit I was thinking the same thing."

"And me too," said Don, thankful for the support, and turning on his headlights. "Thank you all, for that. Now let's carry on. God willing, we'll muddle though this mess somehow. But if any of you are afraid of something we're about to do in the next few hours, this time don't keep it to yourselves."

They did not know it at the time, but it was probably the wrong decision. The dune tongue was only a quarter mile wide. As Don had guessed, it was actually two smaller dune tongues that had recently locked head to tail near the road, two of those tongues that slowly came and went over the decades in the labyrinth. The lead dune tongue, crawling along the valley, had managed to jam its head against the escarpment of a long mesa on the valley's southeast side. The trailing tongue had jammed its tail against the escarpment of a shorter mesa on the northwest side of the valley, where they were parked, the combination tongue blocking the valley obliquely.

If they had taken the time to be careful, they might well have been able to scramble safely across that dune tongue, in an hour at the most, to find help on the road on the other side of it. On the other hand, unaware of their direction, they might have clambered along the tongue instead of across it. The question is academic, however, for they did not attempt it. On Earth, the question was much discussed later, in hearings on the events of that evening.

*

It was just after eight thirty when they set off in their buggies again, headed away from Leaf Valley, their headlights illuminating the rock-strewn terrain. The best they could do in the dark, over the rocks, stones, sand patches, and rolling, misty terrain, was no more than six miles an hour, a mile every ten minutes.

For some twenty minutes, they traveled back along the edge of the escarpment, without seeming to veer much to the right or left. The terrain continued typical of Martian valley floors, rolling gently up and down, with angular rocks and stones everywhere. They frequently passed small dune fields lying to their right, but none close enough to the escarpment edge to block their way. Then the escarpment edge began to curve quite decidedly to the left, as Astrid had predicted it would. Before long, as far as they could estimate, they were traveling northwest, in a direction perpendicular to the road.

For a while there seemed to be no end to this direction of travel, in a direction they would have preferred not to go, deeper into the labyrinth. The terrain was very rough too. Their anxiety intensified and their impatience grew. They continually passed small dune fields lying to the right, and sometimes traveled over sand at the edge of the dunes, but nothing to block their advance.

They traveled in this direction, seemingly, for about thirty-five minutes, keeping near the edge of the escarpment to their left. Then, the escarpment at the left began curving to the left, again as Astrid had predicted. At this, there was a general feeling of hope.

Soon they had every reason to believe they were traveling southwest, in the same direction as the road, and thus parallel to it, but about three or four miles to the northwest of it. Their spirits rose a little, as this became clear. The terrain was smoother now too.

There was now a quite large dune field lying to the right, and as they progressed, it got closer to the escarpment edge, threatening to block their way. Then it was so close that they were driving in between three and nine inches of sand all the time. Their worries intensified. Another wall of sand dunes blocking their way would be the end of them.

About five minutes after they had turned the corner of the escarpment, to travel southwest, the sand got so deep they could not go forward. Don's headlights showed the crest of a dune ahead, but only about four feet high, growing higher to the right. It was right up against the escarpment.

Jose jumped out of his buggy, without asking permission from the expedition leader, and literally charged up the escarpment edge beside the dune, carrying his flashlight. The beam showed only two low dune crests reaching up onto the escarpment. Beyond, the way was clear.

"Everybody out!" he shouted. "There are two shovels in the trailers. We can clear the sand away with our legs too—only about ten meters of sand. No time to waste."

Don did not argue, for Jose was the only one with desert experience. For nearly fifteen minutes they did as he said, Jose and Don shoveling, breaking up the structure of the two small dune crests, while the other four brushed the very fine sand aside with their boots. Finally, they were ready to drive the buggies through the still very sandy opening between the mass of the dunes to the right, and the escarpment edge to the left.

Don's buggy did not get more than three meters before it got stuck. There was still too much sand. Jose ordered everybody out again, except Don. They finally got the buggy through, with Don driving and the other five at the buggy sides, pushing and pulling for their very lives. They got the other buggy through the same way. This cost them another five minutes.

At last, they could carry on, but they were increasingly worried about their way being blocked again, for there was nearly always a dune field close by to their right. They had good reason to worry. After all, they were in the Kasei Valley labyrinth, where sand dunes abound in the small intersecting valleys between mesas, and where entire valley floors are often filled with huge dunes. If Astrid's theory was correct, however, the escarpment edge at their left should soon begin curving to the left again, to take them in a direction back to the road, to meet it at a point well past the dune blockage.

About twenty-five minutes of slow travel later, past one threatening dune field after another, the escarpment edge did just that, as expected. It seemed as if they were traveling along the escarpment edge of an approximately square mesa, about three miles long on each side. If so, they should hit the road after another four miles, five at the most. It was now ten eighteen.

"I think we should turn on the emergency beacons," said Jose. "If we are where we think we are, it should be open terrain ahead to the road, between two mesas."

"Don't you think we're still a bit too far away?" said Don.

"Probably," said Jose, "but you never know, and we're not short of power for the beacons. They will keep transmitting for three hours even if the main batteries are dead."

"All right. Let's turn them on," said Don.

So they began their advance in this new direction, still along the rugged escarpment edge to their left, dunes to the right, their emergency radio beacons sending out the call for help.

Now, hopefully, they were moving perpendicular to the road, in a direction that would take them straight back to it. The frequent dune fields lying to the right, though, constantly threatened to block the way up ahead. The terrain still rolled gently up and down too, and they still traveled over the ever-present, angular rocks and stones, and through random shrouds of ice mist in hollows in the rolling terrain. The ice mist often reflected the buggy headlight beams back in an icy white glare.

Within minutes of taking this new direction, they began to succumb to worry again, for it was now ten twenty. Even if they had every reason to believe they were headed straight for the road, at their crawling rate of advance over the rolling and rocky terrain, doing only a mile every ten minutes, it would likely be near eleven before they reached the road. Their air would run out by about eleven thirty at the latest. So, if a rescue party missed them, there was no way they could make it to the compound in Leaf Valley before they ran out of air.

The emergency beacons were now their only hope. They could make the difference, if only the rolling terrain would let the signal reach the road.

There was also the increasingly worrisome problem of how much longer the main buggy batteries would last. They were good for only eight hours at thirty miles an hour on a road over flat terrain, or for about two hundred and forty miles. They might last a few hours longer going slowly over rocky Martian terrain. They had been driving with the batteries now for over eight hours. There could not be much more than an hour's driving left in them. The batteries and their air could give out at about the same time.

They drove on, anticipating and hoping for the expected encounter with the road. Then, starting a minute later, came a series of ominous warnings.

Between ten twenty-one and ten thirty-three, one by one, an alarm went off in each of their suits, as the main air flask emptied and the air supply system switched to the reserve flask. The alarm was a simple message, warning that there was air for only another sixty minutes at best. Sheila's alarm went off first, followed by

Claude Bertrand's. Astrid Larsson's alarm went off last, just after Don Carruthers'.

The radio link between the suits enabled them all to hear each other's alarms, as the suits switched to their reserve air flasks.

Sheila's alarm went off first because that was what had always happened in training. Sheila consumed oxygen at a greater rate than any of the others, something that had made her more pronc to worry about air supply. Astrid and Don consumed it at the lowest rate. Astrid and Don had the best survival odds, Sheila the worst.

They were now passing fewer dune fields in this stretch of valley. Nevertheless, fifteen minutes later, they encountered a dune field that ran so close to the edge of the escarpment that they were forced to drive through the quite deep sand at its edges for nearly ten minutes. During this time, they barely covered a quarter mile.

Then their way was clear again. Once more, there were only infrequent dunes to their right. They made steady progress. The road had to be close. Hope began to rise again. A few minutes before eleven the escarpment edge began curving to the left again, exactly as predicted. Confirmation!

Now they were sure the road was close. This time they did not follow the curving escarpment edge to their left. They continued on, in the direction they had been traveling, hopefully straight toward the road. Don tried to sight odd-shaped rocks up ahead, where the ground rolled up, to use as markers, to keep him in a straight line. There were still no stars in the sky to help with navigation.

Ten minutes of steady travel later, having passed only a few dunes, there was no sign of the road. Where was it? They should have hit it by now. Then a few minutes later, at about eleven ten, they got a shock. Looming up ahead out of the ice mist was a wall of sand dunes.

"We have to go around them," said Jose, in a forced business-like voice, trying to hide his disappointment.

"Which way, left or right?" asked Don, almost in despair.

"Left, I think," answered Jose. "We have been keeping left as we went around the mesa. We have probably gradually turned a bit too much to the right in the last fifteen minutes, since we left the mesa. It's safer to go left. At least we should come back to the mesa."

Don turned left, with Jose following, and traveled on.

"I don't think now that it's going to matter for me," said Sheila, three minutes later, in a tone that was unusually despondent for her.

The others could hear her breathing. "I think my air is starting to run out. I always use it up faster than anybody else."

"Try to hang on, Sheila," said Jose, but with a note of panic now sounding in his voice too. "We have to be close to the road."

They continued on, traveling with the edge of the dune field to their right. The edge of the dunes was straight at first, but then veered strongly to the right. Another three minutes later, the dunes ended, but where they did, a new escarpment edge began, running almost in the same direction as the edge of the dunes, except for a slight bend to the left.

"I don't understand," said Don.

"I don't either," said Jose.

"I do," said Sheila, her heavy breathing now very audible. It was clear she was beginning to suffocate. "We're lost. God help us… Help us! Please God..."

It was now just after eleven sixteen.

"We can't be lost, Sheila," said Jose, beginning to sense his own air getting very stuffy. "We must have gone too far to the right and run into the next mesa to the southwest. If we keep going along this escarpment edge, it should soon bend to the right, and take us to the road."

Jose was beginning to experience feelings of desperation too, but was determined not to show it.

Don had no idea any more where they were, but they pressed on, hope almost gone, traveling now with an escarpment edge to the right, and still over rolling terrain. Four minutes later, the escarpment edge did turn to the right, as Jose had predicted. But just after they had followed it around to the right a little, as they began going uphill out of a shallow misty hollow, Jose's buggy lost power. The time was eleven twenty-one.

"Don, our batteries are dead," said Jose, vaguely remembering he had used his buggy for ten minutes or so that morning to visit the landing pit. He noticed his breathing getting quite labored too.

"Then this is as far as we can go," said Don, about to stop.

"No," said Jose, but with an effort. "You must keep going. It makes no sense to stop for us. Just try to reach the road, even somewhere near the road. Keep your beacon on. They have to be out looking for us. If you are found, we will be found."

"You're probably right," said Don. "All right, I'll do my best. Wish us luck. But cheerio, old chap, if we don't meet again."

"*Adios, amigo,*" said Jose to himself, as Don's buggy disappeared over the rise ahead, headlights illuminating ice mist beyond. He knew it was hopeless. He was already beginning to suffocate.

Don Carruthers pressed on, driving as quickly as he dared, faithfully keeping the escarpment edge to his right. He drove past the tip of a dune field lying to the left. That escarpment edge to his right was his only guide—his last shred of hope. It had to take him back to the road.

After another five minutes of driving over that rolling, rocky and misty terrain, his head began to fog, as his breathing became labored. He tried to recall what was supposed to happen next. He had to think about what he was supposed to do. The other three were depending on him to reach the road. That's right, he thought, the escarpment edge should turn to the right again, and when it does, I go straight on, and then I should hit the road.

He noticed that he was now breathing heavily, and that his head was beginning to swim a little. Five minutes later his buggy lost power too, and his headlights went out. It was eleven thirty, nine minutes since parting with Jose's buggy.

Just before the lights went out, he had time to notice wheel tracks in a patch of sand up ahead. His already partly disoriented mind suddenly understood that he was traveling back the way he had come. They had gone in a circle since leaving the mesa edge earlier! He began feeling sick inside.

"Sheila, Claude?" he cried in the darkness. "How are you? We have to face the truth…We've no chance of being found now…You were right, Sheila… We're completely lost…My air's going too…I think we should say our good-byes now, before we black out… Oh, my God…I'm so very sorry…What a fool I've been…" His consciousness was tortured beyond description. His despairing cries to his companions were a testimony to his suffering.

There was nobody to hear his words. Claude had lost consciousness eight minutes earlier, at about the time Sheila had died.

"Sheila!…Claude..." he cried in agony, unable to see his two companions sprawled over their seats. "No… No…not this way …"

Don Carruthers was breathing much more heavily now, as these final minutes passed. Yearning images of the green Yorkshire moors, where he used to wander as a schoolboy, passed in and out of his now semi-delirious mind, as well as images from his childhood, and of his mother and father too.

Unlike Richard Derk, who had grown up in a large manor house on a great estate, Don Carruthers had grown up in a modest house in a small town, the son of very ordinary people. His mother, who had died a few years earlier, had worked in a bakery in the town, where his father still worked as an auto mechanic.

Then he thought of his years as a student, funded by scholarships, where he had excelled in planetary science, and then of his rapidly advancing career as a planetary geologist, marred only by a disastrous marriage, since terminated. Then his mind became more peaceful. Suddenly, his nebulous surroundings lit up, and everything seemed to be getting brighter and brighter.

So this is how it is to die, he thought. Then he too lost consciousness. It was eleven thirty-eight.

*

Had they but known, they had been very close to the road. Astrid Larsson's theory about the mesa northwest of the road, and their navigation around it, by sticking close to its escarpment edge, had been very good. They had actually done very well, given that they were traveling in the dark, in the most treacherous labyrinth on Mars, more filled with sand dunes than just about anywhere else on the planet.

Where they had unexpectedly run into the wall of sand dunes some thirty minutes earlier, the road was less than three hundred meters to their right. They had in fact gone right around the mesa northwest of the blocked road, and had run into the dune tongue blocking the valley from the other side, very close to where the road emerged from under the sand. They had thus succeeded in getting around the blockage.

They had not understood this, and had been partly disoriented, when they ran into the wall of dunes. Instead of turning right toward the nearby road, they had turned left, keeping the dunes to their right, to eventually meet the mesa escarpment edge. By then continuing on, with the escarpment edge on the right, they had headed back into the labyrinth, traveling further away from the road. Jose's dead buggy, lying in a hollow about a mile and a half from the road, lay about a mile closer to the road than Don's.

That was where the search party from Leaf Valley eventually found them. It did not help that the distress signal from Jose's buggy was severely muffled by the buggy's location in a shallow hollow, partly behind a long corner spur of the mesa's escarpment. Nor could the search party on the road hear any distress signal from Don's buggy. His dead buggy lay even further from the road, hidden well behind the mesa spur.

CHAPTER NINE

Distress Signals

JUST AFTER nine twenty that evening, a rover left Tip Valley, at the north end of Leaf Valley, and entered Tip Canyon, and the start of the Tip Canyon road. This road led northeastward, through the labyrinth that started about fifteen miles further on, and then on into Hazard Valley.

Dr. Sato drove as fast as he dared, at little more than twenty miles an hour. Any faster was too dangerous that night, given patches of ice mist, the rolling and winding road, and ugly, angular rocks lying on the canyon floor on either side. The hot air defrosters were full on, keeping the cold insides of the front windows clear of condensation frost from moist air inside the rover.

The Zen master knew the lower reaches of the road intimately, and had a map of the terrain on both sides of the road inside his head. He could instantly recall the shape and size of every valley, canyon and mesa on each side of the road. He thus had no need for the terrain map and perspective screens on the dash in front of him, and these were turned off. He merely had to be mindful of the reading on the odometer, to know exactly where he was with respect to adjacent valleys, canyons, and mesas—second nature to the Zen master, with his extraordinary Zen awareness of the planet.

Denise Lavoisier was further back, in the living area in the front half of the rover. She was sitting in a red swivel chair, facing a computer screen, unaware that in a few hours she would once more be the only doctor on Mars. The windows on either side of her had frosted up, and she could not see out.

Denise was wearing her light-blue pressure suit, except for the gloves, helmet and backpack. She was using the computer to help her order and prepare items in a medical kit on her lap—syringes and stimulant drugs, as well as powerful antioxidants. Earlier she had laid out an array of facemasks attached to oxygen bottles. The masks and bottles lay on one end of the adjacent bunk over the driver area. Denise was preparing for a best-case nightmare scenario—six half-alive, oxygen-deprived, carbon dioxide poisoned patients. No preparation was needed for the worst-case scenario.

Further back, to her right, beyond the airlock door and pressure suit closets, just in front of the back bunk, Jurgen Eindorf was sitting on a copper stool. He had his light-green pressure suit on, except for backpack, helmet, and gloves. Like Denise, he was ready to go outside at a moment's notice.

Jurgen was wearing a set of earphones and a mouthpiece, and was working with communications equipment that sat on racks above a storage area. He was configuring the equipment to pick up an array of frequencies emitted by the distress beacons on his mission's buggies. It was not a particularly difficult task for him. The chief flight engineer knew everything about the buggies, including their distress beacons.

He had not had time to do the work before the rover left the glass compound, ten minutes earlier. He had been busy configuring the communications equipment on the other rover, so that Captain Derk could listen for distress signals too. John and Derk had set out in that rover, to drive out through Stem Gap. They would first pick up Ursula Schneider and a medical kit at the ESA habitat, and then drive northeastward down Kasei Valley, in case the missing six had decided to come back the way they had set out. Ursula, the biologist from Austria, had some medical skills.

Emma Grant had remained behind at the compound. Derk had instructed her to see to communications with the habitat, with Mission Control, and with the rovers to the extent possible. Denise had also asked her to see to the two children, if necessary.

The horrific disaster at the NASA landing site in 2038 had taught everyone at Mission Control, and almost everyone on Earth, it seemed, just how easy it was to lose a whole crew on Mars. They were all anxiously following the drama of the missing six, waiting for any snippet of news. In Toulouse, it was just after seven o'clock in the morning, one day and just over fourteen hours behind.

Satisfied that she had everything ready, Denise got up and carefully made her way back to the communications area, holding on to the airlock side of the rover as it trundled along the road.

"Do you have it working yet, Mr. Eindorf?" she asked, holding onto the equipment rack with one hand.

"Yes, it is working, ma'am," said Jurgen. "I have just finished triple checking it." He was very correct with her. He had already learned to respect Denise. As far as he was concerned, she was in charge on this expedition, and he intended to do as he was bid.

"If it's only a simple frequency beep, couldn't some electrical disturbance in the upper atmosphere interfere with it, and mislead us?" she asked. Denise knew Mars.

"Yes, it could, if the signal was just a single frequency, ma'am," he replied. "But it is not. It is an array of six frequencies. If we get a signal, it can only come from a buggy. You can be sure of that."

"Can we expect a strong signal?"

"If they were on high ground relative to us, ma'am, we might pick up a signal from as much as five miles away. But, as you know, Mars has a high curvature, and even flat ground rolls a lot—if they were in just a shallow hollow only a mile away, or if we were in a hollow, we might get only a weak signal. If they were behind some large outcrop, like a mesa or mountain, we would pick up nothing."

"In that case, I'd better stop talking to you and let you start listening," said Denise. "They could be anywhere in this region. So maybe a very faint signal is all we'll get—if we get anything."

"Yes, ma'am."

Denise backed away, carefully making her way to the driver area. Memories of the night she had spent lost in the labyrinth some years back streamed into her mind. And that time, she had had a rover to hunker down in for the night. She shuddered at the thought of being out in that labyrinth at night in buggies, with the air supply near to running out. We have to find them soon, she thought; it's just too horrible to think of what will happen if we don't.

*

It was now nearly ten twenty-five, and Denise was sitting beside the Zen master in the driver area, as it sped along, both of them with eyes intently concentrated on the road.

In the past hour or so, they had come almost twenty miles, had left Tip Canyon behind, and were now in a wider valley. There had been no sign of anyone on the road, nor any faint radio signal that could even hint at the buggies' distress beacons. There had been only the occasional small dune fields on either side of the road, a few of them straddling the road for a hundred meters or so, requiring that they drive off the road for a few brief intervals, to get around them. These few dune obstacles had not delayed them by more than about five minutes. A compounding hazard had been the patches of ice mist that lay here and there on the rolling and winding road, on that dark, starless night. It meant that the driver had to take great care, since mist and sand could obscure the road, cause them to run off it at speed, and hit a rock and damage the axle housings.

"At least the clouds are keeping some heat in. The temperature close to ground is still above the frost point," said Denise, mostly to herself. "Their suits should be able to keep them from freezing."

Because of the low pressure air on Mars, normally frost did not form on the ground above a temperature of about minus 58 degrees Celsius. The air temperature a few feet above ground could easily be well below surface temperature, however, allowing ice mist to form instead of ground frost, depending on the level of moisture in the air.

The Zen master just nodded at Denise's remark. He would not talk while driving. Lack of concentration on the road for just an instant on a night like this could mean an accident.

His caution was justified, for a few moments later, just after the road climbed out of some low-lying terrain, suddenly, a wall of sand dunes loomed out of the mist in front. The Zen master braked hard, but the heavy rover did not respond well, and did not manage to stop before running into it. The machine ploughed into the fine sand.

"*Mon Dieu*!" cried Denise.

The deepening sand acted as a brake, fortunately, and no damage was done.

The Zen master said nothing, as he reversed out of the sand.

"This could be the problem," said Denise, after he had extricated the machine. "It could be blocking the whole valley."

"It looks like a big dune tongue, running forward to the left," said Dr. Sato, as he reversed further. "Two dune tongues could have locked together somewhere near the road." He then turned the rover off the road to his left, to travel along the edge of the dunes.

"Mr. Eindorf," said Denise, "hold on, it's going to get bumpy. The road's blocked by dunes. We're going to try to drive around them. Driving over rocks. Any signals?"

"No, ma'am, nothing," came the reply from the back of the rover. Jurgen could not only listen for buggy distress signals, he could communicate seamlessly with the driver area of the rover.

The huge machine went quite fast over the rocky terrain, at about ten miles an hour. Each of its six very large wheels was attached to a large flexible elbow joint, much larger than on a buggy. This enabled a rover wheel to rise up more easily when rolling over a rock, allowing the rover to travel faster over rough country than a buggy. As they moved forward, the dune tongue to their right continually veered right.

Some five minutes later, about a mile from where the road disappeared under the sand dunes, with the dunes now veering to the left, they came to a steep escarpment, with the sand right up against it. Where the sand ended, the escarpment edge continued on in almost the same direction as the edge of the dune field.

"No doubt about it being completely blocked on this side," said Denise. "Let's check out the other side."

The Zen master merely nodded as he concentrated on turning the rover. Moments later they were bumping over the angular rocks and stones of the rolling terrain again, headed back to the road, this time with the dune tongue to their left.

After they crossed the road, the dune tongue veered to the right. Some ten minutes later, about a mile from where they had crossed the road, they came to another steep escarpment. The sand had advanced some fifteen feet up the side of it. The Zen master stopped his machine.

"At least now we have an explanation," said Denise. "Two dune tongues must have joined up to form a blockage like this in such a short time. This road was open four months ago. Mr. Eindorf! The road is completely blocked. Impossible to go around the dunes. This is probably what has caused all the trouble. Any signal yet?"

"No, ma'am, nothing."

"What do we do now?" asked Denise, looking at Dr. Sato, and with a feeling of hopelessness coming over her.

"If they did not turn back, they probably tried to travel around this dune tongue," said the Zen master. "The escarpment edge here is part of a long narrow mesa that runs along the south side of the road for about eight miles. The escarpment we saw on the other side of the road is part of a nearly square mesa that's about three miles long on each side."

"So there's a chance they're trying to work their way round one of these two mesas," said Denise.

"Very likely," said the Zen master calmly. "The only problem is that there are more similar mesas on the other side, along the past eight miles of road. The next one on the other side is about two miles long, and the one after that on that side is about four miles long. If they tried to get around these dunes on that side they could come back out onto the road between any of those mesas."

"But I suppose it's quite possible they tried the long mesa on this side," said Denise.

"Yes, the gap between this mesa and the next one, on the other side of these dunes, is much closer, and quite flat. The gap on the other side is farther away and rougher."

"So there's no telling which gap they're likely to come out of as they try to get back to the road, or on what side of the road," said Denise anxiously. "They could be stuck in any of the gaps, or lost behind any of at least four mesas."

"It's not possible to search around all of them before they run out of air," said the Zen master. "It's already ten thirty-five. They likely have air left for only another hour at most. And while the rover is searching around one mesa, they could come out of another gap and reach the road. Two vehicles would have been better. One to patrol the road, while the other searched the mesa gaps."

"Maybe what we should do is drive back down the road for a few mesas," suggested Denise, "and listen carefully for any distress signal in the gap between each pair. And then come back this way again, listening again at every mesa gap—I mean just patrol up and down the road listening until about twelve."

"It seems like the best thing to do," agreed the Zen master.

They retraced the distance along the dunes to the road. Once on the road, they drove back along it. They stopped about a mile later, at a high point of the gently rolling and winding road, and opposite the first mesa gap, to see if they could detect a signal. They picked up nothing, and so they traveled on back as fast as they could, stopping and listening at a high point opposite each pair of mesas. But each time it was the same—nothing.

At a mesa gap about eight miles back, they decided it was unlikely the buggies could have traveled any farther off the road. So they turned and drove back toward the dune blockage, again stopping for a minute or so, at each mesa gap. They could not see the gaps between the mesas on each side of the road, of course, but were relying on the Zen master's calculation of where the gaps where, based on the odometer readings and his knowledge of the terrain. With the machine stopped on higher ground, and quiet, Jurgen had the best chance of hearing even a whisper of a signal. But he detected no signal at any of the mesa gaps on the way back either.

When they reached the dunes blocking the road a second time, at a final high point of the road, the Zen master stopped for a minute, before turning around to go back again. Both he and Denise were wondering if there was something better they could do, although neither could think of anything better than continuing the patrol up and down the road. It was now just after eleven twenty and still they had detected no signal from the missing buggies.

"I can't believe this," said Denise, almost in despair. "If they didn't turn around and go back to base the way they came, there must be six human beings suffocating out there, and we have no idea where they—"

"Dr. Lavoisier! Ma'am!" said Jurgen suddenly, clearly excited. "Signal! Very faint. I can barely make it out. This high point on the road must be just letting us hear it. It is a buggy signal, for sure, anywhere between a mile and four miles away."

"Which side?" cried Denise. "Can you tell?"

"No, I can not, but it is repeating every ten seconds, as it should. Seems to be only one signal though—from a single buggy."

The Zen master already had the buggy moving off the road to his left. He would try and see if going that way would increase the distress signal strength. He figured there was a better chance the missing six had decided to go around the mesa on his left side of the road, the side they would have been on when they found their way completely blocked. If he was wrong, the distress signal would get rapidly weaker.

"We're on our way," cried Denise.

Keeping the dune field to his right, the Zen master traveled as quickly as he dared over the rocky terrain at night, almost at twelve miles an hour.

"Ma'am! Signal getting stronger," said Jurgen, after four minutes. "Definitely coming from a single buggy. Hold this course."

The Zen master had picked the correct side of the road, and sticking to his present course suited him fine. It meant he could travel in the direction of the signal and keep the dunes to his right at the same time. He knew that off the road he had to have some reference guide, like the dunes, to be sure of finding his way back to the road. Without some physical marker as a guide, he could get lost in the labyrinth too, on such a starless night.

Soon they came to the escarpment edge that continued on, almost in the same direction as the edge of the dune field, but in a direction a little more to the left. Dr. Sato continued along the escarpment edge, still going as fast as he dared. He knew that every second would count. Then the escarpment edge turned sharply to the right, and Dr. Sato did too.

"Much stronger signal, all of a sudden, very strong—we must be very close," cried Jurgen.

It was eleven twenty-seven.

"Get your helmet on, Mr. Eindorf," exclaimed Denise suddenly, a minute later, as they came to the top of a small rise in the rolling terrain. "I see it. Over there, down in the hollow. Looks bad. One on the ground."

She jumped out of her seat and ran to the airlock. "We both need to go out. In the airlock together. You don't need a backpack."

In the remaining half minute it took the Zen master to come up alongside the stricken buggy, Denise had her helmet on, as did Jurgen. Her gloves had been already on. A few seconds later, as the stair was going down, they had both squeezed into the small airlock, able to take one with a backpack on, but just able to squeeze in two without backpacks.

The rover had stopped with its airlock door facing the buggy front, and the rover stair landed only a few feet away from it. As Denise and Jurgen came down the steps, all outside stair lights were on, and wisps of ice mist hung in the air, reflecting the light.

One of the three was lying motionless on the ground alongside the buggy, on its driver side. The other two lay sprawled in their seats, but one of them, in the middle seat, managed to lift a hand and wave weakly. It was Astrid Larsson, the only one still conscious. They rushed to her first.

"Thank God you have come," was all she managed to say, in a weak, breathless voice, as they got to her from the buggy driver's side. They had to watch to avoid trampling the body on the ground. Astrid was breathing very heavily and fast.

"Can you stand up?" asked Denise.

"I think so … if you help me."

"Come then. Inside you go."

Jurgen and Denise dragged her across the driver seat and out the buggy. Each of them held her firmly by an upper arm, and helped or pulled her the few feet round the front of the buggy to the rover steps. A few seconds later they had her in the airlock, and in the care of Dr. Sato.

"The one on the ground next, Mr. Eindorf," said Denise, as they turned back to the buggy.

The body was lying face down, and they could not see who it was. Each grabbed an upper arm and lifted the body almost vertical, and Jurgen could now see it was Jose Montoya. They dragged him to the rover and up the steps. The airlock door opened as they got to the top. They pushed him in, left him to Dr. Sato, and rushed back to the buggy.

The remaining one, Monique Montpellier, lay in the outside seat on the other side of the buggy, partly sprawled over the side. Her two rescuers were as brutal as they were fast. Jurgen took only a few seconds first, to switch off the buggy's distress beacon. Then they grabbed her by the upper arms, pulled her out of the seat, carried her around the front of the buggy to the rover steps, with her boots dragging the ground, and then up the steps and into the airlock.

The rescue completed, less than two minutes later, both Denise and Jurgen squeezed out of the airlock, and back into the rover, as the stair motors whined, pulling up the stair.

A few seconds later, the rover was moving again. Astrid Larsson had already pointed the Zen master in the direction the other rover had gone. He was hot on its trail at once, driving along the edge of the escarpment, a trail confirmed every so often by clear buggy tracks in patches of sand.

When Denise and Jurgen stepped out of the airlock, taking off their helmets, they found Astrid on her knees, between Jose and Monique. She still had her pressure suit on, but with helmet and gloves off. She had just started attaching an oxygen mask to Monique. Both Jose and Monique were lying on the floor near the driver area. Their helmets were off, and there was a purple tinge in their faces. Jose had swollen lips. They still had their backpacks on, and their heads were propped under folded pillow rolls from the rover's bunks. Oxygen flasks lay on the floor beside them.

A thin layer of frost had formed on the very cold exteriors of the light-green pressure suits of the three rescued astronauts. The frost came from moisture in the air inside the rover, and would evaporate soon, as the suit exteriors warmed up.

Astrid had Monique's oxygen turned on by the time Denise got her gloves off. Denise was quickly on her knees beside Jose. She began attaching a mask, while Astrid continued to work with Monique. Denise was breathing fast. Her lungs had been damaged years earlier and she no longer had full use of them. The exertion outside, without a backpack, had been almost too much for her.

Suddenly, Monique opened her eyes. The oxygen had done its job quickly, for she had fallen unconscious less than half a minute before the rover arrived. She seemed to want to talk, and Astrid lifted her mask, to let her.

"*Mon Dieu*," she said, "they've come."

"Yes, Monique," confirmed Astrid, "they got here, just in time."

"Yes, you're going to be all right, Monique," said Denise, still rather breathless, but looking over at Monique and trying to smile, as Astrid replaced the mask. "You can't have been unconscious long. Just lie still for now, and relax, and try to breathe deeply. I have to tend to this man. What's his name, somebody?"

"Jose Montoya," said Jurgen, "and we have a new signal."

He was again sitting on his stool by the communications equipment, with only his helmet off, monitoring the distress signal from the second buggy. He would inform Dr. Sato about the signal strength every so often, as the rover lurched along.

Denise returned her attention to Jose, turned his oxygen on, and carefully watched Jose's purple-tinged face, now beginning to swell. After a few seconds she looked up, and turned to Astrid.

"Young woman," she said, "I don't remember your name, but your head seems to be working just fine. That was a good job you did with Monique. Whatever the reason, you seem to have recovered very quickly. Now, I've something else for you to do to help. Can you go outside with Mr. Eindorf, and bring the next three in when we find them? I'm going to have a lot of work to do, and it's better if I'm inside when they come in. I fear the next three will be in a lot worse condition, especially if we don't get to them soon." She looked at her wrist display. "It's eleven thirty-five. We found you three at eleven twenty-eight."

"My name is Astrid Larsson, ma'am," said Astrid. "And yes, I can go outside again."

"Take your backpack off, Ms. Larsson," said Denise. "You don't need it for the short time you'll be out—the airlock can take two with backpacks off. One other thing. Can you remember how long ago Mr. Montoya lost consciousness?"

"I am not sure, but it was certainly not much more than a minute before Monique. He was standing beside the buggy, and was trying to talk to us when he collapsed. I tried to get out to help him, but I did not have the strength."

"Good," said Denise. "If that's true I should be able to save him."

"My backback is no good anyway," said Astrid, as she stood up, loosening the straps of her backpack. "No air in it."

"Sorry, forgot," said Denise.

Denise felt for the pulse on Jose's neck again, and frowned. "You have to do better than that," she said, almost to herself.

"Ms. Larsson," she said urgently, still kneeling beside Jose, "can you pass me the medical kit on the red chair—put it on the floor beside me."

Astrid did as she was bid. "Anything else I can do, ma'am?" she asked.

"No," said Denise. "Just get ready to go out again."

The distress signal was getting very strong now. Jurgen informed the Zen master, then took off his headset, got up, helped Astrid remove her backpack, and moved to the airlock. Meanwhile, Denise took some items from her medical kit and bent over Jose, studying his face and measuring his pulse again. In spite of the oxygen, his pulse was still weak, as was his breathing.

Quickly but carefully she prepared a syringe and gave him an injection in the neck. In the syringe was a cocktail of drugs designed to fight the effects of suffocation on the brain and circulatory system. She turned the oxygen up further, and waited. Then she prepared another syringe, loaded with an even more powerful drug cocktail, but before she could use it, Jose too opened his eyes, and muttered something in Spanish. Denise breathed a sigh of relief.

"Mr. Montoya, can you hear me?" she asked, removing his mask for a moment.

"*Si*," came the weak answer.

"Good," said Denise. "You're safe now, in a rover. Just lie still, relax and try to breathe deeply. Will you do that?"

"Yes," said Jose, with a sigh. It was an effort for him to speak, and Denise replaced the mask.

"Looks like we got here just in time," she said a few moments later, as she closed her kit, and got up off her knees. "These two will be all right, but they had better stay on oxygen for a while, and keep lying down until they get their normal color back."

"Where do you want us to put the next three, ma'am?" asked Jurgen. "There is not much space, with two bodies on the floor already."

"You're right," said Denise. "We can't leave them on the floor. We'll need the space for the next three, if we find them. Help me get their ice suits off and get them in the bunks." By now, a thick layer of white frost coated each of the suits of the two on the floor, and Astrid's suit too.

Meanwhile, Dr. Sato was closing in on the other rover. He had kept on following the escarpment edge to the right. A message every so often from Jurgen about a strengthening signal, and a buggy wheel mark on a patch of sand every few minutes, had kept him on the right trail since leaving the first dead buggy.

About five minutes after leaving the first buggy, at almost eleven thirty-eight, he spotted the second buggy. The dead buggy was a good twenty meters from the edge of the escarpment. The Zen Master was traveling quite close to the escarpment edge at the time, between the escarpment edge and the buggy, and had almost passed the buggy before he spotted it. He swerved sharply to his left, and brought the rover round, to come at the buggy from the front, headlights shining on the faces of three obviously unconscious astronauts sprawled in the buggy seats.

The brightness Don Carruthers had seen as he finally lost consciousness had not been some heavenly light, but the light from Dr. Sato's headlights.

Less than ten meters from the front of the buggy, the Zen master turned the rover sharply to the left again, stopping with the rover airlock facing the buggy front. He began lowering the stair the instant the rover stopped, and it hit the ground less than two meters from the buggy front. The rover's airlock and stair were on the rover driver's right side, between its huge front and middle wheels.

Meanwhile, inside the rover, Jurgen and Denise had lifted Jose into the front bunk, his oxygen mask still attached. He was still weak. They had just finished lifting Monique, also still weak, into the back bunk, when the rover stopped, and the stair began going down. Astrid and Jurgen were inside the airlock together, almost at once. It was eleven thirty-eight. Dr. Sato came back from the driver area, as the airlock door closed on the pair.

Shortly after, Denise and the Zen master took the first body out of the airlock. It was Don Carruthers. They dragged him to the front of the rover, near the driver area, and beside the red swivel chairs. Working together, they had him on the floor with helmet off in less than thirty seconds, to reveal another purple-tinged face with slightly swollen lips. They had him on oxygen in another forty seconds, just in time to receive the next limp body from the airlock.

It was Sheila Bell. They had her on the floor beside Don Carruthers, helmet off and head propped, in less than thirty seconds too. But, as Denise knelt down beside her, feeling for a pulse and examining the badly swollen face with a professional eye, and as Dr. Sato brought up the oxygen mask, Denise was suddenly overwhelmed with emotion, and tears came to her eyes.

"We're too late," she said, her voice shaking. "She's been dead for a while. There's no pulse, no sign of life at all. I'll try and start her heart anyway. But I think she's been dead too long."

She applied oxygen at high pressure, to fill her lungs, released the pressure, increased it again, half a dozen times, to stimulate breathing. She also injected a powerful drug designed to restart a stopped heart. Neither measure had any effect. Sheila was dead. Nevertheless, when the airlock was activated again, she asked the Zen master to continue with the oxygen treatment, and got up to take the third body out of the airlock.

Denise had Claude Bertrand's body on the floor at the feet of the other two, with helmet off and head propped, and was on her knees beside him, before Astrid and Jurgen came in through the airlock.

As soon as Astrid got her helmet off, she knelt down beside Denise, and helped her with the oxygen.

"How are they, doctor?" she asked anxiously.

"Much worse this time," muttered Denise, shaking her head. "Your mission doctor's dead. We're still trying—don't think there's any hope—must have lost consciousness quite early on."

"She was the first to have breathing problems," confirmed Astrid, as Denise continued to work with Claude. "She is just the opposite of me—big boned with a fast metabolism. That is why I lasted longer than any of them. And the two men? How are they? This one is Claude Bertrand, from France. The other one is Don Carruthers, from England."

Denise studied the unconscious Claude Bertrand with a professional eye. His face was purple and lips were livid and swollen.

"This one looks very bad too," said Denise, straightening up. "He's alive, but barely. Vital signs very poor. Looks better for Mr. Carruthers—not much worse than Mr. Montoya was—think we can bring him round. Somebody pass me my medical kit. No more talking, please. I need to be in two places at once."

She moved on hands and knees back beside Don Carruthers, injected a drug cocktail into his neck, and turned up his oxygen.

"Keep your eye on him, Ms. Larsson, while I tend to Monsieur Bertrand," she said as she crawled quickly on all fours back to Claude. She bent over him, feeling his pulse again.

Dr. Sato was still trying to restart Sheila Bell's heart. He continued for another five minutes without success, until Denise told him to stop.

Denise worked on Claude Bertrand for nearly fifteen minutes. But in spite of all her best efforts, Claude's condition did not improve, and he remained unconscious, but breathing.

It went much better with Don Carruthers. Less than a minute after Denise had given him the injection, he too opened his eyes, to look into Astrid's long face. "By Jove, it's you, Astrid," was the first thing he said—in a muffled voice through his oxygen mask. Denise moved over beside him at once for a few seconds, further checked his vital signs, adjusted his oxygen flow, and told him to just lie still, breathe deeply and relax—he was going to be all right. As she spoke, he closed his eyes again.

About five minutes after that, with Denise still working on Claude, the Zen master got up from beside Sheila Bell, and went back into the driver area. He got in the driver seat, withdrew the stair, turned the rover around the dead buggy, and began the nearly one and a half hour drive back to the compound.

As he did so, Astrid went over to where Denise was kneeling, bent over Claude. She spoke to Denise in very low tones, apparently worried about something. Whatever she said had an effect, for a few seconds later Denise was back beside Don Carruthers, with a syringe in her hand.

"Just relax," she said to Don, whose eyes were open again. "You're going to make a complete recovery. This is just a sedative. I want you to sleep on the way back to Leaf Valley."

"Can you just tell me how Sheila Bell is?" he asked her weakly, when she had finished, but in a muffled voice, speaking through his oxygen mask. His tone betrayed an obvious anxiety. "Is she going to be all …?"

Don Carruthers was asleep before he could finish his question, and Denise never lifted his mask to let him talk.

As they began the journey back, Jurgen and Astrid helped Denise remove the frost-covered pressure suits of the two patients on the floor, and helped make them as comfortable as they could. They would have to lie on the floor all the way back.

Although they removed Sheila Bell's backpack, to enable her to lie flat on her back, neither of them had the heart to remove her frosted pressure suit. Astrid thoughtfully put Sheila's helmet on again, but without fastening it to her collar. She put it on back to front, to cover Sheila's face. Only Sheila's wavy brown hair was visible through the helmet's transparent plastic underneath.

Sheila Bell was thus left in her pressure suit where she lay, on the rover floor beside the red swivel chairs, next to the sleeping man she had fallen in love with, and who did not yet know she was dead.

*

Jurgen and Astrid sat with Dr. Sato in the driver area on the long way back, while Denise sat on one of the red swivel chairs, looking at the body of Sheila Bell, and thinking about her, but every so often tending to the needs of her living patients.

By the time they were half-way home, Jose and Monique, in the bunks, were fully conscious, but looking a little pale. Denise ordered them to continue to lie as still as possible, however, and to continue breathing deeply, through their masks, which she now arranged to deliver air that was only a little oxygen enhanced.

By the end of the trip back, Jose and Monique could easily get up, and walk out of the rover without help, leaving Don Carruthers still asleep, lying on the rover floor beside Sheila.

It was very late, half past zero in the morning, when they reached the glass compound—on Mars midnight is at nearly 12:40, which is also hour zero of the next day. As soon as the compound's airlock garage had filled, its inside exit door opened, and the Zen master drove the rover through it. He parked it on the pad beyond, with greenery sloping down at the front, and on both sides.

The rescued three from ESA emerged first from the rover, stepping wonderingly onto the parking pad of the compound. The area was lit up by short, vertical fluorescent lights at the corners. Jose, Monique, and Astrid walked around the pad, staring with astonishment at a very different world. It was a world of Martian greenery, where they could breathe the air and smell the plants—Mars as it could be. They were apparently none the worse for their near brush with death.

With Claude Bertrand it was different. His condition was still critical. Denise helped Jurgen carry Claude out, around the front of the parked rover, up the steps on the west slope beside the parking pad, and directly along the garden path westward to the house, followed by the other three ESA astronauts, and the Zen master.

They carried him along the entrance hallway and up the stairs at the end, with the Zen master close behind, and laid him on a narrow copper frame bed in Denise's surgery.

At that moment Denise could do nothing further for Claude until she had more information about his condition. To this end she asked the Zen master to set up electronic monitors and displays, sent by both ESA and NASA in compliance with mission stay agreements.

Jurgen Eindorf, standing at the surgery door, with the others, now asked Denise what she thought they should do with Sheila's body. Denise had had time to think about that on the journey back, and had already decided what to do for the time being. She would keep the body in her custody, and release it to Captain Derk only for burial. She had even decided where it should be buried, although she knew that was not for her to decide. Overnight it would be treated with dignity, and laid in a place of honor.

Tomorrow she would take it to another place, whether Derk agreed with her or not. Denise had liked Sheila a lot, and it was Derk who had stupidly sent her to her death, and possibly Claude Bertrand too. Inside Denise was possessed by a cold anger toward Derk. He could go hang.

"Come with me, all of you," she said.

Carrying a folded sheet of light green parachute cloth she had taken from the surgery, Denise walked quickly back downstairs, and along the entrance hallway to the communications room. There she placed Jose, Monique, and Astrid in the care of Emma Grant, with orders to make use of the bathrooms and laundry room to freshen up, to get their clothes washed and dried, and to get some food from the kitchen. Then Denise asked Jurgen to come back to the rover with her, and the pair went outside.

Inside the rover, they found Don Carruthers still sleeping on the floor. The first thing Denise and Jurgen did was lift him into the front bunk. Denise had actually given him enough sedative to keep him sleeping till morning.

Given what Don Carruthers had been through, after Astrid had informed Denise of his close attachment to Sheila, Denise had thought it would be better if he got a good night's sleep before being subjected to the shock of Sheila's death. She had even decided on something for him to do in the morning, to keep his mind occupied until the abandoned buggies were back in Leaf Valley, and the ESA astronauts could return to their Elbow Hill habitat.

Having tended to the living, they next removed Sheila's pressure suit, and carried her out of the rover and up the steps on the south slope to the path above the parking pad, with the green parachute cloth draped over her. They did not take her to the house. Instead they made their way along a garden spoke path that led down to the hub of the compound—the patio in front of the pool, surrounded by large flowering plants, and with broad steps leading up to the lower front balcony of the house.

The area was lit up modestly by short vertical florescent lights, partly immersed in plants at the four corners of the patio. Here, Denise and Jurgen carefully wrapped the body in the green cloth, and laid it out on the patio, feet nearest the edge of the pool, and in the dead center of the patio and the entire compound.

After they had positioned the body, Jurgen stood up, and went and stood at Sheila's feet for a minute, facing her, head bowed, and deeply moved. Memories of her alive crowded into his mind.

Sheila had had no enemies on the ESA mission, and was liked by all of them. Her good humor, cheerful smile and vivacious character had been a lightening and morale boosting positive on the long journey from Earth. And as mission doctor, she had had occasion to treat every one of the other eleven, for one minor thing or another. Her loss was a severe blow. As the flight engineer stood there, in front of Sheila, he wondered how the Captain and the others would deal with it.

This placement of the body on the patio by the pool was the best Denise could think of doing with it for the present. It would stay there until tomorrow, when she would move it to the more appropriate place she had in mind for it, something the Zen master had already agreed to.

Meanwhile the needs of the living, especially Claude Bertrand, had to be tended to. It was now nearly one o'clock in the morning, and Denise was almost exhausted. There was still more to do and arrange, however, and she continued working.

Jurgen Eindorf had radioed the result of the rescue expedition to Emma Grant from the rover, as soon as communications were possible, at about zero fifteen, and some fifteen minutes before the rover reached the house. Emma Grant had not been idle since. She had sent the news direct to Mission Control and to the habitat at Elbow Hill. At the Elbow Hill habitat, Vince Cassoni had relayed it to John's rover on its way back up Kasei Valley. John's rover was at that point only about five miles from the Elbow Hill habitat. Denise was not expecting her husband home until about three. This would be a long night for everybody.

They entered the house by the front door. As they passed along the hallway, headed for the stairs, they could see Emma working in the communications room. Denise paused by the door.

"Any reaction from Earth?" she asked.

"Mainly thanks it wasn't worse," said Emma. "Shock about Sheila's death everywhere in Europe, but especially in Ireland, and there's great concern for Claude. The President of the European Union has sent Captain Derk his condolences. The President of the United States has sent his condolences to the E.U. President and to the President of Ireland." Emma Grant was always accurately factual. It had been almost eleven o'clock local time on Monday morning, when the news of Sheila's death reached Mission Control.

"That's it?" asked Denise.

"Yes," said Emma. "Have you anything new about Claude's condition I can report?"

"No, not yet, but Dr. Sato's setting up the electronic monitoring equipment," said Denise. "I should be able to get a better reading shortly."

With that she walked on down the hallway toward the downstairs living area and the stairs at the end of the hall, still followed by Jurgen. What Emma had said bothered her, or rather what she had not said. Didn't anyone in Europe appreciate the effort she, her husband, and the Zen master had made to rescue the six? 'Thanks that it wasn't worse', indeed. Without the efforts of the three of them it would indeed have been worse. There would have been six corpses instead of one. A word of thanks to them for their efforts could have been expected.

Monique, Jose, and Astrid were sitting in the downstairs living area, all three wearing bathrobes, and drinking tea and munching cookies. Denise waved to the three but did not join them. She went straight past the living area and briskly up the stairs to the surgery, followed by Jurgen.

As she entered the surgery, the Zen master had just finished setting up the heart and brain monitoring displays. The heart monitor revealed a regular but weak heart beat, as expected. But what she most feared was confirmed by the unit monitoring and displaying electrical brain activity. There was some activity displayed on the screen, which the Zen master had amplified, but it was only a small fraction of the activity of a normal human brain. It looked like Clause Bertrand was brain dead, a conclusion the Zen master had already come to.

Nevertheless, with the Zen master's help, Denise checked all the displays, and cross checked them, just to be sure, and she checked his other vital signs too. Then she treated him as best she could, for nearly half an hour, before standing back from the bed. The former purple face was now a deathly pale.

"How is he, doctor?" asked Jurgen anxiously. He did not have the skills to interpret the patterns on the screens.

"His condition is very poor," said Denise.

"Can you save him?"

Denise did not believe she could, but was not yet prepared to admit that publicly. "It doesn't look good, Mr. Eindorf," she answered, "but I'm doing the best I can."

"Excuse my asking so many questions," persisted Jurgen, who had not grasped the true seriousness of the Frenchman's condition, "but the mission, and even the world, can not afford to lose a man of the skills and reputation of Claude Bertrand. He is the most famous structural engineer in Europe. I saw you were able to bring Jose and Don around with an injection, and I have noticed that you have not tried to do anything like that with Claude. Is there not some way you can try to revive him?"

"I understand your concern, Mr. Eindorf," said Denise, "but there are sound medical reasons why I can't attempt that, at least for now. I'm just too tired to explain. We'll see how he is in the morning." She looked at her watch. "It's nearly two o'clock. I think now we should all see what we can do about getting some sleep. We've done everything we can this evening."

Jurgen had to be content with that.

The Zen master had already gone out of the surgery and was standing patiently in the hallway, just outside the door.

"Goodnight," was all he said, bowing to them politely, as they came through the door.

"Goodnight, Dr. Sato," said Denise. "A man your age should have been in bed long ago. Thank you for all the help this evening."

The Zen master just bowed slightly again.

Jurgen Eindorf, suddenly realizing his mission's debt to this old man, also thanked him, occasioning another bow. With that, the very tired, seventy-six year old Zen master retreated down the hallway to the visitor's room he used when staying at the house.

Denise and Jurgen now went back downstairs. Neither could get to bed just yet. There was a problem with sleeping arrangements. There were beds in the house for only Denise and John, the two children, the Zen master and the patient in the surgery. Now there were five extra bodies to sleep. There were the three remaining bunks in the two rovers, when John got back, but that still meant two missing beds.

Jurgen solved the problem by deciding to return to the habitat with Emma in their buggy, actually the Zen master's buggy, loaned to the ESA mission.

For a moment, Denise was concerned—another buggy out on Mars at night.... But when Jurgen assured her that he knew the road, and when she considered that they would pass her husband on the road, probably about half way down the valley, and that those in the habitat could see the approaching buggy's headlights when it was still miles away across Elbow Plain, Denise agreed. It would be three thirty in the morning before they reached the habitat.

Five minutes later, they set out, after Emma had informed the habitat of their departure and expected arrival time, and John had informed them that he was already inside Leaf Valley, and would watch out for their buggy. The other three astronauts came with Denise to the compound's airlocks to see them off.

This gave Denise, always tidy, an opportunity to get the three to tidy up the six pressure suits from the ESA mission. She also showed them how to set the main air flasks and power units from four ESA backpacks under charge, two sets in the rover's pressure suit-closet and two in the pressure-suit closet near the compound's small airlock. They had some difficulty here, for the main air flasks in the ESA back packs were not removable. Only the reserve air flasks could come out. But they managed.

Astrid then asked permission to sleep in the rover in which Don Carruthers was sleeping, on the parking pad. She undertook to break the news about Sheila to him in the morning. Denise agreed. Denise was not prepared to do it herself, since she did not know Don Carruthers. One of the three surviving ESA astronauts would have to break the news, and Astrid Larsson seemed to Denise to be the most sensitive and tactful.

Denise now invited Jose and Monique to take a stroll around the garden for forty-five minutes or so, until her husband brought the other rover home. She then bid them goodnight and went back to the house.

She was so tired she could hardly stand, and her breathing was labored. This evening had been just too much for a person with her limited lung capacity. Even so, before she went to bed, she checked Claude Bertrand's condition again. She came out of the surgery looking even more saddened, and even anxious, shaking her head. She then went straight to bed, and when her husband came home, just before three o'clock, she had long been asleep.

*

As he drove on the road back up Leaf Valley, John's mind was pondering the new state of affairs the events of the evening had created. Unlike Denise, John was not personally acquainted with Sheila Bell, and although he was sorry to hear of her death, he was not grieved. He was more upset at the person who had sent her to her death, and reflected on what he expected to be Derk's much reduced prestige and authority when the truth came out.

It was clear to him that Derk was entirely to blame for the tragedy. In his mind, ordering six inexperienced crew members on such a dangerous expedition in buggies was the height of irresponsibility. And this from a man who was supposed to have a head for strategy second to none—a strategy mastermind.

Indeed! Some mastermind, thought John. He got some satisfaction from the thought that it would now be much harder for Derk to remove them from Mars.

Had he but known, his satisfaction was entirely misplaced. He was underestimating Derk, as he had done before. That strategy mastermind might have suffered a severe blow, but it was not a fatal blow. Derk had already conceived a plan that would deflect all blame from him, and direct it convincingly where, in Derk's opinion, it properly belonged. And this plan would do more than just ensure the removal of his three opponents from Mars. It would allow him to remove them in a manner that would enhance his reputation and prestige, and cause him to be honored in all the capitals of the

European Union. It would even allow him to be honored in Dublin, Ireland, a capital city which at that very moment was reeling from the shock of the death of Sheila Bell.

*

Emma Grant and Jurgen reached the habitat safely, just before three thirty in the morning. The sky had cleared of washboard clouds by then, the stars were out, and the temperature had fallen further, enabling ice mist to be deposited as frost. The fast-moving moon Phobos, about to set soon, shone on a frost-covered habitat, as the pair got out of the buggy and went inside.

Derk had been busy communicating with Mission Control for almost two hours, ever since John had dropped Ursula and him off at the habitat. He had managed to continue giving the impression that he was in charge of all rescue operations. John Erway, Denise Lavoisier, and Dr. Sato were all acting on his orders.

Before Derk had left the glass compound in Leaf Valley, on his fruitless trip with John Erway eastward down Kasei Valley, he had placed Emma Grant in the compound's communications room. She was to handle the link with the habitat, and most importantly, the direct link to Mission Control via the ESA comsat and the dish antenna on the slope of Mount Tip. He had explained to her, without being overheard, how the three at the compound had agreed to act on his orders. He informed her of what he had ordered, and what the rescue plan was. Emma had reported all this factually to Mission Control. She did it truthfully in fact, and therefore very convincingly, for she did not know that Derk had misled her. She would have done the same even if she had known, but probably not as well.

When Mission Control in Toulouse had learned, just after two thirty, Kasei Valley time, that Emma and Jurgen were on their way back to the habitat, it had sent a message requesting a report from Jurgen Eindorf, as soon as he got back. Toulouse was particularly anxious to have a report from Jurgen, since he had personally taken part in the rescue.

Just after three thirty in the morning, Jurgen and Emma stepped into the communications room, but all Derk was prepared to do was transmit a message to Earth that confirmed their safe arrival, together with news that Claude Bertrand was still in critical condition. He also stated that Toulouse would have to wait until tomorrow for a full report of the rescue, since they were all too tired to think, and had to get to bed. At that point it was mid afternoon at Mission Control.

Being too tired was not why Derk would not allow an immediate report from Jurgen to Mission Control. One reason was that Derk intended to edit Jurgen's report beforehand. It would have to be a report that at least did not deny his leadership role in the rescue effort, and which preferably would affirm that role.

Another reason was the shock in Europe at the news of the death of Sheila Bell, and of the poor chance for the recovery of Claude Bertrand. He knew that not only did it put his mission in doubt, it meant that some one other than him would have to be blamed. He was determined that Toulouse, and everyone on Earth, see things his way, particularly with regard to the assignment of blame.

When Derk finally went to bed in his confined cubicle that night, he had largely recovered from the shock of the events of that evening. He also had reasonable grounds for believing that things might soon be back under his control, and that the tragedy might well turn out to be a blessing in disguise, at least for him. He was also becoming convinced that he would soon sleep in a large room in a large comfortable house, a house befitting a man of his position and prestige, and that he would soon drive around in a rover too, a vehicle whose suitability for getting around on Mars had impressed him that evening.

*

Thus ended one of the most dramatic evenings ever on Mars. Not since Denise had pulled her husband from his grave ten years earlier had so many events telescoped into one evening. That evening long ago had ended with Denise in a state of euphoria. She had ended this long evening worn out, in a state of shock, sorrow, and anxiety about the possible repercussions.

CHAPTER TEN

Aftermath

WHEN THE sun rose over western Kasei Valley next morning, in a clear, pink-red sky, just after six fifteen, there was not a single conscious soul on Mars. One lay dead, on the central patio, beside the pool, in the glass-enclosed compound on the side of Mount Tip. Another lay close to death, in the house within the glass compound. Everyone else on Mars was asleep, some in the house, some in the rovers inside the compound, and the rest in the habitat on the shelf at Elbow Hill.

They remained asleep, that Wednesday morning, as the sun rose higher, and its warming rays penetrated the glass walls of the compound at Mount Tip. Soon they were shining through the spaces between the branches and leaves of the bushes and plants surrounding the patio, and shining on the patio floor, and on the body of Sheila Bell, lying wrapped in green parachute cloth.

Tens of millions of miles away, on Earth, this unconscious Mars was frustrating a very large number of people, especially in ESA and in the media. That summer day in Toulouse, the time was running one day and some thirteen and a half hours behind local time in Leaf Valley, and it was early Monday evening at Mission Control.

Everybody was waiting for news. Everybody wanted to know the details of the ill-fated expedition of the previous day, and the details of the near midnight rescue that was just a little too late. They wanted to know about the condition of Claude Bertrand, and about what was being done about Sheila Bell. They were also curious about Captain Derk's visit to the industrial complex early the previous evening, and about what had transpired at the dinner with Denise and John afterwards. On top of that, they were wondering what was happening on Mars that morning.

In contrast to the previous evening, however, early that Wednesday morning there was nothing happening on Mars. Everybody was sleeping late.

*

Emma Grant, at the habitat, was up first, just after nine. She went straight to the communications room from her cubicle in the command section, which was on the west side, almost opposite Richard Derk's.

Overnight, the center had been inundated with messages from Mission Control. The most urgent was a request for detailed information about Claude Bertrand. Doctors at Mission Control wanted his exact condition every thirty minutes, specified in exact medical technical language. Emma's first act was to send a message to the compound in Leaf Valley, asking for an update on Claude's condition, with medical technical details, if available.

There was no reply until just after nine thirty, by which time Captain Derk had joined Emma. The message was from the Zen master. He had got to sleep before anyone else, except for the drugged Don Carruthers, and had been up first at the house.

His message reported that Claude's condition was 'apparently unchanged from the previous night'. It also contained detailed technical data from the electronic equipment that was monitoring Claude's condition, data that neither Emma nor Derk could interpret.

On Derk's instructions, Emma forwarded the message to Mission Control, but without the accompanying technical data. Derk also sent Toulouse a second message, tactfully requesting that Mission Control wait a further few hours for responses to their other requests. He knew it was eight o'clock in the evening at Mission Control, and that it would not be necessary to send the requested information until next morning in Toulouse, which meant that evening at the habitat. He would thus have plenty of time to consider carefully just what information to send about recent events.

Just before ten, there was another message from Leaf Valley, this time from Monique Montpellier, who was manning the communications room at the house. It stated that Don Carruthers and Jose Montoya had left with John Erway in a rover, a few minutes earlier, to travel in along the Tip Canyon road and fetch the two abandoned buggies. She expected them back around twelve. As soon as the buggies were back and charged up enough, she, Astrid, Don, and Jose would be driving back to the habitat—expected arrival time around two o'clock. In the meantime, Astrid was helping with the schooling of the two children, while Denise and Dr. Sato tended to Claude Bertrand. The message also confirmed that there was no change in Claude Bertrand's condition.

Derk immediately had Emma send a message to Monique, requesting that they return to the habitat immediately the buggies were operational. Derk then instructed Emma to send another message to Earth. It stated that Derk had arranged for John Erway, accompanied by Don and Jose, to drive out and fetch the two buggies abandoned in the labyrinth region. It also stated that Derk had ordered his four absent crew members to leave the compound in Leaf Valley, and drive back to the habitat, as soon as the buggies were back and operational. He also communicated that Dr. Lavoisier had stated that Claude Bertrand's condition was no better. The message neglected to state that Denise and Dr. Sato would be tending to Claude that morning, while Astrid looked after the two children.

In the course of the next hour, the four others at the habitat appeared, and all six had a late breakfast sitting at a table in the eating area in the central module. The morning sun slanted in through the window at the end of the table, but there was no good humor, and almost no conversation.

Afterward, at about eleven, Derk, Emma, and Jurgen sequestered themselves in the meeting room next door, in the command section. Derk gave strict orders to Vince, Karl, and Ursula that they not be disturbed. He also prohibited them from sending any messages to Earth about the events of the past twenty-four hours. They were to send routine habitat and weather information only.

While Derk was in the meeting, the other three performed routine chores, and manned the communications center. The routine habitat information they sent to Mission Control increased the frustration of just about everyone in ESA and in the media, most of whom, by now, were past their bedtimes and almost beside themselves with impatience.

The closed meeting lasted until one o'clock. Derk questioned Jurgen about every detail of the rescue the previous evening. He was particularly interested in everything Denise had done: every action, every syringe applied, where and when. And then he wanted to know every detail of what had happened when they got back to Leaf Valley after the rescue, particularly every action performed by Denise.

Jurgen was surprised by the details Derk wanted to know about, and was puzzled as to the reason. But Jurgen was by nature a loyal subordinate, who would never question his chief's motives, and so he did not ask. Nevertheless, Jurgen noticed himself feeling more and more uneasy during the meeting.

Jurgen Eindorf had always known about the true nature of the ESA mission. Before his arrival on Mars, he had had no problems with the mission's unofficial goal of rescuing the three in Leaf Valley, whether they wanted it or not. Although he did not know any of the three personally, he had been led to believe that isolation on Mars might cause them to be reluctant about being rescued. He could clearly see too, that they were in the way of legitimate progress that would result in a large and important European colony on Mars.

Since meeting the three, he had begun to have doubts. He admired competence and perfection, and took personal pride in his own technical competence. But the previous evening he had seen in one place, and observed in action, the three most competent people he had ever encountered. Previously, Derk had held that number one spot in Jurgen's estimation. As for what these three had accomplished on Mars—what he had seen with his own eyes—it blew his mind. He would not have thought it possible for just three people to accomplish so much.

He had thus, in a very short time, come to respect these three, and admire them. He admired Denise in particular. She was about his age, and never in his life had he encountered a woman like her. Had she not had a husband, whom she obviously was deeply in love with, and had he not had a quite strong liking for Ursula Schneider, the rather quiet and reserved but very clever biologist, he would have allowed himself to fall for Denise. In the days to come, the encounter with Denise would cause him to become even more appreciative of Ursula Schneider, who resembled Denise in many ways, and who liked Jurgen in return.

Jurgen's uneasy feelings were probably the result of knowing his chief well enough to know that Derk was contriving some deviously clever plan. He could not guess what it was, but whatever it was, and no matter how detrimental it was to the three inhabitants of Leaf Valley, particularly Denise, nor how much he might disapprove of it, Jurgen knew he would have to play the part in it that Derk decided.

*

As Monique had reported, a rover left the glass compound at Mount Tip just before ten that Wednesday morning, and headed along the Tip Canyon road toward the labyrinth, to retrieve the two abandoned buggies. John was driving, with Don and Jose sitting in the passenger seats.

Jose was in a somber mood, shaken by the death of Sheila. He had liked and respected Sheila, and had got on well with her. Nevertheless, the sight of the huge walls of the immense canyon they were driving through, the northwest wall glowing in the morning sun, did something to replace those somber feelings with the feeling of awe and wonder at the sheer grandeur of Mars. Jose, for all his resilience, determination, and discipline, was not blind to the splendor of the planet.

Don Carruthers, in contrast, was grief stricken at the loss of Sheila. His mind, which in normal circumstances would have been fascinated with the journey through Tip Canyon, hardly even registered it. He could think of nothing but Sheila. He blamed himself for her death, and knew now that he had been in love with her. He could not stop his mind from dredging up every detail of the previous few days, and brooding on all the what-ifs. Denise, aware of his state of mind, had asked John to take him along, out of sight of the body of Sheila lying in the compound.

The trip through the canyon was uneventful, as was the remainder of the journey, and they reached Don's abandoned buggy just after ten thirty.

By ten forty-five, the rover, with Don's buggy attached on a short tow line, was sitting in a shallow hollow near a mesa spur, in bright sunshine, and a little in front of Jose's buggy. It was in this hollow that Jose Montoya's buggy had run out of power the previous evening. John and Don were outside, busy attaching a towline to Jose's buggy.

Jose was also outside, and had just begun ridge walking up the slope of the spur of the nearby mesa. He was carrying Astrid's video camera, which he had retrieved from his buggy.

The long orange spur descended all the way down from the top of the mesa, and protruded to the west, forming a kind of corner between two of the mesa's escarpments, adjacent to each other. One of these two mesa escarpments faced south, and thus the road as well. The other mesa escarpment faced mostly west.

The ridge slope on the spur was much less steep than the escarpment slopes on either side of it, and Jose was determined to walk up it, to see the lie of the land, particularly the layout of the dune tongue that had nearly cost him his life. He also knew that his chief, and

Mission Control, would want to have a bird's eye view of the place where the tragedy had occurred.

John was interested too. When he and Don completed the towline attachment, Jose was not more than fifty meters away, but already some twenty meters above the hollow.

"Mr. Montoya," said John. "Hold your horses, we'd like to come with you."

Jose waited the few minutes it took John and Don to catch up with him, and the three of them then walked carefully up the orange ridge for another ten minutes. It was wide enough for them to walk side by side, and had only quite small angular rocks and stones lying on it. It posed no danger if they kept away from its steep orange-brown flanks, on either side, both of which looked unstable.

Where they stopped, and turned around to survey the rolling, red valley floor below, they were nearly two hundred and fifty feet up, and had a breathtaking view. The labyrinth region of Kasei Valley might be treacherous, but it was also a place of captivating beauty. Even Don Carruthers, hurting intensely inside from the emotional pain of the loss of Sheila, could not prevent his geological mind being mesmerized by the sight. Jose was more practical, and concentrated on recording the view in every direction.

From their vantage point, they could see dune fields everywhere, in every direction, in every valley, and in every gap between mesas. Some of the light orange dune fields were small, some very small, but some were quite extensive.

It was also apparent that the valley floor below, to the south, where the road lay, was different from other Martian valleys. Although the valley was rolling, and covered with the usual small rocks, eroded craterlets were sparse, evidence of the eroding power of the abrasive, sand-laden winds that scoured it every so often.

The floor of the mesa gap to their right, to the west of the mesa they were standing on, where the vehicles were parked, looked much like the floor of the valley where the road was. Looking west, past the buggies and rover, they could see the mesa on the other side of the gap, its escarpment glowing bright orange in the morning sun. Several large dune fields lay up against its escarpment edge.

Turning more to their right, looking to the north now, well through the mesa gap where the vehicles lay, there was a complexity of mesa escarpment walls in the distance. There were many small dune fields not far away, and a huge dune field in the distance.

On the valley floor to the south, the road could be seen as a gently winding orange ribbon. It was just over a mile away at the nearest point, which happened to be the point where it emerged from the dune tongue blocking the valley. It was now obvious that the long tongue had formed from two tongues that had joined near the road. It began about a mile to their left, beginning at the southern escarpment of the mesa they were standing on, and ended about a mile to their right, at the mesa on the other side of the road.

The orange-brown mesa on the other side of the road, directly opposite, started about two miles up the valley, to their left, on the other side of the dune tongue. It ran southeastward down the valley, to their right, for about eight miles. It had a highly irregular, but exquisitely sculpted, escarpment wall.

They could see through the mesa gap well to their left, on the other side of the road, where the long mesa began. There was a very large dune field well inside that gap, completely blocking it. Beyond this large dune field, through the gap, they could see another more distant escarpment wall.

"Last night we came around this spur we are standing on," explained Jose. "We thought we were headed straight for the road. Actually, we were turning to the left a little as we went, and hit the dune tongue first. But if that tongue of dunes had not been there we would have hit the road. We were not that far out."

"I see," said John. "You must have been darned close to the road when you hit the dunes." Anything involving risk was especially interesting to John. He was anxious to analyze this disaster, to understand exactly what had gone wrong, and why

"Yes, we were," said Jose. "The road would have been just a bit to the right, maybe only a few hundred meters away. We did not realize the dunes were the ones blocking the road. We thought they were just another obstacle. Maybe we had seen too many dunes. We had certainly come to dread running into them, and forgot we were actually aiming for the dune tongue blocking the road. So when we ran into it, we did not realize what it was, and we turned to the left to get round it—exactly the wrong thing to do. That decision took us back here, well away from the road."

"Bad guess," said John, in sympathy. "But a guess was probably all you were capable of. You were probably worn out and disoriented—eleven hours outside in pressure suits—and probably already getting less oxygen than you should."

"I know," put in Don Carruthers, sick to his heart, his mind seizing on yet another what-if. "If only Providence had guided us to turn right along the dunes instead. In minutes, we'd have hit the road and been headed along it. Jurgen would have picked up the distress signal at least fifteen minutes before he did. Sheila would still be alive—and Claude wouldn't be lying near death."

"I'm very sorry about Dr. Bell and Mr. Bertrand," said John, and paused. Then he added: "But you two are both very lucky to be alive, you know. I'm surprised you managed to get around this mesa at all. There was a very good chance the way round would have been blocked by dunes too. As you can see now, in daylight, there are dune fields everywhere."

"Our way actually was partly blocked by dunes," said Jose.

"Had it not been for Jose," explained Don, "we might not have made it round." He related the episode where some small dunes, at the edge of a large dune field, had blocked their way, and how Jose had got them all out to shovel and clear the sand with their legs, and then push the buggies through.

"Awful predicament to be in," said John, shuddering at the thought. "It was a good thing you didn't try to get round the mesa on the other side of the road. You can see that gap yonder is completely blocked by sand dunes further in. If you'd tried that first, it would've cost you another hour at least. Then you probably wouldn't have had enough time to get round this mesa. You'd never have been found in time."

"Going round this mesa was Astrid Larsson's plan," said Don, understanding now just how lucky they had all been, and thinking how he had come close to being responsible for even more deaths. "We were on this side of the valley, right beside the mesa, when we decided to drive around the dunes. I suppose Astrid figured it was safer to stick to the edge of the mesa in the dark, even if it meant driving a bit further back up the valley to get to the gap. The devil you know …. We never discussed going round the mesa on the other side of the road."

"Well, she got that one right," said John. "But I don't understand why your chief sent you on such a dangerous mission. The odds of it going badly wrong were very high. Didn't any of you object? Weren't you aware that this region is full of dunes? After all, it's a Mars mission you're on, not some do-or-die military expedition in wartime. Didn't you each have a say?"

"We knew there were dunes," said Don, broaching a subject he had been brooding on all morning, "but the terrain database maps showed only large dune fields here and there, nothing like what's really here. But that wasn't the deciding factor, as far as I know. I thought the trip was quite safe, and Captain Derk did too, because of the existence of the road. We were given to understand by your wife that it was a good, safe road, like the roads in Kasci Valley. It was that understanding that caused the Captain to send us this way."

"Your chief said something along the same lines yesterday evening," admitted John, frowning. Then he added quickly: "Are you saying that Denise told Captain Derk that there was a good, safe road through here?"

"Well, not exactly," said Don. "She told Sheila, and Sheila told me, and I told the Captain."

"But it's impossible that she could say such a thing," maintained John firmly. "Denise knows that this road is anything but safe. It's a proper road, and it's spectacularly scenic, but it's certainly not safe, especially for a buggy. Even in a rover you need to budget a lot more time than you might think on this road. Denise once got lost around here herself. Lucky for her she was in a rover. She was doing what you had to do last night—trying to get around a mesa to avoid dunes blocking the road. Denise knows this road well—and she always tells the truth. She wouldn't lie about a thing like that. And she liked Dr. Bell too. I know that for sure. She would never have said something to put her in harm's way."

"All I know is what Sheila told me on Monday," said Don. He was now puzzled though, because his gut told him John was speaking the truth. Could he have misinterpreted Sheila's words? If only he had discussed it more with her. He tried to think back to his last evening with Sheila, his mind searching for her words. Then he remembered that it was earlier that day, just after Sheila had treated Denise's dental problems, when she had told him about the road.

"I have to admit I don't remember Sheila's exact words when she told me about the road on Monday morning," he added. "I do remember I had a long conversation with her that evening. I remember mentioning that the expedition yesterday would be safe because there was a good safe road, and Sheila did not contradict me."

"Maybe she thought then that you had found that out from somewhere else," suggested John, suddenly worried about the possibility of the blame for the entire tragedy descending on his wife.

"Could be," said Don. "I suggest that you talk to your wife about it. She's the only one who can clear this matter up now."

"She has already clarified it, to Captain Derk himself," said John. "I heard her tell him last night, before she set out to look for you. She is sure that all she said to Dr. Bell was that there was a proper road through here, and that it was spectacularly scenic. Just one thing though, that I'd like to hear your side of. When my wife talked to Dr. Bell about the road, was that before or after Dr. Bell knew you were going to be driving this way?"

"It was definitely before Sheila knew anything about that," said Don. "It was only after the Captain discovered what your wife had said, that he decided to send us on the trip."

"I see," said John, a little relieved. "That agrees with what Denise said to Captain Derk yesterday evening. There has to have been a misunderstanding somewhere, or an exaggeration…" He was about to add 'on Dr. Bell's part', but thought it better to speak no ill of the dead.

There was silence for a moment, as all three of them reflected on the consequence of a few pivotal words, allegedly from Denise.

Then Don Carruthers spoke again, changing the subject, but still focussing on Sheila. He had thoughts only for Sheila and the circumstances of her death.

"May I ask a favor?" he said. "I know I've no authority to ask, but I would like you both to help me build a small cairn on the valley floor at the tip of this spur. It would have been there, more or less, where Sheila died. I would like to recite a prayer at the spot too. Sheila would have liked that, I'm sure. At least she died in a beautiful place, even if she never saw it in daylight. She had a passion for beautiful places when she was alive."

"I guess that's the right thing to do," said John, as Jose also nodded in agreement. "I'd been thinking we should mark that spot one day, if nothing else then as a warning to others."

Some twenty-five minutes later, the three men were back down on the valley floor, and had built a cairn of black stones at the tip of the mesa spur, about five feet high.

"Sheila was quite religious—a Catholic," said Don, when they had finished. "Do any of you know the Catholic *Our Father*? The Protestant version wouldn't be quite right. What about you, Jose?"

"I only know the words in Spanish," said Jose, somewhat absently. His thoughts were elsewhere.

"I believe it's the same as the Protestant one, if you leave out the last sentence," said John. At that moment, the thought of another funeral on Mars flashed into his mind, along with the thought of a big service on Earth to go with it. These thoughts brought back memories of the burial of his eleven NASA companions, ten years earlier.

"All right," said Don, "I'll use that. But I'm going to change a few words, so that it fits Mars better."

"Hold on a minute," said John. "I think we should record this."

"I should have thought of that," said Jose, whose mind had been elsewhere. He had listened intently to the earlier conversation between John and Don about Sheila and Denise, and was still memorizing it. He knew that Captain Derk would be very interested.

Putting that subject out of his mind, Jose walked to his buggy, lying just north of the cairn, and fetched the video camera. He then walked a few meters south of the cairn, made a small pile of stones, fitted the camera on top and turned it on, with the audio facility and radio antenna set to record Don's voice with the images.

The three then stood beside the cairn, facing the sun and the camera, as Don Carruthers recited the prayer. This is what he said:

'Our Father, who art in Heaven, Hallowed be Thy Name.
Thy Kingdom come, Thy will be done on Earth,
As it is on Mars, and as it is in Heaven.
Give us this Mars day our daily bread,
And forgive us our trespasses,
As we forgive them who trespass against us;
And lead us not into temptation, but deliver us from evil,
On Earth, and on Mars ... Amen.'

Building the cairn at the place where Sheila had died, and reciting the prayer there, did serve a useful function. It helped the living. In particular, it helped Don overcome a small part of his intense pain, and so heal a small part of the wound. And the video recording of the simple ceremony would also help many of his companions on the mission, and many on Earth who had loved Sheila Bell, to come to terms with her death.

The cairn these three built that day remained standing, untouched for many decades, except by the abrasive, sand-laden, labyrinth winds. In time, a monument to the early explorers of Mars would be built on the spot, and would stand watch over a major transportation artery that ran down the valley, protected from errant dune tongues by huge glass sand guards.

An hour later, just before twelve, the three were back at the compound on Mount Tip. John parked the rover outside the rover airlock, and the three of them went outside in pressure suits to unhitch the buggies from the rover, and the trailers from the buggies.

They then pushed the buggies through the airlock, one of them as far as the parking pad close to the other rover, to enable them both to be inside. In a few minutes, John and Jose had them both under charge. In an hour, their batteries would have more than enough charge for the short trip back to the habitat, where there would be ample time to charge them fully.

*

It was nearly twelve twenty, noon on Mars, that same Wednesday morning, not long after the rover had returned from the labyrinth, towing the two dead buggies. Denise was just completing an hour-long series of measurements on the residual electrical activity in the brain of Claude Bertrand. The patient lay on the bed in the surgery, an array of wires and tubes attached to his body. His general condition had not improved.

Denise, with the assistance of Dr. Sato, and his electronic monitors and displays, had checked out every part of Claude's brain that was amenable to electrode probes on the cranium. She was now certain that recovery was impossible.

John was standing near the door, just inside the small surgery. Jose, Monique, and Don crowded the doorway looking on. Astrid had remained with the children in their playroom downstairs, to keep them out of the way.

"Your expression tells me you think there's no hope," said John.

"No, I'm now certain there's none," said Denise. "For all practical purposes, he's already dead. There's no brain activity to speak of, other than the little needed to keep his basic bodily functions operating—circulation and breathing. He's what a lay person would call brain dead."

"Are you absolutely sure, Doctor?" asked Monique, from the doorway. "This man is very important to us—and the most famous structural engineer in Europe. If there is even a faint hope, perhaps there are doctors on Earth who might know of a treatment that could save him."

"I was sure last night," said Denise, "and I've just spent the last hour trying to prove myself wrong, which I failed to do. The brain activity readings are conclusive. There's no chance whatever that he will ever regain consciousness. His brain is damaged beyond repair."

"So what will you do now?" asked John.

"I'm going to disconnect everything, and neutralize a mild stimulant I gave him this morning, and let Nature take its course," said Denise.

"How long before he dies if you do that?" asked John.

"Fifteen minutes to half an hour," said Denise.

Nobody moved away, as Dense administered an injection, after which she and Dr. Sato removed all the wires, electrodes and tubes. Then Denise excused herself and went out of the surgery, and downstairs, to the children's room.

"Claude Bertrand is dying," she said to Astrid. "You may want to join the others."

Upstairs, Dr. Sato remained by Claude's bed, motionless, as if meditating. John moved closer beside him, arms folded. A minute later Astrid appeared, and maneuvered her way into the room, beside John. The other three stayed near the door, in silent vigil, watching the last few minutes of the life of a fellow astronaut they had all known intimately.

The minutes ticked by. At twelve forty-two, Dr. Sato drew the pale-blue, parachute-fabric sheet up over Claude's face.

Some fifteen minutes later, following a brief consultation with Denise, the four survivors of the expedition along Hazard Valley wrapped the body in light green parachute cloth, and carried it outside, to lay it on the patio by the pool, beside Sheila's. It was all Don could do to keep himself from breaking down and weeping, not merely over the death of Sheila, but over the fact that his leadership of a simple geological expedition had resulted in this, after only two days on Mars. How could he ever hold his head up again? He felt not only anguish, but deep shame.

A few minutes before one o'clock, Don and Jose, together with Astrid and Monique, left for the habitat in the two recovered buggies. Just before, Don Carruthers had excused himself, to make a final visit to Sheila Bell, lying beside the body of Claude Bertrand, at peace on the patio, surrounded by greenery.

Before the ESA four left, they thanked the three who dwelt in Leaf Valley for all that had been done to help them, indeed, if truth be told, for their very lives. Each of them understood very well, that without the efforts of those three, their bodies too might now be lying on the patio beside the pool.

Denise then went to the communications room and sent a message to the habitat.

At the habitat, after Derk's meeting with Jurgen and Emma ended, just after one, Derk went across the hallway to the communications room, to discover that a further message had just arrived from the compound at Mount Tip. It was from Denise. It stated that the four survivors were medically fit, and had just left for the habitat, five minutes earlier. It also stated that Claude Bertrand had died twenty minutes earlier. The message contained an expression of condolences from John and herself, and from Dr. Sato, to Derk and his mission, to Claude's family, and the people of France, and to Sheila's family and the people of Ireland.

Derk had Emma forward her message to Mission Control in Toulouse two hours later, omitting the condolences.

Denise had not yet grasped the true nature of the man she was dealing with. If she had, she might have made an effort to send the message direct to Toulouse, herself, via the ESA stationary satellite. It would have been difficult for her to do this, unfortunately. She did not know the access codes and protocols needed to use the dish pointed at the ESA satellite, to communicate directly with Mission Control, as Emma had done, and was sure Derk would not let her have them. She was right about that, for exclusive control of communications between Mars and Toulouse was important to Derk.

Neither Denise nor John had ever communicated directly with ESA Mission Control in Toulouse. Before the ESA mission had left Earth, John had dealt with a different ESA body, the mission planning and negotiating group in Paris, and John had also communicated with the ESA mother ship on its way to Mars. Nevertheless, Denise could have tried to persuade Derk to grant her just a temporary channel to Toulouse that day. But she was just far too tired to go to that trouble, still exhausted after a long night, little sleep, and a busy morning. She did the most convenient thing instead.

She did not yet understand that she could not even trust Derk to convey a simple expression of her genuine sorrow at the deaths of two of his crew. She was genuinely saddened by the fact that one of them was a fellow citizen of France, a man who had left the world a better place than he had found it, and that the other was a much loved doctor, whom she had liked too.

The message arrived in the middle of the night in France, and the people of France woke up to the news of Claude Bertrand's death on Tuesday morning. The news had not been unexpected, but the nation, and indeed most of Europe, did receive a shock. The French were also upset that no expression of condolences had accompanied the message from Denise. The Irish were similarly upset that Denise had not expressed any sorrow at the death of Sheila.

Later that afternoon, after the buggies had arrived back at the habitat, and they had all eaten a late lunch, Derk sequestered himself with Monique Montpellier, questioning her about the events of that morning in the compound, especially about the activities of Denise. At an even later meeting that afternoon, with all four survivors of the Hazard Valley expedition, Derk listened intently to their account of the expedition along Hazard Valley, and viewed Astrid's video recordings.

At first, Derk did not closely question either Jose Montoya or Don Carruthers about their rover trip with John Erway that morning, to fetch the abandoned buggies. He was satisfied with a brief account of the trip and the location of the abandoned buggies with respect to the dune tongue blocking the road, and with a brief viewing of the video from the scene, recorded in daylight.

However, when he discovered that a lengthy exchange had taken place between Don and John Erway, about what Denise had told Sheila about the state of the Hazard Valley road, he became intensely interested. He sequestered himself in the meeting room alone with Jose for ten minutes, and got Jose to relate every detail of the conversation. Jose, knowing his chief would be very interested, had carefully memorized just about every word of it.

In the course of that afternoon, Derk was primarily concerned with the facts surrounding the deaths of Sheila and Claude. Neither his expressions nor his words betrayed any sign of personal grief at the deaths, something noticed by every one of the four expedition survivors, but particularly by the very observant and astute Astrid Larsson.

*

After Denise sent the message about Claude's death to the habitat, she retired to her room. She was still exhausted, and slept for nearly two hours. Dr. Sato, also very tired, retired to his room to rest and meditate.

John, meanwhile, took the two children with him through an airtight door at the south end of the garden. This heavy door in the compound's foundation wall was low down, and opened into a short, buried tunnel that quickly became a plant-lined passageway that descended to the greenhouses and laboratory on the valley floor. John often took the children with him on visits to the greenhouses.

The orange-concrete passageway down to the greenhouses was below ground level, but had a glass slab roof set in aluminum frames, to let the sun shine in on the many plants growing along it.

Originally, when they had first built the greenhouses, John had kept the inside pressures at only half of Earth's atmospheric pressure. Later, with more experience, tests had showed that they could easily tolerate a much higher pressure, some ninety percent of Earth's, which was the same as the much higher pressure inside the glass compound and connecting passageway.

John spent the next few hours tending the greenhouses, listening to his children's shrieks of laughter and joy as they played hide and seek among the plants. Eventually he gave in to the children's demands and joined them in their game.

When they returned to the compound, around three, Denise was up again, and needed assistance in the next and obvious task.

A short time later, John and Dr. Sato were in the workshop of the industrial complex, busy making two copper caskets. They worked efficiently, Dr. Sato making the copper frames, while John cut out sheets of thin copper to fit.

They had a good supply of sheet copper in readiness, for which they had a variety of uses. They had made it using the same simple electrolytic process used on Earth to produce sheet copper.

The workshop was bright, with copper framed glass-slab windows, and was pressurized, but only with Martian air, which they could not breathe. This allowed them to work without pressure suits, merely requiring that they use a small backpack and a mask to supply breathable air.

When they had finished the caskets, Dr. Sato skillfully embedded a small aluminum cross in each of their copper lids. The heritage of the two dead would be respected.

Denise, meanwhile, in her workroom upstairs in the house, had not been idle. Using parachute cloth of various colors, she had sewn together four small flags, each flag about two feet square. She had made the flag of the European Union—two of these, the flag of France and the flag of Ireland. The yellow stars on the European flag had given her the most trouble, but she had persevered and had made four very fine flags. She had also collected three bunches of flowers from the garden.

*

The sun was low above the west wall of Leaf Valley, just before five fifteen that afternoon. A procession of two rovers approached Outlook Shelf, which lay just inside Leaf Valley, near its southwest corner. The late afternoon sky to the west, above the nearby western escarpment wall of the valley, was beginning to turn from pink to a deep purple red.

Outlook Shelf lay high up, where the southwest wall of Leaf Valley ended and the north wall of the smaller Stem Valley began. The two adjacent walls formed a promontory with a commanding view of the south end of Leaf Valley. From this promontory, you had a view of Leaf Valley, Stem Valley, and Stem Gap, and even out through Stem Gap and beyond, to the high escarpment wall running along the northwestern edge of Elbow Plain. From the promontory, as well, you could clearly see that there was a unique rampart lying on top of this escarpment wall.

The commanding view would not have made this promontory so very special, had that been all. Other places on Mars have commanding views too. But it was not all. A flat shelf protruded from the promontory, several thousand feet below it, but still several thousand feet above the floor of Leaf Valley. There was a commanding view from this shelf too.

This was Outlook Shelf, over a square mile in area, and almost as sheltered as Leaf Valley. The three had built the first monastery on Mars at the eastern end of this shelf, close to the escarpment falling away down to the valley floor—it was a Zen Buddhist monastery, and the home of Dr. Sato.

Dr. Sato was driving the first of the two rovers, as they approached the shelf. John drove the second rover, with Denise and the two children beside him. In the trailer of the second rover lay two empty copper caskets, and lying in the two bunks inside the rover were the wrapped bodies of Sheila and Claude.

They were taking the bodies to the monastery, to lie there until the burial, which Denise also had very strong ideas about. It had been Denise's idea to take the bodies to the monastery, an idea with which Dr. Sato and John were in complete agreement.

Just before they had left home, twenty minutes earlier, Denise had sent Captain Derk a message, informing him where the bodies would lie until their burial, and stating her opinion as to where they should be buried too.

Denise had always lamented the makeshift way the bodies of her eleven companions had been buried opposite Funnyface Mesa after the explosion ten years earlier. She and John had simply taken the bodies from where they lay, in the aftermath of the rocket explosion that had killed them. They had wrapped each of them in a sheet of bedding, placed them in the rover trailer two or three at a time, driven them to the gravesite, and put them in their graves.

She had always thought that those eleven had deserved better, but, at the time, that was the best they could do. Since then, they had done more. In addition to a cairn at the head of each grave, there was now a slab of orange concrete, between cairn and grave, giving names, dates, and religious heritage of its occupant, as well a reference to the Mars mission of 2038. Each grave of those with a Christian heritage now had a copper cross as well.

Denise would see to it that Sheila and Claude were treated better. She owed Sheila a favor anyway, for the dental work she had so willingly carried out. And Claude was a famous man, and a fellow citizen of France. She was in a position to give Sheila and Claude far better treatment than the ESA mission in the cramped habitat at Elbow Hill could do, and was determined to do so.

Denise was not religious, but as a scientist, she had a profound knowledge of natural processes, particularly biological processes. She had also developed a deep understanding of Buddhism, particularly Zen Buddhism, through her curiosity, learning, and ten-year association with Dr. Sato. This knowledge of both natural processes and Zen had imparted to her a grasp of the mystery of human existence … the mystery of the human consciousness, of its coming into being and going out of being. It was a mystery that science and reason so far had been unable to unravel, and which to her was the basis of all religion.

It thus seemed to her that the dead could best be honored among the living by allowing them to lie, prior to burial, in a special place set aside for the contemplation of this mystery. There was only one place on Mars where that was possible—the Zen monastery on Outlook Shelf, and Denise knew just the place inside the monastery where Sheila and Claude should lie.

The road up to the shelf from the valley floor was the most daring they had ever built. John and Dr. Sato had used the minicat, years earlier, to cut this road out of the steep escarpment flowing down from the shelf.

The road began nearly a mile inside Outlook Cove, which was an embayment in the west wall of Leaf Valley just north of Outlook Shelf. The slope of the escarpment down from Outlook Shelf was gentler at Outlook Cove than anywhere else.

There was a road into Outlook Cove, for it was in this embayment that they extracted their raw volcanic rock for making cement. Instead of continuing westward along the road, deeper into the cove, the procession now turned left, at a point nearly a mile past the entrance, onto a road that curved back almost one hundred and eighty degrees, and then began to go sideways up the escarpment toward the east. The road continued sideways up the escarpment in this way, getting steadily higher above the valley floor. It was quite steep, about one in four, and climbed steadily for a full mile and a half before reaching the top. A string of light stones marked the edge of the road on the left, all the way up, on the side sloping down to the valley floor.

The drive up along the road was quite something. It was a favorite with the two children, and as they drove carefully up, the children tried to stand up, to see down the sloping escarpment to their left.

When they reached the top and could drive onto the flat shelf, a huge escarpment wall became clearly visible about three quarters of a mile away to their right, across the shelf and toward the west. This was the promontory escarpment, where the west wall of Leaf Valley ended and the north wall of Stem Valley began. It lay shadowy and foreboding, silhouetted against the deepening purple red color of the early evening sky behind it, to the west.

The shelf was red and littered with angular rocks. It rolled a little, and had the occasional small crater, like a Martian valley floor.

The road led well away from the edge at first, and then turned to head almost east, towards a glass and orange-concrete building, glowing and gleaming in the late day sun, about a half mile away.

About a hundred meters from the building, the procession stopped. Dr. Sato stopped because he knew John would. John always did when he came there. It was the sight. It overwhelmed, no matter how many times you had seen it in the past.

The building was very near the eastern end of the shelf. From where the rovers stopped, it stood out against the backdrop of magnificent views, particularly the view across Leaf Valley to the high rampart on top of the escarpment opposite. But there was also the view of Stem Gap to the right, and the view of the now much shadowed Stem Mountains to the far right.

The building itself was simple, and resembled the Parthenon of Ancient Greece somewhat, not by intent, but by necessity. It was a rectangular building, but with rounded corners, with orange concrete pillars around the outside, each about six feet apart and about twenty feet high. Glistening brown copper frames were embedded between the orange pillars to hold glass slabs, sealing the inside from the outside, and maintaining the huge pressure difference.

They stopped only for about thirty seconds. The business at hand was too solemn for sight seeing.

They drove on to the south corner of the west wall, where there was a driveway down to an airlock door, about twelve feet below the level of the shelf. It was similar to the rover airlock at the glass enclosure at Mount Tip. Dr. Sato stopped his rover to the left of the driveway, while John drove down, and into the airlock. Inside the huge airlock, normally occupied only by the Zen master's buggy, there was room for only one rover with a trailer. John waited before closing the airlock door behind him, until Dr. Sato had walked through the door, clad in his white pressure suit.

The airlock pressurized, Dr. Sato removed his suit, and placed it in a closet in the wall of the airlock, while John and Denise took the body of Sheila out of the rover and placed it in a casket. They carried the casket through the wide door at the front of the airlock, and up some wide concrete steps to the ground level.

The enclosed compound was modest in size, one hundred feet wide by two hundred long, the long length running east-west. It had some twenty pillars of copper and concrete to hold the glass roof down, against the enormous air pressure trying to explode it upwards, just as in the glass-enclosed compound at Mount Tip. There was a wide assortment of bushes and plants thickly covering the grounds, and here and there you could see rocks. Dr. Sato's idea of a garden on Mars was somewhat different from Denise's, but had in common with the garden at Mount Tip that it manufactured necessary oxygen.

The monastery had four small buildings within its enclosed grounds. There were two along its long north side, first a small meditation hall, and then a small prayer hall. There was a bigger one in the southeast corner, the Zen master's small residence. The fourth building lay in the southwest corner near the airlock. That was the monastery workshop.

Each of the small buildings was made of orange concrete, with glass windows set in copper frames. Climbing plants grew over all four buildings, as well as up the central concrete and copper pillars, supporting a double glass slab roof. As much greenery as possible was essential for the production of oxygen. Water circulated between the glass slabs of the roof, to protect the plants and humans from radiation, in case of a strong solar flare.

A path led from the airlock, past the workshop, and eastward along the middle of the compound, between high bushes and plants. There were also paths branching from this central path to the other three buildings. The central path stopped at a somewhat raised patio at the center of the enclosure's east wall, from which you could practically look over the edge of the escarpment just outside.

John and Denise carried the casket along this path to the patio, as the children followed along. The children were somehow aware of the solemnity of the occasion, and did not run off to play their usual games in the monastery garden, and among its buildings.

They laid Sheila on the left side of the fifteen-foot square, orange-concrete patio, which was almost right up against the glass of the east wall. Ten minutes later, Claude's casket lay on the right side of the patio, beside Sheila's. The caskets lay almost touching the wall's central glass slab, framed between two huge orange pillars. Branches and leaves of green plants hung over the raised patio on either side.

Next they draped the flags over the caskets, leaving the crosses visible. Then they placed one large bunch of flowers on the concrete between the two caskets, and a small bunch of flowers at the foot of each casket. It was about six o'clock when they finished, and the sun had not yet set.

Behind the caskets, through the glass of the monastery's east wall, was the most magnificent view in the whole of Kasei Valley, possibly on all Mars. The top of the high rampart to the west, as well as the eastern wall of Leaf Valley, and the tops of Stem Mountains to the south, the precipices at Stem Gap, all lay glowing in the light of the setting sun. The bright orange color of these tops contrasted vividly with the lengthening shadows lower down.

A video camera was soon in place on a small tripod at the feet of the two caskets, in time to record the sunset scene—and the sunrise, noon day, and sunset scenes the following day too.

That evening's video of the glowing mountain and escarpment tops, with lengthening sunset shadows, and with the two caskets in the foreground, each adorned with flowers, flags and a Christian cross, and lying in a peaceful Martian monastery, would be seen and appreciated soon on every media outlet on Earth.

Shortly afterward, Denise and John were headed back across the shelf to the escarpment road down to the valley floor. They had a rule that the escarpment road was never to be driven after dark. It was simply too dangerous—one mistake and a rover or buggy would be tumbling down the steep escarpment.

It was nearly six twenty when they arrived at the start of the road down the escarpment. It was still quite bright, for the sun was just visible, beneath its pink-blue sunset fan, above Leaf Valley's western escarpment wall to their left, a little south of the promontory. Before driving down the escarpment road, John stopped the rover, as he often did, to survey the valley below. This time the children did not jump up to see down, as they usually did. They were both fast asleep in the large seat beside Denise.

From this height, they could see all of Leaf Valley lying to the north of Outlook Shelf, to Mount Tip, some ten miles away, and beyond, to the small Tip Valley at the tip of Leaf Valley. The large glass walls enclosing their home and garden on the shelf on Mount Tip looked tiny in the distance, but still managed to reflect the pink, pink-red, and purple-red colors of the sunset sky.

The sun had now set, and as they sat there looking out at the valley, and the brilliant sky above it, a tear began to trickle down Denise's face. "It makes me sentimental just looking at it, John," she said, a minute later, after she had wiped the tear away with her hand. "I can't bear to leave it. It'll break my heart if we have to. Do you think we still will, after what's happened?"

"Last night I had thought that Derk had shot himself in the foot, and that we were safe," said John, "but I've been thinking a lot about it today, and right now I don't think we're safe at all."

"What's caused you to change your mind?"

"A lot of factors," said John. "The first is that I think Derk can manage with the reduced manpower. He was planning on keeping a garrison of eight here, and sending us back to Earth with a crew of four. Now he's lost two. I thought last night he would still need to send back four, so that he'd have only six left, and no doctor, which might not be enough. However, I think now he could get away with sending back only two, so he would still have eight people left to carry out his plans for here."

"And since that Austrian biologist, Ursula Schneider, has human biology training, she could serve as mission doctor," said Denise.

"Right," said John. "You need somebody with medical skills on Mars."

"But he's lost Claude Bertrand," said Denise. "I've been puzzled about why they sent such a famous structural engineer. They must have some big construction plans in mind we don't know about. Without him they may be crippled."

"Possible," said John, "but I doubt it. That young Swedish woman is also a structural engineer, as well as a geologist, and so is the Italian, Vince Cassoni. I was talking to Derk about the skills his people had last night. Perhaps those two are not as good as Claude Bertrand, but with some help from experts on Earth, they may well be able to take his place."

"Astrid Larsson's no fool," said Denise. "Actually I quite like her. She appears to be quite cold and detached, but she's really quite a considerate and reasonable person. She's definitely not a hardened military type, like Jose Montoya."

"Jose's also the second flight engineer," said John. "I lay you odds it'll still be him who's supposed to fly us back to Earth, although it could be Karl Mannhardt, the third flight engineer."

"But wouldn't two on the mother ship be just too few to keep the three of us under control on the way back? Wouldn't Derk be worried we might overpower a crew of only two, take over, and bring the spacecraft back to Mars?"

"No, not at all," said John. "If we were on board, once that lander left the ground, there'd be nothing we could do to avoid going back to Earth. When the lander was back in orbit, there'd be no way to get it down here again, since the fuel would be nearly all gone. As well as that, once the mother ship had blasted out of Mars orbit, there wouldn't be enough propellant left to turn that ship back to Mars either. And even if any of that could be done, it would take an expert flight engineer to do it, and neither of us has any spacecraft flight engineering skills worth talking about. Once that vehicle lifts off, and we're on it, that's it. All we could do is help the crew ensure a safe journey back to Earth. Any funny tricks would just endanger everybody's lives, for no good reason. On top of that, if we were nuts enough to try any tricks, and we weren't all killed, they'd probably throw us in jail for endangerment when we got back to Earth."

"I hadn't realized it was that bad," said Denise.

"It's that bad."

"So if only one person were needed to fly the lander and mother ship, our presence wouldn't matter, and that single crew member would be enough."

"It would," said John. "We'd still be powerless, although I'm sure the ship needs at least two to fly it safely. In a pinch though, they could also get our help to carry out assigned tasks. It would not be in our interest to refuse."

"I see," said Denise.

"A drop in Derk's standing with the top brass in ESA, as a result of what's happened, could have been a big positive," said John. "I was thinking last night that they would probably lose confidence in him, when they found out that the whole thing was his fault. But now I don't think so. That's the second factor I've changed my mind about. I'm sorry Denise, but prepare for a shock. I think Derk's going to try and blame you."

"Me!" cried Denise. "How? I had nothing to do with it. In fact, it's just the opposite. Not only did I have nothing to do with it, but without my help, and Dr. Sato's, and yours too, Derk would have lost all six of them. And he knows that very well."

"Take it easy, Denise," said John, reaching over to take her hand. "I know. But I'm beginning to think this man's a bigger devil than either of us ever would have thought possible. I think he's going to accuse you of deliberately misleading his mission into believing that there was a good, safe road through Hazard Valley and Tip Canyon, and in that way absolve himself of all blame, and lay the entire blame on you."

"But I never said any such thing," cried Denise. "You know very well I would never have said such a thing."

"I know it only too well, and I'm sure by now that Derk knows it too. But the only person who can actually confirm that you never said it is dead, and that's what I think he'll rely on, to blacken you and excuse himself."

"But if they're fair minded in ESA, they'll investigate and the truth will come out," protested Denise. She was shaken to her soul, at the thought of being accused of being responsible for the deaths of Sheila and Claude, however accidental.

"I've been thinking about that too," said John, "ever since this morning out in the labyrinth." He recounted the conversation he had had with Don Carruthers about what Denise was purported to have said to Sheila. "Don Carruthers believes that you told Sheila there was a good road, because he believes that's what Sheila told him. The top ESA brass is more likely to believe the members of its own mission than believe you. On top of that, even if they suspect the truth, they may still not want to investigate. They may be quite happy to crucify you, even if they know the charges against you aren't true, as long as the public in Europe thinks they're true. A lot of people in Europe are going to be hopping mad at what's happened, and if you don't get the blame, then Derk, and ESA too, to some extent, will get it. ESA will likely be quite happy to deflect the blame somewhere else."

"You think they're that bad?" said Denise. "I find that hard to believe. I was once part of ESA, and everybody was honest and dedicated then."

"That was ten years ago," said John, "when ESA was primarily concerned with science and the exploration of space."

Denise said nothing for a while, as she reflected on this.

"Maybe," she said eventually. "I hope not, but you may be right. ESA is now being used to achieve the colonial ambitions of the E.U. And when there's big money involved, I'll admit little ethical niceties won't have a high priority. Outside of the technology world, and sometimes inside it too, ambitious people don't usually get into positions of power by being all that ethical."

"My only problem is understanding what's driving all this," said John. "Why are they so anxious to get control of this valley—but without us? No matter how it works out, the whole thing looks to me like it's just one big cost for the E.U., or the U.S., if the U.S. had got here first. Is it just political prestige? Are the U.S. and the E.U. behaving like two spoiled kids—each one wanting to say to the other: 'Ha! Ha! Ha! I've got a Mars colony and you haven't'?"

"Europeans have never gone after colonies just for prestige," said Denise thoughtfully. "They've always been after the resources they could get from them. Don't forget Europe's relatively resource poor. It's always come down to the money and profits they could extract from their colonies."

"But there's no way you can make money out of a Mars colony," said John. "It's just one big expense."

"I'm beginning to wonder about that; profit could be what's at the bottom of it," said Denise. "Remember the very first thing Derk did when he got here. He drove down to Chiselhead Mountain to inspect the copper deposits. You can be sure his geologists have figured out how much copper's there, and that ESA now knows too."

"But the amount doesn't matter," said John. "Even a tiny fraction of what's there would be enough for any Mars colony for centuries to come."

"Is there any way they could get large quantities of copper back to Earth cheaply?" asked Denise. "If they could, it would explain everything."

"No," said John, "you'd need some lifting vehicle that was a hundred percent energy efficient. A rocket is hopeless. At launch, most of the energy in the fuel goes to the velocity of the exhaust gases. The rocket payload gets only a tiny bit of the energy. That's why it takes so much fuel to launch a rocket into space. For example, it takes two thousand tons of fuel and oxidizer on Earth to launch a conventional space shuttle. It'll take over a hundred tons in the tanks to get that ESA lander back up into orbit."

"Remember I asked you about the project Sheila Bell said ESA was working on in southwest Ireland," said Denise, "what she called 'reel launches', and you said you'd never heard of anything like that. I'm wondering if it could have anything to do with that copper?"

"You mean a reel launch for launching copper into space bound for Earth," suggested John. "Makes no sense to me, I'm afraid."

"I know, but it must be something like that," said Denise. "That reminds me. Maybe 'reel launch' is the wrong name. Remember that video recording Sheila Bell gave me for the children?"

John nodded.

"Well," she continued, "it has two cartoon movies in it for small children. I was watching bits of it yesterday evening with the children, between times, while I was getting supper ready for our guests. One of the movies is about a secret railroad run by leprechauns, for transporting their gold from one place to another. The cartoon characters all have strong Irish accents and I couldn't help noticing that they called a railroad a 'reelway'. Could Sheila Bell's 'reel launch' have been a 'rail launch'? Does that mean anything to you."

"A rail launcher, or rail gun, you mean!"

"Rail launcher? Is there such a thing?"

"There certainly is," said John. "It's a device with a pair of twin rails, and a big electromagnetic energy source. An object can be accelerated along the rails and come off the end at a speed greater than the escape velocity of Earth, and certainly of Mars."

"I suppose it must waste a lot of energy, just like a rocket."

"On the contrary, it's one hundred percent efficient," said John. "All the energy goes into the projectile. In theory you could launch a one-hundred ton space projectile with a rail launcher for the same energy it would take to launch a one-ton payload in a rocket."

"Then why haven't rail launchers replaced rockets?"

"For two good reasons, at least," said John. "First, on Earth, anything launched at escape velocity, about twenty-five thousand miles an hour, would come shooting off the rail launcher like a meteor, so fast it would likely burn up, at least partly, going up through the atmosphere. On top of that, you couldn't have human beings inside a vehicle shot out of a rail launcher. The acceleration along the rails would tear them apart—enormous G forces."

"What about on Mars?" asked Denise. "The air's a lot thinner here, and the escape velocity's a lot less."

"Yes, it could work here a lot better. In theory, you could use it to launch large copper blocks into space. If a copper block was shaped something like a bullet, or better still, like an arrow head, with a thin coating of ceramic heat shielding tiles at the tip of the arrow head, that would be enough to keep it from burning up as it shot up through the thin air here."

"Could that be it?" asked Denise. "Could that be what ESA is working on in that secret facility in Ireland?"

"Well," said John, with puckered brow. "I'll admit that if you were testing a rail launcher, the southwest of Ireland would be the best place in Europe to do it. You'd need a good slope to lay the rails on, such as the side of a mountain, and a good expanse of ocean, down range. They have some reasonable mountains there, and the Atlantic Ocean to the south. In theory, if you could solve all the problems, you could launch into polar Earth orbit from there."

"Sheila Bell said there was no political fight in Europe over where to locate that ESA research facility, as there usually is," said Denise. "If it was a rail launch facility, that would explain it, if what you say is true. There's no other place in Europe with a good mountain and a good down-range ocean, and a decent climate. It seems to me that it has to be a rail launcher ESA is developing."

"I admit the evidence supports a rail launcher development, at least on the surface," said John, "and if it's true, it explains everything. It would also explain why they had Claude Bertrand on the mission. If they were intending to build such a thing on Mars they'd want the skills of the best structural engineer available. I've just one problem. I don't believe it."

"Why not?"

"I'm speaking now as an engineer, Denise," said John. "I know the theory of rail launchers. It's good. All the energy gets converted into propulsion energy for whatever you launch. So in theory, it's ideal for launching heavy objects from the Earth's moon, and good for Mars too. But you need lots of energy. You'd need a big nuclear fusion power plant to supply electrical power. A fusion reactor for the energy supply could be built here. It would be a big engineering project, but it could be done. You'd also need a suitable slope for the rails of the launcher, about twenty miles long. And it would have to slope up toward the east to take advantage of the planet's rotational speed. But I suppose we have that—"

"Like on the rampart over there, on the northwest wall of Kasei Valley," said Denise, looking over at the high rampart, only five miles away, to her right. The rampart was now darkened, but still clearly visible against the eastern sky in the now fading light.

"Hold your horses," cautioned John. "I agree that the thing is possible in principle. But it's impossible in practice. The problem is with the operation of the rail launcher itself. The energy has to be released very quickly, in something like sixty seconds, because that's all it takes for the object to accelerate along the rails and fly off at escape velocity. An enormous electrical energy would have to be produced and released in just a few seconds, to power shooting a large copper block off the rails at escape velocity. That block would be coming off at six times the speed of a rifle bullet.

"Can you imagine that? No pretty pictures of the launch—just a split-second streak going up into the sky. No power plant could ever provide the power at the rate needed. That's why a big rail launcher has never been built. You can build small ones, by storing up energy in racks of conventional batteries, and then releasing the lot almost at once. The U.S. military even has tanks and ships armed with small rail guns. I just can't see how you could do it for launching something like a 100-ton copper block—I imagine you'd need to launch blocks at least that big to make it pay. I would say it's well beyond the technological level of either the U.S. or the E.U. Anyway, if the E.U. was developing that, the U.S. would be onto them. They couldn't keep it a secret. There'd likely be rumors floating around about it, especially on the computer networks, and we'd likely have picked up something. But we haven't. And anyway, as I say, it's just not technologically possible at the present time."

"Could the E.U. have made some advance that would make it possible?" persisted Denise.

"I guess that's always possible, but I can't see how," said John, shaking his head.

"Then how do you explain that ESA project in Ireland that looks like it could be a rail launcher project?"

"I can't," said John, "but I'm going to think very hard about it. I promise you that. There's obviously something going on that we probably should know about. But if it should turn out that you're right, and that what the E.U. and ESA are up to is shipping that copper in Chiselhead Mountain back to Earth at a profit, then we're not just talking billions of dollars or euros, but trillions. There's about three trillion dollars worth of copper in that mountain. On Earth, for that size of resource, people would kill, even start wars."

"It would also start a kind of mad gold rush to exploit the planet," continued John, "and a kind of settlement that's the direct opposite of everything we've dreamed of for Mars. The workers would be living in cheap-as-possible accommodations, probably under ground. They'd come here for just a few years to make some big bucks and get back to Earth with a small fortune. None of them would give a damn about this place. It would be all about keeping costs as low as possible, in order to extract as much profit as possible, from the colony governor down to the meanest worker. It would all be for the benefit of Earth, and to hell with any Martians who might have other ideas for the future of Mars."

"John, it's a nightmare," said Denise, "and Derk would be the colony's governor, living in our house."

"Well, we'd better hope it isn't true, with that kind of money involved," said John. "If it were true, then you could be dead sure the person they'd send up to rescue us would be the greatest devil they could lay their hands on—who didn't look like a devil."

"Richard Derk," said Denise. "He'd be ideal. They wouldn't want the ordinary people in Europe to know what was really going on, until later at least, when it would all have become just boring history. With him they could hide a lot. He can look so innocent and convincing when he wants to."

"You could well be right," admitted John.

"It would have been better if there hadn't been all that copper," said Denise. "Just enough for the use of the settlers of Mars, but too little to make it worthwhile shipping it back to Earth. I've always thought of this place as being for the benefit of those who lived here, and did the work, not for the benefit of colonial masters who lived on Earth. I believe in a Mars for the Martians. With such a big copper deposit, you're bound to get temptations that bring out the worst in mankind—absentee capitalists, whether private or government, who care nothing for the terrain they're exploiting."

"It's happened before," said John, "especially with coal deposits that have to be strip mined. That old saying about coal cursing the land in which it lies has a lot of truth in it. Coal deposits always seems to get under the control of outside interests, who care nothing for the local community and its land. I hope that when the history of this planet is written it doesn't say that copper was the curse of this part of Mars. But let's not jump to conclusions. We have to find out if ESA really is planning on getting that copper back to Earth first."

"How can we do that?"

"I don't know," said John, "but for a start I'm going to see if I can figure out a way to get that copper back to Earth myself. I'm supposed to be a good engineer. If there's a solution, at least in theory, I ought to be able to find it. And second, we should keep our ears and eyes open. After Sheila and Claude are buried, we'll be dealing with Derk's crowd a lot, while his lander's being refueled. Maybe we'll hear or see something that's the clue we need. This has been a very productive conversation, Denise. And now, I think we'd better get moving. It's already darker than it should be for driving down this escarpment. We're going to need our lights further down."

"Sorry—it's my fault," said Denise, a little anxiously, glancing at the two sleeping children beside her. "I've been asking too many questions. We could have waited till we got home. Mars always has to be paid its due respects."

"Didn't I hear you say something earlier about all the work waiting for us? There was something about not sitting around talking when we had so much to do, once we get home."

"You did hear me say that," admitted Denise with a sigh. "The place is a mess after all those visitors. We've piles of cleaning to do. Look! The lights have come on inside the compound. I want to go home."

They took one more look at their peaceful valley, spread out below and around them. The sky was still quite bright, and they could still make out Mount Tip in the distance, and the darkened escarpment walls on either side of the valley. The glass compound on Mount Tip was now clearly lit up, although not very strongly. It was a warm light though, and a friendly light, calling them home.

They then proceeded carefully down the one and a half mile long escarpment road, at only about five miles an hour, with the two children still fast asleep, and Denise worrying about the prospect of being accused of the loose talk that had led to two deaths. If she had but known, that was the least of her worries.

By the time they got to the bottom, inside Outlook Cove, some twenty minutes later, the light was fading rapidly. They spent the next half hour driving back up the valley in the gathering darkness, toward the lights on the side of Mount Tip.

*

As John and Denise drove home that Martian Wednesday evening, the video of the two caskets in the monastery had already reached Earth. Dr. Sato had sent it to the habitat, and Emma Grant, on Derk's instructions, had then forwarded it to Earth. At Mission Control, it was very early Tuesday morning.

In the course of the next few days, this monastery video, and later videos like it, would prevent riots in Paris and Dublin, cities where the inhabitants' initial shock at the deaths of their respective hero and heroine was already giving way to a smoldering anger.

On receipt of the first video recording from the monastery, the authorities in those two cities, aware of the intense feelings among the citizenry, each hastened to erect a huge panel video screen. Each of the huge screens was placed centrally, outside the legislature building in each city: outside the Dail in Dublin, and outside the National Assembly in Paris, and each screen showed the peaceful scene within the monastery on Outlook Shelf. The authorities in each city knew they would soon need the screen anyway, as a backdrop for the inevitable funeral service. It was hoped that the images from the monastery would placate the crowds already gathering in the centers of Dublin and Paris.

In this, the city fathers were right. An upset crowd, of one mind, needs a focal point to help turn it into a mob, triggering a full-scale riot. The only focal point in each city was the huge panel screen. However, no one on Earth who beheld those images from the monastery on Mars could entertain feelings of anger for long. The sight of the two caskets lying in honor in the peaceful monastery, with the view of the magnificence of creation lying beyond, quickly soothed the feelings of anger, replacing them with feelings of reverence and awe.

So, by the time the funeral services in Europe were conducted, on Thursday morning, instead of an aftermath of riots in Dublin and Paris, there was a mountain of flowers, lamps, and candles beneath the huge video screen in each city.

Unfortunately for Denise, Derk would manage to take the credit for the soothing monastery videos. As for the initial smoldering anger in Europe, particularly in Dublin and Paris, it was not dead, and when it would later burst into flames, it would not be directed at Captain Richard Derk.

CHAPTER ELEVEN

Laid to Rest

IT WAS just before eight on Friday morning, almost three days after the death of Sheila Bell. The Alpha-October sky was clear over Leaf Valley, and the early morning sun was not far above the high rampart on the southern end of the valley's east wall. On the west side of the valley, opposite the rampart, Outlook Shelf lay bathed in morning sunshine, glowing bright orange. However, befitting the occasion perhaps, a deep shadow lay on the road down from the shelf, along the side of its north-facing escarpment.

Two rovers were making their way slowly down the steep escarpment road. The Zen master was driving the lead rover. John Erway was driving the second rover, with his family beside him. This rover pulled a trailer with its top removed, draped in dark blue fabric. Inside lay two copper caskets, side by side.

Eventually the rovers reached the bottom, made the sharp turn to come around on the road leading out of Outlook Cove, and then headed slightly north of east, on the road across Leaf Valley. This road led to the junction with the road that ran south from Mount Tip to the valley exit at Stem Gap. As the rovers progressed along it, the morning sun shone directly in the faces of those inside.

Ten minutes later, the two rovers came to this road junction, and turned right. The rovers then headed south, just inside Leaf Valley, a valley sanctuary the two lying dead in the trailer had never seen. This road too lay in sunshine. Soon they were traveling through Stem Gap, headed due east, out of Leaf Valley and into Elbow Plain.

Twenty minutes later, the rovers were well out in the sunlit plain, approaching Elbow Hill. Waiting for them at the junction with the Elbow Hill road sat three Mars buggies, shining in the morning sunlight. Sitting in the buggies were the remaining ten members of the ESA Mars mission.

Jurgen Eindorf was sitting in the driver seat of the first buggy, the one borrowed from the Zen master. Richard Derk sat in the single passenger seat. Behind him, on the seats of the buggy's trailer, sat Emma Grant and Monique Montpellier, both wearing radiation umbrellas.

Jose Montoya was at the wheel of the second buggy, with Ursula Schneider and Vince Cassoni beside him. Karl Mannhardt was at the wheel of the last buggy, with Don Carruthers and Astrid Larsson in the passenger seats. Astrid, in the outside seat, was holding a video camera, recording the approach of the two rovers, and transmitting to Mission Control at the same time.

The rovers did not stop at the road junction, but passed on. The buggies then joined in behind, and the enlarged procession carried on along the main Kasei Valley road to the south. The caskets lying on the blue-fabric draped trailer in front, glistening copper brown in the sunlight, were visible to all ten in the three buggies behind, and Astrid Larsson dutifully recorded the image.

Before long, the procession was progressing between the high escarpment walls that bounded the southern stretches of that great valley. The escarpment wall to the left was in shadow, while that to the right glowed bright orange.

Although the escarpment walls on each side were as much as two miles away, so high were they that they shut out a considerable amount of the sky on either side. That morning, the massive walls seemed to sit watching, pondering and puzzled, silent monuments to the eons of time that had shaped them, and the eons yet to come.

Soon the procession reached Finger Gully, and began the slow climb up the winding road. About fifty meters from the top, the procession stopped, and Astrid got out of her buggy, and walked on up to the top. Then the procession resumed, as Astrid recorded its final advance up out of the gully and on down the Kasei Valley road to the south. Fifty meters further on, the procession stopped again, to allow Astrid to catch up and get back in the buggy at the rear.

Today, the satellite communications system on the buggies was working normally, and Astrid's images were transmitted to Mission Control in real time, so that viewers in Europe, where it was eleven o'clock on Wednesday evening, could watch the funeral procession with only about six minutes delay. In the U.S., where it was very early evening, most American video networks also carried it live.

Soon the long line of Kumar Hills, orange-brown in the mid morning sun, formed a new barrier to the left, as they continued due south. Half an hour later, the procession, now headed due east, had passed through a gap in these low hills—Kumar Gap.

The road through Kumar Gap connected the two north-south running sub valleys of Kasei Valley that were separated by Kumar

Hills. Finger Gully lay at the northern end of the western valley of these two sub valleys. The procession, emerging from Kumar Gap, had now entered the eastern valley of the two Kasei sub valleys.

Chiselhead Mountain, with it huge copper deposits, lay in this eastern sub valley, to the northeast of the Kumar Gap exit. Straight ahead of the procession coming out of the gap lay the high escarpment wall of Funnyface Mesa, some twelve miles away, on the other side of the valley. The old NASA landing site also lay in this eastern sub valley, but it was some twenty-five miles farther to the south. Eleven NASA mission members, one of them a German ESA astronaut, lay buried there.

A hundred meters before the road junction that lay just beyond Kumar Gap, the procession stopped again. Astrid again walked ahead, and recorded the procession as it advanced to the junction and turned right, to the south once more, headed toward the old NASA landing site.

The ESA mission had already been to this road junction, four days earlier. On that occasion, they had turned left, taking the road northeast to Chiselhead Mountain. This terrain was all new, however, to Jose and Monique.

The previous Wednesday afternoon, Denise had informed Derk that she intended to have the bodies of Sheila and Claude lie in honor, in caskets at the monastery, until the burial. At the same time, while conceding that it was ultimately an ESA decision, she had also informed Derk that she thought the two should be buried beside the eleven astronauts buried ten years earlier at the old NASA landing site. She had also maintained that a new row of graves, behind the existing row, should be started for the ESA pair.

Derk had considered this carefully. He had eventually concluded that Denise's recommendation was a good one, and that a burial at the old NASA landing site made the most sense.

For one thing, Max Erlanger, ESA's German communications engineer, who had died in the rocket explosion of 2038, already lay buried there. For another, Derk had not been able to think of any other suitable place. Elbow Plain had not seemed suitable, and it was highly unlikely that he could bury the two in Leaf Valley without objections from John Erway and his wife. And there was no way he was going to bury them out in that sandblasted labyrinth that had killed them. That would just serve to remind everyone of the foolish expedition he had ordered.

The gravesite at the old NASA landing site had thus been the only sensible possibility, even though Derk had personally never been there; and it had the advantage of being about as far away from the labyrinth as you could get with buggies. In the end, Derk had communicated this burial idea to Mission Control in Toulouse, but as if the idea had been his.

Mission Control in turn had pondered the question, and had come to the same conclusion Denise had come to, but with one change. They had preferred that the two be buried in front of the NASA eleven, not behind, as Derk, and Denise, had suggested.

On Thursday morning, after Derk had sent a message about this change to the compound in Leaf Valley, along with proposed times for the procession and funeral, Denise had nearly blown a fuse. She had been tempted to inform Derk that they either be buried in the row behind the NASA eleven or she would see to it that they were buried far beyond the range of the ESA mission's buggies.

Instead, having calmed down somewhat, Denise had sent a message insisting that they be buried behind the row of NASA graves. The message also included an explanation. The front row was reserved for the member of the first manned mission on Mars, and the first man to walk on the planet, the second row was for the members of the second mission, the NASA/ESA mission, and the third row at the back was for the third mission, Derk's ESA mission. Denise's mind had lost none of its orderliness for being more than ten years on Mars.

Derk had nearly blown a fuse in turn. He did not like being told what he could or could not do, especially by this witch in Leaf Valley. But in this particular dispute, Denise was holding all the aces, and so he had communicated his view to Mission Control that a front row burial would not be appropriate, but not for quite the reasons that Denise had given him. He had merely explained that since the ESA mission had come to Mars after the NASA/ESA mission, it would be best if the ESA two were buried in the row behind the NASA eleven, to avoid offending the United States. The people in ESA had seen the sense in this, and had not only communicated their consent to Derk, but had given this explanation of the burial arrangements to the media as well, both European and American.

Derk had seen no point in explaining to Mission Control that the front row was reserved for Dr. Sato, since he was intending to see to it that Dr. Sato did not live out his remaining years on Mars.

Thus it was agreed that the two would be buried in a new row, behind the existing row of eleven graves at the old NASA landing site, on that Martian Friday.

There had been further complications, however. A late morning, midday, or early afternoon burial were the only possibilities at the old NASA landing site, given its distance from the ESA landing site in Elbow Plain. But Western Europe was running one day and just over twelve hours behind the local time on Mars that day, which would mean that the burial on Mars would be taking place well after midnight in central Europe.

For this reason, ESA had recommended that the burial services in Dublin and Paris be held some ten hours after the burial on Mars, on Thursday morning. By that time, the video of the actual Martian burial would have arrived on Earth, which would enable the Martian burial scene to be shown on the giant video screens in the two cities, thus providing a suitable backdrop for their services. The authorities in those two cities, and the local Church leaders, thoroughly confused by the shifting time and day differences between Earth and Mars, and knowing only that the logistics involved were complex, had not objected.

*

It was nearly twelve thirty, just past Martian noon at twelve twenty. The sky was still clear, and the noon sun shone brightly down on the gravesite at the old NASA landing site in southwest Kasei Valley. The gravesite lay on a slight incline, facing northeast, across the slightly rolling, red and gray valley floor, littered with rocks and stones and the remains of small craters. The valley floor stretched as far as the crater-riddled, orange-brown escarpment wall of Funnyface Mesa in the distance, some twelve miles away.

A fairly brisk wind had arisen from the northeast, with a speed of just over eighty miles an hour, and eddies of dust and very fine sand were visible on the ground around the gravesite. Because of the thin Martian air, such a wind exerted the force of a wind of only about twelve miles an hour on Earth.

Except for the cairns of the graves, there was no longer any sign that an enormous quantity of Mars mission hardware had ever landed at this place. Over the years, the three who dwelt in Leaf Valley had been busy at that landing site. They had removed everything of use, and buried everything else. The last thing they had removed had been the long NASA habitat, now the ESA mission's habitat at Elbow Hill. They had cut up all the landers and buried them, after removing rocket engines, all kinds of pumps, fuel and oxidizer tanks, and other useful material and parts.

Except for the graves, the valley scene now looked as naturally Martian as when the first NASA lander arrived, back in 2036.

Dr. Sato's rover and the three buggies were parked along the road that ran in front of the gravesite at the bottom of the small incline. They were parked a little further north, so as not to obstruct the view from the incline across the valley. The other rover was parked behind the gravesite, a little higher up the incline. Inside, the two children were standing on the front seats, watching the burial.

The funeral party had already dug two new graves, six feet apart, facing northeast. They had built a cairn of black stones at the head of each grave, with a copper cross on top, and had laid a plaque of orange concrete between each grave and its cairn. John and the Zen master had made the plaques and crosses. Embedded in the concrete were the name, dates, occupation, nationality, and mission.

The many hands had made light of the work to prepare the graves. The trailer of Dr. Sato's rover had carried four shovels, along with ropes, concrete plaques, and copper crosses. John and Don Carruthers had dug Sheila's grave, while Jose and Jurgen had dug Claude's. Everybody, however, even Derk, had had a chance to dig out a symbolic shovel full of red Martian soil.

While the graves were being dug, the others had collected rocks in the buggy trailers, or had piled them up, to construct the cairns. Captain Derk, who did not like to be seen to do manual work, had placed a symbolic rock on each cairn.

There now remained only the task of burying the two caskets, which lay on the ground at the foot of the graves, each casket resting on three short, well-spaced ropes of parachute cord.

The previous evening, Derk had received a message from Mission Control, which he had forwarded more or less unaltered to Denise. ESA had concluded that the Zen master, as the only priestly person on Mars, would be the person most qualified to officiate at the burial, perhaps by reading some psalms, and the *Our Father*. The Irish had been particularly worried about Sheila not having a priest of some kind present to conduct whatever ceremony was performed. A Zen Buddhist was not exactly to the liking of the Irish Church, or the Vatican either, if truth be told, but it was felt that a man of some religion was better than a man of none, and hence the request.

Denise had replied that she thought it unlikely that the Zen master would consent to read such very religious words at the burial, and that if asked directly might well reply with something that those who had no understanding of Zen might consider insulting to Christianity, like a comment that such words 'stink of religion'. She had thought it possible, however, that he might agree to say something of his own, appropriate to the occasion.

Denise had approached the Zen master about this, and it was as she had predicted. He had been unwilling to have anything to do with Christian psalms and prayers, but had agreed to say a few words of his own. If they wanted psalms and prayers, they would have to recite them themselves. And so it had been decided.

Astrid now set the video camera on a mound of stones a few meters back from the caskets, which lay at the feet of the graves. The camera pointed between the two caskets, past the open graves and past their cairns to the mesa escarpment wall in the distance. It transmitted the images direct to Earth via a buggy's satellite link.

The thirteen present then broke into two groups, one on each side of the pair of caskets, so as not to obstruct the camera, and left Derk standing between the two cairns, facing the camera, the noon sun reflecting from his helmet. By now the wind had grown stronger, strong enough to be felt pushing against a pressure suit, and there were quite pronounced eddies of fine sand around the two cairns.

Derk held a prayer book in his left hand, a book that had belonged to Sheila Bell. From this, he read some psalms for the dead, and then, from a small sheet of paper embedded in the book, he recited the same *Our Father* that Don Carruthers had recited two days earlier in front of the cairn in the labyrinth.

Don Caruthers, standing near Denise, beside Sheila's casket, seemed to be particularly touched by this second recitation of the *Our Father*, modified for Mars. Denise noticed him steadying himself, as if he had been about to fall.

Following this recitation of the prayer, Derk bowed his head for a few seconds, then raised it and said 'Amen', a second time. He then lowered the prayer book, and walked the few feet to his left, to join those beside Claude's casket.

There remained only for the Zen master to say his few words. Dr. Sato now walked slowly between the two caskets, but not as far as the spot between the cairns, where Derk had stood. The Zen master stopped with the heads of the two caskets at his feet, just before the open graves, and turned around.

Then he joined his hands, with palms pointed out, facing the camera, and bowed his head. For a full five minutes he stood there in the bright noon sunshine, sand and dust swirling at his feet, head bowed, and saying nothing.

John, although not really surprised, was as mystified as everybody else, except Denise, who just smiled to herself.

Then the Zen master raised his head and said this:

'Fine sand and dust, swirling, low down, driven by the wind.
Blown together, a majestic sand dune, marching on the valley floor.
Fine sand and dust, swirling again, low down. What next?'

Then he bowed to those on his left, and to those on his right, unjoined his hands, and walked back to the group beside Sheila Bell's casket.

At this, Derk breathed a sigh of relief. Even if what the Zen master had said had made no sense, at least the words could not offend anyone on Earth, strange though they might be. Nevertheless, the Zen master's simple words would be taken careful note of on Earth, and their meaning much discussed in the media, for days to come. Eventually they would be placed on the plaques on monuments to Sheila Bell and Claude Bertrand, later constructed in Dublin and Paris.

Derk now gestured to the two groups by the caskets. Each group then surrounded the nearest casket, and lifting it by the six rope ends, carried it forward over an open grave. Seconds later the two groups had lowered the caskets.

For the next ten minutes, they shoveled the red soil of Mars down on top. They all took turns, and Derk placed a symbolic shovel full in each grave, in full view of the camera.

Then the unexpected happened, as Don Carruthers was heaping soil on Sheila's nearly completed grave, with the strong wind blowing the dust off the top of the heaped soil. He fell, on his face, quite suddenly, on top of the grave. Luckily, there were no sharp stones on the slightly heaped soil, otherwise he could have smashed his helmet faceplate, or torn his pressure suit. He had not merely lost his balance though, for after he fell, he lay quite still.

Denise was keeling beside him a few seconds later, carefully turning him over. She was helped by Astrid Larsson, who had been almost as quick to get to him as Denise. When they got him turned over, his head was hanging limp inside his helmet, his eyes were closed, and his face was a deathly pale.

Everyone had gathered round by now, as Denise examined him, checking the data on his wrist display. Among some of them, Derk included, there arose feelings of anxiety and fear, not unlike those experienced on that tragic evening in Hazard Valley. Could it be that Mars had not been satisfied, and was intending yet another victim, or perhaps more than one?

"John!" cried Denise, in a concerned voice, looking up. "We have to get him in the rover. I'll go inside and take him out of the airlock. Dr. Larsson! You come in after him, please. I may need you." With that she ran to the rover steps, as John and Jose lifted Don, and carried him to the rover after her.

*

Some thirty minutes later, at about one thirty, and about fifteen minutes after completion of all work finishing the graves, with everyone standing around outside the rover, Denise appeared at the rover's front window, and asked for Derk to come inside.

Denise was standing by the red swivel chairs, between the two rover windows, when Derk came through the airlock. She had already removed her pressure suit. The two children were beside her, half kneeling, half standing in the swivel chairs.

"This won't take long," she said, once Derk had removed his helmet, and approached her, "but I have to speak to you as a doctor."

Derk had noticed as he came in that Don was lying on the back bunk, with Astrid standing nearby. Derk was genuinely concerned. The whole of Europe, where it was after one in the morning, would soon see the image of Don Carruthers collapsing over Sheila's grave. Indeed, many who had stayed up to watch on the video networks already had.

"Is it serious?" he asked.

"I don't think so," said Denise, "but I'm limited in what I can do here. His collapse seems to have been caused by a mental blackout brought on by a level of emotional stress too high for just about anyone to bear. I mean the stress of nearly being killed in Hazard Valley, combined with the feeling that he was to blame for the deaths of Sheila and Claude, combined with the loss of somebody he was very attached to. As well, when we found him last Tuesday, he was unconscious. He responded to treatment quite quickly, but it's still possible some hidden damage was done, although, as I said, I don't think so. The emotional stress is probably the only factor. But I can't be sure. So it would be prudent to give him a thorough checkout at once, just in case. I need to take him back to my surgery to do that."

"I see," said Derk, relieved. "How long before he recovers consciousness?"

"He's just sedated at the moment," said Denise. "I brought him around a little while ago. He'll stay asleep until we get back. There's no way he should sit in a buggy on the way back."

"How long do you propose keeping him?" asked Derk. He showed no hostility. In private, he knew that Don Carruthers was in very safe hands, and that Denise would act only in Don's interests, no matter how much Derk might be engaged in telling everyone in Europe a different story about her. As far as he was concerned, she could keep him as long as it took him to recover. His only reservation was that the delayed refueling of the lander was to start next day, and he would need every hand, if it were to be done on time. And there was also the very important geological survey work to be done, and drilling samples to be obtained, before the time scheduled for the lander to lift off, about three weeks after it had arrived. The delay caused by the tragedy in Hazard Valley now meant that the schedule was very tight, if the lander was to lift off before the current favorable launch window closed.

"If my diagnosis here is right, he can return tomorrow," said Denise. "I imagine you'll need him to help with the refueling. It'll be best if he has plenty of work to occupy his mind anyway, but nothing too stressful or dangerous. It might be best if he gets heavily involved only with the fuel. The oxidizer's something else. According to my husband it's extraordinarily dangerous. Maybe you can find some geological work for him while that's going on."

"I see," said Derk. "I'll take that into account in assigning his duties. You'll let me know as soon as you've completed your examination? They'll be very anxious at Mission Control, and in England too, when they see the video of the burial."

"Yes," said Denise. "I'll do that. One other thing. It would be best if someone from your mission stayed with him at the house this evening. It should be somebody he's relaxed and comfortable with, who won't upset him. I would strongly recommend Dr. Larsson, if you can spare her. I've found her very helpful in that regard."

"She has permission," said Derk at once. This suited him just fine. He preferred that another one of his people stay at the house in Leaf Valley. That way he could better be sure of what had gone on at the house. There could well be goings on there that he could exploit.

"Good, it's all settled," said Denise. "Dr. Larsson can transfer into the rover when we get to Elbow Hill. You probably want her to ride her buggy back."

"I do," said Derk.

At that, both Derk and Astrid went out, and Denise called John in. Outside, Derk explained the situation briefly to his crew, to the relief of all. The party then got itself assembled, and headed back northward toward Kumar Gap.

The northeast wind was quite a lot stronger by now, and the layer of swirling sand and dust was several inches thick on the ground. But it presented little difficulty after they had passed down Finger Gully, and they had the high, sheltering escarpment walls of Kasei Valley on either side.

Near four thirty in the afternoon, when they reached the road junction to Elbow Hill, they were once more exposed to the wind, which was streaming down Kasei Valley from the northeast. As Astrid switched from her buggy to the rover, the swirling dust and fine sand was almost six inches thick on the ground.

Some twenty minutes later, with the rovers safely back inside the shelter of Leaf Valley, there was no wind at all, and no trace of even the smallest eddy of dusty sand around its rocks and stones.

Outside the valley, in Elbow Plain, it was a different story. The strong wind blew the rest of the afternoon, although it did not stop Derk's crew from completing preparations of the hardware needed for the refueling. John had done his job well, for there was no wind at all down in the landing pit, and by nightfall Derk's crew had the tanks and plumbing ready.

The strong northeast wind blew strongly over the gravesite the rest of that afternoon too, forming sand tails in the lee of the rocks and stones. Gradually, it eroded away the rover wheel tracks on the incline, and the footprints of the thirteen who had buried Sheila Bell and Claude Bertrand.

Those two dead would not remain visited only by the valley winds, and occasional dust storm. There would be two who would visit the site regularly, in the decades to come, until it was their turn to join the two buried there. The visitors would stand at the foot of the graves, looking past the cairns to the mesa beyond, and reflect on what had been, and on what might have been. Human life, for better or for worse, was now entrenched on Mars, and would continue.

*

When the rovers reached the glass compound, just after five thirty, Don Carruthers was already awake, and was able to get out of the rover without help. He was surprised to find himself stepping out into the greenery of the garden, with the late afternoon sun shining on the plants. This time, the pleasant garden atmosphere could help him relax, which it did not do the last time he had been there, given that Sheila had been lying dead on the central patio. But Sheila was far away now, buried, and out of sight, forever.

As they walked along the garden path to the house, Don Carruthers was between Denise and Astrid, who both watched his every move. Denise's first priority was his checkup, and she led him directly to the surgery.

Don Carruthers spent nearly an hour lying on the bed in the surgery, with electrode probes attached to his cranium, as Denise, together with Dr. Sato, performed a series of tests. These mostly involved monitoring the electrical activity in his brain in response to stimuli. It was after six thirty when Denise could disconnect the probes, turn off the electronic displays, and let him get up.

"It's good news, Dr. Carruthers," she said. "Your brain activity and responses to standard test stimuli are completely normal. There's no reason to believe you've suffered any brain damage from that evening in the labyrinth."

Don did not know quite what to say, and just said: "Well, thank you, Doctor. Frightfully sorry I put you to all this bother. I mean, passing out like that."

"No bother," said Denise. "It was the pain, wasn't it, just before you passed out?"

"Yes," admitted Don. "It was very bad. I had no idea it could be so bad."

"Don't worry," said Denise. "You're just human."

"Emotional pain can make you pass out if it's intense enough," she explained. "I know you will want to grieve, and that's healthy. But I would advise you to do it by allocating a short private period for that each day, fifteen minutes at most. After you've done that, have the discipline not to let your thoughts dwell there for the rest of the day. Keep them elsewhere, and try to have an assortment of pleasant things to let your mind dwell on every so often too—anything at all, as long as it's pleasant to you. Human company helps too. Horrible things happen, but a human being can take only so much of that. The mind needs to dwell on pleasant and positive things too, to stay healthy."

"I'll try to do as you say," said Don.

"And one last thing," said Denise. "I want you to sleep in the bed in the surgery tonight. I have to do one last test. I want to record your brain activity while you're asleep. And now, why don't you take a walk in the garden with Dr. Larsson while I'm getting some supper ready? I'm sure everybody's hungry. My husband and Dr. Sato will be happy to show you around, and answer any questions."

"Thank you, Doctor," was all Don could find to say to this.

Astrid Larsson, who had been standing in the doorway, listening, was more forthcoming. "Come with me, Don," she said, with a smile on her long face, unusual for her. She was relieved to hear that there was nothing wrong with Don Carruthers that the passage of time, and possibly a little caring from her, would not cure. "It is a beautiful Martian evening, and the sun has just set. I for one could use a walk in the garden, but I would enjoy some company."

After everyone had gone outside, including the two children, Denise went first to the communications room. There she composed a brief report on the condition of Don Carruthers, and sent it to the habitat. Richard Derk, relieved at the news, ordered Emma Grant to forward it to Mission Control.

Some four hours earlier, before he left the gravesite, Derk had sent Mission Control a message, using a buggy satellite link. It had stated that Denise would be carrying out a thorough checkup on Dr. Carruthers, at Derk's request. When this latest report from Denise on the condition of Don Carruthers arrived at Mission Control early that Thursday morning, there was widespread relief in Europe, especially in England.

*

Later than evening, just before eight, John, Denise, Dr. Sato, Don Carruthers, and Astrid Larsson sat around the table eating dessert in the dining room of the house on Mount Tip. Denise and John had already put their two children to bed.

It was a relaxed group. There was no hostility, and the conversation, what little there had been, was friendly. As usual, Dr. Sato said almost nothing. He listened intently, though, and missed nothing.

Although the conversation so far had been quite light, Don Carruthers had participated very little, and had mostly made merely polite remarks when required to respond to something. To Denise, who had watched him intently without it being obvious, it seemed that he was still brooding.

It was Astrid who had kept the conversation going. She had talked about the ESA mission's long outbound trip to Mars, and Denise in return had talked about the 2038 NASA and JSA missions, in which Astrid had seemed very interested. Astrid, as a structural engineer, as well as a geologist, just like John, had also been interested in hearing about how the glass compound, house, and garden on the shelf on the southeast side of Mount Tip had come to be built. They also talked about the labyrinth rescue, and Astrid and Don discovered that it was John, Denise, and Dr. Sato who had developed the rescue strategy, and had decided on how resources were to be allocated, not Derk, as was believed at the habitat, and in Europe.

There had been silence for a while, when Denise suddenly thought to say: "I was in Stockholm once, at a conference at the university. It's a nice city. I liked the islands, with all those bridges between them. Is that were you got your degrees?"

"No," said Astrid, "I studied at Uppsala, although I was born in Stockholm. I grew up in an apartment on the south side of Stockholm, in a suburb called Farsta. It's quite far from those islands at the city center, but it has a lake nearby."

"What was your degree project, or research?" asked John, suddenly wondering what special skills in structural engineering or geology she had, that had got her on this third manned mission to Mars.

"It was a project related to some development work at the European Space Agency," she answered.

There was silence. Then Astrid said. "I know that tells you nothing. I admit I am being evasive. But that particular ESA project was a secret one, and I am not supposed to talk about it."

"Must be hard to keep something secret among research students in a university," said Denise. Her curiosity was aroused, as was John's, but she quite liked Astrid, and felt uncomfortable about probing. She decided that the best she could do was try and keep on the topic, in the hope that Astrid might reveal something about it.

"Actually, it was not so hard," said Astrid. "It was all simulation work on a computer array. No other student had access. The other students just knew I was simulating a structural engineering project. That was enough to know. Nobody ever asked me about the details."

Denise was even more curious now. What was the structural engineering project she had been simulating? Why was it secret? Did it have anything to do with why she was on the mission? And did it have anything to do with the copper at Chiselhead Mountain, or with the secret ESA project at the southwest tip of Ireland? Denise could see that her husband was very interested. She now remembered what John had said a few days ago, about keeping eyes and ears open when ESA mission members were around.

"What would you have done if anyone had asked?" Denise asked, as if she was forcing the conversation a little. Then, before Astrid could reply, she said: "Oh, excuse me a moment, I'd like to pull the drapes—the reflections on the window glass behind you are annoying me. But carry on."

"Oh, I would just give the name of the project," said Astrid, as Denise pulled the drapes at the two windows on the west wall of the house. "One engineering student I was out on a date with actually did ask. When I told him what the project title was, he asked me what it was about. When I told him it was complicated and would take a bit to explain, he said 'No thanks' and that was the end of that."

"Must have been quite an intimidating project title," said Denise, as she sat down again, facing Astrid and the window. The Zen master was sitting to her right, and John was sitting at the head of the table to her left. Don Carruthers sat beside Astrid, opposite the Zen master. "In my field, when you have only some fairly trivial or peripheral project work, that's when you see an impressive, intimidating project title, designed to keep people from asking too many questions. I suppose it's the same in your field."

"It's the same in every field, I think," said Astrid, smiling at the thought, "but the project I was working on was not trivial or peripheral."

It was now or never, thought John. "Aren't you going to let us hear this intimidating title?" he asked. "You've certainly succeeded in making me curious."

"I suppose it would not do any harm to tell you what it was called," said Astrid. "It was quite a few years back anyway. The name was *Structural Stress In A Gravity Shaft Powered Electromagnetically Coupled Trebuchet*. Don't ask me to explain what it was about."

"Well, that's an carful, and no mistake," said John. "You're not going to get many who would ask you to explain what that was about."

"Is that *trebuchet* as in the medieval siege artillery trebuchet?" asked Denise. "If it is, I can tell you a good story about a trebuchet from my student days in Paris, a real trebuchet, not a computer simulated one."

Astrid was slightly taken aback at this, but now it was her turn to be curious. She was intensely interested in the trebuchet principle. "Actually, it *was* to do with the medieval trebuchet idea," she said. "But now you have made me curious about your trebuchet story."

"I remember it as if it were yesterday," began Denise. "It was a student project at the University of Paris. Four groups of engineering students—ten of them in each group I think—had to build a device working on the trebuchet principle that would fling an old refrigerator one hundred meters across a university football field. Their professor had explained the principle in class, and there was a prize for each student group whose fridge cleared the hundred meters. Anyway, instead of designing their own, one group of students decided to cheat. They went to the university library and dug up a design from the eighth or ninth century, ..."

"I didn't know they had trebuchets that far back," said John.

"They did indeed," said Astrid. "They used them for knocking down castle walls. It was France where they were perfected. But let us hear the rest of the story, although I think I know what you have coming."

"It's very funny, in retrospect," said Denise, smiling, "although the police and a lot of Parisians didn't think it was funny at the time. Anyway, these students built this huge wooden trebuchet according to the original medieval design. They were good cheaters and didn't change a thing in the design. They assembled it on the football field along with the other three trebuchets, from the three other groups of students. The cheaters' trebuchet was the only one that had wheels. The other students knew that medieval trebuchets always had wheels, but hadn't seen any point in putting wheels on, since their trebuchets weren't going anywhere. The cheaters, on the other hand, just copied everything in the original design, wheels and all."

"The suspense is killing me," said John. "What happened?"

"I distinctly remember the day—a gray Saturday morning in November with a drizzle," said Denise. "A lot of students and professors showed up to see the show. There was even a camera crew from one of the networks. Each machine had a long rope attached to a big wooden firing pin. It took about five students at the end of the rope, a safe distance away, to pull the firing pin out and set it off. With the first two machines, the same thing happened when the pin was pulled out, and the big lever in the machine started to move. Instead of firing the fridge, the lever tore the machine apart, and it just collapsed. The third machine managed to get the fridge in the air—it went only a few meters—but that machine collapsed too.

"With the fourth machine, the one the cheaters built, it was different. When they pulled the pin out, and the lever started to move, the whole machine went shooting forward on its wheels, in the firing direction. Then, as the fridge got in the air, but still in its sling basket—it was going in a huge arc—the machine stopped suddenly and started shooting backward on its wheels. Then the fridge went shooting out of the sling, at an enormous speed. The cheaters' machine was the only one that worked. I never understood exactly why myself, but apparently the wheels are essential to the mechanism, to keep it from shaking itself apart."

"And I suppose the fridge went the hundred meters to win the prize," said Astrid.

"Not quite," said Denise. "The machine flung the fridge about three hundred meters, right out of the football field, over a road, and over the roofs of some houses on the other side of the road. It came down several houses farther back, and went right through the roof of one of them. Fortunately, there was nobody inside at the time."

"I'll bet there was a fuss about that," said John, laughing. Even Don Carruthers was laughing, as was Astrid, and Dr. Sato was smiling. Like John, Dr. Sato understood the trebuchet principle, and just how powerful the machine was, when correctly constructed.

"There were no more trebuchet building projects at the university after that," said Denise.

"I think we should have no more talking about trebuchets either, for this evening," said John, still laughing, but inwardly feeling very satisfied. He had the clue he had been looking for—a gravity shaft, with electromagnetic coupling. "If we keep on talking about them, I'll be having a nightmare about a trebuchet on Mars firing big boulders at our glass structures. Let's talk about Mars instead. But we're all finished here. Why don't we move into the living room and make ourselves more comfortable?"

Ten minutes later, they were all seated around the table in the living room, in the corner beside the stairs, drinking coffee and tea, and munching cookies.

"I understand you have some geological survey work to do, after the lander's been refueled," said John. "Anything special?"

It was Don Carruthers who answered. "We've several projects," he said. "But the main project is a detailed survey of the northwestern wall of Kasei Valley at Elbow Plain, including samples from the rampart on top."

"Does that mean your mission intends to get up on top of the rampart?" asked Denise.

"Yes, the original idea was to drive up in the buggies," said Don. He had been holding his coffee mug in his hand, but as he said this it shook, and he narrowly averted spilling on himself. "I'm not sure about that now though," he added, after he had put the mug back on the table, "and I'm not sure how you would do it either."

"Well, I can tell you one thing," said Denise, "and this time let there be no mistake about what I said. It would be madness to try to get up there in buggies. It's far too dangerous. Would you agree, John?"

"Absolutely," said John firmly. "I can't think of a more dangerous trip in a buggy."

"Is there even a way up for a buggy?" asked Astrid, suddenly concerned. If there was to be an expedition to the rampart, Don Carruthers, as the mission's chief geologist, was sure to be on it. And if what her hosts were saying about such an expedition were true ….

"Yes, in theory, there is," said John, "up along the narrow ridge at the rampart's east end, with a steep drop on either side. That ridge starts at the top of the escarpment, right at the edge. You need to have a head for heights. The drop to the left going up is the worst—it falls all the way down to the floor of Kasei Valley, right into Snakepit Crack in fact. The drop to the right's not as bad—just down to the high plateau level—but it's no joke either. Along that ridge—three miles of it—is the only way up."

"Have any of you been up?" asked Astrid.

"Yes, we've all been up there," said John, "just out of curiosity. We used two rovers. It's pretty flat and windswept up there. Going up the ridge was the worst part. Once you're on the ridge there's no chickening out and turning back. You have to go on up. You have to be very careful too, and lucky. If it were to get windy, like it did today, you couldn't go up. And if you were already up when the wind started, you'd have to stay up till the weather improved. But even stuck up there in a rover on a windy day could be dangerous. There's no shelter, and the wind can be a lot worse than down in the valley—it's just like the fast moving air over an aircraft wing. It's possible you could be overturned, even in a rover. Of course, in a buggy, you'd soon run out of air, if you ever got stuck up there."

"Is it a long trip?" asked Astrid. "I mean, have the buggies enough range to get up there and back?"

"That would depend on where you started from," said John. "From the habitat, it's about a five-hour trip up in a buggy, maybe six, and five or six back. A lot of the trip would be over rough terrain, across the plateau east of here—no road. I'd say a trip like that would be just over the limit of the buggy's range if you started from the hab. It might be just within range if you started from here. Good way to kill a lot of people though, going up there in a buggy."

"The view must be spectacular," said Don.

"It sure is—hard to beat. The time we were up, we stayed only half an hour. It was too risky to stay longer. I remember the weather was very good the day we went up. No wind at all. But then, when we were up, a wind began to rise—we got down off that rampart pretty darned fast I can tell you. But why's it so important to get samples up there, anyway?"

Don Carruthers looked at Astrid, as she looked at him. She seemed to read his mind. "I am very sorry," said Astrid. "I know you have been very good to us, but we are not permitted to talk about that. The Captain has issued orders about it. We could get in trouble if we did."

"Well, we wouldn't want to get you in any trouble," said Denise. "But it's obvious that ESA has gone in for secrecy in a big way since I was part of it. I suppose they don't want the Americans to scoop them. In my time, ESA and NASA were cooperating. But let's talk about Mars, and its future, and keep the politics out of it. We just love this planet. I'm wondering what you think of it?"

"I really like the place," said Astrid, "especially since I have seen what it is possible to do here. For example, what you have managed to do. You like it too, Don, do you not?"

"I'm prejudiced, being a geologist," said Don. "It's a geologist's paradise. Just magnificent. An incredibly beautiful desolation, but dangerous too. Sheila said once that ...."

His voice trailed off, and the coffee mug in his hand shook. He put it down on the table. The others waited for him to continue.

Then Denise spoke, a professional tone in her voice. "What did Sheila say?"

He did not answer for a few seconds, and then he said slowly: "She said that being here was like being a fly in the middle of a magnificent spider's web, waiting for the spider to show up. It was the evening before she died...."

"She was right, in a way," said John, quickly. "If a fly wants to enjoy a spider's art and engineering, it should not land on the web. It should keep a safe distance."

"You mean it shouldn't run a risk?" said Don.

"That's right," said John. "Always have a good margin of safety on Mars. Never run risks—if you do the planet will eventually get you."

"Sheila seemed to think that way too," said Don. "The evening before she died she told me she thought our buggy trips so far from base were too dangerous. The worst is that I assured her that it must be all right, and that the Captain knew what he was doing."

"Sounds like Sheila had a sense for the risks on Mars," said John, "but obviously didn't have the authority to act on her sense of danger, and do things more safely. I know what that's like. I've been there. The difference is that I was lucky, while she paid with her life."

Don winced visibly. At this point, Denise thought it time to steer the subject away from Sheila's death. Don Carruthers was still her patient, and she did not want to be blamed for allowing a conversation that brought on another collapse.

"I suppose your chief is planning to have you two remain on Mars after the lander takes off," said Denise.

"Yes," said Astrid. "I have been told that. I was to stay anyway, but after Claude Bertrand's death it is now even more necessary that

I stay, being a structural engineer. And Don is to stay too, as chief geologist."

"Has your chief explained how you're to manage?" asked John.

"Yes," said Astrid. "Our mission will take over the facilities here in Leaf Valley, after you have gone. There will not be enough greenhouse capacity, but we will build some more. That will be our first priority. I will copy your design. It seems to work very well."

"I see," said Denise. "Has your Captain said anything to you about the fact that he won't be able to take over these facilities? This territory here is ours, and we're not intending to leave. After the initial three weeks are up, we'll have kept our end of the agreement with ESA, and will be under no obligation to supply your mission with either food or water, or even accommodation. You'll all have to leave in that lander, unless some of you want to resign from ESA, buy some land from us and settle here. We'd be very reasonable about the price."

Astrid's mouth opened and her jaw dropped. Don Carruthers just stared at Denise in surprise. This was a point of view they had never even heard before, much less analyzed.

"You say you own this land," said Don, a minute later, when he had recovered. "I'm surprised at that. The Captain says it belongs to the people of Earth through the U.N. Mars Office, and that title is soon to be transferred to the E.U. at a suitable price."

"That's incorrect," said Denise. "The U.N. Mars Office simply lays claim to the land in this region. We lay claim to it too. But we were here first, and we settled and developed it, and are in possession of it. So our claim must be the stronger of the two."

"How much land are you laying claim to?" asked Astrid.

"To Leaf Valley and the Kasei Valley lands around it, from the old NASA landing site to the south to just past the end of Hazard Valley in the northeast. We've developed the entire region, built the roads and mines, including the big copper mine at Chiselhead Mountain. We've even staked our claim to those deposits, as you may have noticed."

"I did notice," said Don Carruthers. "Captain Derk was very upset when he found out, and ordered us to stake a claim over yours. I admit I wasn't too happy about that—I've never liked the idea of claim jumping."

"But if all this is true," said Astrid, still trying to grasp the implications, "then our entire mission is on a wild goose chase, as you say in English. There is no point to it. The whole idea was to carry on the development of this region from where you left off, after you had gone."

Neither John nor Denise said anything, but watched the reaction of their two guests intently, in a non obvious manner. It was clear to them that neither Astrid nor Don had any personal stake in the E.U. taking over Leaf Valley and evicting them from their homes. It was a matter that had been decided at much higher levels. Don and Astrid were not intended to be part of the dirty work. Their job would be to make the colony function later.

"I do not understand any of this," continued Astrid. "My understanding was that you would be happy to be rescued and get back to Earth, and that even if you did not want to be rescued it was because being ten years on Mars had affected your brains. If you did not want to go back, that would just mean we had to help you get used to the idea. I mean, it would be because you were just a little crazy. The possibility that you would not want to be rescued and that you were perfectly sane at the same time was never discussed. But I have seen both of you working and functioning here in the last few days, and seen what a wonderful place this is, and I have to admit you are two of the most sane people I have ever met. So something is very wrong somewhere. I can easily see why you would not want to leave all this, especially since it is something you have created yourselves. Do you understand what is going on, Don?"

"No, I don't," said Don. "But it seems to me there's a legal tangle at the root of it, and I'm not a lawyer. It's obvious that our hosts have some rights, given they've created all this. It's also obvious that the people of Earth have some rights to Mars too. And what's more, there's an awful lot of them. If it ever came down to a fight, and I can see how it could, given all that copper down at Chiselhead, you three could not possibly resist an economic and military superpower like the E.U. I mean, you can't stop others coming to Mars and developing it just because you got here first. Nobody on Earth's going to think that's reasonable."

"We do not in any way want to stop people on Earth coming to Mars," said Denise. "The more the better. If people want to come here to build settlements and trade with us, we'd be delighted. The planet's big enough. It's got as much land area as the Earth."

"You mean if the E.U. had sent a mission," said Don, "fully equipped, to start a new settlement outside of your territory, say south or west of the old NASA landing site, you'd have been very happy about that."

"We'd have jumped for joy," said Denise.

"You wouldn't have tried to say you owned that land too and tried to get paid for it?" asked Astrid, wondering about the minds of her hosts.

"Of course not," said Denise. "If the E.U. or the U.S. were to do that, they'd be creating value where none existed before. That land is presently worthless. It's not like the land around here. The land here is the most valuable on Mars, because of the value we gave it by our work and development. We believe in a very simple principle. A man or woman has a right to be paid for his or her work."

"You mean that what you object to is the E.U. trying to get the value you created for nothing?" said Astrid.

"Right on," said Denise.

"I think, however," said Don, "that the E.U., and everyone in Europe, think that they're getting it in return for the cost of rescuing you."

"It takes two parties, in agreement, to exchange goods and services," pointed out Denise. "We never asked to be rescued."

"All right," said Astrid, now very curious, "suppose the E.U. were to accept your prior claim and were to negotiate with you for this territory—and everything you've created. Would you sell it?"

"No," said Denise, "we would not. This is our home, and it's not for sale."

"Well," said Astrid, "suppose the E.U. were to offer to buy a part of your territory, say the land in Elbow Plain, and most of Chiselhead Mountain, would you be willing to sell that?"

"No," said Denise, "although if the E.U. was building a settlement outside our territory, say south of the old NASA landing site, we'd certainly be willing to sell a good chunk of the copper at Chiselhead, for a fair price to both sides. There's far more copper there than this settlement here could ever use."

"But why not Elbow Plain?" asked Astrid. "I thought you said earlier that if anyone wanted to settle in your territory you would be very happy to sell a piece of the land for a fair price."

"To any free individuals, yes," said Denise, "but not to a colony under the direct control of Earth. We'd immediately be in the minority, with Earth calling the shots. It's not the future we want for this region of Mars."

"I am very curious," said Astrid. "How do you see it developing then?"

"It's all very simple," said Denise. "We understand and accept that eventually the big powers on Earth, the E.U., the U.S., Japan, and so on, are each going to found colonies on Mars, each one under the direct control of its mother country. The planet's big enough, and we couldn't stop them if we wanted to, and we would have no right to either, even if we did want to. But we want to keep this region around Leaf Valley free and independent, where the benefits and profits of this part of Mars stay with its people. The settlers of this region could invest their surplus in infrastructure to keep themselves free, independent, and prosperous. We're against Earth getting its hands on any surplus we create. Earth has no right to any part of it. Any surplus should stay with the people of Mars in this region, who, of course, would be happy to trade what they produced with the other colonies elsewhere on Mars, and even with Earth."

There was again silence, as Astrid and Don considered this.

John was leaning over the low table a little, observing the two visitors intently. His right hand was tapping the table gently in time to some music he had selected earlier. At that moment, an old military song, with a determined rhythm, was playing softly in the background.

"And who would be in charge of this independent region on Mars," asked Don, eventually. He was wondering if these two were crazy after all, rebels mad for power.

It was John who answered, no longer tapping the table. "Only one possibility makes sense. The people of this region would have to be in charge. We would put up a building, maybe in the middle of Leaf Valley. In the middle of it, we could have a big round table. Each person in the region, who was of age, would have a seat at the table, where all of them would make decisions on matters that affected them all, the most basic of democratic republics.

"As the settlement grew, we would make the table larger, until eventually, when the population grew too large, the people who were of age would vote to select representatives to sit around the table to decide on matters common to all."

"Each person would have the right to own land," he went on, "to produce and exchange his or her products for the products of others, or to work in the service of others, as that person freely decided. The power to decide, both in matters of government, and in matters of production and consumption, would reside with the people, the first free people of Mars. We would draw up these rules of government, as a Constitution, to protect the settlement from tyranny. Any person wanting to join the settlement would have to accept them, and buy some land."

"So when the settlement was still small," said Don, thoughtfully, "each person at the round table would be equal, as far as entitlement to a seat was concerned, but respected only for what he or she had accomplished and contributed as a free citizen. The Free Citizens of the Round Table of Mars, I suppose."

"Very well put," said Denise.

"And I suppose your flag would have a circle on it, on a pink background, to symbolize your round council building," said Astrid, who was very imaginative. "It could have a brown disk inside, to symbolize your round table, made of copper, I presume."

"Very good idea," said John. "Obviously we'd need a flag, if we were ever to win recognition. Your flag design would also be a symbol of Mars, Dr. Larsson."

"And there would one day be a huge statue, like the Statute of Liberty, up on Stem Mountains, on top of the escarpment wall, overlooking the entrance to Leaf Valley," added Denise.

There was silence again, as the military music in the background continued. Astrid had her head bowed, deep in thought. Then she raised her head. Her long face looked very sad.

"They will never allow it," she said decisively. "The big powers on Earth would see it as a threat to their interests, especially the E.U. They are interested only in colonies, especially colonies they can exploit. Their attitude is: Give us this Mars—all of it, but especially this part of Mars. They would be against even a small piece of Mars belonging to a free people. It would be a constant reminder to their colonists that they would be much better off free, and be an incitement to revolution. You will have to fight for your vision. I am certain our hearts are both with you, but I do not see how we could ever help you. I do not see how you could ever win either, even if justice is on your side. There is a great deal of injustice on Earth, and probably will be on Mars too. We may even be forced to act against you when the time comes, although I, for one, will try not to let that happen. Now, if you will excuse me, I am very tired. It is nearly nine thirty, and it has been a long day. We are all supposed to be ready very early in the morning for the refueling work."

"Yes," said Denise, touched by what Astrid had said. "It's time to get to bed if we're all to be up before dawn." Then she turned to Astrid and said: "You have to sleep in the rover, Astrid, like last time. The house is full. Dr. Carruthers has to sleep in the surgery. I still have some tests to do on him."

At that, they got up, and carried their mugs and plates to the kitchen, as the military music in the background ended and was followed by gentler music.

As Astrid walked along the garden path to the rover, a few minutes later, deep in thought, it hit her that Denise had just called her by her first name for the first time.

She continued to think about this, before she fell asleep, as she lay in the back bunk of the rover in the parking pad, surrounded by greenery. It would be hard for her to accept this hand of friendship being offered her, even from a woman who had saved her life. Her first loyalty had to be to her mission, and the second to her native Sweden, whose people thought she was an extraordinarily clever heroine who could do no wrong. Astrid did not want to disappoint them. The pressures were too great, and she was too conservative—she felt she simply could not do otherwise. She resolved only to do the best she could.

CHAPTER TWELVE

Hostile Intent

EARLY NEXT morning, on Saturday, Alpha-October 20, the refueling operation began in earnest. The fuel was first, and nearly everyone was involved.

A small chemical plant in the industrial complex manufactured fuel continuously. It used the carbon in carbon dioxide in the Martian air, and the hydrogen in water, which is just hydrogen oxide, to produce a fuel made of carbon and hydrogen, thus a hydrocarbon, typical of most fuels. The energy needed to make this uphill process take place came from a small portable nuclear power plant. It was a downhill path when the fuel burned, releasing the energy stored.

The fuel manufactured flowed through a pipe into fuel tanks sitting in a row outside the plant, a little lower down. The fuel tanks were dug into the inside of the rim of a small, shallow crater. The flatbed of a rover trailer, when parked on the floor of this crater, beside the fuel tanks, was about a meter lower down. When fuel was needed, it could flow, under gravity, out of a fuel tank in the side of the crater rim, into portable fuel containers in the trailer.

John, Denise, and Dr. Sato had taken the fuel tanks from the landers at the old NASA landing site, years earlier. The chemical plant that made the fuel had also come from the NASA landing site.

The oxidizer, needed to burn the fuel, was stored in tanks dug into the inside of the rim of a separate shallow crater, near the building housing the chemical plant that made it. Originally, they had used the chemical plant from the NASA landing site to make the oxidizer too, but prior to the expected arrival of the NASA rescue mission of 2046, NASA had sent an additional chemical plant, as a backup. John had put this plant in a separate building, and used it to make oxidizer only. In this way, there could be no building that ever contained even small quantities of fuel and oxidizer at the same time, and so no risk of an explosion.

The fuel and oxidizer had only to come in contact to ignite. The oxidizer was essentially a very reactive form of oxygen. It would burn just about anything that came in contact with it, including all plastics, most metals, and certainly human flesh. It was one of the most dangerous chemicals in existence, and had to be stored in special titanium alloy tanks, and handled and transported with extreme care. John had taken the tanks to hold the oxidizer, and the plumbing for piping, from the landers at the old NASA landing site too.

The separate fuel and oxidizer plants, and the separate sets of fuel and oxidizer storage tanks, both sets sheltered inside separate small craters, made it impossible for the fuel and oxidizer ever to get together, ignite, and cause an explosion. At this time, there was almost a hundred tons of fuel and nearly three hundred tons of oxidizer in storage at the site. This was more than twice as much as needed to refuel the ESA lander.

There was enough fuel and oxidizer in storage to cause an explosion capable of obliterating the entire industrial complex. Such an explosion would be more than twice as powerful as the one that had destroyed the NASA landing site in 2038. However, John had eliminated all the risks, and this simply could not happen. Even if a tank were to accidentally rupture, its contents would be contained in the shallow crater until it evaporated. There was nothing else in the two craters.

During the refueling, each trailer carried four small alloy containers, each capable of carrying a quarter ton of fuel. The ESA mission had brought these containers especially for the refueling operation. They had also brought safe, flexible, heated piping, with pumps if needed, to connect a fuel container on a trailer flatbed to a fuel storage tank embedded in the crater rim. At the other end of things, they had other flexible piping with pumps and heaters, to transfer the fuel from the trailer containers to the fuel tanks of the lander.

Jose and Karl stayed at the storage tanks at the industrial complex, to ensure that the fuel was loaded properly, while Jurgen and Derk remained with the lander, to ensure that the fuel was pumped up into the lander fuel tanks properly. With five vehicles involved, two rovers and three buggies, there was a vehicle to be unloaded or loaded every half hour, a process that took some fifteen minutes at each end. The remaining eight drove to and fro, John and Denise driving the two rovers, and the other six in the three buggies, two to each. Dr. Sato was not involved—he did his part by staying at the house with the two children.

The operation did not go quite as smoothly as planned. On Saturday and Sunday, they moved fifteen tons of fuel each day, but on Monday and Tuesday they transported less than half that. The problem was high winds and dust out in Elbow Plain in late morning and most of the afternoon. John thought it wiser to suspend operations at midday on those two days, and Derk agreed. There was only a modest wind on the following day, however, and they were able to work all day. By midday Wednesday, they had moved the needed forty-five tons of fuel, and the lander's fuel tanks were full.

Moving the oxidizer started on Wednesday afternoon, Alpha October 24. Greater care had to be taken now, and on Thursday and Friday they moved only twelve tons each day. On both Saturday and Sunday, they had to suspend operations once more in early afternoon, because of high winds in Elbow Plain. They moved only eight tons of oxidizer on each of those days. Then the weather improved, and on Monday work proceeded all day.

On Tuesday morning, Derk ordered Don Carruthers, Vince Cassoni, and Astrid Larsson off the job, together with one buggy. The loading of seventy-five tons of oxidizer was nearing completion, and Derk had another important priority. He ordered these three to begin a detailed geological survey of the northwestern escarpment wall bounding Elbow Plain, the part of the wall beginning at Stem Gap, and running due east from there for about thirty miles.

John missed the diverted buggy quite quickly, and began wondering where it was. He asked Derk about it on Tuesday afternoon at the landing pit. Derk would say only that the three geologists had some geological work to do.

Later that afternoon, after emptying his trailer at the landing pit, John was driving across Elbow Plain, on his way back to Leaf Valley, to fetch another load of oxidizer. As he approached Stem Gap, he spotted something metallic, glinting among the rocks a few miles to his right, below the escarpment wall. He stopped and examined the object through field glasses, and saw the missing buggy and three figures, clearly engaged in geological fieldwork. It figures, he said to himself, and carried on into Leaf Valley.

The work transferring the oxidizer now continued with only the two rovers and two buggies. There were no further interruptions because of bad weather, and by early Thursday afternoon of Beta-October 03, the job was done.

At this point, the ESA rescue mission had been on Mars more than two and a half weeks, and was due to depart the following weekend. The orbital dynamics of the mother ship, going around overhead, meant that there were not that many times each day at which the lander could launch and safely dock with the mother ship. One such time was 2:43 on Saturday afternoon, Beta-October 05, and Derk tentatively scheduled the launch for that time. That day was also two days before the Martian Thanksgiving.

*

The previous weekend on Earth, the rage of the people of both Ireland and France had erupted in violence. The disturbances had begun a week after the funeral services in Dublin and Paris.

During the week leading up to the disturbances, Derk supplied ESA with more and more damning evidence of the guilt of Denise Lavoisier in the deaths of Sheila Bell and Claude Bertrand. Derk forwarded the evidence gradually, in a compelling manner. It was impossible not to conclude that Denise had lured Don Carruthers' expedition into the trap in the labyrinth, and later had systematically done everything possible to make sure that Claude Bertrand did not recover after his rescue.

ESA released the substance of Derk's reports to the media in the days after the funeral. ESA also released interviews with Derk on the subject, conducted by Emma Grant. News and media discussions in Europe were almost exclusively focussed on this topic. The media became more and more obsessed with it, and soon began using highly charged language, causing the population of Europe to become more and more upset with the conduct of Denise Lavoisier.

Derk, in all of the interviews, displayed an obvious sympathy for John, Denise, and Dr. Sato. He always appeared reluctant to believe that Denise could be as bad as the evidence he was forwarding might lead one to conclude. He certainly gave the impression that he, for one, was not inclined to lay blame, even where it was warranted, or do anything to bring those obviously responsible for this hideous crime to justice, unless forced. The apparent reality of the situation, as transmitted from Mars by Derk, was becoming all too clear to the population in Europe, and even to most people in the United States.

That summer week in Europe, late Alpha-October on Mars, it was seven weeks past Martian opposition, and the Earth still lay almost on a line between the sun and Mars. That meant that, from the viewpoint of a person on Mars, the Earth was almost in front of the sun, and could not be seen from Mars. In contrast, on Earth, a full Mars could be clearly seen, shining brilliant red in the nighttime sky, a little west of due south at midnight. It was the first star to come out each evening, and by dark was the brightest object in the heavens. Unfortunately, at this opposition, the blood red light of the planet did not incite the usual feelings of wonder in Europe. Instead, it incited anger toward an inhabitant of that planet, and her co-conspirators, who had deliberately, so it appeared, killed an European hero and heroine, and had come close to killing another four.

On Thursday evening in Dublin, early Saturday on Mars, there was a discussion on a popular video network, in which several participants almost lost their tempers. Afterward, a crowd emerged from pubs on the north side of Dublin, in a foul mood. Soon it was headed south, along the main thoroughfare, O'Connell Street, toward the south side of the city and the other side of the river, where the nation's public buildings stood. As it marched, the Red Planet glowed its angry red, due south in the sky ahead of them, reminding them of the loss of their heroine, and intensifying their anger.

As they marched, others joined them. Soon that main thoroughfare north of the river was swollen with an angry mob of at least ten thousand people. The city fathers, aware of the possibility of mob violence, had ringed public buildings on the other side of the river with police in riot gear, but there were far too few of them. The mob surged across the bridge to the south side of the city, and the situation degenerated into a full scale riot. Cars and buses were smashed, overturned or set alight, and the windows of shops and many public buildings were smashed too, before the police could bring in reinforcements and disperse the crowd.

In Paris, the following evening, on Friday, there was a similar display of violence. The crowd began collecting under the trees on the broad sidewalks on the east side of the Arc de Triumph. Soon it was swelling into a great throng of people, spilling out into the roadway, as others arrived along the many streets and avenues leading to the famous circle. Soon an enormous crowd, seething with anger, was marching east along the Avenue of the Champs Elysee toward the city center. At the eastern end of the grand avenue, it met a barricade of police in riot gear. As in Dublin, it was not enough, and a full scale riot ensued, with burning vehicles and damage to businesses along the avenue.

There was a further disturbance in Dublin that evening. There, things went even further, at least as far as Denise was concerned. Like the evening before, just after dark, a crowd of angry citizens grew in O'Connell Street on the north side of the river, and headed south along it toward the bridge. This time the police were ready, and were determined not to let the mob cross the river. Heavy lines of riot police, backed up by an impressive array of anti-riot hardware, blocked the exit from the wide bridge, which was not very long. But the mob did not intend to break windows in public buildings this evening. It would vent its anger in another way.

The crowd now occupied the bridge, and the walled embankment on either side of it, on the north side of the river. It next began to build a heap of fuel for a bonfire, right in the middle of the bridge. Everybody seemed to have been carrying something that could burn—bits of old furniture, old car tires, and boxes of old newspapers. In no time at all, the angry crowd had assembled a mountain of combustible rubbish, as the Red Planet looked on, that summer evening, from a clear night sky to the south.

A stout wooden pole soon appeared, which a group of young men and woman then embedded in the center of the mountain. Then, a huge effigy appeared at the north end of the bridge, held overhead by about fifteen sets of willing hands. The effigy was of a woman, in a long black dress, with brilliant red hair sticking out sideways (straw, dipped in red paint). On her head was a conical black cap, witch style. And on her chest, there was attached a square of white cloth, with the letters in red: *The Witch of Mars*.

The crowd on the bridge parted to let those bearing the effigy through, and the mob soon had this effigy tied to the pole in the center of the mountain of rubbish. The mountain was then set alight. Meanwhile, the police at the south end of the bridge held their ground, but did not interfere, relieved that they were not going to be attacked.

As the flames engulfed the effigy, the anger of the crowd began to abate, as its mood changed. A large throng of young men and woman then began holding hands, or holding on to the ends of each other's clothes, as they danced around the blazing fire, their faces lit up by the flames. Half an hour later, as the fire subsided, the crowd began to melt away, peacefully.

Denise had been burned in effigy as a witch.

The following evening, Saturday evening on Earth, there was a further angry gathering in Paris, in front of the broad steps of the National Assembly. An army of riot police confronted the mob, arrayed ten deep along the steps up to the building. But this time, the mob was not intent on violence, nor did it intend, like the Irish mob, to burn Denise in effigy. After all, Denise was a Frenchwoman, one of them, but one who had killed one of their own. She was one whom they felt they had every right to stand in judgement over.

The leaders of the mob had a list of demands, which they wanted to present to someone high in authority. There was no politician within miles of the legislature that evening, but the Chief of the Paris Police eventually made an appearance, and accepted the petition, promising he would turn it over to the President, in return for the crowd's agreement that it would disperse and go home. The petition demanded that Richard Derk, leader of the ESA mission to Mars, be granted the legal authority to arrest Denise Lavoisier and return her to France, to stand trial. It also demanded the arrest and trial of John Erway, as an accessory, and that any possible complicity on the part of Dr. Ichiro Sato be investigated.

Early next evening, Sunday evening on Earth, very late Monday on Mars, the President of France addressed the nation, and promised that the wheels of justice would start turning immediately. His speech was also listened to in Ireland, with real-time translation.

The people of both countries, as well as those in the rest of Europe, were now satisfied. There was no more violence or unlawful demonstrations, and the damage done by the rioters was soon repaired. Something was being done. The Witch of Mars would be made to pay for her crimes.

*

Denise and John did not find out about these events on Earth until four days later, on Friday, Beta-October 04. Although they could communicate with Earth, they did not have a permanent link, via a NASA comsat, because such a link would have required that NASA always have a large dish antenna on Earth directed at Mars, to pick up the weak signals from Leaf Valley. This was out of the question, given NASA's limited resources. Denise and John did have the ESA satellite link, but they were not empowered to use that.

NASA had put a new set of stationary communications satellites in orbit around Mars just prior to the expected arrival of the NASA rescue mission in 2046. This enabled Leaf Valley to send a message to Earth, or receive one from Earth, at any time of the day or season, provided NASA had a large dish antenna on Earth directed at Mars to either receive or transmit. The weak link in the communications was thus the shortage of NASA dish antenna time on Earth.

The arrangement with NASA was that NASA could send a message to Leaf Valley any time, and have it recorded. But Leaf Valley normally could send a message to Earth only on Sunday evening, between eight and nine, local Mars time and day, when one of NASA's large dish antennas would be directed at Mars and available to the settlement. A typical message from Leaf Valley was a request for specific information, such as a request for a video of a network news program, or information from a database. The requested data would then be transmitted to Mars later, usually not more than a few days later, when NASA dish antenna time became available.

Normally NASA computers on Earth handled such requests from Leaf Valley, and no human intervention was involved. The computers simply allocated the necessary resources, such as dish antenna time, according to complex resource-sharing procedures.

On Sunday evening, less than a day after Denise had been burned in effigy as a witch, John had sent a routine request to NASA for a video of a network newscast that usually gave a fair sample of world news.

John was in the habit of making such a request every two to three weeks, to keep up with events on Earth. However, on this occasion, unbeknownst to John, NASA had a severe shortage of giant dish antenna time. This was due to NASA's exclusive lease of antenna time to the CIA, for eavesdropping on ESA communications between the habitat and Mission Control, and to the U.S. Air Force, for communicating with its Mars mission, now very close to Mars. NASA did not send the requested news video until five days later—Friday, the day before the scheduled launch of the ESA lander.

Thus, on the day the refueling operation ended, Thursday, Beta-October 03, and only two days prior to the scheduled launch of the ESA lander, Denise was unaware of the extent to which her name and reputation had been destroyed in Europe. She was also unaware that the European judicial system, at the very highest level, was in the final stage of charging her with serious criminal offenses.

*

That Thursday evening, when the refueling was finished, there was to be a small party at the habitat, as a celebration of the completion of the arduous and risky task. It was also to serve as a farewell party for those who would be returning to Earth—Jose Montoya, and Monique Montpellier, and, as expected, Dr. Sato, John, Denise and the two children as well.

The party had been Vince Cassoni's idea. He had thought that the mission needed cheering up after the deaths of Sheila and Claude. In his opinion, the ESA mission had become too preoccupied with work, with too little play, and needed a little of the fun, laughter, and good food characteristic of his native Italy—*La dolce vita.* Of course, a party needed a legitimate excuse, and the end of the refueling, and the imminent departure of Jose and Monique, was just the excuse the normally cheerful Dr. Cassoni needed. He had approached his chief with the idea earlier in the week.

Derk had given the suggestion very careful consideration over a period of days, and finally, after seeing some strategic positives in the idea, had agreed.

Derk had come to consider himself as being in a position comparable to that of a disciplined government department chief, required to carry out a deportation order against a family of illegal immigrants, who had some sympathetic support among the population. On the one hand, the government had to be seen to be acting decisively against those who would transgress the rules. On the other hand, it did not want to be seen as a hard-hearted monster, with pictures in the media of grim-faced officials forcing woman and children on board deportation aircraft against their will, kicking and screaming.

Derk still hoped that John and Denise would agree to leave Mars without being forced, although he now knew the chance of that was small. Nevertheless, it could only be to his advantage if the European and American populations saw him treating John and Denise kindly and courteously, by inviting them to the party, with the children and the Zen master. Such images might well go far to offset any later images of unpleasant scenes, which might be unavoidable if the three refused to go quietly. They would also further enhance the image of himself that he had been building on Earth, as a decent and honest man placed in a very difficult situation.

Denise had received the invitation, two days earlier, on Tuesday evening. It had come from Derk, and was worded cordially. A copy had also gone to Mission Control, and had already been released to the media on Earth.

It was John's instinct to refuse the invitation. He had at once suspected a trap. Denise was not so sure, and had thought that it might be a chance to show themselves to be friendly and sociable, and thus make it harder for Derk to use force against them.

John had persuaded Denise to wait a day before replying to the invitation, while he sniffed out the lie of the land. The following morning, Wednesday, he had left the fuel depot much earlier than usual, headed for the lander with a load of oxidizer he had loaded himself. He knew that Don, Astrid, and Vince would be headed out on their daily geological mission to survey the northwest escarpment wall just east of Stem Gap, and he intended to run into them.

John's calculations were correct, and just after seven he had met their buggy, about a mile west of the junction of the main Kasei Valley road with the Elbow Hill road. As their buggy approached, John had slowed and stopped, just off the road. The sun was not long above the boundary escarpment wall to the east, and its rays had lit up John's face.

"Good morning," he had said, as Don Carruthers, who was driving, slowed and stopped just beside him. "I see you're to have a party tomorrow evening. I would never have expected that. I wouldn't have thought your chief was the partying type."

It was Astrid who had replied: "He is not. Don and I were surprised too. But it was not Captain Derk's idea. You can thank Vince Cassoni here. It was all his idea."

"Any particular reason?" John had asked, still suspicious.

"There is a lot more to life than just work," Vince Cassoni had answered, in his pronounced Italian accent and a big smile. "Everybody is much too serious around here, you too, if you will pardon me for saying so. We have to lighten up, or I think we will just go crazy. We all need to have some fun. I am going to make a delicious pizza, redder than Mars. Now just tell me. How long is it now since you enjoyed a really nice Italian pizza?"

John could not help smiling. The Italian geologist was obviously sincere. "Come to think of it," said John. "It's so long I've forgotten what one tastes like."

"So you will come and enjoy some pizza, and bring your beautiful wife, and the children too," Vince had said.

"All right, I'm sold," John had said, suddenly convinced that no harm was intended. "We'll be coming. Maybe we all could use a bit of cheering up."

"But there is one condition," Vince had said, suddenly looking serious. "You leave Mars politics, geology, engineering and work matters outside. It is to be a party—not an excuse to talk shop."

"Fair enough," John had said, with a smile. "I promise. Speaking about talking shop, where are you surveying right now? I haven't seen you for a while."

It was Don who had answered: "We're working quite a bit up the valley, about sixteen miles up, at the bottom of the escarpment a few miles this side of where Snakepit Crack starts."

"Have you much more to do?"

"Another five or six days probably," Don had replied. "We intend to do a thorough survey of the escarpment as far as the eastern end of Snakepit Crack."

"Look guys, be careful working near that pit," John had advised. "It's more dangerous than you would think. The ground at the edge can really be deceptive. There's no clear edge in many places. The ground can just slope away, getting steeper and steeper. You could easily get caught, and slide over, buggy and all. Another thing, the surface layer may look solid enough, you know, near the edge, but in reality, it can be completely eaten away underneath. It can give way without warning."

"Thanks for the tip," Don had said. "We might have been tempted to walk to the edge for a good look down."

"Don't even think about doing that," John had said. "It's not like the edge of the wall of an escarpment. Some weird processes must have gone on to form that pit."

"I've been wondering about that myself," Don had said. "Well, I suppose we should be getting to work. We'll see you at the party on Thursday."

"Enjoy your work," John had said, actually feeling a touch of envy at these three out doing geological survey work, while he had to spend his day ferrying oxidizer. "Oh, by the way, I'm curious about that escarpment myself, especially how that rampart on top of it came to be formed. I may drop by some day later in the week, when we get this refueling finished."

"I don't suppose there's any harm in that," Don had answered. "We might well be interested in hearing your opinion about a few things."

"But say nothing about it to the Captain," Astrid had added, looking very serious, just before the two vehicles had parted.

That evening Denise had sent Derk a message promising to come to the party, and to bring some potluck food, as requested.

*

The two rovers from Leaf Valley turned into the Elbow Hill road just before six on Thursday evening. John, Denise, and the two children were in one rover, and Dr. Sato was in the other.

It was a beautiful fall evening. The sun was sinking toward Stem Mountains to the west, and casting long shadows across the red valley floor, as they drove up the ridge road to the habitat on the side of Elbow Hill. There was a band of thin, white, washboard clouds approaching from the east though, promising a cloudy night.

John and Denise had no pressure suits for their two small children. Instead, they used two pressure dollies, designed and built by Dr. Sato from copper and glass, to allow them to take the children out on the Martian surface. They needed the dollies this evening, to get the children from the rover to the habitat.

A pressure dolly looked like a normal two-wheeled dolly on Earth, except that it carried a four-foot long, pressure-tight box, attached vertically. The box was made of copper, with a thick glass window on either side, and fabric inside for insulation. It also had a small seat inside for a child to sit on, strapped in. The front of the box had a door of thick glass embedded in copper. At the back of the box was a backpack from a pressure suit, to supply the interior with air and heat. The control panel was on top of the backpack. A radio, removed from a pressure suit, enabled communication. Thus a child in the pressure dolly was safe, could see out on three sides, could be heard, and could be conveniently wheeled about. A pressure dolly just fitted inside a rover airlock.

There was a small crowd outside the habitat waiting for them. Ursula Schneider was there, standing beside Jurgen Eindorf. They were both curious to see how the two Martians would get their children from rover to habitat. Don Carruthers, Astrid Larsson, and Vince Cassoni, interested in expressing a welcome, were also there. Emma Grant, was there too, recording with a video camera.

Dr. Sato was first out, carrying a small belongings container. He went up the steps of the other rover at once, just in time to open the airlock door, and take the pressure dolly with the first child out. He did not have to bump wheel it down the stair. Two pairs of willing hands, Don's and Vince's, seeing what was required, grabbed its wheels and lifted the pressure dolly down the stair. A minute later, Astrid pulled the second dolly out of the rover airlock, and Don and Vince provided the same service again.

Soon the children were inside the habitat, in the airlock room, and out of their pressure dollies. They stayed in the care of Dr. Sato, while Denise went back out again, wheeling one of the pressure dollies. The children meanwhile enjoyed the rapt attention of the ESA mission women, with the exception of Emma. After all, these were the first two humans born on another planet, and even Derk would not go so far as to attempt to vilify them. Ursula Schneider was entranced by them, and the children responded to her.

Denise soon stepped out of the airlock a second time, along with her husband. She was carrying a plastic belongings container, and John was pushing the pressure dolly, now filled with containers for dessert, tomatoes, salad vegetables, four transparent plastic containers of Martian white wine, and two plastic containers of Martian fruit juice. Denise intended to do her bit to make the party a success.

When Denise opened the door of the pressure dolly, the sweet smell of good food filled the airlock room, and a dozen hands were there to bring the food to the kitchen, while Denise explained to Vince, in charge of party operations, what the food was.

Astrid now led the visitors into the hallway of the southern science section of the habitat. She led the way, followed by the children, then John and Denise, followed by Dr. Sato. They were to have two cubicles in the science section for the evening, which would serve as their changing rooms. All three of them were wearing the usual body suits under their pressure suits, and had to change. Their clothes for the evening were in the belongings containers they had brought.

Astrid showed Denise and John into Claude Bertrand's old cubicle on the west side, and then pointed Dr. Sato to Sheila Bell's, on the east side, beside the surgery.

"I am afraid it is rather cramped," said Astrid to Denise, as she showed John and Denise to their cubicle. John thought Astrid had seemed particularly keen to make sure they got Claude's former room, which was further along the hallway than Sheila Bell's, something that puzzled him.

"It's space enough," said Denise, as they went in, after the two children, who immediately jumped on top of the small bed.

An unusual device in the cubicle captured John's attention at once. It was a quite large, transparent, plastic cube, about eighteen inches square, with a squat box of control electronics underneath. The device was sitting on the small desk, with a computer on the floor beside it. Beside the device was a 'bird', the 3-D equivalent of a computer mouse. John recognized the plastic cube at once.

It was a three-dimensional computer display unit. Inside the cube was a fine, three-dimensional matrix of normally invisible semi glass wires. Where three of these wires crossed, light could be emitted, permitting the device to display a three-dimensional image of any object or scene, even a human head or body.

John had never seen such a device, other than in media images from Earth. Architects and engineers, and the military too, used such units for displaying images of complex structures, vehicles, and battlefield terrain, in true three dimensions. When John had left Earth, nearly eleven years earlier, such display units had just been appearing. The technology had since been perfected, and they were now in widespread use on Earth.

"Not hard to guess what Claude Bertrand needed this for," said John, after Astrid had gone.

"For the big ESA project, I suppose, whatever it is," said Denise. "Is there any way to display an image of the project hardware?"

"No way," said John. "You can be sure Derk's had this computer's memory cleaned before any of us would be allowed in here."

"You know, I got the impression Astrid wanted us to be in this room," said Denise.

"Did you?" said John. "Well, so did I. I wonder if she's trying to tell us something."

"Do you think she might have hidden a data storage unit with the project's construction plans somewhere?"

"I doubt it," said John. "Derk's got to have made sure this room's clean. But I'll look while you're changing."

There were not many places to look—under the thin mattress on the bed, and in the space between the bed and the adjacent wall. John found nothing interesting, and soon they had changed and left their body suits lying on the bed.

Dr. Sato was waiting for them in the hallway, and they made their way back to the airlock room and on through to the living area of the habitat. Denise was wearing a long green dress, and John was in shirt and slacks, as was Dr. Sato.

When they entered the living area, in the central section, they immediately got the impression of a party atmosphere. The room was full of lights, and decorated with carefully cut pieces of silver and gold paper and foil, taken from kitchen supplies. Even the plant pots on the tables were covered in silver foil, which glistened in the many lights.

The two tables were now joined together to run along the eastern side of the long room, and were even covered by white tablecloths—sneaked on board the spacecraft from Earth by Vince Cassoni for just such an occasion. The long table could seat fifteen, and two of the chairs at the north end were raised up on a platform of plastic belongings cases, to seat the two children.

Astrid Larsson and Ursula Schneider were busy setting plastic glasses and the wine containers and decanters along the table, while Jurgen set out the plastic plates and cutlery. In the northeast corner, Karl Mannhardt and Jose Montoya were busy setting out an array of speakers attached to a computer. There was to be music and dancing after the dinner.

Vince Cassoni, Monique Montpellier, and Don Carruthers were working in the kitchen area, along the west wall of the room. Vince was directing operations, mostly involving preparation of six large pizzas, liberally decorated with Denise's tomatoes. His strong Italian voice was audible above the general buzz.

They were all dressed in their Martian best. Two of the women, Ursula and Astrid, wore long dresses. The other two, Monique and Emma, wore slacks, but with colorful tops.

Derk came up to them as they entered, followed by Emma, still video recording, and transmitting to Earth. He was smiling graciously. The dinner that evening was in his domain, after all. Everything would function to perfection, and everyone on Earth would see it, and would also see him both as a decent man and a competent and gracious host.

"We are so glad you could make it," he said. "It's nice to have everybody on Mars together for such a happy occasion, after what we've all been through." He hoped one of them would say something that could be interpreted negatively on Earth, and was not disappointed.

"I have to admit we did hesitate at first," said John, always direct, "since we weren't interested in a farewell party for ourselves. We're still intending to stay put, as you probably know."

"Come now," said Derk, "let's not quarrel. It's to be a fun evening for everyone. Come and be seated. We're just about to have some drinks. Vince will have the pizzas ready in about ten minutes. We've made places for you all at the end of the table."

He ushered them to the north end of the table, and John and Denise lifted the children into their high chairs. Derk acted the perfect gentleman, and pulled out the chair for Denise to sit down, with Emma continuing to video record from the other end of the room.

At that, the others began to seat themselves along the table. The children were seated at the foot of the table at the north end. Denise sat at the west side of the table, beside Dr. Sato, who was next to the children. Vince sat to Denise's right. John was on the other side, opposite Dr. Sato, and beside Ursula Schneider, the mission's biologist. Ursula, although she had no medical degree, was now serving as the mission's doctor. Jurgen Eindorf sat beside Ursula.

Derk sat at the head of the table, at the south end. Astrid Larsson sat next to Derk, on the east side of the long table. She was opposite Emma Grant, who was next to Don, both on the west side.

Soon they were eating appetizers, prepared by Vince, and drinking wine, as the relaxed atmosphere gradually generated a buzz of conversation. Denise talked to Vince about his appetizers, but John did not have much success with Ursula, who seemed rather quiet and reserved. He spent most of his time seeing to the two children. When Ursula did talk at any length, it was to Jurgen. Denise, on the other side of the table, noticed that Ursula and Jurgen seemed to understand each other, and wondered if there was something going on between them. To her eye, they certainly seemed matched.

Then Vince got up, calling to Monique and Don Carruthers. They went over to the kitchen, and carefully extracted six large pizzas from the kitchen's two ovens. These they duly spirited over to the long table, after which the three would-be chefs sat down, to loud applause. The pizzas looked delicious, and had a mouth-watering aroma. But before anyone could attack them, Derk tapped the table with his fork, and stood up, as Emma got out of her seat and backed away, recording with her video camera. Derk would make a speech.

"I have no wish," began Derk, "to become unpopular—"

"Impossible," interrupted Vince, who was not afraid of Derk, and had a sense of humor, "you already are unpopular." There was laughter at this, a frown from Derk, and then a big smile.

"—to become unpopular," Derk continued, "by delaying this feast before us unduly, which our resident comedian (more laughs) and pizza chef, Dr. Cassoni, with the assistance of Monique and Don, has worked so hard to prepare. But the occasion requires that some things be said."

"We are gathered here," Derk went on, "all of humanity on Mars, to celebrate accomplishment. Our mission, at the behest of the people of the European Union, has traveled safely to Mars, has landed safely, and following the arduous and dangerous task of refueling the lander, is now ready to send our mother ship back to Earth. The refueled lander will bring a large array of geological samples up to the mother ship. These samples are no doubt eagerly awaited on Earth. The lander will also ferry up Jose Montoya and Monique Montpellier, who have served this mission and the European Space Agency with distinction. A toast to Jose and Monique."

They all stood up, toasted Jose and Monique, and sat down, with applause afterward.

"And, of course," continued Derk, "I would be remiss in not saying that it is my fervent hope that three of those present, who have been on Mars far longer than is right for any human being, will be willing to return to mother Earth with the mother ship. No matter, I want to propose a toast to Dr. Ichiro Sato, Dr. Denise Lavoisier, and Dr. John Erway, in recognition of their early contribution to mankind's development of Mars."

They all stood up again, and toasted. Even John and Denise stood up, taken completely unawares. It was the first time Derk had ever said anything even remotely complementary about them. They did not realize that Derk was merely complementing himself, since he had successfully completed all propaganda operations needed to destroy their characters and reputations behind their backs.

"And finally," said Derk, when they had all sat down again, "I have one last solemn request. We must not forget Sheila Bell and Claude Bertrand, who were wrenched from us in so untimely a manner. They would have wanted us to carry on, however—I'm sure of that—in a spirit of hope, optimism, and good humor, which we will do this evening. But they would also have wanted us to remember them sometimes too. I now propose a minute of silence and reflection on the lives and accomplishments of these two, whom we miss so terribly." At this he remained standing, and bowed his head, while Emma continued to video record.

The minute expired, he raised his head and said: "That's all I have to say. Enjoy the party: the food, wine, and music, and the dancing afterwards."

A slice of pizza was soon on everyone's plate, with small slices for the children. Karl Mannhardt got the computer playing recordings of lively Italian party music, at a low volume, and presently there was eating, drinking and a general buzz of conversation.

Ursula Schneider's silence earlier now turned out to be due to her being somewhat overawed by John. She soon began to lose her reserve, helped by the wine perhaps, and began to expound on her favorite topic—life on Mars, or rather why no trace of life had been found so far. Jurgen, who had heard her theories many times before, merely listened, and made the odd intelligent remark.

Ursula actually surprised John, for she turned out to be an enthusiastic scientist, deeply interested in Mars. She thought it possible that Mars did have life, but deep underground. She made much of the fact that, deep enough underneath, the pressure and higher temperature would transform the ice underground to water, providing a sanctuary for life. She and John soon had a lively debate going on the issue—in between John preventing his two children making a complete mess of their end of the table. She mentioned that ESA intended to dig three very deep shafts on Mars soon, in connection with a major engineering project, which she knew next to nothing about. She hoped that a trace of life would be found in these shafts. John now found the conversation very interesting, but found himself puzzled as to the need for three deep shafts. Dr. Sato listened with great interest too, and actually joined in on a few occasions.

Denise spent most of the meal talking to Vince Cassoni. The conversation began with where he had got the ingredients for so excellent a pizza. It turned out that he had planned for just such a party before he left Earth, and had made sure that all the ingredients, various cheeses, meats, and other Italian specialties, were on board, and were not touched during the voyage from Earth.

"I was supposed to be going home with the lander on Saturday," he explained, his normally smiling and expressive face looking a little sad. "My wife and childen were expecting me. This should have been my farewell-to-Mars party too. But the Captain has ordered me to stay, to make up for losing Claude. I would prefer to go, but if the Captain will not allow it, then I have to stay—till the next opposition in two years. I have no choice. I do not like it, but I understand. If I were to go, he would have only Astrid left for the structural engineering work, and there's going to be a lot of that. And please do not ask me about engineering—I will not talk shop this evening."

"Fair enough," said Denise. "It's not a subject I could talk intelligently about anyway. Does your family live in Italy?"

"Yes, of course," said the Italian, his eyes lighting up, "in the most beautiful place on Earth. And how I miss it."

"And where would that be?"

"Lake Como," said Vince. "Have you ever been to Lake Como?"

"No, I'm afraid not," said Denise, "but I've heard it's an enchanting spot."

"Enchanting—beautiful—magnificent," cried Vince, throwing out both hands. "Ordinary words will not describe it. You have to be a poet. When you get back to Earth you must visit it, and my wife too, and give her my love. You will be very welcome."

The conversation continued, and the time flew by, as Denise was treated to pictures of the famous lake, and pictures of Vince's home and garden and family.

Soon the pizzas had been consumed, and Vince, Don, and Monique served Denise's dessert, followed by cookies and some more of Vince's cheese, by which time, fortified by generous amounts of wine, everyone was in a good mood. Even John relaxed, as he concluded that Derk and his military personnel had had too much wine to get up to any funny business.

It was only eight o'clock when the meal ended.

Karl Mannhardt now got the computer to play lively dance music, as many hands pushed the tables against the east wall, to make space for a dance floor in the middle of the room. Almost immediately Jose and Monique took to the floor, followed by Jurgen and Ursula, and Don and Astrid, and then by the two children, causing much laughter.

Apart from the Zen master, who was clearly not interested in dancing, there were seven men and five women, so that it was possible for everyone to have a dance partner most of the time. Denise danced with John, and with Don, Vince, and Jurgen, but never with Jose, Karl or the Captain. John danced with Ursula, Astrid, and Monique, but never with Emma.

Denise noticed Jurgen and Ursula dance together a lot that evening, and Jose and Monique dance together a lot too. So that's how they tend to pair off, she thought.

About eight thirty, John noticed Derk leave the room and go into the command section. About five minutes later Emma followed. They did not return. Some ten minutes later, John, who remained very alert and observant, noticed Astrid disappear into the command section too. She did not reappear until just before nine, when she began dancing with Don again. He wondered what she could have been doing. The other women left the living area once in a while too, but stayed away only a few minutes—probably to go the washroom, he thought. He decided to keep an eye on Astrid. Shortly after, he noticed her disappear into the airlock room, and on into the science section. This time she was back after only a few minutes' absence. Her goings and comings did not seem to have attracted any attention among the others, who seemed intent on enjoying themselves.

Just after nine thirty, the children, who had become tired of trying to dance, and were sitting on the table watching the dancing, fell asleep in each other's arms. John and Denise stopped dancing, took a child each in their arms, and retreated toward the airlock room and the science section, with the Zen master following. Vince and Jurgen would have gone with them, but Denise protested, saying that although they obviously had to go home, the dancing and the party should continue. They would look into the living area to wave good night when they were ready to go outside.

Denise was first in the cubicle and pulled her body suit off the bed to lay her sleeping son down. Lifting the body suit exposed a square object lying on the bed. It was a computer data storage unit. Denise picked it up and examined it.

"John," whispered Denise excitedly, as her husband put his daughter down on the bed. "This wasn't here before. It's got CB printed on it. It must have belonged to Claude Bertrand."

"Quick," said John softly, taking the unit from her, his eyes wide open. "I think I know what this is."

John turned on the computer beside the desk. Within seconds of inserting the storage unit, the cube display unit lit up. A 3-D image filled the display cube, extraordinarily realistic. It was an image of the south end of Leaf Valley, Stem Gap, and the escarpment wall of Kasei Valley to the east of it, with the high rampart on top. It was a perfect three-dimensional model of the terrain.

"Please fetch Dr. Sato, Denise, while I figure this out," said John, in a low voice. "I want him to see this. We've probably got only a few minutes."

Less than a minute later, Denise came back with Dr. Sato, who still had not changed. By now, John had figured out how to control the image using the 3-D display. He had succeeded in getting a row of control ikons to appear at the bottom front of the display, which he could trigger with the bird in his right hand.

"Look at this," said John softly, as he clicked the bird.

The image magnified and a huge structure appeared, running east-west across Leaf Valley, just behind Stem Gap. A rail tunnel ran up the sloping escarpment on the east side of Stem Gap, and along the edge of the northwest escarpment wall of Elbow Plain. It went upward at a steady rate of ascent, reaching the top just at the eastern end of the rampart.

"It must be a rail launcher," said Dr. Sato quietly. "It's at least twenty-five miles long, and climbs about three miles, and aims due east, with the planet's rotation."

"But John," said Denise softly, "you said such a thing was impossible, because you could never get the electrical energy into it. I remember you said the launch vehicle would have to run along that rail in seconds to get enough speed to get into orbit. You said no electrical power plant could supply the energy at the rate needed."

"Watch," said John. "They're not using an electrical power plant to supply the energy. They're using a gravity shaft, or rather three gravity shafts, with electromagnetic coupling—the trebuchet principle on a very large scale, and with a very modern twist."

As he spoke, he clicked on an ikon, and the image changed and magnified. Three large vertical shafts appeared, running deep down into the ground from the top of the rampart, each lined with electromagnets. There was a tunnel into the bottom of each shaft from the floor of Elbow Plain. At the top of each shaft was an enormous, streamlined, bullet-shaped object—essentially a heavy weight.

Then John clicked on a 'Launch' ikon. A large brown object, clearly a large block of copper, with short stubby wings, began to move along the rail tunnel, starting at the western side of Leaf Valley. It picked up speed rapidly as it began a gradual ascent up the edge of the escarpment, and on up to the top of the rampart.

"That's your block of copper, headed for Mars orbit, and then for Earth," said John, in a low voice. "I'm a bit puzzled about the wings though. But watch the heavy weights at the tops of the shafts."

As the copper missile accelerated along the rail tunnel, the heavy weight in one huge shaft was falling ever faster. About half way down the four-mile deep shaft, the weight in the second shaft began falling too, faster and deeper. By now, the magnified image of the copper missile shooting up along the rail tunnel was a blur.

Then the heavy, bullet-shaped weight in the third shaft began falling, well before the first weight reached the bottom of its shaft. By now, the missile was glowing orange. Just as the third weight neared the bottom of its shaft, the missile, glowing like a meteor, emerged from the rail launch tunnel at the top of the rampart, in a streak of light. It streaked up through the Martian atmosphere, and then on up, into space, its trajectory gradually bending over. The image perspective in the computer display cube continued to adjust, as the missile went higher and higher. The copper block eventually ended up in a very high circular orbit, some twenty thousand miles above the planet, along with other winged blocks of copper.

Then the image returned to a close perspective of the launch site, revealing a large nuclear-fusion power plant in the middle of Leaf Valley, generating the electrical power needed to haul the weights in the three shafts slowly back up.

"Wow!" whispered Denise. "Is this thing really possible?"

"Yes it is," said Dr. Sato quietly. "It's consistent with all the known laws of physics. The innovative idea is the gravity shafts. All the energy of the huge falling weights is changed into electrical energy, which then powers the magnetic drives of the rail launcher. A very large energy goes to the launch vehicle in a very short time, in not much more than seventy seconds. And you need the nuclear power plant only afterward, to supply the energy to haul the three heavy weights back up again—it's like charging an enormous battery. Then they're ready for the next launch."

"I see," said Denise, in a low voice. "But that only gets the copper blocks into orbit. You need power to blast out of orbit to get back to Earth. How are they intending to do that?"

"You saw that the copper block ended up in a very high orbit," said John softly. "Only a modest kick would be needed to free it completely from Martian gravity. Then it's downhill all the way to Earth, under the pull of the sun's gravity. Maybe there's a display. Yes. There is. Look!"

An image of a spacecraft appeared, with what looked like the spokes of a huge wheel sticking out from its rear end, all the way around, like a flat topped umbrella. Attached to the spokes were long cables, each one attached to a train of copper blocks. The whole assembly was in high orbit, and looked like a giant jellyfish. Suddenly the steam rocket motors on the spacecraft fired, but for only a few seconds. This was enough to kick the whole train assembly out of Mars orbit, headed for Earth.

"A nuclear-powered space tug," said John quietly, "towing at least a hundred barges of raw copper, bound for Earth—"

At that moment, they heard voices in the hallway. John was quick. In his mind, he had anticipated this eventuality as he worked with the computer. In seconds, he had the computer turned off, and the data storage unit ejected. He grabbed the unit, and had it under the mattress in another second. Then he was bending over the bed, and stroking the hair of his sleeping daughter with the other hand.

"I don't think it's possible," he said, in a louder but still quite low voice. "It's a pity, but we have to wake them. There's no way we can get them into their—"

At that moment, Monique Montpellier knocked on the only partly closed door. "We were wondering if you were all right," she said, as Denise opened the door fully.

"Yes, we're fine," said Denise softly. "We've all had too much to eat and drink, and have been dancing too much. We've hardly the energy to get changed, and it's such a pity to wake the children. It's been a great party."

"Do you need any help?" asked Jurgen, who was standing beside Monique. "We can help you get the children into the rover."

"Thank you very much," said John. "But we can manage fine. We've taken the children in and out of the rover ourselves more times than I care to count. Just give us a few more minutes to get ourselves organized. We'll be in the airlock room ready to go in five minutes at most."

"All right," said Jurgen. "We will see you off at the airlock."

With that Jurgen and Monique withdrew. Ten minutes later, having said their farewells to the group in the habitat, most of them still dancing, the three were in the rovers, under a now cloudy, starless sky, on their way back to Leaf Valley.

*

Later that evening, Dr. Sato, Denise, and John sat around the table in the downstairs living area of the house in the glass compound, discussing the huge ESA rail launcher project.

"I can see how the falling weights in the shafts are the source of energy," said Denise, "but I don't see how that can make the copper block come out of the rail tunnel fast enough to get into orbit. That copper block came out like a meteor. And I don't see how it's all connected to a medieval trebuchet."

"Could you explain it, Dr. Sato?" asked John, "I think you're better at that kind of thing than I am. I'll use too much engineering jargon."

"It's really quite easy to understand," said Dr. Sato to Denise, "if you just try to think like a child. Suppose you have a see-saw, where the plank on one side of the pivot is ten times longer than the plank on the other side. And suppose you sit on the long side, with nothing to balance your weight on the other short side. Then your feet would be on the ground—and the other short side would be up in the air. Agreed?"

"Yes," said Denise, "and I think I see what's coming next."

"Good," said Dr. Sato. "Now suppose a heavy weight, say thirty times your weight, were to fall down on the short end of the see-saw. What would happen?"

"The short end would be pushed down very fast by the heavy weight," said Denise, "and the long end would go up, with me on it."

"Correct, and here's the crucial point," said the Zen master. "Because the long end is ten times longer than the short end, the long end would have to fly up ten times faster than the short end would be pushed down. So if the short end was going down at twenty miles an hour, you'd be going up at two hundred miles an hour at the long end. That's the basic principle behind the trebuchet, and the reason why that piece of medieval artillery could fire a quarter ton block of stone as much as three hundred meters."

"So then, if I understand what you're driving at," said Denise, "when one of those heavy weights in the shafts is falling at one hundred miles an hour, the coupling to the block of copper causes it to move along the rail tunnel at ten times that speed or more."

"That is correct," said Dr. Sato. "You could imagine that the falling weight was connected to the copper block in the rail tunnel by a cable. When the heavy weight falls down the shaft, like with an elevator, the cable pulls the copper block up the rail tunnel—"

"And you get the ten to one speed ratio, or better," broke in Denise, "if you have a pulley system so that when the weight falls down one meter the block of copper is towed up ten meters."

"Except that, in practice, a cable would have to be far too long and heavy," explained John. "So you get the falling weight to generate electric power from its motion energy. The gravity shaft's a rail launcher working in reverse—motion energy in and electricity out. That electricity powers the copper block along the rail tunnel ten or twenty times faster. And that's why Astrid Larsson's research topic was called a *Gravity Shaft Powered Electromagnetically Coupled Trebuchet*. Change the word 'trebuchet' to 'rail launcher' and you have what we saw in that computer display."

"And that's what they've been perfecting in that remote corner of Ireland," said Denise. "So what they've got there is a rail tunnel running up a mountain toward the south and the sea, and a reverse rail shaft down from the top of the mountain, or several shafts, and a power plant to power lifting the weights up to the top of the shafts. But how come the CIA didn't know about this?"

"I suppose they must have kept it well hidden," said John. "They couldn't hide the power plant, but the rail tunnel could be just under ground, and the top of the big vertical shaft could be covered over. And if my school geography serves me well, Ireland's a very cloudy place most of the time, like Seattle in winter. Good place to hide things from spy satellites."

"What about landing the copper on Earth?" asked Denise. "We didn't get to see how they were going to do that."

"It's not hard to figure out," said John. "When that tug spacecraft arrives at Earth, towing its trains of copper blocks, it first gets itself into the right trajectory for a shallow entry into Earth's atmosphere. Then it gets out of the way. It'll probably call in at the moon for a load of water for its steam nuclear rocket, and then head back to Mars for more copper. It could even be manned by a robot crew.

"Meanwhile, the copper blocks all come in gliding like space shuttles. That's probably why that block we saw being launched had wings. Then the blocks splash down in the Pacific, or South Atlantic, or Indian Ocean."

"But wouldn't they burn up on the way down, and even if a block got down in one piece, wouldn't it sink?" asked Denise.

"No," said John. "You could easily prevent that. The copper blocks would have crude heat tiles fastened on the underneath, like a space shuttle, so that they wouldn't burn up. When they splashed down, they'd probably lose their wings, but they wouldn't sink because they'd be just hollow enough to float. So a transport ship with a crane could come and hoist them on board. That block in the computer image looked like it was a thousand tons."

"So each space tug would bring about a hundred thousand tons of copper to Earth every trip, at least," said Denise. "That's about two billion dollars' worth of copper. That's big money we're talking about."

"Yes," said John. "So now we can see what we're up against."

All three were silent for a while. Eventually John spoke. "Why did there have to be so much copper at Chiselhead? A tiny fraction of what's there would have been more than enough for the needs of a settlement here, for centuries to come. Now we've got big money interests on Earth breathing down our necks, determined to get us out of the way, so they can get at that copper. There's no doubt about it, Denise. They'll turn this place into a hell if they get their way—workers living underground, working their butts off in the copper game, all of them hoping to get back to Earth with a small fortune some day."

"With Derk in charge, at least in the beginning," said Denise.

"At least now we know one thing for sure," said John.

"What?"

"Derk means business," said John. "He intends to have us on that lander when it launches on Saturday, even if he has to kill some of us to do it. That's why they have guns. And it could be the reason he was so nice to us this evening."

"You mean to put us off guard," said Denise.

"Yes, so that we won't think to take precautions that might make things difficult for him."

"Who do you think left that data unit in Claude's cubicle?" asked Denise. "Astrid?"

"Obviously," said John. "Claude's data units would likely be hers now. I think she figured I'd already figured the ESA project out myself—which I had actually—except that I had visualized only one gravity shaft, not three. I guess they must have found that three shafts worked better in their simulations. Anyway, I think she's trying to protect us by showing us just what we're up against here, and why it's madness to try and fight it. She's telling us to give up and agree to go quietly, for everybody's sake. She doesn't want any of us to get hurt."

"I'm not going," said Denise stubbornly. "I intend to stay. This is my home, our home." But inside she knew it was hopeless. She could see no way to stop her home from becoming Derk's home very shortly. John noticed a tear in his wife's eye.

"No, we're not going," said John. "We fight it. We defend our homes and this valley—our Plan A, the first line of defense. We start defensive operations tomorrow. The enemy's on our doorstep, poised to strike. But since we're outnumbered and outgunned, we may be overwhelmed, and may not be able to stay here in this valley. In that case, we'll have to resort to our Plan B, if we're to avoid going up in that lander in thirty-six hours. I sure hope we don't have to resort to Plan B. It'll be tough. The only good thing about Plan B is that Derk can't know anything about it, and we had the time to put nearly all the resources in place before he arrived. Everything's ready, except for the bit we do in Outlook Cove tomorrow."

He paused, and turned to the Zen master. "Dr. Sato, circumstances call for a decision. You have to decide what you will do: Stay with us or go back to Earth on Saturday. Staying with us may be dangerous. We've no idea what they may try to do to us in a fight."

"Do you intend to use your guns against them?" asked Dr. Sato.

"No," said John, "that would make matters even worse, anyway. It would be like killing a cop. We'd be hunted down. I would use guns against them only if they were to use guns against us—in self-defense. I've no problem having them think I would use guns against them, though."

"In that case, things can continue to be as they have been since you first came to Ares Valley," he said.

Tears streamed down Denise's face at this. "Thank you," she said. "We wanted you to be with us."

"Then we'd better get down to business and discuss our Plan A options," said John.

And so they talked on, for hours, discussing options and developing plans of defense. It was very late when they all went to bed.

*

Just before eleven thirty that evening, Astrid Larsson let Don Carruthers into her cubicle. She had been in bed and got back in, as Don sat down on the chair beside the bed.

"They saw the data unit," said Astrid, sitting up with the pillow at her back. "I checked Claude's computer—and erased the log entry. No one will ever know."

"You remembered to retrieve the data unit?"

"Yes, I have it here, along with Claude's other engineering files," said Astrid.

"So there's no way anyone could ever find out?" said Don.

"At least nobody could ever prove I did it deliberately," said Astrid. "I could just have left the data unit in Claude's room by accident. I know how you feel about breaking mission rules. Claude's data units are all in my custody now, so I have a right to be working with them."

Don sighed. "I suppose so. I'd rather you hadn't done it though. You could have gotten yourself in a lot of trouble. And I'm still not convinced it was worth it. You still think it was?"

"I can only hope it was," said Astrid. "At least now they know they have no chance. They are both decent people, who have been unlucky to get in the way of big business interests. The news from Earth is terrible. Everybody just about thinks that Denise Lavoisier is guilty of murder. The Captain has been deliberately spreading false information about them."

"I wouldn't go so far as to accuse the Captain of that," said Don. "Maybe he does think she's guilty. I have to admit that for a while I thought she was too. But now that I know her better, and her husband too, I can see it makes no sense. She's just not the kind of person who would do such a horrible thing."

"No, she is not," agreed Astrid, "and the Captain is definitely spreading false information on Earth. I can tell you he knows for sure she did not do it, and he has done nothing to inform the authorities on Earth."

"But how can he know for sure, and how can you know he knows for sure?"

"Because I listened to the conversation between Denise and Sheila," said Astrid.

"What! But you were at the landing pit that morning. How? ...Was it recorded?"

"Yes," said Astrid.

"It's not possible," said Don, shaking his head. "The Captain could not possibly have made a recording of Sheila's conversation, if it showed that Denise had never said anything about a good, safe road through the labyrinth. If it had, then the Captain would not have been so sure the road was safe. He certainly would not have sent us on the expedition."

"It was not the Captain who made the recording, Don. Brace yourself." She paused, looking at Don. "It was Sheila who made it."

"What!"

"Sheila was collecting the material for a book," explained Astrid, "which is why she was always so inquisitive about everything that was going on, about things far outside her medical specialization. She often made recordings of conversations for that reason. She carried a small recording device in her shirt pocket. She was selective though. She never recorded any conversations with you." Astrid looked at Don, with a knowing expression on her face.

Don was shocked. "How do you know this?"

"Emma found the files on Sheila's computer after her death, and the Captain had them all transferred to Emma's computer, for safe keeping. One of the files was a recording of the conversation between Sheila and Denise, on the morning of the dental treatment."

"But how did you know about these files?" asked Don, still amazed.

"I overheard part of a conversation between the Captain and Emma, the day after the funeral. The Captain seemed to be instructing Emma about sending lies to Mission Control about Denise Lavoisier. Ever since, I have been waiting for a chance to break into Emma's computer, to see what was going on. A few hours ago, I got my chance, and I took it."

"You what!" Don was shocked again. "So that's what you were doing when you were away from the dancing this evening."

"Yes. The break-in was no problem. I spent all my time at university working with computers, and my research for ESA was top secret. My computers had all kinds of barriers and firewalls to prevent access by nosy people, and I got pretty expert in that kind of thing. Emma's computer was not that well protected. She was not expecting a break-in from anyone on the mission. She has been in the Captain's cubicle since about eight-thirty this evening, both of them probably a bit intoxicated too. That was my opportunity."

"Do you realize you'd be kicked out of ESA in disgrace for a thing like that, if the Captain ever found out, and that I'd be derelict in my duty if I didn't report it?"

"I do," said Astrid, "but I do not believe you would snitch on me. I did it for a good cause—prevention of injustice."

Don breathed hard. He did not like to be involved in breaking the rules. "No, I suppose I won't—but I should."

"Do you want to hear the part of the conversation where Sheila and Denise talked about Hazard Valley? There is a copy of the file in my computer. You turn it on—I am very comfortable here in bed."

"I should have nothing to do with this."

"But it is very important for you to know the truth about Sheila's death, is it not?"

Don looked intently at Astrid and nodded. He hesitated, but turned on the computer. Astrid gave Don the access codes, and shortly after Don was listening to Sheila's voice. The file was in both text and audio format, and he listened only to the parts where the road out of Leaf Valley through Tip Canyon was discussed.

"So there's no doubt," he said, as he switched off the computer, "Denise Lavoisier is completely innocent, and more than that, she's a heroine, by any standard. If it had not been for her we'd both be dead. Those three don't deserve to be turned out of their homes. What's the Captain going to do? Have you any idea?"

"I actually know," said Astrid.

"Because of something else you found in Emma's computer?"

"Yes," said Astrid. "The French Ministry of Justice and the European Court of Justice have ordered the arrest of Denise, and her deportation to Earth, to stand trial for murder and attempted murder. The court has empowered the Captain to carry out the arrest with whatever degree of force is necessary. John Erway and Dr. Sato are also ordered arrested on charges of being accessories to murder. The indictments arrived this evening, just before eight."

"Heavens!...But that recording proves the charges are false," said Don, "and the Captain knows it, and now we know it."

"But there is nothing we can do about it," said Astrid. "As you said, I would be kicked out of ESA if I ever revealed I broke into Emma's computer. And who am I going to tell? Mission Control? There may well be others in on this in ESA. My whistle-blowing message might not go anywhere, and I might even have an accident. There is very big money involved here. I would not be surprised if the Captain were to release that recording himself later, after the three are safely off the planet. He could say he had just discovered it among Sheila's effects. It would sound plausible enough. The charges could then be dropped before the case ever went to trial. Meanwhile, the Captain and ESA would have achieved their objective, which was to get those three off Mars, without looking bad. There is no way they could ever get back again."

"My God, what a diabolical scam!"

"It would not be the first time," said Astrid, "in a situation like this."

"It's happened before?"

"Yes, it has. Away back in 1500, King Ferdinand of Spain thought Christopher Columbus was getting too much power in the new colony in Hispanola, which Columbus had founded. So the King sent over a new governor to sort things out, a pretty ruthless type. When he got to the New World, he threw Columbus in jail, on all kinds of false charges, and then shipped him back to Spain in irons, in disgrace. After Columbus was safely back in Spain, the charges were dropped, and Columbus was released."

"And that's what's going to happen to these three, and their children," said Don, "and there's nothing we can do to stop it?"

"No, nothing," said Astrid. "All we can hope is that they do not resist arrest and cause somebody to get killed."

"I understand now why you were so anxious this evening that they see Claude's project file," said Don. "It might just prevent them from fighting back when they find out they're to be arrested on charges of murder. If somebody did that to me, I'd be in a mood to commit murder myself, especially if I'd busted my ass trying to save the people I'm accused of murdering."

"Most people would," said Astrid. "But one day it may all work out for the best. In the long run, it turned out a bit better for Columbus. Nobody remembers the name of that governor who threw him in jail, and very few know the name of the King of Spain at the time, whereas everybody knows of Christopher Columbus."

"You may well be right," said Don, getting up. "And now I'd better let you get to sleep. Looks like the next few days are going to be very interesting, maybe even historic."

"Yes, it looks that way. Good night."

"Good night, Astrid. I won't snitch on you. You can depend on that."

CHAPTER THIRTEEN

Prisoners

EARLY ON Friday morning, just after six o'clock, on the day before the launch, the six took their places around the table in the meeting room in the command section. Derk had called the meeting for very early, given it was the morning after the party.

None of the four from the science section were present. Those four were still asleep, unaware that the meeting would take place. Not even Astrid Larsson knew, and she was good at figuring out what was going on when she was not supposed to know.

It was a typical cloudless morning on Mars. The high, washboard clouds of the previous evening had cleared away. The sun was not yet up.

"Look at it as a commando mission, with Jose in charge," said Derk, who was sitting at the head of the table. "Jose is to be obeyed without question. Understand?"

Emma, Monique and Karl nodded. Four were going out on the planned expedition.

"The weather's good," added Derk, "so you should have no trouble on that score."

"What if the old man's there, and does offer resistance?" asked Monique.

"It's highly unlikely he could be there," said Jose. "I talked to Erway about that the morning we all went out to fetch the buggies in the labyrinth. That road up to the monastery is far too dangerous to travel in the dark, and it was after dark when they left here last night."

"But he could be on his way up right now," said Karl. "Monique has a point."

"That's very unlikely too, Karl," said Derk. "But if by some remote chance he were there, you can be sure he won't offer any resistance. But again, if by some remote chance he did offer some resistance, remember that he's unarmed, and a very old man. We don't want a public relations disaster. As I said earlier, he's not to be harmed. I want them all alive and well. You're acting as police officers. You are not authorized to use any harmful force, especially any deadly force, unless there is no doubt you are in danger of your lives."

"And if he shows up later in the day, I suppose we just surprise him," said Monique.

"It would not be wise to assume we could surprise him," said Emma.

"Oh," said Derk, turning to Emma, who was at his left.

"I've watched him," said Emma. "He's like a bloodhound, always sniffing everything out, things nobody else can detect. If he shows up at the monastery, I'm sure he'll know we're there, even before he comes in."

"In that case, you'd better be on the lookout for him," said Derk. "He could turn back without going in, and raise the alarm. One of you had better be outside when he arrives, so you can arrest him and bring him inside, and prevent that."

"Are you sure we should stay inside and out of sight all day, and keep away from the escarpment edge too?" asked Karl, in a heavy German accent. "It seems to me that one of us could keep tabs on everything that is going on in the valley, if we had an observation post right at the edge."

"I agree," said Derk. "We could. But it's too risky. It's best if you stay inside and under cover. Anyway, if my reckoning is right, there's a commanding view of most of the valley from the inside—at the glass wall on the east side, right beside the edge of the escarpment wall. But you can't use that openly either. You could be seen."

"Isn't it likely they'll try to set up an observation post at Stem Gap?" said Emma.

"I expect they will," said Derk. "They'll want to be on the lookout for when we're coming. You should easily be able to see if they set up such a lookout post, even if you're well back from the glass on the east side. All you need to be able to see is the road and the escarpment at Stem Gap. So make sure you keep back from the glass, and stay well hidden, behind some building or bushes. If he spots you, the whole strategy will fall apart."

"What if they've already set up an observation post?" asked Emma. "Erway's not stupid."

"If he has, you just turn back," said Derk. "That would mean a change of plan. But I'm sure he won't be there. I believe he'll wait until the test firing. He'll figure there's no point anybody making a move until we know the results of the test, and he'll assume we'll all be sleeping late this morning, after the party last night. That party was very useful." Then, looking at Jurgen, who was beside Emma, he said: "You're sure Erway knows the test is at eleven?"

"Yes," said Jurgen. "I let it drop casually in conversation with him during the dinner yesterday. He definitely picked up on it. I do not think he suspected anything."

"Good," said Derk. "It looks like everything is taken care of. Divide and conquer never fails."

"There's just one possibility that's bothering me," said Emma, "something we haven't discussed."

"I want every possibility discussed," said Derk. "What's not taken into account is what makes things go wrong. If there's something we've missed, I want to hear it now. What is it, Emma?"

"What's to stop them just taking off in their rovers for a month or so, until after our launch window is closed? Those rovers have unlimited range. They can go anywhere. If they did that we'd never find them."

"They certainly could do that," said Derk, with a sly smile, "but if they did, they'd come back to find us in complete control of all their facilities. And they'd have to come back, because they'd eventually run out of food. When they did, I'd place them under house arrest—in a habitat somewhere out of the way. Not this habitat—that would be too good for them. Maybe that small Japanese habitat they used to live in. Then we'd ship them off at the next launch window. Which reminds me, I didn't see that Japanese habitat anywhere when we were up there. Have any of you seen it?"

"It's there," said Jurgen, "behind the lab beside the greenhouses."

"Good," said Derk. He then continued: "But I don't believe they'll take off in their rovers. There's a very good reason why they wouldn't. It's the two children. It would be just hell for the adults, stuck in rovers for months with two screaming children. No, they'll try to stay in the valley, and hold on to their homes."

"At which they will not succeed," said Emma.

"They will not," agreed Derk. "Any other questions?"

He looked around. There was silence.

"All right, chaps," said Derk, glancing at his watch. "Off you go. It's six fifteen—sunrise in five minutes. You should be at the monastery by seven. Remember. You keep under cover until dusk, and you don't use the radio. Stick to the plan as much as possible, but use your initiative where circumstances demand it. You just abort the plan, and come back, if you don't receive the success signal after the test firing. Listen for it just after eleven, but don't respond. Jurgen doesn't expect any problems with the test. Assuming the test is a go, I expect to see the four of you safely back here tomorrow morning with the prisoners, and their rovers too. By tomorrow evening they'll be on their way to Earth, and out of our hair."

*

A short time later, a buggy set off down the ridge road from the habitat on the shelf at Elbow Hill. The buggy was Dr. Sato's, on loan to the ESA mission.

Jose, the expedition's leader, was driving, with Emma Grant beside him. Behind, sat Karl and Monique. Each of them had military training and experience, and each of them was armed. Emma and Karl had had Special Forces training. They all knew what they had to do, and were prepared to do it. Emma and Karl were capable of doing even more, if called upon.

Shortly after, they reached the junction with the main Kasei Valley road, turned right, and headed along the road to Stem Gap. The huge gap, some nine miles ahead, glowed bright orange in the just risen sun. As they sped along the road on their covert mission, patches of ice mist still lay in hollows of the valley floor, and the scattered rocks and small craters were casting long shadows.

Just before six forty, they reached Stem Gap. Anxiously, they scanned the sunlit cliff to their left, with its small sloping escarpment below it. Nothing. They scanned the huge sloping escarpment to their right, falling down from the bottom of another much larger precipice, still partly in shadow. There was nobody there either, to bar their way, and they passed through Stem Gap unopposed.

Shortly afterward, the commando mission was deep inside Leaf Valley, headed for the road up to Outlook Shelf. The first purely military operation of Richard Derk's mission to Mars was well under way.

*

Later that morning, shortly after ten thirty, the sun was still shining brightly in a cloudless sky, and there was no wind. Two rovers were traveling south, inside Leaf Valley, headed for Stem Gap.

About three miles before reaching the gap, the rovers slowed, and then turned off the road to the left.

An enormous sloping escarpment lay on this left side of the road. It fell down gradually from the bottom of the huge cliff much higher up, on top of which lay the high rampart of Kasei Valley. On the other side of the road, three miles further ahead, at the beginning of Stem Gap, lay the sharp line of Stem Mountains stretching off to the southwest. This mountain chain, separating Leaf Valley from Elbow Plain, began with a near vertical cliff bordering the gap, but with only a tiny sloping escarpment below it. The far larger sloping escarpment, cliff and rampart, at the left or east side of the gap, was much higher than the vertical cliff that began Stem Mountains on the gap's west side.

The only way into Leaf Valley from Elbow Plain was through Stem Gap, unless you were willing to take a long journey round to one of two northern entrances to the valley sanctuary. One of those long ways in was through the labyrinth first and then Tip Canyon, and the other was down through West Tip Gully from the high plateau surrounding the valley. West Tip Gully lay just north of Mount Tip. That was the strategic layout of the land, and John intended to take advantage of it.

The rovers were now traveling along the escarpment slope, at a shallow angle to the road, but still headed for Stem Gap. They got higher and higher above the road as they progressed, the one rover behind the other.

John was driving the first rover, with Denise and the two children beside him. Dr. Sato was driving the second.

By the time they reached the outer end of Stem Gap, with all of Elbow Plain in clear view ahead, they were some six hundred feet above the road running through the gap below to their right. They were still not high enough for the ground to slope really steeply, however, so enormous was the sloping escarpment below the cliff on that side of Stem Gap.

There were craters scattered over the slope, most of them fairly small, and John soon found one that suited his needs, one whose floor was free of fine sand that a rover could get stuck in. Shortly after, they parked both rovers in this shallow crater. They were facing southeast, so that, through the front window, they could just see over the crater rim toward Elbow Hill and the landing pit, some twelve miles away. They could clearly see the landing pit through field glasses. The nose of the lander was sticking out of the pit a little, glinting in the morning sun.

"Good," said John. "This crater will do fine. We can see them, but it's hard for them to see us. They can't see much of the rovers, and we've a good view of the road through the gap as well." Looking at his watch, he added: "It's ten fifty. Jurgen Eindorf said the firing was at eleven. He'll be on time, I'll bet."

"I don't know whether to hope it doesn't work or it does work," said Denise sorrowfully. "If it doesn't, and they can't fix it, I can't see Derk being willing to stay in the habitat for the winter."

"No, he'll want our house," said John, "you can be sure of that."

"And if the lander does work, he'll want us on board tomorrow."

"I want it to work," said John. "But I'll do my best to make sure we're not leaving with it."

John's strategy, worked out with the others the previous evening, was simple. They just had to keep Derk out of the valley, and both prevent Derk from taking them to his lander and prevent him from getting any more food. If they succeeded, they would starve him, and force him to leave instead.

"At least he can't accuse us of trying to kill him and his crew," said Denise.

"No, he can't," said John. "He has no right to any further food from us. We've done everything we contracted to do. Derk has plenty of his own food, only not down here on Mars."

"But if we can't stop him getting into our valley, it's Plan B," said Denise sorrowfully. "I've never liked Plan Bs. They always seem to involve the disaster scenario, like hitting the lifeboats because the ship's going down."

"Better the lifeboats than going down with the ship," said John. "But try not to worry about that. It's Plan A right now. We just have to make sure Plan B is always an option; that's all. There's just those last few things left to do to get it ready—which you'll be doing shortly…Look! Something's happening."

Looking through field glasses, they saw a buggy emerge from the landing pit, carrying two people. It headed down the trail to the road, and then east along the road toward Elbow Hill and up the winding ridge road. It reached the shelf at the habitat just before eleven, and then turned around, to face the landing pit. The two in the buggy did not get out. Instead they both began observing the landing pit through field glasses.

"Jurgen's inside the hab," explained John. "He can control the rocket motors from the communications room—I can almost hear his count down. He's going to fire rocket cylinders one, three and five in the first firing—at about a quarter thrust, for two seconds."

"There he goes!" said John.

Suddenly, three bright flashes of orange flame appeared, equally spaced around the pit. Almost immediately, the flames were engulfed in red dust, strongly illuminated. The display lasted two seconds exactly, at the end of which time there was a cloud of dust and smoke above the landing pit.

"Seems to have worked," said Denise, with a sigh.

"Let's see if the other three cylinders work," said John. "If they do, then circumstances will have decided our next move—I guess that's the kind of thing you usually say, Dr. Sato."

"Perhaps," said the Zen master. "In this situation, it would be more true to say that it is your strong desire to remain on Mars, combined with circumstances over which you have no control, that is deciding."

"I guess so," said John, raising his field glasses again. "Look. The dust has settled. He should be firing again soon."

They did not have long to wait. A minute later, three more flashes of flame appeared equidistant around the lander, differently positioned this time. These flames too extinguished after exactly two seconds, leaving another cloud of dust and smoke above the pit.

"So that's it," said John. "Our fuel and oxidizer burn in those rocket motors the way they're supposed to. That machine is now launch ready."

"So I take it we proceed with our Plan A," said Denise.

"We've no choice," said John, "unless you want a trip in that lander. That test will be the signal for them to put their plans in motion too."

"I don't like you sitting here all alone, trying to defend this valley," said Denise. "I'm no general, but I think any military person would laugh at you. This would be a job for a whole company on Earth."

"The insanity of it is probably what I've got going for me," said John. "I doubt if Derk will be expecting me to defend this gap, but that's what I'm determined to do. And don't forget this isn't Earth. On Earth, even a whole company couldn't defend a gap like this. The enemy would just bring in airpower and pulverize everybody.

But here there's no airpower, at least not yet. It's good old-fashioned cowboys and Indians. I guess we're the Indians—and the palefaces from Europe want our land, as usual. All right, I'm going outside. Push the radio and the detonator controller into the airlock once I'm out. I'll take out the nanogun and the mags myself. You keep the automatic rifle and machine pistol."

Soon John was outside, with two boxes of electronic gear at his feet, along with the nanogun and ammunition for it that he had burgled from the lander three weeks earlier.

One of the boxes of electronics was a small two-way radio, with a long antenna. The radio could be plugged into his suit. Given the height of the observation post, some six hundred feet above the valley floor, it would permit him to communicate with the house and rovers, as long as the rovers were inside Leaf Valley or out on Elbow Plain. It was a modification of a radio from the old NASA landing site. John and Dr. Sato had tested it for an eventuality like this before the Europeans had arrived, as part of their general precautionary preparations.

The other box was a radio controller that could set off remote-controlled mines John had buried at Stem Gap.

"We've a lot to do today, and little time to do it all," said John. "You should have the hab and minicat towed down to Outlook Cove by two o'clock at the latest, if you both get going now. I'd like to help, but somebody has to stay here, just in case."

"You think they'll come?" asked Denise a little nervously. "I don't like this. I don't think Derk has any sense of decency. He's ruthless. I'm sure of it."

"I'm sure of it now too," said John. "But in a way that's a positive—we know he's capable of anything, and so we know we have to be on our guard. He's not predictable either, unfortunately. But my guess is that they won't come until tomorrow morning. If they were to take us today they'd have the problem of keeping us overnight at Elbow Hill—it could be a very unpleasant scene—you crying your head off, and the children screaming. I reckon he'd want to avoid that."

"But he could have some other plan we haven't thought of," said Denise.

"He could, and that's why I'm going to sit here all day today," said John. "All right, you'd better get moving. As soon as the hab's in Outlook Cove, don't forget to come up here and let me have some lunch. Make sure you come up the way we just came up. You have to keep the rover out of the line of sight to Elbow Hill. Better if they don't know what we're up to. And remember to put the hab well inside Outlook Cove, and hide it out of sight of the road."

"We won't forget," said Denise. "They mustn't find that habitat. A lot of my work's in its laboratory."

With that, the two rovers backed away from the crater rim, turned around, and climbed over the rim to the north. Then they began the slow, sideways descent northward, along the escarpment, and back down to the floor of Leaf Valley.

John watched the two rovers descend to the road. Soon they were down, and headed northward toward the glass compound at Mount Tip, to fetch Dr. Sato's habitat. This was the Japanese habitat they had towed all the long way from the JSA landing site in Ares Valley, ten years earlier. They had lived in it while they were constructing their greenhouses and the house on Mount Tip.

John could keep the rovers in sight for only a short time after they reached the road, because of a huge spur on the escarpment about three miles to the north, blocking his view. More importantly, his observation post inside the small crater allowed him to keep a constant check on the road eastward across Elbow Plain. Using his outdoors field glasses, John could keep the habitat on Elbow Hill in view too, and this he did conscientiously. The habitat lay southeast of him, half way across the rolling, red, rock-strewn plain.

John also had a direct view across Leaf Valley to the monastery at the eastern edge of Outlook Shelf, about five miles away to the west, but he never once scanned it with his field glasses—there was no danger from that quarter, or so he thought.

*

Just after five thirty that afternoon, Richard Derk and Jurgen Eindorf were in conference in the habitat meeting room.

"Good. That observation post they've set up on the escarpment is just what I was expecting," Derk was saying.

"The top of the rover sticks out like a sore thumb," said Jurgen. "I would have thought he would have made a better effort to hide it—you can easily see it from here with field glasses."

"Only because I asked you to look for it," Derk reminded him. "If you weren't searching for it, it would be very hard to spot."

"I suppose so," said Jurgen. "But if they are all sitting up there, it could ruin the plan."

"If they all were, it would," said Derk. "But it's highly unlikely they're all there. There's only one rover there right now, and they certainly wouldn't want to have the children up there for very long, possibly in harm's way. My guess is that only Erway's up there. I'm sure the others are home in the compound."

"And you are still planning to drive over and confront him this evening?" said Jurgen.

"Yes, a trip to Stem Gap will serve multiple purpose," said Derk. "The most important is the diversion. We want his attention on us at dusk, and not elsewhere. That reminds me. I assume our geologists are back from their field trip? I want Astrid and Don to come with me, not you."

"Yes, they're back," said Jurgen. "Why do you want Don and Astrid with you?"

"Because it's better if we make it look as if all the people he has to worry about are still out in Elbow Plain," said Derk. "Don and Astrid will be under strict orders to keep quiet. It'll be dusk, so there's no way Erway can know who's in the buggy. Also, if Erway does anything violent, we'll be able to send Mission Control a message about Erway going crazy, and behaving violently toward innocent geologists out on an inspection of the northern wall of Kasei Valley. Don and Astrid's corroboration will be strong evidence."

"Do you expect him to be violent?"

"I don't know," said Derk, "but with all that fuel and oxidizer he's got, he could easily make explosives. We have to be careful there. Of course, I want to have to turn around because of something violent he does. I want him to think he's scared us off, because it'll make him feel a lot more secure about the gap. Later, when we give him good reason to feel very worried about something else at home, he'll do just what we want."

"I suppose it will work. I doubt if he could figure this out."

"There's no way," said Derk, "and the operation this morning seems to have gone smoothly."

"Well, at least this way, nobody is likely to get hurt," said Jurgen, with a sigh. Although he was impressed with his chief's strategic planning skills, he had no stomach for dirty work.

"It is a pity we have to do this to them," Jurgen continued, letting out what was on his mind. "Having met them and seen what kind of people they are, and what they have accomplished, I find it hard to convince myself they deserve to be treated this way. I can not forget they saved the lives of four of us. I certainly would not like to see them hurt. On the other hand, if Denise Lavoisier did what the evidence suggests, she has to stand trial. The indictments are real. We have to arrest them, and this is probably the only way to do it without hurting anybody."

"It is," said Derk, "although it's still a very unpleasant business. But we have our orders, like it or not. The sooner we get it over with the better. I need a bite to eat before we go. We should leave just after six."

*

It was just after six fifteen that evening. John was still at his observation post, but sitting in the front seat of his rover. The sun, beneath its brilliant pink-blue sunset fan, was just above the west wall of Kasei Valley, just north of the monastery at Outlook Shelf, and about to set. John was not looking at either the monastery or the yellow sun. He was looking attentively through field glasses, focussed on the habitat to the southeast. It looked as if something was about to happen.

Nothing had happened during the afternoon, with regard to activity on the part of those who were now the enemy.

Inside Leaf Valley it had been different. He had watched Denise and Dr. Sato tow the Japanese habitat into Outlook Cove, just north of Outlook Shelf. Shortly after, about two thirty, Denise and Dr. Sato had driven up the escarpment to the observation post in the small crater, and they had all eaten a late lunch in a rover.

Then Denise and Dr. Sato, with the two children, had gone back up to the industrial complex in one of the rovers, leaving him the other rover. John had needed to be able to sit inside, in the cold of the late afternoon and evening.

Later in the afternoon, he had watched Denise drive into Outlook Cove with a nuclear power plant in the rover trailer, followed by Dr. Sato, who was driving the minicat. Shortly after, he had seen them drive out again, without either the nuclear power plant or the minicat. The rover had then taken the road back to the house at Mount Tip. That was just after five. Those activities had all been connected with their Plan B, and had gone smoothly.

The minicat was a most important piece of equipment. It had come to Mars with NASA's 2038 mission, and had survived the explosion that had wrecked the landing site. It was a small excavation machine, with a bulldozer blade and claw at the front, and a mechanical shovel at the back. It had been used to construct all the roads in the region, mostly by bulldozing rocks to one side.

At five fifteen, John had noticed a buggy with three occupants drive up Kasei Valley, coming from the northeast. It had turned left at Elbow Fork—the junction with the main Kasei Valley road, the road that ran from Stem Gap up to the old NASA landing site. Then, at the junction of this road with the Elbow Hill road, this buggy had turned left again, headed for the ESA habitat. It had clearly been Don, Astrid, and Vince, returning from their geology fieldwork.

But now, looking through field glasses, he could see another buggy on the move, coming down the ridge road from the habitat. It also had three occupants. I'll bet it's coming this way, he thought. It puzzled him though. Why would they come at this time, he wondered. If they were headed for the compound they wouldn't get there before dark, he thought, unless they're intending to take us this evening and keep us overnight at the house. Well, that's why I'm sitting up here, he thought, just in case they try something like that.

The buggy did not seem to be going very fast, and it took it nearly half an hour to reach the gap, by which time it was getting dark. The buggy had no lights on, as it approached.

John was outside the rover by now, at the rim of the crater, watching the buggy through outdoors field glasses. He had backed the rover away from the crater rim, into its center, where it could not be seen from the road.

He looked at the nanogun lying at his feet. The buggy was well within range now, approaching the gap below. Just one shell from that gun and there'd be three dead bodies down there, he thought. They're lucky I'm not the kind that likes to kill people. Obviously, they don't know we have guns, otherwise they wouldn't just drive up in the open like that, he thought. But even if I did feel like killing them, it would be stupid. The E.U. would have a mission full of cops up here at the next opposition. A shot across the bows is the best we can do. Since they don't know we have guns, maybe it's best if they continue not to know, he thought. Yes, I think so.

He bent down, and pressed a combination of buttons on the detonator control, generating a digital code, broadcast as a radio signal.

Immediately there was a bright flash, about a half mile ahead of the buggy, just off the left side of the road. Rocks and stones flew into the air from the force of the explosion. In the deepening dusk, the explosive flash lit up the whole of Stem Gap.

John and Dr. Sato had made powerful, remote-controlled land mines earlier, before the ESA mission arrived. Each mine was made from a copper box with two glass containers inside, one containing rocket fuel and the other oxidizer. When the radio signal reached the mine's small antenna, it triggered a spring-loaded hammer that broke the two glass containers, causing the fuel and oxidizer to mix, and explode violently. Dr. Sato had agreed to help make the mines only when assured they were for demonstration purposes, to deter entrance to Leaf Valley. Each mine contained some fine electro-mechanical parts that only Dr. Sato had the skills to machine.

The explosion had an immediate effect on the driver of the buggy. The buggy stopped, and turned around, going off the road a little. Then it went shooting back down the road away from the gap, with headlights still off. John estimated it was traveling at about twice the speed with which it had approached the gap.

John smiled to himself, as he watched the retreating buggy. I'll bet that gave them something to think about, he thought. And then he thought, a little sadly: The first shot. I just fired the first shot in a very small war, but the first war on Mars nevertheless. Hardly any-one on Mars yet, and already we have a war, he thought, feeling depressed.

Shortly after, he went back inside the rover, and drove it back to the crater rim, so he could continue to watch the buggy from inside, as it progressed across Elbow Plain, clearly headed for the habitat. Its lights were now on. When it reached the habitat, at about seven fifteen, its lights went out. I doubt if they'll be back here before day-light, thought John, with some satisfaction.

Just then, he heard a very distraught voice on the radio. It was Denise.

"John... John," she cried, clearly in tears.

"What is it?" cried John.

Denise was sobbing, and could hardly speak.

"Denise, try to pull yourself together," said John, very con-cerned. "What is it?"

"It's Derk," she managed to say. "I can't believe what he's done." More sobbing. "The bastard," she sobbed.

"If he's laid a finger on you..." he said. Then, suddenly thinking, he said: "But none of them are in Leaf Valley. I just stopped some of them coming in a while ago. Can you explain, Denise?"

There was a silence, as Denise gradually pulled herself together. "John, it's the news from Earth...it came in this evening. It's awful." She started sobbing again. Then she managed to go on. "There's been an investigation ... I've been formally charged with murder ... with the murder of Sheila Bell and Claude Bertrand ... and with attempted murder ... and with conspiracy to commit murder."

"What!" cried John. "Who did this? Who issued this indictment?"

"It's from the Ministry of Justice in Paris, but approved by the European Court of Justice ... and you and Dr. Sato are indicted as accessories to murder... The evidence against us is from reports Derk's been sending Mission Control about the deaths of Sheila Bell and Claude Bertrand. There have been riots in Europe over them. Everybody thinks I'm guilty." She started crying again. "They ...They've even burned me in effigy as a witch. I feel awful. You can't imagine how I feel."

"My God," cried John. He too was shaken. Both John and Denise had grown accustomed to being held in high esteem on Earth. They were only human, and what human can resist the warm glow of being held in high regard by fellow humans? After all, they had earned it. That esteem had obviously now been lost, and been replaced by contempt and the desire to inflict punishment, at least in Europe. John himself now began to feel the impact of being formally charged as an accessory to a murder. The pain was quite intense, although it was mixed with anger. Suddenly, he understood his wife's feelings, and how badly she must have been hurt—to be a doctor, formally charged with such crimes by the Justice Department of her native France.

"John, I can't bear the thought of it," sobbed Denise. "It's just not true. You have to believe me. I didn't try to kill anybody. I did everything I could to save them."

"Look Denise," said John, "get any ideas that I might think you're guilty out of your mind. Not only do I know you did everything you could to save them, I know you to be completely incapable of such crimes. It's Derk who's the criminal. He'll do anything to get what he wants. Try to stop letting it upset you, Denise. Don't you see? It's all part of his plan. By destroying our reputations on Earth, and getting indictments for serious crimes against us, he'll be empowered to arrest us and send us back to Earth to stand trial. A warrant for our arrest means the right to use force. So now, he can use force against us if he has to, without any repercussions to himself if anybody gets hurt. It's got nothing to do with you personally, Denise. It's just Derk. He's willing to destroy our reputations while we're alive, and he's probably willing to kill us too, if he has to. Maybe I should have killed the bastard this evening—I had him in my sights—sorry, I'm getting carried away too. I don't know if it was him at Stem Gap this evening. It might not have been. Anyway, try to pull yourself together. I need some time to think about this. It obviously alters things—in Derk's favor. We're at war, Denise. It's only a micro war, I admit, but it's still a war. And it's just turned into a dirty war. This guy fights dirty."

This outburst of support for her, and animosity toward Derk, had its effect, and Denise stopped sobbing.

"Thank you, John," she said, almost whispering. "That helped."

"Good. Now, does Dr. Sato know about this?" asked John.

"No, he's meditating in his room," said Denise.

"Maybe you should go and tell him he's being indicted as an accessory to murder," said John. "It won't bother him. Nothing does. But he may have some comforting words to say."

"I think you're right," said Denise, sounding more like her usual self. "I'll go and do that."

"Look. I need some time to think about this," said John. "I'll call you in half an hour, about eight o'clock. We should talk every half hour anyway. I need to stay here for now, just in case. But I don't think we're going to see any more of Derk and company this evening. They'll likely be out in force first thing in the morning though. We'll both have to be down here before sunrise I think, ready for a shootin' war. I'll probably be able to come home later this evening. Try to forget about those indictments. Remember that the first casualty in any war is always the truth. I'll call you at eight."

"All right," said Denise. "Be careful."

"I will," said John.

*

Earlier that evening, about six forty-five, in the deepening dusk, a buggy had made its way carefully down the escarpment road from

Outlook Shelf, and into Outlook Cove. It had no lights on. Jose was driving, with Emma beside him, and Karl and Monique behind.

Once down on the valley floor level, inside Outlook Cove, they followed the road in its huge sweeping curve back out of the cove and across Leaf Valley to the main road running north-south. While making the turn on the road inside the cove, they did not notice the Japanese habitat in the fading light. It lay well hidden in a hollow, a half mile deeper inside the cove.

That morning, Derk's commando mission had come the opposite way, unseen and unopposed, and had driven up to Outlook Shelf. The four had spent the day at the monastery, mostly observing the activities across the valley at John's observation post. Dr. Sato had not visited the monastery during the day, and the four intruders had had a relaxed time. They had not seen Denise either, as she and Dr. Sato hauled the Japanese habitat into Outlook Cove. They had been too far back from the glass wall at the eastern end of the monastery, making sure they were well hidden, as they watched John's observation post.

They were now driving northeastward across the valley toward the north-south road, at about fifteen miles an hour, when suddenly, a bright flash came from Stem Gap. Jose just ignored it, and drove on in the now very dim light. He had been expecting something of that nature, at just that time. His chief was obviously carrying out his part of the plan.

When they reach the north-south road, they turned north, toward the glass compound on Mount Tip. John might have seen them in the dim light, driving down from Outlook Shelf, or on the road across the valley, had he looked carefully, but his attention was fully occupied by the buggy that had just tried to go through Stem Gap.

Once on the road north, Jose's buggy was hidden from John's view by a large spur coming down from the east wall of Leaf Valley, and the four could proceed toward their objective, with no further risk of being noticed.

It was very nearly dark, at about seven forty, when they reached the glass compound, with Jose still driving without lights.

The compound was dimly lit. As Jose drove up onto the shelf in the near darkness, they were just able to make out where they were driving, by means of the feeble light coming through the upper glass wall. He did not drive to the entrance airlocks at the northeast corner. Instead, he drove around the south side of the compound, and over the top of the underground tunnel exit into the greenhouse passageway, keeping close to the compound's enclosing concrete wall.

Jose parked the buggy beside the compound's lower southwest wall, up against the concrete, and hidden well out of sight of the road up to the shelf. Then the four walked back around the building, along the south wall, back over the buried tunnel, until they came to the airlock entrances. Jose then gave his company detailed instructions. Emma did not like what he ordered her to do, but she obeyed, as each drew a machine pistol from its holster, and prepared it.

Inside the compound, there was only an old man, a distraught woman, and two small children.

*

At seven thirty-five, just after talking to John, Denise went out of the communications room, no longer sobbing, but still feeling depressed and upset, and just wanting to sit down and weep some more. She walked along the hallway toward the stairs to the upper level, and the Zen master's room. Just before the stairs, at the end of the hallway, she stopped, and opened the door into the children's playroom to her left. The two children were engrossed in watching a video recording—mostly educational, for Denise made sure that all the recordings she downloaded from archival computer stores were of mixed entertainment and educational value. The children noticed her, smiled, and then turned their attention back to the video. Denise closed the door, and went upstairs.

She walked the full length of the upstairs hallway to the eastern end of the house, and stopped at the door of Dr. Sato's room. She hesitated. She did not like to disturb him while he was meditating. Eventually she knocked and waited.

She had to wait nearly a minute before she heard the old Zen master's voice.

"Come in," he said.

When she came in, she found him standing some eight feet from the door, with hands joined. He was dressed in shirt and slacks. He just smiled at her.

"Dr. Sato, please excuse my disturbing you," she began, "but I have very bad news. For myself, I didn't know whether or not I should tell you, but I've just been speaking to John, and he thought I should. You've been indicted as an accessory to murder by the

Ministry of Justice in Paris and the European Court of Justice, and you have been ordered arrested and brought back to Earth to stand trial."

The Zen master showed no sign of concern. "And what offenses have you and Dr. Erway been charged with?" he asked.

Denise told him, and explained that she had the video of the news bulletin, if he wanted to see it for himself. He shook his head.

"Be not concerned," he said. "Courts of justice in Europe have traditionally favored justice over injustice. You are guilty of no injustice toward anyone. This will become clear in the course of time."

"Thank you," said Denise. "That's what John said. But it also means that they can use this as an excuse to take us to the lander by force, and call it a legitimate arrest."

"That is what they will try to do, no doubt, however unjustly," said Dr. Sato. "But remember that unjust acts carry within them the seeds of the punishment they merit. It remains to be seen—"

At that moment the door burst open, and Karl and Emma were inside the room in an instant, guns pointed at them.

"Freeze!" said Karl. "You are under arrest for murder, attempted murder and conspiracy to commit murder." Neither Denise nor the Zen master moved. Denise just stared at the guns, unable to think, in a state of shock.

"Now, hands in the air, both of you, slowly now. No tricks, and nobody will get hurt," said Emma, as Jose came into the room behind them.

Denise slowly raised her hands. The Zen master took no notice, and his hands remained joined together in front of him. It took Jose only seconds to force Denise's arms together and handcuff them. A few seconds later, he had handcuffed Dr. Sato too.

"All right," said Jose to Karl and Emma. "You can put the guns away now. They are both in custody."

Karl and Emma returned their pistols to their large side holsters.

Denise was still dazed at the speed with which she had been transformed from a free spirit, able to do as she pleased, to a prisoner. When her mind was able to work, her first thought was for her children.

"You bastards!" she screamed. "What have you done with my children?"

"Your children are perfectly safe, downstairs with Monique," said Emma.

"They do not know that you are under arrest," added Jose. "They are not being harassed in any way. We intend them no harm, nor you either, if you will just behave yourself."

Denise calmed down a little. "Bastards," she said again, this time in a quiet hissing tone. "You have no right to do this. You're no better than common criminals, breaking into a peaceful home, armed with automatic weapons, putting our lives in danger."

"I think you have it the wrong way round," said Jose quietly. "I am as sorry about this as you appear to be, but we are only obeying orders. I realize that you have been our hosts in this very house not long ago, and even saved my life, for which I remain grateful. You have my sincere regrets at these events this evening, but we have legitimate orders to arrest you, Dr. Denise Lavoisier, on charges of the murder of Sheila Bell and Claude Bertrand, both citizens of the European Union. We also have orders to arrest Ichiro Sato on a charge of being an accessory to murder. We are simply carrying out these orders."

"Whose orders?" hissed Denise, although she knew the answer.

"Captain Richard Derk gave us our orders," said Jose firmly. "He in turn is carrying out orders relayed to him by the European Space Agency, which has been empowered by the European Court of Justice to act as a police agency in carrying out your arrest and returning you to Earth to stand trial. Your trial will be fair, and, of course, anything you say in our presence may be used in evidence against you. You should therefore understand that we have been granted the authority to act as police officers in enforcing the Law of both the European Union and a member state, namely France. We therefore stand before you as legitimate police officers of the European Union, and have every right to arrest you. The evidence against you has been found sufficiently serious to merit the indictment and warrant for your arrest."

"You know perfectly well that these charges are a fabrication," hissed Denise, looking like a feline ready to tear him to pieces. "Your Captain just made them up in order to have an excuse for stealing everything we've worked here to build up. You're all nothing but a bunch of pirates. I should have let you all die out there in the labyrinth, instead of working myself to exhaustion to save you. You would have deserved it."

Jose winced. Denise had hit home, for Jose was not an evil man, who would do anything to achieve his ends. He knew his chief though, and Emma. He recovered himself quickly. "That threat will be made note of, and possibly used in evidence against you," he said. "Now, be quiet, and come with us." He paused, then explained. "We are only going to seat you in the upstairs living room for the evening, where we can keep an eye on you."

Denise did as she was bid, and her captors led her, along with the Zen master, to the living room at the end of the hallway. Jose pulled the small glass-topped table out from the southeast corner, and motioned Denise and the Zen master to sit in the two comfortable chairs in the corner. The corner was near to the window and sliding glass door out to the patio.

Karl then began searching the rooms along the hallway, and soon he had three light copper chairs arrayed facing the two in the corner, with the small glass table between them.

Jose, Emma, and Karl now sat attentively in these chairs facing their captives, without anyone saying a word. Emma and Karl put their guns on the table in front of them, within easy reach. Then Jose got up, and pulled the drapes across. Denise heard him explain to the others in a low tone: "Just in case. He might see us."

A few moments later the communications room alert went off. There was a message. It's John, thought Denise; he promised to call at eight. Their three captors ignored the alert. Ten minutes later it went off again. They ignored it again. At eight thirty it went off again. Still they ignored it.

Just after that, Monique came upstairs with the two children. Once up the stairs they rushed to their mother.

"Monique's putting you to bed this evening," said Monique, moving to the corner beside Denise and the children, and stretching out her hand.

At this point, the children sensed that something was very wrong, and that something very threatening was in their home. Perhaps it was the two ugly looking machine pistols lying on the glass table. They began to cry loudly.

"Can you help Monique, Emma?" said Jose, irritated "Get these children to bed, now."

Jose's strange and strong Spanish accent and harsh tone did not help, for the children went on crying. When both Monique and Emma tried to lift them away from their mother, the children held on to her fiercely and wouldn't let go, crying even louder.

"Stop it!" screamed Denise. "You bastards! I'll put them to bed."

Monique and Emma backed off. The children stopped crying, but held tightly to their mother, looking very afraid.

"All right," said Jose. "You put them to bed."

Denise held out her cuffed wrists. "Do you expect me to do it with these on?"

Jose said nothing for a moment. Then he said: "Monique! Emma! Check out the children's rooms. Remove anything that could be used as a weapon."

"My God!" screamed Denise. "You think I'd allow weapons in my children's rooms?"

"I have my orders," said Jose, as Monique and Emma disappeared down the hallway.

*

John was puzzled. It was just before eight o'clock, and he was still sitting in the front seat of his rover, in his observation crater high up on the escarpment on the eastern side of Stem Gap. Since talking to Denise half an hour earlier, about the murder charges leveled against her, he had kept the ESA habitat under constant observation using his high-powered field glasses, at the same time thinking about the implications of the murder charges.

Everything seemed normal at the habitat. Most lights were on. There were lights in the living area in the central section; there were lights in the cubicles and the communications room and the washroom in the command section, and there were lights in the cubicles and washroom in the science section. The lights in the cubicles and washrooms went on and off every so often. Everything seemed routine at the habitat. Everybody seemed to be home.

Given the murder charges, it was now obvious to John that Derk was intending to use force against them, to carry out an 'arrest'. What puzzled him was how. The lander was scheduled to launch in about eighteen hours. If there was no activity on Derk's part that evening, and it certainly did not look like it, that meant the attack or arrest attempt would come in the morning. But how?

Derk now knew that Stem Gap was defended, and that one person in John's strategic location, well equipped, could hold off a small army. Derk did not know that John was armed with a deadly nanogun, of course, but he would know that John could easily have mined the road at the gap and the terrain on either side of it. The explosion earlier that evening would testify to that. So how was Derk intending to gain entrance to Leaf Valley? A man of Derk's capability in the military strategy arena must surely have foreseen the possibility of John defending the gap. It was so obvious.

At eight o'clock, he called Denise, as he had promised, intending to discuss the problem with her. Denise had a very good head for possibilities, and John was beginning to worry that there was a possibility he had not taken into account.

There was no response from the habitat. John became concerned at once, but he calmed his concerns with the thought that perhaps there was something Denise had to see to outside the compound, perhaps in the greenhouses, or in her laboratory, and had lost track of the time. At ten after eight, he called again. Still no answer. Now he was worried, and experienced a strong desire to return home at once. But Stem Gap had to be defended, and so he stayed at his post, keeping the habitat under observation, in spite of his mounting concern. At eight thirty, he called again, but got no answer.

At nine o'clock, he called Denise again. Still no answer. Now he was very worried, but again managed to calm his fears somewhat with the thought that Denise must simply be outside the house and had lost track of the time. He could see no other reason why she did not respond. But then, why didn't the Zen master respond?

Still, John stayed at his post, continuing to observe the habitat. After nine, the lights in the living area went out. Now there were lights on in only the personnel cubicles. By nine thirty, there were only two lights on in the cubicles, one in the science section, and one in the command section.

He now called Denise for a fifth time. Still no response from the house. Now John was convinced that something was wrong. Denise could not have lost track of the time for so long. He knew he had to leave his post and investigate. But still he waited.

At nine forty-five, the remaining light in the command section went out, leaving only one light in the science section. They're obviously planning an early day tomorrow, whatever they intend, John concluded. That's what I figured they were up to earlier, he thought. Obviously, nothing was going to happen that evening. And why should it, he asked himself. Derk was not so stupid as to try to get through Stem Gap in the dark, if the terrain on either side of the road, and probably the road too, was mined, with John sitting ready to set off mines by remote control as well. No, obviously, thought

John, he's staying put this evening. It'll be safe to check things out at the house, at least for an hour or so. Better get moving.

And so, just after nine forty-five, John carefully drove back down the escarpment, heading northward. He drove very slowly, without lights, using only starlight to guide him, as he made the sideways descent to the road.

Only when he was about a third of the way down to the road, on the other side of a spur on the escarpment, cutting off the rover from the line of sight to the habitat, did he turn on the parking lights of the huge machine. He did not turn on the headlights until down on the road and well out of sight of any spying eyes at the habitat. At least they won't know if I'm still up there or not, John assured himself. That should help make them think twice about an attempt on the gap this evening.

It had taken John nearly half an hour to get down to the road in the dark. At ten thirty, he was still five miles from the house, heading north, at twenty miles an hour, with headlights full on. At this point, he tried again to call Denise, in the hope that there was a simple explanation for her not answering earlier, and to let her know he was coming. There was still no answer.

He reached the shelf at Mount Tip at ten forty-five. There were the usual few lights on in the compound, and everything seemed normal. John drove in through the airlock as he usually did, glad to be home. The outside airlock door closed, and air rushed into the huge airlock, as John got up from his seat.

As he was about to go up the step into the rover's living area, he remembered the nanogun, which he had left lying on the passenger seat, unloaded, beside a full magazine. He turned, lifted the gun, thought a moment, and then pushed it under the front passenger seats, along with the magazine. Best out of sight, he thought.

As he walked out of the rover and down the step, the inner door of the huge airlock was sliding open, revealing the other rover on the parking pad just beyond. Everything seemed normal there too.

Still concerned about why Denise had not been answering him, he walked quickly along the pad, past the other rover, and up the steps on the western side of the pad to the garden level and the quickest path to the house.

On that path, a few meters beyond the top of the steps, he suddenly felt something sharp stick into his back, and then a voice, in a distinct German accent:

"Halt or I shoot. Hands in the air—slowly. You're under arrest."

John complied, shaken. At that moment, Emma jumped out onto the path in front of him, with Jose behind her. Emma stood in an action stance, pointing her pistol at him, held in both hands.

"Now, lower your left hand, behind your back, slowly now," said Emma.

John did so, and felt a cuff on his wrist.

"Now the other hand, slowly."

Emma's gun prodded John in the chest. Again John obeyed.

"All right," said the voice from behind, clearly Karl's, "we have him."

His arrest happened so fast and so unexpectedly that John could hardly think. When he could, his feelings were a combination of anger and concern, and the humiliating feeling of having been outmaneuvered.

"What have you done with my wife?" he asked, looking at Jose, and trying to remain calm.

"Your wife and family, and Dr. Sato, are safe and well," replied Jose, still blocking the path in front of John, "but under arrest. We intend that you join them presently, in the upstairs living room. As I said to your wife earlier, I am sorry to have to do this to you, but we are only obeying legitimate orders. I do not intend any of you any physical harm. We are empowered and required to arrest all of you, and bring you to the lander tomorrow morning. You and Dr. Sato are charged with being an accessory to murder in the deaths of Sheila Bell and Claude Bertrand. Your wife is charged with murder. You are all going back to Earth tomorrow, to stand trial. I am sure you will get a fair trial."

"Very clever," said John, more relaxed now that he knew his family was safe. He actually believed Jose when he had said he did not wish them physical harm. He had come to know Jose earlier, on the trip to the labyrinth to fetch the buggies, and knew Jose was just a soldier, who would obey orders, but not a cruel or malevolent man.

Jose ignored the remark, motioned with his gun, and said: "Now please walk on to the house, and do not try anything. I do not want to have to hurt you."

There was nothing John could do except obey, and anyway, he was anxious to join Denise.

When John came up the stairs, with Emma and Karl on either side of him, and Jose behind, all of them pointing pistols at him, he was relieved to see his wife and the Zen master, sitting unharmed in the far corner. Monique was sitting facing them, her machine pistol pointed at them. Denise just looked at John, as he approached. Her expression said all.

Emma soon produced another copper chair, placed it beside the two soft chairs in the corner, and directed John to sit down beside his wife, hands still cuffed behind his back. The hands of the other two captives were cuffed in front.

John just smiled weakly at his wife, as he sat down beside her. His feelings of humiliation were intense. He had been badly outsmarted, and had let them all down. What must his wife be thinking of him? And he was supposed to be good at handling risks. At length his puzzlement at how the four intruders could possibly be in the house got the better of him, and he turned to his wife.

"How did they get into the valley?" he asked.

"No talking to each other," said Jose, before Denise could answer. "But I don't mind answering your question. We came into the valley early this morning and spent the day at the monastery. We drove up here from the monastery just after dark, while you were busy watching the road at the valley entrance. This was the Captain's plan for arresting you without bloodshed, and, as you can see, it worked very well. His plans almost always work. You should be grateful to him."

John's feelings of humiliation intensified at this, and he could think of nothing to say. How could he have been so stupid, he asked himself. But Denise, who had been sitting in that corner for more than three hours, had had plenty of time to think, and did have something to say to Jose.

"Well," she said to Jose. "It's obvious that your Captain has won. We're your prisoners and outnumbered, and you have guns and we don't. I'm innocent of the crimes I'm charged with, and so are Dr. Sato and my husband, and I have no doubt we will be found not guilty back on Earth. So obviously, for now, there's nothing we can do but accept our arrest and return to Earth tomorrow, and avoid any bloodshed. I'm very tired, and I've been sitting here since eight o'clock. Do we have to sit here all night, or do we get to go to bed? We're not going to cause trouble now. There's no point. You've won and we have to accept that. But Dr. Sato should be in bed, and I would like to get to bed too. There's no reason why we can't all be in bed, while you sit out here all night with your guns, if you want."

Jose considered this. It was obviously going to be a long night with all of them sitting up like this. If the three prisoners could be locked in the bedroom, then two of his people could sleep in one of the rovers while the other two kept watch. That way everybody could get some sleep. There was also a humane streak in Jose. He could see no reason why his three captives should not be allowed to go to bed. He preferred too, to preserve the respect of the mission scientists, especially Astrid and Don, and would like to be able to say that he had treated his captives well.

"Emma! Monique! Check out the bedroom," ordered Jose.

Emma and Monique were thorough. After about five minutes, they emerged from the bedroom, which was adjacent to the upstairs living room, carrying an assortment of minor objects that could conceivably be used as weapons, such as a pair of scissors, needles, and various items from the adjacent bathroom.

"The sliding door to the outside balcony's the only problem," said Emma. "It's got no lock."

"See if you can find a way to jam it from outside," said Jose. "Karl. You're good at things like that."

At this, Emma went back into the bedroom. Meanwhile, Karl pulled aside the drapes at the living room window out to the balcony, slid back the sliding glass door just beside where Dr. Sato sat, went outside and walked along the balcony to the outside of the sliding glass door into the bedroom.

The three captives could hear Emma and Karl working with the bedroom balcony door. Eventually, Karl came out of the bedroom door into the living area, and walked toward the stair.

"I should be able to find something in the kitchen to jam the runway," he said to Jose as he passed.

A few minutes later, he was back, holding a small copper spoon in his hand. He went into the bedroom, and out onto the balcony. He slid the balcony door closed behind him, and placed the small spoon in the runway under the door, and then tried to slide the door open. It would not budge. Moments later he came back into the living area through its balcony door, sliding the door closed behind him.

"The bedroom balcony door is secure," he said to Jose. "It can not be opened from inside."

"Good," said Jose. "Now, one last thing. Fetch the mattress and bedding from the monk's room, and make up a bed for him on the floor in the bedroom. I want all three of them in the same room."

While Karl was seeing to this, Jose spoke to the captives. “I'm glad to see you've accepted your arrest. I'm willing to let you all sleep in the bedroom this evening, on one condition. Each of you has to take a sleeping pill. I take it you have sleeping pills. I know you gave a sedative to Don Carruthers once.”

Denise hesitated, looking at her husband. John just shrugged his shoulders. “At least it'll make the night pass quicker,” he said.

“All right,” said Denise. “I have some in the surgery. We agree with your condition, on one condition of ours: you take these irons off while we're in bed.”

Jose frowned, thought for a moment and then said. “I am willing to remove your handcuffs, and the monk's, but not your husband's.”

“That's all right with me, Denise,” said John, “if I could have my hands in front of me. It's hard to sleep with hands bound behind your back. There's no need for that, Jose.”

“All right, we can change that,” said Jose.

“Just one other thing,” said Denise. “I'm reluctant to take a pill myself. I don't think it's a good idea for me. I may have to be awake to calm the children. They were very upset this evening. They could easily wake up. If Emma or Monique goes near them, they'll probably scream their heads off. They'll want their mother.”

Jose considered this. “All right, you do not have to take a pill,” he said eventually. “Emma. Take the lady to the surgery to get the pills for the other two.”

When Emma and Denise returned, Jose said: “You go to bed one by one, and the two men will take a pill each before they do.”

Denise went first, accompanied by Emma and Monique. Emma took off Denise's handcuffs, while Monique held a pistol pointed at Denise. Denise then changed into her nightdress.

When Denise was in bed, Karl and Jose brought in Dr. Sato, and took off his cuffs. The Zen master put on pajamas, and then took the pill from Karl and washed it down with water. Jose carefully examined his mouth afterward to make certain he had swallowed it. He then lay down on the mattress on the floor, on the side of the bed away from the balcony door.

Finally, it was John's turn. With Jose pointing his pistol, Karl removed John's handcuffs long enough for him to put on his pajamas and take his sleeping pill. Then Karl put the cuffs back on again, this time with hands in front.

When John got into bed, Denise was not asleep, but she closed her eyes a few seconds later. Satisfied that all was well, and after checking the balcony door himself, and turning off the bedroom light, Jose went out into the living area, followed by Karl, leaving the bedroom door open.

Jose then decided that he and Monique would take the first watch, while Karl and Emma went to bed in the rover.

"Sleep in the rover in the airlock, not the one on the pad," said Jose, in a low voice, "and keep your guns handy. We may as well make sure they can not leave the compound, even if by some miracle they could escape from the house."

Jose and Monique then made themselves comfortable in the two easy chairs in the southeast corner, where Denise and Dr. Sato had been sitting, and resigned themselves to a three-hour watch. They put their feet up on the glass table, beside their guns and the two sets of handcuffs taken from Denise and the Zen master.

CHAPTER FOURTEEN

Fortress

AFTER JOSE and Karl left the room, Denise lay very quiet, eyes closed, all the while listening for movements out in the living room beyond the bedroom door. After about a quarter hour, at about eleven forty, all was quiet out in the adjacent living area. She gently pulled the parachute-fabric bedclothes up over her head, and that of her husband too.

"Are you awake," she whispered, gently prodding her husband.

"Yes," whispered John. "How come the sleeping pill I got isn't working?"

"Because it wasn't a sleeping pill," whispered Denise. "It was a heart stimulant pill. It has the kick of three cups of coffee."

"I see," said John softly.

"Listen," whispered Denise. "I have a plan."

"So have I," whispered John, "but I haven't figured out all the details yet. Sorry about this evening. I guess I blew it."

"Don't be sorry," whispered Denise. "Derk is just very smart. He anticipated our moves. Remember he anticipated our attempt to burgle the lander too. But I don't think he's all that smart. He wasn't smart enough to figure out that we took some of his guns. That's what my plan's about. We have to get the automatic rifle, and maybe the machine pistol too. The nanogun's no good inside the compound. The automatic's what we need. It's under the passenger seats in the rover, the one on the pad. The pistol's there too. Emma and Karl are sleeping in the other rover. I heard Jose giving them strict orders about that."

"That's more or less what I was planning," whispered John. "Karl and Emma obviously haven't found the nanogun, or the automatic rifle. The nanogun's under the front seats in the rover parked in the airlock. If we could get into the rover on the pad we could easily get the automatic and the pistol. That would completely turn the tables on them. They wouldn't be expecting anything like that. The problem's getting out of this room. The balcony door's jammed and Jose and Monique are sitting outside in the corner, watching the bedroom door."

"That's what I think I've figured out how to do, at least how one of us can get out," whispered Denise. "There a good chance it'll work. And if it doesn't, no harm done. Listen...."

John listened. When Denise had finished, he whispered: "Very good, if we get the opportunity."

"I think we will," whispered Denise. "Derk will want to know the result of his operation. Jose hasn't communicated with the hab yet. He has to soon."

"If we do get the chance, the biggest problem will be those seventy seconds," whispered John. "You'll have to try for a hundred seconds, just to be safe, and you can't look at your watch. Monique is bound to notice. Just count in your mind: 'a thousand and one' for the first second, 'a thousand and two' for the next, and so on. How are you going to tell Dr. Sato what he has to do?"

"With a pillow," whispered Denise.

With that, Denise emerged softly from under the bedclothes, and gently pulled her pillow out from under her head with her left arm. Then she stretched it out to the floor, to touch the head of Dr. Sato, lying on his mattress beside the bed, a few feet away. Then she put the pillow back under her head, and beaconed with her left arm, holding it high up. The Zen master, also wide awake because of the stimulant pill he had swallowed, could see the silhouette of Denise's arm against the dim light coming in from the compound outside, through the balcony window and sliding glass door. A few seconds later, Denise could see Dr. Sato very quietly raising himself into a sitting position.

Denise now pulled the bedclothes over her head once again, very quietly, but holding them open to her left, out over the edge of the bed, so that the Zen master, without leaving his bed, was just able to put his head close to hers under the bedclothes.

They whispered together for some five minutes. Then both heads emerged from under Denise's bedclothes, and Dr. Sato returned to a sleeping position.

All they could do now was wait, and hope that the chance Denise expected would materialize.

*

Just before twelve, Denise heard footsteps approaching the bedroom door. Then a figure entered the room, carrying a pistol. Denise winced, but found it hard to believe that the figure intended them harm. The light came on. It was Jose. Denise blinked and looked at Jose. Jose looked at the other two. Both of them appeared to be fast asleep. John was even snoring lightly.

"Not asleep yet," said Jose quietly to Denise.

"Two much excitement probably," said Denise. "Maybe I should have taken that sleeping pill after all. It's not very pleasant lying here thinking of four armed jailers sitting outside."

"You can still take a pill if you want to," said Jose.

"Maybe I'll take just half of one in fifteen minutes or so if I still can't sleep," said Denise. "I really don't want to be completely dead to the world if the children wake up."

Jose did not answer, but turned about, turned off the light and left the room. Denise listened carefully as Jose retraced his steps over to the far corner of the living room, beside the balcony, where Monique was sitting. Denise did not hear any noise from a chair as Jose sat down, and she reckoned he remained standing.

Then Denise heard Jose and Monique talking in low tones. She could not make out the conversation, but she was sure she heard Jose say the word 'Captain', and was nearly certain she heard the phrase 'to the habitat'. Then she heard footsteps head toward the stairs, and descend the stairs. Then there was silence.

Denise waited for about three minutes. Then she got quietly out of bed, walked to near the door, and knocked on the wall gently.

"Jose, Monique," she said gently, but easily loud enough for Monique to hear.

When she heard Monique getting out of the chair, she moved into the open bedroom doorway, and was now able to see Monique and be seen by Monique. Monique was walking toward her with her gun in her right hand, pointed at her.

"Monique, I think I have to have a sleeping pill after all," said Denise, speaking to Monique in French. "I'm wide awake. I'm not going to be able to sleep. The other two are completely dead. Half a pill should be enough for me, in case I have to wake up to see to the children."

Monique said nothing. She was suspicious, and motioned Denise back into the bedroom with her pistol. Monique turned on the light, and inspected the two sleeping men. They seemed fast asleep, with John still snoring lightly. John's cuffed hands were visible above the bedclothes.

Monique retreated out of the room, turning off the light.

"All right," she said, in French. "You can get a pill from the surgery. Don't try anything. I'm right behind you. I wouldn't like to have to hurt you, so please don't force me to. But given what you're charged with, I don't think anybody in France would be very sorry if something did happen to you."

"Now don't be silly, Monique," said Denise. "What could I do to you? I'm a doctor, not a soldier, and I've got two children asleep next door. Do you really think I would do anything that might cause them to be harmed?"

Monique understood the sense in this, and motioned toward the surgery with her gun. Denise then began walking across the living room towards the hallway that split the eastern half of the upper floor in two, followed closely by Monique. Actually, Denise was not worried about a stray bullet in the living area hurting her children next door. She knew the inside walls of the house were solid concrete, which no bullet could penetrate. She was also a courageous woman, with an inclination to run risks.

The pair turned the corner into the hallway, and then turned left into the small surgery. Using her gun, Monique motioned Denise to stop at the surgery door. Monique went into the surgery first, and turned on the light. She scanned every corner for anything Denise could use as a weapon.

Monique was well trained in military and combat matters, and was armed with a deadly machine pistol that she knew how to use. In a combat situation, Monique was a dangerous woman. In such a situation, it would have been impossible for Denise to get the better of her using force. But that was not what Denise had in mind. As soon as Monique entered the surgery to check it out, Denise began counting seconds: *one thousand and one*, *one thousand and two*, ….

Monique now motioned Denise to come into the surgery. "Don't try to touch any surgical tools," said Monique in French. "I know where they all are."

Denise walked slowly to the far wall of the small room, where there was a copper cabinet containing only medicines, above a small copper washbasin. She searched slowly among the plastic bottles, and found the one she was looking for. Denise counted *one thousand and ten* in her mind. She took the bottle of pills down, opened it, and nervously turned it almost upside down to pour a pill out into the palm of her right hand.

Suddenly, she dropped the bottle. Pills spilled onto the floor.

"Oh, I'm sorry," said Denise, almost in tears, bending down to pick up the bottle and the pills. "You're making me nervous with that gun. Couldn't you at least point it at the floor instead of at me?"

"All right," said Monique, backing away a little, and lowering the gun. "Now, hurry up please."

Denise, now down on her knees, fumbled the pills into the bottle; she counted *one thousand and forty-three*. Then she stood up, with one pill in her right hand. She put the bottle down at the edge of the washbasin, and then took a few seconds to snap the long pill in two. Then she put one half pill back in the bottle, and put the bottle back on the shelf in the medicine cabinet; *one thousand and sixty-one* she counted in her mind.

Now she took a plastic mug down from a shelf beside the cabinet, and filled it with just a little water. She hesitated a few seconds, before putting the half pill in her mouth and washing it down; *one thousand and seventy-five*, she counted inwardly. I need more time, she thought. Then she turned to Monique.

"I just need a drink of water too. It won't take me a second."

Actually, she made sure it took ten seconds. It also took her another three seconds to put the mug back on the shelf. It then took her another three seconds to wipe her face with a towel; *one thousand and ninety-one*, she counted.

There was no way she could delay any longer. She now turned slowly and walked slowly out of the surgery and round the hallway corner, with Monique behind her. As she came around the corner, she counted *one thousand and ninety-five*.

*

Ten minutes later, at about twelve twenty-five, back in bed, Denise heard footsteps. Jose was walking across the living room, coming from the stairs. Then she heard voices, and Jose's footsteps approaching the bedroom. When Jose turned on the light to inspect his three prisoners, Denise was lying facing up to the ceiling, eyes closed, her mouth slightly open, faintly snoring. John's handcuffs were still visible, and he was still snoring lightly. The Zen master lay curled up, fast asleep.

Satisfied that he would have no more trouble that night, Jose turned out the light and withdrew.

Five minutes later, with all quiet, Denise drew the bedclothes over her head again, and over John's too.

"Did it work?" whispered Denise.

"Yes," whispered John. "I timed him. He did the whole thing in ninety seconds."

"So the door should open now," whispered Denise.

"Yes," whispered John. "Our Zen master only had to remove the copper spoon jamming the door runway. He managed to slide open the living room door, and get out on to the balcony without making a sound. I couldn't hear him—that's how quiet he was. He'd make a good burglar. I did see him take the spoon out from under our balcony door though. He didn't make a sound coming back in either. If this plan succeeds we'll really owe him one."

"So when will you try?" asked Denise.

"Give them another half hour, maybe a bit more," said John. "They should both be drowsy by then."

By the time another thirty minutes had gone by, Denise had developed a decent snore, rising and falling in a steady rhythm.

Then, very quietly, John got out of bed, holding his cuffed wrists close to his stomach for better balance. Very softly, he made his way toward the balcony door. For an instant, his shadowy outline was visible to Jose and Monique, through the bedroom door. John glimpsed them sitting in the far corner of the living area, feet up on the glass table, but they were not looking at him. They seemed to be dozing. It was twenty past zero in the morning.

Slowly and carefully, John inched the bedroom balcony door open. Each move of the door coincided with the peak of Denise's snore. It took a minute of this gentle pushing before there was space enough for him to squeeze through.

Once outside, John left nothing to chance. He spent an equal amount of time closing the sliding door behind him, just as gently. The temperature was considerably lower outside in the compound than in the house. Cold air coming in through the open balcony door could alert their two captors.

Finally he had the sliding door closed, and could steal away softly. He reached the southwest corner in seconds, only a few meters away.

Once around the corner of the house, he walked briskly along the upper west-side balcony. The balcony floor was freezing cold and he had bare feet. He reached the stair down to the lower level.

He almost ran down the stair, and then ran along the patio on the north side of the house.

A minute later, John was running along the garden path toward the rover parking pad. He then slowed, and crept stealthily down the steep embankment steps to the pad. No sign of Emma and Karl. Once down on the pad, he sneaked around the front of the rover to the rover staircase on the passenger side of the machine.

He hesitated before climbing the rover stair. Still no sign of life. Let's hope Denise was right, he thought, and that she really did hear Jose ordering Emma and Karl to sleep in the rover in the airlock garage.

The rover airlock doors lay wide open. The rover inside air pressure was the same as the air pressure in the compound, making use of the airlock unnecessary.

John climbed the stairs softly. Once inside, he approached the driver area very cautiously. There was a dim light coming in through the rover windows from the parking pad. The front bunk was empty. He breathed a sigh of relief. A few seconds later, he was down in the driver area, under the front bunk. The automatic rifle was still under the passenger seats, undiscovered. He drew it out with his two cuffed hands, together with a full magazine. Then he pulled out the machine pistol and holster.

Who was it that said power comes out of the barrel of a gun, he asked himself, as he stood beside the driver seat, wearing the holster with the pistol. He was holding the rifle, jamming the magazine into its feed well, and experiencing a feeling of grim satisfaction.

Then he went back to the rover's living area, and spent a few minutes practicing holding the gun in his two cuffed hands. He found he could just manage to hold the gun firmly in both hands with a finger on the trigger. They had better not make me use this, he said to himself.

Then he noticed his very cold feet. He turned to the pressure suit closet, and found a pair of copper sandals that he often used inside the rover. The sandals had a rubber lining, both inside and outside. Now, we're in business, he thought.

*

John crept softly along the upper balcony on the south side of the house, until he reached almost to the window at the upstairs living room. He moved his head forward very slowly, just enough for him to see the small glass table through the window. There were two pairs of feet on the table, two machine pistols, and two sets of handcuffs. So far so good, said John to himself.

He quickly backed away, back along the balcony, until he came to the glass door into Dr. Sato's room. Quietly he slid open the door, and a few seconds later he was through the room and in the upstairs hallway. He crept very quietly down the hallway. At the hallway corner into the living area, he put his head forward just enough to see that the two pairs of feet and the two guns were still on the small glass-topped table by the balcony window.

Suddenly, he jumped into the living area, gun pointed at the two in the corner, but keeping well back from the glass table.

"Freeze, or you're dead. Hands in air!" he cried, looking at the surprised pair, with as ugly and as formidable a face as he could make. He was in a crouching stance, right knee almost on the floor.

Jose and Monique obeyed instinctively, their mouths wide open and eyes popping in astonishment. At the same time, Denise rushed out of the bedroom and stood beside her husband, eyeing the surprised pair.

"Take my pistol," said John.

Denise grabbed the pistol from its holster.

He motioned to the prisoners with his gun. "To your right," he said. "Away from the table."

The two edged along the east wall, away from the table.

Denise now slid open the balcony door, with her gun pointed at the two. She took the pistols from the table one by one, and threw them out the door, over the balcony wall into the garden below.

Then she came back, facing Jose and Monique. She held her machine pistol in both hands, as she had learned in the practice session in Tip Canyon, nearly three weeks earlier. She looked quite professional and dangerous actually. She was too, for the gun was loaded and the safety catch was off. She had her left foot forward and the other well back, almost in a crouching position, to counteract the low Martian gravity, as the old Zen master walked into the room. Denise rarely prayed, but right now, she was praying she would not have to pull the trigger.

"Now, Jose, just lower your hands slowly, behind your back," said John. "Very carefully. I'd like nothing better than an excuse to shoot you, after what you put my family through this evening. You dirty rotten bastard. I've a good mind to blow your legs off right now, just for starters."

Denise did not have to be told what to do. She seized a pair of cuffs from the table and had them on Jose very quickly, considering she had never done anything like that before. Half a minute later she had Monique's hands cuffed too.

Denise now disappeared into the surgery, and came out a moment later carrying a large bandage roll, made of parachute fabric. John motioned Jose to sit in one of the light copper chairs in the middle of the room, with his hands over the back of the chair, threatening him with dire consequences if he refused. He did not, and Denise used bandages to tie him to the chair. A few minutes later, she had tied Monique to a copper chair too.

Neither Jose nor Monique said anything. They still had not recovered from the shock of seeing John with an automatic rifle in his hands. That the trio in Leaf Valley could have such a weapon had come as a profound shock to both of them. The three were supposed to be unarmed.

"What are you going to do with us?" asked Jose. He had noticed that John had still not said that he meant them no harm, and had threatened him instead. Jose, for the second time in a few weeks, was in fear of his life. John looked decidedly mean.

John said nothing. He was examining his handcuffs. They had a digital lock with a five-digit key.

"Are you going to give me the code to open these handcuffs," said John threateningly, pointing his gun at Jose's feet, "or are you going to give me a chance for some target practice out on the balcony, like a toe shot off for every digit."

Jose did not hesitate. John looked like he meant it. He told John the key, and the Zen master quickly removed the cuffs and placed them on the glass table.

"So you want to know what's going to happen to you," said John, putting the gun down on the table to rub his wrists. "That will depend on what the judge has to say. You're going to be tried for the string of criminal acts you perpetrated against innocent people this evening. I'm going to prosecute, Denise will defend you, and Dr. Sato will be your judge. I can tell you right now that I'm going to ask for the death penalty. It would give me the greatest pleasure to line the four of you up in the parking pad and shoot you, after what you tried to do to us."

John turned to Denise. "Can you put something in their mouths to keep them quiet?" he said. "We still have to get the other two."

He looked at his watch. It was zero thirty-five.

*

John and Denise were now heading along the path to the airlock garage, having given the Zen master instructions to remove a prisoner's gag only in case of breathing problems. Denise was holding the machine pistol, a pair of handcuffs and some bandages. John was holding the automatic rifle.

When they came to the edge of the embankment down to the parking pad, they stayed on the path running beside the pad, but above it at the garden level. They eventually came down to the parking pad area adjacent to the inside door of the large rover airlock garage. The steps down took them onto the patio where the suit closets were, on the south wall of the rover airlock garage, near the small airlock door.

"Same way as with the other two?" whispered Denise. "We just rush into the rover and say 'stick 'em up'?"

"No, I'm afraid not," whispered John. "That's far too risky. They've probably got their guns beside them. If Emma were to hear you coming in she could have her gun pointed at you in the dark without you knowing it. We can't risk a shootout inside the rover. That might be all right for a movie, but not here. I don't want them harmed, I don't want you harmed, I don't want the rover damaged, and I'm not anxious to get shot myself."

"You did a good job convincing Jose and Monique you wanted to harm them," whispered Denise. "You could have fooled me. You've got those two scared out of their wits. They think we're going to shoot them."

"I haven't the slightest intention of harming them," whispered John. "We can't. If we do, Earth will be charging us with real murders that'll be very hard to defend ourselves against. You'd have Mars crawling with cops sooner than you think, with our faces all over the place on *Wanted—Dead or Alive* notices. We can't risk that."

"So why were you behaving as if you wanted to shoot them?"

"I just wanted to give them a good scare, so they'll do what we want later," said John. "They're only the small fry, obeying orders."

"I see," whispered Denise. "So how are you planning to get these two in the rover?"

"Listen," whispered John.

A few minutes later both John and Denise had pressure suits on. They had spare suits in the closets on the airlock outside wall. The four suits belonging to the four intruders were lying on the patio just beyond the closets, beside the exit from the small airlock, where the four had discarded them when they came into the compound. Where the four suits lay, in a darkened area, they were out of sight of the large exit door from the rover airlock garage onto the parking pad. John had not noticed the discarded suits when he had come out of the large airlock garage, a few hours earlier.

They now crept into the airlock garage from the parking pad, to the right of the rover inside. Bent over, they crept along, between the south side of the rover and the inside garage wall.

Denise stopped at the airlock control panel on the garage wall, but John continued along, round the back of the rover, as far as the northeast corner. Looking around the corner of the rover, along the rover's north side, John could see the stair up to the rover's small airlock, which was lying open.

At the corner of the rover where John was standing, on the low back wall of the machine, adjacent to the engine compartment, lay the outside control panel.

John now slid the small panel door to one side, to reveal the outside controls. The panel had controls and displays for the inside air pressure, for operation of the rover's airlock, for operation of the staircase, and so on, indeed, for nearly all vital rover functions.

"Now," said John to Denise, as he pressed some buttons.

Denise, still standing beside the control panel for the large airlock, pressed the button to depressurize. Immediately, the exit door to the parking pad slid shut, as did the roof door above the rover's shunt radiators. Then a large valve to the outside opened. In seconds the airlock garage interior was at the outside Martian air pressure. Then the outside airlock garage door opened.

Just before Denise had initiated the airlock depressurization, John had pressed some buttons on the control panel, to disable the rover's drive systems and close the rover's airlock doors.

Denise, keeping low down and very close to the rover, now ran around the back of the machine, past John, and along the north side, stopping on the other side of the rover stair. She kept her body low down, close to the rover's side. Her shoulders were actually beside the landing at the top of the stair, and she kept her gun trained on the rover's airlock door.

Then John set off the rover's inside pressure-leak alarm, and waited a few seconds. That'll wake the dead, he thought.

Then he cut off the alarm, and said: "Emma Grant! Karl Mannhardt! Listen carefully. You are in grave danger of your lives. The airlock garage outside the rover has been depressurized, and I have set the rover interior to depressurize in exactly twenty seconds. You do not have time to put on a pressure suit, and anyway you have only one in the suit closet. If you put your guns in the rover airlock, and initiate the airlock's depressurization, I will abort the rover depressurization."

He paused for a few seconds. Then he continued. "You have only two options: obey or die. You now have twelve seconds…eight seconds…four seconds…."

Suddenly, a red light came on at the control panel, indicating that the rover airlock was in use.

John waited some thirty seconds until depressurization of the rover's small airlock was complete. Then he pressed a button on the control panel, to open the rover's outside airlock door.

"Karl! Emma! Your guns had better be in that airlock or you're dead," he said, looking along the side of the rover to the stair, and waving to Denise.

Denise cautiously moved out a little from the rover wall, gun at the ready, just enough to see both if there was anyone at the window in the living area of the rover, almost above her head, and if there were any guns lying on the airlock floor.

Nobody was at the window, and the two guns were on the floor of the airlock. Denise rushed up the stair, and kicked the guns out of the airlock and down the stair. "I have them, John," she said, as she went back down the stair, and turned around to point her gun at the exit from the rover.

John now went to the control panel on the rover garage wall and pressed the pressurize button. The outer door of the huge airlock garage closed, and a valve opened, allowing air to rush in again. Less than half a minute later, the door out to the parking pad opened. John then calmly walked over to join Denise at the stair.

"You can both come out now," he said. "The pressure out here is back to normal. Keep your hands in the air and no tricks."

Emma came first, followed by Karl. They both looked sleepy, shocked, and fearful.

A short time later, the two captives were standing in the parking pad, beside the other rover. Karl was handcuffed and Emma's hands were tied behind her back with bandages. It then took only a few minutes for John and Denise to get their pressure suits off, one at a time. One of them kept the two captives covered, while the other took off the suit.

Ten minutes later, Emma and Karl were also sitting in the upstairs living room, bound to copper chairs, beside Monique and Jose. All four were in a state of profound shock.

*

It was one thirty in the morning, and the trial of the four was in its final stage. It was no doubt primitive, but it was a trial, with charges, prosecution, defense, and judge, and it was the first on Mars.

John had reasoned that a trial, even a primitive one, was a necessary procedure for deciding the fate of their four captives, if their settlement was ever to be acknowledged as legitimate. The trial was taking place in the upstairs living room, with the accused bound to their chairs, but not gagged.

The charges against them were armed entry into two private residences, kidnapping, and intent to do bodily harm. John had acted as prosecutor, while Denise acted in the defense of the prisoners, and the Zen master presided as judge, sitting in the corner beside the stairs.

In his prosecution, John had argued that since the four had been prepared to take their lives if necessary, to achieve their aims, and were a danger to the free people of Mars, they could not be released. Since they could not be held captive either, he had argued that the only thing to do was shoot them. Denise's defense of the four had been that they were merely soldiers obeying orders, and that those issuing the orders where the real guilty party.

Each of the four was given the opportunity to speak in his or her defense. Only Jose did, making the following statement.

"We do not recognize the legality of this kangaroo court," he said. "But since you are armed, and in a position to kill us, and since you appear to be attempting to arrive at some kind of justice, at least from your point of view, I want to say the following. We did not mean you physical harm, and we did not inflict any physical harm on you. In fact, the only reason we are now in this position—that we are now your prisoners —is that I was so considerate of your welfare that I allowed you all to go to bed and sleep. I could just as easily have kept you sitting up all night, under constant guard. Our orders were to arrest you and bring you to the lander in the morning, alive and well, and those orders I attempted to carry out, to the best of my ability, as a soldier. That is all I have to say."

Denise and John had then presented closing arguments. When they finished, it was nearly one forty-five. It was now the turn of the Zen master, who stood up to deliver his verdict and the sentence.

"The court finds that you did knowingly inflict pain and suffering, on three innocent adults and two children. Although the court accepts that you were acting under orders, orders alone do not justify unjust acts. The fundamental issue in this case is whether or not you acted under orders, knowing the orders to be unjust, that is, knowing that the three adults whom you kidnapped were innocent of the crimes of which they are accused, and of which this court knows them to be innocent. The prosecution has not proven that all four of you acted knowing your actions were unjust, but neither has the defense proven that you acted believing you were acting justly. The balance of the evidence shows merely that it is likely that one of you, Emma Grant, knew the actions were unjust, but that it is uncertain that the other three knew.

"Given this, and given that your actions placed innocent people at risk of their lives on this most dangerous planet, justice would be best served if you were punished in a way that you yourselves understood you had earned. The court is unfortunately limited in the sentencing available to it. The court therefore does the best that it can, in ordering you expelled from this compound, without transportation, to march the twenty-four miles between here and your habitat. It is between six and seven hours' march, and since you are all young and healthy, you should be able to accomplish that without injury to yourselves."

*

A short time later, John was standing outside the compound, at the top of the driveway leading down to the airlocks, as Jose came out of the small airlock. A paper-thin layer of white powder frost lay on the ground, and the moon Phobos hung low in the starlit sky, a witness to these strange goings on. John was holding the automatic rifle, pointed at Jose, with the nanogun at his feet.

"Keep your helmet light on," said John. "Keep to the road, and wait down on the valley floor for your companions—with your helmet light on. Now get moving. If you try anything funny down there, you'll have exploding nanobullets to contend with."

Emma was the last one that the Zen master released from her binding to the copper chair, while Denise pointed her gun at her. As she came through the small airlock door, John was waiting for her, and gave her much the same instructions as the others, with this in addition:

"As you march down the valley, stay on the road. Only one of you need have a helmet light on, but the one with the light on should be at the rear. You understand? I want to be able to see all four of you. If you try to leave the road anywhere, I'll have to open fire with the nanogun. Anyway, since you probably don't have more than about eight hours of air left, if you want to survive, you'll have to head straight for Elbow Hill. You can't come back in here. I'm turning off the power to all the airlocks tonight, even the greenhouse airlocks. And there's one last thing, very important, for your own safety. Don't leave the road as you walk through Stem Gap. There are landmines everywhere except on the road."

The four did not try any tricks. Had they been on Earth, they might have, but not on Mars. They did what John suggested, and marched off down Leaf Valley, headed for Stem Gap. They were thankful for the trial, and for Dr. Sato's lenient sentence that apparently had prevented John from shooting them.

John stood at the edge of the shelf in the moonlight, for some fifteen minutes, watching them trudge off down the road. Then he went inside, and sat on a bench on a mound, at the end of a spoke path at the southeast side of the compound. He sat there for half an hour, wiping frost from the inside of the glass wall every so often, and studying the procession outside through field glasses.

When the four were three miles down the valley, he walked back to the house, shut off the power in all airlocks, and went to bed.

Denise had a sleeping pill waiting for him, to counteract the stimulant pill he had taken earlier, and which had kept him very much awake.

*

John and Denise, in separate rovers, arrived at Stem Gap just after seven next morning—Saturday morning, Beta October 05, the day of the planned launch of the lander. The two rovers stopped on the road, just through the gap, and John surveyed the sunlit road ahead through field glasses.

"I see them," said John, "less than two miles ahead. They're straggling. They may not make it. Guess we'd better give them a ride the rest of the way. Keep about a hundred meters behind me, Denise."

They carried on along across Elbow Plain in the bright morning sunshine. Five minutes later, John drew up behind the straggling four. Monique was in a bad way, and was being held up by both Jose and Karl.

"You'd better get in the trailer," said John. "You're not going to make it before your air runs out. You've still got ten miles to go."

The four did not object. Karl scrambled into the trailer first, and helped the others in. When John heard Denise's message confirming they were all in the trailer, he continued across Elbow Plain.

About three miles from the habitat he stopped, and surveyed it through his field glasses. There was no sign of activity. He continued on, turning left into the Elbow Hill road, some five minutes later. At the start of the stretch of road up the ridge to the habitat, which now lay only about a half mile away, John stopped.

"Everybody out," he said. "This is as near as we go. Regard yourselves as released prisoners of war."

He watched as the four filed past the front of the rover, and started trudging up the hill. The short rest had helped Monique, and she seemed to be able to walk without assistance, even if not too well. Those four had just had a load taken off their minds, if truth be told. Fifteen minutes earlier they had all four been both physically exhausted and in great fear of their lives. Now at least they knew they were safe.

John turned the rover and retreated across Elbow Plain, with Denise in front. About fifty yards before Stem Gap the two rovers stopped, and both John and Denise got out. John did not care if they were being observed from the habitat through field glasses. In fact, he hoped they were—which was indeed the case.

John then helped Denise unload two fairly heavy copper poles from her rover trailer. Her trailer also contained a large number of small copper objects, each about nine inches square, each looking like a small hat. The trailer also carried two shovels, various tools, and a large copper plaque. Soon they were hard at work on the road in the sunshine.

It was important that they get the work done quickly, for even though Derk's military people were in no condition to attack them as they worked, if Derk had enough time he could get something organized. They got the job finished just after nine, without incident.

*

Just after twelve the previous evening, Derk received the first word from Jose that all was well, that the plan had worked flawlessly, and that the three prisoners were currently in bed and under guard. Derk was delighted. Jurgen, standing beside Derk in the communications room, had mixed feelings at the news—things could now proceed, and before long, an impressive colony would be the result. Unfortunately, it seemed to him, that colony would be constructed on the foundation of a profound injustice, unless it truly was the case that Denise was guilty as charged. It all bothered him.

During his conversation with Jose, Derk was not merely content with a general account of the current state of affairs at the compound. He wanted all the details—fodder for his strategic mind, as it probed for weaknesses. He kept Jose engaged in conversation for some fifteen minutes.

"There's no need to be in any hurry to bring them down here in the morning," Derk said to Jose at the end of the conversation. "If you get them here by eleven, that will be quite sufficient. Let them bring any items of personal belongings they want, but not more than what will fill three belongings cases each, and one each for the two children. Bring them directly to the lander. Let us know when you leave the compound. We'll expect to hear from you just before ten."

"Well, that's that," he said to Jurgen, after he signed off with Jose. "We have them, and it wasn't as messy as it could've been."

"Thank heavens for that," said Jurgen. "I suppose we should try not to feel too bad about it. After all, we are sending them back to Earth, unharmed. It is not as if we were shipping them off to some frightful place, like the moon."

"That's the right attitude," said Derk. "Earth's a superb planet, compared with this one. They should be grateful they're going home. In time, they probably will be. I'll admit Earth would be an even better planet to live on if it were not for the pressure of the hoards of people it has, most of them landless. I'm sure that's what made those three want to stay here. They certainly had a passion for the land they had here. And there's plenty of land here, as much as on Earth. Some of it just takes your breath away."

"Like the inside of Leaf Valley?" said Jurgen.

"Yes, indeed," said Derk. "Well, it's the E.U.'s valley now, in the E.U.'s possession. In practice, that means it's ours, and in our possession."

"Are you going to let Mission Control have the news this evening?" asked Jurgen.

"I'd prefer to wait till I have them off the planet," said Derk, his forehead furrowed. "On the other hand, they're all sitting waiting for news down there. It's hard to see how those three could possibly escape now. All right, let's send Mission Control a message."

Derk explained what he wanted, and left the details to Jurgen. He went to bed shortly afterward, trying to decide if he should move to the compound immediately after the launch, and take up residence, or wait until Sunday.

Mission Control received Derk's message just before nine thirty on Thursday evening. Toulouse was one day and three hours behind local time in Kasei Valley, and ESA released the news in time for it to be included in the Friday morning newspapers in Europe, where the story got front-page headlines.

ESA did not release the news until just before midnight, local time, and saw to it that the main topic was the arrest of the three, for the sole purpose of bringing them back to stand trial. The ESA news release also emphasized that the arrest had been accomplished with no injury to anyone, not even minor injuries. It made no mention of the way now being open for building a colony, to be supported by copper mining on an enormous scale.

The news was received everywhere in Europe with a sense of satisfaction, that Friday morning. Justice was being done.

In the United States, it was early Thursday evening when ESA released the news, and there was no official reaction in Washington, where most offices were closed. This was convenient for the Administration, for the President and his cabinet were becoming resigned to the loss of the Leaf Valley region to the E.U. The President was having difficulty seeing how the secret military Mars mission, currently only about five days from Mars, could reverse the situation. There was some consolation, however, as a result of certain behind-the-scenes maneuvering.

The E.U. Commission had been anxious that the U.S. be placated over any bad feeling that might be caused by the arrest of John Erway, a U.S. citizen, and the E.U.'s acquisition of title to all the lands and resources of the region, both natural and man-made. As a result, it had come up with a lucrative scheme that appealed to U.S. interests.

The rights to mine the copper on Mars and transport it to Earth were to be sold, very inexpensively, to a conglomerate of European companies. One of them was the British Woomegong Group, with copper interests world wide, the major one being in Australia. The E.U. Commission for Corporate Affairs, with the agreement of the British Government, had informed its Department of Commerce counterparts in Washington that it would look kindly on a merger of Woomegong with the American mining giant, Condor Copper Inc.

This merger would ensure the involvement of the United States in the project, and the flow of U.S. risk capital to Mars. Europe would not then have to shoulder all the risk. It would also ensure that U.S. interests received a share in both the profits and the copper. There was so much copper on Mars that there was easily enough for both the E.U. and the U.S.

Negotiations between Condor and Woomegong were already at an advanced stage, and the share prices of both companies had been advancing steadily all that week. The advance had begun when it had become clear that John Erway and Denise Lavoisier were to be arrested on serious criminal charges and returned to Earth to face trial. The announcement of the merger was scheduled for the end of the following week.

For these reasons, the network media discussions in the U.S. that Thursday evening were generally non critical of the arrest of a U.S. citizen on Mars by E.U. forces, even though panel discussions on the networks were plentiful.

Many panel members were lawyers. They were all of the opinion that the E.U. was justified in carrying out the arrest, given the weight of evidence against the three. They felt that John Erway would receive a fair trial, that the legal proceedings could take years, and that U.S. law firms would likely be involved. Some of those very lawyers, aware of what the publicity could do for their careers, were already laying plans for getting John Erway as a client.

There were, however, some exceptions to the general American acceptance of the arrests that evening.

Throughout the United States and Canada there were societies dedicated to the settlement of Mars by private individuals, and dedicated to supporting the property rights of those who explored, developed, and set up settlements on Mars—people like John Erway and Denise Lavoisier.

That Thursday evening, the leader of the largest of these Mars societies appeared on a prominent network talk show discussing the arrests. The Mars society president was a former NASA engineer with a law degree. She caused an uproar, when she said she suspected that a land grab was under way, that dirty work was afoot. Fifty million people across the United States and Canada heard her.

"I smell a very big rat," she said, "and I'm urging the membership to get out this evening and make their protest at these so-called arrests visible and audible, immediately, while there is still time to affect the outcome."

The membership obliged that summer evening. There was not much they could do, at such short notice, but they did congregate in small groups on the steps of the city halls of the major cities, carrying placards, and making speeches. The police kept them company, but, since their numbers were small, and they showed no inclination to violence, and even offered the police refreshments, they were not interfered with. They made a lot of speeches though, about property rights on Mars. Many of the speeches called on the President to insist that the E.U. release the three on Mars at once, and to insist on an investigation into the charges taking place while the three remained on Mars in their homes.

Later that evening, these demonstrations received major publicity on the networks. On Friday morning, they also figured prominently on the front pages of U.S. newspapers.

The demonstrations did not stop the advance of the prices of Condor and Woomegong, when they opened for trading on the London Stock Exchange, on Friday morning. Share prices of large U.S. corporations with European subsidiaries that would be involved in the development of the E.U. colony also advanced, as they had been doing every day that week. There was still no public mention of the connection between Condor, Woomegong, and Mars, and most investors were mystified as to the reason for the advancing share prices.

*

Derk was not up particularly early the following morning, and the six at the habitat had a relaxed breakfast together just after seven. They sat around one table, with the sun streaming in from the window at the end of it. The leisurely breakfast went on until nearly seven thirty. Derk was in a good mood, and had succeeded in explaining the situation to the four scientists in an apologetic kind of way.

"Of course, we would have preferred that they return to Earth of their own free will to face the charges," he said. "Now everyone on Earth is going to see them getting on board that lander with handcuffs on, as common criminals."

"Is it really necessary that they be handcuffed?" asked Astrid, getting up to fetch some coffee from the kitchen on the other side of the room. "Are they that dangerous?"

"Believe me, they can be," said Derk. "But you don't want to be a witness to anything like that today. Better if you don't see it. I want you, Don, and Vince to continue the survey work on the escarpment as usual today. If you're a reasonable way up the escarpment you should be able to get a good view of the launch from there."

"So we won't get a chance to say our good-byes to the three Martians," said Don.

"Afraid not," said Derk. "I don't think they'll be very interested anyway, and the survey work has to go on. We're going to be swamped with work—"

"Captain!" said Astrid suddenly from the kitchen. She had just glimpsed two rovers through the window, about a mile away, approaching the habitat. "We have visitors."

Derked jumped out of his seat, with the others, as they all rushed to the two kitchen windows.

"They weren't supposed to bring them here till eleven," said Derk to Jurgen, who was standing beside him, looking out the window at the two rovers.

The rovers, bright blue and yellow in the early morning sun, were now approaching the ridge road up to the habitat. Nobody had field glasses handy, and they all continued to stare in surprise, as the two rovers stopped, the blue and yellow unmistakable against the red and gray terrain. Then four figures clambered out of the trailer of the front rover, and began to straggle up the ridge road.

"Get me my field glasses somebody!" shouted Derk. Only Astrid knew where they were. She produced them a minute later, along with another pair, by which time the rovers had both turned, and were headed at speed back to the main Kasei Valley road. She gave the glasses to Derk and Jurgen.

"They're wearing our suits!" exclaimed Jurgen, focussing his field glasses on the group. "It has to be Jose, Monique, Emma, and Karl. Yes, no doubt about it, the big one is definitely Karl, and I can make out Emma's blond hair. *Mein Gott*! They look like they need help. They're in a bad way—hardly able to walk."

Derk was shaken. He could hardly speak.

"Jurgen! Don!" he said at last, in a hissing voice. "Get the buggies out. Drive down and pick them up, at once. Hurry! They may need medical help. Ursula! Get your surgery ready."

As Jurgen, Don, and Ursula rushed out of the room, Derk remained at the window, his field glasses trained on the four on the ridge road. Suddenly one of the four stumbled badly, but was caught just in time by a companion. This one was now no longer able to walk without assistance, and advanced only with difficulty, in the rear, leaning on Karl.

Vince had picked up Jurgen's field glasses, and now stood at the next window, looking out at the four, with Astrid beside him. Astrid was only pretending to look out. She was studying Derk's face through the corner of her eye. The pleasant look she was used to seeing had been replaced by an angry snarl. They won't get away with this, Derk was thinking to himself. Astrid was able to read his thoughts accurately.

*

It was just after three o'clock that Saturday afternoon, and Derk and Jurgen were having a discussion in the meeting room. The scheduled launch of the lander that afternoon had been postponed.

Astrid, Vince, and Don were off on their daily geological survey. Ursula was in the surgery, on Derk's orders, studying the treatment of gunshot wounds.

The four who had had to walk all night were asleep. Apart from Monique, they had suffered only blisters on their feet, which Ursula had treated. Monique had also suffered stress damage to the cartilage in her left leg, near the knee, but nothing that would not heal in a few days of rest.

Before Derk allowed the four to go to bed, he had extracted a full account of what had happened the previous night. In one way he had been relieved. On seeing his people straggle back just after breakfast, minus a buggy, he had suffered a blow to his ego. Never before had he suffered such a defeat at the hands of an enemy, especially such a weak enemy. He could not understand how such a thing could be possible. He understood at once, and his confidence in himself was restored, when he learned that the three had guns.

He did not consider it to be his fault that he had not known that John had actually succeeded in removing a set of guns from the lander three weeks ago. Derk had not known how many sets of guns were on board originally. His superiors had told him that it was best for him not to know, given that they were illegal, and that he should know only that there were enough, hidden inside rock sample cases, with empty cases on top. His superiors at ESA had obviously goofed, and Derk had already let them know.

Half an hour earlier, he had sent a long report to Mission Control, in an angry, blaming tone, detailing the escape of the prisoners, and how missing guns had made it possible. He had also informed Mission Control of the apparent sealing of Stem Gap, as a result of mine laying activities during the morning, and of the apparent conversion of Leaf Valley into an impregnable fortress. He had not asked Mission Control for advice. He was sure the brass would be able to work out the strategic implications themselves, and take some of the blame, for the implications were very serious.

ESA waited four hours before releasing the news of the escape of the three. The release came at four thirty in the afternoon in Europe, after most stock exchanges had closed, but an hour after the opening of the New York Stock Exchange. At the end of the ESA press release, there was a brief mention of the difficulty in re-arresting the three, not only because they were armed with stolen test weapons, but because Stem Gap had been mined that morning. It was this last item of news that triggered the financial carnage.

That Friday, the financial media reported these events on Mars merely as important, but still general, news events, not related to any financial matters. The financial markets, as is usual, always know, however. To the surprise of average investors everywhere, within minutes of the release of the news from Mars, waves of selling hit the New York exchange.

In the beginning, the selling was directed at the companies secretly involved in the huge Martian copper enterprise, especially Woomegong and Condor. The selling quickly spread to other companies, U.S. and European, those involved in construction of the Martian facilities related to the mining and transportation of the copper, including most large U.S. companies with European subsidiaries. Then the selling spread to their suppliers, and then to the market in general, as speculators, traders, and frightened investors, ignorant about what was going on, contributed to the selling. That day, known thereafter as Red Friday, marked the first time events on Mars ever triggered a massive sell-off on Wall Street. It would not be the last.

Meanwhile, on Mars, Derk and Jurgen, unaware of the financial market meltdown that would take place in a few hours, were sitting looking at a computer display, on the meeting room table. The screen showed an enlarged perspective of Stem Gap.

"Is there any chance we could remove them?" asked Derk.

"I doubt it," said Jurgen. "We could build a workable metal detector in the workshop to detect them. You just need a battery, some coils of wire, some logic and a display, all of which we have. I am assuming the mines are made of metal. But digging up landmines of an unknown type would be a very risky proposition. We have no idea how sensitive they are, or even how much alike they are. There is also the sheer number they put down. I estimate they were putting down four mines every five minutes this morning, and they were at it from before eight till after nine."

"That would be over fifty mines to remove," said Derk, looking very concerned, yet still very determined. "That's certainly a lot."

"If it was only one or two, we could probably do it, by taking very great care," said Jurgen. "But fifty. If each of us went out to remove as many as possible before being killed, I think you would run out of people before they were all cleared."

"So you're telling me we have to think of something else," said Derk.

"Yes, trying to move that many landmines is just too risky," said Jurgen. "Do you have another plan?"

"No," said Derk. "Not at the moment. They're holding the high ground, and we're pinned down." He paused here, looking at the computer screen. Then he said: "There's just one thing that puzzles me about those mines." He did not continue, but looked at Jurgen, searching his face.

Jurgen frowned, and said: "Yesterday they showed us they had remote controlled mines buried in Stem Gap, beside the road. We saw one of them go off. Then Emma was warned last night not to leave the road going through Stem Gap this morning. We were even warned three weeks ago that it was very dangerous to leave the road in Stem Gap. That indicates very clearly that they had mined the terrain on either side of the road even before we arrived on Mars. Then early this morning we both observed them laying mines on the road itself. I do not see any puzzle."

"Well, there is one," insisted Derk. "Erway spent most of yesterday up on the escarpment guarding the entrance. When we arrived there, at sunset yesterday, he let off one of his mines to show us he was serious, and that the terrain on either side of the road was mined. But the road itself was not mined at that point, because yesterday morning Jose drove through, and last night Erway ordered Jose's company to march out of Leaf Valley on that road. What puzzles me is why they waited until this morning to mine the road. If it had been me, I would have mined it yesterday. Sealing that entrance at once should have been a priority. There's something about the mind of our enemy I don't understand."

"You have a point," admitted Jurgen, his face puzzled. He thought for a minute, and then said: "But Erway is not you. He does not think like you. He is not a military man. He is an engineer."

"Why would that make a difference? From an engineering point of view, the obvious thing to do is seal the entrance at once. He should have had the mines laid yesterday afternoon at the latest."

"Well, for one thing," pointed out Jurgen, "I think they value their reputations, and, at least up until last night, were very unwilling to hurt anybody. Landmines have a terrible reputation. I think both he and his wife would have been prepared to lay mines on the road only as a last resort. Yesterday afternoon, Erway had two choices. He could stand guard up on the escarpment, with a nanogun, which we did not know he had yesterday, and not lay the mines on the road. Or he could lay the mines on the road and go home, without having to worry that anybody could get in."

"I see what you're driving at," said Derk. "If he had done the second thing, somebody could have gotten hurt, when he wasn't there. So he preferred to sit on guard and be in control, and scare us away, like he did with us yesterday evening."

"That would fit with the way his mind works, and his wife's too," said Jurgen. "And then there is the influence of that Buddhist monk. I can not imagine him condoning laying mines on a road that everybody has to use to get into that valley."

Derk thought about this, and then said: "Yes, I think you're right. It fits everything we know. All right, here's what we're going to do. You and I are going to drive over there to talk to him, as soon as we're finished here. He went up to his observation post after the mines were laid. He doesn't have to stay there now, since the entrance is completely blocked, but I think he'll stay there anyway. He'll want to keep track of everything we do."

"What are you going to talk to him about?"

"Well, as I said, I don't have a plan yet, to get ourselves out of this mess. Probing his mind may help me come up with one. If we can't come up with one, we can't stay here. We'll run out of food soon. He knows that, and I'm sure that's what he's counting on. Anyway, always surprise your enemy, even if you can only do it with words. I'm going to say something to him he won't be expecting. You'll hear when we get there. Now, let's go. You do the driving. Make sure you attach a white flag to the buggy antenna."

Actually, Jurgen's explanation of why John had waited until that morning to mine the road through Stem Gap was dead wrong. There was a far simpler explanation, which, had Derk known it, would have caused him to act very differently. Jurgen's explanation was the one John was hoping Derk would accept.

*

In mid afternoon, Derk and Jurgen set out across Elbow Plain in the buggy. Jurgen was driving. It was a bright sunny day, with no clouds in the sky, and almost no wind. Jurgen had attached a piece of wire horizontally to the buggy's surface radio antenna, and had hung a large strip of white fabric to the wire, to serve as a flag.

They reached the entrance to Stem Gap just before four. There was no sign of life. They stopped a few meters before the large, two-poled copper sign that John and Denise had erected that morning.

The sign's large copper sheet between its copper poles glistened in the afternoon sun. Permanent letters had been formed on the copper sheet by means of small holes. The sign read: DANGER! MINES!

Derk had plugged the buggy radio into his suit half an hour earlier, and had been listening for any communication as they approached the gap.

"We'd like to talk," said Derk, looking up at the sunlit escarpment just ahead to the right, where John had his observation post.

There was no response. Derk waited for some five minutes, then tried again.

"We have something important to say to you," said Derk. "We have discussed this new situation at length, and have concluded that we have no alternative but to admit defeat. We have no way to enter your valley to arrest you now, and we will have no food in five days. We have no choice but to leave. We will be leaving in three days, all of us, on Tuesday morning. In the meantime, we would just like an assurance from you that my people will be free to continue to take samples along this escarpment, without interference from you. They will not try to enter this gap, of course. We know you have a nanogun, and I'm very concerned about the possibility of an accident, where you assumed hostile intent on our part, causing you to open fire. I'm certain you would not want to kill or injure innocent scientists."

Derk briefly caught a glimpse of sunlight reflecting from a pressure-suit helmet high up on the escarpment, behind the rim of a small crater. Then there came a response.

"We've always found that imminent starvation on Mars helped us see things clearly," said John.

"So you would be prepared to starve us?" said Derk.

"Certainly not," said John, evading the trap. "We have no intention of starving anyone. You have plenty of food of your own, on your mother ship. Starvation would be your choice. So would the choice to attempt to enter this gap. There are mines everywhere, both on and off the road. They can be set off in the usual way, and I can set any one of them off, any time, by remote control. They're quite deadly, don't you think?"

At that moment, there was an explosion, not far from the road, about half a mile ahead, on the right side. Rocks and stones flew about a hundred feet into the air, out of a huge dust cloud. Derk and Jurgen heard the muffled thump disturbing the thin air.

"Quite," said Derk.

"Oh, by the way," added John. "I wouldn't recommend trying to clear these mines. They're quite unstable. The slightest touch, you know. The only way to clear them is by exploding them. Of course, to do that you have to have the remote controller, and the digital codes."

"We had already come to that conclusion," said Derk, patiently. "We've no intention of trying to clear them. Now, about this truce. Are you willing?"

"I thought a truce meant merely a temporary cessation of hostilities, after which it was back to war as usual," said John.

"You are accused criminals," said Derk. "I have no power to change that. The indictments against you were issued at the highest levels in the E.U., and there has been no objection from the United States. You would be well advised to surrender and return to Earth willingly, to stand trial. But since I no longer have the power to arrest you, I am asking for a truce. The truce would be for the remainder of our stay, which is three more days, as I said. But you must understand that there will be another expedition, in a few years, and it will have the power to arrest you. Mining this gap will not keep a future mission out of your valley. That expedition will be much better equipped than this one. So, yes, you're right. I can offer you only a truce. Hostilities will resume, but not before the new expedition arrives. Ultimately, your days here are numbered."

John did not respond to this immediately. He was thinking about the trillions of dollars worth of copper, and the fact that the E.U. now had the technology to exploit it. Hoards of developers of every kind would soon be on their way to Mars. Time was not on the side of the trio in Leaf Valley.

John understood only too well that before long, their sheltered valley would be ripped apart to build the rail launcher, rail connections, and the fusion power plant, and other development, including the destructive engineering work on the rampart to build the massive gravity shafts and associated electric power generators.

"You have a point there," said John eventually.

"I'm glad we agree," said Derk. "Now do we have a truce?"

"When are you leaving on Tuesday?" asked John.

There was no answer for a moment. Then, following a nod from Derk, Jurgen answered.

"There's a launch possibility at 10:42," said Jurgen.

"All right," said John. "You will leave at 10:42 on Tuesday morning. You will not destroy or damage anything you can't take with you, such as the buggies. You will leave all your weapons undamaged—eight sets, with their ammunition. You will not attempt to enter Leaf Valley during the three days. In return, we will not interfere with your activities outside Leaf Valley."

"We agree," said Derk. "Now, is it safe to leave the road here, in order to turn?" asked Derk.

"Yes," said John. "The mines begin a short distance beyond the sign."

With that, Derk gestured to Jurgen. The buggy turned around, and Derk and Jurgen headed back to the habitat.

*

John kept watch on the habitat for the rest of the day, but the only activity was what was obviously Don, Astrid, and Vince returning from their daily geological field trip, around five o'clock.

Just after nine, with only a few lights left on at the habitat, John drove his rover down along the escarpment to the valley floor, and then northward, on the road back to his home at Mount Tip.

To gain entrance to the compound, he had to ask Denise to reset the airlock fuse. The control room did not have a master switch that could disable all the airlocks. The house had not been built with facilities for keeping out intruders. It had no locks anywhere. The airlock door motors and valves had fuses, and these were now acting as locks. They could not be surprised again by a break-in like the one the previous evening.

Some time later that evening, there was strategy discussion in the downstairs living room.

"At least we can be thankful there was no conversation yesterday," said Denise, "when that buggy showed up at Stem Gap, and you didn't get a chance to say the road through the gap was mined."

"Sheer good luck," admitted John. "I was all prepared to tell them about our mines, but I wanted to let off an explosion first, to make it look convincing. That was why I never got a chance to talk. They just turned around and bolted. Of course, we know now they weren't there to talk anyway. That buggy was just there as a diversion, to distract me while the other buggy was coming down from Outlook Shelf."

"And the diversion worked too," said Denise. "You had no idea what was really going on."

"No, I didn't. But at least, I didn't get a chance to tell them the road was mined. Derk would have known at once it was a lie, since his men had already driven through the gap early that morning, without us knowing."

"But he must be puzzled about those mines we laid on the road this morning," said Denise. "He would have seen us laying them. He must have wondered why we hadn't done it earlier."

"He'll be wondering all right," said John. "But I doubt if he'll figure out that the real reason we were laying them this morning was that he had destroyed our bluff by getting his men through Stem Gap yesterday morning. This morning's obvious mine laying, with him seeing us do it, was simply our attempt to patch up our mistake. I'm sure Derk was impressed with that explosion I set off today, after the one yesterday. He has to believe there's a minefield now. None of them will try to get through that gap."

"It could be a disaster if they did," said Denise. "But I suppose we've grounds for hope."

"It's more than just a hope," said John. "What he said this afternoon sounded convincing. He does seem to be intending to pack up and go home."

"I don't trust him," said Denise. "I don't believe anything he says. Tell me, John, do you really think he's given up, and is going to leave on Tuesday?"

"What choice does he have?" asked John. "If he sits there, he'll run out of food."

"I just don't think he's going to sit there," said Denise, now looking very worried.

John frowned, and looked thoughtfully at his wife, and then at Dr. Sato. John had thought it safer if they all stayed together for the time being, and Dr. Sato had not gone home to his monastery. The Zen master appeared unconcerned, as usual.

"What do you think, Dr. Sato?" asked John. "Has he any way of carrying out a repeat of last night?"

"He cannot come through Stem Gap," said the Zen master. "But he is a man with a very great sense of his own importance and destiny, and a very large ego. Gaining control of this valley is very important to him. It is unlikely that he will give up if he can see a chance of succeeding."

"So you both think he's trying to trick us," said John. "Trying to give us a false sense of victory, while all the time he's hatching some new scheme."

"That's the kind of man he is," said Denise. "Nothing he says can be believed."

"I've been worried about that myself," admitted John, "although he seemed very convincing this afternoon. I suppose it'll do us no harm to assume the worst—that he's got some plan. Can either of you see what it might be? I'm darned if I can."

"Well, since he can't come in though Stem Gap," said Denise, "he's got only two other ways into this valley. South to Finger Gully, and then northwest across the plateau, and then down into the valley at West Tip Gully. Or northeast to the eastern end of Hazard Valley, then westward along the valley, and back in through Tip Canyon."

"They could never succeed with the southern route," said Dr. Sato. "It's well over two hundred miles, and there's no road across the plateau, and it's very rough and uneven south and west of here."

"That leaves only the Hazard Valley route," said John.

"But he lost two people trying that the last time," said Denise. "I can't see him being dumb enough to try it again."

"It's just possible he could succeed doing it," said John, "if he took all necessary precautions. It would be a very high-risk venture, though, and I've never got the impression he was a risk taker. He's the kind who plans things meticulously, and takes pride in his superior strategic mind."

"That's true," said Denise. "I remember what Jose said yesterday evening when he had us in handcuffs. He said Derk's plans almost always work."

"If he took risks a lot, his plans would fail a lot," said John, frowning. "That confirms that he's not a risk taker."

"So you think he'd never dream of trying the Hazard Valley route again," said Denise, "now that he knows how dangerous it is in a buggy."

"It sure looks that way," said John, "which leaves him no options, which put us back where we started."

"It would still be better to assume the worst-case scenario," said Dr. Sato.

"I agree," said John. "That's obviously the only thing we can do. The best I can think of right now is to sit down at Stem Gap from dawn till well after dusk, with the nanogun handy, until they're gone, so I can keep my eye on them—just in case they get up to something. You two will stay here, with the power off on all airlocks. There's plenty to do here anyway. We can't neglect our normal work."

"You don't think there's any chance he'd try to get through Stem Gap at night," said Denise.

"No," said John. "Nobody in his right mind would attempt a minefield at night. Now let's get to bed. This has sure been a day we won't forget in a hurry."

"There's one thing that might confirm he's really leaving," said Denise, as they stood up. "He'll have to inform Mission Control, and ESA will have to inform the media. So, if he's really leaving on Tuesday, it'll be all over the media on Earth soon. I can send a request to the NASA computers for news tomorrow evening. If we're lucky we could get a reply by Monday morning."

"We might," said John, "but we can't depend on it. It took five days for a reply last time. For now, we just have to assume the worst-case scenario—that Derk has some plan we can't foresee."

*

At the habitat that evening, a similar discussion was taking place. Derk, Jurgen, and the four other military members of the mission were seated at the long table in the meeting room. Their pressing problem now was that the only source of food on the surface of Mars was inside Leaf Valley, so that they had only three choices: get into the valley, starve, or leave.

That evening they discussed their options at length, and like the three in the glass compound, they discussed the southern route into the back of Leaf Valley, and the northern route along Hazard Valley.

There was also the possibility that Erway was bluffing about the mines guarding Stem Gap, and that they should simply attempt to sneak through the gap at night. They did not discuss this. Derk had seen two large explosions set off by John, and was aware of just how much explosive material in the form of fuel and oxidizer lay under his control. He was convinced that a frontal attack on the gap would be suicidal. There had to be another way, but that evening they could not come up with one, although the discussion was fruitful.

It enabled Derk to glimpse a promising tactical possibility that was still too half-baked to reveal at the meeting. His germinating plan was missing an essential component, and he decided to wait and see if he could develop the plan further, before discussing it with his team.

After the meeting, Derk instructed Emma to send a message to Mission Control. The message was brief and stated that the mission would leave Mars on Tuesday morning at 10:42 local time. The message also contained his regrets about the mission's failure to gain control of Leaf Valley and arrest the three who lived there. It stated further that the mission currently had no choice but to leave, since they had neither the food resources to stay longer, nor the military resources to penetrate Leaf Valley, which was now an impregnable fortress.

That night, it was a long time before Derk could fall asleep, as he lay awake pondering the problem. He could not bear to have all his ambitions thwarted by these three, and have his career ruined. Back on Earth, forevermore, eventually even in the history books, he would be known as the man who had been whipped by three Martians, one of them a woman, and another an old monk.

Necessity is well known as the mother of invention, however, and that night, Derk was certainly facing a necessity. Just before two o'clock, the mother of invention delivered the missing piece of the jigsaw puzzle his mind had been working on. Derk's mind wrestled with his new idea for another hour, finding ways around obvious weaknesses here and there. About three, a combined feeling of both relief and tiredness fell over him, and he could sleep on his new idea.

CHAPTER FIFTEEN

Go for Launch

NEXT DAY, Sunday, well before sunrise, John was once more at his observation post, carefully monitoring activities at the habitat. He sat in the front seat of his rover, parked against the rim of the small crater, high up on the escarpment at Stem Gap.

When the sun came up, it shone directly through the rover's front window, onto John's face. In the next half hour, as John watched, it dispersed the ice mist lying in patches on Elbow Plain. Early morning ice mist was a common occurrence in the Martian fall.

Nothing happened until just before seven, when one buggy, carrying three persons, left the habitat. John figured it was Don, Astrid, and Vince, headed out on their daily geological survey.

John watched the survey buggy travel northeastward on the main Kasei Valley road, as usual. He was suspicious, nevertheless, and examined the buggy very carefully through his field glasses. He could easily do so, because the field glasses could support a one hundred times magnification. At the nearest point of the buggy, about seven miles away, it appeared in his field glasses image as if it were only about a hundred meters away. The buggy did seem to be on the usual survey expedition. He could clearly see geological survey equipment in its open trailer.

During the rest of the day, the remaining buggy at the habitat made three trips to the lander, its trailer apparently loaded each time. The buggy was just too far away for John to make out what was in the trailer, but it certainly looked as if the lander was being loaded in readiness for departure.

In late morning, a quite strong wind from the northeast developed, and there was blowing dust and light sand near the ground in Elbow Plain, forming a wind-blown layer about six inches thick. There was no wind of significance up on the escarpment where John was parked, for he was sheltered by the huge precipice that began higher up the escarpment, to the east of him.

By mid afternoon, the wind had intensified, and the blowing sand and dust layer had grown to about a foot thick on the plain below.

Then, around three in the afternoon, the other buggy appeared, the one that had gone on the geology field trip that morning. It was coming back along the Kasei Valley road, headed for the habitat. It was earlier than usual, but John was not suspicious. It would be difficult to do field work in that level of blowing dust, he concluded.

After five there was no further activity.

The time passed. The wind died down, and a sunset fan formed to the west. Darkness fell, and lights came on in the habitat. After eight they began going out, and just after nine, with only a few lights on at the habitat, John left his post, and headed home in the rover. The minefield at Stem Gap would stand guard during the night.

*

Next day, half an hour before the sun rose, John was once more back at his observation post high up at Stem Gap, with early morning ice mist shrouding the floor of the valley below. It was Monday, the day before the scheduled departure of the lander. It was also the second Thanksgiving Day of the 23-month long Martian year.

As soon as there was enough light, John carefully checked the habitat through his field glasses, looking for the buggies. He could spot only one, parked in front of the habitat. Where was the other? He remembered he had not checked where the second buggy had been parked before darkness had fallen the previous day. He cursed himself for being so stupid. All he could do was wait.

Between six and seven, he watched the ice mist below clear off, after a spectacular sunrise over the escarpment to the east, on the other side of Elbow Plain.

Seven o'clock passed, and the valley began to glow in the early morning sun. But this morning, there was no sign of the geological survey buggy. Could it be that the buggy was needed for some more sinister task? He tried to console himself with the thought that the geological survey was probably complete, but continued to worry.

Just before eight, the missing buggy appeared from around the other side of the habitat, and headed down the Elbow Hill road. John breathed a sigh of relief. He had been caught out once, and was determined not to be tricked again. If they're going to try anything, he thought, it has to be today.

He kept the buggy under observation as it got closer. It turned onto the main road, and headed toward Stem Gap. Then, at the road junction a few miles west of the landing site, Elbow Fork, the buggy turned right, and headed northeast on the main Kasei Valley road. It was carrying three people. He inspected the trailer carefully through his field glasses. It seemed to be carrying geological equipment. It was obviously only Don, Astrid, and Vince, setting out down the valley on the usual geological survey, but an hour later than usual.

He sure keeps them working, thought John, wondering what could have caused the one-hour change in departure time. For nearly half an hour, he tried to come up with an explanation, but there were too many possibilities, and he had to give up. That was his mistake. He should have contacted his wife. She had a better head for strategic possibilities than he had.

*

There was more than just geological survey equipment in the trailer of that buggy, and it was not carrying Don, Astrid, or Vince either. Those three were back in the habitat laboratory, ordered to spend the day there, studying and organizing their rock and soil samples, and preparing reports. Instead, the buggy was carrying Derk, Emma, and Jose.

In the trailer, underneath the geological equipment, lay automatic rifles, nanoguns, and machine pistols. The trailer also held a battery from the other rover, one of its three primary power supply batteries. It was fully charged and could propel a rover without a trailer for eighty miles on level terrain. In addition, the trailer held six reserve air flasks, each one good for one hour of normal use.

Derk was intending to penetrate Leaf Valley by means of Hazard Valley.

The distance from the habitat to Stem Gap via Hazard Valley was almost one hundred and seventy miles, when the road was clear, which currently it was not. Derk knew that from the previous failed attempt. But with the extra battery, his buggy would have power for three hundred and twenty miles on a level road, more than enough to get around all known blockages. That extra battery, together with travel in daylight, knowledge of where all the dune blockages lay, fully-charged air flasks and batteries at the moment of departure, an extra two hours of air each, and no time wasted admiring scenery, would give Derk all the resources he figured he needed to carry out his plan.

The intelligence gained from the earlier failed attempt to enter Leaf Valley via Hazard Valley was now invaluable. Without it, Derk could never have developed this plan.

Initially, Derk's rover proceeded northeastward down the Kasei Valley road at the usual speed of the geological survey buggy, about twenty-five miles an hour. Derk knew John would be watching. But as soon as the buggy was well out of the line of sight of John's observation post, at a low point of the road, it stopped, about ten miles from Elbow Fork.

All three got out and walked back to the trailer. There was no talking. Jose and Emma knew what they had to do, and indeed had practiced it the previous day, on the other side of the habitat, out of sight of John.

Together, Emma and Jose lifted the heavy battery from the trailer, and laid it on top of the broad battery compartment at the tail of the buggy. They used metal braces Karl had made in the habitat workshop to bolt it securely in place. Then they attached power cables to connect it in parallel with the buggy's normal batteries. They now had their planned super buggy, with one third longer range.

Then they used more braces to bolt on a large open metal container to the top of the battery compartment, beside the extra battery. Derk helped them load this container with the extra air flasks, and with machine pistols, holsters and ammunition, and handcuffs and leg irons too.

Then they strapped the automatic rifles and nanoguns to the back of the roof-rack framework above the battery compartment. The last thing they took from the trailer was a pair of shovels, which they also strapped to the framework beside the guns.

Finally, they disconnected the trailer, and pushed it into a hollow beside the road. They would travel light to save power, and would have no need for the trailer.

The whole conversion exercise took no more than six minutes. As soon as it was completed, they made a final check to make sure they had everything, and had done everything right. Then they climbed back in the buggy, and continued northeast.

They knew that every minute could count, and traveled as fast as possible down the Kasei Valley road. Emma did the driving on this initial easy stretch. Jose would take over later, when they got near to Hazard Valley. On straight road stretches, she had the buggy up to thirty-five miles an hour, and occasionally up to forty, for the extra battery gave the machine extra power.

Although it was a typical bright sunny morning, they were expecting a strong east wind later in the morning, which would probably cause a six-inch layer of blowing sand and dust on the valley floor. An east wind would be a headwind in Kasei Valley, and they were anxious to be out of the valley before the wind got up. In contrast, on the later part of their journey westward, up Hazard Valley, a wind from the east would be a tail wind.

Derk was feeling confident as they drove down Kasei Valley that sunny fall morning, and passed by Snakepit Crack. The important point was that they had air for thirteen hours, until nine o'clock in the evening, well after dark. He was sure it was enough for his plan to work, and with a reserve margin too.

This time he was going to capture them. There would be no mistakes. He would have them off the planet before they knew what had happened.

*

Just before eleven, they reached the junction with the road that headed north across rough country, to the eastern end of Hazard Valley. By now, not unexpectedly, a quite strong wind had arisen, blowing east along Kasei Valley. It was picking up considerable sand and dust, but the layer of blowing sand and dust was no more than six inches thick on the road.

The trip across the rough country, on the road northward linking Hazard Valley with Kasei Valley, went without incident. Jose was driving now. He knew the road, and so they made good progress, for the most part. The hills along the route sheltered them from the wind most of the way, and they reached the east end of Hazard Valley around twelve.

The east wind had little to blunt its force in Hazard Valley, which, although wide, was considerably narrower than Kasei Valley, and gradually narrowed along its length, which caused the wind to funnel more. Here the wind was generating a layer of blowing sand and dust a foot thick on the road. But now it was a tailwind, since they were headed west.

Jose could always see the road, however, despite the poor conditions, and he progressed at full speed.

Just before one o'clock, they reached the large dune tongue that straddled the road, and a great deal of the valley. On the previous expedition along this valley, Jose and his companions had encountered this dune tongue just as it was getting dark, and had made slow progress driving around it in the encroaching darkness. This time, it was the middle of the day, with the sun shining brightly.

They wasted no time discussing the dune tongue, and turned off the road to the left as soon as it came into view. The blowing sand and dust on the rock strewn terrain did impede Jose slightly, but by one thirty, they had traveled around the huge tongue, and they were back on the road. The worst problem had been loss of visibility every so often, caused by sand and dust blowing off the tops of nearby dune crests.

They pushed on along Hazard Valley, mostly on the road. They were forced to leave the road every so often, to navigate around small dune fields that had strayed onto the road, just as on the earlier journey. The wind strengthened as the afternoon wore on—the valley was getting narrower, increasing the funnel effect. Now the fast moving layer of wind-blown sand and dust was nearly two feet thick on the road, and was causing Jose to reduce speed. Jose knew exactly where they were though, for he had kept his eyes on the escarpments and mesas on either side of the road as they drove along.

Just after two thirty, Jose stopped.

"The big dune tongue, the one that completely blocks the valley, is about three miles up the road," said Jose decisively. "You can not see it from here, because of all this blowing dust. There is no need to drive any closer to it. We have to get around it, and to do that we have to leave the road here."

Jose pointed to a gap between two mesas to their right, lying about a mile northwest of the road. There were many small, scattered dune tongues between the road and the gap between the mesas, with sand and dust blowing off the tops of the dunes.

"I take it you mean drive through that gap, and keep to the mesa on the left," said Derk, who had thought long and hard about this critical part of their journey.

"Yes," said Jose. "That gap takes us into the labyrinth. I had a long discussion with John Erway about this labyrinth, when we came out here with Don two weeks ago, to fetch the two buggies. He said that nearly all of its valleys are full of creeping sand dunes, most of them impassable. It is one of the most dangerous places on Mars, according to him. I can not imagine him recommending it in a buggy, at any time, and certainly not in weather like this."

Jose was worried. The blowing sand and dust would make it even easier for them to lose their way, in a place where all the interlocking valleys looked very much alike anyway. Using the satellite link to let the habitat and Mission Control know they were lost would not help much. Who could help? Only John Erway in his rovers, and he would probably just laugh and let them perish, or just pretend to look for them. He knew too, that if the wind got significantly worse than it was now, they were certain to lose their way.

"What do you think, Jose?" asked Derk. "Can we make it round? Luck doesn't seem to be on our side today. I wasn't expecting this level of blowing dust."

During the past three weeks, there had been quite a few days with blowing sand and dust in the afternoon, but Derk had never seen anything like this, and was just as worried as Jose.

Jose thought hard, before answering the question. The problem was not just the wind. It was the narrow valley that was funneling it; and many of the valleys inside the labyrinth were even narrower, with even more pronounced wind funnels. On level valley terrain, off the road, a two-foot layer of blowing sand and dust would make travel difficult, and would slow them down significantly, but would not stop them. But in the narrow valleys of the labyrinth, sand and dust would be flying off the tops of dunes everywhere as well, so that visibility was bound to be much worse. Jose had had field experience of conditions like that in dune-filled valleys in North Africa, and knew just how treacherous such conditions could be, and how easy it was to get disoriented.

"Captain," said Jose at last, looking at his chief, and trying not to have a concerned expression on his face, "with very great care, and some luck, we could make it. But I cannot recommend it. Going in there today is very dangerous. We are putting our lives at risk. Perhaps you would consider turning around and going back, while there is still time. The mistake we made last time was not turning back when we had the chance, when it was obvious that going forward was very dangerous. We could just make it back to base, or at least close enough to get help, if we turn now."

"Thank you for a frank assessment, Jose," said Derk, looking at the gap between the orange mesas, standing out against the pink of the sky, and the dune tongues in front of it, with sand blowing off the dune crests.

Derk now thought hard. He was being forced to run a risk, something he hated doing, for it was obvious that there was a significant chance they would not come out of the labyrinth alive. On the other hand, turning around and going back to the habitat meant the end of all his ambitions, and return to Earth in disgrace. He could not bear the thought of such an outcome, so painful was it to contemplate. He knew he would rather die on Mars, in a heroic attempt at victory, than suffer returning home a beaten man. This was his last chance to capture the three in Leaf Valley, and he had to take it, regardless of the risks. In a few days, by Thursday, they would have no food left. As for the risk to the lives of Emma and Jose, he never gave that a moment's thought.

"We proceed as planned," said Derk at last. "But we'll be extra careful we don't get lost." He paused, and then continued: "Jose, you will concentrate on driving. You will concern yourself only with the terrain just ahead of the buggy. Emma, you will concentrate on keeping the mesa escarpment to the left always in sight, and will tell Jose when he has to turn. If you get close to losing sight of the mesa, you warn Jose before you do, so that he has time to turn. Let's go."

At that, Jose turned off the road, to the right, and headed for the left side of the gap between the mesas, and the way into the interlocking valleys of the labyrinth. The gap began just over a mile away to the northwest. But progress was slow over the rock covered terrain in the blowing dust, as they traveled around small dune tongues, and it took ten minutes of arduous travel before they reached it. At the entrance, Jose stopped for a few seconds, hesitating, studying the terrain ahead.

Inside the mile-wide gap between the mesas, they could now see a heavy concentration of small dune fields, with fine sand blowing off the dune crests, and filling the air to a height of some twenty feet. Derk said nothing during the few seconds Jose was stopped, and waited for him to proceed. He eventually did, keeping to the left side of the gap, close to the mesa escarpment, just as he had done on the previous disastrous attempt at driving through the labyrinth, an attempt that had taken the lives of two of his companions.

Soon the lone buggy carrying the three soldiers, armed to the teeth, had disappeared into the sand dunes and blowing sand and dust of the labyrinth.

Whatever might be said about the character of Captain Richard Derk, there was no doubt that he was a man of courage. Derk, like all his ancestors, when confronted with a situation where his very future lay on the line, even when the odds were against him, would wade into battle against any foe, with every ounce of strength and strategy at his command. It was not hard to imagine this determined Norman baron, armored in his pressure suit against the elements, sword in hand, slashing and cutting his way through the labyrinth dunes that lay between him and the governorship of the first colony on Mars.

*

All that day, John maintained his watch from his observation post. He was feeling tired, having had only a minimum of sleep for the past few days. That morning he had been up just before five.

After the geological survey buggy disappeared down Kasei Valley to the northeast, there was no activity until just after eleven, when the other buggy made a trip to the landing site, with three persons on board.

John watched intently. A strong wind had arisen by now, lifting a thin layer of blowing sand and dust on the plain, but this did not hinder his observations. The wind was from the east, so that there was no funnel effect out on Elbow Plain, unlike the case at the western end of Hazard Valley, and in the narrow valleys of the labyrinth. On Elbow Plain, the wind was a nuisance, but hardly a hazard.

When the buggy returned to the habitat, half an hour later, it went round to the east side of the long building, out of sight. They must be loading the trailer again, thought John, expecting to see it again shortly. He did not, however. This no show, together with a complete absence of any further activity around the habitat, puzzled him a little, but did not raise any concerns. It's not very pleasant outside; they must be all inside, organizing their data and reports, thought John.

Of course, in that conclusion, John was quite wrong, but had no way of knowing. That afternoon, Derk, Jose, and Emma were battling their way through the labyrinth. Furthermore, unbeknownst to John, the other buggy, parked out of sight on the other side of the habitat, was being prepared for a journey quite different from the further trip to the landing site John was expecting.

At two o'clock, that other buggy, driven by Karl, with Monique and Jurgen in the passenger seats, left the habitat. It pulled no trailer. It headed due southeast, in the direction away from Stem Gap, down the rough slope from the Elbow Hill shelf to the plain below. It kept to the line of sight between habitat and Stem Gap, so that, as it descended to the plain, John could not see it.

Once down on the plain, the buggy veered to the right a little, so as to put the entire Elbow Hill between it and Stem Gap. It then headed due southeast, unseen by John, toward the lower level of the southeastern escarpment bounding Elbow Plain, about twelve miles from the habitat, about twenty-four from John's observation post.

When it reached the eastern edge of the plain, it turned left, to the northeast, and headed down Kasei Valley. It was too far away for John to spot with the naked eye, as it emerged from behind the left side of Elbow Hill, but twelve miles further away. At the level of the road, it would have been over the horizon. John could not even have spotted it through his field glasses, had he been looking for it. That afternoon, small amounts of dust in the air significantly reduced visibility at such a distance. Although the wind was lifting only a six inch carpet of swirling sand and dust on the valley floor, enough dust was also getting higher into the air to generate a red haze at long distances. John was tired anyway, and was content merely to keep the habitat and landing site under observation.

Around four thirty, he spotted the geological survey buggy, or so he thought, headed home, pulling its open trailer filled with survey equipment, as usual. That will be their last survey, he thought. It doesn't look as if anything's going to happen now. They'll be on their way home tomorrow.

He felt a slight pang of regret at this. He had got to know Don and Astrid, and liked them, and would be sorry to see them go. He knew Denise would be sorry too. He thought of how it all could have been, how their fledgling settlement could have been happily expanded, to everyone's benefit, had it not been for that copper, and that bastard Derk.

Of course, that buggy did not carry Don, Astrid, and Vince. It carried Karl, Monique, and Jurgen, instead. They had secretly traveled up the valley to where Derk had left the open trailer filled with survey equipment that morning. Having hitched the trailer to the buggy, out of sight of John, they were now openly returning to the habitat, as if returning from the usual geological survey.

Derk was always thorough in his plans. He knew that every activity on Elbow Plain would be watched, and was making sure that there was nothing that could arouse John's suspicions.

There was no more activity that afternoon.

As the sun was setting behind the west wall of Leaf Valley, John had a call from Denise. She had just received a news video from Earth, in which the headlines were the planned return of the ESA mission, without the arrest of the three on Mars. The news video had also contained a report on a demonstration in Washington by members of various Mars societies, in support of the three on Mars. The demonstrators had been peaceful, but had carried placards with slogans like: *Hands Off Leaf Valley*, *E.U. Go Home*, *The Martians are Innocent*, *God Bless Leaf Valley*, and so forth.

The light faded. Just after seven, to John's surprise, buggy headlamps came on at the habitat, and a buggy started down the Elbow Hill road, and eventually disappeared into the landing pit. Some fifteen minutes later, the buggy reappeared, but instead of heading back to the habitat it headed toward Stem Gap, with its headlights full on. John tensed. Was this it? Was this Derk's final attempt to arrest them?

Suddenly, the buggy stopped, and its lights went out, and John lost sight of it. It had grown quite dark low down, although there was still a pale purple light in the sky, through which the brighter stars were visible. For some twenty minutes, John peered through his field glasses at the spot where the buggy had stopped, trying to see what, if anything, was going on. He wished he could have had a pair of infra-red night glasses. But they were military equipment, and no one had ever thought they could be needed on Mars. John was having visions of three armed Special Forces personnel advancing on Stem Gap in the dark. He was sure they had night glasses.

Then suddenly, three sets of flames appeared, equally spaced around the landing pit, as illuminated sand and dust burst into the air. The flames lasted just one second, but in the brilliant orange light he could clearly make out the buggy, with two occupants, still parked where it had stopped earlier. John relaxed. It was just a final test of the rocket motors.

Some twelve minutes later, there was another burst of flaming dust from the landing pit, again lasting just one second. A few minutes later, the buggy turned on its lights again and headed back to the landing site. John, still sitting in the front seat of his rover, looked at his watch. It was now eight twenty. Fifteen minutes later, the buggy reappeared out of the landing pit and headed back to the habitat.

There had been lights on at the habitat all evening, and by the time the buggy reached it, all the lights were on. John relaxed further. It was clearly just Jurgen doing a final test of the motors, he said to himself. That lander's definitely going to lift off tomorrow, he thought.

But John was wrong about it being a final test. It was nothing of the sort. The motors had been tested the previous week and had worked perfectly. It was all part of Derk's plan, just another diversionary tactic.

John's attention was to be kept focussed on the landing pit and habitat between seven and nine, and Derk had concluded that getting Jurgen to conduct a spectacular test of the rocket motors that evening was probably the best way to do that. Derk had planned on reaching Tip Canyon well before seven, and on being active inside Leaf Valley, in the semi darkness, between seven and nine. He had an air supply until nine.

Just before ten, with only one light on at the habitat, John decided to call it a day, and headed home. The minefield at the gap would do the usual job of guarding the entrance during the night.

He reached home at ten thirty, and sat in the rover a few minutes, on the shelf outside the airlock, looking around. Could there possibly be a trap waiting for him, like a few days ago, he wondered. This was Derk's last chance.

Impossible, he thought. The two buggies had been out in Kasei Valley all day.

Then it hit him. He had never seen the two buggies together all day. Then he thought: But one buggy had gone on the geological survey, while the other went up and down to the landing pit. He shook his head. This is driving me nuts, he thought. When he asked Denise to reset the airlock-door fuse, she responded at once, and the door opened, and he could drive inside. But he decided to be cautious anyway.

He emerged stealthily from the rover airlock, onto the parking pad, a pistol in one hand and the automatic rifle in the other. He did not go straight to the house. Instead, he stole quietly up the steps to the south. Then, bent down, he stole along the outside garden path at the edge of the compound. Then he stole quietly around the inner garden path.

Finally, he came at the house from the back, and made his way stealthily along the east-side patio, and then along the lower front balcony, as far as the downstairs living room, where he could see in through the balcony window. His wife was sitting in the corner, with Dr. Sato, and the corner table was set. Everything seemed normal.

He retraced his steps, stole up the stair to the upper level balcony, and checked the upstairs rooms from outside. Once more, everything was normal. My mind is playing tricks on me, thought John to himself, as he slid open the upstairs living room door, and went inside. He left his guns in the bedroom, and walked downstairs to join Denise and Dr. Sato.

"Come and have Thanksgiving dessert, John," said Denise, as he entered the room. On this Thanksgiving Day, the usual supper was out of the question, but Denise had promised John a special dessert. "You must be bored stiff sitting down there all day. Oh, and I have news too, a message from Earth. You'll never guess who from."

"Who? The Pope?" asked John, as he sat down, suppressing a yawn.

"No," said Denise. "From the CIA. The message just came in half an hour ago. It's the first for over a month."

"Oh," said John, his tired mind suddenly alert. He knew it had to be important.

Every one of the few communications they had had from the CIA had turned out to be important.

"Yes, indeed," said Denise. "We've been asked to be ready for a really big surprise in about six days, and to confirm or deny immediately that we are still in possession of Leaf Valley. They have a big dish directed at Mars, and a channel open, to pick up our reply."

"Have you answered?"

"Yes," said Denise. "I sent the message twenty minutes ago. Have you any idea what the surprise might be?"

"Beats me," said John, relaxing again, as Denise served him some dessert. "Maybe they've decided to send us some guns. If so, they're a bit late. I could use a few tanks though, just in case Derk has a change of mind at the last minute."

"Does it still look as if they're leaving?" asked Denise.

John spent some time giving her a summary of the day's events, including the test firing—in between forays into the dessert.

"That certainly looks like they're leaving," said Denise slowly. "But it looks almost too much like it. I still don't trust that man."

"Neither do I," said John. "But there's no way he's going to enter this valley tonight, and even if he could, he couldn't get in here. There are no functioning airlocks. He'd run out of air sitting outside. And there's no way he's going to destroy this compound—or even the rovers. He wants all that for himself, intact."

"I would like to see the launch, if it's really going to happen," said Denise. "So would the children."

"No problem," said John. "Come down about an hour before. Dr. Sato, I'd like you to come too, if you feel up to it."

The Zen master merely bowed in agreement.

"We should drive over and inspect the habitat, after the launch," said Denise. "I hope they leave it clean and tidy. I'll bring the children's dollies."

"Yes, do that," said John, getting up, after finishing off his dessert. "Now I have to get to bed. I'm dead beat. I can hardly think. Good night. Try not to wake me when you come, Denise."

John left the room, and pulled himself up the stairs, holding on to the stair rail, a very tired man. The continuous stress was beginning to wear him down. He has seen better Thanksgivings.

*

It was just after five next morning, launch day, when John left the compound in his rover, headed for Stem Gap. It was still fairly dark as the rover came out of the airlock. Just before, with pressure suit on, and holding the automatic rifle, John had scouted around outside, but there had been no sign of anything unusual on the shelf.

He reached his observation post just after five forty-five, and began his usual vigil. Just after six twenty, he watched another spectacular sunrise above the very high escarpment wall on the other side of Elbow Plain, a good thirty miles away. Then he watched patches of ice mist on the plain disperse in the early morning sunshine. There was no activity at the habitat.

By nine thirty, there was still no sign of any activity. John was puzzled. At nine forty-five, Denise arrived, driving her rover, with Dr. Sato and the two children in the passenger seats. She parked the rover beside John's, so that all of them could see over the crater rim, and across the sunlit plain, to the habitat and landing site.

Within minutes of Denise's arrival, there was action. John spotted a buggy on its way down the Elbow Hill road. He inspected it through field glasses. It was carrying three persons. He expected it to turn into the landing pit. It did not, but carried on to the junction with the main Kasei Valley road, and then headed northwest, and then west, at full speed, toward Stem Gap. Denise was observing it through field glasses too. They watched it for some ten minutes.

"John!" cried Denise, suddenly. "The children! They're carrying guns."

John had just been able to make out the guns too. They were the large nanoguns.

"Quick!" he said. "We have to back the rovers away from the rim, out of sight. Then everybody out. I'll bring the guns."

Five minutes later, John, Denise, and Dr. Sato were lying on the cold ground, helmeted heads peeping over the top of the crater rim. John was holding the nanogun, Denise the automatic. The rovers, parked at the center of the small crater, could no longer be seen from the road below. The children sat in the front seats, looking on.

The buggy heading along the road toward Stem Gap had maintained its speed. It was now only three miles away. The two in the passenger seats were clearly holding nanoguns. John felt threatened. Why had he been so stupid as to allow his family up here that morning? One nanogun bullet exploding over the crater could kill all of them.

John considered opening fire on the buggy. He did not want to fire first. But with nanoguns, if you did not fire first you might never fire. But then he thought, they haven't used their range finders yet. So they can't open fire yet. He sighted the buggy with his range finder, and injected a shell into the firing chamber.

Suddenly, about a hundred meters from the sign warning of mines, the buggy stopped, and the three jumped out, each of them carrying a nanogun. All three ran away from the buggy—two to the right and one to the left. One of the two that went to the right went much further than the other. In thirty seconds they had all taken cover behind small crater rims, but all well apart. A single nanobullet could no longer kill all of them. John groaned. He was watching military tactics, which he had not thought of, and could not match. They were now in a position to kill him, his entire family, and Dr. Sato, with loss of only one of them, at most. He considered getting Denise and Dr. Sato to run back and shelter in different craters.

Suddenly, John felt a sharp prod at his back, just below his backpack. At the same time they all heard a voice, loud and clear.

"Let go your weapons, and don't move. Please don't give me a reason to shoot you in front of the children. You're all under arrest."

The voice was Richard Derk's. Beside him stood Emma and Jose. All three were armed with automatic rifles, pointed at the three lying on the ground. They also wore side holsters, holding machine pistols. It was just a few minutes after ten o'clock.

*

Twenty minutes after their surprise arrest, Denise and Dr. Sato sat in the living area of the rover, in the red swivel chairs. Neither wore pressure suits. They were both handcuffed and leg ironed, and tied to the chairs with rope—made from parachute cord taken from the rover trailer.

The rover was still inside the observation crater, facing about east, so that the sun was slanting in through the window above the low computer screen. Denise, still in a state of shock, could see her husband through the window.

Her two children were free to move around in the rover. Sometimes they cried, sometimes they sobbed, and sometimes they screamed, either holding on to their bound mother, or standing on the passenger seats at the front, looking out at their father through the side window.

Emma Grant was sitting in the driver seat, and took little notice of the children. She sat somewhat uncomfortably, wearing her pressure suit, backpack and all, awaiting orders.

John was standing near the rim of the small crater, handcuffed and leg-ironed, with Derk and Jose nearby. Derk was still pointing his gun at John, while Jose was bent over, examining the remote controller John had used for detonating mines.

"It's a simple digital remote controller," said Jose to Derk, looking up. "You just need the codes to set off the mines."

Derk motioned John toward the controller. "Why don't you be a decent chap," he said, "and explode the mines for us, especially those on the road? That way we won't need to drive you all back through Hazard Valley. I'm sure you'd prefer us not to do that. Why put yourselves through such an ordeal? There's no chance you can escape now. There's a launch opportunity at two fifty-three this afternoon. A quick trip through Stem Gap must be better than a long drive through Hazard Valley. Come now, tell Jose what to do."

"Get lost," said John.

"Very well," said Derk. "It's your risk. Emma is going to drive through the gap anyway. She'll go very fast, forty to fifty miles an hour. That's twenty to twenty-five meters a second. That way, if a mine goes off it'll damage only the tail of the rover. Of course, the rover will likely depressurize, but Emma's wearing a pressure suit, so she'll be all right. But your wife and children...."

Derk studied John's face. It was expressionless.

"Very well," said Derk. "If your family is killed, it will be your doing."

He turned to the rover and waved to Emma.

As John watched, Emma turned the rover, took it out of the crater, and then drove along the flank of the escarpment, heading down toward the road, along what was by now becoming a well worn trail. The children, no longer able to see their father, clung to their mother all the way down.

Meanwhile, Derk used John's portable communications device to order Karl, Monique, and Jurgen to get their buggy off the road. After the arrest, these three had gone back to the buggy, and had been sitting in it, just outside the gap, waiting for orders. Derk explained carefully to Karl, mostly for John's benefit, that Emma was going to try to get through the gap in the rover, and would be coming at speed.

Some twenty minutes later, the rover reached the road some three miles away from the gap. There it stopped, facing Stem Gap.

"Well," said Derk to John. "How about the detonation codes? You can't possibly want to expose your family to a risk like this."

"Watch me," said John.

"Very well," said Derk, and used the communications device to order Emma to proceed as planned. The rover began to move down the road.

Of course, Derk had to be bluffing. John was sure of that. Derk wanted the rovers intact. He would not risk damaging one, or more likely, destroying it. Their only chance now of evading deportation was to force Derk to take them on the long trip through the labyrinth and Hazard Valley in the rovers. Maybe an opportunity to escape would present itself, although at that moment John could not see any way to accomplish that.

Inside the rover, Emma suddenly had a humanitarian thought, or perhaps it was just a mother instinct, or perhaps she felt the need to tidy up a matter Derk had forgotten to give her instructions about. It caused her to take her foot off the accelerator, before the rover had gone more than a few meters, and get up from her seat and walk back to the living area. Standing between Denise and the Zen master, with the two children clinging to their mother, she removed her helmet, and spoke to Denise.

"The rover's going to execute a dangerous maneuver at high speed," she said. "There could be a sudden stop. Your children could be killed if they stay were they are. I'm sure you would not want that. They should be either strapped into the passenger seats, or lie up against the wall in the front bunk. Which do you want?"

"Bitch," hissed Denise. Then she said: "In the bunk, where they can see me."

Emma was quick. She practically tore the children from their mother, and placed them in the bunk, which was quite close to where Denise sat. The children screamed. The bunk was too high off the floor for them to get down.

"You quiet them," said Emma, disappearing back into the driver area.

As Denise tried to calm the children, and get them to lie quietly against the front wall of the rover, Emma was back in the driver seat, fastening her helmet. She pressed the accelerator into the floor, and the huge machine jumped forward, headed toward the gap. By the time she had the rover's speed up to nearly fifty miles an hour, almost a mile a minute, she was two minutes from entering the gap.

Up above, Derk, Jose, and John watched the speeding rover flying down the road. Sixty seconds from the gap, Derk looked at John. John seemed unconcerned. Thirty seconds from the gap, John still looked unconcerned. Now Derk suddenly looked worried.

"For God's sake man," he shouted, "give up! Give us the codes! You'll kill your family!"

"No," said John, "you'll have killed them, not me."

At this point, Derk lost his nerve. He was particularly worried about something happening to the children. It would look bad back on Earth. He shouted into the communications device: "Emma! Stop! That's close enough."

Inside the rover, when Emma heard the order to stop, she was only ten seconds from the gap. Her foot was on the brake at once, but the brakes were having very little effect. The problem was the rover's speed. Its designers had never expected it would be driven on a road. It was built for going slowly over rough and rocky terrain, about ten miles an hour on average. At nearly fifty miles an hour, the brakes did not work well, and would take some time to stop the heavy machine. A slight downward incline of the road through Stem Gap did not help either.

Emma was nearly a third of the way through Stem Gap before the rover began to slow significantly. The speedometer reading was now down to twenty miles an hour and falling quickly. But now Emma was puzzled, as was Derk, watching, for so far there had been no mine explosions. Emma concluded she must have just been very lucky.

Suddenly, she realized her predicament, in the middle of a minefield. The rover's tracks along the road so far were clearly safe. However, she did not have the skill to reverse the machine over those safe tracks, especially with a trailer attached. Nor could she reverse quickly. A mine explosion was nearly certain, but a mine explosion at very low speed was far more dangerous than one at high speed.

Emma could think tactics very fast. There was only one thing to do. She took her foot off the brake and stamped on the accelerator, and the rover began to put on speed again.

Two minutes later, the rover shot out of Stem Gap at fifty miles an hour, past the sign warning of the danger of mines, and past Karl, Monique, and Jurgen, sitting beside the road in their buggy, to the amazement of everyone, except John.

Suddenly, Derk understood. He turned to look at John, with a sly smile on his face.

"Well, I have to congratulate you," he said. "You had me fooled. There were no mines on the road at all. And we made a long, dangerous journey through that blasted labyrinth yesterday, because we all thought your mines were real. Those mines you laid on the road on Saturday morning were dummies, weren't they?"

There was nothing John could say. His bluff had been called. There was no hope now. He merely nodded in reply.

"And you had a few real mines laid off the road for demonstration purposes, to make us think you had mines everywhere. How many have you got left?"

John did not answer.

"Come," said Derk. "You may as well tell us now, and give us the detonation codes. I'm sure you wouldn't want one of them to kill somebody in the future. It wouldn't go well for you at your trial if that were to happen, now would it? Our little war is over. It's time to get rid of the mines."

John could not deny the truth of this.

"There's only one left," said John, and gave him the code.

Derk nodded to Jose, standing beside the detonation controller. Jose entered the binary equivalent of the code. Immediately there was a huge explosion, about half a mile from the other side of the road, opposite were they stood.

Satisfied that there was no further danger from mines, Derk now ordered Karl to drive his buggy up by the shortest way possible.

"It's perfectly safe now, Karl," said Derk, plugged into John's communications device. "I need one of you to drive our buggy back. It's in a crater a bit above this one."

John, Derk and Jose waited while Karl's buggy made its way up the shallow escarpment. It did not take the gradual route along the escarpment flank, the way Emma had gone down, but came up in a straight line from where it had been parked, and took less than ten minutes.

With the buggy's arrival, just after eleven, Derk began giving orders. He ordered Karl to fetch Jose's buggy, which was hidden in a crater, a little further back from Elbow Plain, and about a hundred meters further up the escarpment.

He next ordered Monique and Jurgen to help Jose get John into the remaining rover. Soon John was out of his pressure suit, and seated and bound to one of the two red swivel chairs in the machine's living area. John had no choice but do as he was ordered. He had a feeling Derk would have liked an excuse to shoot him.

Finally, with John secure in the rover, Derk ordered Monique and Jurgen to drive their buggy back down to the road, and then to the compound at Mount Tip. They were to bring back the third buggy, abandoned by Jose four days earlier, as well as pack some belongings containers for the captives, for their journey to Earth.

By this time, Karl was making his way down the escarpment toward the road, driving the other buggy, the one that Derk had used to journey through the labyrinth. The extra battery at the back did not go unnoticed by John, looking through the rover window. He was now beginning to understand how Derk had outmaneuvered him a second time, or was it a third time?

Soon the rover was following the two buggies down to the road. Jose was driving, while Derk sat in the other swivel chair opposite

John, his machine pistol on his lap. Derk seemed to want to talk, even show off a little.

"Although you had me fooled about the mines," said Derk, as the rover trundled down the escarpment, "I had you fooled about where the buggies were yesterday. My diversions and distractions yesterday worked better than I had hoped. But I really did doubt you would fall for that distraction with the rocket-motor test, yesterday evening. If you had looked over to the monastery yesterday evening, instead of watching the test, you would have seen us going up the escarpment road to spend the night up there. We had to go up to the monastery to get everything recharged after our long labyrinth trip. That was the weak part of my plan. I was afraid you'd have learned from Jose's use of the monastery last Thursday, and would have had that road up defended. One person at the top of that road could hold it against an army. And we couldn't have lasted much after nine o'clock. I must say I was delighted at how negligent you were."

John said nothing. He understood now why the CIA had insisted that this man was extremely dangerous.

"And in case you're wondering why Karl's buggy left the habitat this morning just as soon as your wife arrived," continued Derk, "it was no coincidence. It's remarkable how effective a shaving mirror is for signaling over long distances on a sunny day. I gave the signal as soon as she arrived. My dear chap, you may be a good engineer, but as a general…."

*

Later, just before twelve, Derk was standing by a kitchen window, holding a mug of coffee. He was feeling good about himself. Nothing could stop him now, and the news of the re-arrest of the three had already arrived at Mission Control, where it was just past eleven thirty on Monday morning. Local Toulouse time was running one day and just under half an hour behind Kasei Valley time. ESA had released the news at once, to an astonished world, sparking an explosive rally on European stock exchanges.

Derk was sitting at the dining table, having an early lunch with the others at the habitat. Every so often, he stood up, and walked over to the kitchen, to look out the window and down to the landing pit. The two rovers were parked a mile away, in the sunshine, on the trail leading down to the pit, in full view of the habitat. By now, a moderate wind from the east had arisen, and a layer of blowing sand and dust swirled on the valley floor.

Emma was standing guard inside the rover holding Denise and Dr. Sato, machine pistol at the ready, with orders to shoot Denise if she made any trouble, something Emma was quite prepared to do. Karl was on guard inside John's rover. He too had orders to shoot, if John made any trouble. Derk knew that Karl would do just that, if necessary, and no longer cared if he did.

He wanted rid of them, either back to Earth or dead would suit him fine. These three had almost cost him his life—at one point during the previous day's journey through the labyrinth, he and Jose and Emma had got badly lost. Derk was sure they had found their way out by good luck only.

However, if truth be told, it was Jose's stubborn determination and desert experience that had seen them through, when neither Derk nor Emma could see what to do. In later years, Jose's story of that day in the labyrinth, exaggerated no doubt with the passage of time, would become a classic, a Martian mini version of Hannibal crossing the Alps to invade Ancient Rome by the back door.

Derk returned to the table again. Seated there were Don, Astrid, Vince, Ursula, and Jose. Derk was not expecting Jurgen and Monique back from the glass compound with the two buggies until about one.

"Pity you couldn't go out on your survey yesterday, Don," said Derk, as he sat down again, opposite Don, "but we could not do without your transportation. That messy business with the arrest had to have the highest priority."

Both Don and Astrid wanted to ask Derk about the state of the prisoners, but dared not. They both knew that this was a matter in which they were powerless. Instead Don just said: "It wasn't a good day for survey work yesterday anyway—a bit too much blowing sand and dust. And I see it's much the same today."

"It's not as bad today," said Derk. "Actually, I wanted to talk to you about that. We have to get the survey of the escarpment finished as soon as possible. When it's finished, we still have the top of the rampart to survey—we have rovers now, so we'll be able to do it. There's plenty to do, and I can't afford to waste any more time. We've wasted enough on this arrest caper. For the life of me, I can't see why those three couldn't have just agreed to go home and save everybody a great deal of trouble. Don, I want you, Astrid, and Vince to continue with the survey work this afternoon. Leave the launch to us. There's nothing for you to do there. Can you leave at once?"

"Yes, I suppose so," said Don, both surprised and disappointed, and glancing at Astrid and Vince, who also looked surprised.

"Exactly how far have you come, anyway?" asked Derk.

"As far as the escarpment section opposite the beginning part of Snakepit Crack," said Don, trying to keep from thinking about John and Denise. "We still have to get as far as the escarpment at the northeast end of the crack. The escarpment could be a problem around there. There are signs of instability—Astrid thinks it was the sheer weight of the escarpment, before the rampart on top eroded away, that was the basic force behind the formation of that rupture in the—"

"Well," said Derk, not in the mood to listen to geological theories, "that's why it's important to get an accurate survey done. If we have the complete data, the engineering will be able to compensate for any instabilities. Now I think you should be going. Since you're getting started late today, you can stay out an hour or so longer."

At that Derk got up, and walked over to the kitchen to get some more coffee, and to check that the two rovers with his prisoners were still parked beside the landing pit, which they were.

Both Don and Astrid desperately wanted to say their good-byes to John and Denise, and to Dr. Sato. Astrid also had something she thought it important that Denise should have. But now there was less than three hours remaining before the scheduled launch of the lander, at two fifty-three, and there was no arguing with their chief. They had no choice but to obey his orders. They both understood the real reason Derk was sending them out on the survey mission so late in the day. It was his desire to prevent them being witnesses to any unpleasant scenes that might unfold prior to the launch.

Fifteen minutes later, Don and Astrid were in their buggy, along with Vince, on their way down Kasei Valley to the current survey site, between Snakepit Crack and the northwest escarpment wall of the valley. The wind was still quite strong, with a six-inch layer of blowing sand and dust just above the ground. Just before they left, they had heard Jose assure Derk that the wind was nowhere near strong enough to impede the planned launch.

*

Around one o'clock, Jurgen and Monique arrived back at the habitat with the two buggies. The launch scheduled for two fifty-three was still on.

Things got moving just before two o'clock. Everybody was outside at the landing pit, or near it.

First, Emma drove Denise's rover into the pit. One by one, Monique and Ursula then parceled the children up in their dollies and took them out of the rover, as they screamed for their mother. Jurgen and Derk stood outside watching, Derk holding an automatic rifle. Jurgen was holding a video camera. Under instructions from his chief, he videoed only the scenes of Ursula and Monique wheeling the dollies up the steps and into the lander. He recorded no audio, as the children screamed in terror. There were tears in Ursula's eyes. This was not what she had come to Mars to do.

Inside the lander, on the upper personnel floor, the children began responding to Ursula, as she detached the copper containers from the dollies and fastened them to the lander seats. Instinct told the children she would not harm them, and they quieted down.

Ursula took very great care with them, speaking to them in a very soothing voice, and keeping the thick glass doors of the containers open as she fastened the containers to the lander seats. She talked to them wonderingly about the long journey in a great spaceship they were going on, to see the magical Earth they had heard so much about. She assured them that mother and father were going too, and would be joining them in a few minutes. Soon she had the glass doors closed, and the children lying quietly, almost horizontally, in their small seats, securely strapped into their airtight containers, while she stood in front, entertaining them by making outlines of exotic animals, especially giraffes, with her hands.

Once the two children were inside the lander, Emma backed the rover away, and drove it out of the landing pit again, up the cutting, and parked it on the trail just outside, beside John's rover. Derk and Jurgen walked up the trail behind it. Outside the landing pit, they were exposed to the blowing sand and dust close to the ground.

Ten minutes later, Jurgen, still acting under Derk's orders, was walking backward down the cutting, and keeping to its right side. He was recording a procession with his video camera. The cutting and landing pit were sheltered from the wind outside, and there was no blowing sand and dust to interfere with Jurgen's video recording, as the procession advanced toward the lander, in the bright afternoon sunshine. Jurgen was transmitting the video to the ESA satellite in real time, via the satellite communications system in a buggy parked nearby in the pit.

It was a sorry sight. Three figures walked in single file down the center of the cutting, first John, then Denise, and then Dr. Sato. Each of them was leg ironed and handcuffed, hands in front. Derk and Jose walked in single file on the prisoners' right side. Neither one was armed, but Karl and Emma, walking in single file well to the other side of the prisoners, were armed with automatic rifles.

On Derk's instructions, Jurgen was careful not to include Karl and Emma in his video recording. Derk did not think it a good idea for the public in Europe to see him deploying automatic weapons on Mars. He had also arranged things so that the procession would take as long as possible, to enable a powerful graphic recording of the last minutes of these three on Mars. By the time the procession reached the lander, the video of its beginning had already reached Earth, and was being watched world wide. The world could see Derk in his moment of triumph, bringing these criminals to justice.

There were a few thoughtful observers on Earth, however, who were thinking along other lines, as they watched these images. Some of those observers, particularly members of Mars societies who had championed free settlements on Mars, wept at the sight. Others, among the thoughtful few, were wondering if history was repeating itself, as Astrid had also wondered, a few days earlier. Many of them even looked up the history of the early years of the New World, especially the year 1500, when that ruthless governor of the first settlement, the newly arrived appointee of a greedy monarch, cast a disgraced Christopher Columbus in jail, falsely accused of heinous crimes, and shipped him back to Spain in irons.

*

The minute count-down had begun.

"Launch control: T minus thirty-one minutes. Nose antenna visual confirmation. Do you read?"

It was Jurgen's voice, with his pronounced German accent. He was in the communications room at the habitat, with Derk and Emma beside him. Both Emma and Derk wore field glasses around their necks, every so often looking out the window at the landing pit, a mile away, where the lander's nose tip was just visible above the crater rim, shining in the mid afternoon sun. Karl and Ursula were outside on the shelf, sitting in a buggy, watching the landing site. Ursula was looking at the landing site through outdoors field glasses. Karl was holding a video camera, pointed at the landing site. It's image was being transmitted to a screen in front of Jurgen, and back to Earth too. Karl would record the expected spectacular launch.

There were four full images of the lander on a large screen in front of Jurgen as well. Earlier, Jurgen and Jose had placed four remote-controlled video cameras equidistant around the rim of the crater surrounding the landing site. They were expendable cameras brought to Mars specifically for use in launch control.

"Copy," replied Jose. "Transmissions received. Do you read?'

"We read you," said Jurgen.

Jose, sitting with Monique on the lower personnel floor of the lander, had just deployed a short stub antenna at the nose of the lander, to allow a digital link with the habitat in the crucial half hour before launch. Jose was now the flight engineer on board the lander, but he would not be in full control until the craft left the ground.

Jurgen was in charge of the launch, acting as launch controller. He had complete control of the lander's systems via the computers at the habitat and the digital radio link to the lander. He also had a full visual display of the lander from four directions.

Both the computers at the habitat and in the lander were equipped with extensive checking procedure software, that would check every system and sub system on board the lander, in the correct sequences, looking for any flaw that might negatively affect the launch. Both sets of computers had to confirm each other's findings.

Some seconds passed.

"Launch control: T minus thirty minutes. First auto control check positive. We have a go for launch," said Jurgen.

Inside the lander, the launch control jargon could also be heard coming from a speaker on the upper personnel floor, where John, Dense, and Dr. Sato sat in their pressure suits, without backpacks. Their helmet valves were open to the atmosphere inside, which was at normal temperature and pressure, and was breathable.

They were all three handcuffed to their seats, and were by now resigned to their fates. Denise was sobbing. John could hear her, but could think of nothing comforting to say. She was taking it very badly, broken hearted, all her dreams shattered. At the same time, John was experiencing feelings of despair, shame, loss, and rage all at once, despair because there was now no hope, shame that he had let his family down, loss because of the loss of everything they had worked so hard to build, and rage at the false charges being leveled against them, and the sheer injustice of it all.

The minutes passed, as the computers did their work, checking, testing, rechecking, retesting. Each minute, Jurgen made the cryptic comment: *Launch Control: T minus ...*, usually with a message about the correct functioning of some on-board system.

Everything was proceeding normally. Jurgen, although uneasy in his mind at what was being done to John, Denise, and Dr. Sato, was a first-class flight engineer, and was giving the launch his full attention. At least he would get them safely back to Earth.

Jurgen was confident nothing would go wrong. The lander was well designed, and was a very robust, over-engineered machine. The engineers at ESA had learned the lessons of the failures of 2038 and 2046. Every system was functioning as it should.

Even so, the cluster of three rocket motors in each of the lander's six rocket cylinders ensured that the lander would get successfully into orbit, even if a few of the individual motors should fail on launch. Nevertheless, Jurgen was certain that the lander would be able to lift off flawlessly, and complete docking with the mother ship a few hours later. By next day, John and Denise would be over half a million miles away in space.

"T-minus twelve minutes. All systems normal," announced Jurgen.

John too was counting off the minutes, like the millions on Earth who were watching with a six minute delay. Just about every trader at the major European stock exchanges, where it was early Monday afternoon, was also watching, as were most investors, and trading had practically ground to a halt.

Eleven minutes to launch.

John waited for Jurgen's cryptic message. This time it did not come. He frowned, and waited. Ten minutes to launch. No message from Jurgen this time either.

John's suit earphones were on, as they usually were, and he listened intently for any indication that something was wrong with the lander. If it were to malfunction and explode, it was the end of them all. There was nothing more dangerous than a malfunctioning fully fueled rocket.

Nine minutes to launch. Still no message.

Then at eight minutes to launch there came a monotone, computer-generated message from the speaker:

Automatic Launch Control System. T minus eight minutes. On schedule for launch.

John was puzzled at why Jurgen was no longer calling out the minutes. At least there did not seem to be any problem with the lander.

Automatic Launch Control System. T-minus seven minutes. On schedule for launch.

Then he thought he heard Derk's muffled voice over the speaker on his floor, saying the word 'no'. Then came Jurgen's clear voice.

"T minus six minutes. All systems functioning."

The minutes passed, with Jurgen once more announcing every minute.

"T minus thirty seconds. Clear to launch. Pre-ignition commencing."

"T minus twenty seconds, pre-ignition proceeding."

On the screens in the communications room at the habitat, smoke and flames were visible, streaming from the nozzles of each of three of the rocket cylinders, equally spaced around the lander.

"T minus eleven seconds, pre-ignition completed."

Smoke and flames were now streaming from the nozzles of all six of the lander's rocket cylinders.

"Ten."

"Nine."

"Eight."

. . . .

CHAPTER SIXTEEN

Snakepit Crack

THE NOON hour of the launch day found Don Carruthers, together with Astrid and Vince, driving down Kasei Valley in the buggy, in compliance with Derk's order to continue with the geological survey, in spite of both the launch that afternoon, and the relatively windy weather.

Just after one o'clock, Don took the buggy off the road to his left, about half a mile before the southwestern extremity of Snakepit Crack. The strong east wind, and the shallow layer of blowing sand and dust it raised close to the ground, was not much worse than it had been earlier in the morning. It did not impede their progress, as they traveled across the red, rock-strewn terrain, headed for the lower reaches of the escarpment on the northwestern side of the eight-mile long rupture in the valley floor.

Snakepit Crack meandered northeastward, more or less, between the road running down Kasei Valley and the northwestern escarpment of the valley, at the northeastern end of Elbow Plain. The giant crack thus ran about parallel to both the road and the escarpment. In fact, the gently sloping lower reaches of the escarpment ended right at the edge of the huge rupture.

The entire length of the massive escarpment, bounding the northwestern side of Kasei Valley at Elbow Plain, was a geologist's paradise, a banquet of geological wonders.

At its southwestern end, there was the impressive Stem Gap, whose formation mechanism was still unexplained.

Then, running along the top of the escarpment, from Stem Gap to a point adjacent to the start of Snakepit Crack, was the huge rampart, giving the effect of a double-decker precipice on the Elbow Plain side.

A traveler on the high plateau north of Elbow Plain, headed south across the plateau, would not suddenly encounter a sheer wall, dropping down to where the escarpment began sloping steeply down to the plain. The rampart would block the way. Instead, the traveler would first have to climb up a steep escarpment slope, and then up its near vertical wall at the top, to reach the flat top of the rampart.

The rampart top lay thousands of feet above the high plateau. Only after crossing the rampart top, several miles wide, would the traveler get to view Elbow Plain, from the top of a cliff that dropped down to the top of another cliff, which in turn dropped down to the escarpment slope that descended to the floor of the plain.

What had caused the formation of the massive rampart was another geological mystery, although, mysterious or not, that was the very structure ESA engineers were intending to exploit, in the construction of a gravity-shaft powered rail launcher.

A further mystery was the top of the escarpment in the region adjacent to Snakepit Crack. On the cliff top there, only the eroded remains of a rampart could be seen. There were no explanation for the forces had caused the rampart to erode away here, or for where the eroded materials had gone.

Finally, there was Snakepit Crack itself. The deep rupture in the valley floor, at the bottom of the escarpment slope, was about a mile wide for most of its eight-mile length, but with a few wide embayments on its northwest side. The northwestern side of the crack, where the escarpment ended, was much more sheer than the southeast side, adjacent to the road. The pit sides were generally not vertical, and usually consisted of a sequence of alternating precipices and shelves. In a few places, the shelves were so narrow that the resulting composite precipice fell almost vertically, all the way to the pit bottom.

Some geologists thought that a long carbon dioxide gas bubble under the ground had caused the crack. Others thought it might have been the weight of the rampart above, before it eroded way, pressing down on the Martian crust, that had opened it up.

It was chiefly these mysteries that the ESA geological team had been exploring for the past week. Of course, Mars was not short of mysteries for a geologist, but some understanding of the geology of this escarpment was essential, if construction of the rail-launcher mega project was to get under way. The enormous investment in the project demanded that there be no possibility of a major geological surprise after construction started.

That day, the team was to survey a three-mile stretch of the escarpment, where it sloped down to the edge of Snakepit Crack, just before the central section.

It was about five miles over rock-covered terrain to get from the road to the survey site. You could not just drive over to the survey site on the escarpment slope from the nearest point on the road opposite. The deep pit lay in the way. You had no choice but to drive around the end of it.

By about one twenty, they had skirted around the southwestern end of the giant crack, and around the pit's first embayment too, and were journeying northeastward, along the lower reaches of the escarpment, with the crack to their right.

They were traveling about three hundred meters from the edge. But because they were also about fifty feet higher up, they had a superb view of the pit, and Astrid and Vince could not take their eyes off it. They could easily see the sloping upper cliff wall of the other side. Through their field glasses, they could see sand and dust flying off the rounded edge into the abyss.

Don, who was driving, kept his eyes on the terrain ahead. The thin layer of blowing dust did not bother him much, for he knew what to expect. They had surveyed this section of the escarpment in the days before. The wind-blown dust obscured only the smaller rocks and stones ahead, which the buggy's flexible wheels could easily manage. He could see the ground ahead quite well enough to avoid driving over large rocks.

About three miles from where the crack started, about a hundred meters from the edge of the crack, and at the beginning of terrain they had yet to survey, Don stopped.

"This looks like a reasonable place to start," said Don. "Gradients first. Usual routine. Let's get the gear out."

They usually started by measuring the gradients on the escarpment at lower levels, followed by measurements of the distances to the top and bottom of the sheer wall looming above the escarpment slope. They needed this data for estimating the quantity of eroded materials that had formed the escarpment, and rates of erosion of the precipice above. Later they would make seismic measurements.

The main item of equipment they used for this phase of their work was a computer-controlled theodolite, with laser sighting.

"Right," said Don, after the unloading, "the heavy stuff stays at this end. I'll do a setup one hundred meters from the edge. I have to have the buggy here. You two can take the targets to the other end."

"Keeping a hundred meters from the edge of the pit, or thereabouts, I presume," said Astrid.

"Yes," said Don. "We can adjust the locations at each end when we're set up. It's a pity we can't start closer to the edge, but I think

John Erway's advice is worth following. That edge is not like the edge of a normal precipice."

"What we really need to do this job is a helicopter," said Vince.

"You'll never see one on this planet," said Don. "Right ho, chaps, let's get moving. I should have the laser set up by the time you get over there."

As Astrid and Vince walked away from the buggy, carrying markers, measuring rods, reflectors, and other light-weight measuring equipment, Don busied himself setting up the theodolite, on tripods, about ten meters from the buggy.

Astrid and Vince remained silent as they walked the first thirty meters or so along the escarpment, keeping their eyes on the ground ahead. There was nothing unusual about the terrain, other than being less rocky than would normally be the case near the bottom of such a large escarpment. There were only a few large rocks here and there, not more than eighteen inches above ground, but plenty of smaller rocks. Quite close by, the layer of blowing dust was sufficiently transparent for them to make out the surface quite well. But more than ten meters ahead, the blowing red dust completely obscured the surface, so that smaller rocks could not be seen.

They walked well apart, about twelve feet apart, which was usual when they were out walking in pairs. This give them the freedom to turn this way and that, to avoid a larger rock, without getting in each other's way. Vince was nearest to the edge of the crack, but still a good hundred meters from it.

Most places, the descent from the edge of the crack to the bottom was a sequence of alternating precipices and shelves, but not here. Here the shelves breaking up the precipice were practically non existent, so that there was essentially just one sheer cliff all the way down to near the pit bottom. The two geologists were well away from the ill-defined edge of the crack, and so did not give any thought to the dizzy precipice close by, and the awful drop into the abyss. Neither of them had any intention of going close to the edge. Astrid and Vince concentrated instead on the gently sloping escarpment they were walking across.

Because there being no obvious dangers from large rocks, and because the terrain was quite even, apart from the gentle slope toward the edge of the pit to their right, the two were unable to resist a conversation about events at the landing site that day, which they both found very interesting.

Don could hear the conversation as he worked with his theodolite. He would probably have ordered Astrid and Vince to stop talking, and concentrate on the work, had it not been for the even, relatively rock-free terrain, and the fact that he too found the conversation interesting, and eventually joined in himself. There was simply nothing to alert any of them to what lay in wait.

"About an hour, and they will be weightless. I wish I was on board too," said Vince wistfully.

"Those three would be happy to swap with you," said Astrid. "I think having to leave here will break Denise's heart."

"I can understand that," said Vince. "She could get life in prison, if convicted. Your own home, even on Mars, is a lot better than jail."

"You do not fully understand, Vince," said Astrid. "It is not the thought of going to prison that is breaking her heart. It is having to leave Mars. She really is a Martian. This is her home, where she gave birth to her children. Anyway, I am sure she does not believe she will go to prison, when she gets back. She is certain she is innocent, and that the truth will come out."

"You seem to think she is innocent too," said Vince, in a puzzled tone. "But the Captain thinks differently, and so does ESA. I overheard him talking to Emma early yesterday, before they set out. He called Denise Lavoisier a witch, and a bitch too."

"I am not surprised," said Astrid. "And I do not just *believe* she is innocent. I know she is, although I can not tell you how I know."

"You sound very mysterious," said Vince, taking his eyes off the terrain to look at her. "I must admit, when I talked to her on Thursday at the party, she did not seem the kind of person who would do such a thing."

"Your impression was right, Vince," said Don, who could still join in, even though he was already over a hundred meters back. "I once thought she was guilty too, but now I know otherwise. You've never been inside her house, have you?"

"No," said Vince. "I just saw it from a distance on those trips with the fuel tanks. I admit it looked attractive. It fitted into the landscape, with all that orange concrete and brown copper."

"If you had seen the inside of the house, and the big garden," said Astrid, "you might understand better why she's heartbroken."

"Really," said Vince, surprised. "If you had a house on Mars like that, would you be happy to live here? I don't think even a palace could get me to want to stay here."

Astrid considered this, and was surprised to find the idea of living permanently on Mars quite attractive. That part of her native Sweden where she grew up was beautiful too, with its forests, hills, lakes, and coastal islands. But for some people, the beauty of this part of Mars penetrated the soul. Astrid Larsson was such a person.

"Yes," she answered eventually, as they drew near to where they were to set up their equipment, "I think I could be happy living here."

"I think I could too," added Don. "I could spend my life working on this planet, and never get tired of it, especially if I had a place to live in like what John Erway's got. You can be sure ESA will never spend the money to build another house like that. The Captain will probably get that house as his headquarters—with the rest of us stuck in a cramped habitat."

"Or maybe in quarters under ground some day," said Astrid.

"You would both change your minds if you were back on Earth," protested Vince, taking his eyes off the terrain again to look at Astrid's face. "I am sure of that. Earth has all kinds of far more beautiful places. You must both come and visit us at Lake—"

Suddenly, the ground collapsed underneath him, and in an instant he was gone. Those were his last words. Astrid heard him scream as he vanished, the scream quickly getting fainter and fainter, and then nothing.

But before Astrid could react to what had happened, even before Vince's screams had faded away, the ground collapsed beneath her too, and in an instant she too disappeared. She too screamed, her scream initially getting quickly fainter too, as she fell, just like Vince's, but then stopping abruptly.

Don, setting up the laser theodolite, some one hundred and forty meters back, looked up from his work when Vince abruptly stopped talking. He had not heard the screams, but stared in surprise and shock at the spot where his two fellow geologists had been walking, seconds before. Now they were nowhere to be seen or heard.

There was only the early afternoon sun shining on the usual escarpment terrain, with larger rocks sticking out of the thin red layer of blowing sand and dust that obscured the ground. Mars seemed to have just swallowed Astrid and Vince without a trace.

*

Don approached the spot where he had last seen his two companions. He advanced cautiously, peering at the terrain ahead, still mostly obscured by blowing sand. Suddenly, he stopped dead in his tracks, and even retreated a little, as he caught a first glimpse of the fissure.

He called out to Astrid and Vince, several times, listening carefully in between; but there was no reply. Inside he felt dread. He understood now what had swallowed them, and knew that his two companions were likely dead.

There were a few large embayments, at least a mile across, along the northern edge of Snakepit Crack. Each of these had probably started out as a small fissure, getting larger and larger, with planetary forces wearing it away to the present embayment.

Don knew that what lay immediately in front of him was yet another fissure, still small, in its early stages of growth. It was not yet large enough for the surface layer on top of it to have collapsed on its own. But that surface layer would not be strong, and could well give way if any extra weight was placed on it. It was exactly what John Erway had warned them about, the previous week.

He got down on all fours, and advanced cautiously toward the hole ahead. About six feet from the edge, he could see the other side clearly. The sun, in the sky to his right, was shining onto it at an angle. The hole was about seven feet wide.

At the left, a few meters away, the surface layer over the fissure was still intact, bridging the chasm. He could see how thick the surface layer was—it varied between four and eight inches.

To his right, in the blowing dust, he could not see as far as any intact surface bridging the fissure. He thought he had better find out. He backed off a few meters, turned to his right, and then crawled on all fours toward the edge of Snakepit Crack. He did not have far to go. Ten meters from the other bridge, there was an even wider bridge over the fissure, this one some four meters across. Don just stared at it. It could obviously not take the weight of a human being.

He now crawled back to where he had first encountered the fissure. He did not go closer to the edge than two meters. Straight ahead, he could see the wall of the other side of the fissure. The surface layer had broken exactly at the top of the wall of the fissure, and did not overhang. Was it overhanging at this side? He decided to play safe, and did not go any closer. He would try to approach the fissure from the other side.

He crawled back a few meters, got up, and began walking to his left, away from Snakepit Crack, carefully watching the terrain to his right. Even though the fissure to his right was now completely covered, and bridged by a thin surface layer, he could see where the bridge was. The ground above the fissure was a lighter color, and every so often there was a meter wide hole, obviously where a rock had fallen through.

After walking some fifty meters, the fissure seemed to end, and there was even a good jumble of large rocks to his right. He turned right, across the rocks, and then turned right again, now heading back in a direction toward the edge of Snakepit Crack, but on the other side of the fissure. Eventually, he reached the point where the surface had given way, and walked to within a foot or two of the edge.

He could now see the other side, where he had been down on all fours a few minutes earlier. The other side of the fissure was in shadow, but he was able to make out a small overhang, protruding over the edge by under half a meter. But even that small overhang meant it was unsafe to walk right at the edge on the other side.

He now got down on his hands and knees again. He did not trust himself standing at the edge of the fissure. He advanced until his head was over the edge, and looked down. He was shocked at what he saw.

To his left, far down, he could see the fissure extend right out to the precipice forming this side of Snakepit Crack, about a hundred meters away. There was a fair amount of light coming in from a narrow opening the fissure had made in the wall of the precipice. The bottom half of the opening was V-shaped, about four hundred feet from the top of the cliff. The top half of the opening was also V-shaped, with the V upside down, about two hundred and fifty feet from the top of the cliff, so that the narrow opening in the cliff face was about one hundred and fifty feet from top to bottom.

Immediately below were he lay, he could just make out the bottom of the fissure in the dim light. It was only about a hundred feet down, nothing compared to the height of the boundary cliffs of Snakepit Crack, but still the height of an eight-story building. This meant that the bottom of the fissure was a chute, running steeply downward, at an angle of forty-five degrees, to the V-shaped bottom of the opening in the side of the cliff. Anything that fell down to the bottom of the fissure would slide down the steep chute to the cliff face. It would then come tumbling out of the fissure, to fall thousands of feet down the cliff to the bottom of Snakepit Crack.

Don shuddered in horror. His two companions were clearly dead, at the bottom of Snakepit Crack. They had obviously fallen straight down to the chute below, slid down the chute and shot out of the opening in the cliff, and fallen to the bottom of the giant pit.

He moved back from the edge of the fissure and got up. He found himself barely able to stand. He wandered a bit farther back, to where there was a fairly large rock, about eighteen inches above ground level. He sat down on it, without inspecting it first for anything that could puncture his suit. He was in a state of severe shock, and could not think clearly.

He sat there in the bright afternoon sunlight for some ten minutes, sand and dust blowing about his feet. What had just happened did not seem real. Gradually he recovered enough for his mind to begin working again.

There was nothing he could do, he thought. They would not even be able to recover the bodies and give them a decent burial. He blamed himself. This was the second time he had been responsible for people in his care, and the second time his actions had led to disaster and loss of life. They had been talking, and broken the rule about not talking while out walking on Mars. And he had too. Two more dead! And Astrid too. She had been his best friend since the death of Sheila, and had been an enormous help to him, and he had grown quite fond of her, even though he still missed Sheila. And Vince gone too, the always cheerful Italian everybody liked.

There was nothing to do but walk back to the buggy and use the satellite link to inform the Captain of the loss of two more lives. He began walking back the way he had come, around the end of the fissure.

Just then he heard a voice.

"Help me. Don? Can you hear me? I need help."

It was Astrid's voice. The voice sounded remarkably cool. He turned around abruptly, and in a few seconds was once more lying down, helmet over the edge, peering into the fissure.

"I'm here, Astrid, looking down. I can't see you."

"I can see you," said Astrid. "You are right above my head."

He thought he could make out something immediately below with a slight sheen. He turned on his helmet light. Then he saw her. She was some eighty feet down, about twenty feet above the chute at the bottom of the fissure, wedged between the fissure's two sides. The fissure narrowed as it went down, the narrowing being greater the further in from Snakepit's cliff face you were.

"I can see you now," said Don. "Is Vince down there too?"

"There is no sign of him," said Astrid. "He was walking well to my right, nearer to Snakepit's edge. This fissure gets wider the closer you are to Snakepit. Where he fell down, it was probably too wide for him to get wedged like me. He must have fallen to the bottom, and then slid on down, and right out into the pit."

"I think you're right. I can see no sign of him either. God help him. Are you hurt?"

"I do not think so," said Astrid. "Just bruises. I must have stopped reasonably gradually in this wedge. That must have saved me. I am wedged between my backpack and my chest. My arms, legs, and head are free. My legs are dangling. But I am losing air. There must be small scratches and tears in the suit. I think I have been unconscious. I have a bad pain in my head beside my left ear. I must have hit my head against the helmet as I fell."

What amazed Don was the way Astrid was talking. There was no anxiety in her voice. She was describing her situation calmly and analytically, as if she was presenting a report. You are a cool one, thought Don, suddenly realizing that this was part of the reason she had been picked to go to Mars.

"How do you know you're losing air?"

"I can see the display on my left arm. I should have about nine and a half hours left. But I have now only eight and a half. The air consumption display is showing four times normal too. There must be a small tear in my suit, maybe more than one."

Don could figure it out two. She had lost an hour's supply of air in fifteen minutes. In about two hours, at that rate of loss, she would have lost all of it. And it could take the best part of two hours to get help. There was no way he could get her out of there alone. They had to stop the leaks at once, or at least significantly reduce them.

"Can you join your two hands?"

"Yes, above my head or behind my back underneath the backpack."

"You have tape?"

"Yes, in my right leg pocket. I can reach it."

"All right. Go over as much of the suit as you can with your hands. Make a note of every place where there's a scratch or a tear."

A minute later, Astrid's voice came back.

"Two small scratches at my left knee, one at my right knee, and one at my left elbow, which I can just reach with my right hand."

"All right, tape them. Hold the tape dispenser above your head to eject a piece, and then put the dispenser back in your pocket before you try to stick it on. Remember your training. For heaven's sake, be careful. Don't drop the dispenser."

There was silence. Don could just make out Astrid's contortions in the light from his helmet.

"Done," came her voice, five minutes later. "My air consumption has dropped. Its only twice normal now. There are probably tears in my shoulders, but it is not possible for me to reach them."

"At least that gives us some time. I'm going to leave you now for a bit, Astrid. I'm just going back to the buggy to call for help on the sat link. Maybe Karl will be able to figure out a way to get you up. I haven't got a rope long enough, and even if I did I couldn't trust it. I can see a lot of sharp stones sticking out of this wall."

"Don, we need John Erway," said Astrid. "He was in search and rescue on Earth, and he knows Mars. We probably need Dr. Sato too. And Jose too. It will be very hard to get me out of here. You have to have more than just Karl."

Don looked at the time on his wrist display. It was one forty-eight.

"But those three are on the lander, and it's set to launch in an hour," said Don. "The Captain won't want to stop that now."

"I know," said Astrid. "But you have to convince him. It is my only chance. He may even want to keep Karl till after the launch."

"That means I may have to drive back and confront him, if I can't convince him. I'm sure he won't want to abort. Look, Astrid, if I'm not back in fifteen minutes, I've had to drive to the hab. All right?"

"I understand," said Astrid. "There is just one thing, before you go. I may not be alive when you get back. I am slipping very slowly down all the time. I could slip out of this wedge at any minute, and slide down the chute into the pit, or tear my suit further and lose the air. I just want you to know something about me I have kept secret from you. I have been in love with you for a long time, although I have never dared ask you to return it. And I did not want to cause you unhappiness when Sheila was alive. I was just happy to be near you sometimes. I am glad to have known you, Don. Now go, before I start to get emotional."

"Astrid, I never knew," said Don, both stung and touched, strong emotions beginning to overwhelm him. "I'm sorry, Astrid, but I seem to be blind to everything that's important. My God, I'll strangle the Captain with my bare hands if he doesn't abort that launch."

"You must not strangle anybody. You just have to persuade him."

"I'll do more than persuade him," said Don, getting up, suddenly realizing what he might have to do, "if he won't abort—if I can get back to hab in time. No time to waste. Try to hold on."

He ran up to the end of the fissure, ran across the rocks, and then ran all the way back to the buggy, even though running was something he was forbidden to do out on Mars, given how dangerous it was.

He reached the buggy without an accident, at one fifty-two. He got in the outside passenger seat, not the driver seat. The satellite link could function while the buggy was moving, but could not be operated by the driver. Buggy engineers had thought that was both unnecessary and dangerous, since it took a fair amount of manipulation and skill to operate the link. Astrid had looked after the satellite link during their previous survey trips, and sometimes Vince. Don had not operated it since training, nine months earlier. He was fairly sure he could do it though. It was not that complicated.

It took him a few minutes to get the link set up. Hurry, for God's sake, he thought. He sent the usual request. "Buggy calling Kasei-73. Do you read?"

He got a display. The message had been sent, but no response from the habitat. He tried three more times. Still no response. Was he doing something wrong?

Then it struck him. Sheila and Claude were dead. That left ten. Three had gone to Snakepit. That left seven. Jose and Monique were going up with the lander. That left five. Derk, Karl, and Emma would be needed with the prisoners. That left two. Jurgen was probably making a video recording of events, and Ursula was probably looking after the children. They were all outside, seeing to the launch. There was nobody at the habitat!

He turned off the link and rushed to the back of the buggy. It took him only a few minutes to unhitch the trailer, before jumping in the driver's seat. Seconds later he was driving along the edge of the crack, headed southwest and back to the road.

He went as fast as he dared over the stony terrain, still mostly obscured by that thin layer of blowing sand and dust that had hidden the small surface holes that would otherwise have alerted Astrid and Vince to the presence of the treacherous concealed fissure ahead of them—if they had not been talking, perhaps.

He reached the road just before two twenty. Once on the road, he drove at speed, forty miles an hour on average, his mind concentrated on his driving like never before on Mars. Fortunately, he had driven this road many times and knew all its bends, and the buggy as well. That was a good thing, for the thin surface layer of blowing sand and dust often obscured curves up ahead. The wind was from the east too, a tailwind, and that helped him maintain his speed. He also had the extra battery pack at the back, the one Derk had borrowed from the other rover for the labyrinth trip. That gave him extra power.

His speed was such that he was barely able to keep the buggy on the road as it curved around small craters. His speed was unsafe for the kind of road and weather conditions. He was in great danger of going off the road onto the rocks on either side if he failed to make a curve. If he did, it would likely be the end of him.

But necessity brings out the best or the worst in people, and Don Carruthers was determined. Vince was gone, but they would not lose Astrid too, if he could do anything to prevent it, even if it meant breaking every rule in the book to save her.

The buggy ate up the miles that sunny and windy afternoon, as he sped along the road across the deserted Elbow Plain in the blowing dust.

He considered stopping to try the satellite link again. He figured there was a good chance they were all still outside. He did not know how the launch was to be managed, whether Jose would do it from inside the lander, or whether Jurgen would need to be in the habitat communications room, and if so, how long before the launch. Don decided he could not afford to risk wasting the time. If he kept on driving he would soon be within easy surface radio range. He could communicate that way and drive at the same time.

Every minute could count, given what he had in mind. Maybe every second.

At two forty-two, eleven minutes before launch, he was about six miles from the landing pit. He plugged the buggy radio into his suit, but did not slow down. He recalled the discussion in training about the necessity for a person in a buggy to hard-wire connect to the buggy radio, in order to surface-radio transmit with a pressure suit on. The astronauts had wanted a wireless connection, but the engineers had insisted on the hard wire. It was simpler, cheaper, and much less likely to go wrong, and easier to fix if it did.

"Captain Derk! Jurgen! Can you read. I have an emergency. Over."

Both Jurgen and Derk were in the communications room of the habitat, managing the launch, some twenty minutes into the count down. Don's signal came in loud and clear

"We read you. Jurgen here."

"Vince is dead. Fell into Snakepit Crack. Astrid nearly fell in. She's wedged in a fissure eighty feet down. The fissure has a steep chute at the bottom that comes out in the side of Snakepit's cliff wall. She's slowly sliding down. Her suit is damaged too, and she's slowly losing air. She has air for about three and a half hours at the very most, likely less. Do you read."

"*Himmel*!" responded Jurgen, as he switched the launch countdown from manual to automatic. "Yes, we read. Where are you?"

Don now heard Emma's voice. She was looking through the communications room window with her field glasses, and had picked up Don's buggy.

"He's about five miles away, on the road, headed this way. Going fast. Raising a lot of dust," she said.

"You must abort the launch," answered Don, nearly going off the road, as the buggy curved around a small crater. He was maintaining his speed at just over forty miles an hour, talking at the same time. He was a man obsessed. "Rescue will be difficult. We need the skills of John Erway and Dr. Sato and Jose. Repeat. We need Erway, Sato and Jose. Please abort the launch. Do you read."

"Yes, we read," responded Jurgen. He turned to Derk. "Captain? Abort the launch?"

"Too risky," said Derk at once. "First priority is to get these three off the planet. We'll organize a rescue in a few minutes, as soon as we have lift-off. Karl will be in charge."

"But Captain, we can not afford to lose Astrid," said Jurgen. "If Vince is dead, she is the only structural engineer we have left. And Karl is not our most imaginative crew member. Don is right. We at least need Jose, and probably John Erway and the monk. This is the kind of thing Erway is supposed to be very good at."

"I'm afraid we have to risk the loss of Astrid, chaps," said Derk. "Anyway, it can't be such a big risk. Why should it be so difficult to pull somebody out of a fissure? We must proceed with the launch first. Then we'll see to Astrid."

"Captain, I am against this," said Jurgen, dismayed. "Request permission to abort."

"Captain," pleaded Don, joining in again. "You have to see the fissure. It's very dangerous. She could slide on down, at any minute, and into Snakepit Crack. We need John Erway, Dr. Sato, and Jose. Please! Abort the launch! Please! Postpone till tomorrow!"

There was silence for a few seconds. But Derk could still not see why it would help significantly to involve John Erway and the Zen master in the rescue.

But then, a feeling of cold fear came over him as he began to see the sense in what Don was telling him. Karl was on the mission only because Derk had wanted him. Although he was not particularly imaginative, he was very good at routine tasks. Most importantly, from Derk's point of view, he would obey orders unquestioningly, even orders of a dubious nature, such as the order to shoot somebody. But if very great initiative or ingenuity were needed to carry out the rescue, Karl was not the man for the job.

Jurgen was better in situations like that, but then Jurgen was not a field engineer, nor a geologist, nor a structural engineer, nor did he have any experience in search and rescue, nor did he know Mars well, all of which skills John Erway had in full, and Jose to some degree. And they might need a doctor too. Derk knew that if it were him who was wedged down in that fissure, threatened with both sliding down into Snakepit Crack, and his air running out, there would be no doubt in his mind who he would want handling the rescue.

But still, he had to get Erway off Mars. If he aborted now, the next launch opportunity was the following morning. Then he thought. Suppose we do abort. There was a much better chance of saving Astrid, and it was true the mission could not afford to lose her. And the chance of Erway escaping him now had to be remote. Where could he escape to? And if Erway failed in the rescue, Derk could not be blamed.

These thoughts ran through his mind very quickly in those seconds. But he was still unsure. He needed more time to make a reasoned decision. Just over six minutes to launch. He decided to stay the course, but continued to ponder the issue.

"No," he said, in answer to Jurgen and Don.

And so the count down continued.

Don responded mentally. Damn you, he said to himself, and continued to drive as fast as he could. He was now within two miles of Elbow Fork, the junction with the road running across to Stem Gap. He could hear the count down.

T-minus six minutes….

The road to Elbow Fork was now nearly straight. He increased his speed to over forty five miles an hour. The buggy was doing more than a mile every ninety seconds.

He braked to get around the junction.

T minus three minutes….

Once around the junction he pressed the accelerator into the floor, completely disregarding his own safety. He flew along the road.

He reached the junction with the Elbow Hill road, partly obscured in the blowing sand and dust. He braked hard, and just managed the left turn. Now he was racing along the road to Elbow Hill and the habitat.

A mile from the junction lay the entrance to the trail down to the landing pit. The cutting in the crater rim, leading down into the pit, was only a few hundred meters from the entrance.

T minus 20 seconds….

He reached the trail. Here he braked hard, and turned into the trail, pressing the accelerator hard again. The count down was now in its final seconds.

Ten.

Nine.

Eight….

"Captain!" shouted Emma, suddenly. She had continued to follow the progress of Don's buggy with her field glasses. "He's not coming here! He's headed down to the landing pit."

"*Mein Gott!*" cried Jurgen, lapsing into his native tongue. "Captain! He will be incinerated! He has lost his mind!"

But Don had not lost his mind. He knew the lander was ringed by remote-controlled video cameras, and that the launch was being watched on Earth. He was intending to force Derk to abort, at risk of the loss of his own life, if Derk still refused. He just had to get into that pit before lift-off.

He was now racing down the cutting into the landing pit, already partly filled with smoke.

Five.

Four.

Three ....

Derk did not have to wait to see Don's buggy appear through the smoke, in the images of the lander in the control room. He knew he had no choice now but to abort.

Anyway, in the last five minutes, analyzing the pros and cons from every angle, Derk had already come to the conclusion that on balance, with just a small margin in favor, the best thing to do was to abort.

But whether he would have actually issued the order to abort in those last few seconds, without Don's heroic action, when it seemed only very marginally best to do so, was something not even Derk could say.

Of course, he would never admit to anyone that Don's actions had influenced his decision in any way. In an interview video report transmitted to Earth that evening, about the day's dramatic events, he steadfastly maintained that, after weighing all aspects of the issue, in a very difficult situation, he had independently decided, at the last second, to abort the launch.

Meanwhile, Don was racing down the cutting into the landing pit. He braked hard as soon as he could see the huge lander, glistening in the sun, and snorting smoke and flame from its rocket nozzles, as if anxious to be gone. Through the smoke, Don could see flames to the right and left. He headed between them, just managing to stop about twenty feet from the lander, beside a landing pod, and between two of its belching rocket cylinders.

Two....

Then he heard Derk give the order.

"Abort the launch."

Jurgen had had his finger on the surface of the button, and pressed it in a fraction of a second.

T minus one second. Engine shut down commencing.

T plus nine seconds. Engine shut down proceeding.

T plus nineteen seconds. Engine shut down completed.

In the control room, Jurgen slumped back in his chair, and breathed deeply, while Derk stood behind him, making a cage with his hands, looking down at the floor, with a grim expression on his face.

Inside the lander, Denise had stopped sobbing. John was perplexed.

"Looks like we're not launching today after all, Denise," he said, an enormous feeling of relief coming over him.

Then the smoke outside began to clear, the wind flowing over the top of the old crater rim sucking it out of the landing pit. He looked out the viewport, and saw the buggy down below, with a single figure inside. It slowly backed away from the lander, and then turned, and headed at speed out of the pit and up the cutting.

"And it also looks like Derk has a small mutiny on his hands," he added, as his brain, like Derk's at that moment, began working on possibilities.

*

Meanwhile, back at Snakepit Crack, things were not going so well for Astrid. She had slipped down almost eight feet in the past hour, and she was sure the rate of slip was increasing. The typical pattern was stability for a few minutes, and then a sudden slip of a few inches.

She could see the illuminated display on her left arm. The rate of loss of air had increased significantly. The suit must be tearing a little each time I slip, she thought. It was ten past three. Even if they had not aborted the launch, she thought, they should be here by three forty-five. She figured the air might last to four thirty, if the leaks did not get any worse, although she had little hope of that.

She was still wedged, her chest tight up against one wall of the fissure, her backpack tight against the opposite wall. The wall material seemed to be a kind of soft sandstone conglomerate, cemented sand with small stones embedded in it, some of them quite sharp. It would be easy to chisel it away, she thought, or chisel a statue out of it. That is probably what my back pack and chest plate are doing, she thought. My weight is forcing them to chisel out bits of the walls, she thought, as she suddenly jerked downward about another four inches. She was now just twelve feet above the steep chute at the bottom of the fissure.

She kept trying to get a feel for the distance between the two opposing walls, using both her hands and her dangling legs. She had a suspicion the distance was widening slightly. She realized that meant the two opposing walls of the fissure could suddenly release her from their grip. If they did, she would drop down to the chute. Nothing could then stop her sliding down the steep chute, and out over the cliff edge just a hundred meters away, with a nightmare fall to the bottom of Snakepit Crack. Better not think about that, she thought. Thinking about it is probably more frightening than having it actually happen. At least, if it happens, it will be over quickly.

She tried to think. Maybe she could use her hands and feet to wedge herself better. She tried, but it did not help, for suddenly, she slipped again. This time, it was a long, steady slip, before she stopped abruptly. The fissure is definitely getting wider, she thought. She reckoned she had slipped about four feet.

She kept on trying to wedge herself better between the two walls, using both hands and feet. It will probably tear the gloves, she thought. Pity I was not wearing overgloves, she thought. Too awkward, when handling that measuring equipment.

She wondered where the equipment had gone to. Probably to the bottom of Snakepit Crack. She was thinking of Snakepit Crack again. She had to keep that out of her mind.

She slipped again. Only a few inches this time. She pushed against the two walls even harder, with her hands and feet. She now stayed in the one place for some fifteen minutes. She could see her wrist display. The rate of loss of air had increased further. It was still only three twenty-five. Please come soon, she prayed.

Then there came another long slip at a steady rate. She could not stop it with her hands or feet. Then, suddenly, the walls relaxed their grip, and she fell quickly straight down.

She fell only three feet, however, before she stopped dead, as her left foot hit the steep chute at the bottom of the fissure. Her right foot still dangled in space, for the chute was very steep, forty-five degrees. She could feel her weight forcing her to her right side, trying to make her tumble over, and slide down the chute.

She was still facing the wall, her right hand hard pressed against the wall in front and her left pressed against the wall behind. She pressed even harder against the two walls, and forced her right foot beside the left. This kept her from falling over; but she knew she could not hold this position for long. Her arms were already tired.

Would it help if she tried to turn? Maybe she could wedge the width of her suit between the two sides of the fissure. But to do that she would have to relax the pressure of her hands against the walls. She knew she would fall over if she did that. The bottom of the fissure was wider only meters to her right, further along the chute. If she fell over, she would slide down the chute for sure.

She decided to do nothing, and just keep her two hands pressed against the opposing walls. She figured she might hold out for ten minutes, fifteen at the most. The air supply did not matter now. All that mattered was how much strength she had in her already very tired arms, and whether or not a rescue party would arrive in time. She noticed she was slipping sideways though, down the chute.

*

Astrid did not know it, but at that moment, a convoy of vehicles was not more than ten minutes away, lumbering over the stones and boulders of the lower reaches of the escarpment, adjacent to the southwestern section of Snakepit Crack. Don's buggy was in the lead, followed by two rovers and two more buggies, almost every land vehicle on Mars. Each of them, except Don's buggy, pulled a trailer.

The trailers were filled with just about everything that could conceivably be of use in the rescue. Each rover trailer carried two long lengths of rope, made of parachute cord, something it almost always carried, in case an emergency tow line was needed. The trailers also carried flashlights, together with an assortment of tools and materials that John and Dr. Sato had recommended they collect from the habitat workshop. There was also a spare ESA pressure suit.

There had been no time to decide what would be useful and what would not. They had taken almost every hand-held tool the workshop had, as well as pieces of metal that might be useful. They had also loaded additional lengths of nylon rope the ESA mission had brought for emergency use, as well as some reserve air flasks that could fit Astrid's backpack, each with an hour's supply of air.

John and Dr. Sato sat beside Don in the lead buggy. Don was driving as fast as he dared.The wind had remained strong, and a thin, orange layer of blowing sand and dust, glowing in the afternoon sun, still obscured the smaller rocks and stones.

Denise was driving the first rover, keeping up, just behind the buggy. Derk sat beside her in the passenger seat. Karl sat in the other passenger seat. They were both armed with machine pistols. Derk did not intend to let either John or Denise out of his sight.

Jurgen drove the second rover, with Emma beside him.

Jose and Monique drove the remaining two buggies, bringing up the rear of the convoy.

Denise had been content to leave the two children behind in the habitat with Ursula, after she saw how well the children liked her. The children seemed to understand when Denise explained to them that Astrid had fallen down a dangerous hole, and that their mother and father had to help pull her out before she died. The children did not want to see their parents go off and leave them in the habitat, but agreed that they did not want Astrid to die either.

As they approached the fissure, Don led the convoy around its extremity, at its furthest distance from the edge of Snakepit Crack, so that they could approach the hole as he had done, from the east side, where there was no overhang.

Don's buggy stopped about five meters from the hole, facing it, with the other vehicles drawing up on either side. Don and John jumped out, and almost ran to the edge of the hole. Dr. Sato got out more slowly, but still made his way quickly to the hole.

Denise stayed in the driver's seat of her rover, watching, ordered to do so by John, to be ready for hauling ropes with the rover. Jurgen remained in the driver's seat of the other rover, for the same reason. But Derk got out, carrying a video camera, keeping his pistol in its holster. There was nothing for him to do, except record events, which he did quite thoroughly. John was in charge of this operation.

There was no real-time satellite transmission of the images Derk recorded. People on Earth could not see this rescue effort live, to the profound irritation of the news media. Derk and Emma would edit the video recording, before transmission to Earth later.

Don and John were first at the edge of the hole. In seconds, they were lying down, heads and arms over the edge. The Zen master joined them on the ground a few seconds later. Don and John were already shining flashlight beams straight down, to where Astrid had been. The two beams shone all the way down, illuminating the chute at the bottom. Dr. Sato's flashlight soon added to the illumination.

Astrid was no longer there.

"Astrid!" shouted Don, almost in disbelief.

But Astrid's voice came back, at once.

"Yes, I am still here," she said. "Have you brought help?"

"Yes," said Don. "Everybody's here except Ursula."

"Hello, Dr. Larsson," said John.

"Hello, Dr. Erway," answered Astrid politely, in a matter of fact tone, although the Zen master could sense it was a little forced. "So you finally managed to come and visit us at work."

John remembered that last week he had promised to drop in on the survey team one day, a promise he had not been able to keep.

"I guess so," said John calmly, wondering if he could have kept control of himself as well in such circumstances. "We can't see you. Where exactly are you?"

"I slipped down gradually onto the chute at the bottom, while Don was away," explained Astrid. "I am no longer wedged. I have been standing on the chute for the past fifteen minutes or so. I use both hands to keep myself from falling over, one to the front and one to the back. But I am not strong enough to stay in one place. I am being slowly pulled down the chute, slipping sideways, against my will. I do not know how far I have come, maybe twenty meters."

"My God," was all John could answer, as they all three shone their beams to the left, in the direction of the edge of Snakepit Crack. Sure enough, there was Astrid, a tiny figure very far down, and now well to their left, and no longer underneath the hole she and Vince had made in the surface cover of the fissure. It was no longer a case of pulling up somebody securely wedged eighty feet down a hole, as Derk had been envisioning. This rescue was going to be much more difficult.

Derk had thought it would be necessary only to lower Astrid a rope, which she could have secured around herself, allowing them to haul her up, perhaps with the help of a rover or buggy to free her.

By now Jose, Monique, Karl, and Emma, had joined the three at the hole, carrying the ropes. Jose had lain down beside Don, head over the edge, looking down. He shuddered at the sight of Astrid, so far down, lit up by the flashlight beams, pushing against the walls of the fissure for her very life. He mentally crossed himself.

"Astrid," said John, "we can see you now. If we got a rope down to you, could you tie it around your waist?"

"Sorry, but that is not possible," said Astrid. "If I take even one hand off the wall I will slide down the chute."

"That's what I thought," said John. "Just needed you to confirm. Now listen carefully. We're going to come down for you. I don't think we can risk just lowering somebody on a rope running over the edge. The side's too abrasive, and it's got all kinds of sharp stones sticking out. The risk of one of them cutting the rope is too high. So we're going to have to build a bridge across the fissure, using a buggy. I mean we'll use a rover to pull a buggy across the top of the fissure, so that it forms a bridge. Then we can lower somebody on ropes running across the smooth buggy edge. That way they'll be clear of the fissure walls. Then we'll use a rover to haul you both up, like a crane. Do you understand?"

"Yes."

"It could take up to ten minutes to get that bridge set up. Can you hold out that long?"

There was no answer for a few seconds.

"Yes, I believe I can hold out for ten minutes," she said at last, but her voice had a faint despairing tone to it, which she managed to hide from everyone, except the Zen master.

"All right," said John.

With that they all got up.

"We should use Dr. Sato's buggy for the bridge," said John to Jose and Karl. "It's got the longest distance between its front and back wheels. Jose, can you get it round to the other side?"

Unlike the ESA buggies, Dr. Sato's buggy had its wheels sticking out front and back, like the wheels of the rovers. This had enabled it to roll smoothly down the frame of the frame container lander that had brought it to Mars with the JSA expedition, ten years earlier. The buggy's front and back wheel axles were very far apart as a result, far enough apart to bridge the seven-foot wide fissure.

John then remembered something he had learned to do in situations of dire emergency on Mars.

"Wait a second, Jose," he said. He had forgotten to check with Dr. Sato.

"You agree, Dr. Sato, or have we overlooked something?" he said, turning around to face the Zen master, who had been behind him, only to discover that the old man was tying a rope around his waist.

"What the …," said John, very surprised. "I see you don't agree."

"She did not tell you the truth," said the Zen master quietly, as he handed the other end of the rope to Monique. "Now, Ms. Montpellier, please fasten the end of this rope to a buggy—Dr. Larsson has no more than a few minutes to live, if she is not secured at once."

"What!" cried John. "Are you sure? You can't just go down there like that. You know it's not safe."

"The young woman will die in the next few minutes, unless someone runs the risk," answered the old Zen master, in his usual unassuming voice. "Better it be someone whose life has been mostly lived, where the loss of what is left would be of no consequence."

With that, he put the rope in the hands of John, Don, and Jose, as Monique tied the end to Don's buggy. "The three of you will lower by hand, as quickly as possible, please," said the Zen master.

He then lifted the end of a second rope, and quickly tied it around his leg. This rope he placed in the hands of Karl and Emma.

Then, quite calmly, he jumped over the edge of the fissure, at a spot about four meters to the left of where they had been lying, and so closer to the edge of Snakepit Crack.

Derk's video camera captured the rare exchange with the Zen master, and the image of him jumping over the edge, disappearing into the fissure, although it would not be seen on Earth in the edited version Derk would send to Mission Control that evening.

"Lower more quickly, please," Dr. Sato called out, seconds later.

They reeled out the rope quite fast, at nearly two feet a second. John, looking very worried, could see it grinding against the side of the fissure. A knife-edged stone sticking out, of which there were many, could easily sever the rope, or badly fray it. Even worse, since the fissure was wedged-shaped, at least for the first eighty feet down, the rope would be mostly tight up against the wall of the fissure, increasing the chance of a sharp stone cutting it. He knew the Zen master was right in what he was doing though. He always was.

It took the Zen master almost a minute to get down to the chute.

"More slowly now, please," he called out.

Headlamp on, Dr. Sato walked quickly down the steeply sloping chute at the bottom of the fissure, restrained from sliding on down only by the rope being let out from above.

John was standing nearest the edge of the fissure, reeling out the rope. The light from the Zen master's helmet lamp enabled him to follow his progress, far below. Derk stood close to John, his video camera directed down at the Zen master, recording the drama.

"Very, very slowly now, please," the Zen master called out, when he was three meters from Astrid.

About one foot from Astrid, he called out: "Stop." He dared go no closer. He knew that even touching her could cause her to go shooting down the chute.

He untied the second rope from his leg, and made a large noose. Then he said: "Take a few seconds to make sure your right foot is firmly on the ground, Dr. Larsson. Then lift your left leg."

She managed to lift her left leg, the one nearest the Zen master. As she did so, the Zen master cast the noose under her left foot.

"Now put your foot down again."

"Now raise your right foot ... use it to pull at the rope a bit."

"Now try to put it down—inside the noose."

She succeeded on the third attempt.

"Please hold on tight up there," called out the Zen master.

Up above, Karl and Emma, with Monique now as well, tightened their grip on the second rope.

The Zen master then spent the next thirty seconds gently pulling the noose up around Astrid's legs. Soon he had it around her waste, just below the level of the bottom of her backpack. But then, before he could tighten it, Astrid stopped pushing against the walls of the fissure. Try as she might, she could not press against them any longer. She had no more strength in her arms.

She fell forward down the chute. The noose did its job, however, and tightened around her waste on its own. Up above, Monique, Emma, and Karl felt the sudden jerk, but held on tight to the rope.

"Dr. Larsson is secure now," called out the Zen master. "You can start building the bridge to haul her up."

Up above, John, and everyone else, breathed a sigh of relief, as he and Jose turned their minds to the relatively easy task of arranging a secure buggy bridge over the fissure.

*

They hauled them out nearly twenty minutes later, at four twenty-five, but not before a spare air flask, attached to a third rope, had to be guided down to the Zen master. Astrid's suit, badly damaged, had completely run out of air some ten minutes earlier.

They took Astrid to Denise's rover at once, and Denise gave her a thorough examination. Fortunately, apart from some minor bruises on her knees, elbows and shoulders, and a bad swelling on the side of her head in front of her ear, she was uninjured. She looked rather pale though, as she sat on one of the red swivel chairs in the living area, with Denise in attendance, an ESA medical kit open on the small table behind her. The late afternoon sun slanted in through the window above the computer screen.

"You've had a bad shock, and that knock on the head hasn't helped," said Denise, as she sat down opposite Astrid, in the other swivel chair, "but otherwise you seem to be all right. Still, I want you to rest in the front bunk on the way back. I'll give you something to make you drowsy. I think you should sleep for a few hours as well, when we get back. Then you'll feel a lot better."

"But I feel fine now," said Astrid. "I am just so very happy to be alive. I really did think I was finished."

"You nearly were," admitted Denise. "You can thank Dr. Sato for your life, and Dr. Carruthers too. Apparently, he was also quite the hero this afternoon."

"Really," said Astrid.

"Yes," said Denise, and explained to Astrid how Don had forced Derk to abort the launch by driving his buggy into the landing pit, in the final seconds of the launch, in full view of the launch-monitoring cameras.

"I did not expect that," said Astrid, suddenly feeling weak.

"Now, you are obviously not feeling as fine as you say, after all," said Denise, observing her closely. Denise liked this young woman.

She then took her by the arm, and led her toward the front bunk, only a few feet away.

"I mean it," said Denise. "You have to rest on the way back."

This time Astrid did not object, and shortly afterward, with Astrid dosing in the front bunk, John was driving the rover back to the habitat. Denise and Derk were sitting in the passenger seats, and Emma was in one of the red swivel chairs.

John did not talk to either Denise or Derk during the drive back. His thoughts were elsewhere. There were tears in Denise's eyes most of the way back, as she watched the sun descend toward Stem Gap, the entrance to the valley she loved, where her home was, a home she would never see again. Derk noticed the tears, but said nothing. His mind was made up, and his heart was hard. He would have them off the planet the following morning, a determination Denise understood only too well.

Dr. Sato drove the other rover, with only Jurgen beside him, unarmed. Although Karl sat in the rover's living area, armed, not even Derk considered the Zen master a threat any more. Had he not been so intimately involved in the affairs of John and Denise, Derk might well have been willing to let him stay on in his monastery until he died of old age.

*

It was just after six when they got back. The yellow sun was very low in the sky to the west, a pink-blue sunset fan above it. John, Denise, and Dr. Sato, with Emma and Karl standing nearby, lingered a few minutes on the shelf outside the habitat, until the sun disappeared behind Stem Mountains. For those three, who had seen so many sunsets, in so many places on Mars, this was to be their last.

Once the three captives were inside, Jose assigned each of them a cubicle. He told them that although they were free to move around for the evening, they would be under constant observation. Jose himself was surprised at the relative freedom Derk had granted the three. Actually, it was due to something that was bothering Derk. Nevertheless, they were forbidden from being in each other's cubicles, or from lingering in the airlock room. John got Sheila's former cubicle, beside the surgery. The Zen master got Vince's, which was next door, and Denise got Claude's, opposite Vince's. They were the three personnel cubicles nearest to the airlock room. The two children would stay in Denise's cubicle that night.

Jose also informed them that once they retired to bed, they would be locked in for the night. Karl was already in the workshop, making locks for the cubicle doors.

Denise did not neglect her professional duties with regard to Astrid. As soon as Jose had said his piece, she went to Astrid's cubicle, near the rear end of the hallway, led Astrid forward to the surgery, and examined her carefully again. This time, she checked her brain electrical activity, in case the knock on her head had done some internal damage. As she worked, Ursula stood watching, anxious to learn some medicine. Denise found nothing else amiss.

Denise then led Astrid back to her cubicle, and saw her to bed. Before Astrid would allow Denise to put her under sedation, she insisted on seeing Don in private, apparently to thank him for what he had done. Don then came to her cubicle, and they talked for about ten minutes, with the patient sitting up in bed. After Don left, Denise came and administered the sedative. Astrid had eaten only a light snack, and was not hungry. The last thing Denise told her was that she could eat a proper meal later that evening, when she awoke.

*

The first thing Emma did, as soon as she was inside the habitat, was walk to the communications room, to send a brief message to

Mission Control, as ordered by Derk. She had informed Mission Control of the loss of Vince, and Astrid's plight, before going off with the rescue mission earlier that afternoon, and Derk knew they would be anxiously waiting. He had not wanted to send a message direct from a buggy, fearing that what he sent would be overheard.

Europe had received the news of the accident with shock.

Now it was Italy's turn to mourn the loss of a national hero. Local time in central Europe that day was one day and just under half an hour behind Kasei Valley time. That August Monday afternoon, Italy was reeling from the news of the sudden loss of Vincenzo Cassoni, at the way it had happened, and the fact that there was no hope even for the recovery of Vince's body, lying inaccessible at the bottom of Snakepit Crack.

There were no gatherings or demonstrations in Italy that evening, for there was nothing to protest about. There was only shock, and a deep national sadness.

It was Sweden's turn to worry too. Late that summer afternoon, there was an unusual stillness over the nation, with subdued traffic on its freeway network, a quietness in its streets, and little activity on its many vacation lakes. Most people were home from work, and stayed inside, waiting for news, fearing the worst.

The video news networks did nothing to dispel the national anxiety. They displayed awesome images of the northwest cliff face of Snakepit Crack, every so often blowing up one image, so that the relatively small, narrow exit from the fissure in the side of the enormous precipice, in which Astrid was trapped, deep inside, could be plainly seen. Paradoxically, the cliff face images were those made by Astrid herself, some three weeks earlier, on that ill-fated expedition that had killed Sheila and Claude.

The good news of the successful rescue, when it came, just before six, brought a dead nation to sudden life, with cars honking, boats taking off around lakes, and the unleashing of a general party atmosphere. The population, however, in its mood of overwhelming joy at the news that happy evening, could have no inkling of Sweden's involvement in what was to happen next on Mars.

CHAPTER SEVENTEEN

Fugitive Path

CAPTAIN DERK and Emma withdrew from the company just after seven thirty, and spent the rest of the evening in the meeting room, in front of a computer, making up a video report for transmission to Mission Control.

Derk took very great care with the report. The care he took was in proportion to the deep concern he was feeling, a concern he did not share with Emma. It had not been a good day, in spite of the spectacular success of his plan to catch the three unawares and arrest them, with all their facilities and rovers intact.

He was very worried about Don and Astrid, and to some extent about Jurgen, and possibly even Jose and Monique, and even Ursula. He bitterly regretted not making the decision to abort the launch as soon as Don, and Jurgen too, had urgently requested it.

He knew everybody on the mission believed that it was Don who had finally forced him to abort, by driving his buggy into the landing pit. And aborting the launch had been shown to be the right thing to do. If the launch had not been aborted, Astrid would be dead. That was clear to everyone on the mission, although thankfully, it was not yet clear to the people on Earth.

Don Carruthers had been shown to be right, in a dramatic manner, and Jurgen too, and he had been shown to be wrong. He had trouble understanding how he could have been so stupid. After all, what did it matter if the departure of the three captives had been delayed a day?

A large part of Derk's moral authority lay in his crew's confidence in his superior decision making ability. That was his only skill, for he had no technical skills. He hated being wrong in his decisions for that reason, with its attendant loss of face. Usually, in the few cases where it occurred, he could always find a way to deflect the blame. He could never allow it to be seen as his fault.

But that afternoon, he had made a horribly bad decision, in his anxiety to protect his own future by getting those three off the planet as quickly as possible, at the expense, as his crew now knew, of the life of Astrid. The circumstances were such that he could find no one to blame. He had openly shown himself willing to pay for his ambitions with Astrid's life. He knew he had fallen badly in the estimation of Don and Astrid as a result, and probably in Jurgen's eyes too, maybe even in the eyes of Jose and Monique.

It was this erosion of his moral authority that was the source of his deep concern that evening. Even worse, the part of Derk's moral authority that lay in his crew's conviction that he would always act to shield them from harm, to the extent he could, had also been badly eroded.

His problem was how to repair the damage, as well as prevent the truth ever getting to Earth, with the additional damage that could cause.

The solution, as far as Earth was concerned, was to distort the truth. He and Emma would portray the rescue as fairly routine, one that they could have carried out equally well without the assistance of Jose and the three captives. In addition, he would casually make it clear, but as a matter of minor importance, that he would have aborted the launch anyway, as precaution, regardless of Don's action in driving his buggy into the launch pit.

The video report he sent to Earth that evening was a masterpiece of deception. It contained mostly the truth. Most of what was lies was by omission, and the remaining lies concerned his own feelings and conclusions, which no one could ever check.

The report was complete with video recordings of the countdown images, spliced with clever commentary and explanations from Emma, together with selected video of the rescue, together with further commentary from Emma. Finally, there was a video interview with Derk that evening, conducted by Emma, showing him compassionately concerned for the life of Astrid, and overjoyed at her rescue. It also showed his deep distress at the loss of Vince. There was no mention anywhere of the three captives, or any indication of any urgency in getting them off the planet.

The problem of resurrecting his moral authority with his crew was more difficult. That would take some time. The core of his approach would be fourfold. First, he would act as if his moral authority was intact. Second, he would act as if there could be no doubt that he had definitely decided himself that the launch had to be aborted and the skills of the three captives harnessed. This would be something Emma would publicly affirm from time to time. She would also publicly assert that the decision to abort had followed due deliberation, which had taken some time. That would explain why the abort had not been until the final seconds. Third, he would find a way to mildly reprimand Don for his rash behavior. Fourth, in the remaining hours before the three captives left Mars, he would treat them firmly, yet considerately and even leniently. These actions should, over time, be sufficient to sow doubt in the minds of his crew as to his willingness to sacrifice Astrid for his own ends. Doubt would be enough to reinstate his firm moral authority.

His first step in that direction was to allow the three captives the run of the habitat that evening, without either cuffs or leg irons. He had grounds for hoping that Astrid and Don would not find out about his vengeful parade of the three, handcuffed and leg-ironed, on their way down to the lander that afternoon. This hope would be in vain, unfortunately, because Astrid would get Ursula, who had witnessed the event, to tell the whole story before the evening was out.

*

Astrid slept for almost four hours, and woke up just before ten fifteen that evening. The pain in her head had largely gone, and she was feeling quite rested, recovered from her traumatic experience that afternoon. She was also feeling hungry.

She lay in bed thinking about the day's events for some ten minutes. She knew the things she had to do. It was the sequence in which to do them that she had to think out.

She got out of bed, and still with her pajamas on, went out into the hallway. She saw Jose and Emma, both unarmed, sitting in two chairs in the airlock room, facing down the hallway of the science section. Her cubicle was at the south end of the hallway, furthest from the air lock room. As she passed the former cubicles of Sheila, Claude, and Vince, headed for the kitchen, she noticed that the doors were sporting aluminum latch locks, each a simple sliding mechanism that prevented the door being opened from the inside.

She nodded to Jose and Emma as she approached, but stopped at the surgery door when she noticed the door was ajar, with a light on inside, and heard Ursula's voice, speaking German. She knocked.

"Come in," said Ursula.

"Working late, you two?" asked Astrid, in German, as she entered the cubicle. Ursula had diagrams of the human brain on the computer screen in front of her, together with a brain wave trace on an electronic display. Jurgen was standing beside her. Astrid, as can many Swedes, could speak German fluently. Astrid's German was actually much better than her English. She had learnt it as a child, having spent many vacations in Germany with an aunt who lived in Leipzig, and spoke it almost like a native. In contrast, her English, though fluent, was very proper, with a distinct Swedish accent.

Emma and Jose, sitting at the end of the hallway, not more than twenty feet away, could hear the conversation in the surgery, but they could not understand what was said.

"Afraid so," said Ursula, in answer to Astrid's question. "Having to learn some medicine is keeping me occupied. I was just trying to repeat a simulation of that brain examination Dr. Lavoisier gave you this evening. Jurgen's helping me with the electrode controller. We can expect people to get knocked on the head every so often, and I thought I'd better be prepared. By the way, how's your head? That was quite a blow you got."

"I'm feeling fine, thank you," said Astrid, "just a very dull pain. I hardly notice it now."

"Good. We're very happy you're still with us," said Jurgen. "We're all still shaken at what happened to Vince. It must be even worse for you. You probably knew him better than either of us."

"It's a nightmare," admitted Astrid. "His poor wife and family ... I have to force myself not to think about it."

"Well, I don't want be responsible for making you think about it," said Jurgen, retreating to the door. "It's time I went to bed. You've just about mastered that controller, Ursula. I'm sure you two would like to talk alone. Good night."

After he had gone, Astrid sat down in the only other chair in the tiny cubicle.

"Jurgen's always very helpful to me," explained Ursula, "although he actually came to talk about what happened this afternoon."

"At least you had a much better afternoon than I had," said Astrid. "I hear it was quite a show. Getting the prisoners and the children into the lander, I mean."

"I would hardly call it a show," said Ursula. "I'm not sure you'd have wanted to see it. It upset me—especially the children. Jurgen was upset too, I think. He used to think the world of the Captain. I don't think he does any more. He no longer believes those three can be guilty of what they're accused of either. Neither do I."

"They're not," said Astrid. "I'll explain that another time. Can you fill me in on what happened this afternoon? I need to know? I'll explain why some other time too."

Ursula told the story of the boarding of the children, screaming in terror, and then their parents and Dr. Sato, after a humiliating parade into the landing pit in handcuffs and leg irons.

"Not very nice," said Astrid, when Ursula had finished. "Thank you for telling me. Now I have to go and get something to eat. Can you give me a few sleeping pills? Have you a pill that would put me to sleep for about two and a half to three hours? I need two of them."

"Problems sleeping this evening?" asked Ursula.

"Lots of problems," said Astrid, as Ursula took a bottle of pills from a shelf, and counted out two.

"Thank you," said Astrid, getting up. "By the way, where did you put the children's dollies? I didn't notice them earlier, when we came back."

"They're still in the airlock room, but in the facilities room out of the way," said Ursula.

The facilities room was a small enclosed room, or large closet, in the southwest corner of the large airlock room. It contained all habitat control facilities.

"I see," said Astrid. "Good night."

Astrid left the surgery, and headed along the hallway toward the kitchen, with the two sleeping pills in her pajamas breast pocket.

"How are you, Astrid?" asked Jose, as she passed the two guards in the airlock room, sitting beside the small facilities room.

"As well as normal," said Astrid. "And thanks to both of you for helping get me out of that hole this afternoon."

"Thank that old monk and Don, not us," said Jose, shaking his head. "But for those two, you would not be here this evening." Emma did not look pleased at Jose's remarks.

"So I have been told," said Astrid, as she passed on to the kitchen.

The kitchen area was deserted. Everyone, apparently, except herself, Ursula, and the two guards in the airlock room, had retired to their cubicles for the night.

In a fridge, she found some leftover mixture of whole-grain rice, beans and vegetables, in a light tomato and herb sauce, the products of the greenhouses in Leaf Valley. It was typical Martian food, filling and nutritional, but nothing to rave about. It was very low in fat, so you could eat until you were full, and never put on weight. She took a plastic bowl full and a spoon, and headed back to the science section.

Jose hoped Astrid would stop and chat about her experience in the fissure. He was genuinely interested. He was also bored, for Emma was not one you could pass the time chatting with. He would have preferred his friend Monique as a fellow guard, but Derk had ordered Jose and Emma to take the first watch.

Astrid just walked past the two guards, with the usual serious expression on her long face. Jose knew better than to try to ambush her.

She did not go to her cubicle, but knocked on Don Carruthers' door.

"Come in," said Don.

"Hello," she said, as she came in. Don was sitting at his tiny desk, organizing files on his computer.

"Hello," said Don. "I thought you might be prowling around later this evening. How are you?"

"I am getting tired of being asked that," said Astrid, sitting down on the edge of his bed. "Thank you anyway. I am just fine. Mind if I have supper in here? I am very hungry."

"Not at all," said Don. "I was sitting here waiting for you to wake up. I thought of waking you, but I decided it would be best to let you sleep as long as possible."

"I am glad you did. We need to talk. I have decided to go ahead with it. Today was the straw that broke the camel's back, as they say. What about you? Are you in or out?"

"I decided hours ago," said Don. "I'm in."

"Good. There are just a few details I need to know before we can proceed."

*

Ten minutes later, Astrid was back in her cubicle, constructing a complex, combined video, audio, and text report on her computer. Her mind was resolute, and fully focussed on the task.

This report was unusual and original. It had a garbage scientific title in English: *Geomorphological Dynamics of Alpha Gravity Fractronics*, with both her name and Don's as the authors. The first few paragraphs were garbage science too, in English, completely incomprehensible. Then it continued in Swedish, with six attachments, the first four in Swedish, the last an audio file in English but with the first few minutes in Swedish. The fifth attachment was missing. She had yet to steal it.

When she finished, she took parts of the report and used it to construct a second report, entirely in English, and without the garbage scientific title and garbage introductory paragraphs. This second report was written simply and clearly, and came to the point in the first few lines.

It took her nearly an hour to complete the reports, and it was just before twelve when she finished. She got up, put a blank data storage unit in her breast pocket, and left the cubicle.

She walked down the hallway, headed for the kitchen once more, holding the empty rice bowl in her hand. The surgery door was slightly open, but the light was off. Jose and Emma looked a little drowsy as she entered the airlock room. She paused in front of them.

"You two look like you should be in bed," observed Astrid.

"We're awake," said Emma.

"*You* certainly seem wide awake," said Jose.

"I had a good sleep," said Astrid. "I will get sleepy again later. Right now I am going to make a mug of almond tea. Would you like me to bring you some?"

They both nodded and Astrid passed on into the kitchen and made the tea. When it was made, she left the kitchen, walking very quietly into the hallway of the command section.

The entrance from the airlock room into the kitchen and living area did not line up with either the hallway of the command section or the hallway of the science section. That meant that neither Jose nor Emma could see her, if they turned around.

If the doorway between the airlock room and living area had lined up with the two hallways, a person standing at the far end of the science-section hallway would have been able to see all the way along the habitat to the far end of the command-section hallway. The habitat designers had thought that would not be conducive to any sense of privacy, and so had introduced the misalignment.

She walked very quietly along the command section hallway, past the communications room, as far as Emma's cubicle, almost opposite Derk's. She opened the door and went in, just as stealthily, and soon had broken into Emma's computer. She had done this quite a few times before, and this time did it very efficiently. She quickly found the video file she was looking for, the video of the rescue Derk had recorded that afternoon. Then she took the blank data storage unit from her pocket and made a copy. A minute later she was back in the kitchen.

The tea had cooled a little. Good, she thought, just right for drinking down quickly. She now took the two sleeping pills from her pajamas pocket and ground them up on the counter top. She was a geologist, and knew how to grind things into a very fine powder—almost dust. Then she poured three plastic mugs of tea, two red mugs and one blue. She put equal amounts of the sleeping pill powder in each of the red mugs and stirred.

"Enjoy your tea," she said to Jose and Emma, when she got back to the airlock room, holding a red mug in each hand.

"Great," said Jose, as Emma nodded in appreciation.

"Mind if I join you for a few minutes, while we drink our tea?" she then asked in a relaxed tone. "I would like to hear about the rescue this afternoon."

"Certainly," said Jose, relieved. He had feared she would just go back to her cubicle.

A few seconds later, Astrid came back from the kitchen with a chair in one hand and her mug of tea in the other, and sat down beside the two guards.

She did not have to sit talking long. She drank her own tea quite quickly, and when Jose and Emma had both finished their tea, she got up. Explaining that she should try to sleep now, she took their empty mugs, and carried the mugs and chair back to the kitchen. She spent a few minutes in the kitchen, and made sure the mugs went in the cleanser, where they were cleaned at once.

She then headed back to the airlock room. Emma and Jose were already asleep in their chairs, heads drooped over. She looked at her watch. It was twelve fifteen, and the habitat was sleeping.

She now walked over to the small facilities room in the corner, opened the door and turned on the light. The children's two dollies sat in the middle of the room. She also noticed two automatic rifles and two nanoguns, leaning against a corner wall, with boxes of ammunition on the floor beside them. Two machine pistols in holsters lay on the floor too. Must be Jose's and Emma's, she thought.

It was the work of a few minutes to take out the dollies. She worked very quietly. She came back to the room again, and looked at the guns, thinking. Then she took the guns and ammunition boxes out too, and gently placed them on the floor beside the airlock door. She hardly made a sound moving the weaponry.

Then she walked down the hallway to Denise's cubicle. She slid back the outside latch quietly, knocked, and went in and turned on the light. Denise was in bed, with her two children sleeping at the foot of the bed. She was not asleep, and Astrid could see she had been crying.

"Hello," said Astrid, in a low voice, as she sat down on the small chair beside the bed.

"Hello," said Denise, almost whispering, and sitting up in bed. "Excuse my appearance. I wasn't expecting a visitor. Thank you for coming. How are you feeling?"

"Oh, just fine," said Astrid. Then she explained. "I came because I have debts to repay. You three have saved my life a second time."

"None of us expect any repayment from you, Astrid," said Denise. "We just did what anybody would have done in the circumstances. Anyway, there's nothing much you could do to repay, other than say thanks maybe, and you've done that."

"Maybe I can do something else," said Astrid. "Could you answer a simple question for me?"

"I can try," said Denise, puzzled.

"If you could escape from here this evening with the rovers, what would you do to survive?"

"Are you thinking of helping us escape?" asked Denise, for a moment completely alert, her mind wide open to a whole new range of possibilities—until she thought of the two guards outside.

"Could you just answer the question?" responded Astrid.

"All right. We had a Plan B," explained Denise, "but it was only for the case where we had to flee Leaf Valley, which is what we'd have to do if we could escape from here. There's no way we could survive there any more. We couldn't defend it, even if we had guns. We're outnumbered and outgunned. Your Captain would just capture us again if we went back home. Our Plan B is not a very good plan, but it's all we have left. It would mean a whole new start, and the loss of a lot of development work I've been doing in my laboratory, and the loss of the laboratory too, but I believe we would manage."

"What is this Plan B? I will not repeat it to the Captain."

Denise hesitated, but then, realizing it made little difference any more, since they were to be shipped off to Earth in the morning anyway, she explained the plan.

"Long before your mission arrived, we took precautions. There's another sheltered valley, off the south side of Kasei Valley, about three hundred miles east of here. It's low down, and out of range of your mission's buggies. It's a bow-shaped valley, well below the level of the high plateau to the south. It's got a long, very high escarpment forming the boundary to the south, in the shape of a huge bow. It has two large mesas where the string of the bow would be, to the north, at the entrance on the floor of Kasei Valley. That gives the valley three entrances from the main run of Kasei Valley. There's also another way out, along a gully that climbs up gradually from the valley floor at the southern extremity of the bow. The gully takes you up to the plateau to the south.

"We gave this bow-shaped valley the name Hercules Valley, and we called the two mesas at the northern entrances the Pillars of Hercules. Anyway, we have a nuclear power plant there, and some solar panels and batteries, and a stockpile of food. There's also a large stockpile of cement, as well as refined copper, aluminum and glass—enough material to build two more greenhouses. And there's a source of water there too.

"We hid our Japanese habitat in Outlook Cove last week, because it seemed that we might have to leave in a hurry. We also hid our minicat and another nuclear power plant there. Outlook Cove's the small valley in the west wall of Leaf Valley, just below the monastery. If we could escape from here tonight, we would drive to Outlook Cove, hitch up Dr. Sato's habitat and the minicat, and head east down Kasei Valley to Hercules Valley. If your Captain didn't find out before morning that we had escaped, we'd probably get away. He'd likely come looking for us in Leaf Valley. But when he didn't find us there, he'd have no way of knowing where we'd gone. He'd know only that possession of the rovers would give us a lot of options."

"I see," said Astrid, taken by surprise. This secret stockpile was something she had not taken into account. She realized at once that she should have thought of it, given that these three were skilled in the art of Martian survival. The existence of the stockpile in Hercules Valley meant that all she had to do was tell Denise she was free to go. That was not quite what she and Don had been planning.

"It would be very hard to start all over again," added Denise, speaking as if she were describing a dream, "but I'd rather do that than go back to Earth. Of course, we'd be outlaws. Fugitives.

Outcasts from the society that's going to develop here. But I'd still be happy to take that path, if I could escape from here. I know John would too, and I do not believe the Zen master would desert us. I do wish we could escape. But there's really nothing you can do to help, Astrid, is there? Jose and Emma must be sitting out in the hallway with machine guns, waiting for you to come out?"

"Would you really be willing to stay on Mars, hunted as outlaws, with all kinds of new hardships to face?" asked Astrid, still surprised. "You must be very attached to this planet."

"Yes, we would, and we really are very attached to this place," said Denise. "It's our home. We've been here a long time, and when you build what we've built with your own hands, it tears the soul out of you to leave it. If we could only stay on Mars, I'm sure that sooner or later we'd find a way to show that we were innocent of all the horrible things we've been accused of, and maybe even find a way to win back Leaf Valley. It's being stolen from us."

She hesitated, thought a moment, and then continued. "The biggest problem with our Plan B would have been leaving the laboratory behind in Leaf Valley. When Derk got to find out what we'd been developing in it, he'd have used it to blacken our names even more on Earth. On the other hand, if we were going to be branded as outlaws anyway, for one thing, I suppose it wouldn't have made much difference if there had been a second thing as well."

"Are you going to tell me what you were developing in your lab?" asked Astrid, puzzled, and now curious as well. There was clearly much more to these three Martians than even she had been able to unravel, and Astrid was very good at unraveling mysteries.

"No," said Denise. "You'll find out in the next few days, when Derk and his friends get to see the inside. Ursula and Monique should be able to figure it out. We'll be long gone from Mars by then, I suppose. But when you do find out about it, try to understand that what we were doing was the only sensible thing to do, seen from a Martian point of view. I know everyone on Earth will think we were very wrong, but I do not think we were. This is another world." She paused here, tears glistening in her eyes, her mind far away in a vision she had accepted would never be.

"I suppose this has been a very long answer to your original question," she said eventually. "Yes, I wish we could escape, even to become outlaws."

Astrid got up. "Well," she said, "get ready for a surprise."

She moved toward the door.

"Oh," said Denise, puzzled.

"I am your fairy godmother tonight," said Astrid. "Your wish to escape is granted. You are free to go, or to stay here as you wish. You can tell your husband and Dr. Sato yourself. I have drugged Emma and Jose. They can not wake up before about one forty-five at the earliest. Just be very, very quiet as you leave, if you decide to go, and do not turn on the rover headlights until you are nearly down on the plain. The Captain is a very light sleeper." She glanced out the partly frosted window. "The moon has just come out of the planet's shadow. If you hurry you will catch it before it sets. Close the cubicle doors behind you and reset the locks. Good luck."

Denise's eyes opened wide in astonishment, but before she could say anything, Astrid had left the room. A few seconds later, Astrid put her head back in again. Denise was already out of bed and getting dressed, obviously intending to go.

"There are some guns beside the airlock," said Astrid. "Take them in case you are pursued, but try not to hurt anybody."

*

Astrid spent the next fifteen minutes working on her computer. She first entered the video file of the rescue, which she had stolen from Emma's computer. She used this video file to complete the first of the two reports she had been working on earlier, the one mostly in Swedish with the garbage science title in English. She converted the video file to a multi-sectioned file, by adding the audio of her own voice, speaking Swedish. This audio section in Swedish went at the beginning of the file. She did not edit the video part about the rescue, which made up most of the file, in any way. She then copied the completed report, with its six attachments, on to another blank data storage unit, and placed that in a pajamas pocket.

She looked at her Mars watch. It was just before twelve forty, the Martian midnight. A day lasted twenty-four hours and forty minutes on Mars. She looked at her watch again. It now showed exactly zero hours. A new day, Wednesday, had begun. She had at least an hour and forty-five minutes to carry out the rest of the plan, before Jose and Emma woke up.

She walked to the airlock room, on her way to the kitchen for another mug of tea. Emma and Jose were still fast asleep on their chairs. The children's dollies, and the guns and ammunition she had placed against the airlock door, had gone.

She made the tea in the kitchen, but did not return to her cubicle. She now began to feel uncertain about what to do next, and hesitated, her earlier resolve weakened somewhat.

She stood by the counter sipping her tea, and looking out the kitchen window, more than half of it frosted. After only a few minutes, she saw the headlights of three vehicles come on, about half a mile away. She stood watching, as the convoy got on to the main Kasei Valley road, headed for Stem Gap at speed. She was still standing there, fifteen minutes later, at zero fifteen. The three vehicles crossing Elbow Plain were now half way to Stem Gap.

Any other person, who had done what Astrid had just done, might have been sentimental at the sight, and could be forgiven for having a tear or two glisten in the eyes. But not Astrid. She truly was a cold fish, devoid of sentimentality. She did have emotions, however, like any other woman. But she profoundly respected justice, and considered it, like the Greek philosophers of old, to be the basis of all that is right and good in society. She would lie, on the rare occasions where telling the truth would lead to injustice, and tell the truth, if lying led to injustice, as it usually did.

She had no doubt in her calculating mind that what she had done so far that evening was right and just. Her belief in justice, above all, was also the reason why she had never made the slightest effort to divert Don Carruthers' affections from Sheila Bell, when she was alive, even though she had been deeply in love with him for a long time. It would have been a profound injustice to both of them.

Earlier, she had planned on doing a few more things that evening. One of them was pull out by the roots the weed of injustice that had been flourishing in the midst of this ESA mission to Mars.

But now she was feeling hesitant, her mind no longer clear. Denise's surprise revelation of the existence of the stockpile at Hercules Valley had already caused her to modify her plans. She had thought originally that the three would need a lot more help if they were to escape from Derk. It was now clear that neither her further assistance, nor Don's, was needed. Those three could obviously manage quite independently on Mars, as they had been doing successfully for the past ten years, as long as they were left in peace.

She stood there thinking for yet another fifteen minutes, toying with the empty mug in her hand. Her brow was heavily furrowed. An intuition was telling her something important was not right, causing her to hesitate.

Her mind wandered back to the evening at the house in Leaf Valley, the evening after Sheila and Claude's funeral. That was almost three weeks ago, although it now seemed like very long ago, so much had been happening. She remembered the discussion about Denise's idea for a free people on Mars, independent and proud of their accomplishments, beholden to no power on Earth.

She recalled some of John's words about putting up a building in the middle of Leaf Valley, with a big round table inside. Each person of age in the region would have a seat at the table, where each of them would contribute to decisions on matters that affected them all. And each person of age would have the right to own land and private property, to produce and exchange his or her products for the products of others. The power to decide, both in matters of government, and in matters of production and consumption, would reside with the first free people of Mars. Any person wanting to join the settlement would have to accept their ways, laid out in a Constitution, and buy some land.

She recalled her own suggestion that their flag should have a brown disk on it, on a pink background, to symbolize the round table.

And she recalled Denise's suggestion that there would one day be a huge statue, like the Statute of Liberty, up on Stem Mountains, on top of the escarpment wall, overlooking the entrance to Leaf Valley.

Then she thought of her childhood, growing up living in an apartment in the Stockholm suburb of Farsta, surrounded by coniferous parkland. Her parents had divorced when she was sixteen, and she had lived alone with her mother, an only child. She had never seen much of her father anyway. He worked in the Swedish diplomatic service and was always abroad. Currently he was in Japan. Her mother had remarried after she left home to go to university, and now lived on a farm in the far south of Sweden, south of the Swedish forest boundary, near the city of Malmo, in a region called Scania, with a flat, relatively treeless farming landscape she didn't care for. She didn't care much for her stepfather either, and had rarely visited her mother since her second marriage.

Suddenly, she saw the answer to what was bothering her. It was a principle she remembered from a social science class: *Nomadic societies never build anything, because they can never take much with them as they move.* It flashed through her mind, and suddenly she knew what to do again, her resolve strong once more. She felt much better, even happy. She could proceed more or less as planned.

She remembered that Don was expecting her. He was probably sitting wondering what was keeping her. But now she would be able to lay the whole picture out in front of him, in a compelling way she could not have done earlier that evening. The decision she had come to, which no one could have foreseen, not even Astrid herself, would be epochal in its consequences, and would not only profoundly alter the course of the development of Mars, but the development of mankind itself, although Astrid could not know this on that pivotal night.

She looked at her watch. It was zero thirty. Out the frosted window, she could no longer see any lights moving across Elbow Plain. The three had evidently reached Leaf Valley safely. But for them it was now a valley that was no longer a sanctuary, a valley that had to be abandoned, in favor of starting over far away.

At that moment, Derk appeared in the kitchen, in his pajamas. Astrid froze. Something had wakened him, and he had just been to the washroom in the command section, and had heard a noise in the kitchen.

"Oh, it's just you, Astrid," said Derk. "How are you feeling?"

"I think I have completely recovered, Captain," said Astrid.

"Good. I've been very worried about you."

He glanced toward the doorway into the airlock room, trying to appear as unconcerned as possible.

"Everything quiet back there?" he asked.

"Quiet as a graveyard," said Astrid.

"Good night then," he said, retreating back to the command section, repressing both a yawn and an urge to go and talk to Emma and Jose. "Try to get some more sleep."

"Good night, Captain. I will try. I am just not very sleepy right now." Good example of where telling the truth would result in an injustice, she thought, as she made her way to Don's cubicle.

*

The moon Phobos had just set, out beyond Stem Gap, and Leaf Valley was now pitch dark, with only a feeble light from the canopy of stars overhead. A train of vehicles was just emerging from Outlook Cove, moving slowly, but about as fast as it could go, at only twelve miles per hour.

In front was Dr. Sato in his buggy, headlights on, pulling a trailer with a nuclear power plant inside. The trailer was attached to the minicat. The buggy headlights revealed the usual paper-thin layer of fine, white frost on the road, and on the rock and boulder-covered terrain on either side of it. The night temperature was well below the Martian frost point of about minus fifty-eight Celsius.

Some two hundred feet behind the minicat, John drove the lead rover. It pulled a loaded trailer, which was in turn tethered to another rover, coming behind, driven by Denise, with her two children asleep inside in the front bunk. This rover was in turn pulling another heavily loaded trailer, which was tethered to a fifty-foot long habitat. This was the habitat that had come to Mars with the JSA mission in 2037. Ten years earlier, the three had towed this habitat all the way to Leaf Valley from Ares Valley, some seventeen hundred miles to the east.

"It's just like the old days, John," Denise was saying, a little sadly. She knew it was safe for John to talk over the radio link at their crawling speed on a road. "I never thought we'd have to do this again. But it's good to be free, out on Mars again."

"Not quite like the old days," said John, a very determined expression on his face. "Back then, we didn't have military types with nanoguns after us."

"But we've got two nanoguns now. Won't that be enough to hold them off if they come after us?"

"Maybe," said John, "but only if they're behind us. If they meet up with us before we get to Elbow Fork—before we get on to the road east down Kasei Valley—they'll be coming at us head on."

"Suppose they don't come until after we get past the fork, how will you handle it?"

"I'll just drive the buggy in the rear, and try and hold them off."

"But that means you'd be exposed," said Denise, feeling a deep anxiety. They were not safe yet.

"A little bit," admitted John. "But if they come after us, they'll have to drive with their lights on, so I'll see them. They'll see my lights too, of course, but they won't know it's only me. You and Dr. Sato will keep at least two miles ahead, out of range. They won't want to shoot anyway, because they'll want the rovers undamaged.

I'll just fire a warning nanobullet every so often. That should keep them from getting too close."

"You think it'll be enough?" said Denise.

"There's a good chance," said John. "Anyway, it's all we can do. Without the nanoguns we wouldn't have a hope. Any pursuers in buggies will not be anxious to have a nanogun shell exploding above their heads. They dare not come too close."

"But we have to get past Elbow Fork, and on to the road down Kasei Valley, before that strategy will work," said Denise. "Astrid said Jose and Emma can't wake up before about one forty-five. It's ten to one now. Do you think we can make the junction in time?"

The main road through Stem Gap and across Elbow Plain ultimately curved to the south, up Kasei Valley to the old NASA landing site. They needed to go in the opposite direction, and about eight miles from Stem Gap there was a junction, Elbow Fork, where a left turn put you on the road running northeast down Kasei Valley. This was the road they needed to reach before they were pursued.

"We should be at the fork by about two o'clock," said John, "so we might just make it before they find out we're gone. It's about fourteen miles from here to the fork, and twelve miles an hour is the best we can do."

"Maybe they won't wake up till quite a bit later," said Denise, searching for the bright side.

"Possibly," said John. "If you want to be very optimistic, maybe Jose and Emma won't bother to check inside our cubicles, when they do wake up. The doors are still locked on the outside. And when the second watch takes over, probably around two thirty, maybe they won't check either."

"In which case they wouldn't find out we were gone until the morning," said Denise, "by which time we'd be sixty miles down Kasei Valley."

"But if you take the pessimistic scenario," said John, "somebody in the hab could have wakened just after we left, perhaps to go to the bathroom, and discovered Jose and Emma fast asleep in their chairs, and raised the alarm."

"In which case, right now, there could be two armed buggies on Elbow Plain, headed for Stem Gap—and we'll both meet in the gap," said Denise.

"In which case it's another set of one-way tickets back to Earth," said John.

"You wouldn't try to fight your way through?"

"No," said John. "We couldn't succeed. If we didn't get killed ourselves, we could well kill some of them. Then they could really throw the book at us, when we got back to Earth. No. We'd just have to surrender."

After that there was silence, as they made their way along the road across Leaf Valley, to the main road running south to Stem Gap, at their maximum speed of only twelve miles an hour. It took them fifteen minutes to reach that road, and another fifteen minutes to reach Stem Gap, at one twenty.

The road through Stem Gap ran almost due east, and slightly down hill, so that even low down on the road, in daylight, you could see anything on the road ahead on Elbow Plain for up to two miles away. At night, you could see the headlights of a vehicle up to four miles out on the plain. And that is what they now saw, the lights of two vehicles actually, headed toward them, about three miles away.

Dr. Sato and John saw the two pairs of headlights first. Then Denise, driving close behind John's rover, saw them as the road curved a bit to the left.

"God, no! Not again!" cried John. He made an effort to get control of himself. "Dr. Sato! We'd better stop and wait for them. Sorry, Denise. Be careful back there, I'm slowing down and stopping."

The emotional blow was almost too much for Denise, after the roller coaster of freedom and captivity she had just been through.

"No!" she screamed. "We have no luck. I can't take any more, John."

The long train of vehicles stopped safely, in the middle of Stem Gap. The three now waited to be taken into captivity for the third time, as the buggies drew closer. Denise was in tears.

"We did our best, Denise," said John. "Nobody can say we didn't try."

Denise did not answer, but John could hear her sobbing.

The buggies were coming very fast, obviously doing almost thirty miles an hour, normally a dangerous speed at night on a Martian valley road. That final stretch across Elbow Plain was reasonably straight though, and well known, so that the buggies were not in any real danger.

John expected the buggies to slow down and stop about a mile away, while they negotiated the surrender. But they did not. They just kept going at full speed, and as they got nearer John could make out only one person in the first buggy, lit up by the headlights of the second.

"What the blazes ...," he said, suddenly. "Whoever you are, slow down! Don't you see us?"

But the lead buggy did not stop until it was only a few feet from the front of Dr. Sato's buggy. The second one stopped just a few feet behind that.

"Hello." It was Astrid's voice. She was in the lead buggy. "It's just me again, and Don too. We have come to give you a hand."

John was so shocked he did not know what to say, as was Denise. He was also enormously relieved. It was not Derk and his soldiers after all.

"Well, blocking the road's not exactly the way to give us a hand," said John, when he had recovered enough to speak.

"It is you know," said Astrid. "We have come to let you know you are going the wrong way. You have to turn around, and take your children home."

"What are you talking about, Astrid?" said John. "Did that knock on your head loosen a few screws? We have to get on to the road down Kasei Valley before your Captain comes after us."

"How is he going to do that?" asked Astrid, very softly.

Then it dawned on them.

"He's got no buggies any more," cried Denise. "He can't come after us."

"But ... But the guns," countered John. "We're still outnumbered and outgunned."

"Not any more," said Astrid. "You have two sets of guns, and we have six and a half in Don's trailer. We have them all: machine pistols, automatic rifles, nanoguns and ammunition, except for just one nanogun, and the four machine pistols in your house—the ones you took from Jose's company the night you escaped from them. I think the Captain has the missing nanogun in his cubicle. We had counted on getting all of the guns at the habitat. But even so, the Captain is now outgunned, and nearly matched in manpower—five of us and seven of his, six really, because you could never get Ursula Schneider to shoot at anybody—unless in self defense."

"You see, we've decided to join your settlement," said Don, "if you'll have us. We like Mars and want to stay, and we like your idea of a free people on Mars, and would like to be part of the settlement."

At this, both John and Denise were overwhelmed a second time. They could hardly think. The Zen master just listened and said nothing.

"This is a very big surprise," said Denise, after a short silence. "We'd be delighted to have you; but are you sure you want to do this? We're accused of very serious crimes, even if the accusations are false. If you join us they won't take long to charge you with something too. And what about ESA? Are you free to just quit?"

"I do not think we will be accused of anything criminal," said Astrid. "It is Captain Derk and some faceless people high up in ESA who are the criminals. We have the proof of that. You are innocent, and they will have the proof on Earth soon too, I think."

Astrid now explained how Sheila had been collecting material for a book and had recorded the conversation with Denise the morning Denise had had her dental work done, known to be the last conversation between the two women.

And that recording was already on Earth, on both sides of the Atlantic. Although Astrid had buried the recording in a message to Mission Control, a little under an hour ago, the CIA had intercepted her message. The recording of Sheila's last conversation with Denise was already in a laboratory in Langley, Virginia, CIA headquarters, being analyzed for authenticity.

"And we can quit if we want to," said Don. "There's nothing in our contracts that says we can't quit any time. I suppose ESA never thought there was any chance an astronaut would want to quit in the middle of a mission, so they never put a prohibition clause in the contracts we signed. I've examined our contracts carefully. There's nothing even in the fine print that says we can't quit. Anyway, it's done. Our resignations should have reached Earth by now, and we've even sent our resignations to the Captain."

"We would like to buy some Leaf Valley land from you," added Astrid, "but you have to give us a loan to pay for it. We are broke just now, but we know how to work hard. You once said your price would be very reasonable."

Suddenly a great feeling of joy swept over Denise, and tears began streaming down her face. For a whole minute there was silence, as John and Denise tried to get their minds accustomed to this whole new, unanticipated situation.

"We'll be only too happy to sell you some land," said Denise at last, wiping her eyes.

"And our land and building loans are interest free, with no down payment and no repayments for one year—one Martian year, that is," added John.

"Sounds very attractive," said Don, feeling very relieved.

"By the way, did you say 'we'?" asked Denise. "Does that mean you want to buy the land as a couple? We have some bargain properties for young married couples just starting out, and Dr. Sato has a supply of free marriage licenses."

"Easily managed," said the Zen master.

"And the settlement needs children," added Denise, encouragingly.

"I haven't been asked," said Astrid softly, "but I'm willing."

"You don't get to choose a wife on Mars, Don," said John, persuasively. "Believe me. It's take it or nothing. And if it's nothing, you'll probably get hell."

"Let's see," said Don, accepting the inevitable, "this is Wednesday. How about Saturday, ten days from today?"

"It will be arranged," said the Zen master. "Does five o'clock at the monastery suit?"

Both Don and Astrid answered yes.

"Well, this is an unexpected turn of events," said John, "and no mistake. I guess we can all go home now. Even if Derk were to set out right now on foot, with his single nanogun, he couldn't get as far as Mount Tip before about eight in the morning. And I doubt if he'd be crazy enough to try that anyway, even if he were awake right now, which he probably isn't. His wings are well and truly clipped, thanks to you two. We can all sleep in peace for the rest of the night. Boy, will he ever get a shock when he wakes up. All right, Denise. Let's get this wagon train turned around. We're going home."

They reached the house in the glass compound at two thirty. After unhitching the habitat, they all went straight to bed. Don and Astrid slept in a rover on the parking pad inside the compound, their minds at peace, feeling safe and secure.

When the sun rose the following morning in the pink Martian sky, it shone down on a building with seven sleeping Martians inside. It also shone on a habitat with one Richard Derk in a fit of rage that shocked at least four of the six remaining under his command. For him, however, the worst was yet to come.

CHAPTER EIGHTEEN

Never Again

ONE OF the two operatives on the night shift at Mission Control was a young Frenchman; the other was a young Italian woman. Although both of them knew English very well, neither of them knew a word of Swedish. For both of them, with Latin mother tongues, Swedish was about as understandable as Outer Mongolian.

When Astrid's disguised message arrived, at one o'clock that Tuesday morning, the two night-shift operatives did their jobs, and examined the message with care.

There was a message tag. It stated that Richard Derk had authorized the report, and directed the operatives to file it in an ESA archive for reports of no interest to the general public. The tag also directed them to forward a copy to a Professor Axel Lindstroem, of the Royal Swedish Academy of Sciences in Stockholm.

The two operatives read the initial body of the report three times. It was in English, and even though they both had a technical education, they could make no sense of it. The young Italian woman remarked that it would win a prize for the report from Mars of least interest to anyone, never mind the general public.

Then they looked at the first attachment, in Swedish. Then the second. More Swedish. Then the third. More Swedish. The young Frenchman had seen enough, and gave up.

The young Italian was more thorough. She looked at the fourth attachment. Still more Swedish. Then she listened to the start of the fifth and sixth attachments. Even more Swedish. She then gave up too. They archived the report as requested, and forwarded a copy to Stockholm.

*

Axel Lindstroem was a professor of planetary geology at the University of Stockholm. Astrid knew the professor personally. He was a friend of her Ph.D. supervisor, and she had met him several times during her years as a graduate student at Uppsala University. Uppsala is only a forty-minute freeway drive from Stockholm.

Axel Lindstroem had a reputation in Sweden, indeed throughout Scandinavia, as the deadly enemy of bureaucratic injustice. He had earned that reputation by his successful involvement in cases of wrongful accusations against innocent public employees.

In one famous case, an innocent professor, falsely testified against by a young student, actually went to jail, until Lindstroem turned up irrefutable evidence of his innocence. He was released, compensated and reinstated, and Lindstroem came out of it a hero.

In recent years, his long history of fearless hostility to bureaucratic wrong doing, his prominence in the scientific world, and his election to membership of the Royal Swedish Academy of Sciences, the body responsible for selecting Nobel prize winners, gave him a voice and prestige in Scandinavia that many an ambitious politician envied. Ambitious bureaucrats at all levels in the Swedish Government had learned to be wary of Axel Lindstroem. When the professor spoke out, the media listened.

This was the character of the man to whom Astrid Larsson had directed her heavily disguised report about events on Mars.

*

That week, Professor Lindstroem, now in his early sixties, and not far from retirement, was enjoying a vacation at his daughter's summer cottage, with his grandchildren. He was white-haired, and had a long, kindly, but confident face. The cottage lay beside a scenic lake, about a hundred and sixty miles west of Stockholm.

That Tuesday morning, his secretary arrived for work at the university in Stockholm, as usual. The message from Mars stood out. It was the first time she had ever seen a message from Mars. It was from the Mars mission leader, Richard Derk, authorizing a report from Sweden's heroine, Astrid Larsson, and the mission's chief geologist, Donald Carruthers. It had to be important.

The secretary, an efficient and experienced woman in her mid forties, had spent the previous evening glued to a video screen, as the drama of Astrid's entrapment and rescue unfolded.

She read the beginning of the report in English, but could make neither head nor tail of it. Then she looked at the first attachment, in Swedish. It contained more garbage geological text, but in every paragraph there was a short sentence urgently requesting that the next attachment be read immediately.

She read the next three attachments in astonishment. Then she thought for a few minutes, and then she acted. She forwarded the report to the professor, and got in touch with him by videophone.

Axel Lindstroem got the call at eight forty-four, as he was having breakfast on the cottage patio, beside the scenic lake.

At nine twelve, his daughter was driving him to the railroad station in Orebro, the nearest large city. At nine thirty-five, he was boarding an express train. At nine forty, he was passing Orebro's famous mushroom tower, as the electric train picked up speed on its way east to Stockholm. His computer was on a table in front of him, functioning and linked to the world.

By ten thirty, he had absorbed every detail in Astrid's report, and had talked to the Chief of Police in Stockholm, an old friend, and had sent him a copy. The Police Chief had soon transmitted messages to Police Headquarters in both Paris and Dublin.

By eleven forty, when Lindstroem's train pulled into Central Station in Stockholm, he had confirmation, from police laboratories in Sweden, France, and Ireland, that the recording of the conversation between Sheila Bell and Denise Lavoisier was genuine.

The implication was that Denise Lavoisier was innocent of all charges against her. Worse, it was clear that the basis of these charges was a criminal fabrication on the part of Richard Derk. And it was possible that high-level people in ESA, maybe even in the European Commission, were also involved.

The professor got to his university office just before twelve. Awaiting him was even more conclusive and damning evidence of Derk's systematic campaign of deception.

Derk had sent a careful message to Mission Control the previous evening. It contained his cleverly misleading and distorted report on Astrid's rescue and the aborted launch.

His report had arrived in Toulouse just before ten, local time, while the evening shift was still on duty, and just before nine London time. Since the report was of great public interest, and in no way damaging to ESA, the London office of ESA had cleared it for public release at once.

That Tuesday morning, excerpts from Derk's false report were in the European press, and the video recording of Astrid's rescue, severely edited by Emma and Derk, was being repeatedly aired throughout Europe, but particularly in Sweden. The professor's secretary had a recording waiting for him.

Lindstroem now compared Derk's version of events with the unedited version sent by Astrid. The gross manipulation, distortion and deception that Derk had practiced was glaringly obvious. There could be no doubt of the truth of Astrid's report.

Axel Lindstroem was in his element. The bureaucratic injustice buster had a bureaucratic injustice of European, even planetary, proportions to bust, and he was just the man to do it.

By twelve thirty, Axel Lindstroem had sent a message to all the important Swedish and foreign media representatives in Stockholm. It stated that Professor Lindstroem would hold a news conference in a university theater at five o'clock, concerning 'an injustice of the gravest nature, involving the European Space Agency and the Mars mission'.

By one o'clock, the Ministry of Justice in Stockholm had a copy of the damning evidence. By two o'clock, the Ministry of Justice in every capital city of the European Union each had one as well. By two thirty, the Director of the European Space Agency, Roger Riddleby, also had a copy.

The European media knew that a press conference, involving Axel Lindstroem, ESA, and Mars, meant that a very big stink was in the works. They descended on Stockholm by plane, train, car, bus, and ferry. And a very big stink it was. The theater was packed. Representatives of the American media giants were there too.

The audience sat stunned, as the professor came on stage and began presenting the compelling evidence, displayed on a large video screen. He recounted recent events on Mars as they had actually happened, not as the media had been misled into believing and reporting. He went on at length, revealing deception after deception. It was the impossible situation, he maintained, and the need to reveal the truth, that had forced Astrid Larsson and Donald Carruthers, whose integrity could not be questioned, to resign from ESA.

He then questioned the management of the Mars mission at ESA. Obviously, he told the astonished audience, only a deep seated corruption could have led to this.

He ended by urging the media to ferret out everyone involved, and press for a thorough investigation. He maintained that the public had a right to know which ESA and E.U. officials knew what, and when they knew it.

When he finished, before he could take any questions, the Prime Minister of Sweden appeared on the stage. He was anxious to deflect any criticism from the Swedish Government, and prevent Axel Lindstroem from getting all the credit for exposing these wrong doings.

The Prime Minister had an important announcement. Sweden and his Government were appalled by the revelations, he said. He was personally shocked that Astrid Larsson had felt forced to resign from ESA. He was therefore announcing that Sweden would do likewise. Sweden had no option but to withdraw from participation in the European Space Agency, until such times as the current corruption in the agency was rooted out.

*

That Tuesday evening, the revelations in Stockholm reverberated across Europe. The continent was in an uproar.

At six o'clock, fearing a riot in Paris, the French Justice Ministry, with the approval of the European Court of Justice, announced that it was dropping the charges against Denise Lavoisier, John Erway, and Ichiro Sato.

At seven o'clock, Roger Riddleby held a news conference near Toulouse, in the building where Mission Control was housed. Because the bulk of the important European media representatives were in Stockholm, he did not get anywhere near as many embarrassing questions afterward as he otherwise would have. He acted decisively nonetheless.

First, he announced an inquiry into the conduct of high level ESA officials connected with the Mars mission. Then he declared that he now had no choice but to order the ESA Mars mission to return to Earth at once.

He tactfully omitted the fact that the mission would have to leave Mars anyway, since it would shortly have no food, nor any means of getting any, other than the food on board the mother ship.

He went on to say that ESA was not accepting the resignations of Astrid Larsson and Donald Carruthers for the time being, even though they were legal. He expressed his hope that the two would reconsider, and return to Earth with the rest of the mission.

Finally, he expressed his sorrow and regret at the way the ESA mission had treated the three in Leaf Valley. He hoped that they would accept what was left behind by the mission, especially the two Mars buggies, as compensation.

Shortly after, Mission Control transmitted a message from the ESA chief to Captain Derk. The message informed him that the E.U. had dropped all charges against the three in Leaf Valley, and ordered the ESA mission to return to Earth at once. This message reached the habitat on Elbow Plain at eight o'clock on Wednesday evening, local time, as the moon Phobos rose above Stem Mountains.

*

The financial world, not just in Europe, but in the United States, was in an uproar too. Following the precipitous market slides on Red Friday, at the end of the previous week, there had been a small rebound in confidence over the weekend. Then there had come the news on Monday that Derk's forces had recaptured the three, and had scheduled their immediate return to Earth, leaving the way open for the immense copper venture to go ahead. This had triggered a strong rally, and by Monday's close, share prices had recovered about sixty percent of Friday's losses. On Tuesday morning, they were set to recover the rest, once the three were off the planet.

But that morning in Europe, faint whispers filtered on to the floors of the major stock exchanges, followed by news of Axel Lindstroem's new conference, and the markets fell broadly all day. The declines were most severe in companies directly or indirectly involved in any aspect of exploiting the Martian copper bonanza.

Luckily, the European markets were already closed when Axel Lindstroem began his news conference in Stockholm. Not so in New York. In the hour after the New York Stock Exchange opened, the market fell to just above the low of Red Friday, and held there until mid morning, eleven o'clock, which was five in the afternoon in Stockholm.

But then, as the news came in from the Stockholm news conference, panic set in. Prices dropped at a steadily increasing pace for the rest of the day. The sell-off easily took out Friday's lows, with a far bigger percentage drop and point drop. That day was known thereafter as Red Tuesday.

*

That Wednesday morning on Mars, Tuesday on Earth, John drove down to Stem Gap, arriving just before eight, and drove up the escarpment to the left for a few hundred feet. He stopped, looked out to the west and southwest, and surveyed the road across Elbow Plain through field glasses. No sign of activity. He drove home at once.

The five then spent the day working, tending the neglected greenhouses and garden, and preparing the Japanese habitat for being lived in again. John was back down at Stem Gap around six, as the sun was setting, but still found no sign of anyone on the road across the plain. He was back home just before seven.

At nine o'clock, a call came in from Jurgen Eindorf. John and Denise took the call in the communications room.

Jurgen wanted to tell them that the charges against them had been dropped, and that the ESA mission had been ordered back to Earth at once. Captain Derk had placed Jurgen in charge of the mission until after the launch.

Derk, apparently, was currently suffering from some kind of severe depression. He had not been seen out of his cubicle since he had received the recall order an hour earlier, and was no longer interested in command. Jurgen had decided to launch at the first window next day, at eight minutes after nine.

Jurgen also expressed his regrets at the way the E.U. mission had treated John, his family, and Dr. Sato. He ended by informing John that the ESA buggies were now theirs in compensation, together with some computers and other equipment the mission would leave behind.

John, suspicious of some further cunning scheme on Derk's part, wanted to know where the missing nanogun was. Jurgen assured him that he had not seen it. He had been in the Captain's cubicle an hour earlier, and he had not seen it there.

Jurgen then asked to speak with Don and Astrid. At that, John and Denise withdrew from the communications room, and fetched the surprised pair.

Later that evening, as all five sat in the living room drinking tea, Don said that he had expected Jurgen to try and persuade them to return to the mission. Instead, Jurgen had only wanted to know how they were being treated. In the end, he had simply wished them good luck. The other members of the mission, except Emma and Karl, had then joined in the conversation, and they had exchanged final expressions of good luck and good-bye.

The four, with Dr. Sato listening, talked on for a while about the ESA mission members.

"I know you're very wary of Jose and Monique," said Don, "but actually they're both decent people. You have to forgive them their military training. They'll obey orders, but I'm certain that neither Jose nor Monique would ever have obeyed an order to do something criminal. They drew the line there. I don't think either Karl or Emma ever did."

"You mean Karl and Emma were brought along in case Derk needed some real dirty work done," said John.

"Probably," admitted Don. "But neither of those two have Jose's guts. Jose's tough. He's the kind of person you want to have with you when you're in a jam. Monique's good too. We found that out the day we got lost in the labyrinth."

"I got to know Jose quite well," said John. "I agree he's a tough one, but I can't forget that evening four of them came into this house with their guns, tied us all up, with the kids screaming their heads off. The memory of that's still a bit too strong for me to think any good of him."

"Actually, Jose was bluffing that night," said Astrid. "I talked to him about it next evening. He was sore at you for making them walk all the way back to the habitat. He told me that when they broke in here that evening, they had empty magazines in their guns. He said he was afraid of an accident, and did not want to be responsible for any of you getting hurt. So he ordered the other three to empty the magazines in their pistols before they came in here. He was most worried about Karl and Emma. He thought those two might be a bit trigger happy, get carried away, and maybe shoot one of you in the heat of the action."

"I know," admitted John. "We found that out later, when we collected their guns. Everybody's been bluffing in this little war. But when we escaped and captured the four of them, our guns were loaded."

"And he knew that," said Astrid. "You scared the life out of him. For a while he really did think you were crazy enough to shoot them, although he changed his mind when he got back to the habitat safely, with only sore feet."

"Well, at least all the guns are accounted for now," said John, "except that one Derk has. It bothers me. My gut tells me he's planning to use it."

*

It was a few seconds before 9.08 the following morning. Two rovers sat in the morning sunshine that Thursday, a few hundred feet up the escarpment, on the east side of Stem Gap. John, Denise, and the two children were in the front seats of one rover. Dr. Sato, Astrid, and Don were in the front seats of the other rover. The adults were all staring through field glasses at the landing pit, some ten miles away, except for Astrid, who was recording with a video camera.

There was no wind that morning, and they could already see smoke and dust billowing vertically from the landing pit. John knew that Jurgen would be precise, and was doing the count down in his mind ... *three, two, one, zero, lift off.*

Suddenly, the lander burst out the billowing smoke, all six rocket cylinders flaming. Straight up it went, gleaming in the morning sunshine. It was a perfect launch. Then the silvery space vehicle began curving toward the southeast and the plane of the ecliptic, still climbing, all six engine clusters still flaming. It was the first launch of a manned vehicle from Mars.

Jurgen sure knows his stuff, thought John, as he watched in awe. John did not have the skills to have taken that machine up. He was glad though, that he and his family were not on board.

Nobody was prepared for what happened next, neither the five watching on the Red Planet, nor the millions watching on the Blue Planet. People on Earth could watch the launch, for Jurgen had placed video cameras just outside the habitat. Each camera covered a section of the launch trajectory, and was linked to the habitat communications room, which in turn was linked via the Mars communications satellite to Mission Control in Toulouse.

Inside the lander, Richard Derk sat stretched out in his almost horizontal seat. The seat was designed to limit the impact of powerful G-forces caused by the rocket's acceleration on launch. Unlike those on the floor below, Captain Derk was not wearing a pressure suit as a precaution. He was alone on the upper personnel floor. The others were below, on the lower personnel floor.

Derk's feelings were those he had been experiencing for the past twenty-fours hours. He was in a state of severe emotional torture. He could not face the failure and disgrace, and the inevitable criminal charges to be laid against him. He could not bear the pain of the total loss of standing, esteem and prestige he had suffered, and would go on suffering, as long as he lived, a complete reversal of all he had striven for and lusted after. His ego had fallen off a precipice. There was only one course open to him that would preserve some vestige of his prestige on Earth. He felt some relief at the prospect of taking that path. It would be easy for him to follow it.

Five seconds into the flight, he just managed to lift the nanogun lying across his thighs. The G-force on the accelerating lander gave it a weight some five times its normal weight on Mars, twice its weight on Earth. Earlier, he had programmed the range of eight meters into the nanocomputer inside the bullet in the firing chamber. That was the exact distance from the Captain's seat to the center of the rocket-motor cylinder attached to the outside of the hull, opposite where he sat.

He aimed at the hull, at a point just above the floor, and pulled the trigger. The nanobullet penetrated the hull, and exploded inside the rocket-motor cylinder, at a point between its fuel and oxidizer tanks, badly puncturing both tanks. A few seconds later, the cylinder exploded. All five watching at Stem Gap saw the rocket cylinder explode, and Astrid captured the explosion on video.

The bulk of the crippled lander survived the initial explosion reasonably intact. But now, the propulsion forces awry, the remaining five rocket motor clusters caused the lander's trajectory to curve toward the northeast.

Barely two seconds later, in quick succession, there came four more explosions, each pair a tiny fraction of a second apart, as four more of the rocket cylinders exploded.

A huge exploding fireball engulfed the lander. Then, the sixth rocket cylinder, detached but still intact, shot out of the fireball, flying erratically, toward the east. Two seconds later it exploded too.

Gradually the fireball dissipated, and a rain of smoking debris now curved back down towards Mars, each piece of debris with its own parabolic trajectory, still headed northeast. It nearly all came down along a three-mile stretch of the floor of Snakepit Crack.

The bodies would never be recovered. In time, Mars would bury them under the accumulations of sand and dust that often blew over the edges of the precipices forming the sides of the immense rupture in the floor of western Kasei Valley.

*

About an hour after the explosion, John drove his rover up the ridge road to the former ESA habitat on the shelf at Elbow hill.

Denise and John were feeling very bad, shocked at the horror they had just witnessed. Denise had wept, and was still sobbing. The children beside her were quiet, sensing something very wrong. Denise had not had the heart to explain to them that the lady they had liked, Ursula Schneider, had just been killed in front of their eyes.

John had intended to drive over to the habitat after the launch, to see what had been left behind, to assess if it needed any repairs, and to try to come to some decision about what to do with the building. After the explosion he had decided to stick with his plan. If nothing else, it might help them get over the shock.

As they drove up the ridge road, nothing unusual met their eyes, except an array of video cameras on the shelf just outside the long building. But then, as they drove onto the broad shelf, they got the surprise of their lives. Four figures in ESA pressure suits walked out from behind the north end of the building. Each of them had a hand in the air. They were all unarmed.

"We saw you coming," explained the one in the lead, in a German accent, "and came out to say hello. Four of us decided to stay behind. We tentatively decided last night, but came to a final decision only this morning. The Captain ... he did not know that we were not on board."

It was Jurgen speaking, and the others were Ursula, Jose, and Monique. For the second time in less than two days, John and Denise were so surprised they could hardly speak.

"But…" said John.

"Sorry to give you a surprise like this," said Jurgen, "but, as I said, we did not know for sure until this morning. Astrid's message about everything that had been going on, and about your ideas for a settlement of free people on Mars, was a big factor in our decision to stay on. We have all grown to like being on Mars as well. When faced with having to go back, we found it very hard to accept. We would like to join your settlement. Will you have us?"

Denise was the first to recover, her former sorrow suddenly converted to a great joy.

"Of course we'll have you," said Denise. "We have a few conditions though, which should not present any difficulty. Perhaps Astrid told you about them."

"You mean about being willing to buy some land, and have our own homes, and produce independently? That kind of thing?"

"Yes."

"We would be willing to settle for the same deal Don and Astrid got," said Jurgen. The others nodded as he said this.

"You would, would you?" said John, now beginning to get his mind around yet another change in their circumstances. "Well, we've a further rule. Look, this isn't Earth, and it's a very dangerous place. It makes things a lot easier and safer if we have couples."

"Are you suggesting that ... I marry Ursula, and Jose marries Monique?" asked Jurgen.

"As I told Don, you don't get a choice about things like that on Mars," said John. "Yes, that's exactly what I meant. Wedding bells."

"And the settlement needs children," said Denise, "if it's to prosper in the long run. So our rule makes sense, at least for a while."

"Well, how about it?" said John, noticing a certain discomfort among the four.

"I am willing," said Jose, suddenly, "if Monique will have me. I would not like to live here without her."

"I will have him," said Monique. "And Jose and I would just like to say sorry for roughing you up last week."

At this, neither John nor Denise said anything. It was still a very sore point with John, and with Denise too.

"I should add that we were tried and sentenced by your court, and did the time for the crime," pointed out Jose, noticing John's frown. "We did the seven-hour walk down Leaf Valley. So now we would ask you to consider the slate as wiped clean, so that we can start over on friendly terms."

John reacted to this speech immediately. "You have a point there, Jose," he said. Then he laughed. "What the hell. Welcome on board."

Then he looked at Ursula and Jurgen, who seemed to have come to a decision.

"I will gladly marry Jurgen," said Ursula.

"As you say, John, you do not get any choice on Mars," said Jurgen. "But I will be very happy to marry Ursula."

"Wonderful," said Denise. "Now we can have three weddings next Saturday."

"By the way, Jurgen," said John. "What went wrong with the lander?"

"I do not know for sure," said Jurgen, looking very serious, "but before the first explosion there was no indication of anything wrong. I do not think it was a system failure."

"Did you ever find that missing nanogun?"

"No, and it is not in the habitat," said Jurgen. "You can check it out yourself."

"You think Derk took it with him?"

"There is no other explanation," said Jurgen.

"Which would explain everything."

Jurgen just nodded. None of the four had any regrets about not going on that lander. An instinct had warned all of them that Derk could not be trusted.

"We had been expecting that Astrid and Don would come over here with you this morning," said Jose. "Where are they?"

"Grieving for you four," said Denise. "They were in such a state that Dr. Sato thought he should take them home. They're going to get a pleasant surprise soon. Have you told Mission Control you weren't on that lander? A lot of people in Europe must be feeling pretty sick."

"Yes, I have," said Jurgen. "Mission Control will have the message by now, along with our resignations from ESA."

"Well, I suppose we had better go out and take a look at the habitat," said John, standing up. "We were wondering about whether or not we should just let it sit here, or move it back to Leaf Valley. Now there's no doubt, we have to move it, if you all agree. With so many hands here now, we can get it moved in a few days. You're going to need it to live in until you can get permanent homes built. You'll have plenty of space. One pair of you could have the entire science section, and the other could have the command section, if you want. Don and Astrid are getting our Japanese habitat. And there's lots of scope for knocking out cubicle partitions, to give yourselves some decent size rooms."

"We have to build more greenhouses before we build permanent homes," said Denise. "Food has to get top priority."

"I want a home like yours," said Ursula. "I've never been inside, but I've heard all about it."

"Maybe you should talk to Astrid first," said John. "She mentioned this morning that she had come up with a design that solves the problem of dust falling on the glass and blocking the light. It's a real pain having go up and clean it off."

"I'd like a nice garden home too," said Monique, "although I could do without having to dust the roof every so often."

"See what you've let yourselves in for," said John, looking at Jurgen and Jose, and still standing up in the driver area of the rover, "nothing but work. And for starters, we should start moving the habitat today."

"But before we start with the habitat," said Denise, "let's all go back home and have our first lunch together, and have our first round table discussion too, about how to get things moving."

"Suits me" said John, sitting down again. "It's a while since I had a relaxed lunch. Come on, guys. You're coming home with us."

An hour later, all nine settlers and the two children were having lunch on the patio in the compound at Mount Tip. The atmosphere was euphoric. There was so much to talk about. If any of the ESA six had any remaining doubts as to the correctness of what they had decided, that first lunch dispelled them, as the realization that they had signed on to the construction of a whole new world sank in.

They found it easy to agree on an initial plan of action, and early that afternoon, a convoy of vehicles poured out through Stem Gap, headed across Elbow Plain toward Elbow Hill. There were two rovers and three buggies, their trailers loaded with tools and equipment. One of the buggies was towing the minicat.

It was back to work as usual on Mars, or so it seemed, and the former ESA habitat at Elbow Hill would be back inside Leaf Valley before the sun set. And John, his call to arms seemingly now in the past, was back in his element again, doing what he preferred to do.

John had learned that nobody can be good at everything, and that generalship was not his calling. He understood now, with hindsight, all the things a good general would have done differently.

By that evening, they had elected John as leader, with Jose and Monique as his advisors on the defense of the settlement, and had agreed to devote some man hours each week to defensive measures.

Within a few days, following recommendations from Jose and Monique, they had cratered the ESA landing pit in Elbow Plain with explosives, and had started building the first defensive fortifications at Stem Gap. Never again would an enemy find it easy to land, and capture and imprison the inhabitants of Leaf Valley.

Although the settlers were not aware of it at the time, these defensive measures may have been the deciding factor in the final episode of the early struggle for Leaf Valley. For unbeknownst to those euphoric settlers, a growing threat was circling above, silently working its way into final orbit—the secret U.S. military mission. The President of the United States had only to give the word, and that mission would land, and launch an attack on the settlement.

*

Three days after the loss of the ESA lander, there were funeral services for Vince Cassoni, whose body lay at the bottom of Snakepit Crack, and for the three who had died in the lander explosion, whose bodies also lay in Snakepit Crack. The nine on Mars built a huge cairn, with a plaque and a copper cross on top, to the memory of Vince, beside the fissure that had killed him. They also put up three cairns with plaques and crosses to the memory of Derk, Emma, and Karl, beside the road on the opposite side of Snakepit Crack, adjacent to where the explosion debris had come down.

Of the twelve who had arrived on Mars a month earlier, six were now dead on Mars, and four of the remaining six had narrowly escaped with their lives, one of them twice.

*

The following Tuesday morning, August 11, six days after the loss of the ESA lander, a tense American President was presiding over a secret meeting in the War Room below the West Wing.

The President sat at a large curved table, with his military chiefs on either side. There was a huge map of the Leaf Valley region on a wide-perspective wall screen in front of them.

The only item on the agenda was the U.S. military Mars mission. It's mother ship was now in final orbit around Mars, with a Mars lander attached. The ship had reached Mars only seven days earlier, the day before the ESA lander had exploded on launch.

No one on Mars, or in ESA, was aware of this secret mission. John and Denise knew only that they were to prepare for a surprise.

"A few days earlier and we'd have been the cavalry, coming to the rescue in the nick of time," sighed the Secretary of Defense.

"Yes, and they'd have brought our lander down inside Leaf Valley," said the President, "and welcomed us with open arms."

"And we'd have taken it without firing a shot," said the Chairman of the Joint Chiefs.

"You're certain they wouldn't let us land in Leaf Valley now?" asked the President, looking at his CIA Director.

"Dead certain," said the CIA chief. "There isn't even a chance of a landing site in Elbow Plain. They've cratered the ESA landing site. And the habitat is already back inside Leaf Valley."

"And if we just try to land on our own," said the Air Force Joint Chief, "there's a risk of an accident. We need flat ground and landing beacons for a safe landing. And flat ground for the launch later. Same problem the ESA people had."

"There's a chance we could persuade them to build us a landing site somewhere else—on sheltered, flat ground, with landing beacons," said the CIA Director. "Maybe near the old NASA landing site. What if we try for that?"

"It would mean a long buggy journey just to get to where we could mount an assault on the valley," said the Chairman of the Joint Chiefs, making a dismissive gesture with his right hand. "And don't forget they've got eight people now, leaving out the old man, and nanoguns. That means we'd find every entrance to the valley defended. They've got the manpower and weapons to do it."

"What about those fortifications they seem to be putting up at Stem Gap?" asked the Defense Secretary. "Looks to me like they're preparing for another invasion."

"That's how it looks to me too," said the Chairman, folding his arms. "They're turning the damned place into a fortress. The worst thing is those nanoguns. We'd have ten people out in two buggies. One nanogun bullet could take them both out. Those nanoguns were made for war on Mars. And we didn't bring any. None of us ever anticipated we'd be up against eight smart people with nanoguns, two of them trained military personnel."

"Even so, couldn't our ten Special Forces boys match the eight on their side?" asked the President.

"Maybe yesterday," replied the Chairman, "but not tomorrow. Both Montoya and Montpellier are first class. They're experts at nanogun tactics, and could train the others very quickly. The odds of our mission succeeding in an attack on that settlement are very low. Our boys really don't have a chance against an enemy with nanoguns. And a very smart enemy. Plenty of brain power. Plenty of experience on Martian terrain too, which we don't have."

"They'd also have the strategic high ground," pointed out the Marine Corps Chief of Staff, "behind a fortified position. And we know they can make pretty powerful landmines."

The Chairman of the Joint Chiefs did not respond. He seemed wrapped in thought, one hand holding his chin, as if far away on a battlefield. Then he said: "Even if we did succeed, it would likely be at the expense of heavy casualties on both sides."

There was silence, as they all considered this bloody scenario.

"So we'd end up with egg all over our faces too, just like the Europeans," said the President eventually, "right before the election. I prefer the Europeans with the egg on their faces."

"But even if the odds of military success favored us, it would still be very hard for us to attack them," added the President. "They have the moral high ground. They're super heroes now, after the fight they put up against the ESA mission, not to mention those two rescues. If we attacked, we'd look very bad in the eyes of the world, and in the eyes of most Americans too. Is there any other option we haven't considered? Any way we could still succeed?"

"Mr. President," said the Chairman of the Joint Chiefs, his arms folded again. "There are plenty of ways we could do much worse, and look as bad as the Europeans. There's one way we can neither win nor loose—the neutral option. But there's no option that gives us a reasonable chance of a military success. We just did not foresee these circumstances."

"The neutral option being to simply keep quiet about this Air Force mission, I suppose," said the President, "and just bring the boys home, and be thankful that it worked out in such a way that the U.S. wasn't humiliated."

"That's right."

"There's just one thing that bothers me with that," said the Secretary of Defense. "They're bound to get stronger with time—from a military point of view. I'll bet they'll have artillery before the the next opposition. They've got the brains and the industrial plant. Nothing starts an arms build-up as quick as a near defeat."

The President nodded in agreement, but said nothing.

There was now a long silence. The issues had been discussed. Everything was on the table. It was the President who had to decide. Was there to be yet another small war over land on Mars?

*

It was two days later, Thursday on Earth, and just before nine o'clock on Mars, on the morning of Friday, Beta-October 18.

Two rovers and a buggy sat on the east side of Kumar Hills. The vehicles were facing east, toward the old NASA landing site, a few miles away. In the distance, the pockmarked escarpment wall of Funnyface Mesa was clearly visible in the morning sunlight.

The three vehicles were about two hundred feet above the floor of the valley. John, Denise, and Dr. Sato sat in the front of one rover. Jurgen, Astrid, and Don sat in the other rover. Jose and Monique were in the buggy. Ursula had stayed home with the children.

Each of them, except Dr. Sato, had an automatic rifle and a nanogun, and knew how to use them. Jose and Monique had conducted training exercises the previous evening.

They all had field glasses focussed on a slowly descending lander. It was already low enough to make out that it was similar to the ESA lander in design, except that each of its six rocket cylinders had a cluster of four rocket motors. Radar beacons were guiding the lander down, with only three of the six rocket cylinders firing.

John, helped by Jurgen and Jose, had spent the previous day bulldozing the floor of an old shallow crater to prepare a landing pit. The crater, whose rim was almost completely eroded away, was similar in size to the one John had picked for a landing pit in Elbow Plain. It lay on the valley floor below, a mile east of the three vehicles.

The previous Wednesday evening, John, helped by Jose, had negotiated the landing site with the CIA, after being informed that the surprise they were expecting would be a lander, that would arrive on Friday morning. When informed that the lander was bearing gifts from the people of the United States, everyone had been elated.

However, when the CIA refused to say exactly what kind of lander it was, that elation soon gave way to suspicion, especially on the part of Denise, Monique, and Jose. As a result, Jose had recommended a landing site no nearer than the old NASA landing site.

When the CIA then agreed to the NASA landing site, Jose was still wary. He argued strongly for a landing site some two miles from the old NASA landing site, but only about a mile from Kumar Hills, and John had seen the sense in this. Ever the military man, Jose suspected a trap. He wanted to monitor the landing from high ground on the hillside, within nanogun range of the lander, just in case.

That sunny morning, the lander was in full view, hovering above the landing pit, about a mile away. It was a spectacular sight, its rocket motors blasting long jets of orange flame downward, but that was not what John was focussed on.

"My God!" he cried. "You were right about being cautious, Jose. That's a personnel lander, not a supply vessel. Look at those view ports." Two rows of view ports pointed to two personnel floors, with a cargo floor beneath, just like with the ESA lander.

"It's got a military look about it too." said Denise nervously, as the vessel finally disappeared into the landing pit, in a cloud of red dust. The spacecraft was painted in the oranges, browns, and grays of a military vehicle intended for desert warfare. The mystery lander had no other markings. It was obviously not a NASA spacecraft.

"It has to be a military machine," said Jose, lowering his outdoors field glasses, and looking very worried. "And if there are people on board, they have to be military. God only knows what weaponry they might have, or what they intend. Sorry everybody, but I have to recommend we get in military mode, at once."

John, very concerned, and horrified at the thought of being attacked by hostile Americans, needed no persuasion. In minutes, their vehicles were under cover, well separated along the slope, about a hundred meters apart. In another few minutes, they were all outside, each of them, except the Zen master, carrying a nanogun. They spread out along the slope, along a line about fifty meters in front of their hidden vehicles, and took cover. The Zen master stayed further back, higher up, also under cover, observing intently.

For the next hour, they patiently monitored the landing pit through outdoors field glasses, but saw nothing unusual. There was no sign of any life emerging from the lander.

"If it's a Trojan Horse, they're not supposed to come out till after dark," observed Denise at last.

"I wonder," said Monique. "Trojan Horses appear in the afternoon for that reason, not the morning."

"But the CIA insisted on an early morning landing," said John. "This is very strange. If it's not a Trojan Horse, why would they use a military personnel lander to send us supplies?"

"Perhaps some of us should go over and investigate," suggested Jurgen. "What do you think, Jose?"

"No, too risky," said Jose. "They could have a trap waiting for us. Curiosity is a weakness. Remember, that was what defeated the Trojans. There is actually no need for us to do anything. We can just sit here. Unfortunately, so can they—if their lander is well provisioned. It could easily be a habitat and lander rolled into one."

"So you recommend we just wait them out?" said John.

"Yes, at least till we find out what firepower they have."

"That makes sense," said John.

"How long?" asked Denise, thinking about her children.

"God knows," said Jose.

They went back to waiting and watching, keeping under cover. But ten minutes later, suddenly, Dr. Sato, driving the buggy, went shooting across their line of defense, right between John and Jose.

"They can do no harm to an old man whose life is of little consequence," said the Zen master, as he drove past. "This way you'll find out what's over there without risk to any of you."

Everyone was shocked, but John was first to respond.

"That's the second time in two weeks you said that," he called after him. Then he added. "Your life may not be of any consequence to you, but it's of very great consequence to us. Please come back!"

Dr. Sato took no notice, and drove on down the rough slope.

"Somebody had better get in a rover and keep in contact with him," suggested Jose, as the buggy reached the valley floor.

"I'll do it," volunteered Astrid.

A few minutes later she was back inside a rover, which she drove forward a little, to where she could just see over a low ridge in front. Five minutes later, she watched the Zen master's buggy climb over the shallow rim of the landing crater, and disappear down inside.

"Any sign of life, Dr. Sato?" she asked, before he disappeared.

"No, none at all," came the Zen master's response.

The rover's wide radio range allowed the six out on the slope to talk to Astrid, and to hear the exchange with the Zen master.

"Do you think he'll be able to get inside on his own, John, if there's nobody there?" asked Astrid, a few minutes later.

"If anybody can, he can," said John. "He could cut that lander up into tiny pieces. He has all the tools he needs in the trailer. He once cut up two big Japanese landers all on his own."

They continued to wait and watch, tense and worried. Then, twelve minutes later, Dr. Sato's buggy reappeared on the crater rim.

"You won't be needing your guns," the Zen master announced, in his usual quiet voice. "There are only supplies on board—two big five-seater buggies, pressure suits, power plants, and a lot of other things, and a message of good will from the President of the United States. The CIA told the truth. Come over and see for yourselves. There are some bottles of California wine in—"

The rest was drowned out, as everyone jumped up, arms waving in the air, guns cast aside, in a spontaneous eruption of cheers and shouts of elation.

*

It was Thursday evening, more than ten hours after the Air Force lander had come down on Mars. The historic news conference about the event, held in the spacious East Room of the White House, had gone on until just after dark.

Afterward, the CIA director accompanied the President, as they walked in silence along a hallway, on their way back to the West Wing. The President was tired, after the seemingly endless stream of questions about the surprise landing on Mars. The media still knew nothing about the secret military mother ship, which had already left Mars orbit, headed for Earth. But the news conference had been a success, and both men now felt that things had gone a lot better for the U.S. than the worst that could have happened.

The President stopped at a window that looked out to the south. The Red Planet was easily visible, the brightest object in the sky.

"I look out at that planet sometimes," he said. "It's hard to believe how much money's been spent on it."

"And the only result so far is a successful settlement on Mars that thumbs its nose at the superpowers on Earth, and gets away with it," said the CIA chief.

"Yes," said the President. "It looks like we're going to have to accept their ownership of that part of Mars, for now at any rate. They possess it and can defend it. In practice, that means they own it, no matter what the U.N. Mars Office says."

They were silent a while, as they walked on. Then the President remarked: "You know, that planet puzzles me. It's like a big red sponge. Nothing that lands on it ever seems to come back. No human has ever walked on Mars and come back to Earth. It seems to turn people's heads once they get there. Must be quite a place."

"Yes, it either kills you or converts you, it seems," said the CIA chief.

"You know," said the President, "I didn't want to bring it up on Tuesday, with the brass present, but I was worried about our boys getting bitten by the Mars bug too. They could easily have handed in their resignations, and joined the settlement."

"The thought had crossed my mind," admitted his CIA friend. "Ordering them home was the right thing to do. And if I may say so, that was one great idea you came up with—letting the settlement have the lander as a good-will gesture, I mean."

"It didn't cost us anything," said the President. "We'd have had to jettison the lander anyway. It was too heavy to haul back, with its big heat shield and all. Using it for good will made the most sense. Maybe it'll help us do a copper deal with them some day."

"And maybe that's something we should get working on," said the CIA chief. "By the way, there was something else I thought it was better not to bring up at the meeting on Tuesday."

"What was that?"

"What's going on in that laboratory they built some years back."

"Have you found out?"

"No, not for sure, but from their patterns of database access...we've narrowed it down to only a few possibilities. One of them would not go down very well here on Earth, I'm afraid, if it turned out to be the one they're working on."

"Will you have a report for me soon?"

"We need to do more work before we'd have anything you could act on. I can't feed you speculation."

"Then you'd better keep at it," said the President.

"We intend to."

"The other thing that puzzles me is how that man Derk managed to screw it up so badly," said the President. "He certainly had everything going for him. A brilliant strategic brain, the latest weapons, the settlers completely outnumbered, and our mission still millions of miles out in space, unable to touch him."

"I've thought about that," said the CIA chief. "Took me a while, but finally I understood his mistake. It's a mistake as old as the hills. Shakespeare understood it too."

"Shakespeare? Tell me," said the President. "We don't want to make it ourselves."

The CIA chief took a sheet of folded paper from his inside jacket pocket, and handed it to the President. The President opened it and read the following:

Heat not a furnace for thy foe so hot,
that it do singe thyself.

THE END

APPENDIX 1

Simplest possible Mars Calendar and Clock, as used in the novels *As It Is On Mars*, and *Give Us This Mars*.

[Things should be as simple as possible,
but not simpler - *Albert Einstein*]

Mars Clock

Mars rotates on its axis just like Earth, which gives rise to the planetary phenomenon of day and night, which we experience here on Earth too. However, Mars takes a little longer to rotate than Earth, so that a Mars day is a little longer than an Earth day.

One Martian day, or *sol*, as it is sometime called, lasts 24 hours, 39 minutes, and 35.238 seconds. A Mars day is thus about 2% longer than an Earth day. This gives Martian clock designers a few problems.

Some people have proposed a new second for use on Mars, about 2% longer than a second on Earth. That way, you could keep the convenience of a 24-hour day on Mars, each hour having sixty minutes, and each minute having sixty seconds, as usual. This is impractical, unfortunately, because the second is a deeply embedded unit in all kinds of engineering and scientific units of measure.

Accordingly, there is no choice but to live with a Martian day almost 40 minutes longer than 24 hours.

A Mars clock or watch will therefore run until 24:39:35 at night, or 12:39:35 at night (close to 12:40), at which instant the time reverts to 0:00 of the next day. Thirty minutes later its is 0:30, or zero thirty in the morning, or half past zero. After another hour, it is 01:30, or one thirty in the morning.

Twelve hours after midnight (at 0:00), it is 12:00 in the morning, but not quite midday. Midday is at almost 12:20, at 12:19:48, to be precise. Nothing unusual happens at this point, and time just increases through the afternoon and evening, until midnight at 24:39:35, when it abruptly reverts again to 0:00, or zero hours.

From all this, it can be seen that a clock or watch must be specially designed for use on Mars, the difference being those nearly 40 minutes just after 24:00 hours, or twelve in the evening.

Days of the week on Mars

The days of the week in the Mars calendar used in the novels have the same names as the days of the week in the Gregorian calendar for Earth, namely Monday, Tuesday, etc.

To start things out, since January 01, 2000 is a Saturday on Earth, and since that day is also Alpha-January 01 on Mars, that day on Mars is designated as a Saturday too.

Now, since Earth local time runs ahead of Mars local time by almost 40 minutes each day, and therefore by a whole day every thirty seven Earth days, on any given date, the day of the week on Earth will not necessarily be the same as that on Mars.

Thus, for example, when it was 4:30 in the afternoon, on Sunday, Alpha-October 14, 1089 (about the time, and the day, of the ESA landing) at the Elbow Plain landing site, it was 6:58 P.M. local (daylight savings) time, on Friday, July 10, 2048, in Washington, D.C.

This is the reason some people have proposed using different names for the days of the week on Mars. The author thinks different day of the week names for Mars are unnecessary and dangerous. You may ask yourself if you would have preferred other names for the days of the week in these novels. The author, for one, would have found that too confusing, and an easy source of error.

The Days and Months of the Martian Calendar

Mars goes around the sun just like Earth, and is similarly inclined on its axis, so we get seasons, just like on Earth. The difference is that it takes Mars almost two Earth years to go around the sun, so that a Mars year is almost twice as long as an Earth year.

To be more exact, one Martian year is 668.599 Martian days.

This means we get 23 months in the Martian year, if each of the first 22 months has 29 days, and the last month has 30 days. But that takes care of only 668 days. We have to have a leap day every second year, as well as a leap day every tenth year, to take care of the remaining 0.599 days. The last month is the leap month.

To keep things as familiar as possible in the calendar used in the novels, there are two Januaries, two Februaries, and so on, but only one December, as laid out in the table on the next page.

Note that each of the four seasons is almost twice as long as the corresponding season on Earth.

Martian Calendar data:

1 Martian day or sol has 24 hours, 39 minutes, 35.238 seconds,
or 1.02749118 Earth days.
1 Martian year has 23 Martian months.
1 Martian month has 29 Mars days, except for the last month,
which is 30 days, but 31 days in a leap year.

*Synchronization day is Saturday, Alpha-Jan 01, 1064,
which is Saturday, Jan 01, 2000.*

The Martian months:

Alpha-January: 29 days (Winter)
Beta-January: 29 days (Winter)
Alpha-February: 29 days (Winter)
Beta-February: 29 days (Winter)
Alpha-March: 29 days (Winter)
Beta-March: 29 days (Spring; ***Equinox: Beta-March 04***)
Alpha-April: 29 days (Spring)
Beta-April: 29 days (Spring)
Alpha-May: 29 days (Spring)
Beta-May: 29 days (Spring)
Alpha-June: 29 days (Spring)
Beta-June: 29 days (Spring; ***Summer Solstice: Beta-June 24***)
Alpha-July: 29 days (Summer)
Beta-July: 29 days (Summer)
Alpha-August: 29 days (Summer)
Beta-August: 29 days (Summer)
Alpha-September: 29 days (Summer)
Beta-September: 29 days (Summer; ***Fall Equinox: Beta-Sept 28***)
Alpha-October: 29 days (Fall)
Beta-October: 29 days (Fall)
Alpha-November: 29 days (Fall)
Beta-November: 29 days (Fall)
Alpha-December: 30 days (Fall; ***Winter Solstice: Alpha-Dec 25***)
(Alpha-December, the leap month, has 31 days in leap years--years ending in either an odd number or zero.)

Martian Thanksgivings (from the novel: *As It Is On Mars*):

Alpha-April 07, and Beta-October 07

Synchronization with the Gregorian Calendar.

Saturday, Alpha-Jan 01, 1064 is Saturday, Jan 01, 2000.

By a fortuitous orbital coincidence (see below), the Martian calendar on the previous page synchronizes naturally with Earth's Gregorian calendar, so that Saturday, Jan 01, 2000 Gregorian is Saturday, Alpha-Jan 01 in the equivalent Martian year of 1064.

Technically, at 00h:00m:00s Mean Solar Time at zero Martian longitude (on the Airy Meridian), that is, AMST, on Alpha-Jan 01, 1064 it is (to within a second) 20h:40m:32s UST (or GMT) on Dec 31, 1999 on Earth. Midnight at Airy-0 and midnight at Greenwich, at millennium end, are thus 3h, 19m, 28s apart. (Airy Crater is a small crater on Mars, used for the zero of longitude.)

An orbital coincidence occurred in 1999. A Mars winter solstice in the northern hemisphere occurred on Saturday, December 25, 1999. Since Alpha-December 25 is Winter Solstice day in the above Mars calendar, this gives rise to the natural synchronization. Saturday, December 25, 1999 is the same as Saturday, Alpha-December 25, 1063, and hence Saturday, January 01, 2000 corresponds to Saturday, Alpha-January, 1064.

Thus the new millennium on Earth begins with the two calendars synchronized, and we may call Jan 01, 2000 *synchronization day*. (Note that 2000 Earth years corresponds to 1064 Mars years.)

Mars years in the novels

The dramatic events that launch the story in the novel *As It Is On Mars* all take place in 2038, Gregorian, which is 1084 in the Mars calendar. Mars year 1084 actually begins in 2037 Gregorian, with Monday, Alpha-January 01, 1084 corresponding to Monday, August 13, 2037 Gregorian.

Most of the events in the novel *Give Us This Mars* take place in the summer of Gregorian 2048, which is the early fall of Mars year 1089, or 25 Mars years and about eighteen Mars months past the Earth millennium of January 01, 2000.

Mars year 1089 can also be written as M25, that is, 25 Mars years past the millennium on Earth, with M corresponding to 1064. Mars year 1064, which begins at the Earth millennium, can be written as M0. Note that if we use the more convenient M-notation for Mars years, leap years are still odd-numbered years, but also years ending in the digit 6 (1070 is M06, 1080 is M16, and so on).

APPENDIX 2: Map of Western Kasei Valley

Western Kasei Valley lies in the Northern Hemisphere on Mars, so that, most of the year, the sun is in the southern sky at midday. However, the region is close enough to the equator, between about 500 and 750 miles from it, that in midsummer the sun can be overhead. The region is thus mostly in the Martian 'tropics'. For example, the latitude and longitude location of Leaf Valley corresponds to that of eastern Cuba on Earth.

Key to Map

(Low numbers are in the north, high numbers are in the south.)

1. Hazard Valley
2. Dune Narrows; main east-west Kasei Valley channel
3. Kasei Valley channel; (road) fork north to Hazard Valley
4. Labyrinth region
5. Leaf Valley
6. Elbow Plain
7. Chiselhead Gully
8. Finger Gully
9. Chiselhead Mountain
10. Kumar Gap
11. Funnyface Mesa
12. Old NASA landing site from 2038 (marked as x). It lies a few miles east of Kumar Hills, which run north-south.

Note that the map depicts three distinct altitude levels: the high plateau level of Lunae Planum (to the east), the lower plateau level to the west (shaded), and the main Kasei Valley channel level, lowest of the three. Elbow Plain and Leaf Valley are at this lowest level.

The old NASA landing site is at the middle level, that is, at the lower plateau level. The top of Funnyface Mesa, some ten miles east of it, is at the high plateau level.

Western Kasei Valley

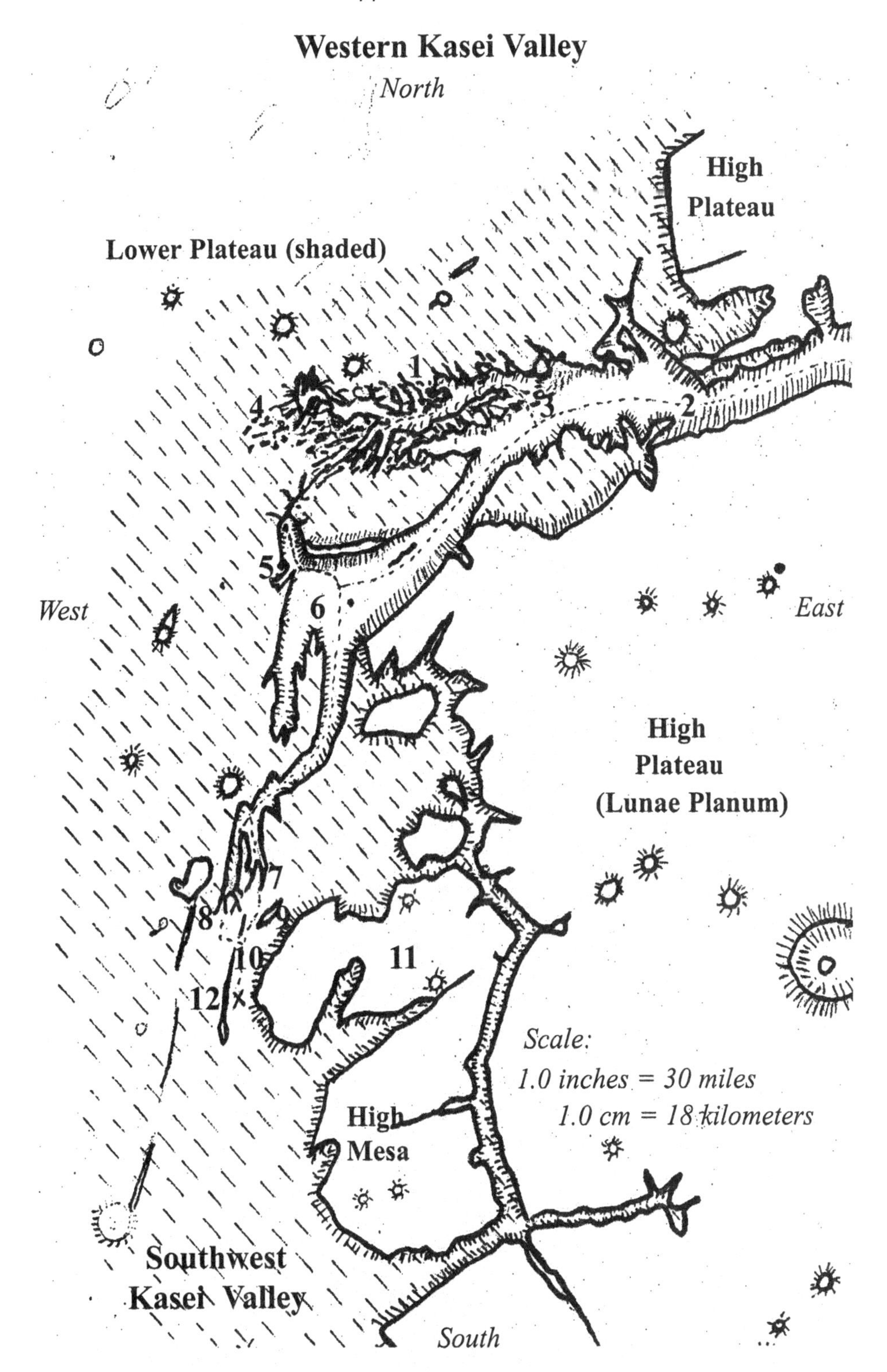

APPENDIX 3: Map of Elbow Plain Region of Kasei Valley

Key to Map

(Low numbers are in the north, high numbers are in the south.)

1. Labyrinth region
2. Tip Canyon
3. West Tip Gully
4. Mount Tip (site of the glass compound)
5. The rampart
6. Outlook Cove
7. Outlook Shelf (site of the Zen monastery)
8. Stem Gap
9. Snakepit Crack
10. Elbow Fork (road junction)
11. ESA landing site (marked as x)
12. Stem Valley
13. Stem Mountains
14. Elbow Hill (site of the ESA habitat)
15. Deadend Arm
16. Main north-south Kasei Valley channel.

Elbow Plain Region of Kasei Valley

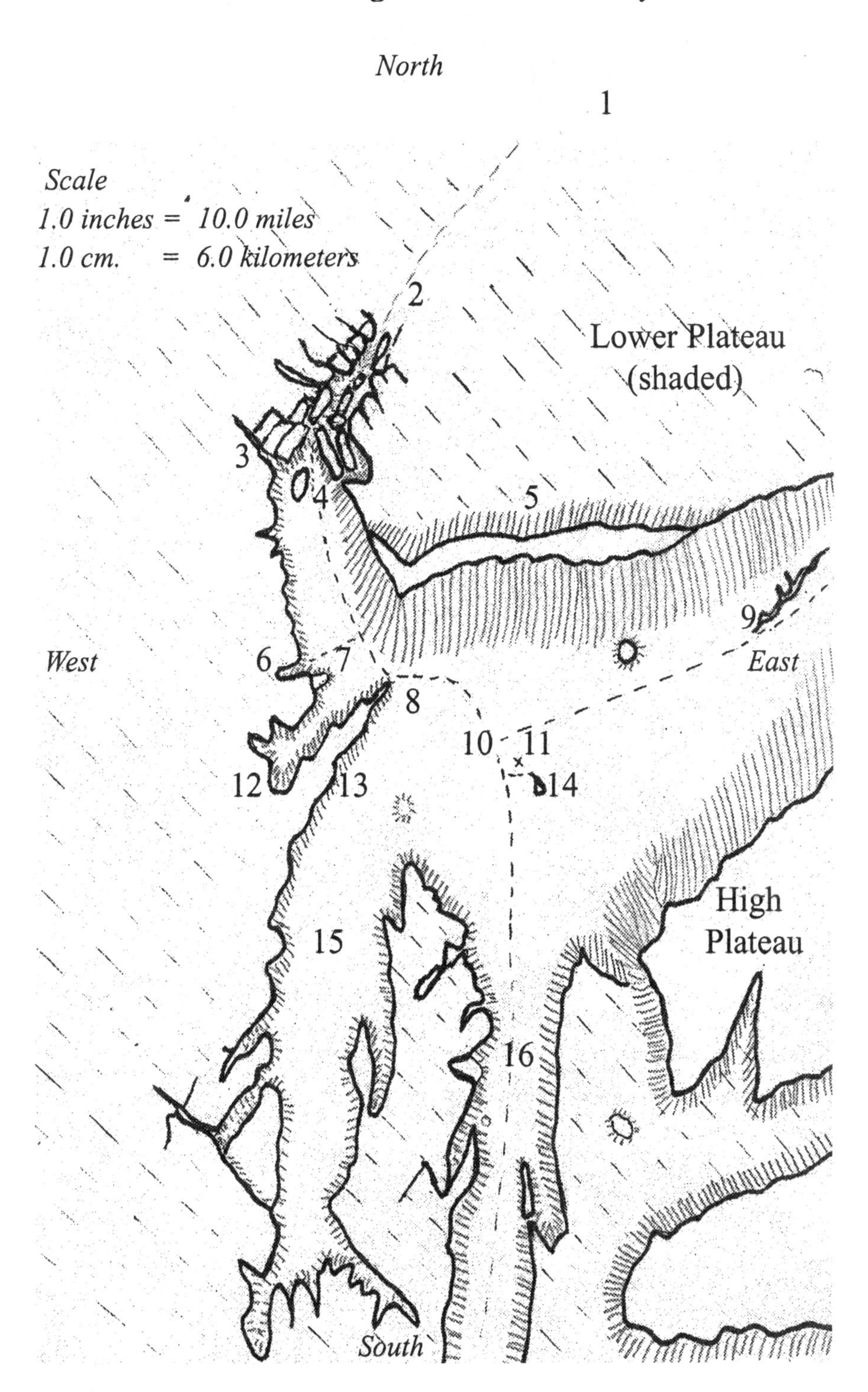

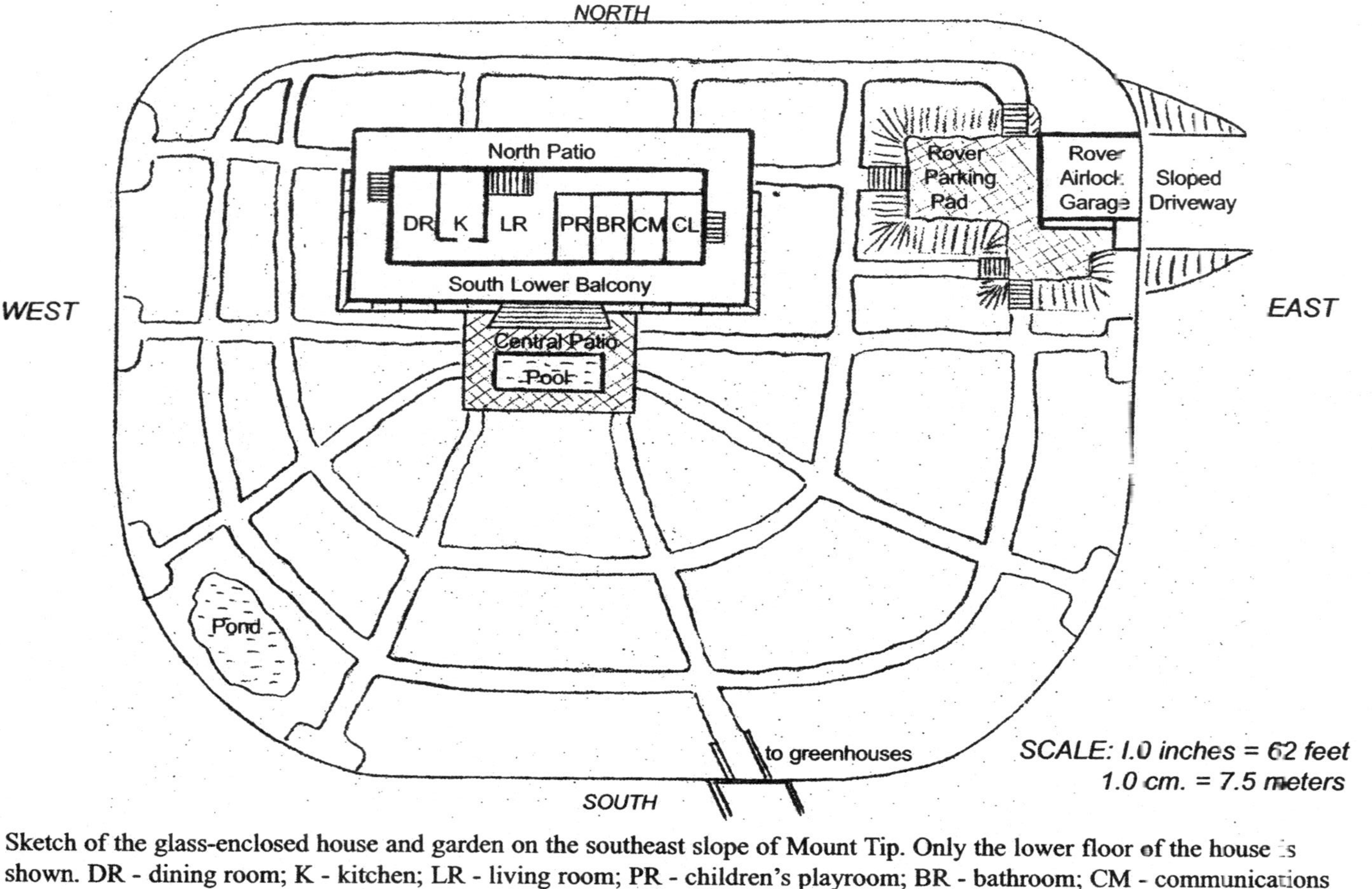

Sketch of the glass-enclosed house and garden on the southeast slope of Mount Tip. Only the lower floor of the house is shown. DR - dining room; K - kitchen; LR - living room; PR - children's playroom; BR - bathroom; CM - communications room; CL - control room. The land slopes down to the south. For this reason, the north patio is at ground level, whereas the south lower balcony, at the same level, is above the level of the central patio and pool, requiring steps down.